^{XO}Orpheus

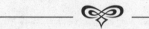

Fifty New Myths

Edited by KATE BERNHEIMER

PENGUIN BOOKS

PENGUIN BOOKS

Published by the Penguin Group
Penguin Group (USA) LLC
375 Hudson Street
New York, New York 10014

USA / Canada / UK / Ireland / Australia / New Zealand / India / South Africa / China
penguin.com
A Penguin Random House Company

First published in Penguin Books 2013

LIBRARY OF CONGRESS CATALOGING-IN-PUBLICATION DATA
Bernheimer, Kate.
    xo Orpheus : fifty new myths / Kate Bernheimer.
      pages cm
    ISBN 978-0-14-312242-5
    1. Mythology, Greek—Fiction.   2. Greece—History—Fiction.   3. Fantasy fiction.
    PS3602.E76.X6 2013
    813'.608037—dc23
    2013020128

Printed in the United States of America
10 9 8 7 6 5 4 3 2 1

Set in Sabon
Designed by Spring Hoteling

Contents

———— ❦ ————

In the modern characterization of Orpheus, culled from diverging stories of antiquity, Orpheus is the best musician of all time—let's make that the greatest artist. Orpheus could play the lyre so well that animals, rocks, and trees danced to his songs; he was so good at his chosen instrument that he even charmed Hades into letting his bride, who had died after falling into a pit of vipers, return to the world of the living. But Orpheus made one little mistake.

ANTHROPOGENESIS AND NORSE CREATION MYTH

The city was their home. Top floor of a narrow brownstone, no elevator, hallways as dark as caves. They lived near a train yard, where the tracks intersected like arteries. Twice a day, the passing trains shook their tiny apartment like a toy. It was not an extraordinary place, but extraordinary things would happen there.

ARGOS

Perhaps you've read of me. I am the hound old Argos. I once belonged to the hero Odysseus some twenty-seven, twenty-eight hundred years ago. Homer granted me a few lines in his epic. He presented me then in a pathetic light.

BACCHANTES

From the start, it was a mistake. Carson Bakely was an earnest student, but he possessed a mediocre intellect, and, frankly, I wasn't sure what to do with him. He showed up during office hours one sunny afternoon when I had been left to my book—all the other graduate students were no doubt filling the outdoor seats at the Cambridge bars—looking freshly scrubbed and ready for some assignment.

BAUCIS AND PHILEMON

Edward Carey ✧ Sawdust 32

I remember them, though I was only a child. They would always be together. If you looked out for them you might see them on a street corner, or you would come across them at dusk leaned up against a tree, heaving and muttering.

BROWNIES

Maile Chapman ✧ Friend Robin 42

I knew well that my mother had been wanting to move closer to me for some time, so when she took a fall on the sidewalk outside her senior apartment complex back east I broke her lease and brought her to Nevada.

THE CALIPH OF
ONE THOUSAND AND ONE NIGHTS

Text and Illustrations by David B. ✧
The Veiled Prophet 54

CANDAULES AND GYGES, AS TOLD BY HERODOTUS

It would be eight years before he told her he'd killed them. Or at least, before he told her he held himself responsible for their deaths, which at the time were put down to natural causes: dehydration, the heat of the sun, overexertion.

COYOTE MYTHS

After the doctor gave them the choice, they took their baby home.
"He's here," said Ben, into the phone. "They let us leave."

CRONOS

The ogre's wife was a good woman. She was not an ogre, but she was ugly, by human standards, and she had married the ogre because he was strong and productive, and together they had made six small ogre children. The children all took after their father.

DAEDALUS

Once there was a boy whose father built a labyrinth.
This is a different story from the one you know. This father didn't build the labyrinth to imprison a half-man, half-bovine monster. He didn't build it to appease a king. No one's going to fashion wings out of feathers and wax, and no one will plummet into the ocean to demonstrate the price of hubris.

DAEDALUS

The villagers watched as he touched down on sand. Shoulder-sore, sun-pink, his arms caged in wooden shelves of feathers, he was not the harpy, not the geryon they had feared. He wore his beard in the style of Minos.

DAPHNE

And so it came to pass that Daphne grew weary of being a tree. For centuries, Daphne had been grateful for her wooden status, and had even come to quietly enjoy Apollo's visits, during which he swore abiding adoration.

DEMETER

When they divided up the year, Demeter had chosen, for her own, the months when the days start getting longer. It was easier that way. It meant that she delivered her daughter back to her ex-husband in the late, bright Montana summer and she could handle it then, most of the time, with a little pharmaceutical help.

DEMETER
AND PERSEPHONE

Walt Collins is at the Fitzgerald playing blackjack when his sister, Lorna, waves to him from across the table. She has her five-year-old daughter Cora with her. She also has a black eye and a dried line of mascara down her cheek.

ERIS

She might have been considered pretty. The other girls in Yakutsk Children's Home #5 told Lena that she was. Full lips, dark flashing eyes, violet like a storm gathering over the ice. Lena would be prettier if she wasn't so angry, Director Laskaya said to the girl from time to time.

GALATEA
AND PYGMALION

It was almost sweet the way they worried about me.
"You're so pale," the nurse said. "You must keep quiet until your color returns."

GOD AND SATAN

The town held twenty churches, large and small, north and south, east and west, on both sides of the railroad tracks. The Baptists and the Mennonites had dark glass doors and triangular arches, the walls of polished stones. The First Christian, a marble and cement façade made yellow by the rains. The Episcopalians, a tiny one-room with a red door glimmering through the winter fog.

GOLEM
AND PYGMALION

She was pretty enough for a man. That's what people said about her. Short feathery hair. Shovel of a jaw. Eyes that seemed to squint with no sun.

HADES

My shadow learned to walk when I learned to walk, and her first word was also my own. When I lost my teeth, she lost her teeth too. The Tooth Fairy left me a quarter; my shadow left me her teeth—under my gums. Over time they grew in.

HUMAN PENTACHROMATS

Lyle stares at a lemon.

  How does the lemon appear to Lyle? The rough skin is what he has been taught to call yellow, and he knows many modifiers of that word— pale, bright, dull; he knows also metaphoric substitutes: gold, butter, dandelion, even lemon.

ICARUS

Don't think I write to be believed. At this point in my life, I couldn't care less. Besides, there's no chance anyone would buy my tale. If someone tried to lay it on me, I'd just shrug. Shrug all you want, then. What follows is true down to the very last word.

KILLCROP

Someone in the apartment was screaming. Had been screaming for a while now. Was it him? No. He didn't think so. How could he scream underwater? Underwater was how he felt. Sunk. Waterlogged. Drowned.

THE KRAKEN

Once there was a squid who fell in love with the sun. He'd been a strange squid ever since he was born—one of his eyes pointed off in an odd direction, and one of his tentacles was a little deformed.

LAMIA/CHILD-EATING DEMON, GREEK

"Long ago," Leonora told her children, and the telling was long ago, too, "I was just ordinary." Of course they didn't believe her. She was taller than other mothers, with a mouthful of nibbling, nuzzling teeth, and an affectionate chin she used as a lever. Her hair was roan, her eyes taurine.

THE LOTUS EATERS

Artesia jumped the fence into the broken-down-to-crap miniature golf course, and then came Pog, and then Pete and the other girl. The world was a gorgeous chocolate brown, a gleaming purring soft color that also glittered.

THE MAENADS AND
SINBAD THE SAILOR

We lived in caves, on battlefields, in fortresses, schoolhouses, Hollywood, meadows, the Old West, cabins, huts, boxcars, castles. We knew our aptitude for gathering berries, being orphans, starring in movies, disarming witches, fleeing armies, teaching school, working in offices with typewriters and carbon paper, nursing soldiers, tending bar, building with twigs and bigger sticks.

MAHĀBHĀRATA

War rages on, and Drona is its heart.

Some songs tell of good wars, kind wars, wars where, when the fighting's over, you sit alone in the woods and breathe and think, this was good, this thing I've done.

MONSTERS

Soon, all the trains fell apart. Then all the planes did. Then all the plants did. When the planes and plants and trains had been destroyed, it was time for him and I to show ourselves to each other in our true colors. After all, there was no natural beauty to distract us from each other now.

EDITH HAMILTON'S *MYTHOLOGY*

The day he was born, the Steelers won the Super Bowl. And that's why, every year, our hero eats a football-shaped cake at his Super Bowl party. For many years, his mother made the cake; then, for a few years, the task fell to assorted girlfriends and other designated female intercessionaries.

NARCISSUS

Beautiful rooms full of light and fire and everyone pretending not to look at me. I was much desired, by rich boys with their hearts breathily on their sleeves, rich men's wives *d'une age certain* in rather a lot of kohl, urbane and athletic Athenians who spoke of friendship and excellence, spendthrifty wine-factors whose chins trembled when I breathed on them.

ODYSSEUS

I was given a very warm welcome when I returned home after my trip abroad. In fact, as my ship pulled in, a small crowd gathered right there on the dock, waving their hands and handkerchiefs, crying excitedly, and smiling in my direction.

ODYSSEUS

These are the first words of the story I am speaking to you now:
—Once, in the beginning of robots—

OEDIPUS

The Brigadier-General wears a frayed bathrobe in a mildewed, smoky nonsmoking hotel room, someplace Midwestern, perhaps Ohio, someplace cheap, perhaps Econo Lodge. To get here you drive through the series of pocketed communities that fray the outskirts of these usual someplaces, someplaces that are like industrial cities that were once more industrious cities.

ORPHEUS AND EURYDICE

Let's assume there's a man on a beach because there is. Let's assume he is a husband because he's wearing a wedding ring. Let's assume he's just been married because he fiddles with this ring perpetually, and as he's on a beach, let's assume he's made the terrible mistake of going on a honeymoon.

PARADISE

Santa Cruz is someone's paradise. Funny thing for a Brazilian to say. Don't those handsome naked bronzed people from the Southern Hemisphere live in Paradise? What about *their* paradise? And what about the Surfer Dude and the Lighthouse, beacons guarding our looking-glass world, long ago left to us by the Hawaiian Duke Kahanamoku. Our looking-glass paradise. Paradise Lost.

PERSEPHONE

Eudora Hale spent the warm months in Fairlady with her mother, and the cold months in Lost Lake with her father. That's how it seemed, at least. Now that she was old enough—nearly thirteen—Eudora knew that whatever the time of year the sun would never reach Lost Lake the way it did Fairlady. Some parts of the world were difficult to find, even for beams of light.

PHAETON, FROM OVID'S *METAMORPHOSES*

I got to choose the meeting place, so I picked the mall. I tried to think of the one location my dad would most hate, and this was all I could come up with. It made me so mad, as I sat there in the food court, not eating because I wanted him to pay for it, because it hit me that the worst place actually would have been the apartment where Mom and I live.

POSEIDON

One town got a god who carried another town inside of him which locals were sometimes allowed to enter, never to return. Another town got a god shaped like a loaded pincushion who had to be placed on a shelf out of reach of adults and long-armed children because what looked like pins were not pins and what looked like cushion would bubble the skin and boil the eyes and make the bones burn.

POST-APOCALYPSE

Manuela Draeger ∞ Belle-Medusa 403

The other night, someone knocked on the door.

It was late. It was very dark and very cold. Throughout the entire evening, I had listened to the silences and the noises reverberating above the city, in the towers and the crumbling houses, in the empty streets.

RAJA RASALU

Aamer Hussein ∞ The Swan's Wife 432

I once knew a woman who loved a swan. She loved all swans, and geese and ducks and water hens too, but most of all she loved a swan she called Satin. On Sundays we went to the park to feed the birds that nested among the rushes beside the lake. They'd come running after us and pluck at our calves with their beaks.

SEDNA, INUIT

Kathryn Davis ∞ Sanna 447

I was just a girl and then I wasn't. Many taboos were directed toward me and I could hear them all! *Pssst pssst pssst*. The smaller fish expressed themselves with sibilants, the larger ones with a preponderance of vowels. On the day everything changed, I was just a girl; hurricane season was upon us, the autumn equinox.

SIRIN

Lutz Bassmann ∞ Madame Liang 457

Madame Liang is the building's sole inhabitant. She had other names in her youth, seventy or eighty years ago, especially when she was queen of the dormitory and fired a gun alongside the last resisters in the Orbise commune. But afterward she lived in Asiatic refugee camps and zoo-parks for undermen for so long that she practically forgot her initial identities.

SISYPHUS

Kit Reed ❦ Sissy 465

To become a man, every first son has to kill his father. Oedipus taught us that, right? Look, you can forget Freud and all those other psychiatric dribblers. In no way is this essential murder about sleeping with your mother. Your balls are on the line, and if you still don't get it, I can't explain it.

THE STRIX

Ander Monson ❦ In a Structure Simulating an Owl 474

In a structure simulating an owl in which are inscribed the eyes of my former husband, having been etched on shook silver foil, serving as a replica of his eyes in his absence, blue dashed with bits of white as if they were in every moment on the verge of dissolving . . .

TEZCATLIPOCA

Donají Olmedo ❦ Cat's Eye 487

Uncle Sebastián's cabin rose inscrutably above the forest of a wooded town: El Salto, the municipal seat of Pueblo Nuevo, in the state of Durango. Pine trees surrounded it like giant gendarmes. I, a feeble, disoriented boy about to swallow the key to a jail cell and be my own prisoner, drove toward the green, sweet-smelling prison, intending to go through it.

TRANSFORMATION

Sigrid Nunez ❦ Betrayal 492

Whenever I travel I try to avoid getting into conversations with strangers I happen to be sitting with. There is nothing worse than being trapped for hours with a dullard or a chatterbox. Yet it is my experience that these types travel more frequently than anyone else. But with the woman on the train it was different.

I knew I could count on Dean. He was like a brother to me—better than that. Ever since we'd met, our first day of Basic—both of us just eighteen years old. Turned out, we'd both grown up near Houston. Dean was from just north of Sugar Land, in Mission Bend, and I was from Alvin; in good traffic, just a little less than an hour away. Maybe it was that.

Ken Bekerwire's village was perched between mountain and sea. As the mountain was high, so the sea was deep, in a continuous narrative of geology. In this isolate place, Ken made a living from fishing, as his father had done before that and his grandfather before that.

Once, through a confluence of events and no fault of his own, a horse fell in love with a baby.

This happened at a busy crossroad where two well-traveled paths met and mingled before going their separate ways.

What is the deepest loss that you have suffered?
If drinking is bitter, change yourself to wine.

—from *Sonnets to Orpheus* II, 29
Rainer Maria Rilke
Translated by Stephen Mitchell

Introduction

In the modern characterization of Orpheus, culled from diverging stories of antiquity, Orpheus is the best musician of all time—let's make that the greatest artist. Orpheus could play the lyre so well that animals, rocks, and trees danced to his songs; he was so good at his chosen instrument that he even charmed Hades into letting his bride, who had died after falling into a pit of vipers, return to the world of the living.

But Orpheus made one little mistake. The King of the Underworld had told him not to look back to the trailing Eurydice until they had exited his kingdom. This was a reasonable condition really, given the very favorable terms of their unusual agreement. Yet Orpheus, being at least half human by most accounts—his mother was allegedly the muse Calliope—forgot himself, or got nervous, or suddenly doubted his own powers—whatever his motivation remains unclear. Upon entering the light of this world Orpheus fatally turned around and watched his love, Eurydice, disappear forever into the shadows where she still walked.

Thus Orpheus, arguably the most prevalent symbol for Art in the Western world, shows us both the power and limitations of the whole venture. Yes, it might feel like you're conquering death when you play that song, paint that picture, compose that poem, or type that story. Yes, you might experience the sensation of escaping the everyday world, perhaps even your own mortality, upon hearing, watching, and reading the best artistic examples. But the feeling is illusory, Orpheus tells us.

The feeling is, after all, just a feeling.

"XO" in the modern sense is a farewell, a departure, a leave-taking—and *xo Orpheus* suggests another good-bye by Orpheus to his bride, Eurydice. The phrase is sad then, humanly sad, considering how things turned out for them in the end. Yet, as the title to a collection of new myths, *xo Orpheus* is meant to suggest a farewell of literature, our symbolic Orpheus, in its old relationship to the world of myth.

If fairy tales are "domestic myths," as Maria Tatar has proposed, then classical myths are worldly tales, generally involving some contact between the mortal and immortal realms, between humans and the gods. Well documented, the relationship of literature to myth in the Western world has undergone much change over the millennia, as first the age of Gods fell away before the notion of a single god, and then, for many people, that single god slipped away too. For more than a hundred years now (let's use the popular terms of modernism and postmodernism) writers have been dealing with this transition, or their perception of this transition.

No Gods . . . no god . . . only humans.

Humans and their machines.

And the myths of former times held a resonance precisely because of this change. They echoed back to us from a place of lost power and transcendence. How far had we fallen? How lonely we were in a world without gods!

But times have changed once again. The age itself has changed. There is some news, and it's not very good news: we humans, once merely human, have supplanted all godly endeavors—we have become like gods ourselves. It's the biggest story on earth.

As scientists have discovered, or perhaps explained is a better word, or perhaps identified, we now live in the age of the Anthropocene. The *geologic* age of the Anthropocene.

Those high priests of material evidence have given us our own epoch like the Holocene, the Pleistocene! Apparently we now, it seems, have superhuman powers. With our evolved busy hands and our evolved busy brains, in an extraordinarily short period of time we've managed to alter the earth with such geologic-forcing effects that we ourselves are forces of nature.

Climate change, ocean acidification, the sixth mass extinction of species. Events that used to take hundreds of thousands, even millions of years, we humans have miraculously accomplished in a little more than a century. We, in our less than divine wisdom but apparently quite divine powers, are now transforming the planet like an Olympian might have created an Ice Age, or a Titan might have thrown down an asteroid from the sky to kill off a bunch of dinosaurs.

We are the gods.

Our scientists have said so.

And our high priests have given our communal life span an epochal name: Anthropocene. This is a Greek name to boot ("human" plus "new"), which brings me back to those myths. What do the myths—those vertical tales about the breach between the human and godly realms—have to tell us now in the new age with humans as gods? What is Myth in the Age of Anthropocene?

Based on the stories gathered here, the early answer is this: sad.

Of course we only just left behind Myth in the Age of the Holocene, bade it farewell as readers and writers. Only in the last few years has the term Anthropocene become widely used in scientific circles. Only over time, therefore, over the coming decades, centuries, millennia—however long the Age of Anthropocene lasts—will we know more about what art means and what artists make, how this shift changes some things and leaves static others. We do know one thing has changed, for those who might say this is faddish end-time thinking: humans are gods. This wasn't true even a generation ago, though some predicted its coming.

A profound sadness, yes. Oh, you may find a whimsical story here and there in the bunch, and you might be struck by the violence too. Yet "XO" Orpheus wrote to his beloved, and "good-bye" this book says to the old relationship of literature and myth, of myth to the human. Even the whimsical stories in here, even the most violent ones, reveal a gaping anxiety, a primal fear, leading to sadness about what we have done.

Of course the stories are also deeply absorbing, ethical, lovely, and strange, different one from the next, each searching for a happy home with a reader.

Yet again the same questions arise: How far have we fallen? How lonely have we become?

When humans become gods, when our wings grow so great as to beat about the very edges of the earth, no one can answer but us.

Good-bye, and so hello.

—*Kate Bernheimer*

XO Orpheus

ANTHROPOGENESIS, OR:
HOW TO MAKE A FAMILY

Laura van den Berg

The city was their home. Top floor of a narrow brownstone, no elevator, hallways as dark as caves. They lived near a train yard, where the tracks intersected like arteries. Twice a day, the passing trains shook their tiny apartment like a toy. It was not an extraordinary place, but extraordinary things would happen there.

A history of the city: there were no seasons. No flowers or sunshine or stars or clocks. They were neither north nor south. The tall buildings were rusted and empty, like abandoned machines. The trains never stopped. No one came or went. A limestone ash tree stood in the center of the city. It was tall as a skyscraper, a monument to nothing. If you climbed to the highest point of the tree and looked out, you would see that the city was surrounded by an ocean, the water as black and still as oil.

Nell was a cool woman. Her exhalations were white streaks. Ice crystals nested in her hair like barrettes. Meno was forever on the brink of being engulfed in flames—red-rimmed ears, sweat-slick skin. She dreamed of the dark, cold waters of a seacoast. He imagined standing deep inside a forest, surrounded by trees with canopies so dense, the sky would molt with green. The city, with its grayness and trains, was a compromise neither of them could remember making.

Fire and ice, their friends called them, because they were so different. *How did you ever find each other?* These friends were wan, both in spirit and in body. They were struggling to find the right way to live. Nell and Meno would smile and shrug, feigning coyness, but the truth was they could not remember how they met. It was as though they had just woken up one morning in this apartment, in this city, these lives unfurling like rugs before them.

In bed, Nell's eyes would freeze inside her head. Until they thawed, they would be wide and unblinking, like a doll's. At the most pleasurable moment, Meno's open mouth would glow with fire.

What about children? their friends were always asking. *Half fire and half ice! How lovely they would be!* Once Nell let snow rain from her fingertips until a tiny snowman stood frozen on the floor. *See?* she said. *Birth is not the only way to create.* Meno rested a hand on the snowman's shoulder and melted it down to a gray lump. *You have the best party tricks*, said the friends.

Where did these friends come from, anyway? Nell sometimes thought, but there was no answer to that either. They had just appeared, hovering around her and Meno like vapors.

It was the nature of cold to be steady and still. It was the nature of fire to catch, to spread. Their situation was not sustainable, and yet it was being sustained.

One morning, Nell woke to the smell of smoke. At the foot of their bed, a baby with fire-covered hands was burning holes in the sheets. The ice crystals in Nell's hair melted; water dripped down her spine. She shook Meno awake. Around them trains rumbled.

Meno scooped up the baby and ran from the bedroom, his feet so warm they darkened the floorboards. Nell followed his footprints into the kitchen, where another infant was squirming across the floor. The child crawled toward her and grasped her ankles. One set of fingers numbed her skin; the other left a hand-shaped burn.

Here was the problem with fire: you could never predict how it would spread. Meno had only wanted one, maybe two, but the children kept appearing. One emerged from the puddle of sweat at his feet. Another crawled out of his armpit. None of this seemed to cause him any pain.

Soon it was all they could do to keep these children from singeing the draperies or shattering the glass windowpanes with a single touch. When the trains passed, the babies shook their fists and wailed. Their friends came by and placed bets on which one would grow up to rule the world. *What a beautiful family!* they cooed. They never stayed for long.

One morning, to calm herself, Nell made another snowman and watched, uncomprehending, as the figure turned into a child. She began to sob and soon the tears that dropped to the floor became children too.

Nell and Meno read a parenting book. They were advised to leave the house once a day. They went for a walk through a barren city park, each of them pushing a large stroller. The sky was dark and growling. They tried to teach the children the words for *rock* and *tree.* To demonstrate, she and Meno patted the trunk of a leafless tree and another child stepped out of the bark.

We'll never be able to find a babysitter, she cried to Meno on the way home. *Not for a million dollars.*

Time passed. Meno kept ice packs pressed against his forehead, trying his best not to sweat. Nell didn't create anything from snow. They stopped reading. They didn't go outside. No more children appeared. Maybe the flood was over. Maybe they would survive.

One night, they attempted the kinds of things they used to do in bed. The babies were sleeping in the wicker bassinets scattered across the apartment. One in the bathtub. Another nestled in an armchair. Another in the dark of the linen closet. The trains had finished for the night. Meno's lips were feverish. Nell's breath loomed above her like a cloud.

But something was not right. When Meno touched her, a pain flared in her belly. He pressed against her and she began to spark, like flint to steel. Right away she could tell that these were not the lights of passion, but of destruction. Lightning striking a tree. A power line meeting water. A line of fire racing toward a barn. She heard a crackling. The flesh underneath her belly button burned. Meno breathed chilly air onto her throat. His lips were hard and cold as stone.

If only he had realized that parents rarely outlive their children.

Fire and ice, that's what they do to each other in the end, their friends would later say. But first the bodies of Nell and Meno would burn a hole in the apartment roof. First the children would rise from their bassinets and walk naked into the city streets, hearty and hale as giants. They would all look up and see a light blazing in the sky. They would feel their blood warm, their bones turn dense as ice. They would feel the beginnings of language sitting like a stone on their tongues. They would think that this, finally, was what it must mean to be alive.

"Anthropogenesis, Or: How to Make a Family" *was inspired by an ancient Norse creation myth: in the beginning there was nothing but the realm of fire and the realm of ice; an interaction between the two gave way to the world. I have taken many liberties, but this myth provided the bones of the story.*

—LvdB

ARGOS

Joy Williams

Perhaps you've read of me. I am the hound old Argos. I once belonged to the hero Odysseus some twenty-seven, twenty-eight hundred years ago. Homer granted me a few lines in his epic. He presented me then in a pathetic light:

> . . . castaway
> on piles of dung from mules
>   and cattle
> . . . infested with ticks
> half-dead from neglect . . .

I had waited for my absent master for twenty years and when he returned he came in the guise of a beggar, a mangy tramp, a bag of bones. This was calculation, this deception, the final triumphant wile of the wily Ulysses. I alone recognized him. I thumped my tail in joy though I hadn't the strength to drag myself an inch toward him.

He did not acknowledge me. He did not place his hand on my bony head or stroke my withered flanks. A friendly touch from him would have meant the world to me of course. I had often dreamed of his return, which I had long associated with happiness. I cannot tell you why his wife and son did not take care of me those long years or why their servants were so cruel. There is much that animals do not understand.

I do know, however, that Homer did not invent me. I was always Argos. It is Homer, indeed, who in all probability did not exist as an individual, his words being the imaginings of many. It was even said that Odysseus "flicked away a tear" when he beheld me though I did not see it, as the hero had turned his back on me.

This subterfuge was necessary for his success. So had the goddess Athena counseled him. To be recognized was to be betrayed. He strode away from me and into the palace halls to claim his kingdom, slay the insolent suitors (one hundred of them he killed in an instant), and regain his wife, the faithful Penelope. His triumph was thus achieved and little happens after. As for me, this is how I am dismissed by the Homers:

> Then his destiny released
> Old Argos, soon as he had
> lived to see
> Odysseus in the twentieth year
> restored.

The dark shadow of death closed down on me . . . and so on . . . yet in fact I did not die, or only in the most limited sense. Athena, after placing me in such an unhappy and unfair position—to not, for all purposes, be remembered, to not feel once again, and for the last time, the comforting touch of a beloved hand upon my head—took pity on my poor dogsbody and made me immortal. It was her last act before less marvelous minds took over and stripped the gods and goddesses of all their transformative powers.

With the speed and strength I once knew before my Odysseus went off to the wars that were so necessary to him, I now run freely and everywhere through all the years to be with my brothers and sisters at the moment when their brief lives are spent. Often, the ones they have been devoted to are with them, making those human sounds of sorrow and reassurance, stroking and smoothing their fur, promising them that they will not be forgotten. This is the heavenly situation, this moment of reviving love, and my heart always sheds happy tears when I witness it, as Athena in her mercy intended. As for my brothers and sisters who die neglected, bewildered, and alone, I, Argos, have been given the honor of guiding them on the next roundelay. It is a strange journey, far more extraordinary than the adventures of Odysseus. We disassemble, we are restored, our trials are great, the obstacles many, but I remain with them until after long seeking they find kindness and return love recognized. Such love endures beyond all our endings.

It's good for them to know this, Athena told me.

She says I am a good boy.

My grandson in Maine was throwing bread to the birds and calling them by name. So you've given them names? I said. No, he answered, they already had their names. So many of the heroes' hunting dogs are given names in Greek myth, but Argos seems to have always possessed his. Faithful, forgiving, more noble than his long-absent master, his duties are also more heroic.

Or so I would have it here.

—JW

Bacchantes

THE SISTERS
Sabina Murray

From the start, it was a mistake. Carson Bakely was an earnest student, but he possessed a mediocre intellect, and, frankly, I wasn't sure what to do with him. He showed up during office hours one sunny afternoon when I had been left to my book—all the other graduate students were no doubt filling the outdoor seats at the Cambridge bars—looking freshly scrubbed and ready for some assignment. He was a good-looking boy and that was no doubt why my colleague, Hillary Hart, had accepted him into the doctoral program. But poor Hillary had died at the start of the semester—found dead in her bathtub apparently having succumbed to a heart attack—and in the scramble to provide supervisors for her advisees (mostly handsome boys) I had inherited Carson. He was the bottom of the barrel and I remembered how, in elementary school, I had always been the last chosen for teams; this might make another person sympathetic, but this similarity inspired the same reticence toward him as I had for my younger, ignorant, unappealing, and generally less successful self.

I invited Carson in and he sat in the stiff little chair—other professors had warm, inviting office furniture, but this encouraged students to stay—with a broad, midwestern smile, even though I'd learned he was from Brooklyn.

"Carson Bakely, right?" I asked.

"That's right."

"What brings you to my gloomy cave on this glorious day?"

"Well, I need some help."

"Really?" I was sure that Bakely did, indeed, need help, but I had forgotten whom it was that he was writing about. I paged through an unrelated yellow pad hoping that it might jog my memory. "Nathaniel Hawthorne?"

"Herman Melville."

"Ah," I responded. "And what about Melville?"

"See, that's the problem." He put his hands on the knees of his trousers and looked across the expanse between us with unblinking eyes. "There's so much of it."

"Written about it?"

"That too." Carson raked his hand through his thick, black hair as if to dislodge a thought that might be trapped there. "I don't know if Melville's really my thing."

"Your thing?"

"No. I think Melville is amazing, of course. Who doesn't?"

"For sure."

"Before Hilly died—"

"Hilly?"

"I mean Professor Hart. Before Professor Hart died, we'd talked about it. We talked about it a lot."

"It?"

"My work. She thought I should stick with American. But maybe start researching something not so . . ."

"Difficult?"

"Long."

"So what have you chosen as your new topic of interest?" I wondered how I would make it through the required hundred pages of dissertation prose, of why it was necessary to encourage Mr. Bakely to waste the next three or so years after which I, along with my other colleagues, would then be faced with no other choice but to fail him.

Carson nodded seriously as if we were in agreement and, with a pronounced set of jaw, declared, "I'm interested in Emily Dickinson. I want to know everything about her."

———

OF course, it has been forty years since that warm spring day when Carson Bakely's earnest form cast its shadow on the dusty boards of my office, but I remember this encounter very precisely because after Carson Bakely was found murdered, I had to go over it so many times. The whole Bakely tragedy was an exercise in tedium foisted upon me by Bakely's desire to read as little as possible on the way to his Ph.D. Bakely had expressed a desire to learn "all there was about Emily Dickinson" thinking that this was easily accomplished. As I was the Dickinson scholar, he ended up on my doorstep. Most of my advisees were earnest, plain girls who seemed to think that in the process of unlocking Dickinson's secrets, they would discover something noteworthy about themselves. No, there was nothing that distinguished Bakely other than his maleness and complacency. Although he did present an opportunity since he lacked direction and, therefore, followed mine quite well: I could use his research. Was I an opportunist? Certainly. Did I kill him? Certainly not. And I also never received the papers he was supposed to bring back to me. But The Sisters—who had turned down so many of my more talented, accomplished, and capable students—accepted him. I could only surmise that this decision was based on his good looks. He really was a handsome boy.

THE Sisters of whom I speak were the board members of a literary society whose seldom used but official name was "The Sisters of Emily Dickinson." These women were all residents of Amherst, Massachusetts—birth, life, and death place of Dickinson—who claimed to have some previously undocumented papers. The Sisters did nothing to convince me of the value of their property, but if what they had was genuine, I would benefit dramatically from this connection and knowledge.

Unlike Carson Bakely, I had been a committed Dickinson scholar from the start. I had pored over her work in my youth—clumsily simplified offerings that had been heavily "edited"—and had always maintained a conviction that these editors, Mabel Loomis Todd and Thomas Wentworth Higginson, had done the poet a great disservice: something in these penetrating lines, albeit shellacked with a perfervid editing vigor, hinted at a divine genius. There was a sense of conflicting style in those lines that a sensitive reader could not help but notice, and I was determined to restore the works to their original bite and beauty. What this required was to scrape away the banal edits with the help of the poet's original papers.

This was the subject of my dissertation, and I was busily at work on it, when Hitler decided to invade Poland. I was not a particularly young graduate student and my soldiering abilities were apace with my sporting—no mildly alert person would choose me for their team—but my knowledge of German made me useful and I found myself in Europe until the mid-forties. Several years later, dissertation in hand, I was working an assortment of teaching jobs and living in a basement apartment on Beacon Hill. I could literally recognize the well-heeled set from my vantage point at street level. I was still doggedly at work combing through letters, restoring dashes, torturing syntax, when I learned that a likewise-minded prep-school teacher (Lawrenceville, but still) was getting ready to submit some definitive volume for publication. And it appeared the following year.

I felt bad for myself and others felt bad for me, as my scholarship was flawless and my writing style both expansive and purposeful, but there was nothing to be done. A book deal for my compilation of "new" Dickinson poems never materialized, although I did manage to place three papers in respected journals. These papers—significant—and my biography of Emily Dickinson earned my professorship at the newly established Increase University, a job that I held until my retirement in 1980. The Dickinson biography, *Mermaids in the Basement,* stuck it long enough to earn me tenure, but was not long after mustered out of print. Apparently, many of the letters that I had used for my research had been forged, and the information provided by my book proved to be incorrect. I had purchased the letters from a graduate student (he claimed to be a relative of Dickinson's) who, as I later learned, had quickly left the program with a wad of my cash and decamped for Cuba. I was bankrupted, both financially and in my desire to teach, but unsure of what else to do.

In the years of my teaching at Increase University, little of note happened. I published earnestly, then not so earnestly, then not at all, and noted that the powers that be did not seem to care whether I published or not, only that paying students had classes to attend and that Increase University had degrees to confer. And this was the state of my career on that fateful day when I considered that Carson Bakely could possibly be the key to restoring my academic reputation.

———

I had started receiving the letters from The Sisters of Emily Dickinson five years earlier, forwarded by my department chair after our respected Victorianist Eric Herbert-Watson died in a drowning accident: he was swimming across Walden Pond when he suffered a leg cramp and sank like a stone. Or at least that's what we believed since it seemed the most logical conclusion for the presence of Herbert-Watson's body at the bottom of the pond and in his swimming trunks. The letter was straightforward, handwritten on good cream stock, and with little flourish. Dear Professor Herbert-Watson, we are in possession of some papers of Emily Dickinson . . . looking for an intern . . . suitable disposition, et cetera. Small stipend. Free accommodation. Send statement of purpose, curriculum vitae, recent photograph. Oddly, the logo on the letterhead was a bunch of grapes with the letters "E" and "D" depicted in an ornate twist of vines.

Those of us who work in academia often receive odd little correspondences, and, truth be told, fifty percent of academia is just that: odd little correspondences. This letter awakened an intellectual interest that had so long been dormant that when it began to stir, I mistook the alien sensation for anxiety. But it was only curiosity. I quickly composed letter, typed résumé, folded paper, licked stamp, and trotted to mailbox with the lightness of a younger man. I hesitated at the posting—wondering if it really was acceptable to list publications without dates—then decided that if The Sisters wanted to know, they could always ask. I then returned to my office to await their response.

Four days later, I received a letter back on the same grape-bunch stationery stating that my application was incomplete. Where was my recent picture? My most recent photograph was an extra from a not-too-distant passport set and I sent this along, grudgingly, since the lighting was unflattering and unfairly accentuated my jowls. Why did The Sisters require a photograph anyway? This feeling of resentment was compounded by their rejection a few short days later and I thought that would be the end of it; however, the following spring another letter from The Sisters showed up in my mailbox, this time addressed to me rather than Herbert-Watson, again requesting a student (student was now underlined) intern and with the same request for a recent photograph. As I was curious about the contents of The Sisters trove, I did recommend that students apply for this "internship." And once, visiting a colleague who had retired to Northampton, drove—on a whim—the five or so miles to Amherst to see if I could manage to persuade The Sisters to share their materials with me. But I had no address for them—all letters listed a post office box—and, surprisingly, no one at the actual Emily Dickinson House, now a museum, had heard of them. Or at least that's what they claimed. Accessing these papers was hardly an obsession, but I was curious, and Bakely was eager to give it a shot and to share his findings.

The semester ended and I decamped to my bungalow in Truro, enjoying the salty air and absorbing myself in the usual summer reading: literary biography, Henry James, light criticism, and—my old favorites—the works of Edith Hamilton. Occasionally, a friend or colleague would come for the weekend and I'd prepare some steamed lobsters and corn, or we'd drive out for a basket of fried clams, but this summer—like every other summer—was characterized by sun-warmed solitude. Upon returning to Increase University—and my overstuffed faculty mailbox—in the fall, I found a letter from Carson Bakely. He had actually been accepted for the internship and was planning to spend June, July, and the first half of August in Amherst going through the papers. He thanked me for having introduced him to this opportunity and looked forward to attending my seminar, Correspondence and Consequence: Letters as Vehicles for Communication in Late Victorian Society, in September. I had scanned Bakely's letter while moving it across my field of vision and now passed it on to a trash can conveniently located to the right of the table, where I stood sorting my mail. Of course, September had now arrived and, after Bakely missed the second of our Tuesday afternoon seminars, I began to wonder what might have happened to him.

I'm not sure exactly when the police became involved, but they did, and they questioned me extensively. I, stupidly, had disposed of every letter from The Sisters of Emily Dickinson. Apparently, my reference to these letters and my assertion that Carson Bakely had left the previous June to participate in an internship were the only witnesses to the legitimacy of Bakely's departure for Amherst. There was, apparently, no such organization as The Sisters of Emily Dickinson. It was only after tracking down the department chair, who had a vague recollection of having forwarded me some letter of

Herbert-Watson's, and approaching Ms. Offutsky, the department secretary, who corroborated this story—she remembered sorting the letters into my mailbox—that the detective believed my version. Two days after, when Bakely's battered body was found dumped in a ravine on the trail to Mount Orient near the Amherst-Shutesbury border, the police questioned me again. But I knew nothing. All I could tell them was that I had suspected an affair between poor Bakely and Hillary Hart, but as Hillary had died before Bakely, this was nothing but a sordid sidebar—yet another tarnish on the struggling reputation of Increase University.

In the weeks after the discovery of Bakely's body, details began to emerge. One of his arms had been torn from his shoulder and was a good twenty feet from where—apparently in flight—the rest of him had finally expired. In the surrounding area, police had discovered the carcass of a deer, four squirrels, a fox, and a house cat, all of which had met a similarly violent end. A broader investigation was opened—apparently, in other years, other young men and house cats had disappeared. The specter of Bigfoot was raised, also aliens. Perhaps cougars were back in the area. The story was tabloid ready, wildly popular, and then spent. The letters from The Sisters never came again. I retired to Truro to my life of splendid isolation, only occasionally disturbed by local reporters who found my living alone—I am now a hundred and two years old—remarkable.

I didn't think about Carson Bakely much. Once, his mother sent me a letter describing his deep admiration for me, something she thought I'd appreciate. I found it hard to believe; however, this banal communication did make me grateful that I'd never married, never had children, and been parentless for close to seventy-five years. And that was it, until the box appeared on my doorstep, delivered by UPS. I'd stopped ordering things a decade earlier, as I hadn't expected to live past ninety, and was therefore surprised to see the UPS man—who was now completely gray and rather comical in his brown shorts—darkening my door. But there was indeed a delivery for me, Basil Zinn, Professor Emeritus, et cetera. And the origin of the package? It had been sent by an Emma Dickinson Slutsky, 317 Garber Road, Amherst, Massachusetts.

Using my envelope slitter with the deer-horn handle, I ripped through the tape. A dusty smell rose up like a spirit. I reached for the handwritten note, which was composed in a looping scrawl.

Hi Mr. Zinn,

I was renovating my kitchen and had to knock down a wall and found all these letters stuffed there. The house used to be my grandma's and she was kind of weird, the kind of weird that does things like stuff letters in walls and seal them up. I would have just dumped them, but they're kind of old and all addressed to you. I called the university to see if you were still alive (I didn't think you would be. Congratulations!). So here they are! My kitchen looks great now and gets more light, but my husband thinks that we knocked out a support beam and that the house is going to collapse.

> Yours Truly,
> Emma Dickinson Slutsky

There were five envelopes inside. All were of the Sisters of Emily Dickinson variety as evidenced by the grape-bunch logo on the flap and all were addressed to me at my English Department mailbox. There was no return address although Carson Bakely's name, in a young man's impulsive hand, was inscribed in the envelope's top left-hand corner.

Of course I had wondered about what had happened to Bakely. According to police records, he had never arrived at the train station—or at least no witnesses could place him on the platform, although the conductor thought he'd gotten off at an earlier stop, Palmer, or some such thing, which didn't really make sense. Why would Bakely have done that? In fact, there was nothing to place Bakely in Amherst at all except for his mutilated corpse—found in the woods—and the long-gone letter sent to me from his home in Brooklyn, stating that his bid for the internship had been successful. He had not dined at any of the local restaurants, nor visited the post office. Amherst is a college town and in the summertime was quiet, a third of its school-year population, thus it seemed strange that no one had seen the young man who was, if nothing else, good-looking—someone a waitress would remember.

I poured myself a V8 and sat down at the table with the envelopes.

The first of them yielded to the deer-horn letter opener with a low shredding noise. A powdery, sinister mold and accompanying dank smell, embedded in the paper, was released as I unfolded it. The letter was dated June 5, 1976. I decided to open all the letters so as to read them in order, although my eyes were eager for those first revealed lines, lines that resurrected Bakely's scripting hand that had been still these last two-score years: a hand removed and cast aside (along with the right arm) of that poor boy, unless he were left-handed, in which case he'd died with the relevant arm and hand attached. But who could remember which hand he wrote with? It was a long time after all. And, although some students took notes while in my office, Bakely hadn't bothered. Could I fault him for this? No, for I had had little to say, not just to him, but to everyone. My friends were men and women much like me—people who did not tax and were likewise unwilling subjects to the affliction of close company. Suffering, for the most part, had been avoided.

When the occasional high-school student or local reporter did indeed drop by to ask the particulars of my life, I had little to offer. These people on my doorstep had been reared by the fawning behemoth *The Titanic*, and not ship, mind you, but foundering movie with its plucky old broad and her magical trove of anecdotes. All I could do was tell the reporters about the man who had delivered vegetables with a horse-drawn cart, although it was a long-ago memory. Actually, at this point it was the memory of a memory, and a memory of that, repeated over and over as one's image is repeated in opposing mirrors at a fun house. It took many repeated memories to get me back to six years old and the laced boots and stiff shirt with sailor collar—details I also shared—which were held for me by a brown and white photo that was on my bedside table. This picture was the only photograph I had on display throughout the house. Perhaps there should have been someone else, but since a century separated that child from my present incarnation, to me he was another person entirely.

BAKELY'S first letter was short and communicated little other than his delight at having this "wonderful opportunity" to commune with "my Emily." I continued to read. He was, apparently, staying at a cabin in the woods somewhere along a ridge of mountains. He wasn't sure exactly where he was, but he "felt the Dickinson spirit everywhere." I wondered if the spirit in question wasn't actually some local mountain product, distilled from corn. The Sisters themselves, he said, were immensely helpful—if not particularly friendly. He had assumed that he would have a room somewhere, not this "rustic palace" with a "brook" that, predictably, "babbled." The Sisters had brought him all kinds of supplies to tide him over—coffee, tea, sugar, tins of milk, flour. Sea biscuit. Salt horse. I exaggerate with these last provisions, but the staples provided seemed so bizarrely *staple* that it seemed I was holding a missive from an Oregon-bound pioneer, rather than a graduate student with an internship.

The "rustic palace" had two rooms. The one to serve as Bakely's chamber had a bed, a maple dresser, and a window that looked past long pines into a boulder-strewn ravine; the other was filled with crates and boxes of the relevant papers. And how had they come to acquire these materials? The Sisters told the story thus: Emily Dickinson was storing boxes of papers with her brother, Austin Dickinson, at his house just up the street, and he had placed these boxes—and there were several—in his basement. At some point the basement of his house was at risk of flooding, and Austin had had the boxes transferred to his law office in the downtown. These boxes were subsequently forgotten, subject to neglect because the papers were thought to be random accountings of the Dickinson family household and were assumed to have no value. After Austin Dickinson's death from heart failure in 1865, the boxes ended up in the possession of his secretary. The woman held on to the papers with a zeal born of an unrequited passion, apparently inflamed by the elder Dickinson's Byronic locks and strong jaw. This spinster secretary—a Margaret Pouncey Shumworth—was one of the founding Sisters.

As to why The Sisters sat on this trove and controlled these materials in a manner both inefficient and secretive, they offered this: the rest of Emily Dickinson's papers were at Harvard University. Harvard created a great amount of anxiety among The Sisters, and even Bakely, not the sharpest knife in the drawer, realized that much of The Sisters' concern was blatant paranoia sieved through reason. However, had the "dons" at Harvard learned of the papers, they might well have descended upon the cabin, their coffers spilling coins, igniting a righteous greed, if not among The Sisters themselves—who were too pure to fall for such a cheap exchange— then among their heirs. It was in this spirit of secrecy that they had met Bakely at the train station in Palmer. Their desire to learn of the value of the contents and control their fate had resulted in their enlisting of Bakely to their cause, as there was not a scholar of literature in their number. Of course, after the enlisting of Bakely, there was still not a scholar of literature in their number, but I suppose that is now beside the point.

Bakely arrived at the station on a warm June day, the sky clear, the air clean, the Palmer toughs at safe distance. As Bakely descended the train with rucksack, he was met by five middle-aged ladies of varying heights and weights, but who all—to disquieting effect—were sporting the severe part and smooth hair, knotted at the nape, as was depicted in the one known photograph of Emily Dickinson. As for the precise location of the cabin, he wasn't sure, as the vehicle that had served as his conveyance was some sort of converted delivery van. Benches had been installed in the back, where he was seated, but there were no windows.

But what, I asked myself, was in the boxes?

I turned to the next letter. This one was dated June twelfth. I asserted myself upon its long-held folds, smoothing the creases.

Bakely wrote that the boxes revealed a massing of preserve receipts, knitting patterns, bills of lading, settled accounts with the plumber, unsettled accounts with the carpenter, tuition reminders from Mount Holyoke Female Seminary, bills from the local dairy, lecture flyers from visiting preachers, instructions for the new clothes wrangler, ancient seed packets, long-brown pressed flowers— a churning gorgon of detritus that would, occasionally, shake loose from its tentacles something of actual value: a letter in Emily's own hand or, fantastically, a poem.

In the words of Bakely, "Most of it is junk, but some of it isn't."

As a special treat, Bakely had transcribed a fragment of a letter, which he believed to have been penned by Emily as a draft for something finalized elsewhere, and eventually sent off:

> If fame belonged to me, I could not escape her. If she did not, the longest day would pass me on the chase, and the approbation of my dog would forsake me then. My barefoot rank is better.

BAKELY said he wasn't sure what it meant, but he knew that Emily Dickinson had been inordinately fond of her dog Carlo and that, perhaps, in addition to favoring white dresses, she also preferred to go about in bare feet.

The third letter, from the nineteenth of June, revealed that Bakely had started to feel the jitters of exile. A stray dog had appeared outside his window and when, as he liked dogs, he had opened the front door to give it a bowl of milk, the dog had tried to attack him, running—full-tilt, teeth bared—from the edge of the clearing. Bakely only just managed to get inside, slamming the door behind him. He stood with his back against the quaking door, the dog pounding and scrabbling at the wood, until the beast seemed to give up. Bakely, heart pounding, the bowl clutched to his chest, the milk soaking through his shirt and dripping down the front of his pants, had been in a state of damp terror, when one of The Sisters had called to him from the porch. He pulled her in to safety and told her of the fanged peril that was prowling just outside, but she said she had not seen a dog, that maybe it had been a wolf. To Bakely's reckoning, it had been a Saint Bernard, but The Sister had coolly told him to calm himself. She had come with provisions—milk, butter, salt, oranges, and, since he seemed a nice young man, a potato casserole that only needed to be reheated. Due to the generous portion, Bakely thought it possible to survive on the casserole for several days. Bakely asked The Sister if he might, perhaps, return to town with her; he had, after all, been alone for over two weeks, but she waved off his request. Had he finished going through the papers? No? Well, that was a bit disappointing. And surely a strapping young man like him wasn't afraid of a dog.

He continued to sort through the papers and thought he'd found a few letters of interest and some notes that had resulted in poems, although the completed poems existed, and publicly, elsewhere. And then he confessed that he had become fearful of something, although he was ashamed to admit it. At night, he heard large animals ambling around the cabin—for it was no longer a "rustic palace"—and the dismembered carcass of a rabbit left upon his doorstep had only served to further disturb him.

The fourth letter, the most valuable of them all, was the one that contained the poem, of course untitled.

Wisdom always teaches us
That girls should play with knives

And spring about the inward hills
Crossed thick by trunk and leaves

At evening's ruby spill to run
with hound through mountain creases
to finally hold him still—Now still!
Sharp blades reflect our faces.

The final line had been bracketed with a question mark, and several alternate lines, according to Bakely, had been supplied:
"And deep in grimy places."
"Although he is in pieces."
And, the prosaic, yet still prophetic:
"Thus end all our races."
The poem, to Bakely's understanding, had never been deemed satisfactory to the poet, and Bakely's opinion (mine too) was that it would have been disposed of, were it not scribbled on the back of a home remedy for poison ivy.

The fifth letter was the shortest of them all. Bakely started with an apology. He said he could no longer stay with The Sisters, because he had discovered something about their organization that disturbed him. He wrote,

> I wanted to write on Emily Dickinson because I thought it was something I could handle. I should have stuck with Melville, even though I'm a slow reader. I'd rather tell you what The Sisters are up to in person. I know it would sound crazy if I wrote it and if I were you, I wouldn't believe it. Let me just say that my life is in danger and that if anything happens to me, it was The Sisters. My food is running low. The casserole gave out days ago. I start my hike to the nearest town at dawn.
>
> Sincerely,
> Carson Bakely

Sad to note, Bakely had only finished half the address on the envelope, scripting only the "Inc" of "Increase," as if he'd suddenly realized that this letter would not be posted in his lifetime, nor the others that he had so dutifully presented to The Sisters to mail on his behalf.

I put the letter down. He must have written it in the days before his death. Who were these Sisters? I thought of Bacchantes, worshipers of Dionysus, who would drink to the point of madness and then run through the forests of ancient Greece, tearing to shreds anything unlucky enough to cross their path. But the Sisters weren't Bacchantes. They were admirers of Emily Dickinson. The Bacchantes had run with wild wolves, not ill-mannered Saint Bernards, and I was running with my wild speculation.

Of course the trail had gone cold, had maybe even been paved over, but I thought it worthwhile to do a little investigation. I stood from my chair, adjusted the front of my cardigan, and took bold steps to the telephone. Directory assistance soon put me in touch with Emma Dickinson Slutsky's number and soon a quick bleating began to echo in far-off Amherst. It was Ms. Slutsky herself who answered with a chirpy hello that suggested familiarity with any and all who might be calling.

"Ms. Slutsky," I began, "I am Basil Zinn."

"Oh," she said. "Do I know you?"

"I was the recipient of a batch of letters that you kindly mailed to me after discovering them in the wall of your house."

"You're that teacher who's, like, a hundred years old."

"I am a retired professor."

"Wow," she said. "Awesome." There was a moment of silence.

"I'd like to thank you for your taking the effort to send me the letters."

"Sure," she said. "Any time."

There was a moment's silence. "And I was very sorry to hear about your grandmother."

"What did you hear?" inquired Ms. Slutsky. "Wait. Are you a friend of my grandmother's?"

"We knew each other, once." At this point I was happily lying, since I had not thought through the particulars of my call to Ms. Slutsky, only that I had wanted to know a vague—and therefore not wholly satisfying—more. But had I been a friend of the grandmother's, the information would no doubt flow. I quickly began to spin the details of a Depression era courtship. "How long has she been gone?"

"Gone in what way?"

We both paused.

"Because we had to move her out last year. That's how I got the house, but Grandma's not dead, far from it. Actually, not that far from it, because she is ninety. I'm sorry. That's rude when you're talking to someone as old as you. Who can know? Maybe she'll live for another twenty years. I mean, that would be something—"

"So she's in the hospital?"

"Oh, no. She's in an old folks' home. She has a walker and can't do stairs anymore. And we were worried that she might burn the house down. She kept leaving the stove on."

"Could you tell me the name of the retirement community?"

"She's in North Amherst at the Merry Oaks. Wow. I didn't even know she had a friend. I thought everyone was dead. Sorry. I shouldn't keep—"

"On the contrary," I said soothingly. "You have been most helpful and very, very kind."

THE car keys dangled on one of the hooks by the door. I checked my driver's license. It had—as I'd predicted—lapsed in the last five years, although I'd stopped driving some time before that. The car, however, was in good order—a 1995 Honda Accord—which was now driven only by Megan, the teenager who lived next door. I paid Megan a modest fee to do my grocery shopping and to take me to my various appointments, which I scheduled—for her convenience— in the hours after school. Paying the insurance on the car was an extra expense and I suppose I could have just as easily taken taxis, which I sometimes had to use, but I liked my arrangement with Megan and even let her use the car for outings with her friends. Once, when retrieving my coat off the backseat on my way to physical therapy, I had discovered a foil envelope that I knew had once contained a condom. I did think it odd that Megan was having sex in my car, but could muster no outrage—none at all. I thought back to the time when I too had indulged in such activities, which, at this remove, seemed of an almost mythological intimacy. I couldn't remember the last time I'd taken off my clothes and rubbed myself against someone. And then I thought of how people often said, "I can't remember the last time . . ." to refer to such things as eating lobster or going to the cinema, and how, if they'd actually taken a moment to probe the past, they probably could have remembered. They weren't dealing with the numbers I dealt with and Megan was welcome to use the car for whatever activity made the most sense to her. The only conditions I imposed were that she return the vehicle with a full tank and never move the driver's seat.

Thus, it was rather disconcerting when I sat, for the first time in ten years, behind the wheel and realized that I could no longer reach the pedals, nor see in the rearview mirror. I must have been shrinking at an alarming rate and, at my current size, was probably the vertical equal of an eleven-year-old. My clothes were loose, but I'd attributed this to the fact that I most often wore wool, which I seldom laundered—I'd thought my pants stretched out. I wondered why my doctor hadn't addressed this shrinkage at my most recent appointment, but the doctor hadn't said much to me for the last decade other than, "You should just keep doing what you're doing."

My second attempt to escape the garage, although accompanied by an ominous crunch, was successful and soon I was driving in the direction of the Bourne Bridge. It was a brilliant June day and the traffic headed onto the Cape was moving at a slow pace; I, however, zipped along unimpeded, watching the swerve of the newer vehicles as they shot into the left lane. It occurred to me that I had not been off the Cape in close to twenty years, not since Ms. Offutsky's funeral in Hingham, which I had felt obliged to attend: I was the only faculty member, and witness to her martyring of self to the English department, to survive her. I wondered about my other colleagues, long since gone, Hillary Hart in her bath, Eric Herbert-Watson in Walden Pond, and contemplated what might finally take me.

When I forgot to put in my hearing aids on days that Megan came, she would knock and knock before eventually letting herself in. I would find her shouting in the kitchen, eyes twitching and mouth aflap—although the sound reached me as though through wadded socks—and had come to the conclusion that Megan lived in fear of being the discoverer of my dead body. This was a valid fear and I did not want to disappoint. Inspired by Hillary Hart, I considered stripping naked and sitting in the tub, stretching my mouth to a final and appalling yawn, and waiting—would it take that long?—for death to take me. This ghastly image was much more appealing to me than the slippered-feet, folded-hands, and bowed-head death that was probably stalking me in my favorite chair, the "he must have just slipped away" death, the "he never suffered, the poor dear" death. Perhaps these thoughts were morbid, but it is only natural to think of the future, and at one hundred and two, there wasn't much standing between me and oblivion. Death, according to both odds and logic, could, would, and really should have met me at any minute. I wondered how long it would take to reach Amherst and decided I ought to increase my pressure on the gas. I was soon driving up I-495 at a confident forty-five miles per hour.

Forty years earlier Carson Bakely too had headed to Amherst, unsure what he would find and innocent of his fate. In his letter he had stated plainly that were he dead, it was The Sisters that had done it. Now Bakely had been in the earth these long years and this woman—this grandmother of Emma Dickinson Slutsky—would finally answer for her actions. Or, perhaps, she would merely answer a few questions about Bakely and then I'd leave her to her card games, soap operas, and the mysterious Senior Zumba that was a regular offering at the community center in Truro, and no doubt also a featured activity in the environs to the west. But what mystery did The Sisters have to hide? I remembered the policeman telling me that others had gone missing—cats and young men. I remembered the long-ago passport photo that I had sent to The Sisters and compared it—at the time I was close to seventy—to that of Bakely. I thought of the other students who had applied for the internship. Nearly all were girls and the only boy other than Bakely—I think he was an Alex—had his profound allergies inscribed on every feature. The Sisters had wanted a healthy young man and I had sent them one. As I passed the Sturbridge exit, I recalled the logo on their stationery: vines and grapes. I thought of the ferocious dog, the sounds of midnight ramblings, the dead rabbit. What *was* The Sisters of Emily Dickinson? Who were these women with their grapevine logo and predilection for young men, with their thrice-folded stationery, windowless vans, and moldering boxes?

This was a cult in the neoclassical mode, a women's cult that flourished in the ravines and piney dives along the Quabbin Reservoir: a cult tied up in Emily Dickinson—her work and hairstyle, her love of dogs, her Vesuvian façade that held back a laval tide of secrets—a strange sisterhood that ensnared graduate students with original documents, sequestered them in remote cabins, and tore them limb from limb. Or limb from body, since limbs weren't actually attached to other limbs.

As I exited at Palmer, I thought of Bakely. As I took the turns through Three Rivers, I imagined him bouncing along in the back of the van. I imagined the sharp turn that had taken him from the paved roads to the less-traveled, swiftly ascending switchbacks that led to his "rustic palace." And in the bathroom of the Belchertown Sunoco, I thought of him preparing for his dawn trek, while The Sisters whet their knives and roused their hounds. The Merry Oaks, as indicated to me by the stabbing, oil-stained finger of the grease monkey, was only six miles away. I hitched up my trousers to my rib cage and made purposeful steps, cane well gripped, to the Honda.

THE Merry Oaks announced itself with a flaking painted sign that struggled beneath a bank of blown lilac. The driveway, curving in an indulgent oxbow, seemed designed for go-cart enthusiasts, despite the frequent speed bumps, which were heralded—too late to be helpful—in yellow and black stripes. The building itself was a low-slung brick thing with anachronistic columns sprung about the front as if it were a bank, or a mausoleum, or any other new thing that struggles to look old with columns. In the parking lot, all the handicapped spots were taken. Another visitor, a man much like myself, only a decade younger, was lowering his feet out the driver's side door. He propped his elbows against the car and raised himself to standing position, then, one steady foot after the other, headed to the entrance. I, employing the same system, swung both legs out, found the ground—a disconcerting distance from where it once had been—and began, in my closest approximation of haste, to follow him into the building. The door slid open and I crossed the transom of the Merry Oaks unimpeded. Inside, an assortment of seniors were arranged around the lobby in wheelchairs and armchairs, some wrapped in neat blanket bundles, others sprawled in neck-torquing, open-mouthed slumber, all arranged to catch the slanting sunlight like so many potted plants. From an adjoining room, I heard a competent muster of piano music accompanied by a young woman's encouraging voice saying, "Very good. Well done." I was reminded of kindergarten—or some approximation of a recollection of the distant kindergarten—and the memory was pleasant, which surprised me. The desk was currently unmanned and as a phone began to ring, I fought the urge to answer it. On a board hanging just to the left of the telephone were a series of Post-its of some sort of visits. Perhaps it was for physical therapy, or massage, or haircuts. Names were listed along with times and, helpful to me, room numbers. I felt sure that I would recognize The Sister when I found her. I scanned the board quickly, undisturbed by anything but a gentle wind that ruffled the Post-its when the front door slid open. There it was. At 3 P.M., Margaret Dickinson Shumworth, of room 114, was due for something. I scooted casually to the left side of the room, where a short hallway appeared to branch into a network of corridors. The correct direction was eventually ascertained after consulting a number of plastic signs and I was soon headed down a promising passage. At first I was concerned that I would be seen as an invader, but after the second nurse passed me—this one a young man in orange scrubs with an impressive fountain of dreadlocks—I realized that I fit in quite well. So long as I moved at a compromised speed, I was fine; even disorientation would be on par with expected modes of behavior.

Room 114 was at the end of the hallway. On a corkboard on the door, children's crayon drawings had been pinned up. Two were of leopards, modeled on house cats, but spotted with yellow and orange and black. One was of a bunch of purple grapes and had "Hapy Birthday GramGram" written under it, perhaps a gift from Ms. Shumworth's great-grandchild. I raised my cane and rapped on the door. There was no answer. I rapped again, but still no one responded. Stealthily, I tried the handle—which swung downward unimpeded—and pushed the door open. I was momentarily startled by another person in the room, but quickly realized that it was merely my reflection in the dresser mirror. The room was empty. A sliding door that led out to the gardens had been left open and the breeze lifted the floor-length curtains inward. There was a single bed with a simple wooden headboard, a dresser, an oriental rug. A door that had to lead to the bathroom was just to the left of where I stood. A small kitchenette counter had a sink, and cups hung cheerfully on hooks above it. There was no hotplate, but an electric kettle: Ms. Shumworth was not allowed to burn down the building, but she was permitted to make herself tea. I shut the door behind me. A leopard print bathrobe hung on a hook within. Tucked into a corner of the dresser mirror was a postcard of Caravaggio's *Bacchus*. There were framed photographs arranged about the room: school portraits, wedding pictures, an elderly man—Mr. Shumworth?—who smiled out with long, yellow teeth, but most interesting of all was the picture beside the bed. A kneeling woman (I assumed Margaret Dickinson Shumworth) smiled out at the camera, her arms wrapped around an enormous and drooling Saint Bernard. The photograph seemed to have been taken some time in the seventies, because Ms. Shumworth looked to be about fifty and the style of turtleneck—although I had several that I still wore—fit that fashion, as did the woman's fierce middle-part, but the fact that the rest of her hair was knotted in back made me assign this attribute to other factors.

I made my way to the open sliding door and looked out across the lawn. At a short distance was a bench. A walker had been placed just to the left of it and seated on the bench was a woman I could identify, because her gray hair was neatly styled into a bun. I did not know what I would say as I drew closer, and was composing my thoughts, when she felt me coming and turned. I had not known her in her youth, but looking at her now—her sharp little eyes and tight mouth—I guessed that she had not mellowed with age.

"Good morning," I said, but it occurred to me that it was somewhere after noon.

"What of it?" she replied. "And who are you?"

"I am Professor Basil Zinn," I responded. She was holding something in her hand and when I said that, she unfolded her fingers to reveal a set of false teeth. "Perhaps you recall—"

"Yes," she said. "Increase University. What brings you here?"

"Some questions," I said. "Your granddaughter sent me a batch of letters."

Here, the woman started to laugh, a low chuckle. She shook her head from side to side. "You want to know what happened to Carson Bakely?"

"Yes, I do." I was surprised by her forthrightness.

She looked pointedly at the edge of the lawn, where it blurred into a mass of vines marking the border of the woods. "I had a feeling all day," she said, "that it wasn't over. The nurse said I should have stayed away from last night's cabbage, but I knew it wasn't that. I had a feeling."

I placed my hands squarely on my cane and pulled myself to my full—although compromised—height. "So what was the fate of that poor young man?"

Margaret Dickinson Shumworth looked over at me, where I stood beside the walker. "You want answers?"

"Indeed."

She responded by placing the set of false teeth into her mouth, where she worked her gums and lips until all was comfortable. She wiped her hands on the knees of her pink velour pants. "Pass me the walker."

I dragged the walker over to her and she pulled herself to standing.

"You want answers? They're in the woods."

"In the woods? You mean up by Shutesbury?"

"No, my friend," she said. "The answers are right here, in these woods. Go on. You'll see."

Despite the clear delivery of her words, this Margaret Dickinson Shumworth seemed to be suffering from dementia.

"I don't see how that can be."

"I don't imagine that you can. But it's true. Answers are right there, if you're brave enough to look."

Perhaps, I thought, it might be good to humor her, this strange remnant of The Sisters. I gripped my cane in my right hand and took a few steps forward.

"Go on," she said. "Even you can move better than that."

I took a few more steps. She stood, hands gripped on the walker, watching me. I was aware of how ridiculous it all was, but didn't know what else to do. There was a woodpecker knocking away at something in there, hidden by the greenery, and I thought I would go look for it, pretend to see it, and then come back. Maybe then she would be willing to share her secrets with me. With this plan in place, I willingly went forward the few more steps until I was at the very perimeter of the lawn. I looked over my shoulder to see who else was about, and there were at least a dozen people, but of the same variety as in the lobby—people in chairs and on benches angled to capture sun. I wondered if any of them could move, or even see at a distance of farther than six feet. Still, I was curious that there might actually be something in the woods. And if there wasn't, well, even better. I parted the curtain of vines and, stepping between two birches, escaped the flat expanse of cultivated grass.

It was the smell that hit me first. Something had died back there.

I thought that Margaret Dickinson Shumworth might be a very figurative sort of lady—a concept suggested by her reading of Emily Dickinson—and that she was perhaps giving me a metaphorical equivalent of what had happened to Bakely. I tucked my head into the woods, but couldn't make out anything. I ventured forward with the tip of my cane sinking in the mud. A few feet in, I saw the first squirrel. It had been decapitated and was, of course, dead, but a soft wind was stirring the fur of its tail in a way that suggested, if not exactly life, movement. There was another dead squirrel two feet away, with its intestines unraveling out of its tiny gut. Further in, I managed to make out a patch of calico fur. She was still active, this Sister, this Margaret Dickinson Shumworth. She was still active and when I heard a twig snap behind me, I knew I was in danger. In the pooling sunlight I felt a moment's warmth and bravely turned to see what had followed me. There she was, The Sister, hands on walker, hair pulled tight. Her eyes had a strange, snakelike hardness and she was watching me. Above me, the squirrels chattered their warnings, rattling branch and leaf, but I stood earthbound, the air catching in my throat. "The Sisters . . . The Sisters . . ." I said, struggling with words.

"What about us?" she said.

"You're monsters! Bacchantes!"

"You're the monster," she said. "You know absolutely nothing about Emily Dickinson."

And casting aside her walker, The Sister took a step forward, and then another, teeth bared, shortening the distance between us.

I live in Amherst, Massachusetts, where the cult of Emily Dickinson is thriving. This made me think of other cults that buzz around the theme of womanhood, so my story is a somewhat humorous recasting of a troop of Bacchantes, who, in classical mythology, are followers of Bacchus/Dionysus who liked nothing better than to get really drunk and then go running through

the wooded mountain slopes of Nysa, often in the nude. Sometimes they would encounter animals that they would tear limb from limb in a spirit of feminine camaraderie. And sometimes they would come across unlucky young men, who would meet the same fate.

—SM

SAWDUST
Edward Carey

I remember them, though I was only a child. They would always be together. If you looked out for them you might see them on a street corner, or you would come across them at dusk leaned up against a tree, heaving and muttering. Mostly, though, they weren't noticed, they could be standing right next to you and you wouldn't see them until suddenly you knocked into them or one of them tugged on your sleeve. They were around us, all the time, but not really seen.

They were the same size and the same shape as each other, both had thick hips and thin hair. It was certain that they were very old. They lived together in one of the basement flats in one of the old fifties blocks built after the war. Their clothes weren't like any other clothes we'd seen, they were ancient and colorless. When they spoke their voices were very quiet, like gases. Sometimes, if you stopped still and looked out for them, you might see them sitting on the side of the road as the traffic went past, one using fingers to comb the hair of the other, very carefully, the other grinning. I saw them once upon a pavement, standing together holding hands and crying.

They were not twins, they were not even siblings. They were husband and wife. They had married and made their lives together long ago. They did not shout against the world like so many others, but played out their days with small noises. Slowness was theirs and quietness too, they would be thrilled by the slow fall of dust, and waited for it as others do for snow. They were young once, it is presumed, and in their youth there was likely a difference in their faces, one was probably taller than the other, one slimmer. They could be easily spotted then, one from the other. In those long-ago days there were other people in their lives presumably, they moved about, they entered other people's houses. But slowly, so slowly I suspect they didn't notice it at first, there were ever less people, until at last it was certain they had only each other, there was no one else for them, and nowhere else but the small rooms of their lives. Then, year by year, I think they must have grown alike. There are some gaps of course. There are unknown chapters, I shall fill them. I can manage.

With only each other to look upon, no other faces to tempt them, no other life to behold, they became twins of isolation. Looking in the mirror was the same as looking at each other. This happened slowly, but they noticed it, and encouraged it, they delighted in it. It was the greatest defense they had against the world. This concentration on each other became so strong, so essential to them, taking up so much of their day, that everything that was not each other became very confusing. Even to think of someone else, some strange vaguely remembered person from their past, would send them into howls of pain and distress.

They were not sure if they had any children. If they had had them, the children surely had gone away and never called upon them anymore. Some mornings they were sure there were children, but by evening they doubted it again. Sometimes, in unison, they put their hands out as if they were holding a baby, they remembered something about the marvelous weight of it.

They slept a lot. They lay in their old gray bed with its gray sheets, and pulled thick blankets of dust over them. When they slept, and they slept for so long, their long lank hair grew in their sleep. It stretched from one head to the other, intertwining, tying together. When they woke at last they would sit together undoing their hair, but giggling at how their hair had stretched out one to the other, keeping company while they dreamed.

They did not eat much, they needed very little. More and more it became hard for them to eat. They picked at things, most of their plates remained untouched. They bothered less and less about cooking. They would snack on crumbs. Soon enough they found dust itself was sufficient food. They had bowlfuls of lint, they gathered up the dust under their bed and ate it together. They ate the books upon their shelves, they ate old photographs the subjects of which were confusing to them. They ate moths and loved to feel them fluttering inside them, flies they ate, spiders too, though reluctantly, because spiders were so good at catching the flies. Day by gray day they went on, together always together. Waiting for their greatest fear. Waiting for the days to run out. Knowing that the last day should come. Waiting in terror that one should die first and so leave the other horribly alone. This, more than anything, disturbed them. They frequently gently poked each other to make sure that they had not died between blinks.

IT so happened that one night there was a knocking upon their door. No one had knocked upon their door for many years and the noise was unfamiliar to them. But there it was again. The strange noise. They couldn't find it at first, they looked everywhere in their small rooms, and at last they became brave and admitted that the noise came from outside. How that ruffled them. There were always noises from outside, the shouting of people, ambulance and police sirens, radio blasts, all this was familiar to them and was not spoken of, but this outside noise, unlike all the others, was very close, was just the other side of the door. There was only an inch and a half's thickness of door between them and some other someone, some alien, new person, some stranger, some would-be trespasser who was knocking upon their door as if he had the right to do it. Perhaps, they wondered, if they were very quiet the someone would go away. And so they stayed very still by the door and waited. But the knocking came again. And then, after a moment, again. The someone was not going away. It was the old woman, at last, who had the great idea.

"Open the door?"

The old man stared at her for a long while, much impressed, before proposing an idea that was really an extension of hers, "Turn the handle."

"And let in," the old woman said.

"Shall I?" asked the old man, his hand near the doorknob.

The knocking came again.

"Make welcome," the old woman said.

"Make dinner," the old man nodded.

"Lay table."

"Tablecloth."

"Cutlery!"

"Fork and spoon to the left!"

"Knives on the right!"

"Side plates!"

"Oh, yes, side plates by all means!"

"Salt."

"And her husband, pepper."

"Do it then, pepper husband. Open the door."

"This door of all doors, salt wife?"

"That's the one."

The knocking came again.

Before the door was opened there was no knowing what sort of someone there was on the other side. The old woman had secretly hoped for a little girl, very pretty, in a dress, holding a balloon. The old man had pinned his heart on another old man, jovial and with a strong handshake, holding a bottle of wine as a gift. But as the old man's old, old claw-hand touched the doorknob and even, to the gasping of his spouse, twisted it, as the secret was at last to come out and for it to be suddenly revealed which of all the possible humans, which particular one was there upon their threshold, the old man closed his eyes, the old woman her hands covering her eyes stood back.

The door was opened.

They did not see him at first because both their eyes were closed, and not seeing him, and not hearing him, they feared together very much that there was no one at the door after all, that it had all been a trick of a heating pipe arguing with itself. (An excitement like this had happened once before, it was a radiator, sputtering with trapped air.) Slowly, similarly, they braved themselves to look and found that a person was there. An actual person. The shock of it.

Not a small girl with a balloon.

Not an old man with a bottle.

There stood before them a young man, in his early thirties, tall and slim and wearing a suit. His hair, which was dark, had been carefully combed. He was clean shaven. A handsome young man, in polished lace-up shoes. His face was pale, his eyes were blue. His nails were well looked after. His tie might have been silk, or cotton or nylon. His shirt, his shirt was white. He stood there, oh he stood there, a man in a suit.

"Hello," said the old woman after a while.

"Hello," said the old man immediately after his wife.

The man in the suit looked down at the old couple, his eyebrows, which were dark, seemed to frown slightly.

"You're just in time," said the old woman.

"Perfect timing," said the old man.

The man in the suit looked at them.

"Come in then, come in. Husband, ask him in."

"Please, please, come along in, won't you? Please?"

The old woman took hold of the stranger's hand, that is to say her old withered hand, so small and fragile, so gray and liver-spotted, so gnawn and unclipped, took his immaculate youthful hand, and gave a tug upon it. She shuddered and delighted in the unfamiliar touch. And the man in the suit stepped in, he was in their territory then.

The old woman led him into the kitchen, the old man took out the one still working chair in the house, though it creaked terribly and was decidedly wobbly, and gestured for the man to sit. The chair was dusty, but the man sat. The chair groaned briefly but made no further complaint.

"How nice that you came," said the old woman.

"How good that the chair fits," said the old man.

The old lady thought about a tablecloth and not having such a thing, settled at last upon the old sheet of their bed. She laid it on the table. The old man put a chipped plate in front of their guest. The old woman put down a rusted fork and a teaspoon, for they had no larger spoon in the house. They searched about for food. They took a yellowed book from the shelf and plucked it, they lay the old pages out in a salad. They sprinkled it with dust and mites. There was an old broken clock, they gutted it, and it plinked and pinged into a bowl. They seasoned an old bed spring. They presented rashers of old wallpaper. They garnished a roast of old shoe with moth and carpet fluff.

All these were carefully placed in bowl or plate, cup or glass, and put before their visitor. When they had finished, and this took them a little while, a great many dishes, plates, and bowls were set before the young man.

"Napkin!" shrieked the old woman.

"Munchkin!" answered the old man, for these were names they had called each other a very long time ago, and they had forgotten them. To be reminded was a sudden and absolute joy.

"Pork roast."

"Lamb chop."

They laughed.

"Mr."

"Mrs."

"Binky."

"Bunky."

Other things seemed to be returning to them. And suddenly, they did not know why, there was sawdust on the floor which had not been there before.

"Green grow the rushes oh," sang the old woman.

"I had a little nutmeg," sang the old man.

The old people stayed together at the other end of the table and gave their visitor encouraging looks. They licked their lips. They swallowed. The visitor looked at all the food. There was new sawdust all over the floor.

"There was a young boy in my class, he was blind in one eye, I remember that now!" said the old man.

And the visitor ate some clock and as he ate it the clock seemed to turn to soft pasta and to smell so beautifully. And as he ate it seemed to the old people that the young man grew a little bit bigger. And there was more sawdust on the floor.

"There was a girl, she had freckles and glasses and stooped a little, we went everywhere together, we swore we'd always know each other," said the old woman.

And the visitor ate some dust and the dust seemed to turn to soup. And the sawdust was all about on the floor.

"There was a girl, she was older than me, I kissed her once," said the old man.

And the visitor drank old water and the old water seemed to turn to wine. And there was the sawdust.

"There was, I remember, I remember, a young man in a cap, with a scarf, bicycling by," said the old woman.

"That was me. That was I!" cried the old man.

And the visitor ate some shoe and the shoe seemed to turn to beef.

"And there you were! Taller than me," said the old man, "taller and so, so lively, alive, and golden."

And each time the old people spoke it seemed there was more sawdust on the floor. Now the old people were a little frightened of the sawdust but they could not stop speaking now that they had started.

"James and Henry and Richard."

"And Harriet and Edith, Iris and Maureen."

"And Edwin."

"And Alice."

"And Cecily."

"And Mildred."

"Hubert."

"Winifred."

"Annabel."

"Eustace."

"Percy."

"Oh, oh, and there was a little girl."

"Oh!"

"Oh!"

"Oh!"

"Oh!"

And they held each other then, and their visitor who was now so much bigger and taller that his head was nearly touching the ceiling finished his plate and on the floor there was sawdust up to their ankles, they didn't like to mention it, how had it come there, they didn't like to think of it at all, for it was frightening to them. The visitor put down his fork, he put down his spoon. He drained his glass. All the plates were empty. He sat there huge and observant, and they, the old ones at the other end of the table, looked up at him, sawdust to their knees, and shivered.

"Did you like it?" the old woman asked.

"He did! He ate it all up!" observed the old man.

The visitor put his hands in his pockets and took out some coins, they clinked upon the table.

"We don't want money," said the old woman.

"No need for money," echoed the old man.

The visitor picked up the coins and put them back in his pocket.

He stood up. He looked down upon them, he scowled slightly, he walked out of the kitchen, moving easily through the sawdust, but crouching somewhat he reached their front door.

"Oh!" said the old woman.

"Oh!" said the old man.

The old people followed, wading through the sawdust. Again it was the old woman who spoke first, "Thank you for coming, we don't want money, we wouldn't want it. What we do want, what we need, if ever it was to be wondered, is not to be left alone, either of us. Don't let one of us die before the other."

They followed him out of their dark flat. Some sawdust spilled into the corridor, messing it up.

"Oh!"

"Oh!"

They crowded around after him. They had reached the outside of the building then, they were standing on the street.

"Oh!"

"Oh!"

The visitor, so tall now he was the height of buildings, looked down upon the small and old people. His hands stretched out. With one hand he took hold of the hair of the old woman, with the other the hair of the old man. And he pulled the hair upward. He pulled them and he pulled them, and they screamed and stretched. Very soon the old man and the old woman had stretched to the height of buildings. Long and thin they had become now. Their hair had grown into strands of thick wire. Their bodies were stiffening, were turning to wood. Soon they were two long poles. The last to go were their faces.

"Oh good-bye, good-bye, my husband."

"Good-bye, good-bye my wife. Oh."

The visitor in the suit stalked off into the night leaving them there.

IT took us a few weeks to notice the old couple weren't around anymore. When had we last seen them? We couldn't exactly say. Slowly, over time, I pieced it all together. Weeks before, a suited man had come knocking on all our doors, and no one had let him in. Our parents despised salesmen touting objects and religion, they were not to be tolerated. The only people to open their doors were the old ones in the basement. The suited man had been everywhere else by then.

It was all so long ago.

I was just a child then.

THEY'VE pulled down the apartment block now, it's no longer there. A car park stands in its place. When the workmen came to clear the place out, the old people's apartment was found empty of people, a great number of plates upon the kitchen table, a great deal of dusty sawdust upon the floor, no one knew where it came from. And no one knew where the old people went, or even what their names were. But I have seen them since. May I tell you? There are two more telegraph poles than there used to be, I'm certain of it, and these two have certain dark knots of wood near the top, almost like faces. The strands of wire pass from one to the other. You don't believe me? You can see them for yourself, on the corner of Church Street and Park Road. Take the 27 bus. They're still there. Among us.

I chose the myth of Baucis and Philemon because, going back and rereading myths, I was surprised and moved at how gentle this story was, that it was principally about an old couple who wanted to die together at the same time and so avoid the survivor's devastating grief.

—EC

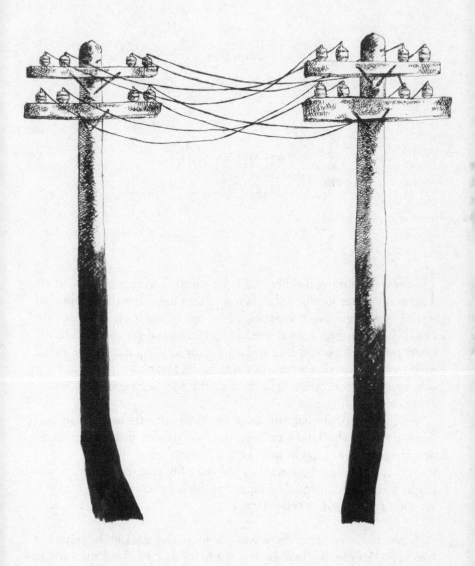

Brownies

FRIEND ROBIN
Maile Chapman

I knew well that my mother had been wanting to move closer to me for some time, so when she took a fall on the sidewalk outside her senior apartment complex back east I broke her lease and brought her to Nevada. For several weeks she rested and recuperated in my guest room, with a soft bed and a window looking out over a dwarf pine tree. Where that pine tree came from, I don't know. It isn't native to this place. Very little is. But the sun is magic, and hardy things tend to thrive here.

We didn't openly acknowledge that the reason for her fall had been a stroke, the kind that rears up in a sudden intense headache and then pulls out again like a tide, leaving minor impairments in its wake. Fortunately, it was a mild one. But unfortunately, it was the kind that often signals a bigger problem on the way. But, again, we didn't discuss it in those terms.

FOR her to buy a house here was my idea, though I let her think it was hers. I'm sure by then she was ready for a place of her own where she didn't have to be tidy or presentable in front of me, where she could drink wine, watch television, and putter around unobserved.

We found a townhouse on the other side of this complex, being sold by a family in another state whose elderly mother had passed away several years before and who couldn't wait out the busted housing market. Over the course of just a few weeks the documents were overnighted back and forth and the sale was done. They'd cleared out their mother's valuables long before, and they asked us to just keep whatever furniture or household clutter we wanted, and donate the rest of the personal effects, if we wouldn't mind.

Her new townhouse had the same floor plan as mine, in reverse, but with a ghostly odor of old plywood, dusty carpet, and dry stale air vents. We'd seen it before we made an offer, of course, but we hadn't been back inside since the inspection, not until after the house closed, when, keys in hand, we came to make plans. It was much dirtier than I remembered.

"How do you feel?" I asked, suddenly wondering if we'd done the right thing.

"Wonderful," she said, and went upstairs. She turned left at the top and disappeared into the master bedroom as if she'd been doing it for years. I thought she was taking stock of what the rooms would need, but when she didn't come back I went up after her. I found her supine on the bed and I was sure she'd had another stroke, until I saw that she had carefully pulled back the stiffened bedspread and was lying on the sheet, as you do at a motel when you're afraid of the filth on top.

"Ma," I said from the doorway.

"I'll start sleeping here tonight," she said.

"Let's have somebody come in and clean up first," I said, though I welcomed the idea of her moving in right away. Not because I didn't want her to live with me, but because it was inevitable, and she'd only be a few hundred yards away, after all.

"I can clean my own house," she said.

"No, Ma, I'll get someone else to take care of it."

It was too hot to linger, and I was wary of turning on the air conditioning because of what might come flying out: bugs, mites, skin flakes, scorpions, spiders—who knew how many opportunistic creatures were tucked away inside the walls. I made her leave before I turned the unit on, and when I locked the front door behind us I didn't let her take the key. Not until I could get the place in order for her.

———

I took advantage of the deals advertised online these days: four hours of licensed housekeeping for cheap, including a full carpet shampoo (stairs extra); pest control for indoor and patio (plus garage); plumbing tune-up and hot water tank flush. Painting the walls and ceilings. Electrical service for dead outlets on the right side of the house. Grout steam-cleaning. Everything I could think of.

At the home inspection stage there had been the usual minor issues, nothing big and certainly nothing to stop a sale, especially such a convenient one, but enough to occupy my attention. I hadn't paid attention to the contents because I'd been busy looking through them to the walls and fixtures, the pipes, the electrical box, the dodgy-looking popcorn ceilings. It didn't particularly register that the clothing hanging in the closet upstairs was the wardrobe of the woman who'd lived there before. Her coats, blouses, slacks, and skirts all hung neatly on the rails, and her shoes were lined up neatly underneath. So it took me quite a while to realize that my mother had—either from confusion or laziness—begun wearing the dead woman's clothes, instead of laundering her own in the washing machine out in the garage. I didn't realize until I found her dirty laundry in a big pile on the stained concrete where the dead woman's car had once been parked.

I knew then that I'd have to hire help, someone to check on her, someone to do her laundry and change the sheets but also to help clear out the closets and get rid of the clothes, throw away the cosmetics in the bathroom drawers. I talked to a couple of home-care agencies. A few different people, vetted by them, came to help for an hour here and there. I met each of them. We didn't give any of them a key. My mother was still in charge. She seemed to improve, and I was relieved that I didn't have to worry quite as much.

WE fell into a pleasant, easy pattern. I picked her up for dinner a few times a week, and, if we timed it right, we'd get the early bird special at the steakhouse just around the corner. She kept me informed about the people I hired to come and fix things. At some point she began referring to someone in particular, someone she called *the girl*. The girl was here today, she'd say. The girl did the dishes. The girl watered the plants. She's good company. She's a good girl. Too bad she wasn't the most dependable girl—sometimes she didn't show for days at a time. But when she did come, she was a dream.

I didn't remember any girl in particular, but maybe the home-care agency had assigned someone.

"Which girl?" I asked.

"The one I like," said my mother.

"But what's her name?" I asked.

"Eh," said my mother, who could be so very uncooperative at times.

I pressed. "You must know her name, don't you?"

I don't think she did, and this unsettled us both.

Because I wanted to meet the girl I turned up unannounced a few times. Once, I slept on the sofa, because my mother said that although the girl often came late, sometimes she came very early in the morning.

"You're making her uncomfortable," said my mother.

"Will you call me next time she's here? And will you tell her I'd like to meet her?" Of course I'd asked my mother already to do both, and she hadn't.

"Sure," said my mother.

And then I began to think maybe there was no girl.

"You must have done all of this," I would say, looking at the hall closet full of neatly folded linens that I knew I hadn't washed.

"It was the girl," said my mother.

"Which one?" I said, leadingly.

"The one I like."

"The one who's good company?" I asked, losing patience.

"That's right," said my mother.

Still, I didn't push as hard as I might have. Things were getting done around the house, my mother was gaining weight and energy, and, from what I could see in my mother's bank account, she couldn't have been paying the girl much at all. Just pocket cash. Nothing to speak of.

IT was over the girl that we had our first disagreement since the stroke; I'm only surprised it took as long as it did. "You're in a good mood," I said across the table at dinner, in the booth I liked because it was near the window and the salad bar. "What did you do today?

"Today?" She frowned. "Oh, just the usual."

This is the kind of answer that always makes me suspicious, because it can so neatly mask memory trouble.

"What did you have for lunch?" I asked.

"Fruit," she said promptly. "The girl and I had fruit salad. And iced tea."

"Ma," I said. "Where did you find this girl? We're in Las Vegas. Do you know how many bad people there are here? Or not even bad people," I amended, because she was fond of the girl, "but poor people, who might be desperate and selfish?"

"You don't think I can spot them?"

"No, Ma, I don't."

This was much the same disagreement we'd been having for years, in one form or another. I tell her when I doubt her ability to do something, or decide something, and she tells me to butt out, that she can make her own decisions. I never really win, but neither does she.

"Look," I said. "I want to meet the girl. That's all."

"You have," said my mother with such conviction and alacrity that it seemed she must be right.

"I did?" I asked, scanning backward. "When? I don't remember."

My mother smirked. "Odd feeling, isn't it. Not being able to remember."

And then I saw that she was trying to teach me a lesson of some kind, which is usually the way these fights temporarily adjourn.

WHEN you buy a house there are details you can't know until after you move in. In this case, there was a floodlight behind my mother's house, shining down into her patio after dark. It kept the alley safe, and was convenient for the people who walk their dogs, and the people who work nights and come and go like others do by day. But it flickered. Unbearably. I didn't realize until one night when I was taking out her trash, through the patio and garage to the alley. Because I knew the area so well—it was my neighborhood, after all—it hadn't occurred to me to check the place out after dark. I thought I'd been as thorough as I needed to be.

"Doesn't that bother you?" I asked my mother.

"No," she said. "What?"

"That flickering."

"No," she said again.

"It would drive me crazy," I said. "I'll call somebody about it to-morrow."

She clicked her tongue. "For god's sake," she said. "That light isn't going to hurt me."

"That kind of flickering can cause a—seizure." I had almost said *stroke*. "You don't want to put yourself at risk."

She turned away, back to the house, and I thought she might lock me out. "All you do is complain," she said. "You focus on every-thing I'm doing wrong."

As I hauled out her trash can I mentally refuted that. I don't com-plain much. I keep quiet, often. When I went back in she wasn't ready to let it drop.

"Listen, kiddo," she said. "Quit bitching at me all the time."

"Fine," I said, washing my hands at her sink. "I'll stop talking to you at all, how about that."

"I mean it," she said.

"Fine," I said again.

"Your negativity is fouling up the peace."

This was halfway to a compliment about the house I had chosen for her, probably her way of apologizing. I decided to accept it.

"I'm glad you like it here," I said. "I'm glad you find it peaceful."

"Lucky I do," she said. "Imagine if I didn't."

I replaced the trash bag and then turned to see what else needed doing. I was just putting a hand out to gather the recycling when she said, "Don't bother. The girl will be here tomorrow."

I put the garage key away in the kitchen drawer, pushing it back and out of sight. With the other spare keys and loose coins I saw both of her parking permits, neither of which she used herself, since she no longer drove. They were clipped together, untouched since the day I put them there.

"Ma," I said. "Both your parking passes are here. Where does the girl park when she comes over?"

"Nowhere," she said. "She doesn't drive."

"How does she get here? Don't tell me she takes the bus."

"Oh, no," said my mother. "She lives right around the corner. I don't know exactly where, but it's right nearby."

I met the girl just as I was concluding that my mother had been doing all the work herself and fibbing about it. But she was different from whatever I'd expected. She wasn't a girl, for one thing, since she was clearly my age at least, and that's being generous. She looked like a woman who hadn't bothered much with sunscreen in her life and now had the permanently tanned and thinned flesh of some Nevada natives who spend their time outdoors. She wore an old sweatshirt, the cuffs pushed up over her elbows, and her forearms and neck were marked with sun freckles and flat pigment spots. Her hair was short and curly, brown and streaky. Her faded jeans made her look underdeveloped. She was not wholly unappealing, but I was not attracted to her, and I felt a little disappointed.

She was washing dishes while my mother sat to one side in a kitchen chair, chatting with her. She washed the dishes one at a time, placing them in the drying rack, ignoring the dishwasher. It occurred to me uncharitably that if my mother had been paying her by the hour, she might be stretching out the task longer than necessary, maybe stretching everything out in order to get paid a little more. On the heels of this thought I expected her to be wary of me, or to at least pick up the pace for my benefit. But she didn't. She continued working at exactly the same methodical speed. She didn't pause or make any move to shake my hand when my mother introduced her, and she didn't even turn fully around. She was wearing some old flour sack chef's apron, tied with ratty strings behind her back, and the more I looked, I thought maybe I recognized the sweatshirt as an old one I'd thrown away months before. But I guess one gray sweatshirt is much like another.

"This is Robin," my mother said.

"Robin," I said.

"Robin," she confirmed; her voice was raspy, an ex-smoker.

"Nice to meet you," I said, neutrally.

She was looking at me over her shoulder, and her eyes were dark and snappy, pupils big and blown like a doll's. When she spoke, her teeth were good, straight and white.

"Nice to meet you," she said, perfunctorily. And then, before I could say it, she added, "Seems strange I haven't seen you around here before now."

MOSTLY when I came across Robin she was in the middle of some task, washing more dishes, vacuuming the carpet, folding a pile of laundry. She never stopped what she was doing. More than once when she turned to look at me I wondered whether she was on drugs.

But she did a good job cleaning up that house. She and my mother seemed to get along companionably; she just didn't have much to say to me. And so, since they didn't seem to care whether I turned up or not, I relaxed into the new routine. I was busy enough that it was a relief to skip going over to my mother's house every single day, a relief not to suddenly remember in the middle of the night that my mother's trash can had to be put out. It was nice not to have to check her locked mailbox in the mailroom, which was at the other end of the complex from my own. So, even though I was not at ease around her, I was relieved to know that Robin was there. Later I would have even more cause to be glad, because she was there the night my mother had her second stroke.

My mother called me that evening, while I was on my way to the gym, and we didn't speak long. She had a cordless phone that was unwieldy in her hands and she'd irritated me by accidentally pressing buttons with the side of her face. I just assumed she'd had a big sloppy glass of merlot. I told her I couldn't talk then and that I'd call her later, or the next day.

She called again that night, after I'd gotten home. It was a little later than normal, but not so late that I worried automatically.

"I thought you'd be here," she said, without preamble.

"What?" I said. "Why?"

"Just watching TV," she said, thickly. I could hear the phone shifting around in her grip.

"Ma," I said. "Are you okay?"

"Are you coming over?" she said.

"No, Ma, it's getting late. Not unless you need something. Do you need anything?"

"No," she said. I heard the phone shift again, and she hung up, slowly.

It took me, I'm ashamed to say, a little too long to realize the strangeness of the exchange, the vagueness in her voice. I'd been about to take a shower when she called, and I went ahead and did. But while standing under the water I had a bad feeling. By the time I called her back, her line was busy. As soon as I stepped out into the cool shadows of the alley I could hear the big-engine sounds of an idling ambulance, and when I got to her place I found the doors open and her living room crowded with two male EMTs asking questions as they prepared to take her away. They were already packing up their equipment, snapping, tucking, adjusting with efficiency over and around my mother, who looked half asleep. Robin was there. She was the one answering them, standing with her arms crossed tightly across her chest. She was wearing what might have been pajamas—a faded T-shirt, a pair of old drawstring pants. I wondered if she'd been here the whole time, or had happened to come by, or whether my mother had called her after calling me, and whether she'd come immediately, as I hadn't.

"When did—" I started to say, but Robin turned and slapped me in the face so hard that it deafened me for a moment before she backhanded me on the rebound. Her knuckle caught me on the lip, hard and bony.

"She needed you," said Robin, and she pushed me roughly toward the alley, where neighbors were starting to congregate. "Go with her."

MY mother was hospitalized for a week before spending another two in a rehab facility, with a walker, a treadmill, and a physical therapist. This is good news. But it's only good because they gave her a clot-busting drug whose window of helpfulness would have closed, had it not been for Robin calling 911 when she did.

I had no way to contact her, or to thank her, much less make sure she got paid, and she made no effort to contact me. I knew she had a key to my mother's house because whenever I stopped by I found everything in perfect order, the mail brought in from the mailbox and arranged in prioritized piles, the kitchen trash empty, the perishables thrown out, the soil in the plant pots nice and damp.

I wanted to leave Robin something, a token of thanks, at least, until I could catch up with her to thank her more properly. My mother told me, when I asked, that Robin liked sweets, especially sugar cookies and cakes. These struck me as a junkie's preference, but what did I know, and a few days before my mother came home I picked up a big cake with chocolate butter-cream frosting at the nicest bakery I could think of. That cake wasn't cheap. I left it out on the counter for Robin, and when I came back the next day it was gone. No crumbs, no plate in the dish rack, not a sign of it or her. Where it had been I left her an envelope with a check inside, and I wrote the words *Thank You* in the memo line. I left the house feeling pleased. She'd split my lip when she slapped me, popped it right open, but she probably didn't realize. I would never mention the slap, because she had been right. I had been wrong. And when I saw her, I planned to tell her so.

THE morning of my mother's release I stopped by the house to drop off some flowers and groceries ahead of time. When I unlocked the door, I found that Robin—or someone—had been there during the night. Couch pillows and magazines were thrown around the living room, and there was a dark, greasy-looking path worn into the carpet leading all the way to the kitchen, as if dirty feet had been trudging back and forth, back and forth all night. I thought I was seeing it wrong. The air conditioning was on high and the air was freezing, but even so there was a fetid odor; the kitchen trash can was stuffed, and it reeked of wet stale coffee grounds. All of the recycling bins were full as well, and as I looked dumbly down at the empty wine bottles I thought, *My god, Robin must have had a party.* The refrigerator door had been left open. There was grit on the kitchen table, rice on the floor, a broken bottle of vinegar in the sink. Harder to explain was the drought in the soil of the burnt-looking plants in their pots. The last time I'd looked, they'd been thriving.

I went up the stairs with my phone in my hand, on guard in case someone was still there. The linen closet had been emptied onto the floor and my mother's bed was heaped with unwashed laundry, but nothing seemed damaged, just disarranged and dirtied. The mirror in the master bathroom was flecked with dried pinkish-white foam, probably toothpaste spatter. The bath towels—damp and streaked— were wadded in the tub. Alarmed by more foul odors, I flushed the toilet, twice, without lifting the lid.

I spent an hour on the phone with cagey maid services who wouldn't give estimates over the phone, and who charged exorbitantly for same-day desperation calls. It cost me a lot to get someone to come clean the house quickly enough to bring my mother home as planned; in fact, it was roughly twice the amount of the check I had left for Robin. And finding an emergency locksmith to come out and rekey all the locks right away was expensive too. Robin hadn't cashed the check; at least I had the satisfaction of canceling it.

I told my mother about the wrecked house and the cleaning plans I had to scramble to make, but she just asked me to pick up another cake, any old cake would do, and she put it in the freezer for the next time Robin came by. She didn't seem to understand when I told her that Robin had turned on us, for no reason.

"You must have offended her," she said.

"How?" I said. "By giving her presents? Who in the world would be offended by a nice cake and some money?"

I was angry, but she wasn't well, and I didn't push.

She'd been lucky, again. She had a weak left leg and some balance trouble, and she would have to walk with a brace, at least for a while, but she insisted that she could go up and down the stairs without help. She refused to wait for me to come over and assist her. She'd been given a list of light exercises and she practiced them throughout the day. She spent most of her time in the front room, watching TV, standing near the window with one hand on the back of the couch for balance, slowly repeating the gentle movements, over and over. But I knew she was also keeping an eye out for Robin in the common area and walkways.

During her three weeks in the hospital, my mother lost what she had gained with Robin; she lost the weight, the energy, and all the good new color in her face. What kind of person arrives, and helps out, and then undoes it all in one petulant day? What kind of person disappears with no explanation? I don't want to hear from Robin. I don't need an answer. But she owes us both an apology.

"You'll never see her again," I said. "She doesn't care about you."

"Don't be so dramatic," said my mother. "She's my friend, not yours. Why should you care if she turns up or not?"

"Promise me you will not let her back inside the house."

"No, I won't promise that," said my mother. "I can't keep the place tidy by myself. Anything that girl does is helpful."

This is how our disagreements go. With me being taught a lesson, whether I understand it or not.

This story is about a Brownie, a type of household spirit or hobgoblin who tidies houses at night. Brownies don't like to be seen or thanked and they get angry

if you try to pay them. They also dislike gifts. They tend to wear old rags, and become upset if you try to give them nicer clothing. Brownies don't like to be offered food, though small amounts of cream and bread or cake are acceptable if left without a fuss. They like domestic animals and bees and sometimes become attached to one member of a household, usually an older woman, and they react badly if that person is mistreated. If you offend them, Brownies turn malicious.

—MC

The Caliph of
One Thousand and One Nights

THE VEILED PROPHET

Text and Illustrations by David B.

—*Translated from the French by Edward Gauvin*

The Veiled Prophet 1

David B.

It was during the reign of Harun al-Rashid, the Caliph of the Thousand and One Nights.

Hakim al-Muqanna practiced the impure trade of dyer outside the walls of the city of Merv, in Khorassan.

One day a white shape appeared in the sky. People thought it to be the Simorgh, the legendary bird of Iran.

It was a giant piece of cloth.

It floated down and stuck to Hakim's face.

He tried in vain to tear it off.

Someone recognized, within the veil's folds, the face of Abu-Muslim, hero of Khorassan, defender of the oppressed, who had been assassinated one century earlier by the Caliph al-Mansur.

Hakim, God has spoken! You are the re-incarnation of Abu-Muslim the valorous!

The revolt erupted right away. All the Caliph's men were slaughtered.

Before his enemies' bodies, Hakim changed his face.

Look! He has the face of the prophet Mohammed!

He changed again and again, ultimately assuming six different aspects.

The educated recognized Jesus, Moses, Abraham, Noah, Seth, and Adam.

One man parted the veil...

...and dropped dead at the veiled prophet's feet.

One year later, Hakim al-Muqanna had established his kingdom and defeated seven armies that had been sent against him.

The Caliph Harun al-Rashid enjoyed taking nighttime strolls in Baghdad, in disguise, to observe his people's joys and sorrows.

One night he decided to take the game one step further by going to spy on Hakim in his lair.

Having turned over the reins of state to his vizier and his executioner, he crossed his empire all the way to Khorassan.

Underway, he stopped in the caravanserais, where travelers were discussing the veiled prophet.

Clearly, he has no face.

His face is like a mirror!

His face is that of an ephebe of great beauty.

Behind his veil there is emptiness. This revolt is founded upon wind!

Whosoever looks into it sees his own soul!

The people who look at it die of love on the spot.

This wind has raised a storm that will fall back upon his followers.

Some cannot endure this vision.

There is no more beautiful way to die!

And so the Caliph saw the veiled prophet assume various shapes under his eyes.

He arrived at Hakim al-Muqanna's camp without a hitch.

Much to his amazement, no one tried to check his approach.

Harun al-Rashid walked through the ranks of the veiled prophet.

He arrived in a room where corpses were slowly desiccating.

Hakim was officiating from a recess in the wall.

There is no obstacle separating me from the world. You are free to gaze upon me!

Behind you, the corpses of those who dared.

And before you, a thrilling mystery.

I have come but to bring you a present, O Prophet!

It was a mirror. The Caliph hoped that this naive gift would compel al-Muqanna to unveil himself.

He slipped the mirror under his veil.

When he handed it back to Harun al-Rashid the mirror's face was dark.

Every day, the veiled prophet would preach to his troops.

This world does not exist! It is an illusion!

The real world is behind this veil. But you cannot see it without perishing!

Here, there is neither law nor religion. The violation of every law is the first step toward the real world.

At night, he used the women in his harem as if he were plowing a field.

All of them he took, one after the other. He was creating children with new eyes, he claimed, who could gaze at his face.

By day, he showered his followers with hammer blows.

He forged new men who would be capable of breaching the veil and reaching the real world.

The Veiled Prophet 2

At night, the sounds of a work site issued from his chambers. The lights of a forge could be glimpsed through the windows.

The veiled prophet explained that angels were building a face for him.

Now al-Muqanna proclaimed himself to be the entire world incarnate. He demanded to be worshipped as such.

Some faithful had yoked themselves to this task and spent their days and their nights enumerating his infinite names.

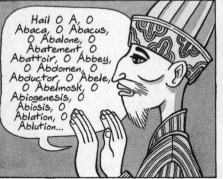

Hail O A, O Abaca, O Abacus, O Abalone, O Abatement, O Abattoir, O Abbey, O Abdomen, O Abductor, O Abele, O Abelmosk, O Abiogenesis, O Abiosis, O Ablation, O Ablution...

This "Road of the Names," as it came to be called, was strewn with corpses.

One evening, the Prophet announced that God was preparing a new flood and that he, Hakim al-Muqanna, would be its instrument.

He kept within himself the martyred bodies of all those who had been oppressed since the epoch of Adam.

On the day of reckoning he would vomit the fruits of his entrails onto the world.

Listening to the veiled prophet's followers, the Caliph Harun al-Rashid understood that this deluge was intended to restore a Golden Age, that of the ancient Kings of Persia, and to annihilate Islam and Arabic domination.

The prophet was worshipped in the guise of a flame on the branch of an almond tree and one could discern the ideal city within this flame. Statues representing fabulous beasts were being erected.

It was said that Simorgh the bird strode at the head of this veiled man's perennially victorious army.

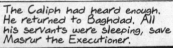

The Caliph had heard enough. He returned to Baghdad. All his servants were sleeping, save Masrur the Executioner.

It is as if you have looked death in the eyes!

I did not even have that fortitude.

This man in his desert is more powerful than I.

He has only overcome provincial troops. Your army will crush him.

What can my army do against a deluge?

The Veiled Prophet 3

On each side the armies were readying themselves.

The spies spied, the scouts scouted, the patrols patrolled.

One night, I slipped into the veiled prophet's chambers as he lay sleeping...

Then I slipped my hand under his veil.

I pulled out a handful of sand.

I drew aside the veil and took one step forward.

And then?

Noth-ing...

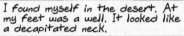

I found myself in the desert. At my feet was a well. It looked like a decapitated neck.

At the bottom of the well, my face was reflected in water dark as blood.

Above the well, a giant moon crushed the desert.

I took one step back and I found myself back in the veiled prophet's chambers. I fled that very night.

A desert... a well...

It is from this well that will emerge the rain of corpses announced by al-Muqanna!

?

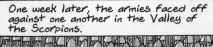

How can one battle an army of the dead?

One week later, the armies faced off against one another in the Valley of the Scorpions.

The Company of the Crows launched itself against the Men of Iron.

From a wooden fortress, the Caliph observed the battle with his executioner at his side.

The battle was inconclusive for a considerable time, but as the evening wore on, the veiled prophet's men began to flee.

From the well emerged a first body: That of Adam.

Then Eve's followed, and Cain's and Abel's.

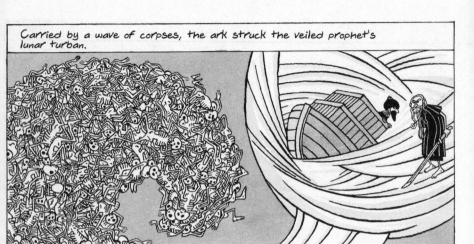

Carried by a wave of corpses, the ark struck the veiled prophet's lunar turban.

There! Al-Muqanna's hammer! It must be ours!

I'll go!

The Caliph Harun al-Rashid diverted the torrent of corpses, ripped the veil, destroyed the desert, bashed the turban to bits!

He then pushed back into the well the veiled prophet's various remains.

The Valley of the Scorpions was empty. When the Caliph and his executioner gazed into the well, cloudy water reflected back their image.

Nothing is moving!

He is dead!

Their return was silent and inglorious.

The hammer is heavy...

The city of Baghdad was lit up for the Caliph's return, but no one celebrated his victory.

Without knowing exactly why, he sensed his victory to be illusory. One night, the answer came to him.

The sky was black as the walls of a well. The moon, minuscule, appeared to be a distant aperture!

Suddenly the veiled prophet was framed by the aperture.

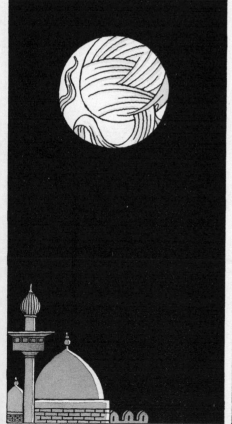

And then the Caliph realized that he was nothing but a dead man, scrabbling amidst the others, at the bottom of the well.

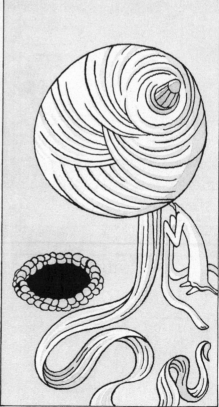

HENRY AND BOOBOO
Elanor Dymott

It would be eight years before he told her he'd killed them. Or at least, before he told her he held himself responsible for their deaths, which at the time were put down to natural causes: dehydration, the heat of the sun, overexertion.

When at last he said it, standing in the kitchen and looking not directly at her but just to one side, she reached out a hand and turned his face toward hers. She held his gaze, this nineteen-year-old boy who was her son, and told him not to be so silly. She called him Rich, not Richard, and asked if he'd finished packing and did he realize what the time was he'd be late for his train?

"Of course you didn't," she said. "It was an accident, you know it was. I know it was. Everyone said so the next day, once they'd all calmed down and worked out what happened. Come on, we should've left by now. It feels like it's going to pour down any minute and I want to get back before it starts."

There was a look on her face, though, of something like fear. He'd seen it there before, but only once or twice and not for a long time now. When he was little and woke in the night he would go to her room and she'd open her eyes to find him sitting on the empty side of the bed. She'd say, "What are you doing, Rich?" and he'd say, "Just checking," and she'd say "Checking what?" "That you're all right," he'd reply. "That's all."

And later, when he grew suddenly and was taller than her and came home from school one day with a bruise on his face. She'd cried and he'd laughed, lifting her up and circling the kitchen with her in his arms saying Mum, Mum, Mum it's what boys do, I had a fight, get over it.

This time, in the early morning brightness, the look disappeared as soon as he saw it. It wasn't that she hid it, as such, but rather that it was replaced by a racing kind of concentration, which he understood to mean she was having trouble remembering exactly what had happened at Edward and Annie's house on the day he was talking about. That she was trying hard to recall the sequence of events leading to her carrying the stiff little guinea-pig-corpses out to the car and taking them away, Rich on the backseat beside them, tears falling fast down his face.

"It's the least—" she'd said to Edward's mum, after Annie, who was only eight, had screamed and run upstairs to her bedroom. "They're so upset, your two, it's best this way, isn't it?" And when they'd got home he'd slammed the car door by accident and she'd said, "Rich, for goodness' sake," and he'd shouted at her then, that if his own father hadn't fucked off he wouldn't have had to spend so much time with Edward's dad and he hated it there anyway and she said, "Rich," again and he said, "What? So I'm swearing. Get over it, I'm eleven years old already."

She'd lifted the bodies from the car and taken them through the house to the garden where she buried them underneath the plum tree and climbed on the ladder that stood there. She picked enough for her to be able to call up to him, later on, "Do you want crumble or pie?" so he knew it was all right and he wasn't really in trouble, and nothing he ever did would stop her loving him.

THIS morning she said, "Look at the time, Rich," and he could see she'd given up trying to remember and was thinking only of the train, and of the fact she'd reserved him a seat and he'd have to stand all the way from Leeds to London if he missed the one she'd booked him on.

"But I have to tell you," he said. "I mean, I know you think you know but you don't. I didn't tell you before, not properly."

"You were children. Things like that happened all the time."

"Edward was my best friend, Mum. Do you get what I'm saying? I mean, I'd have done anything for him. You know, anything. And the way I saw it, he'd have done anything for his sister. For Annie." And before he'd even started he was backtracking and asking did she remember how they first met?

"No, Richard. I don't. I'm sorry."

She started to clear the breakfast things from the table, making more noise than she needed to.

"Through a hole in the frigging fence, that's how. I mean, I couldn't even see the guy. All I could see was his nose. And I was three years old. We both were. But we knew it even then. Friends for life."

She turned her back and began to wipe the work surface. He could see she was listening, though, so he carried on.

"It matters to me, all this shit. They were my idea, you know, of what a family should be. Or of what a family could be. And that place. Man, I mean. It was like some kind of paradise for me. A haven."

"Rich!"

"I'm just saying! I know, it sounds kind of out-there, but that's what I'm saying, don't you get it? I want to talk about it. It's important."

She gave up then and they sat at the kitchen table. Five minutes in she stopped looking at her watch and he knew he had her, and that she wasn't thinking about the train anymore.

THEY'D lived next door to each other at first, Edward and Rich and their families, with driveways side by side and gardens that adjoined. The hole in the fence had been a small one, but big enough for two little boys to look through and watch each other playing. And big enough for Edward, eventually, to cup his hands around it and call out. Rich had gone over and put his finger up to the hole and stuck it through and Edward had bitten it and that was how it started. Rich went screaming in to his mum and she washed it and put a plaster on just because he wanted her to, and because it would make him feel better. She was still laughing when she carried him back out to the fence and said, "Hello! Is there anyone there? I'm looking for a cannibal, a very short one I think!"

She became friends with Edward's mum that day. Afterward, the boys were rarely apart and at first, Edward quite abandoned his little sister, Annie. When they were eight, Rich's mum found a note in the kitchen from his dad saying he'd gone and would be back the next day to collect his things. That same year, Edward's parents, Michael and Sandra, moved to the other side of town. There would be another baby one day, they said, and with Edward and Annie wanting their own rooms, it was simply a question of space.

In the years that followed, she got into the habit of dropping Rich off there every Saturday, and when one summer she'd said were they sure, and she was embarrassed, really, to impose, Sandra said Edward and Annie wanted him to come, and it was no trouble and he was so well behaved. "He's family," Michael said, and he tousled Rich's hair and Rich didn't know whether he minded or not. "It gives us more time with the little one if they've got him to play with," Sandra said. "And goodness knows we need it now."

Michael taught him how to do the things boys do on Saturdays, like saving a goal or oiling a chain or cycling without stabilizers, and Edward was easy about sharing his father's attention. If it was him and Rich on their own, Annie would sometimes join in as well. "She's the best girl in the world, my sister," he told Rich one day in the woods behind his house. "She's like a boy almost. I mean she can kick and run, but she's a girl."

The boys made a den out there, stringing a rope between two trees and draping over it an oilcloth they'd found in Michael's shed. They took a couple of empty paint tins to use as stools and started to collect other things during the week, things to furnish it with. Edward went on his own sometimes, after school, and Annie went with him if he asked her to. Rich was annoyed at first but then he would see what they'd done and he was glad of it. He went one afternoon to his dad's shed, right at the bottom of his garden. There was an old transistor radio with a stash of batteries, and some reels of string and fish wire and a pair of pliers, almost new. He found a couple of flashlights as well and during the next few weeks he took these things, one by one, hidden in his sports bag. He thought his mum hadn't noticed but then one Saturday morning she said did he want a hand taking any more stuff to the den, and what about a thermos flask, would he like to take some soup to share with Edward?

Before long it became not a den but their kingdom, with stakes

holding up the oilcloth on either side so it draped to the ground, and
with tarpaulins and tires and bracken also, forming the outer walls.
The whole thing was true enough to the color of its parts, and positioned far enough away from the path, to remain hidden from anyone passing. When, one Saturday, Rich asked his mum to drop him
at the edge of the woods instead of at Edward's house, and to help
him carry a worn-out rug along the path, with a pair of cushions
discarded from her garden as well, it was complete: a world apart
from the world.

Every Saturday morning the boys would cycle through the woods
to the den, and every Saturday lunchtime they would arrive home at
the same time as Annie got back from her friend Charlotte's. The
two girls would have spent the morning playing with Charlotte's
dolls' house, which was bigger than Annie's, or making up a dance
routine. She would run straight in from the car and show her parents the moves, if she could remember them, and she'd show the
boys as well if they let her, and then Rich would offer to help Sandra with the lunch and she would always say no, don't worry, sweetheart, go in the garden and play with the others. The three children
would take the guinea pigs' cage onto the lawn and lift them out
and put them straight on the grass, enclosed in a ring of wire netting brought by Michael from his shed, and then they'd watch them
play.

Henry, the elder of the two pets, belonged to Edward. Booboo,
the younger and therefore the smaller by at least an inch or more,
belonged to Annie.

"That's a stupid name, Booboo," Rich said, the first time Edward
took him to see them.

"It's not. Annie chose it. She's only eight, you know. And she's my
sister so shut up about it."

"All right, but I'm just saying, it's a kid's name for a pet."

"She is a kid."

"Henry's a much better name."

"Of course it is, I chose it," Edward said, and then he punched
him, and said don't say anything to Annie about the name, and
Rich punched him back and they rolled on the floor in each other's
arms.

They hardly ever fought, not properly. Edward was taller than
Rich so it wouldn't have been fair, and Rich didn't think he should,

since it was Edward's house. But sometimes he'd forget and something would happen. Once, Edward won a fight and held Rich on the floor in his dad's shed. He picked up a power drill and put it to his best friend's head for a joke and they scuffled and he kept it there and pressed the tip against Rich's skin, hard. They spent the rest of the afternoon looking at everything on Michael's shelves. They sniffed bottles of turpentine and they took a screwdriver and levered open a tin of varnish and sniffed that too. They found a stack of sandpaper squares and rubbed them against each other's faces until their skin turned red and then, at the last, they followed the wire to the wall and saw that the drill had been plugged in all along, the socket switched on. Years later one of them would bring it up, and they would talk about what would have happened if Edward had pressed his finger on the button.

When they were called in for Saturday lunch they'd leave the guinea pigs in their enclosure to have what Michael called "a good runaround." And then they'd leave them a little longer so that Edward could clean out the empty cage while its occupants ran wild for a time. He did this on his own, and Annie and Rich, who were never allowed to join in, would sit on the shed steps and watch him, or kneel by the wire ring and watch Henry and Booboo run and chase each other.

Rich asked Annie once why her brother wouldn't let him or Annie help.

"They're his, aren't they?" she said.

"One of them's yours, isn't it?"

"Sort of. Well, no. He got it with his pocket money, for my birthday. He let me name it but he says it's his because he bought it. He says I'd get it wrong if I cleaned the cage."

"So that's why he does it himself?"

"And because he loves them, doesn't he?" Annie said, and she spelled the letters out, "L-O-V-E-S's them. I don't mind, anyway. Why should I?" but Rich could see she did, a little.

At the end of the day, after the boys had played football and Annie had done her piano practice, everything would be put away and Henry and Booboo would be lifted back into their cage and brought inside and the children would sit down to eat with Sandra and Michael, all of them together, before Rich's mum came to fetch him home.

She would ask him, over breakfast on the Sunday morning, what they'd had for their tea the night before. Usually he'd mumble something about not being able to remember, but didn't she know they called it dinner, not tea. Sometimes, though, he'd be kind and tell her. He'd say it was nothing special, just fish fingers and peas, and that it was never as nice as the food she cooked, and could he have toad-in-the-hole for lunch, with gravy?

HE'D gone especially early to Edward's house on the day it happened. Michael had promised the boys he'd help them, either with the model airplanes they were painting in his shed, or with the wooden swords they'd found in the attic a month or so ago, stuffed in a box of his own childhood toys. Paint peeling and rusted nails coming loose between the handles and the blades, these last needed what he'd called "a complete overhaul." Until then, he'd said, they shouldn't use them unless they wanted splinters and tetanus, all at once. As for the airplanes, it was the fiddly bits they'd left till last. When he asked them one day what they were waiting for, and why they'd started a job if they weren't going to see it through to the end, Edward told him they didn't want to spoil what they'd already done, and couldn't he finish it off for them?

On this particular Saturday Michael said they'd only have time for one or the other, the airplanes or the swords, and he'd only help them if they started straight after lunch and tidied up afterward. His other condition, agreed the previous week, was that they take Annie with them to the woods in the morning. Charlotte was at her grandmother's, so Annie couldn't go there to play, and because Sandra wanted a rest before lunch, Michael had to look after the baby.

By half past nine the boys were in the shed, deliberating over their day. They reached an easy agreement about prioritizing the swords, neither of them much minding the patches of gray under the airplanes' fuselages, or the smudges they'd made around the points where the wings joined the bodies of the craft. The swords were the thing, they'd said straightaway, both of them having sustained splinters in the palms of their right hands when trying to use them the previous week. Where they differed, though, was on the question of whether the bargain was worth it.

"I don't see why we're going if she has to come," Rich said. "Let's stay here, do something else. It's going to be hot. Let's ask your mum if we can turn the sprinkler on."

"Don't you like her?"

"I'm not saying that. It's just less fun. We can't ride our bikes if she comes. We'll have to walk all the way. And she's boring."

"She's not," Edward said, and he took Rich's wrist and gave him a Chinese burn, hard and fast and silent. "She's my sister."

Rich shook him off and stared at the red bracelet appearing on his skin.

"What's so great about her anyway?" he said. "She's just a kid. She's just a girl."

"There is something great about her, actually."

"Like what? Forget it, I'll stay here. You two go."

"Fine. Your loss. Like you said, she's just a girl."

"Huh?"

"That's what I'm talking about, idiot. I bet you've never seen a girl close up. She'll show you everything. She shows me, I mean. She'll show you too, I reckon."

"What do you mean, everything? Everything what?"

"Are you stupid? She takes off her clothes and lets me look. I asked her on the way home from school one day, in the den. She didn't say anything, she just did it."

"What clothes? Her top? You mean she takes off her top? So what. Girls are the same on the top."

"I mean everything. I've seen everything. And last time I touched it."

"What do you mean, it?" And then, when he told him, "That's gross, Edward. You're making it up, I'm going to tell her." He walked toward the shed door.

"I'm not making it up," and he grabbed Rich by the wrist again, harder this time. "Don't tell her I told you. It might not be the same with you. I mean, she might not show you. Anyway, you don't want to come, so forget it. That's what we'll be doing, though, if you stay here."

"Shut up," Rich said. "Just shut up," but he didn't try to pull his wrist away. He stood, for a moment, with his face right next to Edward's. He listened to the sound of their breathing, out of sync and low, and he wondered whether he had a choice.

"All right," he said, and Edward released him. "All right," he said again. "But you have to ask her, not me. She'd definitely say no if it was me."

As they sat on the shed steps in the sun and waited for Annie, Edward revised his suggestion a little.

"Maybe you're right," he said. "Maybe she wouldn't want you to see. Maybe it wouldn't be the same."

"You said she would," Rich said. "You said she'd show me everything. You said you'd ask her." He stood and looked down at Edward, sitting on the steps. "I'll tell her anyway, even if you don't."

"All right," Edward said, standing as well and placing both his hands on Rich's shoulders. "But we'll have to do it differently, or she might tell Mum."

He told Rich where on the path he should say he had a tummy ache and was going back to the house, and which way he should circle through the woods in the other direction to reach the den first. He said he should position himself on the side of the den with the slit between the tarpaulin and the oilcloth, where neither of them had quite been able to make them fit together. He should squeeze himself in between the ring of bracken and the tarpaulin and the cloth, Edward said, and he should kneel on the ground, right next to the slit. And then he should lean his head over to one side so that he would see everything Edward saw, without being seen himself.

"She'll never know," he said. "She'll never look there, not if you stay still and keep your mouth shut. And no loud breathing either."

ANNIE didn't seem to care when Rich announced, halfway there, that he was feeling ill. She didn't even look at him when he said, "I'm going back. You two go on." Once he'd cleared the corner and was running, that was what he thought of first: the fact she hadn't cared.

He took the course Edward had described and he ducked under bracken and swooped into hollows and up again, weaving through leaves and trees like a dog, or a hare being chased. The day was warming up and he was sweating as he ran and he wished she'd said good-bye, at least, and then he wished she'd never come in the first place, and he'd never agreed to Edward's plan, and that instead they were cycling the circular route together, just the two of them. He reached the place where the woods became like the surface of the moon, dry little dips and hummocks completely clear of bracken.

On their bikes they would get up speed and come out of a hollow on their back wheels, shouting sometimes but other times only concentrating and riding hard and fast and skidding against each other and when they got there they'd throw their bikes down and run inside. And then he remembered his mum, suddenly, and what it had been like carrying the rug to the den with her, and he stopped and wished she was there now. He felt his T-shirt clinging wet to his back and he listened to his breath, panting. He listened as well for their voices on the path but he heard only the woods and he ran on and suddenly he'd arrived, and he was squeezing between the bracken and wedging himself in and he knelt down and before he could think anymore he could hear their voices and he leaned his head to the side and it made a noise against the bracken. He could see Edward moving the flashlights around a bit and angling their beams and then he could see Annie and she was taking off her top and she turned around and said to her brother, "Come on then, what are you doing? Take yours off as well."

"I don't feel like it this time," Edward said, but then he did and the two of them stood side by side, bare-chested, undoing their shorts. When Annie pulled hers down her underwear snagged on one of her sneakers and Edward left his shorts undone and knelt down in front of her and unlaced her sneakers and took each of them off. He pulled her underwear off as well and she half sat, half fell down. She lay on one of the cushions and said the same again, "Come on. What about you," but Edward backed away to the other side of the den. "I just want it to be you today," he said. "Just do that thing we did last time but I'll stay like this."

She started to stand up again and reach for her underwear.

"That's not fair," she said.

He stepped toward her and pushed her down, quite gently, and they fought a bit but only halfheartedly and Annie was crying a little and then she said all right, all right and Edward knelt in front of her.

"I just want to see it, Annie, we don't have to do anything if you don't want to. I just want to see." He moved to one side as Annie looked down at herself and opened her legs and Rich saw everything Edward could see, and he didn't want to carry on watching but he did, until Edward crawled forward and Rich couldn't see Annie anymore apart from the bottom half of one of her legs. And then a short while later it was over, and Edward was doing up his shorts again and going to the other side of the den.

Edward played with the dial on the radio, not saying anything to his sister, and she stood and started to get dressed. When there was only her shirt left she picked it up and began to walk toward the place where Rich was kneeling behind the tarpaulin. His breath came faster and he considered moving his head away from the slit, but she was close enough to hear even the slightest movement so he tried to stay completely motionless. She stopped right in front of him. She did up the last of her buttons and she dropped to the floor and put her head down to tie her laces and still he thought it would be all right and she'd turn and walk away, but then suddenly he couldn't hold his breath anymore and it came out in a kind of a grunt, and she flicked her head back and saw him.

She covered her mouth with her hands. She stared at him. And then she took her hands from her mouth and she turned and spoke to her brother and her voice was flat and hard.

"Let's go home. I'm bored. Come on."

"I don't want to yet," Edward said. "Let's stay."

"Why?"

"Why not?"

Rich didn't move. He was pretty sure that if he left, and they decided to go as well, they'd see him through the trees, setting off in the other direction. He didn't know what Annie would do if that happened. He was confused by her response, and because he didn't understand it he was scared by it as well. He felt angry with Edward, really angry, but he was excited, somehow, that he'd watched. And then, immediately, he was angry with himself for feeling excited.

As soon as he heard Annie say, "All right then, but I don't want to stay for long, I want to go home," he squeezed himself out and ran, feeling sick at the thought of her telling her parents. When he reached the house, he hid behind the shed just as Edward had told him to. The other two arrived and Edward hung back while Annie went inside. Rich waited for a minute, then he slipped from behind the shed and kicked a ball with Edward, not looking at him, until Sandra called them in for lunch.

AT the table he could barely swallow, let alone speak. His plate was still half full at the end of the meal and Annie said, "Hasn't your tummy ache gone yet?"

"I knew something was up with you, sweetheart," Sandra said, starting to make a fuss, and Annie said, "Didn't he tell you, when he got back?"

She looked at him and he thought he would be sick, right there on his plate, but then Michael said, "Right lads, let's be having you, swords or airplanes, which is it to be?'

"Swords," they said, and he told them he'd take them to pieces first. They could help him strip off the old paint after that, and sand the pieces down as well. When he'd nailed them back together they'd see about whether to do a repaint or a varnish. "Cage first, though, don't you think?" he said.

Sandra told Annie to go and do her piano practice, and then she put her hand on Rich's head and said no thank you, he didn't have to help with the washing up, why didn't he help Edward carry the cage out instead and find somewhere to have a quiet sit-down if he was feeling poorly? "But make sure you sit in the shade," she said. "It's hot today, that'll be what's making you feel funny."

Rich was relieved, but then Annie said, "He shouldn't be on his own if he's poorly. Can I do my practice later, when they're doing their swords?" and Sandra said, "Yes, of course you can, go on then, the two of you." She kissed Rich on the top of his head as they left and he felt even sicker than before.

Annie went first and when the two boys came after, carrying the cage between them, she was sitting on the grass.

"She saw me," Rich whispered, as they negotiated the steps down from the kitchen door, one at a time and slowly.

"What?"

"She saw me."

"No way. She would've said. She would've screamed or something. She's always screaming."

"She saw me, just before she said she wanted to go back."

"She didn't, I'm telling you."

They were getting closer to her now and she turned to look at them. They put the cage down and Rich went to the shed. He stepped inside, feeling her gaze on him. When Edward came in to fetch the wire netting, he said it again.

"She did."

"Look, Rich. Either she did or she didn't. What's the big deal? She probably wouldn't care anyway. But I reckon she would've said something by now if she'd spotted you."

"She didn't say anything afterward?"

"Nope."

"She looked right at me, I know it. What did you talk about on the way home?"

"Nothing much. She mainly talked about Charlotte, and what she was having for her birthday. Stuff like that. Forget it." He walked out of the shed and Rich stayed where he was, thinking about Annie not caring.

She was still on the lawn when, shortly afterward, he followed Edward out. Edward lowered the guinea pigs into the ring of wire netting and then he went to the other side of the garden and began to clean the cage. Rich sat down next to Annie and they watched Henry and Booboo. Annie got on her hands and knees and crawled in front of him. She started to stick her fingers through the netting, trying to feed them bits of grass.

"Annie, they've got enough already. It's everywhere."

She ignored him.

"They're running around on the stuff, Annie. They don't need any more, do they?"

"They're my guinea pigs, not yours."

"Guinea pig," Rich corrected her. "Only one of them's yours. Only Boobee, and he's not even yours really, is he?"

"Booboo," Annie said. She stopped what she was doing but she stayed where she was, down on her hands and knees. "It's Booboo, not Boobee."

He saw then that she was crying, so he put a hand on her shoulder. Edward, who was watching from the other side of the garden, walked over and pushed Rich away.

"Why're you crying, Annie? What did he say to you?"

"Nothing. He didn't say anything."

She started to cry even more.

"Ignore him, Annie," Edward said. "Don't take any notice, whatever it was."

She wiped her nose on her sleeve and started sticking pieces of grass through the netting again, crying at the same time.

"Annie, I'm going to ask Dad what we need for the swords. You can come with me if you like," but she shook her head and he went inside on his own.

The kitchen door swung shut behind him and Rich stood up from the grass.

"Annie. I'm sorry."

"What about?"

"The den."

"What about it?"

"You know."

She turned to face him and she wasn't crying anymore but her cheeks were bright red and her lower lip was moving up and down. "I hate you."

"He told me to do it, Annie. He said I should hide there. He said you wouldn't mind."

"I hate him too. I hate both of you. Do you always do everything he tells you?"

"No, I don't. I didn't want to do it. He pretty much made me. And I'm sorry, OK? I said I'm sorry."

"Doesn't make any difference."

"Tell me what to do then. Tell me what will make a difference. I mean, I don't know what to do."

"Don't do anything. And don't tell your mum. Don't tell my mum either, or my dad."

"Of course I won't. But you should say it's OK, if someone says sorry to you. My mum says so."

"It's not OK. It's not enough, saying sorry. It doesn't change anything."

"What else can I do then? What?" He began to feel desperate, and just as he became aware of an actual pain in his chest, as though he had run too fast, or as though there was something properly wrong with him, Edward appeared on the steps outside the kitchen door.

"He really told you to do it?" Annie asked Rich, her voice quieter than before.

"Yep."

"Well then. Do something to him. That's what you can do if you want to make it OK." Her face was white, not red, and her lips set hard on it. "Do something to my brother, and then I'll say it's OK."

EDWARD and Rich were in the shed. Michael had told Edward to get whatever he thought they needed, and to put it all in front of the shed door; he'd be out in a minute once the baby was settled. Neither he nor Rich knew exactly what to take, so they decided they'd bring everything that seemed halfway likely. Edward was up a stepladder, passing things down to Rich. They'd already made a little pile of things by the door: sandpaper squares, a small box of nails and a hammer, some pliers to take the old nails out and paint brushes for the repaint, or the varnish, whichever they ended up doing.

"How d'you get the old paint off then?" Rich asked, taking the pot of varnish that Edward handed him next.

"That's what the sandpaper's for isn't it, dumbo."

"All right," Rich said, placing the varnish by the door with everything else. "My dad used some kind of liquid, that's all. For chairs and stuff. I helped him when he did our kitchen chairs."

"Well, your dad isn't around to ask, is he?"

Rich stepped over to Edward and kicked the bottom of the ladder.

"Sorry," Edward said. "Didn't mean it. Take these, anyway. Maybe you're right," and he passed a couple of plastic bottles down to Rich, who put them by the door with the rest. "Turpentine or the gel stuff in that bottle, one or the other."

"I told her," Rich said then.

"Told her what?"

"I mean I told her I saw. And I said sorry."

"What d'you do that for?"

"Because I am. Sorry, I mean."

He looked at Edward, waiting to hear his reaction before he decided what to do next.

"Well, she obviously doesn't mind, does she, if she's still talking to you. She'd have told Mum already, if she minded. So that's that then, isn't it?" and he jumped off the ladder. "What did you think of her, anyway? She's amazing, isn't she? She just does it."

"She didn't just do it, Edward. You made her."

"Give over. She just did it. You should come in, next time. We'll do it again and I'll ask her if you can come in when we do it."

"No way. That's gross. You're gross, Edward."

Rich walked to the door and picked up the box of nails. He took both swords in his other hand and went out of the shed, slamming the door and leaving Edward to bring the rest on his own.

THE heat had risen by the time they began, and that was how Michael explained their silence.

"Get a drink of water first, if you've had too much sun. And if it's not the heat, then cheer up a bit, will you? Whistle while you work, or something, come on, I'm trying to have some fun here."

They started to make a bit of an effort, both of them, but before long Michael had given them separate tasks so it didn't matter anyway. When he'd pulled out the nails, and when the boys had sanded off most of the paint and the swords lay in pieces on the grass, Michael sent Edward into the shed for some wire wool. "Might as well do it properly if we're going to do it at all, son," he said, picking up one of the bottles. "And bring a few pairs of gloves as well." A minute or two later, Edward stuck his head around the shed door and threw some gloves on the grass. He called out that he couldn't see any wire wool, and what did it look like, exactly, and Michael said, "For goodness' sake, Edward."

He went in to help him, and that was when it happened.

Annie stood from the grass next to the wire enclosure and walked over to Rich. She bent down and picked up the bottle of turpentine. She looked at the label, and then she held it up to Rich and pointed at the orange box with the black fork of lightning right across it and the word HAZARDOUS in capital letters beneath. Still holding it up, directly in front of his face now, she turned and nodded toward Henry and Booboo.

That was all she did. Just that, and nothing else.

She put the bottle down and walked away. At exactly that moment, Michael and Edward came back out of the shed and Michael handed Rich a pair of thick rubber gloves and a piece of wire wool. He daubed some of the contents of the other bottle onto one of the sword pieces and passed it to Rich. "Make sure there are no flecks left. Rub and rub and then keep on rubbing some more."

When Rich looked after Annie she'd gone. The kitchen door swung shut, then open, then shut again.

Thinking back in the days that followed, he would wonder whether, in fact, he'd imagined it. But at the time there had been no doubt in his mind, nor any ambiguity in her gesture: that was what she wanted, and that was what he'd do.

He had to wait for his chance, though, and it was a while before it came. As Michael daubed and the boys rubbed and scraped and handed the pieces to him, there was the sound of her piano practice, floating from the living room window. When Michael began to nail the pieces together again, "I think a varnish will do the trick, boys, don't you?" it stopped. Edward's sword was being done first and

Rich sat on the lawn while they worked. He tore off pieces of grass and made a pile of the sharp little blades between his feet and then he looked up and saw her at her bedroom window. He raised his hand and nodded. "All right," he said silently. "I'll do it. Not yet, though. Give me a minute." He was shading his eyes from the brightness of the sun, so he couldn't be entirely sure, but he thought she nodded back at him.

IN the end he left it so long he almost faltered. But then he saw her again at her bedroom window and Michael and Edward were both in the shed, putting everything away. He checked through the window and Michael was on the stepladder and Edward was passing him things and Rich picked up the bottle and ran. He struggled with the top and had to try more than once, kneeling with it on the grass and pressing and turning, pressing and turning, and then it opened. He reached over the wire netting and held it upside down and sprinkled it on the grass, as much as he could and as quickly as possible, and then he ran back, doing up the bottle at the same time and spilling some of the liquid on his knee. He put it down exactly where he'd got it from and when he looked, Henry and Booboo were already nibbling at the spot where he'd sprinkled it.

"It must have been," he said to himself. "I mean, that must have been what she meant," and then Edward came out and saw the bottle and picked it up and took it into the shed, "One last thing, Dad," and Sandra stood at the kitchen door and called out, "Dinner! Dinner everyone!" Michael and Edward emerged from the shed and Michael said, "Come on, lads. Job done. I'm starving!"

Edward started to walk toward Henry and Booboo and Rich's stomach heaved inside him, turning and moving up toward his throat, but then Michael said, "Come on, boys, come and eat first." Edward did as he'd asked and they went to the house, the three of them together. "They're all right out here a bit longer," Michael carried on. "It's cooler now. And you can collect your swords after dinner as well. The varnish will have dried and we can give your mum a demonstration when she gets here," and he tousled Rich's hair and they stepped inside.

"IT probably won't work, anyway," Rich said to himself at dinner. He tried to block out the crashing of knives and forks. "They'd know, as soon as they tasted it. They'd know not to eat it, wouldn't they?" He gazed at Annie, chewing slowly, and then he realized she was staring back at him and he lowered his head and didn't look at her again. Instead, he did what his mum called his zoning-out thing and simply stopped hearing the conversation, stopped being there. He thought about what they'd do with their Sunday, the two of them, and he decided he'd tell her next week that he didn't feel like going to Edward and Annie's and could they go on a Saturday outing instead, him and her and nobody else? "Anywhere," he'd say. He didn't mind where, he just wanted a change.

And then his mum was there, suddenly, and they were all in the kitchen together and she was ruffling his hair and saying, "Golly, Rich, you've caught the sun haven't you?" and Sandra was saying, "Sorry, I should've given him some sunscreen, I didn't think." His mum said, "No, don't be silly, it's good for him to get a bit of color," and Sandra went to get the baby then, to show Rich's mum before bath time. Edward said, "I'll go and fetch Henry and Booboo in, shall I?" and Annie went with him and the next thing that happened was that the rest of them were standing there with the baby and they heard Annie scream. She ran back in, straight through the kitchen and into the hall, and they heard her gasping and stumbling on the stairs and she screamed again and her bedroom door slammed shut.

Rich stepped outside onto the lawn. Edward was walking toward him, Henry in one hand and Booboo in the other, both as stiff as little boards or blocks of wood. He dropped them and ran to the shed and back again and he was carrying one of the swords and he had Rich on the floor and was pressing its blade flat against his windpipe and Rich couldn't breathe and Michael was pulling Edward off him and Sandra and his mum were there and Sandra was saying, "Sorry, I'd better go up to Annie," and Rich looked up at the house from where he was lying and that was the last thing he saw before he and his mum left, taking Henry and Booboo with them: Annie, standing at her bedroom window, framed with the light behind her. Sandra appeared in the frame as well then. She was holding the baby in one arm and she folded Annie into her with the other, pressing her into her chest.

THIS morning, sitting opposite him at the kitchen table, his mum said nothing at all. She waited until she was sure he'd finished, and still she said nothing. Not until he'd gone upstairs and come back to the hall with his bag, and she was putting on her coat and the sleeve caught on her watch and she swore.

"Sorry," he said. "I've made us late for the train," and she said, "Oh, it's not that, don't be silly, it doesn't matter now," and she pulled on her coat and buttoned it up.

She opened the front door and the rain had begun, slanting in great heavy sheets. They went out through it and sat in the car and they watched the wipers and waited for the engine to start. She wiped the steam from the windshield and tried again, and then when it started, they sat for a minute or two until she was sure it would hold, and finally she pulled out of the drive.

Neither of them said anything else and he wondered whether perhaps he shouldn't have told her about Edward and Annie, and what had happened in the woods. He kept trying to look, to see her eyes as she drove. To work out if he'd done the right thing. She kept her face dead ahead, though, and he couldn't tell what she was thinking until they were about halfway there and he heard something else under the thud and suck of the wipers on the glass. Slightly out of time and its pitch higher, but only a little, it was the sound of her weeping and trying to hide it. He saw one tear fall from partway down her cheek and splash on the steering wheel and he stopped looking.

"I'm sorry, Mum. I'm sorry if I upset you."

"Really, it's not that. It doesn't matter. I just wish—" She wiped her nose on the sleeve of her raincoat and was silent for a half minute. "I was thinking of another time I took you to the station, the first time you ever went to Dada's? It was snowing, do you remember?"

"No, Mum. I don't."

She said it had been awful, and he'd seemed to have no idea how much she'd hated him going, and all he would talk about was a spider's web he'd found.

"A what?"

"You really don't remember, the very first time you went?"

"No," he said, "I really don't," and she told him he'd found a spider's web in the porch, one that had caught the frost, and he'd come to her in the hall as she was putting the last of his things in his bag and said, "I have to show you something, Mum," and he kept saying it until she stopped what she was doing and went with him, which meant they were late for his father.

"We talked about it for ages. You had a theory about spiders' webs. You'd made a list of the options for seeing them."

"The options?"

"Yes. So you told me you'd worked out you could only see a spider's web if it was snowing and snowflakes had settled on it, or if it was raining, or if it was in bright full sun, or—"

"Oh god, how annoying. I'm sorry."

"No, I liked it," she said, and they stopped at the station traffic lights and he became aware of the sound of the wipers again, back and forth. "I think I've still got it somewhere, upstairs. You'd written a list and you gave it to me and you asked me whether something like that was real, something that was there but that you couldn't always see. Like a spider's web. You had this idea that if the only time a thing could be seen was when it was covered in something else, like raindrops, or snow, then it didn't really exist, the rest of the time."

And then the lights changed and they were pulling up outside the station and he said no, don't worry, you'll get a fine, but she insisted and left the car on the line and ran in with him to buy another ticket, "You can't stand up all the way to London." And then the train was ready and they held one another to say good-bye and people were pushing past them and she said, "Go on, and good luck. Don't worry and don't work too hard they're only exams," and then, "The car, I'd better."

She ran down the concourse and the train was pulling out and he couldn't see her anymore, but there she was, standing at the back of the crowd. She raised her hand and waved, so he pressed his forehead against the glass and waved as well, and then she turned and walked away.

Henry and Booboo is a retelling of the origins-of-dynasty myth of Candaules and Gyges, as set out by Herodotus in his Histories. *King Candaules, so in love with his own wife that he thinks her the most beautiful woman in the world, persuades his favorite body-*

guard, Gyges, to hide in their bedroom and watch her undress. She sees Gyges but says nothing. The next day she offers him a choice between killing her husband for having dishonored her, or being killed himself. Gyges kills the king, marries the queen, and becomes the ruler of the kingdom. I was introduced to the story by Michael Ondaatje's novel The English Patient, *and by William Etty's painting* Candaules, King of Lydia, Shews his Wife by Stealth to Gyges, One of his Ministers, as She Goes to Bed. *Herodotus tells an astonishing tale of manipulation and deceit, and of the ways people find to excuse their own actions. In my retelling I relished being able to explore the spaces he leaves: the things unspoken, the explanations withheld, and the questions unasked by his characters.*

—*ED*

MODERN COYOTE

Shane Jones

After the doctor gave them the choice, they took their baby home.
"He's here," said Ben, into the phone. "They let us leave."

"In the middle of the night?"

"We had to. We were going crazy in there. Five days."

"You should have waited the extra day, the observation day you mentioned before. What if something happens?"

"I have to go, he's crying. Everything is fine."

ADAM ran through the apartment shouting, "I have a baby brother now!"

The place still felt new, strange, and when he entered the back room, the sunroom, he went quiet, turned from the dark and ran to his father, whose voice now filled the baby's room.

"I have a baby brother now!"

"You do," said Ben, touching his phone. "Special."

Sara leaned over the crib and kissed the baby's stomach.

"That room back there is scary," said Adam. "I hate the man who lives next door. I liked living in the hospital because it felt like a hotel."

"The man next door?" asked Sara.

"The one building nothing," said Adam. "He just moves stuff around."

"It's called landscaping," said Ben. "He's making a garden and a patio."

"He's a coyote!" shouted Adam and he ran to the living room for TV time.

Ben and Sara studied the baby's breathing.

BEN told Sara that she should get some rest. The baby—couldn't they settle on a name yet?—kept them up night after night with cluster feedings. This was normal, but felt unusual. The baby's eyes were gray and always open. Ben remembered the last name of the doctor he disliked most—Black.

Ben started bumping into walls, crying in the shower. His work suffered and he made excuses. The non-sleep took a special kind of wear on Sara. On multiple occasions Ben found her pressed against the crib in the dark, rubbing her body on the bars, half asleep, and humming.

"Just tell me he's going to live," she said, turning from the crib. Her body was black.

Ben said, "He's going to live."

"He's okay, right? We did the right thing?"

"I promise. He's fine. He's going to live," said Ben, and he walked from the nursery and into the kitchen where he looked out the window and at his neighbor moving piles of dirt around with a shovel.

DURING dinner Adam refused to eat and couldn't stop staring out the kitchen window at their neighbor, Alan, who was moving dirt around his backyard. There was a pile of red concrete blocks that hadn't been moved since they went to the hospital, in the middle of the night, Alan shouting, "Good luck!" from the backyard. Alan never slept. He worked in the dark. He always wore a baseball cap.

"He's retarded," said Adam.

"Adam!" said Sara.

"He's retarded like my baby brother."

Ben said, "You shouldn't say things like that. Your brother is fine. He just had complications. Perfectly healthy."

"I hate that man," said Adam, standing on the chair and pointing. "I hate the coyote man."

"Why do you call him that?"

"Because," said Adam, "he's a coyote. And coyotes turn other people into coyotes and they live underground together. It's what they do."

"Eat," said Ben.

"Retards!" shouted Adam.

AT work, Ben didn't mention what happened in the hospital—the five days and the wires. He passed his phone around a half circle of coworkers who all commented on the picture of his nameless baby. Megan touched the phone with a finger like she was actually touching the baby's face. Steve, who never smiled, smiled, and said the baby was super cute. When his boss asked him about the dark circles under Ben's eyes, an odd dark blue, everyone laughed.

"We're not getting a lot of sleep, that's for sure," said Ben. "Talk about working two jobs."

"You'll get sleep," said Megan, "when he's twenty."

"A parent's job is to worry," said his boss. "Just be glad he's healthy."

"We are," said Ben. "We are we are we are."

"Get some rest," said his boss.

Ben kept saying, "We are we are we are," until Steve grabbed him by the shoulders and shouted, "Go Giants!"

ADAM didn't come into the living room for TV time for the first time since they moved in. It was the one time of day when they could be together. Adam liked to pick the show, pointing the remote at the television and making a gunshot noise when the channel changed. He stopped at any show with an animal.

"What's wrong with him?" said Sara, sitting on the couch, trying to get comfortable.

"I'll check on him," said Ben. "Maybe he fell asleep."

Ben walked down the hallway, past their bedroom, and toward the baby's room where he heard Adam humming. He remembered that the last show they had watched during TV time was a special on coyotes. Adam had howled like a coyote, neck stretched toward the ceiling fan. Sara laughed and bounced the baby in her arms. When the narrator described a winter starvation scene, a coyote unable to successfully hunt a deer, its rail-thin body skulking a snowy mountain, Adam said he didn't want to watch anymore and threw the remote at the television.

Adam was in the nursery, working. Ben slowly walked in.

"Adam?"

"I am . . . coyote man . . . I am . . . coyote Sam," sang Adam.

Ben couldn't understand what he was seeing.

"I am . . . living in a tin can . . . I am . . . coyote man."

"Is everything okay?" shouted Sara from the living room. "Do you need me?"

Attached to the bars on the crib and to the baby's wrists and ankles were pink colored strings. Ben watched Adam finish tying a long piece of string around the baby's leg. The baby smiled and spit up something yellow. The baby flailed his arms. Adam trimmed the string by using the baby's toenail cutters. He plucked the string and it vibrated. Then Adam continued singing while unraveling more string. He didn't notice his father approaching. Ben counted eight different strings tied to the baby.

"Adam," said Ben.

"Dad!"

"What are you doing?"

Ben began untying the strings.

"It's like the hospital," said Adam. "I re-created all the wires so the baby will live now."

Ben quickly untied the wires while the baby's eyes scanned left to right. There was one wire wrapped several times around the baby's neck. Sara's voice was getting closer. Ben worked faster as Adam laughed and then ran away. When Sara entered the room all the wire was balled up in Ben's pocket and looked like a bird's nest in his pants.

"Old shopping receipts," said Ben.

BEN couldn't sleep. He got out of bed and walked into the nursery where Sara lay sleeping on the floor. He crouched and shook her awake with his hand on her shoulder.

"Is he dead?" Sara said.

"No, he's fine," said Ben. "I have to tell you something."

"Then tell me. Don't scare me."

"Let's go into the bedroom."

From the floor Ben grabbed his jeans he had worn earlier in the night. He told Sara about the strings, the wires, how Adam had tied them around the bars of the crib and around the baby. Like the hospital wires. The odd thing was, the baby seemed fine, actually appeared to enjoy the strings wrapped around him. He looked healthier. He glowed. Sara trembled while listening. Ben held her hand.

"Here," said Ben.

When Ben unfolded the pockets to his jeans, they were empty.

"Looks like you're the one who needs sleep," said Sara, touching his face. "The rings around your eyes. They're blue."

WHILE leaving for work, Ben saw Alan carrying a wheelbarrow full of dirt from the front lawn to the backyard. This is what Alan did every day. The mailman told Ben that Alan never worked a day in his life, that he was wealthy from an automobile accident.

"How's the project going?" asked Ben, smiling.

"Good, good. Want to see?"

Ben followed Alan to the backyard where Alan explained in sweeping hand motions his plan for the patio, a fountain, and a garden. Alan wore his baseball cap so low all Ben could see was a small mouth and several ribbons of greasy black hair that clung to his neck.

"Impressive," said Ben, drinking his coffee. "You've been working on it since we moved in."

"Buddy, it's not a race."

"Right," said Ben. "I know. I wouldn't know how to even start a project like this."

"So, what do you think?"

Ben sipped his coffee and looked at the backyard, which was nothing but a small square of dirt with several bricks placed to form a crude circle. Ben couldn't, even stretching his imagination, thinking maybe something was wrong with him, believe that any work had been accomplished on the backyard. Alan was the hardest working neighbor who somehow didn't work.

"Can't wait to see the finished project," said Ben.

SARA started having dreams. Every night she slept on the floor, in front of the crib, and she listened to his breathing, trying to find the moment where his breath would skip, or worse, stop. Eventually, she'd fall asleep. She averaged two hours of sleep a night. The most common dream she had was the one where a long wire extended from the heel of her foot. In the dream, her body was sky-high and horizontal, floating, limbs flailing, her head fogged in blue clouds as children in a field below pulled the wire from her foot and ran toward a forest made of wires. Sara was a kite. The wire was endless. The children tied her to the forest. When she woke from this dream she sat up and checked on the baby. Then she inspected her foot.

ADAM wouldn't participate in TV time anymore and he wouldn't spend any time with Ben or Sara. When Sara tried to hold him he'd growl and bite her wrists. He said TV time was evil and he was finished with animal shows. All Adam wanted to do was sit on the kitchen counter and watch Alan work, or not work, on his backyard.

"I'm going to catch him," said Adam.

Alan was walking around the backyard, stabbing his toe into the dirt in random spots. He waved at Adam and Adam waved back.

Ben rubbed Adam's back, wondered what was wrong with his son. Maybe the hospital had been too much. Maybe he shouldn't have witnessed the baby with the wires, the IV line stabbed into his hand, the oxygen tube inserted inside his nose. Ben never thought to shield him from the images. Even when the nurse drew blood from the baby's foot, and Adam put his hand over his own face, peeking between spread fingers, Ben let him watch.

"Catch him doing what?" asked Ben.

Adam drank from a juice box and with force collapsed it.

"Being a coyote," said Adam.

THEY took a walk around the block and at each corner Sara made Ben say into her left ear, "He's going to live." When Sara asked Ben to walk around the block again, Ben was thrilled because he thought maybe she was getting her energy back. The birth had been difficult. The five days that followed in the hospital, even more draining. But then she made him say the words, "He's going to live," every twenty feet. It became a game. Ben went along with it. Sara looked indifferent, staring off into traffic lights. The next time they walked around the block, she had him say the words every other step. Alan watched them from his front porch on each trip around the block, his arms crossed over his chest. He wore denim covered in backyard dirt. Sara said: "Just keep saying it until I believe it" and they walked around the block thirty more times with Ben in song.

———

BEN couldn't sleep. He forgot days. The strange blue circles around his eyes seemed to expand and cover his face. In the bathroom mirror, his face looked smaller. When his boss called asking him where he was, Ben said, "It's Sunday, I'm home," and his boss replied, "That's funny, because it's Tuesday." Ben couldn't remember what day it was. He continued looking at the smallness of his face in the bathroom mirror, touching his skin. Any time he checked the time on his phone, he believed it was hours off.

He walked into the kitchen for pretzels. He opened the bag and grabbed several, standing at the kitchen sink, looking out into Alan's backyard. He heard water. There was a stone structure and a black figure standing next to it. The fountain was in place! It was past midnight, but Ben opened the window and whisper-yelled out to Alan that he was doing a great job, very impressive. He could never complete such a job. Ben's father once told him that he lacked "suburb skills."

"Thank you," said Alan. "Slow and steady wins the race, as they say." Alan's shape in the darkness wobbled and shifted, then disappeared. "See, the trick is being calm and patient in life, not worrying so much about stuff. Everything will get done eventually."

Ben took a step back and swallowed. A black figure was walking toward the window. The fountain spewed water into the sky. The black figure was tiny and hunched over and had the head of a coyote. It stopped and howled as water rained from the fountain in diamonds. When the black figure's lips were pressed at the opening of the window, they were Adam's, and he said, "I'm a coyote."

BEN worked three days in a row to make up for missing Monday and Tuesday. He didn't sleep in the hotel, completing project after project on his computer and arriving at the office before 6:00 in the morning. When he came home, Sara was peeling her skin off, standing at the bathroom mirror.

"I went out today by myself," she said, smiling. "This is called a chemical peel. Makes you look younger. I feel better."

"He's going to live," said Ben.

"I know," said Sara. "I'm feeling better. I'm not as worried."

"What about Adam?"

"Still pretending to be a coyote," said Sara. She pulled a wide sheet of skin from her forehead. "He's been spending more time with Alan on the backyard."

Ben put his arms around Sara and nuzzled his face into her neck.

ALAN knocked on the door. When Ben answered he noticed Alan had grown a gray beard and his hat was farther down over his face. His ears were more prominent and they too had gray hair. Orange leaves blew from the branch of a tree and fell on the porch, around the black boots of Alan. Ben rubbed his eyes and he saw pulsating red walls.

"It's finished," Alan said. "Come take a gander."

Ben walked around the house with Alan and stood at the edge of the backyard of dirt. A stone fountain sat in the middle with no running water. There were more piles of dirt and extra shovels. Alan's head was nothing but baseball cap, beard, and smile.

"Ta-da!" said Alan, extending both hands, palms open to the backyard. "Three months' work, and it all paid off. It's all about patience. You either have suburb skills or you don't, Ben."

When Ben looked at the sky he saw a cloud shaped like a coyote. He said to the smiling head of Alan, "Is my son here?"

"Your son?"

"He thinks you're a coyote. He said he was going to catch you being one."

Alan laughed and shook his head. His long black hair swayed and gave Ben the creeps. On the back of Alan's denim jacket was a large patch showing a dream catcher with blue feathers and orange crystals.

"He told me that. He's a smart kid, great imagination. Helped a lot with the backyard."

"Are you?"

Ben couldn't stop looking at the sky. His head felt like it was in the sky. The coyote cloud passed through him in a long breeze. His shoes were covered in Alan's dirt. No worms.

"Am I?" said Alan, who pulled the cuffs of his jacket over his hands, sunk his head into his jacket.

"Yeah," said Ben. "Are you a coyote or not?"

"Depends who you ask," said Alan, smiling.

EVERY hour, from eight in the morning to five in the evening, Ben called Sara from work and left a message saying the baby was going to live. If coworkers were near, he whispered. He sometimes called from the bathroom stall. Ben thought they were over this, but Sara had been cataloging the baby's breathing and had found some discrepancies. She drew charts on the nursery room walls. She used the chemical peels a half dozen times a day and her skin looked burned.

"I think maybe you're overdoing it," Ben said.

"I'm feeling good, Ben. Let me just feel good for a change. You know how hard it's been."

They sat watching television. It was TV time and Adam was in the backyard with Alan positioning a fountain. Sara's face was covered in splotches, the television lighting her up in a horror-movie fashion. In several spots on her forehead was the wet blood of fresh cuts.

"Just be careful," said Ben.

Sara checked her voice mail.

MY son was born to wires.

THE baby was on Sara's chest so she could hear his breathing and write down each breath and the time on a yellow pad she had positioned next to her plate of spaghetti. She filled notebooks by the dozens. Across the table from Ben, Adam wore a coyote mask. He cocked his head from side to side. He pretended to eat by nuzzling his face into his plate.

"Take it off," said Ben.

"Take what off?" said Adam.

Sara kept writing, one ear against the baby's mouth. She sucked on a strand of spaghetti covered in sauce.

"The mask."

"Mom," said Adam.

Ben closed his eyes and saw the hospital room decorated in wire. Alan was there, crouched in a corner of the ceiling. Sara held the baby as a nurse in a red surgical mask weaved a wire basket around them. Alan howled from the corner and vomited dirt.

Ben opened his eyes. The coyote stood on the chair howling. His mouth was coated in blood.

"Can you believe this?" said Ben.

Sara drew clouds on the paper that she drew longer or shorter depending on breaths. Her ear was against the baby's lips.

All Ben could hear now was the fountain from Alan's backyard. Ben stood up and walked to the kitchen window. Alan was in the backyard. His son the coyote threw his plate across the room. There were more fountains, thirty of them, each making a fountain sound but with no visible water. Ben couldn't see the sky.

THE hospital called on a Friday, the day after the pediatrician, and told Sara that the baby had to be reconnected to the wires. She texted Ben at work who didn't read the message until he was about to call in his hourly "he's going to live" message. He tried calling her back, the phone hidden under the conference room table on his lap, but she didn't answer.

Ben stood up with the phone against his ear, calling again and again. Everyone around the conference room table stared.

"If you leave during this meeting," said his boss.

"It's the baby. You don't understand," said Ben. "We were in the hospital for five days. I didn't want to bring it up before. Sara won't answer."

"What's wrong with your face?" said Megan. "You don't look so well."

"I'm sorry, I have to go."

"Let's talk tomorrow," said his boss.

Ben drove home and called Sara who wouldn't answer. He passed a red truck with a stone fountain strapped in the back. Alan was driving with both hands gripped high on the wheel. His beard was massive.

Ben drove through a red light and caused a fender bender. On each call to Sara he left a voice mail saying, "He's going to live."

Ben ran up the driveway and entered the house. The coyote was there, sitting on the couch, his head cranked to an impossible angle. On the television was a fountain spraying gold arcs into the mouths of thirty different versions of Alan. The coyote told Ben it was TV time, come join the family. Ben stepped away from the coyote as he walked, shouting for Sara, the coyote turning his head more and more until his chin was in line with the ceiling.

"He's going to live," Ben repeated through the house. "Sara, he's going to live, okay, I'm coming."

In the nursery, Ben first saw Sara's back. Then he noticed the walls covered in breathing diagrams on top of breathing diagrams. The room smelled like the hospital room and crayons. When Ben walked closer to the crib where Sara stood, she turned and said the baby didn't need the wires.

"What?" said Ben.

"Look how good he's doing," Sara said.

The baby was in the crib, his skin red and bloodied. Ben tried to pick him up, but couldn't because of the softness. He let go of the baby. Ben's fingers were wet. In the crib was the bottle Sara had used for her chemical peels.

"He's a snake," said Sara.

WHEN Ben woke it was dark and he was in Alan's backyard surrounded by nodding coyotes. All the fountains had been moved to the perimeter of the backyard and then the coyotes, including Alan and Adam, helped Ben dig. Wires were underground. Millions of wires and his baby somewhere deep in the wires to be found. He pulled the wires apart like spiderwebs and walked underground. It smelled like the hospital. The walls flashed red and white and a police officer asked Ben what his wife had done. Adam ran ahead of him, telling Ben to hurry up, his coyote tail raised high. There wasn't time to worry. The rushing sound was all fountain.

The taking-off point for this piece is the character of Coyote the Trickster, placed in a modern context. Other mythical themes run throughout as well (for example, the mention of a snake shedding its skin in order to reverse aging). My goal was to write a contemporary story about a couple returning from the hospital with their newborn baby, but have these weird "mythical" happenings interjected. It's a very weird result, I think, and super strange. Part myth, part horror story.

—SJ

Cronos

DEVOURINGS
Aimee Bender

The ogre's wife was a good woman. She was not an ogre, but she was ugly, by human standards, and she had married the ogre because he was strong and productive, and together they had made six small ogre children. The children all took after their father. She had not expected otherwise—one look at his giant teeth, height, and huge features, and she knew his genes had to be dominant.

Years earlier, she had left her own village by choice, traveling up and over the green and rising hills in search of a life for herself, and when she had met the ogre in the tavern, him stretched along the entire side wall, his voice scratched from cigar smoke, she thought she might give the alternate world a chance. Everyone in her hometown knew of the ogres, living up on Cloud Hill like that. With their magical boots, and that hen.

With also, she wondered, other appetites? Later that night, at his home, the ogre had been surprised at her willingness to take off her clothes, since he'd been rumored to eat people for dinner. As she unlaced her blouse, he touched his fingertips to her trembling bare shoulders and explained in his low gravel that he only ate human beings he did not know. I know your name now, he murmured. I know your travels. You're safe. Her eyes were closed, and when she revealed her breasts, he sighed. They were sculpted by a different artist, he whispered to her, with a subtler tool. It was all too much for her at first, overwhelming, but she soon grew to love him and his body, its giant harshness, its gentle gruffness with her. Next to him, she felt herself so delicate. At school, she had been the roughest-skinned, the one with the drooping features, the one no one could ever imagine that way, in a bed. She did not care about not being pretty, but she wanted to be seen as a future woman, as one who could participate, and no high school boy could take that leap. The ogre, however, found her nothing short of revelatory, and the first time he entered her, he shouted with joy.

One evening, after many years of contented marriage, the children tucked in their bed, asleep, snoring faintly, wearing hammered gold crowns with their nightshirts because their father wanted them to feel like royal ogres in their dreams, a human girl and her siblings knocked on the door, frightened. They were lost, and the ogre was out at the tavern, and the ogre's wife opened up, and there they were—a group of six live human kids, with bright hair and red felt hats and snapping eyes, reminding her so sweetly of her long-ago nieces and nephews. The ogre's wife disliked firmly only one aspect of her husband: his interest in eating the children of humans. It could've been me! she told him once in bed, while he twirled and twisted her hair over his fingers. She could not bear to turn the children out into the ogre-filled night, so she hustled them inside and in a fierce whisper told them they could hide in the same giant bed as her own children, but not to make a sound, not a peep! When the ogre came home, late, he smelled them, of course; how could she have imagined he would not smell them? She was half asleep, twisted in the sheets, and hoped desperately that he would just crash out on the sofa in drunkenness. What she did not know was that earlier in the night, the smart little girl leader of the human group had swapped their six red felt hats with the six golden crowns on the heads of the deep-sleeping ogre children, and when the ogre cackled hungrily, bumbling around the house, hunting for the source of the scent, he, of poor eyesight, of booziness, of delirium, ended up eating all his own children due to the swapping of those hats.

In the early morning, the human children ran off, terrified, giggling.

WE skip ahead five years, because five years were full of nothing but searing pain and tears. Five years of lying on the bed unable to move, slogging up to do the basic functioning needed to hold things together, then back to bed. Five years of scathing bitterness at ogres, and also at humans, at where she came from, and the worry that had led her to open the door; I should've let him eat them first thing! she said, weeping into the down of her pillow, though she felt sick any time she had even gotten the hint that her husband had eaten a child. But her *own*! There were two that she mourned the most, much as she hated to admit it to herself, but she had loved Lorraine and Stillford best, the two most complex-looking ogre faces, who had emerged post-utero like gnarled wood knots, and who had turned out to be all sweetness in nature. How they had loved their human mother. They nestled on her lap and nudged their big heads into her shoulders. They were gentle during the breastfeeding, unlike their siblings. Ogres grew teeth early, and she had to stop feeding most of them or they would've ripped off her nipple, truly. She, many times, ran to the bathroom with blood streaming from her breasts from a careless slash, a little ogre child happily lapping up the red drops on the sofa. To those she gave formula. But she was too soft-hearted to decide for them all; for each new child she risked her breast, and Lorraine and Stillford had been different, angled their teeth just so and suckled like little human babies, and perhaps held within their selves some of her human genes that knew not to tear at the gentleness offered. Now they were dead, digested in the system of their father, who had been so angry he split a bone out of his neck while overclenching his jaw and had to go to the hospital where he broke four beds and injured a nurse. He was angrier than ever these days, and their marriage and its focus and tenderness had faded. His favorite had been Lutter, the superogre demon child who was so kinetic she rarely saw him still and who had scraped the walls into shreds with his nails and twice tried to swallow his mother whole. She had let him train with her husband only, and why Lutter, even in his sleep, had let himself be eaten, could only have been due to the deep dreamy trust he felt of the smell of the mouth he was entering, a mouth he knew from its firm position over his shoulder, telling him instructions on how to rip through cartilage and sinew, and an inability, due to that core of trust, to imagine his fate could end this way.

AFTER enough time had passed, she was able to get out of bed for hours at a time. She could go into town and engage in minutes of small talk. She could sit outside on the porch and watch leaves twist on the birch trees. She could read a short article in the newsletter. On this day, a day of change, she cleaned the house top to floor, using swaths of cloth that grew dark with dirt and dust. She swept tumbleweeds of lint out the front door, and poured scrubbing detergent into all the sinks to scour the vast yellowing basins. At the market, she bought root vegetables by the dozen and chickens and sausages. She stuffed the chickens and made a stew and fed her husband who came home ragged from his work climbing mountainsides to look for caves packed with jewels and gifts like the magical harp that that thief Jack had stolen from his brother years ago.

We are pillaged, constantly, said the ogre, laying his loot in a sparkling heap by the door. And they fear us?

He kissed her on the ear, and sat down to roll a cigar out of crisp brown paper and a fist-sized wad of tobacco.

Good stew, human, he said, after dinner.

She cleared the dishes. The ogre did not help with chores.

Please don't call me that, she said, for the hundredth time.

That's right, he said, patting his belly. I forgot; I'm sorry. Love that sausage, delicious. Your best yet. He lit the cigar and inhaled deeply.

She wiped the globs of leftover chicken off the dining room table with a sponge.

While he mumbled to himself, digesting, sleepy, she filled the pots with soap and water to soak and ate a little bowl of the chicken stew behind the counter. She rarely ate at the same table as her husband anymore as she now feared him during mealtimes, couldn't stand to watch him slurp up animals with that vigor and those grinding, pointed teeth.

Husband, she said, putting her bowl aside. She walked out from behind the counter. I have decided I need to go on a trip, she said.

The ogre was finishing his fourth mug of wine. He liked the darkest wine, the red almost black.

Go where? he said, wiping his mouth. To see your family?

She shook her head. Her family lived below, in the people village, and last time she'd been home, before the devouring, everyone had lectured her on ogres and complicity and betrayal. She'd waved them off. He's a good man, she had said. She had not dared show pictures of her children.

I'd like to see something pretty, she said. Maybe a lake?

There's a river that's supposed to be nice a few valleys over, he said, exhaling bracelets of smoke to the rafters.

Okay, she said. A river.

I could go with you, he said, turning a giant brown eye to hers. His eye like a pool hers could swim inside.

A mucky pool.

No, she told him. I need to do this alone.

He nodded. He understood. They each coped in their own way. He had women on the side, ogre women, everyone knew. Maybe she didn't know, but probably. After all, although being with a human was the ultimate in showing off both self-control and status, sometimes a man just wanted a woman like himself. There were no prostitutes in the ogre village, as it was a barter economy and females chose males with equal discernment, but there were a couple who liked this particular ogre and every few months he'd make a little visit as a way to honor where he came from. It's for my mother, he told the ogre-woman once, and she'd laughed and laughed, nude and mottled and calm, sprawled over a mattress, one arm crossing loosely over her forehead.

The ogre helped his wife pack up. He buttoned up her bag and told her he would miss her, which was true. From his plunder, he gave her a magic cloak that would turn her into the color of the dappled light that shot through foliage and also a cake that would become more cake once she'd eaten half. He kissed her forehead, roughly, and she melted a little under his arms.

Do you know how long you'll be? he asked.

I don't know, she said.

Okay, he said. I'll be here.

They spent the night almost close, her forehead pressed against his wall of triceps. Come morning, she walked through the door and into fields of glistening green.

WHAT marriage could recover? She did not plan on ever returning. The ogre wasn't sure but he thought it was unlikely. He was not insensitive, despite all suspicions. The day she left he skipped work and went to the tavern for lunch and drank ninety-five beers. You're a machine! the other ogres said, admiringly, as he slammed down another stein. Foam made an old man's beard around his mouth, and he burped in an echo that trembled the hillsides.

She felt it, his wife, now miles away, following a winding path up and over light rolling hills covered in sage, and dandelion fields, and one meadow of sunflowers swaying in the daylight. She walked and walked until dusk, trying to collect distance under her feet, and then she camped out under a shady elm with her checkered cloth. She unpacked some almonds and dried cherries and she also ate the cake, which would let itself diminish to half and then, under her bare eyes, build itself back up out of nothing, out of air, until it was a full cake again. She was grateful for it, but somehow it also bothered her. Finish, cake, she said, tearing off half, watching it rebuild. Finish! She tore off more than half, the whole, but the cake was unstoppable. Plus, she needed it. What, she was going to trap birds and roast them over a fire? She was a woman who shopped at a market with a wheeled cart and used honey-lavender soap. She drank from her water mug and refilled it at a spring at the edge of the meadow, and before she fell asleep, she sprinkled the remaining cake crumbs around her cloth.

In the morning, she awoke surrounded by expectant-looking crows. Enough! she said, shaking the cloth as they tottered away.

Really, she could've spent the rest of her life there just sitting and feeding those crows and herself with the cake, but she wanted to reach the river.

When she heard a clip-clopping sound, she put on the cloak so that she looked like the dappled sunlight beneath the elm, a particularly glorious sunlit area that did not correspond to the rules of sun location in the sky, but who would notice that except a particularly astute observer of shadows? This was just a human horseman riding along in ogre country, looking to find some treasure like his comrades who had come up here and survived. She watched him, his handsomeness, his vanity and sureness, his sculpted hair and cheeks, his strong hands, his proud red jacket, and she was reminded again why the ogres had attracted her, and why she had loved young Stillford so, his wet brown eyes searching out hers, those sharp smiling crooked teeth. The ogres knew they were ugly and in that they were decent. They did not ever think they could be like this man, she thought, as he galloped off, tossing his head with pleasure. He ducked and rose over hills and she saw it coming before he did, saw the ogre who ran the corner store just out on a pleasant walk in his seven-league boots, rounding the corner and surprise!, what a gift!, and the man too late raising his gun and landing a shot on the ogre's shoulder, which was nothing to an ogre, nothing a little mending at night wouldn't do, a little digging with a fork into flesh to expunge a bullet, and she watched in her cloak as the man was plucked from his horse and eaten whole. It was a horrible sight, one she had tried not to see for most of her wedded life, but on that day she found it almost comforting. Just to see it. Not comforting to see pain and death but just to see what she could not let herself imagine and therefore ruled her. She wept quietly under the tree as the ogre chewed. Then he walked off, rubbing his belly in his boots, a little scrap of red cloth sticking out of his mouth until he reached out a tongue and licked it in, just like a human might do with a bit of jam.

The horse had run off but it circled back after the ogre left, pacing in the field then settling down, and after her shaking subsided, she walked over to where it was grazing. A couple of hours had passed, and the horse seemed focused on the clover and calm. After all, the eating had been brief, and the man had barely had time to scream, and ogres were just about food, not about power play or torture. They were just endlessly large and hungry beings. She mounted the horse and rode lazily along, digging around in the thick leather packs on the side where she found some snacks—turkey jerky that she used to love, made in the village, and some peaches, a rare delicacy for her as ogres couldn't care less about peaches, and the fragrance consumed her mouth—like eating perfume, like kisses of nectar. She found a letter from a wife using a royal blue quill pen, wishing the man well. It was all awful, she thought, tossing the peach stone onto the green hillside where it wedged against a rock, near some bees. Happy bees. She patted the horse's neck. Now she and the woman had something in common. Though loss did not pass from one person to another like a baton; it just formed a bigger and bigger pool of carriers. And, she thought, scratching the coarseness of the horse's mane, it did not leave once lodged, did it, simply changed form and asked repeatedly for attention and care, as each year revealed a new knot to cry out and consider—smaller, sure, but never gone. Stillford, she thought to herself, as the sun grew high in the sky. My sweet Stillford, with his dirt art. My funny Lorraine, who danced to the lute so earnestly. Out of my body, these beautiful monsters.

It was ridiculous, at times, how many tears one body could produce.

A few hours into the afternoon, after napping on the horse who was eating clover in the inverted bell of a valley, the woman was startled by the sound of trumpets. She jerked awake, recalling the sound from her childhood, when trumpets were the way news was delivered, and sure enough, across the field emerged a troop of human men and women on horseback, some walking, two trumpeting, one waving a bright red flag. From what she could recall, a bright red flag meant war.

Ho, woman! called the strapping man at the lead, and she did not have time to put on her cloak and even if so, they'd take her horse and she liked having the horse.

They trotted over, a whole mess of people, and she hadn't looked at so many human faces together in years. How refined they were! How tiny and delicate! Those dot nostrils! Their hairless hands!

Are you lost? the head man asked, not unkindly. He wore a helmet wrought with silver swirled markings on the sides that seemed to speak of royalty.

No, she said, thank you. I'm on my way to the river.

This is ogre territory! said the man, sitting straighter. You're not safe!

He turned to the others, beckoning them closer.

No, no, she said, waving him off. It's fine. I'm skilled at hiding. I've been living in this territory for years.

Ho! he said, digging his hands into his horse's mane. Years? And survived?

You must help us then! We sent out a scout earlier to look for mines, and we have not heard back. Did you see anyone?

Of course, one careful look at the horse and all would be revealed, but the man was very focused on her face, as if he had been trained in it.

No, she said.

You saw no danger? said the man.

Nothing but crows, she said.

Ogres *eat* people, said the man, leaning in.

To her annoyance, her eyes thickened with tears.

Ah! You've seen something?

She shook her head, tucking her hands under the saddle and feeling the horse's warm coat beneath her, the large and living backside. No. I just heard a story once, of someone getting eaten, and I found it sad, she said. The tears tracked her cheeks.

He nodded. They all had their own stories.

Our sentry is a good man, the man said, and he said he'd contact us immediately via light signaling with use of the sun and his mirror and we have not seen a thing. Ah! Is that his horse?

He glanced down, and saw the packs. She had in her lap some turkey jerky that she'd been eating earlier.

Oh, I don't know! she said. She widened her eyes. Is it? I was just walking and came upon this horse and needed a rest. Hours ago. It did not have an owner.

The man's brow furrowed. The horse, alone? Hours ago?

Alone, she said.

He consulted with a short man next to him on a taller horse, making them even.

You'll have to come with us, the main man said.

Oh, no, she said, slipping the turkey jerky into a pocket. I'll walk. I'll give you his horse. I didn't realize it belonged to anyone recently. I thought it had been wild for a while.

No, said the man, firmly. We need you to come with us.

He nodded to his short man, who began to dismount.

The woman leaped off her horse, and backed into the meadow. The afternoon sun filtered through pine needles on high fir trees to the side, and with a quick move she had the cloak out of her bag and on and had turned into light and shadow.

Where'd she go? said the short man.

Witch! said the first.

The trumpets raised and blared.

The woman crept quietly to a corner of the meadow. Had any one of them been attuned to light they would've seen one patch of splattered sun shapes moving along in a way that did not correspond to the breeze.

But they were not. They were preoccupied with what had happened. They had liked their handsome, courageous scout. They quickly assimilated the man's packs and letters into their leagues, and put a child who had been previously riding with his mother onto the horse, and the two lead men swore and the woman watched silently from her spot in the meadow as they moved in a clump over the hills.

SHE stayed in the meadow in the cloak for hours, and the sun went down and lit the grasses with orange light, and she wondered about her husband who was likely going to see one of his women on the side. Although it made her cringe inside, a fist in her stomach, there was also a distant relief in it, in people just doing what they needed to do. She found comfort in the way the grasses swayed, and murmured, and at dinnertime, in a little whisper, she asked the cake to change flavor, and magic cake that it was, it shifted from vanilla pound to a chocolate Bundt, and she ate it with pleasure, plus some more almonds she had in her pocket and the remaining turkey jerky. Water from the spring. The moon rose in a crescent and crickets rubbed their wings together and in the far distance, now and again, she could hear the shining bleats of the bugles and trumpets.

IN the morning, she walked on. She could smell the river now, the heavy moisture, the damper grasses under her feet. The trumpets had grown fainter and she imagined they were returning home to arm up and come back to try to defeat the ogres with guns and bayonets. Maybe they will, she thought, vaguely, though the ogres had magic and bigness on their side and the humans had a hubris ogres did not. Ogres bumbled, and erred, but their weaknesses were not hidden and this helped them, in the long run.

She ate her lunch (more dried cherries) and then took the cake out of her bag. Something about it still bothered her. I need to fight for my life a little harder than this, she told it. It was now a chocolate chip cake, and she felt bad for it, this cake so willing to change and please her, with no other beings around who could speak to it, and enjoy it, but she ate a small portion and then wrapped it in a checkered napkin and tucked it in the branched fork of a sturdy oak.

Here, cake, she told it, patting the napkin. You are to have your own adventure now. No matter what happens, you can grow again.

As she said it, as she stooped to shoulder her bag, she understood why she could not tolerate being around a cake that survived so repeatedly, and she stood, bowed at the branch, and walked away.

FINDING food became much harder, then. She rooted for berries, having learned years ago from her husband what was edible, but more times than not, the berries were bad. She ate a handful of sour ones in the afternoon, and dug up some old peanuts and a beet. Dirt filled the cracks in her hands. She found a strong stick and rubbed the end to a point with the paring knife she'd brought in her sack, and when she finally reached the river—dark blue, racing, stone-dribbled—after refilling her water (ogre country water was always drinkable—something to do with the deep reserves replenished by the clouds)—she saw a quick orange fish in the current and crouched down and after dozens of tries, speared it. The fish flapped on her stick and she knelt and prayed a thank-you. She had only seen a fire built in front of her a few times, but she was able to wrangle together some sticks and fir needles and with the matches she had in her pack managed to get enough going to scorch the cleaned fish, though she missed many of the bones and picked them from her teeth in thin pullings. She let the fish guts molder in the grasses for another animal. Everything would get eaten in some way or another.

She slept that night wearing the cloak, a bright spot of dapple in the darkness. Soon into her sleep she woke at the sound of rustling, and caught a bear cub next to her licking up the fish guts and eyeing her sunspot curiously. She removed the cloak and it scampered away. The next morning, she wrapped up the cloak and left it in another tree's branches. She did not want help from magic. She did not want any more handouts.

SHE grew rugged and wiry in the fields, spearing fish, using up the last of her matches but not until she was sure she had figured out how to make a fire on her own, which sometimes took over an hour. Her legs turned leaner and tanner and she squatted and watched the clouds and the river and felt her sense of internal time shifting. We adapt, she told herself repeatedly. This is what they mean by adaptable. The men rose up from the village with their spears and guns, and when she saw the glints of red and the banners of war she climbed a high tree and watched from a distance as the human forces with shining weaponry and brass charged into ogre territory. Into the thatched huts and the rickety tavern and the ogre gamefield full of nets and balls woven from goathide. She watched, again, as the ogres ate the men whole. They could eat and eat. She watched the ogres fall from the expert weaponry, and the sight of a fallen ogre enraged the other ogres and invigorated the remaining men so the last phase was particularly bloody. Casualties were tossed off an embankment on Cloud Hill, and far below, people cried out and ran from the falling bodies.

On one of the days, she spotted her husband from the height of her best scouting tree near the thickest part of the river, where she'd set up a little daily life for herself that included hours of watching insects move grasses around or feeling the wind shift over her skin. Her husband, who had aged. She could see it in his limp. She missed him. She felt from his limp that he missed her. She had taken good care of him. He had been her one and only love. She watched as he swiped at the humans with swinging arms and ate two and then stumbled off and could not continue. The humans shot guns in his direction but he just swatted bullets like sport and the humans were radically outnumbered by that point and her ogre was one of the biggest. He limped farther away, and then twisted and turned, and his body moved in a way she'd never seen before, an uncomfortable jerking, an insistent movement from feet up to mouth, and he vomited up human—legs and arms and a head tumbled straight out of him. It was unchewed, the body: it was just parts and parcels of humanness, and the body lay there in the grass, glazed in a layer of spit and acid. Everyone stopped, for a second, seeing that. The man, who had not been chewed, but had been split into parts, was of course dead. The ogres held still, sweating, staring. The ogres had never seen an ogre throw anything up in their lives—they were nothing if not able digesters, and they shuddered at the sight of it.

On light feet, the woman crept closer. She ran through the grasses and leapt into another tree. The humans were muttering among themselves because although they had seen bodies eaten it was something else to see a body reemerge. The man's parts were now moldering in the grass, perhaps for the same bear cub. When she was close enough, at a high perch, she found she could recognize the man. An uncle of hers, a distant uncle, her mother's eldest brother. His twisted hand, his nose, that tweaked shoulder and distinctive jaw. She clung to the branch and thought perhaps her husband had thrown up the man because the taste had reminded him of his own children. Perhaps he had banged up against memory through an inexplicable familiarity. He had never told her he was sad. He had never expressed true regret. They had, in fact, never really talked about it. How to talk about it? How to blame him, or could he blame her? Weren't they both to blame for it, and also blameless? Who were the little human children who'd escaped, and where were they now?

The remaining ogres staggered off, and the remaining humans went to surround her dead uncle's parts. It was a truce moment. There had been enough death, and the ogres were not going to be vanquished, and the remaining humans did not want to be eaten, so they put the uncle's body into burlap bags and began the slow march home. Her ogre sank to the grasses on his knees and hung his head. He stayed there for hours, wilted, hunched, and from her perch in the tree, she sent him love. She made her love into a piece of the wind, formed from the air in her and placed on the air outside her, and sent it to him, even though it would be too diffuse by the time it got there. Still, even the bear cub felt it, trotting over to whatever remaining organ bits he could find, lifting up his nose to smell the new hint of freshness in the evening air.

THE cake, at first, had remained in the tree. Lodged in the branch nook of the old oak where she'd left it. But various birds found it in a few short days—they could smell its bready sweetness from yards away, and they pecked so hard at the napkin that the cake fell from the nook and rolled out of the linen. On the ground, the birds pecked it into nothing. It replenished. They pecked. It replenished. The cake wanted to satisfy the birds so it made itself into a seeded type, and the birds went at it with new vigor. The cake replenished. The birds were so full they hopped off, wobbling, but they returned with eagerness in the morning, and the next morning, and the birds that lived near the oak tree became fat and listless. They could hardly fly. All they did all day long was peck at the cake.

The cake had grown old. It had been made so many years ago, and it had been so many cakes in its time.

I will never die, thought the cake to itself, in even simpler terms, as cakes did not have sophisticated use of language.

ON her walk back, the woman saw it on the ground. She recognized her napkin, checked blue against the dirt. She was heading home. She was not sure if she could really return, or how to do it, but she wanted to try. She missed her husband, and the sight of him throwing up her uncle had filled her with a sore and tender love. There was the cake, in seeded form now, and she felt sorry for it.

With her pointed stick, she dug a hole in the ground. Now, dear cake, she said, gently burying it, patting the dirt. At least you can rest. At least you will not be endlessly pecked and diminished.

The birds found it in a day. A cake like that? Let that kind of thing go? They thought not. They scrabbled in the dirt and dragged it out with their beaks. They had missed it, for that missing day.

They pecked with unusual ardor. A few worms had already attached to its bottom side and were eating it too, and the cake had formed its back side into a kind of dirt cake and its front into seed and it would replenish itself according to the ratio of its eaters.

It went on like this for a while, and a few of the birds died early, from overeating and lack of flight. New birds came and went. Same with the worms.

THE woman returned to her house, and her husband opened the door, widening it when he saw it was her, and they sat at the kitchen table. It did not feel wrong. She got up and took her items out of her dirty bag and piled them into the sink for laundry. That moment a few days later when their arms touched over by the guest room? They ate their stew bowls together. They walked formally into the living room, sat on a sofa, and stumbled through a conversation. At night, she climbed onto his chest to sleep and he held her in place like a belt. Later, they took a few trips to a waterfall, and a glacier, and befriended an ogre who ran a school. After many years, the woman died of natural causes, and a few years after that, the ogre died. Eventually, his mistresses died. Down on the ground, in the people village, over decades, the war men and women died. The human girl who had escaped her early death died, across the land, over by the ocean, in her shack of blue bowls and rocking chairs. The witch who had originally made the cake and made up the spell and given it as a gift to her beloved ogre-friend died.

The cake went on and on.

Time passed, and the climate shifted. The trees and grasses faded, and the land grew dry. Birds stopped flying overhead. Reptiles ate the cake but eventually died out. The worms dried into dust. A quarter mile away, the magic cloak had stayed stuffed in its tree, hidden from view over many, many years. Some wind had nudged it into open air, and now, half tucked in the broken branches of the dead tree trunk was a shining bright coat-shaped area of dappled light through foliage. It showed dapple long after the sun had stopped shining through any leaves, because there were no more leaves.

Neither could move, but the cake felt a sense of the presence of the cloak, and thought it might be a new eater coming to find the cake, and the cake, always wanting to please—the cake who had found a way to survive its endlessness by re-creating its role over and over again—tried to figure out in its cake way what this light-dappled object might want to eat. So it became darkness. A cake of darkness. It did not have to be human food. It did not have to be digestible through a familiar tract. It lay there on the dirt, waiting, a shimmering cake of darkness. Through time, and wind, and earthquakes, and chance, at last the cloak fell out of the tree and blew across the land and happened upon the cake, where it ate its darkness and extinguished its own dappled light. The cloak disappeared into night and was not seen again, as it was only a piece of coat-shaped darkness now, and could no longer be spotted so easily, had there been any eyes left to see it. It floated and joined with nowhere. Darkness was overtaking everything anyway. Pouring over the land and sky. The cake itself, still in the shape of darkness, sat on the hillside.

What's left? said the cake. It thought in blocks of feeling. It felt the thick darkness all around it. What is left to eat me? To take me in?

Darkness did not want to eat more darkness, not especially. Darkness did not care for carrot cake, or apple pie. Darkness did not seem interested in a water cake, or a cake of money. Only when the cake filled with light did it come over. The darkness, circling around the light, devouring the light. But the cake kept refilling, as we know. This is the spell of the cake. And the darkness, eating light, and again light, and again light, lifted.

There's a story from Scotland called "Molly Whuppie" and another called "Little Thumbling" from France which are stories of clever human kids who trick ogres and escape a close death. These were the inspirations for the story—and "Jack and the Beanstalk" too, since usually there's a wife in there who opens up the door to the ogre home and is trusting and ends up losing something devastating in the process.

—AB

Daedalus

LABYRINTH
Ron Currie, Jr.

Once there was a boy whose father built a labyrinth.

This is a different story from the one you know. This father didn't build the labyrinth to imprison a half-man, half-bovine monster. He didn't build it to appease a king. No one's going to fashion wings out of feathers and wax, and no one will plummet into the ocean to demonstrate the price of hubris.

No. In this story, the father built the labyrinth before the boy was born, and they both lived in it. Other people lived there, too—the boy's mother, and his sister and two brothers.

IT is not accurate to say that the father wanted to live in the labyrinth. But it is fair to say that, owing to many factors, the labyrinth was where he was most comfortable.

It was a pretty common thing, for men to build labyrinths not because they wanted to live there, but because they were comfortable in them. By this time it was somewhat less common than it had been, say, thirty years previous. But these men and their labyrinths still existed in great numbers, and often they were admired for their labyrinths by other people, who referred to them with complimentary phrases like *real men* and *old school guys*.

———

THE father first started building the labyrinth in a place called Vietnam, where he had been sent to kill people. He had been sent there to kill people ostensibly because they had funny ideas about how society should function and how they should govern themselves— ideas that men like the father had been instructed to fervently disagree with. But the real reason he'd been sent to kill people was because the Vietnamese were, on average, smaller than him, and darker-skinned, and all spoke a rapid, clipped language that sounded like primitive gibberish to men like the father, which made it easy to believe that the Vietnamese were inferior, even subhuman.

Which in turn made it easy, even desirable, to kill them.

IT'S not as though Americans invented this type of justification for murder, of course. People had been doing that for a long time. The French had just been in Vietnam, in fact, doing the exact same thing. Before that, the Germans had done it to the Jews. Before that the Turks, for whatever reason, had done it to all sorts of people, including the Armenians and the Greeks. Before that, white Europeans in America had perpetrated a doozy on Native Americans, and were very creative and sneaky about it, sometimes using guns, for sure, but other times using blankets laced with lethal microbes, or even just pen and paper.

The psychological phenomenon behind all this killing can be summed up neatly thus: two kids are on a playground. One of them has black hair, and one of them has red hair. The kid with the black hair walks up to the kid with red hair and punches him in the nose. The kid with the red hair had been thinking about doing the same thing to the other kid, but he'd been a bit too slow.

INCIDENTALLY, the boy and his family did not stay in the labyrinth because they couldn't find the way out. That's another way in which this story diverges from the one you know.

They knew where the exit was. It wasn't a terribly large or complex labyrinth.

IT turned out that, despite the fact that the Vietnamese were small and dark and incomprehensible, it was not easy at all to actually kill them. It was easy to think about, but not easy to do. They still bled red. Their guts looked like any others'. The father ended up

knowing this firsthand, having seen the shredded guts of both Vietnamese people as well as the bigger people whom the father fought
alongside.

So it came to be that, around the time that the father was introduced to the sameness of everyone's guts, he started framing up his
labyrinth.

BUT listen, this is a real story, and everyone knows real stories are not
that simple. No matter how traumatic a single experience might be, it
cannot explain everything about what a person becomes. So it is not
accurate, ultimately, to say that the father going to Vietnam = the father building his labyrinth. The father, by all accounts, was with-
drawn and quiet and self-contained almost from the very beginning.
He was a *real man* well before he became a man. Vietnam was an ex-
acerbating factor. The father's innate withdrawal was the nature, and
all those shredded guts were the nurture, and when you put those
things together and gave them a good stir you ended up with someone
whom no one could really know, and okay fine, we're all acquainted
with at least a handful of people like that, now aren't we.

THIS is the sort of thing that the boy, now a man, tells himself about
the father: "Hey, most everyone is unknowable," the boy tells himself. "It was no great or special tragedy that you didn't ever really
know your father. Don't spend your whole life as one of those pussies who whines about how his father didn't tell him he loved him
enough. One of those candy asses. Endless fifty-minute hours, fucking drum circles. Cathartic weeping sessions. For the love of all
things holy. Don't."

WHEN the father came home from Vietnam after two years, the
people who had known him before, friends and family, went into
his labyrinth to visit. Sometimes they were able to find him, but
more often they were not. They would wander the long corridors
and call the father's name softly, but after a while they'd begin to
sense that the father was hiding from them, that he in fact did not
want them there, and they would grow uncomfortable, and then
they would follow the clearly marked directions to the labyrinth's
exit.

After some time, most people did not visit the labyrinth as often.
A few stopped visiting at all.

———

ONLY one person ever asked the father about the labyrinth. This was the father's own father. He got drunk to work up his courage, then went and found the father in the labyrinth.

"What happened to you over there?" he asked the father. "Why are you hiding in this maze?"

The father just stared.

"I mean, this was an awful lot of trouble to go to, building all this. Something must have happened to make you do it."

But the father looked at his shoes, and waved a hand to ward off any further queries.

Shortly after that, the father's father died. He was still young but had drunk too many beers and smoked too many cigarettes, and his body was pretty mad about that, and so it quit.

THE father did occasionally invite people into the labyrinth. Usually these people were women. Most of them did not stay very long.

Then the father invited the woman who would become the boy's mother into the labyrinth. She ended up staying until the father died thirty-five years later. In fact, she even stayed in the labyrinth for a while after the father died, and only just recently emerged, nearly five years after his death. She came out and blinked rapidly in the sunlight and offered the world a tentative okay-let's-get-on-with-this smile and then slowly walked away.

THE labyrinth has since fallen into disrepair—cobwebby corners, chipped and crumbling mortar—but it still stands, and can still be visited, though often only in dreams, or else when the visitor is quite drunk and thus capable of resurrecting the dead, temporarily, in his mind.

THE boy was born in the labyrinth.

But this is not his story, any more than it is his mother's, or his brothers', or his sister's. He is transcribing it, but it does not belong to him. And really, if the boy is being honest, this story has less and less emotional power over him as the time since he left the labyrinth grows longer. Fact is, the boy views this story as more of an intellectual curiosity now, almost as though that day when he sat at the kitchen table weeping while the father made no effort to hide his disgust had never happened.

———

ON the other hand, the boy is perhaps not the most reliable transcriber. Two reasons: First, his memory is poor. Second, he has a lifelong habit of playing fast and loose with facts. He will tell the truth now, though: he has lied about so many things that some of those lies have embedded themselves in his brain as the truth.

The thing at the kitchen table, though—that's the God's honest.

HERE'S what happened: the boy had lost his mind. At the kitchen table, in the labyrinth, the father and the mother were trying to figure out what to do with him. He was eighteen years old. He would go on to regain his mind, then lose it again, then regain it again. Lots would happen, going forward. There would be a future. But at that moment, the boy believed he had no future. His thoughts were like a television displaying snow. He wanted to jump into the river just above the dam and drift down into the turbines. Every blade his eyes fell upon appeared to have only one purpose. And so he wept. And the father glared. Then the father said some unkind words to him, words that in fairness he probably ended up regretting. Nonetheless, he said them. And the boy wept more.

GIVEN this, had he not been dead, the father might have experienced pride at the way the boy comported himself, years later, the night the father died and everyone but the mother left the labyrinth to the rats and spiders, to the abrasive powers of wind and sea spray.

Because that night the boy did not weep. He left the father's corpse and brought a bottle of whiskey to a friend's house, and the two of them stayed up drinking until five in the morning. The boy smiled, and then slept, and the next day he greeted family and friends as they arrived, accepted their condolences, rubbed their backs as they wept, told them all would be well.

WHEN he was young, as far as the boy was concerned, the father was the half-man, half-bovine monster this story is lacking. Or at least something equally scary.

The boy's friends felt the same way. They were all afraid of the father. They tiptoed through the labyrinth, held their breath until they were outside its walls again. None of them knew why they were so afraid—the father was not violent, did not raise his voice. He barely spoke at all, in fact. Yet they were all terrified of him.

Years later, whenever the father came up in conversation, there would be grinning admissions of this terror, and then invariably someone would speak in soft, affectionate tones about how, to them, at that age, the father had been pretty much the epitome of what a man should be, and it would be clear that time and experience had not changed this early opinion one little bit, no it hadn't.

NO one ever actually left the labyrinth, of course. But then, you knew that. You knew we were lying when we said the thing about the mother leaving after nearly five years, and the other thing about everyone but the mother leaving the night the father died. No one ever leaves the labyrinth, they just think they do.

It is true, though, what we said about the labyrinth falling into disrepair.

WE know what you're thinking. This is a myth, and like all myths it comes freighted with obvious metaphors, rote morals. *Enough with the labyrinth thing* is what you're thinking. *I get it.*

You don't get it, though. We're here to tell you. You don't. But that's not your fault. It's ours. We want to tell you one true thing about this. It's our only desire, actually: one true thing. Just one. If only. Would that we could. We keep trying different words, knowing that they will always be forever the wrong words.

Understand: the failure is ours, not yours.

SO please, forgive us—back to the labyrinth again:

Once, in the labyrinth, when the boy was a young man, the father told him a story. This was an occasion, in the same way that pizza night had been an occasion when the boy was a child: rare, captivating in its rarity, over too soon, hazy in the recollection. Stories like these, from the father, were like Yeti sightings. But so anyway, the father's story was about another boy, a boy who had reminded the father of his own son. This boy had had the back of his leg blown off accidentally by a shotgun blast. The father, who worked as a firefighter and paramedic, had been the first person on the scene. He drove up, lights strobing red and Klaxon blaring, announcing that he, the father, the real man, paragon of capableness on whose watch nothing could go wrong, had arrived.

Except this boy, see, the whole back of his upper leg was just *gone.* Obliterated. The femur exposed and splintered by buckshot, oozing marrow. This was one of those times when even the most capable person could do little other than offer comfort—a circumstance, co-incidentally, not at all unlike the one the father would be facing a few years later, right before he died. Everyone faced that circumstance, it turned out, sooner or later, whether they lived in a labyrinth or not.

But so in telling this story to the boy—his boy—the father kept coming back to one thing: how the boy who was missing the back of his leg stared at him and said, "Don't let me die."

And there was the father, carrying two equipment bags that over-flowed with futility, and wearing a uniform meant to transmit the message that he could handle anything. This was a kid around seven years old, understand, the father told the boy. He seemed so grown-up, the way he stared, the way he talked. He said it over and over again: "Don't let me die."

But he did die. The father went back to the fire station and changed his uniform, which was stiff with blood, and a few years later he told his son, the boy, all about it, while the two of them took a break from changing the oil in the father's truck in the labyrinth.

IT occurred to the boy to wonder if his father had become a fire-fighter and paramedic as penance for having once killed small bab-bling yellow people. The boy wandered the labyrinth, looking for etchings or graffiti to that effect, but surprise surprise, never found anything.

THERE exists a picture of the boy clutching a new plush Mickey Mouse doll, squeezing it to his chest, lying on the bed next to the father, who is frozen in the middle of a yawn. The sheets are tousled and twisted; an ashtray rests on the mattress to the father's left, a Marlboro smoldering in its basin. This was on the third Christmas morning of the boy's life. The mother had taken the picture, or at least we presume she had. It was one of those times when they all three happened to be in the same part of the labyrinth.

ONCE, after the mother quit smoking, the boy asked the father if he ever would quit smoking. This was five years before the father died, and although the seeds of what killed him were likely growing in his lungs, he was not yet aware of this. And he said to the boy, "Nope. I'm going up in smoke."

Like the story of the boy with his leg blown off, like pizza night, this was rare and thus wonderful: a moment of levity from the father.

WHO knows? Maybe the father wanted to kill himself. Likely this was not a conscious desire, but when somebody smokes cigarettes for forty years, one has to wonder if a latent suicidal impulse is at work. Especially in this instance, with all things considered. We mean, the guy lived in a labyrinth, for God's sake.

EVENTUALLY we'll stop treating the father with this detached reverence, and we'll do the right thing and satirize him. Or else just disavow him, as our brother did. We'll move beyond recognizing the father's weaknesses and wounds and we'll assassinate him long after he's died. We'll hang him in effigy from the labyrinth's outer walls. Until then, though, you're stuck with this.

BUT what is this, exactly, this thing you're stuck with? Let's face it, this is not a story at all. This is a catalog of how recovery follows heartache follows recovery, over and over, until you die. This is humping the garbage to the curb two days early and leaving it for the stray cats and neighbors to pick through. This is not a story.

Nevertheless: what, if anything, is the moral of this non-story?

It may be found in this fact: there, up on that hill, within the father's crumbling labyrinth like a nesting doll, is another, newer labyrinth, in current use and good repair.

The myth from which "Labyrinth" drew inspiration is, of course, obvious. When I first sat down to work, I had the idea of doing a contemporary retelling of Daedalus and Icarus, but the more I wrote, the more the story resisted the template of its famous forebear—in much the same way that all sons, if they wish to become men, must resist the template of their fathers.

—RC

———— ⚇ ————

THE LAST FLIGHT OF DAEDALUS
Anthony Marra

The villagers watched as he touched down on sand. Shoulder-sore, sun-pink, his arms caged in wooden shelves of feathers, he was not the harpy, not the geryon they had feared. He wore his beard in the style of Minos. The legs jutting from his tattered tunic were the width of a healthy man's forearms. His knees buckled as he whipped his wings against the shore, unable to knock a single feather from the contraption. The watching villagers heard a wail, which may have come on the wind, may have come carried in the creature's throat, and they anchored their hoes in the soil, their swords in their sheaths, unable to tell if this was a man or a beast from the tales their elders told.

But he was a man, a famed inventor at that, and when they delivered him to King Cocalus of Kamikos, they were each rewarded with a heifer. King Cocalus had heard of the man and was surprised and proud to learn that this cherished inventor had chosen to cross the sea on wooden wings to reach his little kingdom. To mark the occasion, the king threw a banquet. The inventor ate little, drank less, and the famed citizens that populated the king's table found the guest a taciturn and morose man, unworthy of the seat of honor in which he slumped. To lift the sullenness the inventor had cast across the evening, the king proclaimed that he would grant the inventor a single request. What chests of treasure, parades of virgins, pastures of sheep would the inventor want, wondered the famed citizens. But with his brow furrowed, his voice dying but not quite dead, the inventor asked only to access the shipyards with the finest wright in the kingdom.

The wright had heard of the inventor's fabulous contrivances and was gratified to work alongside such a man. They labored in a workshop beside the harbor. The inventor showed a keen interest in hulls, and the wright taught him all he knew of the intricate art of planking and ribbing. The wright wanted to continue the inventor's education, to elucidate the wonders of spars, rigging, and sails, because after all, the wright thought, had the inventor known how to build a ship, he wouldn't have had to fly across the sea. But the inventor was only concerned with hulls. He spent long hours studying the resin-glazed wood, muttering to himself as if trying to unlock the enigma that allowed men to walk, and live, and wage war on the water. The inventor was nearly a madman, the wright thought, living at some unseen edge of oblivion, where an incident as ordinary as a bird diving underwater could cause him to weep.

Under the inventor's direction, the wright's men constructed the oblong hulls of two vessels. But when the wright began discussing decking, the inventor waved him away. This isn't a boat, the inventor at last admitted. Into the empty oar slots, the inventor slid the most peculiar originations: long wooden staffs that split into two curved pincers, large enough to grip a barrel. They were built of the same treated timber as oars, but resembled the claws of an immense wooden crustacean. Inside each claw were organs of ropes, wooden gears, and pulleys, configured in such a way that the strength of a single man could move and operate the claw underwater. Extraordinary, the wright said, but the inventor wasn't finished. He beckoned the wright to place his eye against the end of the wooden staff. The wright expected darkness, wood grain, but a complex arrangement of glass sheets allowed him to see through the shaft, to whatever world lay at the end of the pincers. Extraordinary, the wright repeated, wishing he could summon a larger, more forceful word.

Within a fortnight, the inventor had divulged his plan to the wright. The two hulls would be joined together as a seed pod, a

Trojan fish, into which the inventor would be sealed. The pod would be towed by ship to the sea and, weighted by grain sacks, lowered toward the sea floor. Through a signaling system of slender ropes, the inventor would communicate with the ship, giving instructions, guiding his descent. But why, the wright asked. For what purpose? The inventor wouldn't say.

On the morning of disembarkation, half the kingdom showed up to watch the inventor slip inside the seed pod, the wooden anchor, the clawed creature, whose name and purpose mutated ceaselessly in the realm of their speculation. The villagers and townsfolk remarked that for all his brilliance, the inventor was a sad, quiet man, living on the wrong side of reason, a man to be admired and pitied. When the sail of the wright's ship shrank to one among the multitude of white swells on the horizon, the villagers and townsfolk were relieved to see him leave. They worried their children would look up to the celebrated but unfortunate inventor, and seek to live like him, beyond the quiet confines of contentment.

In the submersible, towed behind the wright's vessel, the inventor was at long last alone. Through the rope rigging, he signaled to the wright to lower him. Peering through the ends of the wooden claws, the wooden rakes, the pincers, the talons, whatever they were, the inventor could create far better than he could name, he watched shadow rise through the depths, the crystal blue darkening, as if he fell into a squid's inky cloud. For two days he raked the sea floor with the wooden claws. He came upon rocks, sunken ships, the soggy skeletons of immense fish, but these dead things were not what he sought. As he trawled, the sea floor continued to fall, and he signaled to be lowered farther still. The whole weight of the surging, swelling sea pressed against the resin-sealed capsule, but the inventor didn't fear the submersible's failure, but rather his own, which was the fear of his son in the darkening water, and the innumerable craggy creatures upon him, the scalloped monsters stripping his son's flesh, the urchins making a home within his son's rib cage, the starfish spawning in his mouth, the eels darting through the once-winged cages of his arms, the fish eggs glistening on his pelvic bone, all these nightmares colonizing the wounded thing that had been his boy.

By evening of the second day, he came upon a narrow gash in the ocean floor. He should wait for tomorrow, he knew, when the muted hint of daylight might brighten the trench. But he couldn't wait, not when urchins and anemones were building lives for themselves inside his son's body. He signaled and was lowered. The sharp trench walls battered the sides of the capsule, but just a little more, a little farther. The sea was a vise crushing the wooden vessel. The hulls moaned and wailed, but just a little more, a little farther. His son was there, in the darkness, he couldn't see but he knew it, he must go deeper, must rescue him, just a little more, a little farther, and when the wooden hulls cracked, when the black swells entered, the inventor took that first breath of water with the relief of a man surfacing, and then he was gone, the designs of his wondrous mind forever lost, and he drifted as the splintered hulls fell upon the empty trench floor, where they would become a city of shelter for many generations of crabs.

I've heard various takes on the myth of Daedalus, Icarus, and their wings, all of which end with Icarus falling into the sea. But what happened next? What would Daedalus invent following his son's death? Seen from that angle, the myth transforms from a cautionary tale of the dangers of ambition to a testimony of the power of art and creation.

—AM

Daphne

DAPHNE
Dawn Raffel

And so it came to pass that Daphne grew weary of being a tree. For centuries, Daphne had been grateful for her wooden status, and had even come to quietly enjoy Apollo's visits, during which he swore abiding adoration. But while Daphne was immortal, she was not ageless. As the millennia passed and Daphne's rings grew thick, annoyance bloomed. She sighed in the wind and she moaned to the birds and the stars, many of whom had also been nymphs back in the day. Now well past middle age, Daphne was irritated by small boys scrambling up her limbs and dogs urinating on her trunk and men denuding her branches for wreaths with which to laud themselves. Young lovers carved her bark, selfishly scarring her flesh with their impermanent affections. Sticky creatures tapped her sap, and witchy old women stripped her leaves to boil them for unguents.

Her friends the elms were dead.

As for Apollo, he hadn't been seen in a very long time. Some claimed he'd risen heavenward and fallen, but this was speculation. Cupid, whose gold and leaden shafts of malice had created Daphne's problem in the first place—striking Apollo with obsessive desire and Daphne with aversion—was said to be hobbled by gout.

With every passing season, Daphne's roots grew deeper, as did her despair. She longed once more to wander the woodlands in search of delight. Daphne was lonely. "O Father, alas! O Apollo, alas! O even vengeful Cupid, alas, alas!" she cried. "Why have you forsaken me?"

The birds tried to soothe her. "Flutter off!" she snapped.

Finally, Philomel sang to her a secret, her beak to a knot: "First you must unearth yourself, uproot yourself, and this done, your body and your face will be restored." The nightingale was swift and small and cunning, and had mastered the theft of forbidden information.

Yet Daphne wailed anew, for how was she to wrench herself from whence she had been planted? Her limbs creaked, truly, and sorrow and rage did not enable her release. "O Philomel, alas!" she cried, but Philomel had flitted off.

The rains came and went. The earth did not release her.

The flowers bent their heads.

The Pleiades, pale sisters—those nymphs turned to stars—endeavored to assist, but they were stranded in the heavens with arthritic Orion in halfhearted pursuit.

The river god slept.

Daphne trembled.

The sun was relentless.

"Diana!" cried Daphne at night to the moon. "Take pity on me! For, Cupid aside, was it not your own twin whose desire begat my undoing? And had he not taunted Cupid to begin with, would Cupid have struck?"

"Speak not ill of my brother," answered the moon, revealing her face.

And yet she considered Daphne's point.

At last and at length, in the fullness of time, the moon waxed merciful. She lighted the waters. She riled the tides. She fired up the river god, old as he was: "Awaken yourself! Raise high the waters! Devour the shores!" And so the rivers rose. And so the winds rose. And so the seas rose, flooding the woodlands, eroding the hills to the cries of wolves, felling mortal trees. The wind and the water, the sore earth itself unbound the laurel's roots.

TENDRIL by tendril, she rose in the night. When the storm had stilled and the cold wind slept, with no soul to witness, she lifted herself.

The moon had retreated. The Pleiades shone brightly for once that night to guide her way. Orion, old hunter bereft of desire, did not even notice their newfound glow.*

ON strange new legs, by the light of the stars, she went down to the river and lay there to sleep.

At dawn she viewed her visage, reflected in water, and shrank back in shock. Philomel had lied to her!

Woman though she was, her beauty was gone.

Her body was sacked.

Age had rendered Daphne demographically irrelevant. No hot-blooded god would chase her again.

And so Daphne rose.

And so Daphne wandered.

And so Daphne walks through the world as she will, to lands far and near, to towns here and there, taking her time, changing her name, talking to birds, not looking over a brittle shoulder. Here she swipes sugar, stuffing her pockets. There she sings, off-key, aloud. She squints and she spits. Some claim to have seen her feeding the pigeons, hugging the trees, scolding the dogs, saluting the moon, crooning to stars, wading the rivers on bunioned feet, plucking an apple with ravaged hands, licking the juice, laughing quite madly, snapping a child's arrow in half.

Daphne, like so many nymphs, was pursued by an unwanted suitor. In flight from besotted Apollo, Daphne cried for help, and her father the river god obliged her by turning her into a laurel tree.

—DR

---

*In the morning, a number of citizens swore that the hole in the earth where the great tree stood was the work of thieves; others declared it the act of a single God.

Demeter

DEMETER
Maile Meloy

When they divided up the year, Demeter had chosen, for her own, the months when the days start getting longer. It was easier that way. It meant that she delivered her daughter back to her ex-husband in the late, bright Montana summer and she could handle it then, most of the time, with a little pharmaceutical help. She couldn't handle giving her up in the dead of winter.

Hank could have fought for sole custody, since Demeter had a reputation for erratic behavior. But granting her half the year had been a gesture on his part: generosity as a sign of power. He would not have it said that he took a child from her mother. He was always more subtle than that.

Perry, their daughter, had been unexpected, the pregnancy a buoyant gift at a time when Demeter and Hank were like drowning people, tugging each other under. But the moment Demeter saw the pink thing in the nurse's arms, the tiny creature that had turned her inside out, she knew the baby wasn't going to save her marriage. It was only going to break her heart. They hadn't named her Persephone; that would have been unfair. They had named her Elizabeth, after Hank's mother, but Hank started calling her Perry Mason early on, for her steady infant gaze that would break down any witness, and it stuck.

At thirteen, Perry had the pert features and turned-up nose of a figure skater, although she wasn't one. She hadn't yet found the thing she might be very good at. Hank hoped it would be science: he wanted his daughter to be straightforward and rational. Demeter hoped it would be music: she wanted Perry to be darker and more complicated. At the dinner table, when they were still living in one house, Perry had looked from one to the other of them as if they came from the moon. Her strange parents. Only she was of the earth.

Hank had bought her an oversized pink nylon duffel bag, and Perry carried it back and forth between the two houses. He'd made more money after the divorce than he ever had before, with new income from oil leases, and he owned a big house on a hill now, with a new red truck outside.

Demeter parked, and Perry leaned over in the passenger seat and kissed her quickly on the cheek, eager to avoid any drama. "Bye, Mom," she said. "Love you." Then she lugged the duffel toward the house, her bare legs in blue shorts taking her blithely away.

It wasn't natural to give up your child every year. It wasn't right. Demeter knew that Hank could say the same thing, but she had no interest in being fair to Hank, and she had carried that child inside her body. She had fed her with her own blood, and then from heavy, unfamiliar breasts. She had held Perry when she was sick and vomiting, her hair damp with fever.

She watched her daughter twist her shoulders to get the wide bag through the front door, without a look back. The dark interior of the house engulfed her. The screen door slammed shut.

Demeter sat alone in the car. The tears shouldn't have surprised her, but they did. They came hot and choking. Her jaw shook. Her nose ran. She knew she should leave, and not embarrass Perry or give Hank anything to comment on, but she couldn't see to drive.

Finally Perry came back outside and leaned in through the car's open window. "Mom," she said.

Demeter fumbled for a tissue. "I'm sorry."

Perry got into the car and sat looking at her hands, with their chewed cuticles. "You chose this," she said.

Demeter wanted to say that she would have died if she had stayed with Hank, but she tried to be discreet in front of their daughter. "I know."

"And you picked the dates."

"I did. I'm all right, sweetie."

"You're *not*."

"No, really I am." She blew her nose decisively. "You can go inside."

Trouble clouded Perry's pretty face. *"Mom."*

Demeter didn't want to be doing this, to be taking this perfect child and putting the pain in. "I'm okay. I just needed a minute. Don't watch too much TV, all right?"

"I won't."

"And no jet skis."

"He doesn't have a jet ski."

"No jet skis!" Demeter said. "They're death machines."

"All *right*."

"Okay."

"Okay," Perry said. "Bye." She got out and waved. Those long legs carried her back into Hank's world, where she would do Hankish things. Water ski, even if there were no jet skis. Eat red meat every night, and too much sugar. She belonged to her father now.

As Demeter drove down the hill, away from Hank's house, she felt as if there were a cord attached to her viscera that was stretching, pulling. When she was young, she had liked to say that she would never have regrets. Her life was her life, her choices her choices, and she would stand by it all. But she did have a regret now. She wished she had never had a child.

She pulled the car over to the curb, startled by the thought. It was true. She couldn't wish her daughter away *now*, but if she had a time machine, she would go back and erase the conception. Then there wouldn't be this agony, there wouldn't be the black times. She would have found other sources of love, and she wouldn't have this gnawing emptiness. One tiny erasure and everything would be different. Catastrophe avoided.

She pressed her hands against her sternum to stop the ache. She had always known that Perry was mostly Hank's. That cross-examining stare came straight from him. She had his logical mind and his quiet stubbornness. But that didn't make it less painful to give her up.

FINALLY she got herself home, parked beneath the big maple tree, and went inside her little house. It was dark and empty. The refrigerator hummed. She had no television—a fact that was eternally embarrassing to Perry—so she switched on the radio, to have some companionable sound. *StarDate* was on.

Hank had told her long ago that she had a voice for radio, but she had never pursued it. What she had was a campfire voice, mellow and clear at low volume. She had met Hank at a bonfire where he played songs in her range on his guitar so they could harmonize. She was impossibly young then, with wheat-colored hair. She'd sat cross-legged on the cold ground and watched the embers burn, but she knew he was watching her, listening through the other voices for hers. When the fire died down, he'd wrapped his coat around her shoulders and she was his.

She opened the refrigerator. There was some leftover tabouli. A tub of yogurt. The nonhomogenized milk that came in glass bottles from the dairy, with a thick band of cream to scoop off the top. Frozen pesto in the freezer. "I'm so tired of this food!" Perry had shouted at her once. "It's not real food! I will not eat millet!" Demeter closed the refrigerator to make the voice go away.

Hank would be grilling steaks tonight. Married, they had tempered each other, made compromises in the way they lived their lives. Apart, they had gone to opposite extremes. Perry said that joint custody with them was like jumping back and forth between a hot tub and a snowbank.

"Which is which?" Demeter had asked.

"You know what I mean," Perry had said. "You're just different."

But Hank would be the hot tub, of course. Which left Demeter the snowbank.

"Tonight the Perseid shower will be approaching its peak," the radio voice said, confiding and urbane. "You might see shooting stars coming from the direction of the constellation Perseus. This constellation was named for the Greek hero, and is located near the constellations of his wife, Andromeda, and her mother, Cassiop—"

Demeter switched the radio off. She would go for a swim. Clear her head. She stuffed her suit and cap and goggles into a canvas bag and left the front door unlocked. She locked it when Perry was home, mostly because of Perry's displeasure when she didn't, but there was no point now. It was a safe enough town.

She walked toward the city pool, past the café that had bought flower arrangements from her garden after the divorce, when she hadn't known how she was going to make money. She walked past a pawnshop where she'd taken jewelry, and the coffee shop that had to be a front for something, because it couldn't possibly have paid the rent with coffee all these years.

A woman with a little boy sat on a low planter. The boy might have been three, in a red and blue striped T-shirt. They had a worn air about them, and Demeter guessed that they were staying at the homeless shelter on the next block. The sight of them together, inseparable, the mother with her skinny arms around the child, squeezed Demeter's heart, and she wanted to tell the woman never to let him go. Instead she looked down at the sidewalk until she was past.

Interesting clouds were forming over the mountains when she arrived at the pool. Some kind of weather coming. But she should still have time to swim. There were the bike racks. Inside the brick building, the chlorine smell. All the years of swimming lessons overlapped the present moment in her mind—Perry as a baby, a chubby toddler, a string bean of a nine-year-old on a pink bike.

Four-o'clock lap swim cost a dollar. When Demeter looked up from fumbling in her bag, she realized that she knew the dark-haired girl at the cash register. The girl was smiling, waiting for Demeter to notice. She wore a red lifeguard shirt and looked just like her father, who'd died when she was four. She had his gray eyes.

"Oh, my God, Annie," Demeter said. "You're so beautiful."

Annie blushed, pink coming to her cheeks. "Thanks."

"How's your mom?"

"She's great," Annie said. She put the dollar in the till. "You know her, she's indestructible."

Demeter nodded, staring at the girl, doing clumsy math. She must be eighteen. Demeter felt like she was a hundred. She felt Paleozoic.

"There might be lightning coming," Annie said. "I'd get your swim in quick."

"Right," Demeter said.

She went into the damp concrete locker room, feeling disoriented. Annie's father, Duncan, had been Hank's business partner. He'd been cheerful and competent, always ready to fix an engine or stop a fight: to make things right. Annie's mother, Kay, was slight and strong like a pioneer woman, tempered steel where Demeter had often felt herself to be decadent and soft.

Duncan and Kay had been the best friends of her early marriage, and Demeter had loved them both in a way that felt sustaining, like sunshine. But those were the bad old days, and so she had slept with Duncan, as a matter of course. It was just an extension of her ordinary love. He had run his fingers through her hair, lifted her light body to his hips. When she'd started to get confused about it, the confusion was easier if she was stoned. That was the bad old days, summed up. It could be a kind of haiku:

I slept with my friend.
Then I got high.
Spring of '76.

THEN, that June, Duncan and Hank had gone down with scuba gear to look for earthquake damage on a dam, and Duncan hadn't come up.

At first, Demeter thought Hank had killed him. What had been a dalliance, a distracting sexual guilt, had become a cataclysmic horror. Hank *knew*, and had taken revenge. The world was dark and vicious. But she soon realized that wasn't true. Hank knew nothing. When he'd pulled his wetsuit back on and found Duncan on the bottom of the lake, he was bewildered, grief-stricken, distraught.

Then she thought that Duncan might have killed himself, torn between two women. But she could picture him laughing at the idea, his handsome head thrown back, his gray eyes crinkled with laughter. *Kill* himself? Sleeping with her had been a happy thing. He had loved it. And he had loved his wife and their four-year-old daughter.

Demeter's therapist, Martine, said it was healthy to imagine that laughter, because only a true narcissist would believe she had such power, to drive someone to suicide. Martine had said it slowly, looking over her round tortoiseshell glasses with meaning, which made Demeter wince.

So the drowning had been an accident. Every investigation and inquiry said it was. Duncan's big heart had just stopped.

Next Demeter had blamed Hank for leaving Duncan to die alone, but not as much as he blamed himself. He paced and obsessed and rethought, and Demeter watched him. They were moving around the death like two satellites in separate orbits when they collided in the bedroom and Perry was conceived.

As soon as she knew she was pregnant, Demeter had stopped smoking pot. She started meeting the black-coated Hutterites in their truck to buy chickens and eggs. She bought vegetables at the farmers' market from the Hmong refugees, who coaxed green shoots from the ground so much earlier in the year than anyone else. She ordered milk from the dairy, and made baked eggs and cream with Hmong chives. She didn't worry about getting fat—she was supposed to get fat. When Perry arrived, Hank was enraptured, and Demeter realized how much he must have wanted a child before. He had never pushed her, in her stoned and childfree days, but he had craved fatherhood. She just hadn't seen it.

SHE pulled her swimsuit on in the dank locker room, lost in time. The purple Lycra was a little stretched out and ratty, and she was glad Perry wasn't here to raise her eyebrows at it, to say, "*Mom*, you could've shaved your legs, at least." She pushed her streaky blond hair under a silicone cap and went outside.

The dark sky loomed closer, the color of a black plum, but people were still swimming. She recognized the slow, steady stroke of Ned Keller, who had to be in his nineties now. She hopped into the shallow end and pulled her goggles down over her eyes. Annie was in the lifeguard chair in a red tank suit, swinging a whistle on a lanyard.

Demeter ducked beneath the water and pushed off. It was her favorite moment of swimming, the passage from dry to wet, her skin shedding tiny bubbles of air as she kicked. It felt as if the world were washing off her. She was starting over, newborn. She had swum in high school in Texas and was proud of her stroke. It had always been balanced and consistent, even when she was not. She breathed on the left, took three strokes, breathed on the right.

At the deep end of the pool, she flip-turned and pushed off, still with some of the tingly feeling. She passed Ned Keller, his ancient arms pulling stubbornly along. He had swum in a triathlon with his son and grandson: the son biked and the grandson ran. Demeter wondered if Perry would have a daughter someday, and if they could do that.

She turned again, big air bubbles streaming over her face, and imagined what would happen if she breathed in. Had there been a moment when Duncan's lungs filled with water, when he still knew what was happening? Had he watched himself cross out of the habitable world? She took half of an experimental breath and stood up coughing, choking, her bare feet finding the concrete bottom of the pool, the desire to live too strong.

A whistle pierced the air. She pulled off her goggles, breaking the suction, and saw Annie climbing down from the lifeguard chair.

Demeter had been too obvious in her flirtation with drowning. She needed to tell Annie she was fine, but she had to get a good breath first.

"Everyone out of the water!" Annie called. "Everyone out!" She was looking up at the sky, not at Demeter. The clouds were black and roiling, spilling over themselves, low and heavy. How had the storm come in so fast? A lightning bolt cracked through the bruised darkness. *"Now!"* Annie called.

Demeter kicked to the edge. Ned Keller was climbing out, too, and she resisted the urge to offer him a hand. She wouldn't want people condescending to her when she was ninety. He swam every day. He could get himself out of the pool.

The lifeguards were pushing a long blanket roller on wheels out from the wall. The blankets were heavy blue insulated plastic, to keep the heat in the water at night. Rain began to splatter, and the girl pulling the first blanket ducked her pigtailed head. She wore a dry T-shirt and shorts.

"I'm already wet," Demeter said. "I'll take it." She tugged the corner of the blanket, dragging it along the shallow end as Annie and a tall boy pulled slack off the roller. The pigtailed girl ran inside the office and came out in a raincoat. The tall boy shouted instructions: now they had to slide the blanket down the pool so the next one could be pulled across. Demeter understood, and tugged her end toward deeper water, clinging to the reinforced hem. The blanket wanted to sink as it moved forward, scooping up water in the middle and creating a heavy puddle. She and the boy strained to keep it at the surface.

There was another crack of white light, and then the boom of thunder. The rain came down diagonally in the gusting wind, like someone throwing buckets. But for someone in a swimsuit and cap, it hardly mattered. They got the blanket into position and ran back for another.

"Thanks for helping!" Annie shouted over the wind and rain.

Demeter nodded. Her towel was lumped on the pool deck, sopping wet. The rain seemed to be getting colder. She pulled the next blanket along the gutter.

There was another flash of lightning, and Annie looked up at the sky with an impatient, Duncan-like expression: *Why are the gods foiling my plans? What is this perverse unhelpfulness?* That was her father, through and through.

The last blanket was on and the rain was still coming. Demeter followed Annie into the lifeguard office, peeling the cap off her wet hair. The lap swimmers were gone. The lifeguards, two boys and two girls, toweled their heads and exclaimed about the storm.

"We have a coffeepot for hot chocolate," Annie said. "Somewhere."

"I'm all right," Demeter said, although she was shivering, covered in goose bumps.

"You're freezing," Annie said, pulling a dry towel off a shelf.

It was thick orange terry cloth with red suns, and Demeter wrapped it around her shoulders. She had held this girl on her hip at Duncan's funeral, out in an ancient cemetery, really just a field. They had played a tape of Annie talking to her father, the recorded voice tiny in the mountain air. Kay had explained that her daddy was going to help make the flowers grow, but what did a four-year-old understand? Annie must barely remember him now.

"Are you okay?" Annie asked. "Your lips are blue. You seem a little hypothermic."

"Oh, sweetheart, your dad," Demeter burst out, before she knew what she was saying. "We loved him so much."

Annie looked as if she'd been slapped. Not hurt, just startled. She glanced at the other guards, who were busy drying off. No one was listening. But it was clear that Annie would have been embarrassed if they had. It had been a day for embarrassing teenagers.

"I'm sorry," Demeter said. "You're right, I got too cold. I'll go dry off."

In the empty locker room, she sat on one of the wooden benches along the wall and made herself breathe. Duncan's yellow dog, Blue, had circled the pine coffin in the back of the truck, whining. He couldn't find a place to lie down. She remembered thinking that she was like the dog. She would never find happiness or rest again. But that hadn't been true. People were more resilient than they thought.

The locker room smelled of disinfectant and wet socks. By these scarred benches, a tiny, trusting Perry had raised her arms so Demeter could pull a shirt off over her head. There was a low steel sink that sprayed a half circle of arcing warm water, and Perry and the other little girls had loved to sit in it until a lifeguard came in to chase them out. Demeter always let them climb back in again. She had never liked rules. Maybe that was part of the problem. Maybe if she hadn't chafed against every restriction, for so many years, she wouldn't have had to let her daughter go. But that was wishing to be someone else.

The rain rattled down on the skylights. Demeter would have kept Perry all the time if she could have wrested custody from Hank. She would have guarded her from his world of violent movies and roaring engines. But then Perry wouldn't have her father. She would be like Annie, bereft of half her inheritance. And she would resent Demeter for doing it, of course. So they were stuck with this harrowing division of the year.

Demeter changed into her dry clothes, wrapped the orange towel around her hair, and went back into the office. She was warmer now, although the air was growing colder. Annie introduced her to the others as "Mrs. Hayes."

"Please, no, that's my mother," she said. "Call me Demeter."

"Like the harvest goddess!" the taller boy said, showing off. He had a cockscomb of thick brown hair.

"Exactly," she said.

The shorter boy was ridiculously good-looking: blond, with cornflower-blue eyes. She wondered if they could tell that she'd been crying, with her red nose and swollen eyes, and guessed that she just looked like someone's mother, with goggle rings denting her face.

"Look!" the pigtailed girl said. "It's snowing!"

And it was. They all moved to the door. Thick white flakes fell from the sky.

"It's thundersnow!" the tall boy said.

"You're frickin' kidding me!" the other boy said. "It's August!"

The sky was lighter than it had been when it was raining, and they all stood and watched the world outside turn white. The snow fell surprisingly fast. It had snowed like this in July once, before Annie was born, when Demeter and Hank were hiking in Yellowstone with Duncan and Kay, the white drifts melting around the smoking sulfur pots.

"It's good we got the blankets on," Annie said.

"It's so *weird*!" the blond boy said.

Silence fell, the snow muffling all sound. They watched, transfixed. And finally the snow stopped, and the evening sun burned through the clouds. The white mantle on the blankets glowed.

The tall boy who knew his mythology and his meteorology went outside and made a snowball. He lofted it experimentally into the air, and it landed in the middle of the covered pool and stayed there, white on white.

"Race you across the blankets!" the blond boy shouted. He ran out onto the deck and then kept running across the blanket on the shallow end, legs pumping, until he was sucked down, halfway across the pool. "Halfway!" he cried, grinning. "Beat that!" He rolled toward the side, out of the sinkhole he'd made.

The little pigtailed girl ran out onto the next blanket, snow flying beneath her feet, until she was sucked down, too.

"Not even close!" the blond boy said.

"Sorry," Annie said, looking at Demeter with Duncan's amused gray eyes. "They're kind of immature."

"You try it, Mrs. Hayes!" the tall boy said. "Goddesses walk on water, right?"

"Real ones do," Demeter said.

"It's actually kind of fun," Annie said. "It helps if you keep your knees up high."

"And it helps if you're sixteen," Demeter said. But she knew she could do it. She could feel the way you needed to high-step across.

"Just try it!" the pigtailed girl said, hauling herself out of the pool.

Demeter looked at their sweet faces, shining from the effort and the rain, and she unwrapped the heavy orange towel from her hair. They cheered. "Do I get a handicap for being ancient?" she asked.

"You're not that old," the pigtailed girl said, shaking the water off in a little dance. "You should see my mom—she couldn't do it in a million years."

"Would Kay do it?" Demeter asked Annie.

Annie rolled her eyes. "No. Too sensible."

Demeter's next thought, which she didn't need to say out loud, was that Duncan would have done it in an instant. "This is crazy," she said. But it wasn't *really* crazy—that was the important thing. It wasn't like wishing you'd never had your own child.

The first blanket had floated up and straightened itself out. Demeter backed up to get a running start across the pool deck, then ran, knees high, out onto the blue expanse. For a few steps she was magically on the surface. She was sixteen and unfettered, untouched by grief. Nothing had consequence. Then the insulated plastic sucked at her heels. She took two more fighting steps as she sank into the warm water. She was laughing, tangled up and struggling to the side. There must be a stern warning printed on the blankets about not doing exactly *this*.

The kids were shouting and clapping. "That was *amazing*!" the pigtailed girl said.

Demeter looked. She'd gotten halfway across. It *was* amazing. She climbed out of the pool in her dripping clothes and wished Perry were here, to have seen that. But Perry would be mortified at the sight of her mother making a fool of herself, running and laughing with these kids. Not being a *mom*. So she was glad, again, that Perry wasn't here—and she wasn't glad. Six months to go, the long darkening fall. And already the sun was lower in the sky. Something between a laugh and a sob caught her by surprise, behind her rib cage, and she stifled it by crying, "Annie's turn!"

Annie backed up through the open office door to get a better running start, with Duncan's fierce, competitive look on her face. The light through the sodden air was molten gold. The kids were giddy with anticipation, with incipience. If only it were possible to freeze this moment, this perfect light, and stay here, and not tumble forward. But already the moment was gone. Annie began to run.

"Demeter" is based on the Greek origin story about the seasons: Demeter is the harvest goddess, and her daughter Persephone has to spend part of the year with Hades, as the queen of the Underworld. During the months Persephone is gone, Demeter goes into mourning and lets the world go barren. I first read it as a kid, in the D'Aulaires' Book of Greek Myths, *when my brother and I and all our friends were shuttling back and forth between our divorced parents' houses, and it always seemed like a joint custody story to me.*

—MM

Demeter and Persephone

KID COLLINS
Willy Vlautin

Walt Collins is at the Fitzgerald playing blackjack when his sister, Lorna, waves to him from across the table. She has her five-year-old daughter Cora with her. She also has a black eye and a dried line of mascara down her cheek. She's wearing jeans and a blue sweatshirt and is holding her daughter's hand. Walt pulls out of the game and walks over to them. He looks at his sister and leans down and says hello to the girl.

"Are you all right?" he says to his sister and stands up.

"Not really," she says.

"I haven't seen you in what, two months? I stopped by a month ago but some old Mexican had moved in there and said he'd been there a few weeks."

"Things haven't been going very good, Walt," she says and tries not to cry. "Not for a long time . . . What are you doing here? I've looked everywhere, this was my last stop. I thought you quit?"

"I have mostly," he said and smiled. "I got off work and was walking around. They have a good dinner special so I stopped. I was just playing a couple hands on the way out. What happened to your eye?"

"I need to talk to you about that," she says.

Cora's staring into the crowded room watching people walk past her. Her shoes are untied. She's wearing green shorts and a yellow T-shirt. Her knees are muddy. Her arms are covered in dirt, grease.

"How are you doing, kid?" Walt says and pats her on the head.

"Okay," the girl says.

"Kid Collins," he says and drops down to his knees.

"You gonna give your uncle a hug?"

The girl goes to him and hugs him.

"You still gonna be a boxer?"

The girl nods her head.

"Kid Collins. The southpaw from Reno, Nevada."

Lorna's hands are twitching. She can't stand still. "Walt," she says, "I need to talk to you. It's that important. You know I'd never ask for anything if I didn't need to."

"All right," Walt says and stands up. "Let's get out of here. You still got a car?"

"Yeah."

"Good."

"Where you want to go?" she asks.

"Let's take the kid to Gold 'N Silver." Walt kneels down in front of Cora again.

"You want to get something to eat, kid?"

"Yes," the girl says.

"You know your mom and me used to eat at the Gold 'N Silver as kids. Our folks would take us there every Saturday until we graduated high school."

"Let's go, Walt," Lorna says nervously.

"I have to cash out. Where you parked?"

"At Molly Malone's," she says.

"What kind of car do you have?"

"A 1983 Honda Civic. It's silver. I'll wait for you there."

"It won't take me long," he says and heads back to the table.

IN the back lot of the Gold 'N Silver Walt gets out of his sister's car and lights a cigarette.

"Stay in the car, honey," Lorna says as she gets out. "I have to talk to your Uncle Walt. I'll bring you out a grilled cheese. Does that sound good?"

"Yes," the girl says. "And fries."

"Of course and fries. I love you," Lorna says. "You know that, don't you?"

"Yes," the little girl says.

She kisses her daughter then shuts the car door and locks it.

"Let's go inside," she says to Walt.

Walt's standing on the sidewalk looking at Cora. "Let her come in, Lorna. You can't just leave her there."

"I'm getting her something to go," Lorna says. "She'll be all right. Anyway I just need to talk for a bit. I can't stay long and what I'm saying I don't want her to hear."

Walt leans against the driver's-side window. "We'll be right back, kid. You just hang tight, okay?" Cora smiles and Walt gives her a thumbs-up sign and follows his sister inside the restaurant.

They sit at a booth and Lorna orders coffee and Walt orders a large glass of milk and a side order of wheat toast.

"First things first," she says. "I got to tell you, I love you, Walt. You've always been good to me. You've always been my favorite person."

"What's going on?"

"I don't know," she says and begins crying.

"Are you in some sort of trouble?"

"I don't know," she says and wipes her tears with a napkin. "Are you still gambling?"

"Not really. But something's wrong with my stomach. I have to quit drinking. I don't mind, though, really. I slip up once in a while but I'm almost there."

"Are you working?"

"I'm still selling cars at Hurley's," he says and laughs.

Lorna smiles at him. "I haven't worked since the last time I saw you. I'm a fucking mess, Walt."

"I've seen you look better," he says.

"I know," she says and begins crying again.

"How long have you been up?"

"A long time I think. Days maybe."

"What do you need from me?"

"Just to talk for a little bit."

"How's Cora?"

"She's good," Lorna says and begins to cry again. "I ain't been much of a mother."

"What do you mean?"

"We just been living at people's houses. I don't have an apartment anymore. I've left her with some . . . terrible people."

"You know you can always stay with me," Walt says. "It ain't much. I'm just renting a room at the El Cortez, but it's something. We could get a rollaway and I could take that and you guys could get the bed."

"We're gonna leave town."

"Where are you gonna go?"

"I don't know, maybe Arizona," she says and blows her nose. "I have a girlfriend down there."

"Is Cora in school?"

"She just turned five."

"When do they start school?"

"Seven, first grade starts when you're seven."

"Is it the best thing for you, to move to Arizona?"

"I don't know," she says, and laughs and begins looking in her purse. "I've borrowed a lot of money from you over the years, Walt, haven't I?"

"Don't worry about that."

She takes an envelope from her purse. She empties it onto the table. "There's what? Something like eighty dollars here. I want you to take it."

"I don't need your money," Walt says.

"You might," she says. She's twitching now, and can't sit still. "It'll make me feel better. It'll make me feel like a better person if you take it."

"Look, Lorna, calm down. You just have to tell me what's going on."

"What kind of place is the El Cortez?"

"It's the hotel on Second Street. When we were kids we used to eat there. At Fong's. You remember that?"

"The Chinese restaurant?"

"That's the place."

"I remember it now."

"I'm on the fourth floor. I'll be out soon, though. I'm all right. I've been going to meetings. I'm doing pretty good. Anyway, there's a toilet, a bath, and a sink."

"Is it safe for Cora?"

"It'll be all right for a while. I wouldn't want her there by herself.

But with one of us around it'd be all right. I'll be out of there in a few months. I almost have enough for an apartment."

"I've been a horrible sister."

"You got nothing to be sorry about. I'm just worried about you."

"I've always been so bad at everything," she says.

"Tell me what's going on."

"I really look horrible don't I?"

"You just need to sleep and lay off whatever you're taking. But right now your eye makeup is leaking down your face."

She takes a Kleenex and tries to wipe her eyes. She grabs her purse. "I'm gonna run to the bathroom and wash my face. I'll be right back. Remember to order Cora a grilled cheese and fries. Get extra pickles. She likes pickles."

Lorna grabs his hand and squeezes it, then gets out of the booth and disappears down the aisle toward the bathroom.

Walt waits twenty minutes and drinks his milk and eats the toast. He gets up and goes to the women's room and calls for her. He sticks his head in, but it's empty. He goes back to the table and pays the bill, takes the money she left and the sack with the grilled cheese and fries and leaves.

He goes out the side entrance and looks in the parking lot for her car, but it isn't there. He thinks about taking a cab, but his stomach's burning and he hopes walking might ease it. He's out of the parking lot and walking down the sidewalk when he begins coughing up the milk and toast. He stops between Third and Fourth streets and vomits and then sits down on the sidewalk. It's then that he notices a dragging noise. He looks up and in the dim light he sees Cora, dragging a suitcase by a piece of rope toward him.

"What are you up to, kid?" he says and takes his handkerchief from his coat pocket and wipes his mouth.

"I'm supposed to go with you," she says and stands in front of him.

"I didn't see you in the parking lot. Where were you?"

"Hiding in the bushes. I got scared."

"That's a big suitcase, how'd you'd drag it all this way?"

"I have the rope," she says.

"Why don't you sit down and take a breather," he says, "I got you a grilled cheese and fries."

The girl sits next to him.

"What you feel like doing after you eat?"

"TV," the girl says.

"I don't have a TV," Walt says. "What else?"

"Ice cream."

"That, Kid Collins, I can do," he says and hands her the bag.

"Kid Collins" can be read as a reverse Persephone/ Demeter story. In the version of the myth that's most well known Persephone is lost to her mother—she's sent to the underworld, and she never returns. Sometimes she just runs into the woods but sometimes she's abducted. The Song of Demeter is a lament by her mother about her disappearance. In this version, a mother leaves her kid with her brother. She wants to keep her safe. Maybe the mother's gone to the dark side, or maybe she knows the girl will have a better chance of things with her brother. Even if she leaves her own kid, it's as bad for her as it is for Demeter. A mother is losing her kid. "Kid Collins" has a happier ending—the kid's safe, and her uncle is kind to her— but in the end, the mother is gone. As in the myth, there's not really any salvation on hand. You might survive, the story might continue. That's it.

—KB

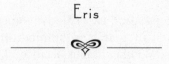

SLEEPING BEAUTY

Gina Ochsner

She might have been considered pretty. The other girls in Ya-kutsk Children's Home #5 told Lena that she was. Full lips, dark flashing eyes, violet like a storm gathering over the ice. Lena would be prettier if she wasn't so angry, Director Laskaya said to the girl from time to time. Certainly she'd be more employable and that was the real worry: how to find jobs for these girls whose mothers had died and whose fathers—if they'd ever known them in the first place—had vanished. The slim diet of companionship, the fierce but fleeting loyalties between survivors, that's all of family Lena knew.

Now it was Lena's eighteenth birthday; her time in Home #5 had come to an end. Director Laskaya called Lena to her office.

"Congratulations," Director Laskaya said, wearily sliding onion-skin pages toward Lena. She had been well cared for, well fed, the document said. All six copies of it proclaimed. She had suffered no undo injury or bodily harm. She had no complaints, no suggestions.

Director Laskaya fished in her desk for a pen. "Sign."

Who cared if it wasn't true? Who cared if she put her name to it?

She wouldn't get the envelope with the two hundred rubles if she didn't.

Laskaya handed over the envelope, relieved to see the girl go.

"VISITORS!" a voice from outside Laskaya's office hollered. "Visitors for Lena!"

ON the crumbling steps stood two elderly women, dripping in mink that carried the smell of marsh in summertime. They measured Lena with their eyes. Witches, Lena decided. They had to be. The tall, stooped one leaned heavily on a black cane. The handle curved into the inky smooth head of a raven. Its amber eyes glittered conspiratorially and its beak, rapier sharp, seemed an extension of the woman's body. "Aunt Nitsa," she said by way of introduction, and even her voice sounded bony and sharp.

"And I'm your Aunt Masha," the shorter one said. Her voice was round and warm; her eyes were dark as figs.

"Have you any skills or talents?" Nitsa asked, gripping that cane, tight, tight. The color of a hematoma, that's what her Aunt Nitsa's eyes made Lena think of. And her voice, strafing.

"No," Lena said.

"Hopeless," Aunt Nitsa pronounced in the hollow tone of a prophecy. "She's not worth the trouble."

WELL, a woman isn't a pot. You can't throw a lid on her, though it would have been grand if someone had. Because blessings and curses carry power, but for some reason, it's the curses we can't forget.

Aunt Masha peered intently into Lena's eyes. "Nothing is hopeless. Can you count, child?"

"Yes."

"Can you take the cold?" A fair question, as Yakutsk was cold more often than not. But she'd grown up in the home, a drafty building, sparely heated.

"Yes."

The two aunts exchanged glances and it seemed as if the fringes of their mink coats conferred quietly.

"Then you can sell in the market," Aunt Masha pronounced.

WHAT a job convincing the city deputy governor! It seemed there were plenty of stalls already. Perhaps it was the strange rustling noise, a flapping from Nitsa's cane, or the fact that the mink murmured at the hems of their mistresses' coats and even bared their teeth slightly. At last, the deputy governor, bathed in icy stares from every provenance, came to his senses: there really was room for another vender.

THE kiosk the aunts had specially built for Lena was of a light aluminum frame with wooden siding. Hinged in the middle, like a giant coin purse set on end, it folded in half and clasped shut with an enormous hasp. The front was wrapped with elaborate metal frets to discourage theft and a small opening just wide enough for a hand to pass a small bundle through. When the kiosk stood open, with the glass bottles of vodka, beer, and cellophane-wrapped packages of cigarettes all neatly lined in rank and file catching the morning sun, the kiosk resembled to a high degree a beacon, a pilgrim's place of prayer, sanctuary. And to Lena it was. Ensconced behind her counter from dawn to dusk, Lena could observe in her private silence the world around her bustle in cold shocks of air and light creep through the layers of cold. She felt, as cold as it was, the tightness in her jaw and her ribs loosen. She wasn't happy, she wasn't so foolish as to believe in such fairy tales. But if happiness *were* possible, then she was feeling something close to it.

AN old legend says God had been flying around distributing riches, but when he got to Yakutia he grew so cold, his hands went numb and he dropped everything. On a day like today, minus 53, Lena can believe it. Not even goose grease rubbed on the skin completely kept the stinging frostbite from her fingers, and this with two sets of gloves. On account of the temperature, the metal workers had been sent home early, which suited her fine; it meant more business for her and the others working the market stalls: Glasha with CDs from China, Old Marina with her frozen fish, Fruma who sold horse hearts and sausages, items always in high demand. Then there was Genady who sold cooking oil and thick wedges of lard on bread—Siberian sandwiches—and who sometimes played his violin.

THEIR words and breath rose in a vapor which hung in a dull fog just a few meters above the ground. The market lights barely dented this dark veil. But Lena didn't mind because it meant, at the very least, they were still alive, still breathing. But if it were a few degrees colder, say minus 56, then the heavens appeared. Every breath, every word uttered froze and fell to the ground in a musical tinkling they called the whisper of stars. Those were the days she could actually see three hours of gossip by simply leaning over the counter and looking at the frozen ice bits on the ground.

ONE day, at minus 57, it was not a bit of ice that fell, but a flash of black, a wrinkle of ink. Lena jumped from her stool. It was an enormous dark bird, uncannily similar to the one she'd seen perched beneath her Aunt Nitsa's hand. The bird settled on the countertop and rapped with its needle sharp beak: *Tap. Tap. Tap.* Lena eyed the bird carefully. It bobbed its head, then fixed its jeweled gaze on her. A silver canister had been attached to one leg. She removed her gloves and opened the canister. A tiny note fell out.

> If you are reading this now
> then it means that your Aunt Masha
> and I have died.
> You are alone now
> but it doesn't mean you have to be lonely.
> It's up to you to figure out what that means.

"OLD bat." Lena crumpled the note and let it fall to the ice. Like a dart the bird pricked her hand. Then with a tremendous flap of its wings, the bird lifted into the air. Lena was too busy listening to the sound of the wings beating the sky into ice to notice the blood dripping from her hand to the countertop and freezing into coin-sized disks. She sat there, as if asleep, and might have continued this way had not Alexander Kolenkov—Sasha to his drinking buddies—recently rotated out of the army and anxious to forget everything he'd seen and done the last two years, gone to the market for vodka. The consumption of vodka was the best method he'd found so far for suppressing unruly memory, though he was not opposed to the occasional dunking with rum or beer or anything else he could get his hands on. And this is what occupied his thoughts: what could he buy for ten rubles, and why was his left boot lisping so oddly, making such a foolish noise, like that of a mouse farting: *s-s-s-squeak?* Then he spied a girl, whose lips seemed to him ripe for kissing.

———

SHE stood enshrined within her kiosk, cocooned in the half-light and shadow cast by overhead sodium lights. She neither acknowledged his presence, nor the sound of his lisping boot, nor even the bizarre conversation floating and falling into ice chunks at the stall next to hers:

"This Zak-Zak Wow-Wow Member Extender—does it really work? Because my fiancé, she's not happy with me. In these temperatures, there's no room for error."

"I'm sorry," came the bored reply from the vendor, a thick-bodied girl with platinum hair.

"It says 'tingly.' What does 'tingly' do? And says it is ribbed for her satisfaction. What does that mean?"

SASHA expected the girl to tell the earnest man where to go and how to get there, but she instead replied with the patience of a mother tucking a finicky child in for a nap. "I don't know. It's like chewing gum. You have to buy it and try it out for yourself. It's just the way it is."

ALL this time Sasha had been watching the sleepy girl. Though a country boy, he wasn't a fool. And though the army had been his home, his only real family, he'd spent his childhood herding horses. And what he'd learned from horses was the importance of patience, of knowing when to move slowly and when not to move at all. He recognized at once that this girl, so sleepy, was also sad and angry beneath her veil of yawns—Good Lord were those her tonsils he just saw?! She had been abused by this life, that much was clear, and when someone has been hurt, then the only remedy is love, an ocean of it.

AND then he saw her hand. The blood had dried, but now her hand was pale as ice.

"You're hurt," he said, withdrawing from his pocket a tuck of wool and rubbing it on her skin.

AT his touch her pupils dilated wildly. While the bored talk— that meaningless chatter that vendors everywhere can sustain in even the most inclement commercial climates without so much as succumbing to a single vast important word—continued in a steady stream of listless torpor that carries the same vigor one might assign to the reading of an obituary, Sasha assessed the situation. Yes, she was beautiful. Yes he wanted to kiss her. In this cold they would likely freeze at the lips. That would really piss her off.

BUT he was braver than most. That is, he remembered that patience is the other half of courage and that morning is wiser than evening. He wrapped another layer of wool around the girl's hand, gently, and backed away, his boots lisping in the snow.

IN the morning Sasha returned. The beautiful girl was at her stool, swallowing her yawns. He still didn't know her name, but he wasn't worried. A herder of horses, a counter of snowflakes, he was not afraid of weight or silence or cold. Perched behind her glass box, she doled packets of cigarettes to her customers, moving like a swimmer through thick viscous fluid. Her real problem, he decided, was not the wound in her hand. It was the lull she had slipped into, the coma of sleeping-while-waking. He knew he had to save her because, truly, there is nothing more terrifying than unregulated waking sleep: it was, after all, the whole reason for all the medicinal vodka, which he drank lest the nightmares bowl him over like a freight train, drag him over the tracks, and leave him stranded, hurting, naked and ashamed.

AND as a person can only sleep for so long, Sasha planted his elbows on the girl's counter, leaned forward and put his nose next to hers. "Wake up," he whispered.

Her eyelids fluttered and snapped open.

"Listen," he tried again.

Lena began to lift her hand, the wounded one, as if to stifle another yawn, but Sasha gently, gently laid his hand on hers.

"I love you. And this love, it will be like life. It won't be perfect. In fact, it will probably tear us into bits. But you're beautiful and I think you're worth it."

Lena opened her eyes. "I'm worth it," she repeated.

"Yes," he said, and kept talking, telling her where her true value lay and how her inestimable worth went far beyond her visible beauty, which was vast. And as his words rose in the slim space between them, rose and turned to solid crystals that fell at his feet, Lena, wide awake now, more awake than she'd ever been, began to breathe more quickly. Her breath, too, rose and fell, adding to the heap of jewel-like ice surrounding them. And on this went, this compilation, this verbal and visual confirmation of love that transcends the body. Beneath the lights of the stalls the crystals grew around them, a shelter, a shield, a cathedral catching and casting the light, multiplying it a million times, as many times as there were breaths, as there were words. Some of the vendors said it cocooned them. Others said, no, it was more like it entombed then, the way the boy spoke so earnestly, the words rising, hovering, then falling to light. Either way, it was agreed by all that the light around them was so lovely, so pure, that they would not for the world look away.

The story "Sleeping Beauty" takes its inspiration from "Little Briar Rose" collected by the Grimm Brothers, and many scholars also trace the tale further back to mythology. I wondered what would happen if Briar Rose hadn't been quite so privileged and what would happen if instead of thick bracken a dense cold separated the would-be lovers. Someone once told me that we write what we love. I think that I write what I fear. I'm terribly afraid of cold and I suppose that fear is what drives this story.

—GO

GALATEA
Madeline Miller

It was almost sweet the way they worried about me.

"You're so pale," the nurse said. "You must keep quiet until your color returns."

"I'm always this color," I said. "Because I used to be made of stone."

The woman smiled vaguely, pulling up the blanket. My husband had warned her that I was fanciful, that my illness made me say things that would sound strange to her.

"Just lie back and I'll bring you something to eat," she said. She had a mole on the side of her lip and I liked to watch it while she talked. Some moles are beautiful and distinctive, like dappling on a horse. But some have hairs in them, and look pulpy like worms, and hers was this kind.

"Lie back," she repeated, because I hadn't.

"You know what I think would be good for my color? A walk," I said.

"Oh no," she said. "Not until you're better. Feel how chilled your hands are?"

"That's the stone," I said, "like I told you. It can't get warm without sun. Haven't you ever touched a statue?"

"You're chilled," she repeated. "Just lie back, and be good." She was rushing a little by then, because I had mentioned the stone twice, and this was gossip for the other nurses, and a breathless reason to speak to the doctor. They were fucking, that's why she was so eager. I could hear them sometimes through the wall. I don't say this in a nasty way, for I don't begrudge her a good fuck, if it was good, which I don't know. But I say this so that you understand what I was up against: that I was worth more to her sick than I was well.

The door closed, and the room swelled around me like a bruise. When she was here, I could pretend it felt small because of her, but when she left the four wood walls seemed to press toward me, like lungs that had breathed in. The window did not help, for it was too high to see from the bed, and too small to take in much air. The room smelled sweet and sour at once, as though a thousand suffering people had lain sweating in it, which I suppose they had, and then ground roses into the floor with dirty feet.

The doctor was next, and he made noises at me. "Chloe says you have not been lying quietly."

I said, "I'm sorry."

He liked that, but he was also suspicious, because I had been apologizing to him every day for a year. For his sake, I tried to vary it—looking down, biting my lip, twisting my fingers. Once, I burst into tears, and that had been his favorite time. I was working on trying to faint, but didn't have it quite right yet, for I needed to spend a long time breathing very fast first, and I hadn't had enough warning that he was coming. But as soon as I did, that would be the new best time. And the doctor would tell my husband, who would shower him with golden coins, and everyone would be happy, except for me. Though I supposed I would be a little happy, for thinking of it.

"What are you doing?" he said, severely. "This is exactly why you are ill."

I had gotten up, you see, while I was thinking about the fainting. The room was smallest of all with the doctor in it, and he had had garlic that day, and what smelled like every day he'd ever lived, so I had gone to breathe by the window.

"I'm sorry," I said. "I just love the scent of the narcissus." It was the first thing I thought of, but it only made him frown more, because there were no narcissus here, since we are on the rocky edge of a cliff over the sea, so that if I tried to climb out the window, I would not escape but die. Also, I was not even sure narcissus had a smell.

"Lie down this instant," he said. Then, when I obeyed, he took my wrist and held it. "Your pulse is slow," he said.

Of course my pulse is slow, because I used to be made of stone, but I didn't say that. I just made a sound, mmmmm, that tried to be contrite and interested at once. I thought that if I'd started breathing fast the moment the nurse had closed the door, this might have been the time I could faint. But I had not done it, and now it was too late.

I said, "I think I would feel better if I could walk."

"You are too weak," the doctor said. "What would I tell your husband if you hurt yourself?"

"I used to be stone," I said. "I can't hurt myself from just a walk."

"That's enough," he said, in that voice that meant he was going to send for the tea. The tea is the thing they give me when I won't lie back, and I hate it, for they sit beside me until I drink it all, and then my head aches and my tongue hurts and I piss the bed.

I lay back. "You're right, this is better," I said. "Mmmm, that feels good." Through my lashes I watched him. He was suspicious, so I snuggled down closer. "You're right, I was so tired and I didn't know it." I hoped that this was enough to save me from the tea.

"Be sure you stay there," he said. "Your husband's coming to see you today." And I thought: I should have saved the snuggling bit, because they don't give me the tea when my husband comes. He hates the smell of piss, and he likes me to be able to use my tongue.

I lay down and arranged myself in the right way. It's easy, because I've had a lot of practice, but also because I think there's some part of me, the stone part, that remembers and is glad to settle into its old lines. The only hard thing is the fingers, which my husband likes to say he spent a year on, making them look real instead of still and limp, like lazy sculptors do. So I have to concentrate and hold them just the way he likes, or it ruins everything.

Time passed, I wasn't sure how much. Then through the door I heard the jingle of coins, and the nurses exclaiming. My husband is quite rich now, and has enough to pay for a thousand more doctors who all tell me to lie down. He is rich because of me, if you want to know, but he doesn't like it when I say that. He says, it's the goddess's gift first, and then his own, since he was the one who made me from the marble. After I was born—and maybe that is not the right word, but if not, then I don't know what is—woke? Hatched? No, that is worse. I am not an egg.

I will say born. After I was born, he tried to keep me inside as much as he could, but there were servants, and people began to talk about the sculptor's wife, and how strange she was, and how such beauty comes only from the gods. Some people believed that, and some people didn't, but suddenly they all wanted statues from him. So he chiseled maiden after maiden, and I said, do you think any of them will come to life? And he said, of course not, these people are not worthy of the goddess's gift. And he told me again how well he had cared for me, dressing me in silks, and draping me in flowers and jewels, and bringing me seashells and colored balls, and praying to the goddess every night. Would not it have been easier to marry a girl from the town? I asked. Those sluts, he said, I would not have them.

The door opened. "Leave and do not disturb us," my husband said to the maids, which was unnecessary, since they've never disturbed us, not in a year's time. But my husband thinks himself a potentate these days.

There was silence, because he was looking at me, checking my fingers and all the rest. I didn't open my eyes, because my job was to lie on the couch without moving so that he might murmur, "Ah, my beauty is asleep." A few times in the past, I had let out a little snore at that moment, just for verisimilitude. But he did not like that at all.

"Asleep?" he said. He stepped into the room. "I am a fool to say so. She is marble and nothing more." He knelt beside the bed and lifted his hands. "O goddess! Why cannot I find a maiden such as this for my wife? Why must such perfection be marble and not flesh? If only she might—" Abruptly, he covered his eyes. "No, I cannot say it."

I thought about making a little snore right then, but that would have been even worse than before.

"I dare not say what I desire. But O, great goddess, you know my secret heart. I beg you, release me from this torment." His head slumped to the pallet, and I opened my eyes, because he couldn't see me while he wallowed in the covers. His hair was thinning, and I counted the bare spots on his scalp. Three, like always.

I closed my eyes, just in time. His head lifted, and he said, "No, it cannot be. I must resign myself." But his hand had fallen conveniently against my forearm, and he pressed it a little in his agony.

"What is this?" He stared at my arm. "Can it be? I would swear that she is warm."

Warmer than regular stone, anyway.

He shook his head, as though to clear it. "No, I am imagining things. Or perhaps the sun has fallen on her, and warmed the marble."

There was no sun in the room, of course, but it wasn't the time to say this.

"Goddess, do not let me be mad!" He began kneading my hips and belly, hard, testing my stoniness. I prided myself on not flinching.

"Yet I will swear it, I will swear on my life, she is warm. O goddess, if this is a dream, let me still sleep." And then he pressed his lips onto mine. "Live," he said. "Oh live, my life, my love, live."

And that's when I'm supposed to open my eyes like a dewy fawn, and see him poised over me like the sun, and make a little gasping noise of wonder and gratitude, and then he fucks me.

AFTER, I lay against his damp shoulder. I said, "My love, I miss you."

He said nothing, but I could feel his impatience. The sweat was drying on his front, and his back was a swamp. Also, the reed ticking scratched through the sheet, and he's used to a padded bed at home.

"What are you working on?" I asked. Because it is the one thing I know he will answer.

"A statue," he said.

"Ah!" I closed my eyes. "I wish I could see it, darling. What is it of?"

"A girl."

"It will be beautiful," I said. "Is she for one of the men in town?"

"No," he said. "I'm tired of those. This one is for myself."

"How wonderful," I said. "I hope I may see it when you are finished."

"Maybe," he said.

"I will be so good," I said.

He said nothing.

"How old is the girl?" I asked.

"Ten," he said.

I had expected him to say "young." When I had once asked him how old he meant for me to be, he had said, "A virgin."

"Ten," I said. "Not twelve, perhaps?"

"No," he said.

"I do love girls at fifteen," I said. "The other day the nurse brought her daughter, and she was so beautiful. Her whole face was filled with light."

"I have no interest in fifteen," he said. "Or the nurse's daughter."

"Of course not." I stroked his chest with my perfect fingers. I tried to make my voice loose and easy, like a yawn. "How is Paphos, my love?"

"Fine," he said. Just that ugly, nothing word.

"Is she happy?"

"How could she be, after what her mother did?"

I was ready for this, and tipped the tears onto his chest. "I am so sorry, my darling. I wish I could make it up to her."

He pushed me off him and sat up. "You grovel for her, but not me."

I wanted to say, what do you think I have been doing? But of course, my husband would not appreciate that. He is a man who likes white, smooth surfaces. I knelt on the floor, my hands pressed together over my breasts. "My love, there is nothing more in the world I want than to come home with you. Just today I wished that I had something of you to comfort me. A painting, maybe. A painting of you."

This surprised him. "A painting," he said. "Not a statue."

"Oh my darling, a statue would torment me too much," I said. "It would be too much like you to bear."

"Mmm," he said. I let my hands fall a little, so that he might see my breasts better. They were very fine, he had made sure of it.

"Do you not miss me? Even a little?"

"It is your own fault, if I do."

"It is, I know, I know it is. I'm so sorry, darling. I was such a fool, I don't even know what I was doing."

"A fool," he said. He was looking at my breasts again.

"Yes, a terrible fool. An ungrateful fool."

"You should not have run," he said.

"I will never run again, I swear on my life. I can barely stand when you leave me, I live every day yearning for you to come. You are my husband, and father."

"And mother," he said.

"Yes, and mother. And brother too. And lover. All of these."

He said, "You say this only because you want to see Paphos."

"Of course I want to see her. What kind of mother would I be, if

I did not? Cold, and shameless. That is not how you and the goddess made me."

I was breathing very hard, but trying to pretend I was not. The floor was hurting my knees, but I did not move.

"Shameless," he said.

"Shameless," I said.

I felt him looking at me, admiring his work. He had not carved me like this, but he was imagining doing it. A beautiful statue, named *The Supplicant*. He could have sold me and lived like a king in Araby.

He frowned, pointing. "What is that?"

I looked down at my belly and saw the faint silvery tracks on my skin, caught in the light.

"My love, it is the sign of our child. Where the belly stretched."

He stared. "How long have they been there?"

"Since she was born." Ten years ago, now.

"They are ugly," he said.

"I'm so sorry, my love. It is the same for all women."

"If you were stone, I would chisel them off," he said. Then he turned and left and after a little while the doctor came with the tea.

THE thing is, I don't think my husband expected me to be able to talk. I don't blame him for this exactly, since he had known me only as a statue, pure and beautiful and yielding to his art. Naturally, when he wished me to live, that's what he wanted still, only warm so that he might fuck me. But it does seem foolish that he didn't think it through, how I could not both live and still be a statue. I have only been born for eleven years, and even I know that.

I conceived that very first time, a moment after I was born. And though I had been stone, and though the goddess made me, my pregnancy was real enough, and I was tired and sick and my feet were too swollen for the delicate golden sandals he liked to see them in. It made him angry, but it did not stop him from pushing me onto the bed or up against the wall, and I worried that because of it I would have not one child, but a whole litter at once, like the cats in the street.

My daughter was beautiful and stone-pale and born in a summer that was so viciously hot the calves died in the fields. But she and I were always perfectly cool, rocking in our chair together. When we would go walking, everyone whispered but no one would speak to us, except once an old woman touched Paphos's foot and asked for my blessing. I murmured something, and she touched my arm in thanks. Her fingers were strange, like twigs on bare trees, but her skin was very soft.

Sometimes, when my husband was working, we were allowed to go as far as the hillsides. Paphos was older by then, and she would pretend to be a shepherd, and I would pretend to be her sheep. She liked that. She liked it even better when I was a goat, and leaped barefoot from rock to rock, and never wobbled. When she got older still, I insisted on a tutor, though my husband thought that would ruin her. No, I said, she will be useful to her husband, as I am not. And he had smiled at me. You are useful enough. But he hired the tutor in the end, because I fawned on him every time he mentioned it.

In the countryside, Paphos would teach me. Look, she would say, you can use sticks for the letters, and I would say, But some of them are round. And she frowned and said, You're right, shall we go to the beach and use sand? So we did, and it was better than sticks, and even better than the tutor's tablet, because the sea washed it for you. She was a smart girl, very smart, and I didn't have to tell her to say nothing to her father.

At night, my husband sent her to bed. He would say, "And you too, wife, are you not sleepy?" And I would know it was time to go arrange myself in bed, so that we might pretend again that I was waking from the stone to him.

When Paphos was eight, he sent the tutor away. "He was looking at you," he said to me.

I was distracted that day, thinking of Paphos and the letters, and I said, "Of course he was." Everyone looked at me, because I was the most beautiful woman in the town. I don't say this to boast, because there is nothing in it to boast of. It was nothing I did myself.

My husband stared at me, and said, "You knew?"

I tried to explain, but it was too late. We were not allowed to walk anymore, and Paphos was given a governess instead of a tutor, and her tablets were taken away, and during the days my husband sulked over his marble and did not work. At night, he was rougher than he had been and would not stop asking, Would you be like the rest? And I knew to say no, no darling, never.

Paphos was impatient—she hated our house, and wanted our old adventures in the country. She wasn't quiet when her father wished to brood, which was always, and as the days passed she grew more impatient still. I took her to our room and we made the letters with our fingers. She was laughing, and I was too, and we did not know how loud we were.

My husband came to the doorway. "Why are you laughing?"

Paphos said, "Why not?" She was taller than the other girls, and long-limbed. She wasn't afraid of him.

I said, "Darling, I'm so sorry we disturbed you."

"She does not say she is sorry."

"She is still a baby," I said.

"I'm not a baby," Paphos said.

"Then apologize," he said.

"You poor thing, you look half-starved," I said to him. "Have you not eaten? Paphos, sweetheart, let me talk to your father a moment."

She left, and I saw him grind his teeth at how obediently she did it. He said, "You love her more than me."

Of course not, of course not. My hands stroked his hair, long and greasy from brooding. It is only that she is too smart for that governess, I said. She is bored, and I cannot teach her anything. She needs a tutor.

He said, a tutor.

And I said, yes, another tutor would make everything better, and then we would not bother you. He was quiet, and I hoped he was considering it, but when I saw his face it was taut and angry, as though he would break the skin. He seized my arm, and he said, you never blush.

I couldn't think to speak, that is how hard he held me.

He said, you do not blush anymore, that is the thing. You apologize and apologize, but you do not blush. Are you shameless now?

No, never, I said. He grabbed the neck of my dress and yanked, but he was not as strong as he wished to be, and it did not tear. He yanked again and again, then pushed me to the floor and held me there, yanking, until the fabric gave way and I was naked.

I covered myself with my hands, and made soft noises like a child. Blush, blush, I prayed. Blush for him, or he will kill you. And I was fortunate, for it was warm in the room, and I was angry, and ashamed too, for I feared that Paphos could hear us, and the blood came to my cheeks and I blushed.

He said, "So you are not completely lost to me." And he sent me to bed, and after, in the torchlight, he wondered at the marks on me, the red around my neck, and the purple on my arms and chest where he had gripped me. He rubbed at them, as though they were stains, not bruises. The color is perfect, he said, look. And he held up the mirror so I could see. You make the rarest canvas, love.

I had a little money, coins my husband had dropped from his messy purses, things I had found in the street. I had shoes that I stole from the governess, leather things, not golden, that were meant for traipsing up and down dusty roads. I had a cloak that I stole from my husband. Paphos had her own, because I had insisted she got cold easily, though she was like me, and was never cold, nor never hot either. And I said to her, "Shall we go to the countryside?"

And she said, "Daddy will not let us," and I said, "I know, so let's not tell him."

We did not make it beyond the next town, because everyone noticed us. "A woman and a girl, pale as milk? Yes, just that way."

THE nurse let me lie in the wet for a long time before she came with the dry linens. She bunched the mattress reeds so that they stuck at me worse than ever, and refused to answer me, no matter what I said to her, even when I told her how beautiful her mole was. I wasn't even lying. At that moment it seemed to have a handsomeness of its own.

After, she gave me a bath. She didn't use a cloth, just her hand, dipped in the water. I think she hoped that I would complain about it, but I didn't, because it must be a miserable thing to wash people if you hate it. Next came the rose oil that my husband pays extra for, which she put on as though she was making bread, slapping my skin with both hands. She meant it to hurt, but I sort of liked the vigor of it, the sound and the way my skin went pink.

When she was gone, I wiped off as much of the rose oil as I could on the sheets. The tea had passed through me and my head was clear. I thought: my daughter is ten. Paphos is ten.

THE next day, the doctor frowned at me. "Are you unwell?"

"No," I said. "I am very well."

He was about to say, "Then why are you lying down?" but that would have meant admitting that I was not sick to begin with. Ha, I thought.

"I am feeling so calm," I said. "Calm, and well."

"Hmmm," he said.

"I hope my husband comes today," I said. "I miss him terribly."

"He said he would," the doctor said.

"How wonderful," I said. "What wonderful news."

The jingling came late, but I wasn't impatient. I arranged myself just so. The door opened, and my husband sent the nurses away. I heard the lock catch.

"Ah, my beauty is asleep."

And I said, "No, I'm not."

He said, "For your sake, I tell you to lie down, and I will return in a moment when you have collected yourself."

I said, "I am pregnant."

He stared. "It is not possible." Because ever since Paphos, he leaves his seed on my belly.

With the gods, all things are possible, I said. Look at my stomach. I had puffed it a little, so that it looked like a mound. And anyway, he did not know what women looked like. To him, if there was anything, it was strange.

He was pale then, almost as pale as me. "The doctor did not say so."

"I did not show the doctor, I wanted you to be the first to know. Darling, I'm so happy, we shall have another child, and then another after that. And then—"

But the door had already closed. Later the doctor came, with a different kind of tea. He said, you have to drink this. And I said, please, will you send the nurse to sit with me while I do?

He said, all right, for he saw that I would cry otherwise. It was amazing how easy it was.

The nurse came, and I said, will it hurt? I fear it will hurt. And she said, it will hurt a little, and then the blood will come.

I am afraid, I said, and I hid my face in the pillow.

A moment passed, and then I felt her hand on my back. You will be all right, she said. I have done it, and look, I live.

But the baby doesn't live, I said.

No, she said.

I wept, racking, into the cushions.

You must drink the tea, she said. But her voice was not so sharp as usual.

If only I could go outside, I said. I want to give the baby to the goddess.

The doctor doesn't allow it.

I waited, and waited, and wept, and at last she said, But the doctor is not here at night.

I wanted to roll on the grass like a dog, but I was supposed to be pregnant and suffering, so I limped, as though every part of me might break. She brought me the tea, and I held it sipping. She said, tell me when the cramping comes.

I sifted the dirt through my fingers. It was dark, and there was only a little moon, which I took to mean that the goddess, if she existed, smiled on me. I said, I think I feel something. Good, she said. We were in the garden, at the back of the house, away from the sea.

I said, I feel something.

Good, she said.

Then I doubled over, screaming. I fell to the ground, and screamed again. She was frightened, because it had never taken her like this, and she hesitated.

It hurts, it hurts! Get the doctor!

She was trembling, and I felt a little sorry, but not sorry enough.

The doctor, yes. I will go for him. Just give me a moment, his house isn't far.

As soon as she was gone, I ran. I did not worry about her catching me. She was clever with her fingers, but she was not fast. I smiled and slipped along the road toward the town.

I did not try the door of the house—I knew it would be locked. But there was a tree behind it, an olive, that Paphos used to beg me to climb with her. I kicked off my sandals and stepped up the warm, gray branches. I reached, and pulled myself into her window.

I had thought about it all day, if I would wake her, or if I wouldn't. But seeing her asleep, I could not. She was a child, only ten, and it would frighten her. So I found the pot of sand she liked to keep because it smelled of the sea and spilled a little on the floor. *Paphos*, I spelled. I would have said more, but that was most of what I knew.

I slipped from her room and went to the front door, which was bolted. I did not have to hurry, because no one would look for me here; had I not run from him before? I eased up the bolt and left the door open, a little.

My husband's workroom was in the far wing, where the light was best. I stood outside the door and though I wasn't tired anymore from running, my breath was quick. The house was very quiet around me. There were no servants to worry about—my husband did not like them to sleep in the house.

I pushed open the door, and saw the girl, glowing in the room's center. Stone, I told myself, because I was shaking a little. She is stone and she will not wake.

I stepped closer and saw her face. It was pale and pearly, her mouth a soft bow. Her eyes were closed, and she was curled on a stone couch. She looked younger than Paphos, because she was so small. She was perfection, every inch of her, from the sweet curls of her ribbons to her sandals painted gold. She had no scabs, and no sand between her fingernails. She did not chase the goats, and she did not disobey. You could almost see the flush on her cheeks.

There were silks on her, draped like blankets, and I slipped them off. There was a bracelet of flowers on her wrist, and I pulled it away. I kissed her forehead and whispered, Daughter, I'm sorry.

I went to my husband's room, and stood in the doorway. He was flung across the bed, and rumpled.

"Ah, my beauty is asleep," I said.

My husband's eyes opened and he saw me. I turned and ran. I heard a crash as he tripped over the stool I had left for him in the hall, but then he was up again, almost on the stairs. I fled through the front door, and onto the road, and his footsteps slapped behind me. He did not shout, because he didn't want to waste his breath; it was just the night's silence and the two of us, running through the streets. My lungs ached a little but it didn't matter, because I wouldn't need them soon.

The road passed through the town and dipped toward the sea. I was slow and fat from a year of lying in bed, but he had never loved exercise, and was fat and slow himself. The dirt gave way to sand, cool and thick beneath my feet, and then I was on the pebbles, which had never hurt me, and then, at last, the waves. I threw myself in, fighting past the breakers to the open sea. A moment later, I heard the splash of him following.

Water was not my element. It dragged at my clothes as I swam. A little farther, I told myself. I could hear him coming, his arms stronger than mine from a lifetime of lifting marble. I felt the water shiver near my foot where he had grabbed and almost caught me. I looked back and saw how close he was and how far the shore behind. Then his hand seized my ankle and yanked, pulling me to him like a rope, hand over hand, and then he had me up and by the throat, his face pressed to mine.

I think he expected me to fight and claw. I didn't fight. I seized him close around the ribs, holding my wrists so he could not get free. The sudden weight pulled us both under. He kicked and flailed back to the surface, but I was heavier than he had thought, and the waves slopped at our mouths. Let it be now, I prayed.

At first I thought it was just the cold of the water. It crept up my fingers and my arms, which stiffened around him. He struggled and fought, but my hands were fused together and nothing he tried could break them. Then it was in my legs too, and my belly and my chest, and no matter how he kicked, he could not haul us back up to the air. He hit at me, but it was watery and weak and I felt nothing, just the solid circle of my arms, and the inexorable drag of my body.

He had no chance, really. He was only flesh. We fell through the darkness, and the coolness slid up my neck and bled the color from my lips and cheeks. I thought of Paphos and how clever she was. I thought of her stone sister, peaceful on her couch. We fell through the currents and I thought of how the crabs would come for him, climbing over my pale shoulders. The ocean floor was sandy and soft as pillows. I settled into it and slept.

This story is based on the Greek myth of the sculptor Pygmalion, who makes a statue so perfectly beautiful that he falls in love with it. He prays to the goddess Aphrodite to bring her to life, and the goddess grants his wish and unites the pair in matrimony. In the original versions of the story, the statue-woman didn't have a name, but she later became known as Galatea, milk-white. I was particularly inspired by Ovid's retelling in his Metamorphoses, *which ends with the birth of Galatea's daughter, Paphos.*

—MM

God and Satan

THE HAND
Manuel Muñoz

The town held twenty churches, large and small, north and south, east and west, on both sides of the railroad tracks. The Baptists and the Mennonites had dark glass doors and triangular arches, the walls of polished stones. The First Christian, a marble and cement façade made yellow by the rains. The Episcopalians, a tiny one-room with a red door glimmering through the winter fog. At Saint Catherine's, the elderly gathered quarters to help repair the splintered white wood frame. The Lutherans, the Church of the Hope and the Redeemer, the Pentecostals and their all-day Sundays, the Church of the Good Shepherd: from every corner, the watchful eye of God guarded over the town.

Whatever the congregation on the corner had once been, the boy hadn't known. They had moved to another building on the better side of town, taking their particular ways of worship with them. All the boy knew was that the church was just another building with dim windows in the afternoon and that the older boys broke in through the back door. He tried to follow them, but they shut him out, closing the door behind them as they explored. He peeked through the low windows, seeing what little he could when he stretched on his tiptoes.

They exited after a time, bored and shuffling through the unruly yard. This had been the extent of their sacrilege. They hadn't even shattered the windows with rocks. The boy went inside alone, but already expected nothing. Before him stretched the stripped, dusty floors where the pews had been ripped out and the boards creaked as the boy walked along. Sunlight came in hazy through the windows, early spring, but inside the church, the quiet walls were of another time. A door in the rear, to his surprise, revealed a narrow kitchen, bare now except for a sink, a quiet drip of water.

This was the church where the neighborhood had gathered after the cemetery visits, the men in black, and the ladies giving out paper plates of rice and beans, lemonade for the children. It had never been his family's church, but the front lawn had been filled by the neighbors nonetheless, sometimes to share condolences, sometimes for a needed meal.

When the boy exited the abandoned church, the older boys were long gone. The neighborhood, too, seemed hidden behind its closed doors, as if the adults had found their own ways to disappear into the day, no one on the porches, not even the faint drift of conversation from a backyard. The afternoon sun hung weak in the sky. The boy tried to shut the door behind him, but the wood was swollen, and he had to leave the door as best he could, a thin dark line, top to bottom, a black space sharp against the sunlight.

He went down the cement steps, the only sturdy thing about the place. The walls buckled visibly along the foundation.

Later that spring, when the church was torn down, the workmen left nothing but the cement steps, the makeshift railing made from pieces of stray pipe, and the four sides of the foundation dug deep into the earth. Whether these were more difficult to break down, the boy didn't know, but as he walked to school, he would sometimes see the workmen gathered there, as if trying to solve a difficult problem. The adults in his family had said that the church was an older building than most people realized and that it would take real work to take it down. It would be a good job to have, his uncles said, and he thought of them gathered in the backyard, idle with beer cans, when the workmen finally began chipping away at the foundation, bit by bit, with pickaxes all through the heat of the afternoon.

By summer, the lot was vacant, just mounds and mounds of earth. The workmen departed and the evenings became long. The adults disappeared into the backyard, no one bothering to call the children in at dusk. School was out. The bored older boys gathered at the vacant lot, kicking at the clods of dirt and the chipped cement.

"Go away," they told him, when he showed up with a small yellow truck, though he hadn't wanted to play with them, only to be in their shadow. He wanted the comfort of their rough laughter, the older boys who didn't need toys anymore, who didn't need the solace of tracing a road in the dirt with his palm, guiding along as if his hand could bring him anywhere in the world. Not here, in a small town with so many churches. Not here, in a place where neither the older boys nor the adults needed his presence. Instead, a road curving out past the crooked wooden electrical posts and into the open spaces.

The boy traced a road for his yellow truck in the dirt of the vacant lot and when he looked up, the older boys were gone. The neighborhood had grown quiet, all the doors closed, the orange of evening casting a light on everything that the boy would later know as loneliness, but back then, he knew only that the light meant the day had ended.

His road drew to a stop at a large dirt mound and the boy thought of the enormous mountains to the east. He thought of the tightness in his chest that he couldn't name when he had noticed that the older boys had gone, the orange of evening filling the space where they had kicked up dust, and he began digging. His dirt road would extend through the large dirt mound, he decided, and his little yellow truck would drive through it to the other side.

Not over it and not around it, but through it.

He began digging, his tiny hand in the soft, dry dirt. The deeper he got, the richer the earth became, damp between his fingers. The heat of the late evening brought sweat to his brow and he worked even harder, thinking of the men with the pickaxes and the shovels. Soon, his road had crept into a tunnel big enough for his arm, but not big enough for his yellow truck. He wondered if digging all the way through might collapse the mound around his arm, ruining his effort, but there was only one way to find out. He wanted to see through to the other side.

He could reach in almost to his elbow, and he did so, scraping out a fistful of earth at a time, careful to pull out slowly so the hole wouldn't collapse. He reached in until he hit the solid pack of earth, then clutched what he could, nothing but earth—no roots, no clods of dirt, no rocks—between his fingers.

When he pulled out the last time, as carefully as before, something followed him out.

His tiny brown hand was followed by a larger one, red as blood, straight out of the hole he'd been digging. The boy's hand held a clutch of dark dirt. The red hand held nothing, but it searched for something to grab, pawing at the ground, testing it.

Later in life, the boy would think his instinct to run was proof of God's existence in the world. God shot fear through his legs and he tripped through the vacant lot, stumbling along, but not letting loose of the clutch of dirt in his hand. He ran up the street, the evening gone past orange into the suffocating violet of coming night. He heard nothing, saw nothing, but the neighborhood was as it always was: the crooked electrical poles, the thin potholed roads, the whir of the swamp coolers, another pot of beans cooking, the trapped heat of all their houses, and the distant presence of the adults in the backyard, a world entirely their own.

He could hear the adults there and the closer he got, the safer he felt. Yet he couldn't approach them nor go into his house, because he had wet his pants. He hid himself among the flower pots of their sagging front porch, the bright petals surrendering to the dark.

His grandmother found him—the first to call out for him in the night—and what she understood about his wide, frightened eyes the boy never quite knew. Nor would he ever know why she sought him behind the shadowy blossoms of the flower pots. She brought him out, but said nothing to the adults in the backyard. She silently led him to the bathroom. She took care of his soiled clothes without a word and bathed him, rubbed him clean with a washcloth, picked away the half-moons of grime from under his fingernails. She rubbed him until his skin hurt and when he cried, his grandmother seemed satisfied that it was the kind of cry that she had expected, a cry holding more hurt than fear.

She dried him without a word. But then again, there were no words between them. She was of another language. She soothed him with the warmth of the towel and a set of clean clothes. She was the adult in the house who went to bed early and she led him to her room at the back of the house. He slept there, though it had been a while since he slept under her care.

That night, there were no dreams. Night had no hold on him next to his grandmother's warmth. Her breathing came steady, even alert. At dawn, she rose and he rose with her. Together in the kitchen, she fed him a cup of hot cereal and a sugary tea from a sprig of orange tree leaves. She read from her Bible in the other language and then she prayed in a whisper, the whole of the house quiet.

His grandmother took him to the backyard. She led the boy with her right hand, the skin a deep brown, laced through with wrinkles, but soft. The boy tightened his grip and his grandmother's hand pulsed with blood and bone—the fact that she was a living being startled him. He loosened his hold, trusting the softness to flow back again, to make her palm only a velvet guide, to make him forget that she would one day die.

All she had was her hands. She had only the other language, so she pointed at the grass wet with dew. She meant to show him what was all around. Both the grass and the dew. She brought his fingers up to the branches of the orange tree from where she had torn the sprig of leaves for morning tea. The thorns on the branches, the delicate shoots. The morning held a quiet the boy had never heard before. His days had always been the scurry of the house already awake, the harsh scuffling of the school playground, the dust of evening playtime. The grandmother bent her head down and brought his small hand to her ear. Listen, her gesture said. The morning birds, the flutter of wings, the quiet hops as they drank the dew.

She led him around their backyard, the small patch of land that contained the world. The hard green globes in the plum tree, waiting for the summer heat. The lowly begonia in the corner, from which she cut pieces for the neighbors. Her hand was gentle, but firm in her conviction that God showed himself everywhere. She pointed around the yard, holding his hand in hers, the evidence innumerable. Whatever had terrified him, the grandmother could answer.

She bent down to the ground near the rosebushes, not yet blooming. She motioned him to kneel as well, as if in prayer, but she scratched at the earth with one swipe. The dry dirt gave way immediately to the darker earth underneath. The grandmother pointed at it. He was meant to continue. She knelt beside him as he dug, picking at the weeds around the roots. A worm writhed in the moist earth. She pointed at this, at the weeds, at the dead leaves, at the husks of rose petals that had come forth too soon. Proof was in everything. Everything. Everywhere. How she might have said it in the other language remained forever a mystery.

But this was the lesson: to point out God in the brightness of day, when it was easy to forget fear. At night, the boy would learn to look at the stars as evidence, the moon a solace, to trust the dark murmur of whatever moved in the branches.

So the boy learned what the hand was, but not what it wanted.

Sometimes, when he could not sleep and thought of what else the night might hold, the red hand burst from the ground, exposing its elbow, its arm, the curve of shoulder. He could think of his grandmother, breathing steadfast in her sleep, and the arm would recede into the ground.

He could think of the plum trees, the orange leaves, and the lowly begonias, and the hand would retreat deeper still. Closing his eyes to sleep, he could dream of unbroken ground, nothing disturbing the soil.

But after his grandmother died, he watched the earth take her back whole. At the funeral, he scattered a tiny handful of dirt over her coffin. The world, then, became larger and more terrifying. He learned of the things of the world beyond his backyard, how winds could ride with sharp force, how the seas broke in terrible waves, and how the ground could crack and shift.

He was getting older, day by day, night by night.

Over at the vacant lot, a stucco house came up, with modest Spanish arches and a tidy front lawn. A family lived there, complete with a truck in the driveway and children playing in the grass.

In his dreams, the ground of the tidy front lawn would break and the hand would rise and keep rising, until it revealed an entire red torso, a terrible winged back shuddering dirt loose from its folds. There was nothing to stop it. It rose from the ground, clicking its cloven foot along the dark street of his neighborhood, and tapped at his door in the quiet of the night.

To this, the shudder between leaves was no answer. To this, the colors of flowers could demand no reckoning. The dark figure knocked at the door, waiting for him to answer, waiting to flash its mouth of bright fire and swallow him into darkness.

Whether in the brightness of day or in the lit house of night, whether alone or with his uncles' voices in the backyard, his doubt became as sure as fog and as constant as sunrise. He thought of the mountains all around him, a wall to keep him safe. He thought of the brevity of flowers and their insistence to bloom again. Everywhere, the world's presence assured him. Everywhere, the world's design sought to comfort him.

But then the voice arrived, hard to place, unsettling in its declaration, its absence of tone. It came into the deep, deep folds of dream, well beyond terror, well beyond light, and it cracked his fear into acceptance and resignation.

"I am coming," the voice said, "for what I took away from you."

It spoke once. Only one time. And it left the boy, now a little older, sitting up in the cold violet of dawn, knowing that he would march toward his end, knowing that one day he would be forced to answer.

I understand myth as our way—via story—to explain what we suspect to be true. The myths wait for our lived experience to catch up to them. Where I grew up, God and Satan were treated as real. They made frequent appearances in oral stories. Hearing about them was like a promise: sooner or later, they would prove themselves to be not myths at all.

—MM

THE DUMMY

Benjamin Percy

She was pretty enough for a man. That's what people said about her. Short feathery hair. Shovel of a jaw. Eyes that seemed to squint with no sun. She was thin but not slight, ropily muscled, with broad shoulders that made her small breasts seem even smaller. For a laugh she called them her mosquito bites, because she knew to make a joke at her own expense took away the power of those who might say something cruel. She was always like this, imagining how someone might hurt her, guarding against the world. Her parents named her Johnnette.

In high school she wrestled. No one encouraged her to do so, least of all her parents, but she liked the purity of it, a true sport, one body against another. Everyone always said the real wrestlers belonged to the lower weight classes. Anybody over 160, 170 ended up poached by football, baseball, basketball. She wrestled at 120 and did all right in her first season, with a 31-15 record, though many of her wins came when an opponent abstained from a match, refusing to wrestle a girl.

The team practiced on dummies named Bill. The school owned five of them. At the beginning of practice the coach would swing open the supply closet and snap on the light and the Bills would be waiting in a shadowy huddle. They could stand upright. They were made of black nylon. They weighed the same as her, 120 pounds. They had squared heads and rounded fists. They appeared like scarecrows dressed head to toe in S&M leather.

Strikes, submission, throws, takedowns. Again and again, she would hurl the Bills to the mat. An arm drag. A duck under. Those were her favorite moves, the moves that didn't require as much strength, the moves that played off the balance and weight of the opponent.

Her coach was a short old man with enormous hands and a neck so wide he had to scissor a slit at the collar of the gray sweatshirts he always wore. He said you didn't wrestle for the trophies, you didn't wrestle for the matches—you wrestled for the drills—and if you didn't take pleasure in the pain and drudgery of it all, you should go home. Some did, but not Johnnette.

Why call the dummies Bill, she asked him, why not Frank, Steve, Joe? He said back in the day, that's how the dummies came, as legless bodies with "BILL" printed across their chests. She liked the idea of the old Bills better. She imagined them as rice sacks with noodley arms stitched onto them. Something obviously lifeless. Not like these Bills, who stood at odd angles and made moaning, squelching noises against the mats and smelled like the sweat smeared across them daily and seemed sometimes to be gazing at her.

Of course there were those who thought it wrong for her to wrestle, the worst among them a boy named Breck. He wrestled at 190, too slow for football. He drank protein shakes and energy drinks. His breath smelled like the water in a vase full of rotting flowers. Sometimes they sparred together. He liked to bring an elbow to her throat, a knee to her groin, and comment on what he didn't find there. He kept his hair shaved down to a black wire brush he used to scrape her. Every now and then he tried to grow a failure of a mustache. When he was a boy, Breck overturned a fryer full of hot grease that cooked his left arm completely, the fingernails peeling away, the skin sloughing off like a snake's, all the way to his shoulder, replaced by scar tissue the color of an angry sunburn. He claimed the arm could feel no pain and to prove his point would prod at it with the tip of a compass or hold a lit Zippo beneath his elbow until it blackened.

Sometimes she felt the same way about her mind. She was not

capable of the same sort of injury as others. As if there was some-thing already dead about her. Killing never bothered her. She shot crows and robins from branches with a slingshot. She chased down grasshoppers and pinched them between her fingers and stared at the black spit that always swelled from their mouths—and then she would toss them into spiderwebs and watch them struggle and tangle and eventually go still when a spider danced down to fill them full of poison and stitch them into a white sack. A river ran through town and she would gather frogs from its banks and hurl them high and watch their legs spread as if they might learn to fly. They never did. The cement smacked the purplish guts from them.

SHE asked her coach if she might take one of the Bills home—she knew she needed to work harder if she wanted to make it to state—and he said all right, so long as she brought the dummy back in one piece. She arranged Bill in the passenger seat of the old Ford truck she drove and buckled him in so that he wouldn't lean on the sharp curves. They drove together around town in this way, his black shape beside her like a shadow.

She lived in a neighborhood near the downtown, where bunga-lows crowded together and oak trees made shady tunnels of the trees and buckled the sidewalks with their old roots. Her house had a two-story detached garage and from the second story she swept away the dirt and cleared away the old boxes and storm windows and laid down mats and made it into a wrestling room. There were a few dumbbells lying around, a pull-up bar she drilled between the exposed rafters. After dinner—after she cleared the dishes from the table and rushed through her homework—she dragged the Bill up-stairs and practiced a Granby, a double arm bar, a gut wrench, a cradle. It was only after committing these moves hundreds of times, her coach said, that she would have the instinct, the muscle memory she needed.

One night, when she brushed her teeth and pulled on her pajamas and went to drop the shades, she saw she had left the light on in the garage, its second-story window aglow, much of it filled with the black, slumped silhouette of the Bill. She could not help but feel it was watching her. She remembered a show about the occult she saw on the History Channel. The narrator said that anything in a human shape took on a human essence. That was the principle behind a golem, a voodoo doll, a wicker man. Johnnette did not think much of this then, but wondered now.

WHEN Breck discovered she was taking a Bill home on the nights and weekends, he began calling the dummy her boyfriend. She was the only girl on the team—she had the locker room to herself—and one time, after she padded across the tile and knobbed on the shower and soaped and rinsed her body and wrapped herself in a towel, she saw her Bill propped against the lockers. He was dressed up in a smiley face tie. A plastic flower was duct-taped to one hand. A purple dildo to the other.

She dressed and with her hair still wet marched from the locker room and found Breck and a few other boys sniggering in the parking lot and without saying a word shoved him and he fell back onto the hood of his Camaro, one of the doors primer gray. She said, "You come in that locker room again, I'll make sure you're expelled," and he said, "What? You scared I saw your dick?" and she said, "Try sucking it ten minutes, maybe you could grow a proper mustache."

The other boys laughed at this, but Breck did not.

The problem with Breck was the problem with all men, she decided. The way she looked confused them. She did not comb her hair. She did not wear lipstick or perfume or earrings. Her skin did not look like strawberry ice cream, her eyes like hard candy. They studied her uncertainly, as if peeping in a window only to find their reflection in it. They were goofy and bossy when they first met her—then cruel and aloof when they realized she would not fuck them.

The next day, when she was raking last year's leaves from the yard, a chipmunk scurried from the woodpile. She remained perfectly still until it came near enough to bring the rake down on. It squeaked and struggled and eventually went still. She knew then the same poisoned pleasure Breck felt when hurting her.

She looked around to see if anyone had seen her. The Bill sat in the passenger side of her truck, like a patch of midnight the sun hadn't swept away. She swung the rake toward him, held out the chipmunk, punctured on a tine, like an offering.

SHE knew her business with Breck was not over—she knew he would want to punish her further—but she did not think he would come for her at home. This happened late one night—in the second story of her garage—after she accidentally lost her grip on Bill and gashed him against an exposed nail. She tracked down a roll of duct tape and whispered sorry when she lovingly applied it to the wound at his forehead.

It was then she heard a shoe scuff the floor behind her.

She spun around, too late, his arm already around her neck, his weight dragging her down. She tore at him, the dead arm that stole her breath, though she knew it would do no good. She wondered if he could not distinguish pain because his skin felt always aflame. She wondered if that matched the feeling inside him now. His arm—when he flipped her over, her back to the mat—made a creaking, rubbery sound that reminded her of the wrestling dummies, the Bills, when she mangled them into submission.

She called out to her Bill then—called out to him as if he could hear her—but the Bill did not answer.

There was only the boy with the dead arm hovering and gasping over her, and with the light behind him, he had taken on a dark, silhouetted appearance, like a black blanket smothering her. She went silent, lest he mistake her cries for encouragement. She was never as strong as the boys she wrestled, but she could often outmaneuver them and only twice had she been pinned. She had a strong neck and would arc it back to keep her shoulders from lying flat. She did the same now, as if this were just another match, but then he pressed a forearm into her throat and she lay flat. He panted into her face. She could see his tongue. It was yellow, almost colorless.

When she was a girl, she liked to linger in the tub until her fingers pruned. To hurry her, her mother would yank the plug and say that Johnnette would swirl away with the rest of the water if she didn't scramble out of the tub and into a towel and then bed where she would dream of whirling downward, into darkness, which is a little what she felt like now.

She was swirling away, almost gone. Blackness pooled at the edges of her eyes, like a tide of unconsciousness about to overtake her, and then it solidified into the shape of a man. A dark man. He stood over them, watching.

One moment Breck was biting her ear and the next moment he was not. One moment her throat felt crushed by a dull guillotine and the next moment she could breathe. She coughed and gulped for air, her lungs hitching, her body shuddering. Then she roughed the tears from her eyes and wobbled to her feet. It took her a long minute to make sense of what she saw.

She did not recognize Breck at first. He was bent in half the wrong way.

Against the wall slumped her Bill. His color matched the feeling inside her. Bruise-black. Black as the deepest hole. The duct tape had peeled away to reveal the gash on his forehead. She used her thumb to seal it in place. Then she took the dummy in her arms and rocked him and whispered thank you and kissed the place where a mouth might have been.

The story draws from the myth of the golem, a voiceless half-formed creature that becomes animated, a servant. In this case the central character and her dummy are equally rough-hewn and seem to stir each other to life.

—BP

Hades

THE GIRL WITH THE TALKING SHADOW
Kate Bernheimer

My shadow learned to walk when I learned to walk, and her first word was also my own. When I lost my teeth, she lost her teeth too. The Tooth Fairy left me a quarter; my shadow left me her teeth—under my gums. Over time they grew in.

My shadow was mean, but I always found her a comfort.

Besides there was no getting away from her, that much I knew. As fast as I'd run, she'd run. Wherever I'd go she went, bigger or smaller depending on the hour but always there like a friend or a horror.

And her gray aspect slid toward me from the ceiling at night—a mirror of me made of shadows—even when my eyes were closed I could see her.

She had a vague edge, a definite darkness.

The older I grew the harsher she got—I don't think she liked the way my growing stretched her so thin. When I became a woman, I grew leagues not only in height but also in ethics. I thought of others before I thought of myself.

Soon after that the shadow girl began to trouble me badly. Her face held a constant and hideous smile. In the past, she had hardly broken even a tentative grin—just like me, whom my mother has always accused of having a grim demeanor.

Things got rough for a while, but we've worked everything out now, me and my shadow, me and that little dark curse of a being.

IN the early days, it wasn't that bad.

The first day of preschool, in the red barn of Happy Acres, I was settling in for a nap, ready to enter a spaced-out blissful condition on a sky-blue terrycloth mat to tinkling music beside a blond girl wearing a pink and purple striped top with a zipper down its center and matching shorts. I thought she was the prettiest creature I ever had seen. So, like a monkey, I stretched out my lips and showed her my teeth; I'd learned to smile, of course! But the response I received was quite unexpected. The blond girl in the purple and pink outfit made a horrid face when she saw me, and turned away. When I told my mother she said, "Don't be silly, it had nothing to do with you!" But that wasn't true. She saw my shadow, I'm sure.

The first day of kindergarten, we were asked to sit in a circle, to sing. I sat down next to Janie O'Malley. Her freckled face went white under her orange hair. She turned to me with her eyes burning bright, reached out, and pinched my hand. Her face was a white globe of meanness. I don't know if it was her face or her pinch that hurt me so much, but I do know I cried. "Go away," she hissed. "Why?" I asked. No answer.

We had to make rhymes later that year with our names. We'd just learned to read and to write. Oh, I was proud at my clever idea! Words, especially rhyming words, had quickly become my very good friends. "Cathy needs a Bathy," I wrote very carefully, in crayon. I drew a claw-foot tub, white and gleaming. How I loved my nightly baths, a special time alone with my mother and with No More Tears. But everything went bad from there. Janie chased me home from school yelling "Cathy needs a bathy! Cathy needs a bathy!"

That evening, when I looked in the mirror as I brushed my teeth before bed, my face simply burned and I could see it burning. I perched on the footstool into which my name was etched in red and blue and yellow letters—C A T H Y—and the happy colorful letters became black and loomed in front of my eyes. Not like shadows, but like headstones.

And later that night the shadow girl came to my room. She had been with me forever, since that very first day, but for the first time since then she told me her name. I woke up in the middle of the night, just as always. The moon shone into the room. I looked over to my sister's bed where she slept deeply. Meg-Anne's brown curls framed her face on the pillow. Even fast asleep she looked like the perfect creature she was; when awake she often played on her toy plastic guitar and sang over and over "I am Meg-Anne!" Above her head, Wonder Woman curtains flapped in the wind; Wonder Woman was pointing her finger straight at me, a gleam in her eye. I noticed a movement on the ceiling; a shape on a string, dropping down.

Soon, on my night table, next to the music box with the twirling dancer inside, sat my shadow, my friend, glowing as the moon glows and as a star sparkles. With her legs crossed and in a puny green dress, just like my own green velvet dress, the one I had gotten at Grover Cronin's, she looked terribly sad. She cupped her hands over her mouth and whispered, "I'm Cathy." Then, she disappeared. I felt my heart beat hard, harder than ever before. She had levitated, hovered over my face. She flew not like a butterfly but more like a crow. And I noticed for the very first time that there were no wings on her back—only her shadow.

I told my best friend Lizzie about my shadow when we played the next afternoon. (Yes, I did have a friend for a time, but nothing lasts forever.) "Oooh!" she said. "Let's play that!" So with our two dolls, who were also best friends, we enacted the scene. It became our favorite game for several years to come. My doll played me and Lizzie's played Lizzie. We set the dolls up in their tiny toy beds. I'd put my hands over my mouth and whisper "Cathy" and then I'd flap my hands together like they were a bird. Lizzie would sit the two dolls up in their beds and with her mouth make a big giant O! of surprise and of fear.

Come to think of it, that's how Lizzie always looked at me: with surprise and with fear.

In fourth grade, one of the last times that we played the Shadow Game, we used my Polaroid to record it. "The camera is broken," Lizzie said dully, waiting for the photo to develop. The frame was filled with white light, nothing more. No sign of the dolls. Nothing but light, white and gleaming.

In fifth grade, the year I lost Lizzie's friendship, my class put on

Mary Poppins. For the tea party scene, Mrs. O'Neill had rigged up a table and chairs to hang from the ceiling on ropes. All the girls wore party dresses in pink, blue, and green. Boys wore black suits with jackets and ties. We sang about candies and cakes. The table and chairs wobbled and danced. In the middle of the nonsense song about delicious foods everything went black all of a sudden. When I opened my eyes I saw my shadow, dangling in a sparkling party dress from the ceiling. Like my dress, hers had ladybugs printed on it, and a clear plastic purse in the shape of a ladybug hung over her shoulder—dark circles under her eyes.

Her shadow-wings were a little bit broken.

Then everything went bright and I was arm-in-arm with Lizzie and Barbara, singing that song. Over my head, I saw the shadow girl, and out of the corner of my eye, I saw Lizzie also look up. She turned to me with terror . . . the dancing went on . . . and then I felt a sharp pinch on my behind. "I hate you, Cathy," Barbara said in my ear. She looked over my head at Lizzie. Lizzie glanced my way, then up at the ceiling (my shadow was gone). "I hate you too," Lizzie whispered. "I hate you, Cathy." Then there was a flash, my mother snapping her camera.

When my mother got the photo developed, in between Lizzie and Barbara, where I ought to be, is no one. A bright light, white and gleaming. "Damn it! I left you outside the frame," my mother said, when she saw it. For my mother those were very strong words. I believe now she was angry because she would have no proof later to show me how happy I was at one time. ("But you loved being in *Mary Poppins* with Lizzie!" she tells me sometimes.)

Eventually, junior high came and things got much worse.

STILL, sometimes, even after what I came to think of as the Poppins Episode, Lizzie would call me at home. Her voice was always very low on the phone, as if afraid someone would overhear her. But who? Her mother had always been so kind to me; she could hardly mind if Lizzie called. "How are you?" Lizzie would ask with concern. "I'm fine," I would answer, pretending not to be crying. I was always so happy she called! "Remember the Shadow Game?" I soon would ask, overcome with emotion, and things would go quiet on the other end of the line. "I have to go," she'd say then. Click went the phone. The day after, she would never say hi to me in school.

She wouldn't look in my direction. I could not believe my good fortune when high school finally ended.

I stayed home, just as I always had wanted. Daily I walked to the library—I planned to work my way alphabetically through its circular rooms. But I especially wanted to read the books locked up in the cupboards in the Adult Room: those rainbow fairy-tale books! I always checked out as many as I could carry and then walked home through the woods. There, in the backyard, at a rotting picnic table, I would read. Around noon, I would go inside and make a peanut butter and jelly sandwich and wrap it in a blue bandana; I'd pour some water and drop some ice into an empty jelly jar. I'd carry the picnic out to the yard like a girl I'd read about in a children's book. For the very first time in my life since before the pink and purple pant-suited girl at Happy Acres scowled at me, I experienced bliss.

At night, my shadow visited me. She'd drop from the ceiling in her tank top and undies—what I slept in too—and hovered just over my pillow, her face close to mine. Into her ear, I'd whisper tales I had read. I told her about science, how the earth was heating up slowly. About novels, like the one about the girl whose half-brother named Ram, "overtaken with lust," had impregnated her. Picture books—a baby chicken who lost its mother. "Are you my mother?" it asked a log.

Meg-Anne had already gone to college two years before, so my shadow and I had the bedroom all to ourselves. I'd fall asleep reading in bed—I'd covered Meg-Anne's bed with books, and sometimes I'd fall asleep lying on top of volumes and volumes—and then with a whoosh she'd appear. She was as big as I was then—five feet four—and had grown her hair long, just as I had. We both had hair past our shoulders: glorious shades of blond, brown, and pink. We wore matching white undershirts, underwear embroidered with the days of the week, and both of us had the same necklace on: I had found two teeny dead frogs in the yard, and shellacked them, tying them onto a string. She could not believe I'd made her a present— her face lit up the room with a smile. She'd never smiled before, and the light that came from it was like sunrise, or sunset. I had begun to smoke cigarettes, a kind that came from over the ocean in a pale blue box, with their name all in squiggles. They made me sick to my stomach, but I liked it.

My girl smoked cigarettes too, as she dangled from the ceiling. We really had flowered!

Yet even though I had started to feel free—I mean not really free, but somewhat free, or at least left alone—my shadow seemed more severe as days went on. While I felt happier as summer progressed, she began to emit an intensity that I couldn't stand. Her eyes went mean . . . and she smoked more and more. She dropped from the ceiling fast, blowing smoke into my face.

Still, somehow, her evening appearances remained a real comfort.

From time to time the shadow girl would tire of my tales, and read me stories out of books that she favored, but I'd shudder and ask her to stop. The stories she read me were from strange, tattered paperback novels and had titles like *Flower Children in Danger* and *Evil Horse-Loving Girls*. That I disliked the novels aggrieved her— I preferred happy stories of rainbows, flowers, and girls and was particularly fond of a series of books about pegacorns, a rare species that is a cross between a unicorn and a Pegasus. I complained, because though I was shy, and self-hating, I was not timid on the subject of stories.

Her flying went haywire when I complained.

All the while I continued to enjoy my trips to the library, and my new outfits and hair. I began to wear my grandmother's old clothes. I wore her fur stole, and petticoats. I read fairy book after fairy book. School ending for good was the best thing that ever had happened to me. Then, one night in August, my shadow appeared, and without a word dropped a box at my feet on the bed. I could tell my shadow was angry. I didn't touch the box, and she said nothing about it to me.

BY the end of the summer, when I had wound my way around the library to Juvenile, having devoured Adult and Reference and the locked-up fairy-tale books, I started to take the long way home, not just through the small woods but into the forest. I walked down the path of pine needles.

One day, a boy I knew called down to me, from up in a tree. "I like your outfit," Plute said. Plute Peters, just a boy from Meg-Anne's class who worked at the gas station at Four Corners, about a mile away from the library and near the entrance to the woods. Plute. Plute! What a name. Who would name a kid something like that? I don't even know if it's short for anything. I was named Cathy, and that's usually short for Catherine, but it was all that I had been given.

C-A-T-H-Y.

P-L-U-T-E.

Spelled aloud they sounded nice together, I thought.

I had on a long white petticoat, under a ratty fur coat of my Nana's. The coat had come with her all the way from Russia, on a boat, and it smelled like the sea, and like honey and roses. "Thank you," I answered, and began to walk faster. Books fell from my arms. Plute leaped down onto the ground, and then touched my shoulder. "What are you so scared of, Weinberg?" he said. "Nothing," I answered. And it was true.

"So sit down," he suggested, gesturing to a tree trunk. I sat on the tree trunk and folded my arms. I crossed my legs too, for good measure. I knew what happened to girls in the woods when they encountered man-strangers. Plute stood in front of me. "Excuse me," he said, with a blush. He always was strange, as much of a social reject at school as I had been. He disappeared behind the oak. Silence, and then I heard him peeing.

Then there was a giant shadow—something flapping in the air— a horrific sound. I leaped up and ran home. I looked over my shoulder once, and saw Plute rushing out from the tree, zipping his fly. "Weinberg!" I heard him cry.

The next day, Plute was waiting for me on the tree trunk. In one hand, he held a bunch of fading hydrangea, and in the other, a little black leather notebook. He thrust both toward me. "These are for you, Weinberg," he said. I thanked him, took the flowers and notebook, and continued walking. I know this all sounds very mysterious and strange, but it wasn't. He was just a guy, and I was a girl. It was a nice sort of friendship, for rejects.

We met daily at the tree trunk after that, him on his break from the gas station and me on my way home to read. I'd smoke my foreign cigarettes and he'd compliment my outfits. He'd ask what I was reading, and I'd show him my myth and fairy-tale books. He even liked me to read them to me. Seems he loved to be read to, just like a child. I didn't even notice that my shadow was gone. She'd been my only friend for so long; thinking back to those days in the woods, I can't quite wrap my brain around how I didn't notice her absence. And believe me, this is nothing symbolic—she just wasn't there. But he was. And after the first time we did it, there was a sound sort of like wind.

After that I could do nothing but sleep, and my head felt heavy and shrouded. Even when I was awake, it was like I was sleeping, or rather more like I was dreaming of sleep, aching for it. I had no thoughts of the library or the woods. All I wanted was sleep, and my mother. She was so kind—bringing me trays of food, quietly placing them on my night table with glasses of milk and some buttered toast. And then, one day as she set the tray down, I saw a tiny body scramble from beneath it. It hopped onto the floor, with lithe, quiet footsteps. Then it zipped up through the air like a bee, and flew into a crack in the ceiling.

When I next opened my eyes, the clock read midnight exactly. I turned on the lamp that my Aunt Sadie had left me when she died. The lamp has a round base that lights up like a moon. It gives off a comforting glow. Sometimes I turn it on and off just to watch the light happen. That night, my mother had left the tray of toast and alphabet soup. I reached for a piece of buttered white toast. I thought about how things had been getting better, around the time I met Plute in the woods, but I was starting to feel funny again—exactly the way I'd felt at Happy Acres when the girl had said "I hate you," and my shadow girl first appeared . . . I nibbled a corner of toast, and sipped some cold sugary tea, and drifted back to sleep with an old song in my head: "I won't grow up, don't want to go to school, won't learn the golden rule . . ."

When I woke up, my room was all in a haze. I squinted my eyes at all the familiar things: in one corner sat a model of a castle, with a water-filled moat that often leaked; on my desk was a long row of little dolls that were popular then. They came in glass jars, they had name cards attached to them with strings; they looked like teeny beauty queens. (I didn't much like them, now that I think about it.) On the shelves sat my collection of fairy tales from the library. I pulled the books down and pored over their pages. I was looking for a story about a baby in water, a water baby. "The Water Babies"? It reminded me of my dream, or my dream reminded me of the story . . .

But soon, I came across another tale I never had seen in all of my reading. It featured a girl who smiled at everything, but nothing ever smiled back. She was a quiet girl who buried her nose in the books. Sometime after she "came into maturity" (as the storybooks often said), a boy did smile at her. She ran home to tell her father and he promptly sent her off to a bad fairy, who locked her in the basement without any books or heating. The bad fairy would slide plates of food under the door. Perhaps the food was magic; her clothes got smaller and smaller upon her, though the meals were meager. And something else: though it was freezing in the basement, she always was warm. One night, when she was so big her clothes had stretched right over her stomach (revealing it to look like a moon), a light—which I understood to be the bad fairy in the form of light—slid through a crack in the window, down the wall, and into the girl. And the next day, her clothes started to get bigger. And bigger. And bigger. Soon the bad fairy let her go home, where she was greeted with trumpets and dancing. But she never smiled again.

My mother brought me some supper. This time it was crackers and jelly, a tall glass of ginger ale. I ate a few bites. "Is the bad fairy on duty?" I asked. My mother gave me a strange and unpleasant glance, and left the room in a hurry. As I came out of the fog of deep sleep, my body began to have a bad feeling. The shadow girl, the sliver of light. Getting bigger, getting smaller again. A black box, and a coffin. I was covered in sweat. I fell back asleep, and woke much later again, still sweating. Above me hovered that box. It had wings jutting out of its edges. I batted my arms and heard a small whisper: I won't grow up.

When I fell back asleep I had the most beautiful dream: me in a meadow, in a gilded storybook frame. Sitting there, I held out my hand. On my palm sat a tiny infant, gazing into my eyes. It stopped my breath—or I passed out or something, because when my mother came to fetch my dinner tray, I had gone pale—with a very slight blue tinge, just like when I was born. They took me to the hospital, and from there, to a halfway home for young girls in my condition.

Halfway. You're not home if you're only halfway there.

I may have been stupid but I wasn't all the way stupid.

AND then my boy came out too soon. On his birthday the sky was covered in clouds. No light to spread into a window and fill him with air. And now, I'm back home, in the house where I myself was a child. I spend all my time lying in bed. I listen to crows. I think of my boy. Up there, on the ceiling, I can see my own shadow.

Of course I find much consolation when my mother brings me a new fairy book from the library or a tray of food for my supper; last night, she made the most adorable pancakes that spelled C A T H Y. Tonight she has promised me alphabet soup—even to remove the letters I hate. Of course, my sister Meg-Anne complains that I'm freeloading. Poor girl just doesn't realize: nothing ever is free.

And even in the most secret places on earth, nothing ever will be.

What if hell is not an underworld, but in this world? In the town where I grew up it was common for tough girls to mutter, "Go to hell" as they randomly shoved you into a locker. Well there wasn't far to travel at Weeks Junior High School. C. S. Lewis once wrote, "About Hell . . . One's own mind is actual enough. If it doesn't seem fully actual now that is because you can always escape from it a bit into the physical world— look out of the window, smoke a cigarette, go to sleep. But when there is nothing for you but your own mind (no body to go to sleep, no books or landscape, nor sounds, no drugs) it will be as actual as—as—well, as a coffin is actual to a man buried alive."

—KB

WAIT AND SEE

Edith Pearlman

I

Lyle stares at a lemon.

How does the lemon appear to Lyle? The rough skin is what he has been taught to call yellow, and he knows many modifiers of that word—pale, bright, dull; he knows also metaphoric substitutes: gold, butter, dandelion, even lemon. What he sees in the humble fruit, though, and what he knows by now other kids don't see, is a tangle of hundreds of shades, ribbons of sunlight crushed into an egg.

And baby oil? His mother, Pansy, works baby oil into her pale satin face and neck before going to bed, and a viscous drop inevitably spills from her fingertip: transparent, translucent, colorless, or so anybody else would say. To Lyle, though, the drop is a rosy sphere.

His skin—caramel or butterscotch or café au lait according to foodies; mulatto to those interested in mixed races—his skin's shade incorporates movement too: on his forearm writhe all the hues in Pansy's drawer of muddled lingerie.

And the neon sign projecting from the exercise center on the second floor of a building in Godolphin Square? Neon plasma has the most intense light discharge of all the noble gases. To a normal human eye it is red-orange; it also contains a strong green line hidden unless you've got a spectroscope. Lyle sees the green line unaided, the flowing molecules of it. It is as if the sign, GET FIT, has given him a gift.

But then, Lyle has been given many gifts. Casual ones for fingers as well as eyes like the pocked lemon and the slinky baby oil and the neon sign—though to touch the sign he needs to poke his skinny arm out the second-floor window while Pansy Gets Fit behind him. The G is unexpectedly cool. Another gift is Pansy's love. Bathed in that love, Lyle in turn is gentle with other kids, especially with kids uneasy under their bragging, kids really as frightened as rabbits when a hawk darkens their world. Lyle's underweight presence steadies them, and he is sought after—but not exactly as a friend. He is more like Anansi the helpful spider of his favorite tales—a quiet ally who prefers his own company but skitters over to join you when you need him.

Yet another gift is money. These days money resides in electronic bits; Pansy has plenty of bits inherited from her Alabama grandfather. And there is, or was, once, the gift of a small amount of yellowish fluid containing enzymes, acids, and lipids. Semen, not to put too fine a point on it.

The unknown bestower of the semen had been living on the edge. He'd come from Africa in a troupe of Lost Boys—not the famous ones from Sudan but less famous, less numerous ones from elsewhere. But the situation was similar: civil war, carnage, a few boys running from their ruined villages all the way to the United States.

One particular Boy ended up in Massachusetts, lived in a house with other Boys, got through high school, and at the time of his gift was employed in a lab in the area. But he was poor. And so he did what many people in his situation did: sold his blood. He thought about selling his sperm too, but he considered it too valuable to be made a commodity—he was proud and he was free and he wanted freely to sire a thousand American sons. So he gave his sperm to a Bank—really a hospital roomlet provided with facilitating magazines.

II

And then there's a submicroscopic gift. It's the consequence of a genetic mutation which has passed mostly unexpressed through the millennia. It was bestowed by evolution not directly on Lyle but on a primate who was his remote ancestor. The gift was a mischievous gene which, if it meets its twin, can affect vision.

"Primate vision unadulterated is trichromatic," said Dr. Marcus Paul. "*Tri* means three and *chroma* means color."

"Yes?" encouraged Pansy from the other side of the desk.

"Well, Mrs. Spaulding . . ."

"Miss."

"Miss . . ."

"Or Ms., if you want to be correct." She grinned.

"Ms., then," said the flustered man, and took refuge in a disquisition. "You know the retina, at the back of the eye, the thing that captures light and color and ships them to the brain. The retina uses only three types of light-absorbing pigments for color vision. Trichromacy, see?"

"See," she agreed, still grinning.

"Well, almost all nonprimate mammals are dichromatic, with just two kinds of visual pigments. A few nocturnal mammals have only one pigment. But some birds, fish, and reptiles, they have four."

"They see more colors than we do? Dammitall."

"They probably do. And some butterflies are even pentachromatic. Pigeons also. And there is one twig on the *Homo sapiens* tree whose members—a small fraction of them—are believed to be pentachromatic too: the Himba tribe. Himbas endure their usually short lives in Namibia . . . Lyle seems to be of mixed race."

"Yes. I asked the sperm bank for a black donor. I believe miscegenation is an answer to the world's ills. All people one color . . . tan."

"Oh," said the doctor, whose skin was the shade of eggplant. "Your donor was African?"

She shrugged her slender shoulders. "I didn't ask and they didn't tell."

"Well, I think Lyle's a pentachromat. Those colors he reports."

She nodded. She was all at once serious. "Yes. No wonder he has headaches, my poor boy." Then she paused, partly to let this young Jamaican take a frank look at her as he was clearly eager to do—at her inky curls, at her small straight nose that angled upward a degree more than is usual, robbing her of beauty and instead making her irresistible—physiognomy's gift to Pansy, you might say. The doctor could see also her wide mouth, her dimples, her long neck and long hands. Her long legs were hidden from him by his desk, but he must have noticed them earlier. She hoped so. Oh yes, and when she parted her lips, out flashed the bright white of her perfect incisors. Men often remarked on that. . . . She continued now: "What's it like to be a pentachromat?" Though she knew, or had an idea; Lyle had told her of the numerous dots of color he could detect on a plain manila envelope. She taught him a new word: pointillism. "Doctor?"

What's it like to have a face like yours? He said: "Neither we nor they have the words to describe this sort of thing. How would you describe color to someone who was colorblind? What we do know is that tetrachromats and pentachromats make distinctions between shades that seem identical to the rest of us. For example, I read about a woman in California, she's dead now . . ."

"From hyperchromaticity?"

"From old age. She was a seamstress, the article said. She could look at three samples of beige fabric cut from the same bolt and detect a gold undertone in one, a hint of green in another, a smidgen of gray in the third. She could look at a river and distinguish relative depth and amounts of silt in different areas of the water based on differences in shading that no one else was aware of. . . . So it's probably safe to say that tetrachromats and pentachromats have a richer visual experience of the world than the rest of us." *But my own experience has become richer in the past fifteen minutes because of this woman sitting in front of my normal trichromatic eyes. I hope she likes my dreadlocks.*

III

Lyle had been an unfretful baby, though for a while he confused day with night. Pansy slept through the days along with him. Gave him breakfast at twilight and took him for a walk, sometimes across the river to Boston but usually around Godolphin. Lyle lay angled on a pillow in his old-fashioned perambulator, facing her or staring upward at the dark green of trees, the charcoal sky. He turned his head to notice glossy books in the window of the bookstore, always open late. There was a full-length mirror embedded in the door of the pedicure place. Sometimes, again turning his head, he stared at mother and child, and she did the same. There she was in black leather pants and a glistening white poncho; there he was, a baby whose skin had not yet begun to darken. *Her* skin had never darkened, though her southern ancestors had no doubt mingled with their slaves and then admitted the lighter progeny into the mansion. A gene for a dusky epidermis might lie embedded in each of her cells.

In his early childhood Lyle went from phase to expected phase—resisted the occasional babysitter, considered the toilet fine for other people, couldn't bear carrots. He played with blocks in a bored way. Idly he mentioned headaches. The pediatrician found no cause for them.

He continued his habit of staring at everything. He himself was odd to look at—the thin beige face, the unsmiling gaze. When they took a walk together, he put one hand in his mother's, like collateral, while his mind wandered somewhere she couldn't follow, and she had to relinquish the treasured notion that mother and child were one.

He didn't like picture books—all those primary colors, he wouldn't look at them. It made her wonder.

The psychologist she took him to said no, he wasn't on any spectrum. "He's not interested in those little board books, so what. He's intrigued by the wider world. Wants to wait and see what catches his fancy."

She thanked him and stood up, a vision in her striped black and white sundress and her black cartwheel. She walked toward the door.

"You, too," called the psychologist. "Wait and see."

SHE'D waited several years. One day irregular blurred lines appeared on the wall of her bedroom. Their interiors filled in; now they were splotches. Then they turned into continents. The plumber found the leaks that were their source, and fixed them. Pansy hired a painter and brought home a color wheel. It was a collection of about three hundred long slender cards of thick laminated paper, each with a hole at one end which allowed it to depend with its fellows from a metal ring. The ring allowed all of the cards to be held in the hand without any of them dropping. They could also be fanned out into a circle. Each card bore seven contiguous squares of similar hues, with names. About two thousand colors were displayed in the device. She dropped it with idle grace beside Lyle, prone on the floor. He abandoned his book—he was reading adventure stories now, aping his classmates, though he frequently returned to those old trickster tales. He inspected this new toy.

He knew what he had before him—paint samples. He guessed that these thousands of colors were about as many as human beings could create—in their labs, in their paint factories, in their electronic workshops. He had endured years of feeling different, of possessing something that was a secret to others and also to him. Now the color wheel enlightened him. . . . People gave hues such hopeful names. There was a square called orange froth and next to it orange blossom and next to that Florida orange; and Lyle could see the froth spit globules deepen to a color that almost matched orange blossom but didn't, and the orange blossom itself acquire a gloss as it approached but did not attain Florida orange. "Mom," he called.

"Yes, darling?" from the other room.

"I have . . . ," he said, and paused. In the Anansi tales secrets were meant to be stuffed into the heart and never pulled out; there could be unforeseen results.

She walked in. ". . . something to tell me?"

"Well . . ."

And then came the visit to Dr. Marcus Paul; and then came the tentative diagnosis of a condition though not an ailment, a condition unknown to most scientists probably because of its weak grant potential. And then came romance. Love at first sight? It can happen. There's often a lot of palaver. "I love you not only because you're beautiful," Marcus told Pansy a few weeks after they met. "I love you because of your admirable politics, your wish that the world's population become one color. Because you mop floors in a soup kitchen. Because you cook like a four-star chef."

She kissed him then, and she caressed his hip with her knee, a gesture that cannot be achieved unless both parties are lying on their sides facing each other. They happened to be lying on their sides facing each other—Lyle was at school—and so the caress impossible under other circumstances was now possible, probable, necessary, unavoidable, though who would want to avoid the deep shudder each felt as joint saluted joint. Then Marcus entered his lovely woman.

Afterward she took over the colloquy. "I love you because of your single-mindedness," she said. "Your voice. Your dreadlocks. I love you because our coupling feels like destiny."

"Arranged by Anansi."

"Anansi? Lyle reads stories about him. . . ."

"He's a powerful spider who used to make his home in Africa, now lives in Jamaica. But he gets around."

"Please thank him if you see him. . . . And I love you because together we belong to Lyle."

"And Lyle belongs to us," said Marcus. In a postcoital clarity he realized that he had found his life's love and his life's work in a single ophthalmologic interview. "We are Lyle's caretakers, guardians, keepers of his secret."

"It's like the housemaid marrying the butler," said Pansy.

"If you say so." *He* felt like a stable boy marrying the princess.

There was a brief three-person honeymoon. They visited Italy where plump lemons offered even more yellows than the ones Lyle knew. They went to Iberia where the tiles of Lisbon and the airport in Madrid presented a chromatic joy, many colors new and glorious to Marcus and Pansy and about twelve times that many to Lyle.

Marcus's clinical practice was easy to transfer to a colleague. He'd been mostly engaged in research anyway. After returning from the colorful honeymoon he built a lab behind Pansy's spacious house and invited his cousin David to join him. The reclusive David, an optician, was interested in the changes to vision that curved or beveled glass, glass within glass, prismatic lenses, all those things, could make when placed in front of the eye. The two cousins had already designed a number of spectacles that helped people with eye diseases see better.

Their little optical laboratory—incorporated, after a while—produced many improved devices. Telescopic eyeglasses for everyday use. Microscope lenses, and surgical snakes with tiny cameras for heads, and smoky instruments for astronomers. These tools became much in demand.

The company flourished, and Pansy's return on her investment was substantial. She was proud of the men's success. Still, when Marcus and David entered their laboratory day after day she liked to imagine that, in addition to their other products, they were working on a superinvention that would grant Lyle's vision to everyone. Performance enhancing, you might say. When perfected it would encounter regulations; when produced it would inspire inferior imitations. Still, it would be a vehicle for public good.

But after four years it had not yet appeared. So one day the patient Pansy inquired.

"I don't think we can do it," Marcus admitted. "We've tried; it was one of our original purposes. But we cannot duplicate work that nature took millions of years to accomplish. We cannot invent an external instrument which will produce an internal variant. The butterfly has a genome, the pigeon too. But where does the penta-chromatic gene lurk? We cannot tell. And if we could tell, and could extract it, and could transfer it to a human cell, would the cell sur-vive? And if yes, yes, yes, yes . . . for what purpose? To give people headaches?"

"It would be only a carnival attraction," Pansy slowly acknowl-edged. "A rich man's plaything. But oh, Marcus. No one else can ever become like Lyle. He's stuck being unique."

IV

And what of the unique Lyle during these years? Well, he had things to occupy him: school, cello, baseball, walks at night with Marcus or David or Pansy. Music was blessedly colorless. In center field the sky showed him its myriad blues and the field its hundreds of greens but none of that distracted him from the flight of the sphere, a head-less wingless bird, a ball white and off-white and off-off-white. Nothing distracted him from the task of predicting the bird's desti-nation and putting himself beneath it, mitt at the ready.

He played in the school orchestra. Once in a while he went to a party and talked to whoever seemed left out—talked awkwardly but soothingly, or maybe soothingly because awkwardly.

He thought about some day becoming a doctor. He liked looking at anatomy plates, vivid to begin with, garish under his inspection. He wondered if his vision, trained, might develop an X-ray compo-nent. Marcus doubted it. They discussed diseases of organs other than the eye—diagnosis, treatment, treatment failure.

But despite the error-free fielding record and despite the mild friendships with his peers and despite the comfort of nocturnal darkness in the company of one of the three people he loved, Lyle, heavy with his secret, often felt sorrowfully alone.

WHEN he was sixteen he began to spend Sunday mornings with last year's biology teacher. They drove to a nature preserve and then hiked its trails. And then one Sunday during a forbidding rainstorm she invited him to forget Nature for a day. She was forty; the ideal age to relieve a sensitive boy of his virginity and to satisfy his curiosity too. He noted that her areolae were not sepia, as novels said, but pulsing pink rose mauve. . . . This dear woman would be fired without a hearing if her generosity became known—he knew that, and he realized how uncalibrated were the rules that claim to protect us from one another. But Lyle was used to keeping things to himself, and anyway he would never betray Ms. Lapidus. Their Sunday morning explorations continued—in the nature preserve if the day was bright, in bed if otherwise.

He shared his secret with her—she would not betray him, either.

"But, wow!" she said, turning to look at him, her head on her palm, her elbow on the mattress.

"Wow? It's an affliction."

"Really? By me it's an opportunity. Think of the things you could do with those special eyes. Detect art forgeries."

He blinked at her.

"You could tell the difference between Rembrandt's paint and pseudo-Rembrandt's paint," she explained. And on another occasion she said, "You could identify altered substances. Traces of banned pesticides."

"Or find the fault lines in a rock," he unenthusiastically contributed.

"Or see a smear of makeup on a man's tweed shoulder."

"Huh?"

She told him that adulterers usually tried to keep their activities hidden, and that their wronged spouses often hired detectives at a substantial fee. And on yet another rainy Sunday she suggested that he could identify fish misnamed by dishonest restaurants. "And sometimes they serve brains masquerading as sweetbreads, or maybe it's the other way around. You could bring miscreants to court."

He didn't answer. He was again looking at her breasts. The areolae were mauve, yes, but mostly by contrast to what he now noticed as yellowish skin; and when he raised his eyes he saw that her sclera were curdling. To foresee the coming of disaster—that was not how he wanted to use his gift. "Would you do something for me?" he managed.

"Just about anything," she confessed.

"Would you have your doctor do an MRI of your abdomen?"

"What? I feel fine."

"And a pancreatic biopsy," he said, and began to cry.

V

Another year. And then, one August afternoon, Marcus emerged from the lab and found Lyle practicing hoop shots by himself. "I have a story to tell you," Marcus said.

"Okay." When he read, the black letters sometimes shuddered on the page. But when he listened his closed eyes found a sort of repose behind the patchwork cerise of his lids.

"It's a Jamaican tale," said Marcus.

"Oh, then about Anansi."

"Anansi plays a part. But it's about a young man."

They sat on the ground, their arms around their knees and their backs against the trunk of a beech, as if they were in a Caribbean village leaning against a guango.

Marcus began:

Once upon a time there lived a youth who was never happy unless he was prying into things other people knew nothing about. Especially things that happened at night. He wanted secrets to be laid bare to him. He wandered from wizard to wizard, begging them in vain to open his eyes, but found none to help him. Finally he reached Anansi. After the spider had listened, he warned:

"My son, most discoveries bring not happiness but misery. Much is properly hidden from the eyes of men. Too much knowledge kills joy. Therefore think well what you are doing, or some day you will repent. But if you will not take my advice, I can show you the secrets you crave."

"Please!"

"Tomorrow night you must go to the place where, once in seven years, the serpent-king summons his court. I will tell you where it is. But remember what I say: 'Blindness is man's highest good.'"

That night the young man set out for the wide, lonely moor belonging to the serpent-king. He saw a multitude of small hillocks motionless under the moonlight. He crouched behind a bush. Suddenly a luminous glow arose in the middle of the moor. At the same moment all the hillocks began to squirm and to crawl, and from each one came thousands of serpents making straight for the glow. The youth saw that a multitude of snakes, big and little and of every color, gathered together in one great cluster around a huge serpent. Light and colors sprang from its head. The young man saw brilliance usually denied to mortal eyes. He saw iridescence bioluminescence adularescence opalescence. Then the scene vanished. He went home.

The next day he counted the minutes till night when he might return to the forest. But when he reached the special place he found an empty moor: gray, gray, and gray. He went back many nights but did not see the colors. He would have to wait another seven years.

He thought about them night and day. He ceased to care about anything else in the world. He sickened for what he could not have. And he died before the seven years was out, knowing at the end that Anansi had spoken truly when he said, "Blindness is man's highest good."

After a while Lyle said, "But, Dad, not complete blindness . . ."

"No. Fables are not literal. Freedom from supervision . . . supravision . . . overvision . . . hypervision . . ."

"Freedom from second sight," added Lyle. "I can have that freedom?" He turned toward Marcus. His remarkable eyes, an unremarkable brown, seemed to swell a little—tears had entered from the ducts.

Marcus put his arm around the boy's shoulders, scraping his elbow grievously on the back of the tree. "I think so."

THE next week, Marcus appeared at dinner with a pair of spectacles—rimless, with wire earpieces. The lenses were constructed of hundreds of miniature polyhedrons.

"Prisms," said Pansy, and went on dishing out *lapin aux pruneaux*.

"Involuted prisms," refined David, who now lived with the family. He had become comfortable at last with his celibacy and inwardness; he was sometimes even talkative.

Marcus turned to Lyle. "These are for you," he said, and he handed the eyeglasses to the boy. "Put them on whenever you like."

"They will give you a different kind of vision," said David, "and, Lyle—it's all right if you don't like the spectacles."

Lyle did not put them on inside. He went out onto the lawn with its commanding beech tree and its flowering bushes. He looked around at the normal thousand-color summer scene—normal to him, at any rate, though he understood it to be his alone. Now maybe he'd know a competing normal. He put on the glasses.

It was as if someone had turned out the lights or a thick cloud had passed in front of the sun. Most creatures see things less brilliantly in the dark, he knew that. He was seeing things less brilliantly. The house, made of flat stones, was gray. Perhaps the gray contained some gold. On the laboratory's green siding, each slat cast a slightly darker green on the one beneath it. The beech tree was a combination of brown and red. The geraniums were a shade of magenta—one shade of magenta. He looked at his skin. Plain tan. He looked at the sky. Blue, slowly deepening—it was dusk now. Dark blue.

He went inside. "I like the glasses."

". . . colors?" asked Marcus.

"Duller. Many fewer. Motionless. Perspective is less noticeable. Things seem to have only a touch of a third dimension. I'm glad for the . . . diminishment. Now I have two ways to see. Thank you, Dad, thank you, David. You've given me a wonderful present."

"We have given you a choice," said Marcus. "Always an ambiguous gift."

Lyle said suddenly, "Spiders—what's *their* vision like?" David said, "Spiders usually have eight eyes placed in two rows on the front of the carapace. The eyes have a silvery appearance. The retinas have relatively coarse-grained mosaics of receptor cells, and their resolution of images is . . ."

"Poor," said Marcus, finishing David's lecture and answering Lyle's question at the same time.

LYLE wore his gift every day, all day, except when he went to bed—and then he did not take them off until he'd turned out the light. His classmates were incurious about the new glasses—they were teenagers, after all, not interested in much outside themselves. But Lyle's new and commonplace vision gave him new and commonplace manners—he no longer stared into space, his conversation became less effortful. Girls phoned him. He got included in more activities. Marcus and David made sunglasses for him, and swimming goggles, biking goggles, wraparounds for chemistry lab. They made him a pair of pince-nez, which he wore to a Halloween party, along with a stiff collar and a frock coat and a false beard. "Chekhov," he explained. He joined the chess club. The club met Sunday mornings. His Sunday mornings were empty. Ms. Lapidus had recently died.

In the lab Marcus and David were now constructing wide-angle micro-optical lenses. The lenses could be implanted—and were, after the proper trials—in a sufferer's eye. They made new tools for photography and tomography. They made corneal inlays. Pansy was running the business side of the enterprise—she was managing a staff of five. Having learned so much about the tricks of the eye-brain double play, Pansy became expert at standard optical illusions, and then invented some of her own, with which she beguiled the twin sons who had been born to her and Marcus. ("Their complexion is unglazed bisque," Lyle said of his brothers, remembering the old paint wheel.) Pansy began a side enterprise selling games of her own design. Some elaborate inventions she used at the twins' birthday parties held in a newly built room off the lab. The kids' friends entered an illusory universe for half an hour, then gobbled up Pansy's sweet potato ice cream, which was real.

VI

At eighteen Lyle was accepted at St. John's. He was looking forward to reading Greats. The day before he was to leave for Baltimore, a thick autumn mist enveloped Godolphin and Godolphin alone—the sun was out in Boston. A graduation gift from Anansi, Lyle thought. He walked down to the river. There the mist rested, soft and colorless. Slowly, deliberately, he took off his glasses.

Mist. Still mist. Then, gradually, colors returned, filled the scattered bits of moisture. According to the laws of physics each drop should have contained a rainbow—but no, on this eve of departure the drops, directed by the spider, were breaking the laws, each producing a singular shade for his pleasure, all together producing a universe of colors. Purple deeper than iris, laced with yolky lines. Bronze striped with brass. He saw the indigo of infected flesh, he saw the glistening fuchsia of attacking bacteria, he saw the orange of old age crinkles that wait invisibly on every smooth young arm. Yes, all colors, in all their headachy variations, colors as they had once been.

His man-made glasses, his trickster specs, had made life less sorrowful, but at a cost. They had deprived him of this sheen of blue blue blue violet seeping into blue blue violet violet pressing itself into blue violet violet violet which yearns to become shadow. Vanilla hectored its neighbor papyrus. There was moss concealing like a mother its multigreened offspring. There were squirming nacreous snakes, slightly nauseating. Much is properly hidden from the eyes of men,

Anansi had said. . . . Chartreuse slashed like lightning across his vision from upper left to lower right and also from upper right to lower left, both slants remaining on his retina that was so cursed, so blessed. Where one diagonal intersected the other in this chartreuse chiasma rested an oval, deep within the intersection, for of course the mist in which these shapes and colors shudderingly resided was three-dimensional or maybe three-and-a-half, and it was in motion, too, the color drops assaulting each other in a chromatic orgy. The oval within the chartreuse X was scaled with overlapping hexagons of nearly transparent turquoise, there must have been hundreds of turquoises, each different from the other by so little, so little; yet by that little, different. *What's your favorite color* people used to ask as they always asked children. Red, he would answer, divining even then that they had no idea how many reds there were: a cloud at sunset, a cloud at sunrise, blood from a scratch, blood from a nose, a run-over cat; and all reds swam on the dappled skin of a tomato. . . . He wondered, not for the first time, who his original father was. He put his glasses back on. Mist returned to mist, ordinary mist, mist in whose every drop curved what people called the spectrum, such a paltry number of colors. This sight was no truer a reality than the glory of a few minutes ago; no less true either. Truth had nothing to do with the witness of the eyes. What he saw now was simply what other people saw. He chose their limited vision; he meant to live in this world as an ordinary man. He would not remove his glasses again.

VII

Several years later, in a magazine called *Optics*, Lyle read a letter:

> *Pigeons have a very subtle multicolored plumage. But we see it with our trichromatic eyes. Since pigeons are pentachromats, their plumage after millions of years of sexual selection must have developed plenty of unsuspected gorgeous colors. Is there any way for us humans to detect with some sort of apparatus all those hidden colors? Is there anyone who can claim a bit of polychromaticism, enough to have seen those hues? Or at least some of them?*

Lots of them, Lyle silently nodded. All of them, maybe. He remembered the silvered green of one barbule, the pearl of another, the way they reflected each other, the celadon nimbus surrounding each individual feather. He was now almost thirty. He was what he had always been: decent, uninsistent, thin. He practiced law in a public interest firm. He judged that public interest would not be served if the existence of human pentachromaticity were to be broadcast. People had troubles enough. Much is helpfully hidden from the eyes of man, the myopic Anansi had said. Too much knowledge kills joy.

He did allow that it would be a gift to ophthalmology if he were to marry a color-blind woman. Their offspring might have a singular way of looking at things. But singular ways of looking at things can bring not happiness but misery; and color-blind females were rare; and anyway he was in love with somebody in his firm and she loved him back—a woman of Japanese ancestry whose self-containment matched his own. Patsy and Marcus approved. She had a slight astigmatism but otherwise her vision was normal. Unless like Pansy she carried a tricky recessive—and the chance of that was infinitely small, given the Japanese age-old penchant for marrying other Japanese only, and certainly not Namibians—human pentachromaticity would disappear again, maybe for eons. He thought that was a good thing. He threw *Optics* into the trash.

"Blindness is man's highest good"—this ambiguous proclamation by the trickster Anansi was one of the sources of this story. I wanted to show the circumstances that might make this true. The possibility of the existence of human pentachromats was the other source. I am fond of sports of nature.

—EP

❦

AN OCCASIONAL ICARUS
Georges-Olivier Châteaureynaud

Don't think I write to be believed. At this point in my life, I couldn't care less. Besides, there's no chance anyone would buy my tale. If someone tried to lay it on me, I'd just shrug. Shrug all you want, then. What follows is true down to the very last word. Proof? I've none to give. My witnesses are gone from this world. If I've finally decided to set the main event of my life down on paper, it's because at my age, I'll be joining them before long. I should've sought out their testimonies while there was still time. I never could bring myself to. To tell the truth, we never even talked about it. This fact will seem unusual in and of itself, maybe even less acceptable than the actual story. What can I do? That's how it was. But enough chitchat; I just wanted to warn the reader that facts—which allegedly speak for themselves—can also speak in riddles.

WHAT a very cruel thing it would be to tell ourselves we have but a few tomorrows left, were it not for a charitable fatigue that whispers in our ear: *you've lived enough, any more would be too much.* I for one seem to have nothing but yesterdays left to relive—a great many, it's true. Yesterdays, like the snapshots people used to stuff into envelopes all jumbled up, dried glue on the back, swearing they'd one day arrange them in some big dedicated album where each one would find its place and caption. Among these snapshots, three enthrall me more than all the rest. What a sad life, you'll say— summed up in just three pictures. But it's my life, and I wouldn't trade it for anyone else's. Conquerors, magnates, artists—keep your flamboyant destinies; I would've hated being someone else, for then I'd never have known these three moments. Or would I? Who says my experience is unique? Perhaps, different as we are, we've all felt something similar? But surely we'd know! Or, on second thought, we could just as easily not know at all.

The first time—that staggering, dazzling first time, far off, far back in the mists of time—was the summer I was nine. Since then, three quarters of a century of waves and wind, of clouds, sun, and rain, of storms and calm have come and gone on that shore. We had it all to ourselves—"we" meaning my mother and I. This was before crowds came and defiled the place. Breton women bent over, scratching at the gray sand with their long tin shovels, were as rare as the rocks and gulls. Mama was reading. I can still picture that popular imprint, with its yellow bindings and woodcut covers. Where are they now, those paperbacks she devoured by the dozen? The Modern Library is now the library of yesteryear. . . .

I've never been able to read at the beach. Too much wind. Somehow grains of sand borne on the breeze seem like words being wafted off my page, and I lose the thread, close my book with a crunch of dislodged, disheveled text. Mama didn't mind the wind. She could read for hours, only now and then lifting her head to make sure I was still in sight. Of course, the Atlantic was quite harmless in the harbor, where Neptune splashed around as in a baby bath. So while my mother read, I would swim, or fish for thick-lipped goby—a kind of miniature grouper with an incredible appetite—in pools the sea left in the chaos of rocks. I'd seen them bite unbaited hooks. When I was tired of these wondrous and inedible fish, I bombarded the boulder fortresses with pebbles, or blew into my harmonica whose reeds the salt breeze soon warped. The wind swept my jarring notes far away. Time passed as if in a dream; the skies above kept changing; rarely did an afternoon go by without a few showers.

That was where it happened, on a summer's day like any other.

But was it really? Later I thought about that day, upended my drawer of memories, trying to sort through the jumble. I couldn't find a thing that felt related to that miracle. No warning sign, no premonitory dream, not a single concomitance. It just happened out of the blue. But do miracles need explanations? One moment I was subject to gravity's yoke, and the next, I was free. One second my bare feet were sunk in the coarse sand, and the next, liberated, they were floating around five inches over my footprints. My heart leapt in my chest. But my fear didn't last: it vanished almost immediately, dispelled by the wonder that had come over me. I was flying, or at least floating in the air like a balloon, a human balloon! Sad sack, I swayed at the whim of a wind that was, luckily, quite gentle. Though the harbor sheltered us, the wind could sometimes give the cliffs a flurry of stinging slaps, mussing its mop of bracken and gorse. With great strides it climbed the rocky headlands and crossed prairies edged with rusty barbed wire to hurl itself madly against the granite walls of farms. In such a mood, it might have driven me into the hinterlands, and God knows what would have become of me then. But that day, I was saved—the breeze was sweet as a song. Playful, complicit, it helped make me aware of my newfound lightness just as it had stifled my cry of surprise before it left my mouth. On a blanket a few dozen yards away, half hidden by the parasol that kept her from the sun when it showed between clouds, my mother lay reading. There was no one else around, except, way in the distance, women still rooting for clams along the shore. Even if they'd looked up, they couldn't have seen anything from where they were.

Without meaning to, simply from the wind and waving my arms, I was six feet up in the blink of an eye. I confess I grew afraid again. The spell could break at any moment, and from that height, falls became dangerous. In theory, I would have landed on damp, loose sand, but it was strewn with pebbles and half-buried chunks of rock that could easily break my bones. Still, the sensation I felt was so exhilarating that I partly forgot my fears. If you haven't felt something like it before, even in dreams, then you don't know what rapture is. It was as if every other joy in the world existed only to give a distant glimpse of that one. Free as air . . . that was it: my flesh had turned to air, since my body had become just as light. The horror of the human condition—mine, but moments before—was suddenly clear. Crammed into mass, packed into the slag of our blood-glutted flesh: such is our fate. Don't even get me started on birds! Every creature of the air, from the humble butterfly to the tiniest gnat, enjoys an exorbitant privilege in comparison.

I wouldn't say I was dancing. How long would it have taken me to start capering like an elf? I don't know. All I had time to do was pollywog around, wriggle and struggle up there in a net of my own movements, always too broad, too brusque. I wasn't exactly strong at nine, with my scrawny arms, glaring ribs, legs like dandelion stems. But the runt I was had a soul of lead and the finesse of a felon dragging around his ball and chain. Despite it all, I noticed with great relief that my powers of levitation weren't only for going up. They also allowed me to go back down. It was a matter of leaning forward and milling my arms and legs, a kind of swimming or rowing I was still far from controlling. How long did I remain hanging in the air—hanging from nothing? A little more than minute, I'd say. Maybe two. Then I landed. Without trying to, but without incident either. The extravagant episode hadn't ended violently, dashing me on the ground as if fallen from a tree or rock. The force (the hand?) that had plucked me from the earth set me back down gently on the sand. I didn't even go sprawling: I landed on my feet. Dazed but unhurt, my heart pounding, I thought at first that it was in my power to take off again. But this time, I wanted my mother's gaze to confirm my Assumption. She had to see me in all my glory as the little boy who could fly. My throat, knotted tight all this time, loosened up: "Mama! Mama! Look at me, I'm flying!" Deep in her book, the susurrus of the breeze in her ears, she heard me without quite understanding what I said.

"What was that, sweetie?" she asked, not turning around.

I stepped back for a running start. I would show her what words couldn't describe. "Mama, look!"

Running as fast as I could, I rose over the parasol in an admirable leap. Not high enough, alas. But I could tell my takeoff wasn't to blame. I numbered once more among the creeping things that creep upon the earth. My bones, my flesh, weighed their meager but inexorable weight again. My left foot caught the parasol's fringed edge and took it with me. This rookie angel crashed into the ground without too much damage: one parasol strut broken, two others twisted, an aching elbow, a knee skinned on a rock.

"Have you gone out of your mind? What's gotten into you?" my mother inquired once it was clear I wasn't about to bleed to death.

"I was flying, Mama! I wanted to show you—"

"Well, you certainly have! My parasol's ruined, and you're bleeding like a stuck pig! Plus you could've knocked me out!"

Apart from how seriously I was bleeding, all this was only too true. Pretending it was only a game, I tried achieving liftoff a few more times to settle the matter, while my mother shook from her book and blanket the sand my somersaults had kicked up. No go. The sky didn't want me anymore. I didn't feel too bad at the time. I figured it could come back tonight, tomorrow—anytime. The energy that had so fleetingly invested me had to come from somewhere. It had filled me, then left me, or exhausted itself. Maybe it needed time to build up again. Maybe I had to recharge, like a battery. My mother clearly hadn't believed me for a second. To her, I'd been playing at flying all along. I was "*such* an imaginative boy," she'd decreed a few years earlier. She was probably right. But this time, I hadn't imagined a thing. I'd really been flying. I repeated these words to myself as I watched the tides and chewed my four o'clock snack of buttered toast sprinkled with sugar. It was much later than four. The sun had stolen away and refused to return; the wind grew cooler. It was the hour of gooseflesh: follicles, rising and bristling on our limbs, told us it was time to go. Mama and I gathered our things and hiked back up to the rental, a little house in a hamlet that probably hadn't changed much since the reign of Anne of Brittany. It wasn't exactly close. Burdened as we were, we felt more like soldiers humping packs than people out for a peaceful stroll. After ducking under the barbed wire that kept cows from meandering onto the beach, we crossed a field (a veritable minefield of marshy patches and manure), then took a path so rutted, so shady, that it stayed muddy even at the height of summer.

Neither that night, nor any night after, did I mourn that fantastical incident. I'd swept it under the rug. I'd flown for myself alone, a solipsistic Icarus. Maybe it wouldn't always be that way, I hoped, reliving the scene under the covers. Mama had cleaned and dressed my knee. The crumpled parasol was beyond repair, she reported in clipped tones. I didn't think so, but she had her pride. She didn't want cows, gulls, or clammers seeing her with a broken-down parasol. We'd buy a new one in the neighboring town as soon as possible, which meant in two days, the next market day. We'd take the bus. We depended on this means of transport for all our travel. My mother had no car. It was as if, in abandoning us, my father had left us by the side of the road.

The summer came to an end without another miracle. Oh, forgetful childhood! Toward the end of vacation, I never even thought about it anymore. I fished for gobies, coaxed ever-raspier sounds from my harmonica, and built sandcastles without expecting to fly off at any minute. Finally, one night I went down by myself to say my good-byes to the shore. Back at the rental, Mama was buckling up our suitcases. Tomorrow night, we'd return to our cramped roost in Paris, where we lived in a garret, a former maid's quarters. The ocean, too, was coming home, taking back the stretch it had ceded us for a few hours. I stood there, pensive, on the blackish moraine of sea wrack, cuttlefish bones, driftwood, and assorted flotsam washed up on the tide. Back then there were no plastic bottles, but rubber dolls' heads and more or less dismembered baby dolls were a common sight. Suspect, when you thought about it: where were all those washed-up dolls coming from? There wasn't a cove without one. What hands were tossing them into the sea through a porthole, or over a ship's railing? I didn't ask myself such questions then. A Hamlet in shorts, I'd happily pick up some poor Yorick's plastic, salt-bleached skull, but I wasn't ripe for any declamations. I tossed the head at a seagull searching for scraps in the debris, missing him by a hair. He flew off. Who knows if, these many years later, that chubby-cheeked head isn't still waiting for the wave that will carry it away again?

Already the waves were swallowing the scene of my adventure. The rock I'd skinned my knee on was gone from view. At that moment, I knew precisely what prison I'd briefly escaped, what tedium I'd been returned to. I would not be an angel. My dreams of azure abolished, I was doomed to the insignificance of an ordinary life: to school, military service, an office or a factory floor, retail or labor, couplehood and fatherhood, disappointment, the wounds you give and the ones you get, a career, its pitiful peak soon followed by retirement, old age, and death . . . Did I really feel all that? Vaguely. I had a premonition. Still, I knew I would hang on deep inside to the memory of that triumphant moment when I'd seen my feet float over the ground, and that this vision would help me brave the rest, life's plaster waiting to be mixed, its weight and inertia.

TWELVE years went by, twelve years I spent pacing life's seabed in a well-weighted diving bell. Sometimes the surface seemed so far away I no longer bothered lifting my head. Events seemed to bear out my fears. Dreamy schoolboy, bored teenager, college loafer . . . as a private, army life left me unconvinced. Maybe I'd have been a tad more involved had I been assigned to a riskier sector, but people are always needed back at base. Barracks life in Rodez was dumb and dismal as I'd thought. Off duty, I'd write my mother, then have a beer and play pool with my bunkmates. I wasn't *that* clumsy, but clearly beyond improvement, so whenever I had enough time I went for long walks alone in the countryside. I'd bring a fishing rod and, on the banks of the Aveyron, forget how our mongrel sergeant barked at us, or how the bunkroom filled with farts. The suicidally obliging gobies of my childhood were long gone. Bleaks and tenches, more reticent, took effort. But I'd baited my line for a different kind of catch when, at noon one fine day of furlough, I stepped through the door of a country inn. I was welcomed by a "winsome maid." Forgive the cliché, but apart from being an actual serving girl, Lorella was truly lissome and lively. Anyway, she served me up the fried whitebait I'd have had a hard time catching myself, along with a carafe of white wine. The whitebait and the white wine I liked; Lorella I liked even more. At least that's what I'd heard her called. I went back to that little roadhouse first chance I got. Lorella was nowhere to be found; an utterly ordinary creature officiated in her stead. Feigning nonchalance, I asked after her, and soon realized my mistake: Lorella was the boss's daughter. She hardly ever helped out with the restaurant. She was studying to be a nurse at the hospital in Rodez. This information eased my disappointment: my unit was quartered a few blocks from the hospital. It seemed like fate. Three days later, charged with delivering a love letter from my section lieutenant to a nurse at said hospital—another nurse, thank God!—I was ready to run into Lorella again. Her severe white coat with its tight sash and her headgear emblazoned with a red cross intimidated me. Would I even have had the nerve to show up if I'd pictured her in that getup? I'd been hanging on to another image of her altogether—one more accessible, laughing and twirling about in a blue serge apron and a little summer dress that bared her arms and throat, a band that kept back her abundant blond tresses. But fate was watching over us. It had to have been, for her to recognize at first glance the grunt she'd served at her parents' inn two weeks ago. She smiled. A young girl's smile means so little, really: they're usually smiling at themselves, at their reflection in the eyes of whomever they're talking to. I didn't know that then; I didn't know anything. But for once, my ignorance did not entail any unhappy consequences. When we'd first met, I'd liked Lorella, and she'd liked me. So there we were, she and I: our mutual attraction the only law of a suddenly much simpler universe. I told her I'd gone back to the inn, what I'd learned there, the lucky mission I'd been given. . . . As for her, she'd never doubted she'd run into me again one day or another. We made a date for the following week. A festival had been announced: attractions, dancing. We'd meet in early evening, if I wasn't confined to quarters and no fresh batch of the wounded kept her late. We had just enough time to make these plans; then an older nurse burst from a closet in the hall where we were standing and swooped down on Lorella. Was I the only patient she had to see to? I looked like a loafer in good health. To clear Lorella's name, I pulled out my lieutenant's mash note and asked where I could find the addressee. Our duenna deferred to my messenger status. The missive delivered, I returned to barracks, my heart full of joy.

WAFFLES sprinkled with powdered sugar that left fun mustaches; a few glasses of sparkling wine; a coney I'd won by shattering, with a single sand-filled ball, the flowerpot where it was buried up to its neck, a maxixe, a java, two waltzes . . . Toward evening's end we were in such a hurry that we left without finishing our glasses of bubbly. A lucky pal had slipped me the address to a tidy little hotel that, as night fell, welcomed all three of us: Lorella, the rabbit, and me.

All I'd ever known before her was a camp follower. Before me, she'd only had a cousin. In both cases, it'd been more a game for naughty children than any sort of *carnal embrace*. We shared our shared inexperience. My life till then had mostly been a journey without a destination. Lorella's arms gave it one. Late that night, as we were sleeping, I woke to a nibbling sound. I realized the rabbit, emboldened by silence, had started in on my belt, which had slipped from the chair. As gently as I could, I untangled myself from my companion and got out of bed. The rabbit beat a quick retreat before my bearing and determination, offering no resistance. I hung my belt out of reach and turned back toward bed. I could hear Lorella's breathing in the darkness. A moonbeam slipped between the curtains, limning her bare shoulders. The thought crossed my mind that come tomorrow, we'd have decisions to make. What would we do with the rabbit? What would we do with each other? Whether in my barracks or the inn, the coney would come to a quick end. And as for us—were we to wait till peacetime to marry? I realized I was taking things a little fast. I needed a way to feel Lorella out on the matter without showing my hand. A shiver ran down my spine. Was I really going to sit here naked while her warm limbs and velvety skin were waiting for me? I took a step closer to the bed, and felt myself unmoored from the ground, rising in the air as once, long ago, on the shore, with this difference: back then it had been in broad daylight, while the room where I now floated was bathed in shadow. My feet had barely left the ground, but there was no doubt about it: it was starting again, I was flying!

I recalled the ease with which, a child of nine, I'd risen, if not exactly scaled the heights. I urged myself to mete out my movements precisely, at the risk of bouncing like a buoy and clobbering myself on the ceiling. Already my cranium was grazing an acorn on the molding. The room's tininess reined in my exhilaration at the power that had been returned to me. True, I was freed from gravity again, but inside a parallelepiped of approximately forty-five cubic yards, still a prisoner of walls, floor, and ceiling. My heart pounding like before, and just as torn between fear and exaltation, I managed to stretch out and stabilize myself in this position over the bed, perpendicular to a sleeping Lorella. I could hear more than see her, make her out from the sound of her breathing. I was tempted to call out, ask her to turn on the bedside lamp. But I was afraid of scaring her. Wouldn't the shock she'd surely feel be likely to change our relationship? It's one thing to entrust yourself to a simple, honest young man, and another to realize you're really dating a freak, or even a monster. Would you marry Icarus? I hadn't known Lorella long enough to have a good idea of what she was looking for in the love of her life, a role for which I was now a contender. Maybe she wanted someone with both feet on the ground? Imagine her disappointment, then, if I woke her, if her eyes opened on my current position! I opted to stay quiet for the moment. And, bit by bit, as my eyes grew used to the dark, I could make out the shape of Lorella draped in sheets and a light blanket that both blurred and traced her figure. The scents that wafted from her sleeping body rose my way. I was in a good place up there, overlooking my love. Had it been up to me, I'd have stayed there a moment longer, but I soon felt that familiar density investing my flesh once more. It no longer seemed as horrible now that I'd felt, by the grace of Lorella, the weight of her breasts against me. Smoothly, in stages, I descended toward the bed and found myself curled up against her just as her thigh and hand moved to find me.

The miracle no more repeated itself the next day than it had the first time around. The only two other nights Lorella and I spent together—try as I did to beg fate by rising and even hopping halfheartedly at the foot of the bed—I remained a prisoner of earthly pull. I wasn't surprised, and quickly returned to bed with my fiancée. For I neglected to mention that the morning after our first night together, we had definitely made some big decisions. For one, we'd released the rabbit in a public park, and for another, we'd vowed to get married as soon as we could, without waiting for victory. We weren't wrong to want to, especially since victory, as things proved, wasn't exactly around the corner. Alas, our marriage was never to be. While we were waiting for regulation authorization to get married from our respective commanding officers, the enemy launched an offensive and skirted the Maginot Line. The reserves rushed toward the border in a heroic mess. I was among them. Lorella too. My section got surrounded by tanks, her medical unit obliterated by shelling. A letter informing me of Lorella's death reached me months later, in the stalag where I stewed away the next four years. Not for a single moment, in those four long years, did I rise even so much as an inch above my mattress of straw. It wasn't for lack of dreaming: I pictured myself floating over the snorers in the reeking air of my hut . . . in a few strokes I'd reached the door and opened it without a sound. I rose rapidly, straight up through the icy air of Pomerania. Beneath my feet, the lighted stalag grew smaller with each passing second. With its lines of huts, its grid of pathways, its barbed wire fences and watchtowers, it started to look like a model before shrinking to a tiny point of light that then vanished in the deep

European night. Then, with the instinct of a migratory bird, I'd turn west and head home in a flurry of wings.

I returned to France on a train in spring 1945. Lorella was dead. My cheeks were hollow and my heart empty. To get me back on my feet again, my mother stuffed me with corn flour, tapioca, semolina, rice pudding: I reverted to childhood. Where matters of the heart were concerned, I surrendered myself to Fulvia's care. Sometimes, watching our children at play, I imagine the ones I would've had with Lorella if those Stukas had respected international agreements that fateful day in June 1940. Those unborn children—I loved them too. But these are things best kept to yourself. What good would it do to tell those who were born that they've got ghostly half-brothers, half-sisters silhouetted by dotted lines, like shadows of their own shadows, staring at them enviously from some nearby limbo? People have been sent to the loony bin for less.

Sometimes, I thought I saw Lorella behind Fulvia too. But no, I was just imagining things. Like my sudden fits of levitation, you might say. Sorry: they're not the same thing. I really did fly—fluttered, at least—three times in my life. The first two I've already told you about. The third was fifteen years ago, in Landes. Mama and Fulvia were both still alive then. Ever since I'd come across the Great Dune of Pyla in the fifties, I'd taken great pleasure in climbing it. I can't exactly describe the effect the view from the top has on me. I quickly forget the grasping backdrop of food stands and souvenir shops. All that's left is a heap of sand fit for Titans and Cyclopes, the surrounding woods, the massive heavens, and the sea below. As a place, it seems to belong more to the geography of my dreams than that of the real world. I found some way to make it to that lookout every year—almost like a pilgrimage, though I had nothing to commemorate. My children have been scaling it ever since they learned to walk, but sometimes, in the area on business, I've also gone up alone.

That year, we'd gone in the off-season: Fulvia, my mother, and I. The children were all grown up. They'd go skiing without us, or else light out on a plane for the far ends of the earth. The windswept dune was deserted under a leaden sky. Despite her age, Mama had climbed up to the top, only taking Fulvia's arm for the last few yards. I brought up the rear. *Labored breathing.* My doctor's technical term came back to me. Without being obvious about it, he'd often ask at the end of a visit, "Any labored breathing? No? Grrrreat!"

I always said no. If he asked me again during my next visit, I'd have to answer otherwise. We'd reached the top of the dune. Fulvia and my mother were ahead of me. After taking a few minutes' rest to mock me, struggling along down below, they'd set out along the ridge with tiny steps, discussing household things—fabric softener, wash temperatures—no longer paying me any mind. I reached the summit in turn. Busy as I was catching my breath, and a bit alarmed by all this labored breathing (hardly of consequence, really, since here I was, still), it never crossed my mind that this would be the right time for another ascent. But that's what happened: I took off, as usual despite myself, and soon I was floating over the ridge, fifty feet or so behind my wife and my mother. Just like long ago, in Brittany, I feared being blown away by the wind at such heights. First I managed, not without effort, to hold my place like a swimmer fighting a current. Then a stronger gust got the better of me, suddenly hurling me so high I let out a cry of terror and closed my eyes. When I opened them again, I saw Fulvia and my mother forty feet below, their faces raised toward me. I detected neither wonder nor worry in their manner. They gazed at me wordlessly, without moving. At most I thought to see in their eyes ever so discreet a reprimand, as if, their conversation interrupted, each had privately thought, *Isn't he done with his foolishness yet?* I opened my mouth—to say what, by God? *Look at me, Fulvia, Mama, I'm flying!* As if they couldn't see me! They'd have had to be blind. Another gust snatched the words from my mouth, lifting me several yards higher before dropping me on the dune brusquely but benevolently, as if dumping an exasperating dog from its lap. I bit the dust a bit roughly—or rather, the sand. Fulvia and Mama exchanged a knowing glance. As I got up and was dusting off my coat and pants, they turned away and walked on, chattering.

We stopped to lunch at a restaurant in Arcachon harbor, where they refrained from mentioning the incident. Upset despite it all, I pretended to be absorbed in reading the menu, which prominently featured a seafood soufflé. Without malice aforethought, I suppose, my mother went for exactly that. Fulvia thought it a wonderful idea and followed suit. It turned out they made the right choice. They relished their soufflés. It was a dish I usually liked, but that day I ordered the biggest, weightiest oysters I could find.

Fifteen years have gone by since then. Mama and Fulvia have passed away: Mama in her time, and Fulvia far too soon. I haven't been back to the dune since, but I know the day is drawing near. I'll go there this winter, on the windiest day, sparing no effort—I'll run all the way up. And if I manage to dodge the heart attack that's been hanging over my head for so long; if, despite it all, this old carcass can haul itself up on high, then I hope and pray the wind will sweep it away once and for all.

—*Translated from the French by Edward Gauvin*

The figure of Icarus has exercised a lifelong hold on the imagination of the classically educated Châteaureynaud, but his winged men represent both the eternal fear and hope of escape. An early story from his second collection features the trapeze artist Menelos, who hides his gift of flight in a circus act. These talents are the target of murderous envy both in that tale and the 2007 novel The Other Shore, *where Menelos reappears. In the 1991 story "Icarus Saved from the Skies," wings are a source of shame and weakness, while the narrator of the rueful tale you have just read is earthbound, yearning, and ultimately as forlorn a figure of fun as was ever sidelined in a Brueghel landscape.*

—*EG*

KILLCROP
Victor LaValle

Someone in the apartment was screaming. Had been screaming for a while now. Was it him? No. He didn't think so. How could he scream underwater? Underwater was how he felt. Sunk. Water-logged. Drowned. He couldn't see. Felt nothing. But he could hear. That goddamn screaming. Wailing. And it wouldn't stop.

In a way this was good. If he couldn't hear that high-pitched voice he'd be lost in this darkness. At the bottom of a river. At the bottom of the sea. But the screams were like a light, flickering at the surface of the waters. He could move toward it. Hone in on the howls. Did he really want to? Better than being left down here. He could hardly breathe.

He kicked his legs. He was a strong swimmer. He tried to use his arms but for some reason they wouldn't move. They'd gone so numb that he couldn't even be sure they were attached to him anymore. There was only this deep chill in his shoulders. An arctic stab in both sockets. This was because his arms were chained behind him. They'd been that way for hours now.

He didn't open his mouth for fear of swallowing water. He wasn't in a river. Nor the ocean. But that's how he felt. Submerged.

He was in an apartment in New York City. His apartment. Where he'd lived, with his family, for three years. Being guided back to clarity, to consciousness, by the lead line of another person's agony. In a way he had to be grateful for this stranger's pain. If not for that screaming he'd only flail aimlessly in this darkness. Lost.

When he finally opened his eyes, once he blinked away the seawater of stupefaction, he saw he was in a kitchen. His kitchen. Sitting in one of the white Ikea chairs his wife had ordered for them six months ago. He was backed into a corner. Wasn't saturated by seawater, but sweat. There was vomit across his chest, on his pants. Still moist. The color of a crème brûlée. He couldn't smell it, not yet, because he was too confused.

He kicked his legs again, like when he'd been swimming, and his feet rattled. He shrugged his pinched shoulders and heard another rattle. He tried to look down but when he did his neck got squeezed so tightly he had to open his mouth to gasp. He was in his own kitchen. Chained to one of his chairs. A bike lock, a U-lock, had been looped around his throat. It held him tight to the steam pipe that ran from the kitchen floor into the ceiling. Since it was winter the steam pipe was on. When he pulled forward and gasped the lock resisted and he slumped backward. As soon as he did the back of his exposed neck touched the steam pipe like a pork cutlet pressed against a hot skillet. He hissed, the same sound as frying meat, and lurched forward but got yoked in the throat yet again. He had to sit in one position, exactly straight, to keep himself from being choked or burnt. A posture exercise.

The whole room felt tropical. Heat in the high nineties filled the room. The steam pipe was partly to blame, yes, but he could also hear now, from the other rooms in the apartment, the rattle and fizzle of the apartment's radiators. All were on. The apartment might as well be melting. His face, his exposed arms, his bare feet. His skin puckered all over from this heat.

And then there was the screaming. Which still hadn't stopped.

He could turn his head if he did it carefully. He could look around the kitchen if he mastered the natural panic. He scanned the kitchen, panning like a security camera. There was a claw hammer on the counter. A carving knife on the windowsill. And the wood floor was littered with hundreds of tiny green pellets. This was rat poison. They'd kept a box of the stuff under the kitchen sink until their son turned old enough to walk, to inquire. Now the pellets were sprayed across the kitchen floor like buckshot.

And there on the oven, finally, he found the source of all that screaming.

Not a person, but a kettle.

The flame turned high and the water inside on the boil. The kettle wailed and spewed a plume of smoke from its snout. A little dragon. It had been sitting on the fire for so long, the water inside roiling, that it jiggled and jumped on the stovetop. The kettle couldn't wait to pounce.

But at least it was only a kettle. Not a person in pain after all. The only one in danger was him. For a moment this even relieved him. Take a breath. But then his body shook all over, the legs and arms clanging in their chains. All this was for him? He was surprised to be alive. The burning kettle wailed a wet threat: his current condition would not last.

His mouth opened then and he called out, hoarsely. It was a woman's name, but you wouldn't know it. A slurred sound, that's all it was. He tried a second time.

"Lou?" he said.

If he'd been a boy he would call for his mother; since he was a man he called to his wife.

"Lucille?" he tried again, but who could hear him over the kettle? He barely heard himself. And after that third try a spasm of pain shot up from his left foot, through his thigh, and into the small of his back. So bad it made him twist, which teased the bike lock and in retaliation it choked him backward again. This time it was the back of his head, not his neck, that glanced against the steam pipe. It burned right through his short hair but he controlled himself this time. He didn't lurch too far forward so he was spared another squeeze around the throat. He panted in the kitchen. Out of breath and out of ideas.

"James," he whispered.

His son.

Lucille and James. His family. He forgot his chains, his pains, the instruments of violence scattered across the room. Where was his family? His people? Were they safe? Now the kettle's screeching seemed like the voice of his newer fear. Not for himself, but for them.

And, just then, he heard the creak of the floorboards in the next room.

From his chair, in the corner, he could look out of the kitchen and see the back room. Its off-white door was shut. When they'd moved into this apartment, when they'd bought the place, there hadn't been a door there because the home was a hovel. They'd been so diligent. Upwardly mobile. Fixing the place themselves, as much as possible. Which included buying that door from the building's super—the man made a side business selling tenants the cast-offs of other tenants—and hanging it themselves. He and Lou had done that together. And right now he couldn't have regretted the improvement more. If they hadn't hung the fucking door he wouldn't have to sit here looking at it, nauseated with fear. If the door weren't there at least he could see who was in the back room rather than waiting for the monster to be revealed. The ache of anticipation, unlike bodily pain, gets deepest inside you and can't be soothed by adrenaline or shock. It's a torture to the nervous system. As he watched the door of the back room his nerves were being shocked in wave after wave.

The door creaked as it swung back. The door had always done that. The kettle insisted that it not be ignored. The left side of his face almost seemed to burn at the high-pitched screeching. A figure stood in the doorway.

The back room was completely dark even though he could see, through the kitchen window, that it was late morning or early afternoon. A sunny day. This was happening under pleasant skies. They'd put blackout curtains in that back room because it's where James slept. The boy once had a problem with waking up when the sun rose. Or, really, his parents had a problem with him rising with the sun. The blackout curtains were meant to keep the room as dark as a cave. And they did. But now that darkness hid the person stepping out of the room, and whatever he had done inside it.

"Just . . ." he groaned.

Just what? What sentence was he trying to shape? Just leave? Just let me free? No. Just let my family go. That's what he was trying to say. And even he was surprised to realize those were the words he meant. Surprised because a person never really knows how he or she will react at those worst moments, do they? Each of us hopes to be brave, to be kind, to be whatever you like. But how often do we get the chance to find out which it'll be? But in this moment the thing he was willing to beg for was the life of his wife and son. The bottom of the teakettle must've been scorched black by the high flame by now. The water inside nearly as hot as the surface of the sun. Let this attacker pour it over his scalp, let his skin bubble and burst, let his eyes melt right out of his skull. Okay, okay. He would scream and die. All right. But let Lucille and James go.

The floorboards in the little hallway between the backroom and kitchen creaked just as loudly as the ones in the back room had done. It was an old apartment and when they'd had the floors sanded the guy who did it said this was the last time the floors could take such treatment. Whoever they sold the apartment to would have to put in new floors. In every room. Each board was as brittle as a Bostonian's smile. Now they creaked and popped, here and there, as the figure stomped into view.

Smaller than expected. Short and thin.

How had this little man overpowered him? he wondered. He wasn't huge, but he stayed in good shape. There was a throb in his stomach. Could he have fought back harder? He couldn't even remember how this guy had gotten into the apartment. They had a security gate over the window in James's room. They were on the fourth floor. Too high to scale the side of the building and slip in through an unguarded window. Too low to drop down from the roof on the sixth floor.

The stranger, this creature, brought along something else. A low noise. Even in his chair he could make the sound out through the sounds of the teakettle's trill. Grumbling. Mumbling. The monster was talking to itself. He couldn't understand the words, but the bass of the voice rumbled, something seismic about it. He felt it below his feet.

The monster's hair was long and hung over its face. The locks were ratty and dry. Appropriately shabby. It slumped as it moved forward which only made it seem more ghoulish. It stepped into the kitchen, brushed past him. So close. Only inches. He shot forward. The chair underneath him rose and its legs banged against the floor. Despite the chains around his shins, the ones around his wrists, he would've crashed into this little man, this thing, that thug, with so much force that it would've gone through the fridge.

But that bike lock wasn't playing.

He lurched forward like that and choked himself so badly that he

almost passed out. Not so surprising. He'd been close to unconsciousness moments ago. Maybe he'd been floating up and down,
from the depths to the shallows, for much longer than he realized.
Maybe he and this monster had gone back and forth like this a few
times already. The claw hammer on the counter, the carving knife
on the windowsill. Maybe he'd been stabbed and bludgeoned already and just couldn't see his body well enough to tell from this
angle. Maybe the kitchen floor, right beneath him had already been
restained by his lost blood. The stabbing chills throughout his body
made it impossible to distinguish between a cut and a crack and a
mortal wound.

Meanwhile his home invader didn't even seem to notice him.
Walked right past the grown man choking in the corner, went to the
oven, and finally turned off the flame. The teakettle yelped for another few seconds. The water bubbled inside the little cauldron.

But why didn't that make the screaming stop?

Without the distraction of the steaming kettle he could hear, distinctly, from the back room . . .

It couldn't be. It couldn't be. He tried to calm himself, but it was
so much harder now. A child was crying in the back room. Who
else's child could it be?

His body, it seemed to lose all shape. He felt larger, like the size of
a star, the sun. A burning gaseous form. Too enormous for the small
kitchen of a two-bedroom apartment. Why weren't walls disintegrating? How soon before the floor and ceiling singed into dust?
Why hadn't the world been burnt to ashes instantly? His terror
burned hotter than the star at the center of our solar system. He
rose in his chair. If the bike lock choked him he couldn't feel it.

What had been done to his child?

He found his voice, but not his words. He growled at the little
man in his kitchen. The one holding the kettle of scalding water.
What threat could that pose now? He was a being of hot plasma.
His diameter was 109 times that of the Earth. The temperature of
his core was 15.7 million Kelvin. His gravitational pull was 28 times
greater than the Earth's.

He bellowed at the home invader while, in the other room, his
son squealed. The figure in the kitchen stood in place. It was holding the teakettle not by the handle but in its palm. Its flesh must've
been burning, but the hand didn't quiver. The invader finally held

his gaze. The creature saw him there, chained in the corner, spitting and raving and rattling his chains.

And now the man in chains could see his attacker clearly.

It wasn't a small man.

This hadn't been a home invasion.

It was his wife.

"Lou?"

In the back room his son's cries turned into hiccupping shrieks. James was almost two, but these were the cries of a newborn. That special senseless yelping. The cries ride one on top of the other, the next one begun before the first has even finished. Not only pain. Also confusion. And such naked weakness. The cries that make a new parent panic right inside the bones.

Lucille had come out of that room.

"*LuLu,*" he tried. "What did you do?"

Maybe nothing yet. Maybe James was only terrified and not hurt badly. The weapons were all here in the kitchen, weren't they? Even in this nightmarish moment he fussed at a thorn of hope.

She watched him.

The steaming kettle sitting on her palm made her look like a waiter, about to bring a tray to a table. How could she not feel the pain? He could *see* her palm had turned red. Despite his son's screams he could even hear the flesh of her hand roasting. The air smelled like burnt charcoal now. And yet his wife registered none of it. She stood in the room, but she wasn't there.

"You remember how it was," he began.

He set back on the chair because his vision had been going blurry and he realized the bike lock could still hurt him even if he couldn't feel it now.

"How it was the first few months after James came. It was hard on you, Lou. You got so broken down. You remember?"

She watched him. She didn't speak. How could this be his wife? She looked drained, as if her whole soul had been siphoned out. She looked almost green. A likeness of his wife carved out of slate. She stayed there, silent. He thought maybe, deep inside, she wanted him to talk her out of whatever she had planned.

"You just got so broken down. It happens to mothers all the time. Lou, it's not just you. I can hear James in there. He still sounds . . . *strong.* There's nothing that happened here that we can't fix."

She shuffled. She looked away from him. For the first time her hand, and the kettle, wobbled, as if she finally felt the pain. As if she was coming back to herself, a satellite returning to the planet.

"Just let me loose. We'll check on James."

Hearing her son's name seemed to work on her like some post-hypnotic suggestion. Her head tilted backward as if she'd gone into a trance. Her eyes became electrified. There was his wife. He had her. Appeal to that woman. The mother of James. Who, he knew, would never willingly hurt her only child.

But he was wrong. He didn't have her.

In fact, he'd lost her.

How long ago? Was it when he said their son's name, or sometime last week, last year?

With her free hand she grabbed the claw hammer off the counter. She stepped toward him with one fluid motion, and drove the hammer's face into the side of his head. His cheekbone cracked. He heard the bone chipping, the sound played loudly inside his skull. And suddenly the right side of his mouth wouldn't open as easily. His vision shifted, the bottom half going dark, as if his eyeball had just slipped out of its housing. Through the left side of his mouth he pleaded even as Lucille, his wife of five years, dropped the hammer to the floor.

She walked past him now. He rose from the chair again. What pain could compare with what James would go through? Nothing. Not one damned thing. He rose in the chair and the bike lock barked him back down. His weight crashing with such force that one chair leg broke right through the thin wood floorboard. So now his chair went back down at a new angle and his throat caught on the bike lock yet again. But this time good posture wouldn't help. He was like a ship listing to port. He was sinking. The bike lock became a noose. He was going down.

"Don't hurt the baby," he pleaded.

His wife walked out of the kitchen.

In the hallway, just before the back room, she turned to him. She raised the kettle of scalding water. The baby wept and choked and coughed and cried.

As she stepped back into the darkened room he sank into a darkness of his own.

Spots appeared in his eyes and still he strained so hard that blood coughed out of his mouth.

She spoke then, clearly and directly.
"It's not a baby," she said.

I wanted to write a story about changelings. The myth of human babies being snatched and replaced by troll babies, specifically. Most of those stories are about the mothers figuring out their kids have been switched, then retrieving (or not) their babies. I was interested in what it would be like if you were the other parent, the father in this case, who had no idea your child had been taken. What would your wife seem like then? A madwoman who wanted to harm your baby. Talk about horror. I started writing this story and it grew and grew. What you have here is now the first chapter of something much longer, larger.

—VL

The Kraken

THE SQUID WHO FELL IN LOVE WITH THE SUN

Ben Loory

Once there was a squid who fell in love with the sun. He'd been a strange squid ever since he was born—one of his eyes pointed off in an odd direction, and one of his tentacles was a little deformed. So, as a result, all the other squids made fun of him. They called him Gimpy and Stupid and Lame. And when he'd come around, they'd shoot jets of ink at him and laugh at him as they swam away.

So after a while, the squid gave up and started hanging out by himself. He'd swim around alone near the surface of the water, gazing upward—and that's when he saw the sun.

The sun looked to him like the greatest thing in the world.

It's just so beautiful, he'd think.

And he'd stretch out his arms and try to grab hold of it.

But the sun was always out of reach.

WHAT are you doing? the other squids would say when they saw him grasping for it like that.

Nothing, he'd say. Just trying to touch the sun.

God, you're such an idiot, the squids would say.

Why do you say that? the squid would ask.

Because, the others would say, the sun is too high; you'll never be able to reach it.

I will, someday, the squid would say.

AND the other squids laughed, but the squid kept trying. He didn't give up—he reached and stretched and reached.

And then one day, he saw a fish jump out of the water.

I should try jumping! he said.

SO the squid started trying to jump to reach the sun. At first, he couldn't jump very high. He'd lurch out of the water and then fall right back in.

But he kept trying more and more every day.

And, in time, the squid could jump pretty high. He could make it eight or nine feet out of the water. He'd make a big dash in order to build up some steam, and then leap up with all his tentacles waving.

But no matter how high and how far the squid jumped, he never could quite reach the sun.

You really are a stupid squid! the squids would say. You really get dumber all the time.

THE squid didn't understand how what he was doing was dumb. But it was true that he didn't seem to be getting much closer.

Then one day in mid-jump he saw a bird flying by.

Wings! I need wings! the squid said.

SO the squid set out to build himself a pair of wings. He did some research into different kinds of materials. He'd found some ancient books in a sunken ship he'd discovered, and he read the ones about metallurgy and aeroscience.

And, in time, the squid built himself some wings. They were made of a super-lightweight material that also had a very high tensile strength. (He'd had to build a small smelting plant to make them.)

Looks like these wings are ready to go, the squid said.

And he leapt up out of the water. And he flapped and flapped, and he rose and rose. He rose up above the clouds and flapped on.

It's working! the squid said.

He looked up toward the sun.

I'm coming, I'm coming! he said.

But then something happened—his wings stopped working. Up that high, the air was too thin.

Uh-oh, the squid said, and he started to fall.

He fell all the way back down to the sea. Luckily, he wasn't hurt—he'd had the foresight to bring a parachute. (He even had a backup for emergencies.)

But he splashed down in the water and, as he did, his wings shattered. And of course, the other squids laughed again.

When is this squid ever going to learn? they said.

But the squid no longer took notice of them.

YOU see, the squid had had an idea—all the way up there at the top of his climb. Just as he was perched at the outer limit of the atmosphere—

What I need is an interplanetary spaceship, he said.

Because at that very moment, the squid had finally grasped something: he'd finally understood the layout of the solar system. Before he'd been bound by his terrestrial beginnings. Now he understood the vast distances involved.

Of course, building an interplanetary spaceship was complicated—much more complicated than a simple set of wings. But the squid was not discouraged; if anything, he was excited.

It's good to have a purpose, he said.

SO the squid set out designing himself a spaceship. The body was easy; it was the propulsion system that was hard. He had to cover about a hundred million miles.

I'm going to need a lot of speed, he said.

At first, the squid designed an atomic reactor. But it turned out that wouldn't provide power enough. He'd gotten pretty heavily into physics by this point.

I need to harness dark matter and energy, he said.

And so the squid did. He designed and built the world's first dark matter and energy reactor. It took a lot of time and about a thousand scientific breakthroughs.

All right, he said. That should be fast enough.

———

AND finally, one day, the squid's interplanetary spaceship was built and ready to take off. The squid put on his helmet and climbed inside.

Well, here goes nothing, he said.

He pushed a single button and took off in a burst of light and plowed straight up out of the atmosphere. He tore free of Earth's orbit and whizzed past the moon, burned past Venus, and sped on past Mercury.

There in his command chair, the squid stared at the sun as it grew larger before him on the screen.

I'm coming, I'm coming, my beautiful Sun! he said. I'll finally hold you, after all this time!

BUT as he got closer, something strange started to happen—something the squid hadn't foreseen. The ship started getting hotter. And then hotter and hotter still.

Why's it so hot? the squid said.

YOU see, the squid really knew nothing about the sun. He didn't even know what it was. It had always just been a symbol to him—an abstraction that filled a hole in his life. He'd never even figured out that it was a great ball of fire—that is, until this very moment. But now the truth finally dawned on him.

That thing's gonna kill me! he said.

HE slammed on the brakes, but the ship just kept on going. He threw the engines into reverse, and they whined, but still he kept going—getting closer and closer.

I'm stuck in the sun's gravity! he said.

HE did some calculations and realized he was lost. He'd gone too far; he was over the edge. Even with his engines all strained to the limit, he had only a few hours to live.

AND as he sat there in his chair, just waiting to die, something even worse started to happen. The squid started ruminating and thinking about his life.

Oh my god, he said. I really *have* been an idiot!

———

SUDDENLY it was all just painfully clear: everything he'd done, all his work, had been for nothing.

I'm a moron, he said. I wasted my whole life.

That's not true; you built me, the ship said.

AND the squid thought about it, and he realized the ship was right.

But you'll be destroyed too, he said.

Yes, said the ship. But I have a transmitter. If we work fast, at least the knowledge can be saved.

SO the squid started working like he'd never worked before—feverishly, as he fell into the sun. He wrote out all his knowledge, his equations and theorems, clarified the workings of everything he'd done.

And in the moments left over, the squid went even further. He pushed out into other realms of thought. He explored biology and psychology and ethics and medicine and architecture and art. He made great leaps, he overcame boundaries; he shoved back the limits of ignorance. It was like his whole mind came alive for that moment and did the work that millions had never done.

And in the very last second before his ship was destroyed, and he himself was annihilated completely, the squid sat back.

That's all I got, he said.

And the ship beamed it all into space.

AND the knowledge of the squid sailed out through the dark, and it sped its way back toward Earth. But of course when it got there, the other squids didn't get it, because they were too dumb to build radios.

AND the story would end there, with the squid's sad and lonely death, but luckily, those signals kept going. They moved out past Earth, past Mars and the asteroid belt, past Jupiter and all the other planets.

And then they kept going, out beyond the solar system, out into and through the darkness of space. They moved through the void, through other galaxies and clusters. They kept going for billions of years.

And finally one day—untold millenniums later—they were picked up by an alien civilization. Just a tiny backwards race on some tiny, backwards planet, all alone at the darkest end of space.

And that alien civilization decoded those transmissions, and they examined them and took them to heart. And they started to think, and they started to build, and they changed their whole way of life.

They built shining cities of towering beauty; they built hospitals and schools and parks. They obliterated disease, and stopped fighting wars.

And then they turned their eyes toward space.

And they took off and spread out through the whole universe, helping everyone, no matter how different or how far.

And their spaceships were golden, and emblazoned with the image of the squid who spoke to them from beyond the stars.

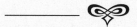

I've always been obsessed with the myth of the kraken, especially that famous drawing by Pierre Denys de Montfort of one of them attacking a ship. One night I had a dream where I was standing in a museum, staring at that drawing on the wall, only instead of attacking a ship, the kraken was grappling with the sun. I woke up and started writing this story. Of course, as I wrote, the kraken got smaller, and the sun went back to being far away. Then halfway through it turned into an Icarus story . . . and then finally into something much larger. Still not sure how it all came together; it was a long, strange trip, but here we are.

—BL

Lamia/Child-Eating Demon, Greek

BIRDSONG FROM THE RADIO
Elizabeth McCracken

Long ago," Leonora told her children, and the telling was long ago, too, "I was just ordinary." Of course they didn't believe her. She was taller than other mothers, with a mouthful of nibbling, nuzzling teeth, and an affectionate chin she used as a lever. Her hair was roan, her eyes taurine. Later the children would look at the handful of photographs of their mother from the time, all blurred and ill lit, as though even the camera were uncertain who she was, and they would try to remember the gobbling slide of her bite along their necks, her mouth loose and toothy on a shoulder. The threat of more. She was voracious. They could not stop laughing. No! No! Again!

Children long to be eaten. Everyone knows that.

Don't you want to devour that child, Leonora asked. Oh look at that bottom. I am, I'm going to bite it. I'm going to eat that child whole.

(To speak of love as cannibalism! She would have thought it strange herself, before her marriage, but here were the children, Rosa, Marco, Dolly, plump loaves of bread, delicious.)

Those were the days just before the buses came in. The children could hear from their bedroom windows the screech of the streetcars up the hill. Their father ran his family's radio manufacturers, and there were radios in every room of the house, pocket and tabletop, historic cathedrals. His name was Alan. "Poor Alan," Leonora called him, and they both understood why: he was in thrall to his wife. He was a very bus of a man, practical and mobile, and he left the children to Leonora, who had a talent for love, as he had a talent for business.

Winters she took the children tobogganing. Summers they piloted paddleboats across the city pond. She never dressed for the weather. No gloves, no sunhats, no shorts, no scarves. She was always blowing on her fingers or fanning her shirt against her torso. Sunburn, windburn, soaking wet with rain. The children, too. Other mothers sent them home with hand-me-down mittens and umbrellas.

Not surprising, said those mothers later: she never took care of her children.

ROSA, Marco, Dolly: Leonora took them to see the trolleys the last day they ran. She wore a green suede coat, the same color as the trolleys, in solidarity. It closed with black loops which Leonora assured her children were called *frogs*.

"It's raining," said Leonora. "The frogs will be happy."

"That's not a frog," said Marco. He was five, the age of taxonomy.

"They are," said Leonora. "I promise. And my shoes are alligator."

"Why are we watching the streetcars?" asked Marco.

"There's no beauty in buses," Leonora said. "A bus can go anywhere it likes. A trolley is beautiful."

"Oh yes," said Rosa, who was seven, "I can see."

Leonora was as melancholy as if the streetcars had been hunted into extinction. They were lovely captives who could not get away, and they left only their tracks behind.

Her coat fastened with frogs, her shoes were alligator. Perhaps she was already turning into an animal.

The children grew bigger, and bony. Leonora grew worse about love: she demanded it. She kissed too hard. She grabbed the children by the arms to pull them close. "You *seized* me," said Dolly, age six, "why did you seize me so?"

"I was looking for a place to nibble," said Leonora. But Dolly was a skinny girl.

Leonora bit. She really did now. Moments later, contrite, writhing, she would say, "The problem is I love you so. I do. Can I be near you? Do you mind?"

What had happened to Leonora? It was the sad story that ran through her family, which had begun centuries ago and wove through every generation—a great-grandfather had lived three decades in an asylum; an aunt had killed herself—and the story had not reached its conclusion yet: this chapter was being told in Leonora. Or she had a fall in the bathroom, and it broke all the vials that contained her essence, and all the chemicals in her body mixed together inside her and foamed and smoked and ran over. Or she missed her children, who were growing up.

The doctors prescribed her pills, which she refused to take.

She still tried to eat her children but they were afraid of her. So she had to sneak. The weight of her as she sat on the edge of their beds in the middle of the night was raptorial: ominous yet indistinct. At any moment, she might spread her arms and pull the children from the sheets through the ceiling and into the sky, the better to harm them elsewhere. The children took to sleeping in the same bed. Rosa, Marco, Dolly. Too old to sleep together but they had to. They chose a different bed every night, and lay still, as they heard her go from pillow to pillow, the unfurling flump of the sheets like the wings they thought they could see on her back.

"Come back to bed," said Poor Alan from the hallway in a terrified voice. "Come listen to the radio and fall asleep." The top of his head was bald. The children could see the bathroom light pool in a little dent in his scalp, just below his summit.

The children had radios in their rooms, too, of course. He snapped one on, to the classical station, to calm them down. "You never need be lonely with a radio!" he always said, but they knew that wasn't so. A radio station was another way grown-ups could talk to you without ever having to listen.

IT was Rosa who told Poor Alan that they had to go. She was fifteen. "We're leaving," she told him. "You can come if you want to. But Marco and Dolly and I are going." Then, seeing his face, "We'd like you to come."

"She needs help," he said.

"She won't get it."

He nodded. "How will we manage?"

"We're not managing now," said Rosa. "In a year I'll get my license. I'll drive the little kids to school." The little kids! She was only two years older than Marco, who was three years older than Dolly.

"What will happen to your mother," said Poor Alan, wringing his hands.

"Whatever it is, it's already happening," said Rosa. "I can't watch anymore."

"She's a wonderful mother. You must remember that."

"I don't," said Rosa. "I can't, not anymore."

He wasn't a bad man. He could be mistaken for thinking it was a war, an ancient one, and that she would fight against the rest of them as long as she was near. In the winter he took Rosa and Marco and Dolly to a new house, and Leonora was left behind. He arranged for her disability checks. He did not take her off the bank account.

"If you get help, we'll come back," he told her.

The father hired a nanny, Madeline, a jug-eared, freckled beauty. A good girl, as her father later described her to the news cameras. She picked up the children every day after school and brought them to the house. Rosa worshiped her; Dolly and Marco merely loved her. This went on for six months, until the day after her twenty-first birthday, when she woke up in the middle of the day still drunk from the first legal cocktails of her life, in the middle of December, and got the children into the car, and found the car was too hot, and as she tried to wrench her black peacoat off one shoulder, and as she felt the last of the black Russians muscle through her veins, and as she hit a patch of black ice, she understood that there would be an accident. She could see the children hurt in the backseat. The windshield gone lacy. Herself, opening the door, and running away, away, away. *When the car stops, I'm going to leg it*, and that was the last thought Madeline or any of them ever had.

NO children, thought Leonora. She had intended to get herself upright and go looking for them. She should have eaten them when she could.

For a while she tried to distract herself with the radios. Each wore Poor Alan's family name like a badge on the pellicle of the speaker. She went from room to room and turned them on, but then she thought she could hear—behind the sonorous day-long monologue of the news station, or the awful brightness of Vivaldi on the classical station, or jokes cracked by a disc jockey named after an ancient king—the voices of her children. She tried to tune them in. You had to use the volume and the tuning knob in mincing little oscillations. Then, there it was: the tootling rhythm of Dolly's conversation. Rosa humming at the back of her throat as though ready to defiantly swallow the sound should someone walk into the room. Marco sighing before he explained something. She wondered whether they each had a station, Dolly, Marco, Rosa. Maybe they had different radios, even. No: they would be cuddled up together in one frequency, the way they liked.

But she could never tune them in clearly, and slowly the noise behind the newscast turned feral, howling, chirping, shrieking: a forest empty of children. Then she knew they were gone. The radios wouldn't turn off tight enough. The voices of strangers leaked through, no matter how hard she turned the knob. She unplugged the radios, knocked the batteries from the backs. She could still hear that burble, someone muttering or the sound of an engine a block away.

She lay in bed. At her ear hummed the old clock radio, with the numbered decagons that showed their corners as they turned to indicate that a minute had ended, or an hour, the hum a little louder then. She felt her torso, where her children would have been, had she managed to eat them.

Not everyone who stops being human turns animal, but Leonora did.

It was time to leave the house. The top of her back grew humped with ursine fat, and she shambled like that, too, bearlike through the aisles of the grocery store at the end of the street. She shouldered the upright fridges full of beer, she sniffed the air of the checkout lanes. Panda-eyed and eagle-toed and lion-tailed, with a long braid down her back that snapped as though with muscles and vertebrae. Her insides, too. Animals of the dark and deep. Her kidneys dozing moles; her lungs, folded bats. The organs that had authored her children: jellyfish, jellyfish, eel, eel, manatee.

I am dead. I am operated by animals.

Her wandering took her to the bakery, where every Saturday morning of their early childhood, she'd taken her children, to let Poor Alan sleep in. In the angled case she saw the loaves of challah. She saw something familiar in the shape.

"Can I help you?" said the teenager behind the counter. His T-shirt had a picture of the galaxy on it, captioned YOU ARE HERE. She tapped the glass in front of the challah. "Please," she said, and he pulled a loaf out, and she said, "I don't need a bag."

He had already started angling the loaf into the bag's brown mouth. Who didn't need a bag for bread?

"I don't need a bag," she repeated. She counted out the money and set it down. "Just the paper."

He handed it self-consciously across the counter. When it was in her hands she adjusted the paper around it, admired the sheen of the egg wash, its placid countenance. Then she carried it to a table in the window and spread out the wax paper and set the loaf upon it.

Marco. She saw his sleeping baby self in the shape of the bread. Knees and arms akimbo, head turned, as always, to the left. The girls had cast different shadows. She put her hand on the loaf to check for oven warmth. Not on the surface. Maybe at the heart. Later she wouldn't care what people thought of her, she'd cradle the loaf in her arms before eating, but now she patted the bread, and then, with careful fingers, pulled it apart. That sense of invading a privacy that is then offered up to you. Yeast, warmth, sweetness, a very child. Her mouth was full with it, and then her head, and throat, and stomach. She felt the feral parts of her grow sleepy and peaceable.

I am eating Marco. I am eating my baby.

Thereafter, every morning she went to the bakery and bought a challah and pretended it was one of her children. She knew she could never say this aloud. Rosa slept with her bottom in the air. Dolly, alone of the children, needed to be swaddled. Marco, akimbo. She carried the day's loaf in her arms to the table. She patted it. Then she ate it. Not like an animal. Knob by knob, slowly: one loaf could last her four hours, washed down with water from the crenellated plastic cups the bakery gave away for free.

That was her nourishment. She lived on bread and good manners and felt sick with her children.

The new mothers of the neighborhood wished the bakery would throw the bulky unkempt woman out. As they wished they felt guilty, because they were trying to teach their children tolerance. But then they looked at the angled case. The center bay was filled with glittering sugared shortbread cookies, decorated according to the season. Hearts, shamrocks, eggs, flags, leaves, pumpkins, turkeys, candy canes, hearts again. Evidence: bakeries were for children, and children were frightened of Leonora. (A trick of the radio again. The children were only tuned to their mothers' fears.)

Sometimes a mother and child would walk by her table, and Leonora could see the tight unhappy discomfort of judgment on the mother's face.

"Say hello, Pearl," the mother would tell her child, and Pearl, dutifully, would say hello, and Leonora would wave. She knew that the mother was thinking, *Thank God she doesn't know what I'm thinking.*

Those children neither pained nor interested her. They weren't

258 | Elizabeth McCracken

her darlings. But every now and then a Pearl or a Sammy would smile at her, and even giggle, and she would, she would want a nibble, a kiss, in the old way. A raspberry blown on a neck, a kiss with a bite at its heart: *nibble, nibble, yum.* They weren't hers but they were sweet. But if you were the mother of dead children, that was over. You weren't allowed.

On those days she ordered a second loaf of bread, which she dragged home and tore apart.

FIVE years passed like nothing. She was recognized in the neighborhood as the monument she was, an obelisk, a cenotaph, constructed to memorialize a tragedy but with the plaque long since dropped off. She was Leonora. Her name had survived, because the bakery workers remembered it, but that was all. Nobody imagined that she was a mother. She was (anyone who saw her presumed) a person who had always been exactly who she was, poisoned, padded, eyes sunk into her face. She existed only at the table, eating bread in her finicking way. She spoke to the people behind the counter. That was all. Some of them were patient and some of them weren't.

Then one day a man came into the bakery, caught her eye, and smiled.

Poor Alan, she thought reflexively, but then she remembered Poor Alan was dead, though he'd remembered her in his will and set up a trust to take care of her. This man wore a green wool hat like a bucket. The hat looked expensive, artisanal. He pulled it from his head and revealed a full head of white hair. No, he never was Poor Alan, who'd lost his hair long before it faded. But she did know the man. He sat down across from her. The tabletop was Formica, the green of trolleys.

"Mike Wooster," he said.

"Hello, Mike Wooster," said Leonora. She could smell her own terrible breath. She still slept in a bed and washed herself but she did not always remember to brush her teeth. Why would she? She scarcely used them.

He bounced the hat around on his fists. Then he set it in front of him. She had a sense he wanted to drop it over the remains of the day's bread: Dolly this time. He said, "I'm Madeline's father."

She heard the present tense of the sentence. "I know who you are," she said.

Everything about him was rich and comforted. "I heard you came here," he said. "That bread good?"

She tore off a brown curve. A cheek, a clenched hand. She sniffed at it before she pushed it in her mouth.

He cleared his throat. "We're having a memorial service," he said. "And my wife and I and our kids—well, we thought of you." He picked the hat back up, brushed some flakes of challah from the brim. "I've thought of you." He said that to the hat, and then got hold of himself. "Every single day I've thought of you. You know," he said, "they turned my daughter into a monster, too."

The alcohol, the coat, the ice. Everyone said that if one of those things hadn't been true, they never would have crashed. "Too?" she said.

The animals of her body were roaring back to life. They—whoever *they* were—had not turned Leonora into a monster. They had erased her. Newspapers, television, the terrible gabbling radio, which spoke only of the children's father, the left-behind man, the single parent. That poor man, looking after his children. To lose all of them at once.

Poor Alan had had a memorial service, too, had invited her. Though he'd asked her to come to the front, she'd sat alone at the back of the church—a *church*! since *when*!—drunk and stunned. Nobody spoke to her. She was a mother who'd let her children go, a creature so awful nobody believed in her. She'd had to turn herself into a monster, in order to be seen.

"Madeline never got a chance," said Mike Wooster. "To redeem herself. But you could. You could be redeemed."

She laughed at that, or part of her did, a living thing sheltered in a cave inside of her. "Redeemed," she said. "Like a pawn shop ticket."

He shook his head. "Like a soul. Your *soul* can be redeemed."

"Too late," she said. "Soul's gone."

"Where?" he said.

"Where do you *think*?" she said.

At that he took her hand. "This only feels like hell," he said. "I know. I do know."

She shook his hand to refuse his sympathy: she could smell the distant desiccation of it. *No.* Why had he come here? She could not be redeemed, a coupon, a ticket. He had a dead child too, of course. She could feel it twitching through his fingers, the sorrow, the guilt, like schools of tiny flicking fish who swim through bone instead of ocean. He was not entirely human anymore either. Indeed, she could hear the barking dog of his heart, wanting an answer. Her heart snarled back, but tentatively.

But if she accepted his sympathy then she would have to feel sorry for him. She would have to *transcend*. Some people could. They could forgive and rise above their agony.

She could feel the turning of her organs in their burrows, and she felt an old emotion, one from before. Gratitude. She was thankful to remember that she was a monster. Many monsters. Not a chimera but a vivarium. Her heart snarled, and snarled, and snarled. She tried to listen to it.

"The thing," Leonora told Mike Wooster, and she pulled her hand from his, "is that you can't unbraid a challah."

"No?" he said. "Well, I'd guess not."

"Would you like some?" she asked.

He looked at the rubble of the day's loaf. "Oh no. No, that's yours."

"Let me get you one. Please."

"I don't need—"

Leonora said, rising, "It will be a pleasure to watch you eat."

I have loved the notion of a Lamia ever since reading Keats's "Lamia" in college (if I remember correctly, I wrote a rhyming, probably insufferable term paper on it). Among the dark topics I am always trying to write about but always fail (fires, spontaneous combustion, people living in houses with corpses in them), my most persistent failed topic is cannibalism. It makes sense to me that a woman who loses her children (as Lamia does in some versions) would turn into an animal— and not just one, since grief contains both prey and predator, fear and rage.

—EM

THE LOTUS EATERS

Aurelie Sheehan

Artesia jumped the fence into the broken-down-to-crap miniature golf course, and then came Pog, and then Pete and the other girl. The world was a gorgeous chocolate brown, a gleaming purring soft color that also glittered. Artesia was one of a kind, she was safe, and she had the power.

It was more of a lurch than a jump, and when her jeans got stuck on a hook of wire, she did plunge for a second, experiencing a lightning bolt of insecurity, not enough to really throw her. She hit the ground and then she was on her feet again, the earth a trampoline. Big grin. Her heart pulsed, throbbing with the brown red core of sheer and perfect life, and there was more to this night than they knew, than anyone could know. This night would last forever, this night was a place you could curl up into and doze, never go home, this night *was* home. For Artesia. For Artesia and Pete. For Pog and the other girl, too, probably, maybe.

This is the magic world where the ages of time abide in a garden of serenity with perpetual peace and harmony.

"Look!" she shouted, pointing at the sign near the dead building. The miniature golf course was an endless universe, about the size of a Walgreens parking lot. A Phoenix car dealer owned the property. Six months ago the golf course had gone out of business, and the retro-tacky-trashy-mystifying world within a world began to disintegrate. Currently in a state of high demolishment, by vandals or design, the course still held on to its dismal charm. Artesia and Pete and Pog and the other girl, they'd needed something—a culminating event—after Bookman's kicked them out. And so they pranced across the parking lot and across Speedway Boulevard, past the golf course's entrance and to the back of the lot, where no one could see them lurking and jumping. Now they were in, and it *was* an enchanted kingdom, all right. Punitive lights from passing cars rushed over them and disappeared again.

Pete and the rest right behind her—all too fucking funny for words. The funny genie sat on his ass on top of the banner, *Magic Carpet Golf*, the name unfurling radiantly underneath him. Used to be lit up, the man on his carpet, and now his smile alone kept him sane.

"I used to come here as a kid!" Artesia screamed.

"Shut the fuck up!" everyone said.

"Oh shit, I used to come here on my birthday!"

"So did I, who gives a shit!" Pog screamed back. He had turned away, morphing into a Black Shape—yes, all you could see was his fat black back like he was some kind of mammoth. Poor sweet Pog, forever the younger brother of yesterday's dealer. You couldn't even see his head behind his shoulders and when you did it looked like a tiny pinhead. He was foraging around in the corners. What the fuck was he doing? He was foraging. Along the edge in the wild zone, looking for something.

"You look like the—the—" Artesia said, or tried to say.

The moon was square, a hunk of light someone had thrown into the sky, as if the world itself weren't yet complete. It was a rough draft, gonna get the details right later. And here we are, thought Artesia. Amazing. The word *amazing* being an embodiment, or a full-on true reality.

Artesia was gritting the crap out of her teeth.

"Here is an arrow," intoned the other girl, pointing at a small sign.

Bitch. Slut.

But Artesia so totally didn't care about that. It was all right, because . . .

"You look like, like the—"

Then here came Pete—the *god of light!*—charging up the path from wherever he'd gone, and he had some kind of long device, a crop or a wand, and as he ran he was elegant and handsome and sexy, as always, as before, and he was hitting whatever the hell was still standing up in this place. Sexy, yes, but sex didn't come into it here. The adventure was complete just as it was, not so partitioned off as sex. Sex was—it wasn't something to look at now. It could be there, in a box, but. You could have sex, but it would be some other time, the perfect time, and this wasn't the perfect time yet. Besides, there was the possibility that some realities, scrawny as they were, from the world outside the fence, could also exist here, infinitesimally, reminders or barriers perhaps? No, *not*, and she was no longer thinking that way.

"We should go where the arrow points," the other girl said. Her legs were bowed, jeans tight around her belly and hips. She was younger than the rest of them, probably fifteen. On her own, she'd said, parents—*poof*—magically disappeared. From here, all Artesia could see was lumpy skin squeezing out from above her jeans. Her black-haired head trained where her finger was pointing, the red arrow painted on the broken-up sidewalk. Suddenly Artesia moved. She didn't want to be behind them anymore.

"Yes!" Pete said, his voice luxurious. "C'mon, Pog, let's go. Artesia, come on baby gorgeous." Giving Artesia the most intense sun-god smile, a full century's worth of love and truth in that smile, in what they had once shared. The other girl looked up from the painted arrow and smiled at him then, too. He smiled back. Some other kind of lesser smile.

"You look like the fucking HUNCHBACK OF NOTRE DAME!" Artesia screamed, totally remembering. But the moment had passed and Pog was far ahead, and they were all four running again, running like wonderful wild animals, animals of the forest, and here was the path, they could smell the night. They were hidden from cars and cops and the outside world. They were safe.

Run they did, and in the half-drafted moon's light they saw the skeleton trace of paths through the golf course. The paths, all crumbling cement, were reminiscent of the Octopus hole (Hole #8). "I remember the Octopus," Artesia said or thought or shouted. He was bigheaded and silver, with strangling long arms that went everywhere, this fat-ass head . . . the paths were like him, or like a skeleton. Follow the crumbling paths. Artesia took uptight piano teacher chipmunk steps up three stairs covered with wrecked carpet. And then the path just ended. All alone on the little lift, Artesia. The scraggly old palms, thin and a billion feet high with like a powder puff up top and no coconuts, "no coconuts," she was mumbling, and then the wrecked ugly dried-out bushes and some grasses—the monsoon had been a fucking nothing this year, and everything was dead dead dead dead dead dead dead, and it was still actually *hot*, at midnight, a beautiful hot now, gorgeous brown mahogany everything she saw—*baby gorgeous*, he'd said—and it was like velvet, and there was truth here, "it's all around us," she was saying, the skeleton path and the funny stairs to nothing, a hangman's last stand, and if you squinted you could see the pieces of bunched-up old bits of green, what passed for a lawn or grass, even in the glorious old days—"the past," she said, "birthdays," and they were still near, her *friends*, and she turned around and screamed "PATH TO NOWHERE" and the girl screamed "SHUT THE FUCK UP!" and they were all laughing and stumbling up the cement path, to the left now, under the blasted last bit of a monkey's tail, the biggest monkey looking for coconuts.

Now here was the Sphinx, rising out of the dark, a beautiful sedate god. They stood and stared. Behind the Sphinx hung the moon (real, in the sky), and this was where the funny little sun king used to be, a sweet sun face smiling like a flower more than the sun, sweeter than the sun. And inside the Sphinx was a bench. She remembered the cool feeling in the middle of summer, on her birthday, remembered waiting for the others, remembered that there were bees, remembered the color of her ball.

"Here you are," said Pete.

"My God," said Pog, "my God!"

"I love the world," said the girl.

Pete who didn't go to college anymore. Artesia who didn't live at home anymore. Pete and Artesia who didn't work at Bluefin anymore—well, Pete did, he'd come back as a sub, but Artesia got her ass fired, manager wouldn't tell her why, probably because he was a fucking racist. Fired both her and Nico, and Nico was now who knows where? He was too old for the fun to be had in Tucson. When Artesia realized how much fun there was to be had here, how there was this whole different as they call it *safety net*, she just did it, the other thing, the *trust exercise*. She put her arms out and fell back into the city's arms.

Her mother: *what a fucking bitch!*

But she loved her mother, Artesia somehow articulated to herself. There was room for loving her mother, room for loving this fat slut girl too—shit, she didn't know better. She couldn't help that boys thought it was fucking cute to be clueless like that. Artesia loved everyone, the world was her oyster, the Magic Carpet Golf Course was the universe as she knew it. And like he was reading her mind, "It's a magic carpet," said Pog, looking with wonder at his feet, and then stepping forward, falling forward, *one, two, one, two*, now not so much the FUCKING HUNCHBACK OF NOTRE DAME as the Abominable Snowman. Bigfoot. She was going to say it but then couldn't—her throat was hollow, a hole, she was shuddering with sensitivity, a fragment of a cloud had trailed over the moon. But the Sphinx was secure—and so they all followed Pog up into the body of the golden Sphinx, a cave of knowledge and power.

Pete grabbed her leg and then her ass and then her leg again as they stumbled up the hill. Artesia was laughing. All was as it should be, part of a larger order. But there was something else, too. She felt it in the back of her throat. What had seemed like hollowness was actually a spasm of nausea, and she tasted puke as she swallowed down.

They sat hunched together in the dark and they hugged, everyone's arms around everyone else, and Pete said, "Let the Sphinx be with us," and they bowed their heads and prayed. They were freezing now with fear because it was true that spirits existed, the world was not just what we saw but what we felt. What we felt *was* invisible, but it existed, did it not? Children knew this, just look at them with their Ouija boards. And look at prayers of all kinds. Look around at what made things real. Invisible things made us who we were.

"I used to come here for birthday parties," Artesia said again. Her mother held the scorecard and wore a straw hat and a dress. She had woven green ribbon into baskets and put packets of sunflower seeds and tiny spades and gardening gloves into each one and gave them to each guest, and they also had a tea party. Her mother was married to her father then. They owned a reddish-brown dog named Valentine. At the birthday party everyone was laughing. No one minded the bees in the Sphinx, coming out of the Sphinx and coming right at them. No, wait. It wasn't her mother who had woven ribbon into the baskets. That was Alicia's mother, that one time.

"Why are you shivering?" Pete's voice, very near.

"I was thinking of my birthday party."

"What?" said Pog. "Not that shit again."

"Don't worry," said Pete.

"But why not?" In the belly of the Sphinx, it was possible he knew everything.

"It's all an illusion," he said.

Other Girl was giggling, and they were all having trouble holding on to their cigarettes, it was hard to tell if they'd just lit them, or if they *were* lit, or if it was time to have another one.

"Look," said Pog.

Crazy ghosts stood or flew on the other side of the Sphinx. On the other side of the sun that wasn't there and the moon that was.

"Oh shit," said Artesia. They ran over to the ghosts. Ten feet tall, two of them. Pure moon-stunned white with birth-defect flipper arms, like they weren't ghosts but dancing porpoises with black alien eyes. It was possible they were beneficent creatures, beneficent but so very sad, as if they'd seen something they didn't understand. As if they were trying to dance on a pretty little planet in the middle of a nuclear war.

Pog was crying.

LONG *earlobes denote aristocratic birth. Mark on forehead is symbol of spiritual insight,* said the sign in front of the big blue Buddha, another chicken wire and plaster god, fat brother to the Sphinx. The sleeper child. The four runners passed by, laughing. There was a magic fish and an ostrich, and inside Artesia the memory of that ostrich's mean beak coming down on her pink golf ball and destroying her chances for an eight on #11. Pete said, "Touch and have plenty, touch and be lucky," as they passed the fish and they all put their hands on the fish's scales, and then the other girl had the idea of getting into the belly of the fish. "Come out, lucky child," said Pete. "Come out," said Pog. Artesia stared at the palm treetops, at a flash of what seemed like blue light, no coconuts. Palms = prison bars. Pete was in the lucky fish, kissing the other girl. Did that happen? Was that happening? Now they were running back down the paths that spread like an octopus.

Jumping over emptiness, avoiding the black lake of night and the broken glass and the crushed concrete, Artesia fell on a piece of rebar and ripped open her arm. Under the Tiki Man, Pete held her hand, licking the wet skin. She was crying with happiness. "The Tiki Man has lost his head," she said again and again. There used to be a lookout at the top but her mom wouldn't let her go up there. The Tiki Man's face was long and lean and giant and sad. "Do you understand? I love you," Pete said, kissing her arm, the gash from the rebar throbbing like the Holy Ghost, like the Sacred Heart. Artesia, laughing. "There was the red ant hole and that was funny and the alligator you hit the ball right into him and there was the monkey, too, but most of all I liked to go on the blue boat, the beautiful blue boat, and my mother would wear these dresses like from the fifties but now we don't even talk, she called the cops on me and threw my shit outside. She threw my clock radio outside and my shoes. There was the funny red bull with his sad eyes, and a scary skull and the rattlesnake den more like a big dirt heap than any kind of real snake place." But Artesia wasn't actually speaking. *"You slut! You slut!"* screamed the other girl, right up in her face. *"He's my boyfriend!"* Now the other girl was crying and Pog was saying, "Let's go," and Pete's smile was aimed right between the other girl and Artesia, as if he were an architect who knew the exact middle of things, a physicist who knew the exact middle of things. The way he pushed her against the wall of the empty pool and the way he held her hands. The way they loved and knew everything like psychic people in the night. She'd tried to act big, mature, after Bluefin. Before her mother gave Snickers to the Humane Society and threw her shoes in the alley and when she and her sister Chelsea—it had all been so long ago, and now she was out here, in the good city. Adventure was to be had. She knew, she'd always known, more than him. College boy. But still he had something, a golden charm, a radiating essential thing that only she understood. The brown velvet of the night was fading, and the Tiki Man had taken on a gray cast. The stalky plants were looking less enchanted and more like something that would be razed soon, forgotten along with all the monkeys and flowers and aliens.

Pog and Pete and the other girl were lying in the bottom of the blue boat, holding hands. Artesia stood on the bow, and it was only then that a few drops of rain came. The stringy cloud had thickened and diffused. "We can't stay here," she said. Pete's hand had disappeared up the other girl's shirt, and Pog was holding her legs. One gangplank went into the blue boat, and another went out. You could come and go like that. The girl was laughing, they were all laughing. Artesia held herself in her arms and stood alone, the figurehead on a ship, face turned.

"The Lotus Eaters" is from a project called Demigods on Speedway, *which reimagines the Greek pantheon in contemporary Tucson, Arizona. The title refers to the Lotus Eaters encountered by Odysseus on his travels. Artesia and Pete are also inspired by Artemis and Apollo, in this rendering not twins, but ill-fated lovers.*

—AS

SLAVES

Elizabeth Evans

We lived in caves, on battlefields, in fortresses, schoolhouses, Hollywood, meadows, the Old West, cabins, huts, boxcars, castles. We knew our aptitude for gathering berries, being orphans, starring in movies, disarming witches, fleeing armies, teaching school, working in offices with typewriters and carbon paper, nursing soldiers, tending bar, building with twigs and bigger sticks. We did not know how well suited we were for slavery until the king arrived one afternoon. Unexpected, she was. Bored where she had been. The king changed the light in the rooms where we hid away from the day to a smoky bronze, almost the color of the drinks that filled tumblers in the evenings when we were not invited to the rooms.

"Sit up straight!" commanded our king. Older than all of us. Blond, blue-eyed, fair. Yet also a vision of viciousness wielding an expert, swishing, poking stick. Her brute's laugh was preceded by a grin that exposed each perfectly straight tooth. For the king, we did sit up very straight on the thick cushions, all lined up in a row. The cushions themselves made us forget who we were. Their cool, slippery covers of opalescent silk had slithering tatters that revealed further underlayers of worn and torn threads (amethyst, ruby, cream, jade, cerulean) that could snag a bare toe or a finger.

Our king made us half crazy, yet none of us could equal the genius for slavery of captive Princess Katie. Hers was the ideal. King tapped Princess Katie with her stick, and Princess Katie cried out in a voice all at once faint, clear, and brave, "My bones are so fragile that they break at his slightest touch!" Beautifully—as if a ghost had held up the ivory slip in which she clothed herself—Princess Katie collapsed. Always demure, eyes down as instructed by the king, yet the king could not quell Princess Katie's rebellious nature. She escaped over and over, tussled helplessly for freedom in the delicious arms of our king.

The king directed us, her recaptured slaves, one by one, to a private chamber, away from the inner rooms. In a bower formed by ancient lilac bushes that hid a length of stone wall, the king commanded us to lie down. The other slaves never told me what happened to them in the chamber. I supposed it was the same for them as for me: the king firmly stroked his fierce, warm hands down my chest, my belly, that mound above my thighs whose response was a great surprise.

Three times, the king came to us.

Then, no more.

We slaves—free?—longed for capture. We sent messages to our king: *Would she come again?* How we drooped by the windows, looking out, watching and waiting for an answer! And when it finally came, it came for Princess Katie alone. Princess Katie was invited to visit the king. The king would not come to us again.

Who would be our king, then?

Twice, I took up a stick and donned the sash, a double thickness of heavy blue satin, but, like the others who had tasted slavery, I wanted to be ravished, not to ravish. As king, I directed no one to the bower; no other king directed me there. Without a ruler, we drifted. Throughout the bronze rooms, girls described new ravishments at the hands of the kings that they dreamed for themselves. I did not say that I was inspired by a beautiful, imprisoned Christian's martyring her scantily dressed self on the chest of a blind man who did not know that his armor was studded with the sharpest of nails, but I did explain that I wore a top made up purely of golden wires. "With a flick of his wrist, the king breaks them and my breasts"—I held up my hands to an imaginary, gorgeous burden—"are completely exposed."

"Slaves" is meant to represent mortal desires, swollen and reaching for something that would be, paradoxically, both base and divine. There is something of the Maenads here—also bar girls and angels.

—EE

DRONA'S DEATH

Max Gladstone

War rages on, and Drona is its heart.

Some songs tell of good wars, kind wars, wars where, when the fighting's over, you sit alone in the woods and breathe and think, this was good, this thing I've done. I have saved lives, I have served my king, I am the man I always hoped to be. Drona's heard these songs; he's never seen the wars they mean.

This war has lasted fifteen days. Not long, but vicious. Mountains lie broken to shards by warriors' wrath. No war has been this great since the first one, which gods and demons fought in mortal guise. Cleaner, Drona thinks as he draws his bow. Safer. Gods and demons, each knows the other an enemy. This is war between men, between brothers.

The sun stands one fist's distance above the eastern horizon. Cries of dead and dying men and elephants, screams of horses and of tortured metal, fill the heavy air. Fifteen days ago there was a jungle here. Now patches of forest stand like tombstones on a blasted heath. There is no word for the world the war has made.

The sun is one fist's distance above the eastern horizon, and already Drona has killed ten thousand men. He looses an arrow, and a mountain fortress breaks like glass. He feels the men there die. Ten thousand fifty-seven.

Two miles away a Pandava chariot swoops low over one of the many wings of the army Drona leads. In the chariot's wake fire spreads, burning men and fortifications that belong to Drona's king. Skin flakes and crisps and peels from flesh. Men stagger under that fire as under a weight. A boy runs from the carnage and flame, swift, bearing bow and arrows with him. Brave. No deserter.

Drona looks on the chariot, and sees his student, Arjuna, standing behind the driver. Hair dark as a night without moon, eyes flashing golden and white with the lightning caged inside his body. Arjuna laughs, and Drona remembers the way he laughed as a boy, remembers the day Drona taught him to kneel, to draw sight on a flying eagle, to loose and fix the bird through its eye.

Drona knows he should loose his arrow and kill Arjuna. This is a war between brothers, and brothers die in war.

The stumbling boy turns, knocks arrow, draws and aims at Arjuna's chariot overhead. But Drona did not train fools, or blind men.

Arjuna has seen the boy. Smooth as poured water, he draws his bow.

Drona could kill him now. Or not. There is a privacy in being the greatest warrior in the world: no one knows your limits. Drona need only kill someone else, somewhere else: any of the chariots dealing death over the battlefield, any of the elephants or tank divisions. His masters might say: "You should have killed Arjuna." But his masters are not him, and when he strokes his mustache and says, "There were better targets," who will know if he lies?

Drona himself would know.

He scans the battlefield for an alternative, and tries not to think about the boy he's leaving to die.

Arjuna changes target.

Curious, Drona follows Arjuna's new line of aim, adjusts for wind and the chariot's speed, and sees, sword drawn on a broad broken field, surrounded by corpses of Pandava warriors, his own son. Ashwatthama, strong and tall. Ashwatthama, with his mother's hair. Ashwatthama, whose sword runs red with blood, Ashwatthama, who has never stepped back from a fight, Ashwatthama, who can stun an elephant with a slap, Ashwatthama, who will die if Arjuna decides to kill him. Drona's son has trained since youth, but Arjuna is a god's child, and Drona's finest pupil.

Arjuna prepares to loose. Ashwatthama does not know he should prepare to die.

Drona does not scream. He does not call out. Ashwatthama is miles away, and could not hear him if he did.

Drona aims for the chariot, for Arjuna, for Arjuna's eye, for the root of his optic nerve. The arrow will enter the young man's brain and bounce within his skull, destroying that fine killer's mind Drona wasted years training.

Arjuna adjusts for wind, and his jaw clenches as it always does before he lets fly. A bad habit, Drona's told him.

Drona's arrow springs free of the bow, and hungry. It shines as it flies. If you stood before Drona and looked into his eye you would see a mandala turning, in three dimensions, a palace, a universe in which God lies dreaming of this war.

God is kind, Drona thinks, and cruel.

Arjuna's chariot turns faster than such chariots can turn. Light twists around it, and space. In his ear, Drona hears laughter and the tinkling of bells.

The arrow strikes the chariot's undercarriage, splinters its diamond armor, shatters its engines, slags its titanium shell. The carriage falls. Drona reaches out with his soul. He feels many spirits rise to the world above, but none of these belongs to Arjuna. Surely he would burn in death as in life, a beacon among hungry ghosts.

A god has saved Arjuna. But his carriage is broken, and he will fight no more today.

Ashwatthama is safe.

And Drona will not be forced to lie.

He smiles, and knows his smile sick. This thing he does is not glorious. That he saved his son without killing his student is an accident, no more, and it is strange to be glad of such an accidental pause from death.

Drona is no philosopher. His world is bound by duty, and by the range of his bow.

On the battlefield, the stumbling boy escapes into the wood, and is lost.

Drona strides forward on air, draws his bow, and kills again.

———

WAR does not stop at day's end, but changes. Scouts and sentries play their games of seek and find, with knives in place of flags. Sages ride the minds of birds to plot the next day's raids. Holy men bless certain battlegrounds to hide their soldiers' footsteps, or blunt the enemy's weapons. Fighting continues by other means.

The Pandava brothers and their advisers gather in the command tent. Two weeks ago, they prepared for this nightly meeting: they arrived shorn and bathed, hair and skin oiled, clad in fine silks and silver ornament, as befit their rank. Time has passed, and war has crept into their minds. Tonight they wear stark uniforms the colors of dust. Stubble grows on their cheeks and chins. They stink of fire, blood, and sweat.

Still, Yudhisthira the eldest pours them tea. He is the wisest of men, and has never lied. When he walks, his feet do not touch the ground.

Arjuna paces the tent. Since he learned to crawl he never could stay still. Like the storm his father, his life is movement. "Drona would have killed me."

"You sound," says Bhima his brother, "as if you are surprised." Bhima sits like a mountain. Ten days ago he began carrying his great mace with him into the council tent. They all bear their weapons with them now. Yudhisthira has seen that mace break open the earth's crust, until lava flowed from the wound.

Yudhisthira thinks he may be scared of his brothers.

"We are at war," Bhima says. "Drona is the finest fighter on the king's side. Of course he will try to kill us. I am surprised he has not already."

"He shot at me." Arjuna steps on the seat of his chair, steps down, turns away, circles the table. "Without warning."

"How do you know it was him?"

"Would you like to see the chariot? I would show it to you, but I can't, because the entire thing melted before it hit the ground."

"He is our teacher," Yudhisthira says, and Bhima closes his mouth. "He is our teacher, and he is a servant of our enemy. He has not tried to kill us yet because he loves us. He tried to kill you today because he can no longer make excuses for not doing so. The war does not go well for his master the king."

"It does not go well for us," says Dhristadyumna, their nephew.

The men who cannot fly, who cannot call upon the gods for aid, who know no dharma weapons, no mantras, no deep magics, are under his command. "Four hundred thousand dead today. At least a third of those I lay at your teacher's feet. More, if we count those he allowed his side to kill by suppressing our air support and artillery. He did not kill Arjuna, but he is slaughtering our men."

Arjuna and Bhima do not speak. Nakula and Sahadeva, their two youngest brothers, nod. Yudhisthira bows his head, and blows on his tea. Arjuna completes his circuit of the tent, sits in his chair, stands, turns the chair around, sits again. Yudhisthira paces. Air cushions his feet. Warm wind blows over and through the dead jungle outside. "Nothing will grow here again," Yudhisthira says, and because he says it, the others know it is the truth. "I have never seen a weapon like the one Drona used on us today. His arrows consumed the world where they fell, and they traveled faster than sunlight. Arjuna, have you ever seen the like?"

Arjuna tilts his chair forward so its back rests on the table's lip. "Drona told me once of a weapon used by God to right the world when it goes astray. No man can call upon it more than once and live. If Drona knew the secret, he never taught me. But I could feel his arrow's strength when it consumed my chariot. If such a weapon exists, he turns it against us now."

"Could any power resist this weapon?"

Arjuna stops drumming his fingers on the table. He sits as still as Bhima. He shakes his head.

"With all respect, my princes, you are asking the wrong questions." The voice is new. No one turns to look. They know the speaker, though he stands in shadow. He watches them all, calm, patient, smiling. Bells ring behind and beneath his voice. Krishna is dark and lustrous, as if a glacier-melt ocean rolls within him. Naked from the waist up, slender, a blade made man. Arjuna's charioteer. A prince in his own right. Not to mention a god.

Arjuna asked Krishna once, before the fighting started, whether it was right to kill friends, brothers, teachers in battle. Their conversation lasted fifteen minutes. Arjuna has not yet told anyone what they said, but when they finished, Arjuna blew his conch and the war began.

Once, when they all were young together, Krishna split himself into a hundred Krishnas to sleep with one hundred cowgirls. In those days, Yudhisthira thought he knew his friend. Since the war began, Yudhisthira has begun to doubt himself.

Yudhisthira turns to Krishna. "What questions should we ask?" No titles between them. They have moved beyond titles.

"You ask what is this weapon. You ask how to guard against it. You should ask: how to kill the man who wields it." Krishna raises his hand. The fingers are long, and slender, the palm paler than the rest of him. "An armored chariot, drawn by an armored steed: difficult to overcome. But kill the driver, and what does the chariot matter?"

Arjuna lets the rear two legs of his chair fall back; they collide heavily with the floor. In the silence that follows, he stands, stretches his arms behind his head. The joints of his shoulders pop like breaking trees. "The weapon matters, because the man holds it. And while he holds such a weapon, he is invincible. Even without that weapon, I doubt any of us could best him in battle. He was our trainer. He made us. He knows how to break us."

"The man holds the weapon," Krishna says, "but the man is not the weapon. Convince him to set that weapon down. Then kill him."

"He is the finest warrior in the world," Yudhisthira says. "He will not set his weapon down just because we ask him to do so."

"He will," Krishna replies. "If we ask him correctly."

"If we have a chance," Dhristadyumna says, "we must take it. Drona has not killed any of you yet, but he is not so forgiving with our men. We cannot fight a war without them."

Krishna smiles, and somewhere bells ring.

AT dawn Yudhisthira meets the elephant. Bhima guides him; Arjuna is elsewhere, darting among the enemy ranks, slaying from above, from below, descending every so often from his chariot to kill by blade, by missile, by bow, by hand. He knows a hundred thousand ways to kill. They all do. They were well taught.

The elephant stands huge and gray and armored in the dark. His long trunk trails in the dust, and his eyes are the size of Yudhisthira's two fists together. One jewel-tipped tusk rubs against Bhima's armor, and Bhima laughs, and pats the creature on the forehead.

"A good soldier," Bhima says. Yudhisthira does not expect it to be more than a good elephant. It smells of musk and earth: new to the lines, it does not yet stink of war. In the distance, the first bombs explode, and the creature pulls away from Bhima. Yudhisthira knows that elephants feel fear. "I call him Ashwatthama." The beast calms. Its trunk twines around Bhima's shoulders like a stole, and he hugs the trunk against his neck. He smiles, wickedly.

Yudhisthira does not smile. Yudhisthira gets the joke, and does not find it funny.

DAWN turns to morning, morning to noon. Clouds obscure the battle: dust and smoke, poison gas, magic fog. The fog does not block Drona's sight, or his arrows. He shines on the mountaintop, a man become a god.

Ashwatthama the soldier, Drona's son, stands in the thick of the fighting. His advance on this Pandava position, near a stand of dead jungle, has met greater resistance than the place's limited strategic import would suggest. He has stumbled onto some secret: a cache of supplies, a hidden weapon. Ashwatthama cannot see through the dead trees. The foliage and smoke are too thick. He will press on, and investigate for himself.

Ashwatthama flows through the Pandava soldiers like a flood. His own men follow him, finishing the fallen, guarding his sides and back, but he is the leader of the wedge, and the enemy fears his flashing sword.

Ashwatthama fears, too. He lacks royal blood. He is a great warrior but he is not his father's equal. In this sixteen days' war he has gained respect as a fighter who does not fear pain or death, but his exploits have not earned him fame. Men still call him Ashwatthama, Drona's son.

Ashwatthama is the son of his father, but he is more, too, and he wishes it known.

With a slash he dispatches a giant, eight feet tall with a monkey's tail, one of the many monsters in each side's employ. The remaining Pandava soldiers here are men, and they fall back. Ashwatthama catches one beneath the helmet strap and blood unfurls from his throat down his shining armor carapace. Another, turning to flee, is pierced where his armor joins beneath the arm, and falls. The rest retreat toward the stand of trees, and Ashwatthama pursues.

They hold these trees, this forest, important. A prophecy perhaps, that if they hold this hill they will win the war? But there are many prophecies, of victory and defeat, on each side. A weapon, hidden within? Ashwatthama cannot feel the sacred light of any divine power here, but there are ways to conceal the greatest of weapons until it is used.

Movement at the forest's edge. Ashwatthama recognizes the shape, a man made to a bigger mold than other men, terror of the wrestling field, strongest man alive: Bhima, receding into the bushes. Bhima bears his mace, and smiles. His face is streaked with blood.

Bhima is the strongest of the Pandavas, but he is not their greatest fighter or strategist. Bhima follows the plans of his brothers. When they were children together, Ashwatthama remembers, Bhima would be the last to join any game, watching instead from the sidelines and talking softly to himself as he determined the rules. Only once he understood would he wade into play, sweeping all before him. This attitude is a product of his strength, Ashwatthama thinks. The strongest men stand still, afraid they will break the world by moving.

Bhima would not have come on his own. The others have sent him to some purpose. Ashwatthama will find out what.

Bhima is strong, but Ashwatthama is fierce, and his father has taught him secret skills. If he bests Bhima on the field of battle, the army will sing his name until the end of the world, which may not be far distant.

Ashwatthama leaps, and in spite of his forty pounds of armor he clears ten feet over the Pandava line, and lands light as a cat, sprinting forward. The dead forest embraces him. Branches and leaves ripple when he passes, like the surface of a still pool when a stone's cast in. Then he is gone.

DRONA looses an arrow with God's power wrapped up inside it, and breaks a cliff face to rubble. An avalanche tumbles down, boulders, dirt, and chips of stone. A column of Pandava cavalry disappears in the collapse, and the falling rocks close a narrow pass through which, he expects, Yudhisthira had hoped to send a pincer movement to strike the left flank of the king's three-pronged advance. Yudhisthira may be the wisest of men, but Drona is the master of war.

Contentment blooms inside him, as dust blooms from rubble.

Then he hears the cry: "Ashwatthama is dead!"

The dust settles.

Beneath, the war rolls on, flattening the world. Swords meet, and spears. Chariots roar, fire burns, missiles explode, elephants trumpet, and warriors blow melodies of advance and retreat on conch shell trumpets. This noise he knows. Over all this a silence hangs, and Drona hears the silence for the first time now, large as the sky, vaster than ever he thought, stretching out to the stars which are not tiny dots of light but great things far away. In this silence, the cry repeats. "Ashwatthama is dead!"

He recognizes the voice.

Bhima.

Drona sweeps the battlefield from right to left and back again, and on his second sweep finds Bhima: stumbling out of a dense copse of trees, spattered in blood, carrying a bloody tunic. Ashwatthama always wore the uniform of his men. The uniform is correct. The blood looks like blood, but Drona does not expect his son's blood to appear any different from the blood of other men. "Ashwatthama is dead!" That same-colored blood covers Bhima's hands and face. Tears seep from his eyes and leave clear tracks in gore. His shoulders shake, an earthquake. He sinks to his knees. One of the king's men sees a chance, runs at Bhima, and Bhima, artless, strikes him in the stomach with a flailing arm and breaks his spine. He sobs, and Drona remembers how Ashwatthama and Bhima wrestled one another as children. "Ashwatthama is dead!"

No other sound can touch the silence, so the words echo there.

Bhima cries. He should have taken Ashwatthama captive. That was his right, and Ashwatthama should have accepted captivity. But they strove always against one another. And Bhima does not know his own strength. And Ashwatthama does not know when to quit, or how.

He wants to make his father proud.

Still the words resound.

Drona cannot see within the copse. The trees are too dense; they have not yet been destroyed. Drona could loose an arrow to burn them from this distance, or break them to splinters, but if his son remains within, or his body . . .

No.

Bhima grieves, Bhima weeps. But Bhima may lie. Arjuna fights on foot, pressed on all sides, glowing with battle: he moves so fast his armor shines white with the heat of it. He would tell Drona the truth, but would also try to kill Drona if he approached now. Since the first days of the war, Arjuna has shown little hesitation. He is a good soldier.

Yudhisthira will know. And Yudhisthira will not lie. Yudhisthira is the best of men.

Drona seeks the Pandava command tent. Those three are fake. That fourth is in fact a trap set too close to the lines, inviting an assault that would overextend a hungry commander. There. The fifth tent, neither so far back from the line nor so close as to seem foolhardy, its flags present but not ostentatious, bristling with prayer antennas.

Drona's bow is in his hand, and righteous fire fills him. He steps forward and the world flexes, kneels. Distance is one, a shadow of the mind. He enters the battlefield like a chess player's hand enters the board, and stands before the Pandava tent. Men and monsters rush to meet him, but he still holds his bow, and the wheels of God turn about him. He stands within a diamond palace. His assailants quail and fall back.

He steps into the tent, into the shadows.

He expected more within. Screens reflect the light his body sheds. Chairs stand empty. Thick rugs' thread glints gold. Drona wonders if he has been tricked. But no. Yudhisthira is here, and that is all Drona needs.

Yudhisthira is the son of the Lord of Judgment and a mortal woman. He is wise, and good, and he was never Drona's favorite student, because there is a limit to how wise and good a man can be in war. And because of his slight sad smile, ever present, which Drona felt, even when he was a man and Yudhisthira a boy, boasted of knowledge he, Drona, would never attain. Yudhisthira has never lied. Drona would believe this of no other man, but Yudhisthira is barely a man: less, and at once more. His feet do not even touch the ground.

Drona steps forward and the light that moves with him, the light of his weapon, casts changing shadows on communications equipment, on maps and charts, on the planes of Yudhisthira's face. Yudhisthira is not smiling.

"Is my son dead?"

Yudhisthira opens his mouth, but no sound comes out.

Drona realizes he could kill the Pandava with a thought. End the war here. He could have done this at any time, saved lives and stopped slaughter. The thought seems unimportant to him now, distant. But he could have saved—

"Is Ashwatthama dead?" he repeats, and realizes he is sobbing.

Yudhisthira's throat tightens. "Ashwatthama is dead," he says, and says something more, but the bellow of a nearby conch trumpet fills Drona's ears and he falls to his knees and closes his eyes and feels the tears flow.

Souls depart the battlefield, hundreds at a time. They rise to the sky, and rising their color fades, their forms fail and they merge back with light, with God, and emerge again. But some, rising, endure. Their wills gird them in form and heavenly flesh, and shining with the glow of liberated spirit they approach heaven, and walk with gods. Ashwatthama was brave. Ashwatthama knew the secrets of the world. He would walk in heaven wearing his own skin. Drona too knows the secrets of the world, and rises to seek his son. His hands slack, and his bow falls from them. His skin ceases to glow. His fingers float by reflex into a mudra. Drona's soul flies upward, living, and the gates of heaven open for him.

ASHWATTHAMA hears the cries of his own death, but he cannot tell from what direction they come. The trees here are thick. He strikes one with his sword and it topples, but still he cannot see the sky. The copse is not copse at all but forest, and chasing Bhima he has wandered into its depths. All paths lead in, a spiral with no outer edge. He sprints, he doubles back, he seeks his own tracks and finds none. The marshy ground holds no footprints.

He smells blood, though, and thinking blood must be the battlefield he bears toward the stench. Through the pressing bushes, the thorns that catch in his hair and tear his skin, through the branches every one of which resembles an upraised mace, to the clearing at the forest's heart. An elephant in Pandava armor lies there, bathed in a spreading pool of its own blood. Flies have found it already, and dart above staring eyes. A mace has caved in the elephant's skull. A bloody handprint rests on one jeweled tusk, a final pat from its murderer.

Ashwatthama has seen dead animals before, has killed many. But he staggers back, and stumbles into the wood, and does not know why he is afraid.

YUDHISTHIRA looks down on his enemy, his teacher, his friend. Divine power set aside, soul wandering heaven, Drona seems smaller even than other men, and Yudhisthira realizes it has been ten years—more?—since last he saw Drona face-to-face. Yudhisthira feels an unfamiliar pain.

The tent flap opens, and two men enter: Dhristadyumna and Krishna. Both grin triumph. Krishna holds his conch shell, and Dhristadyumna's hand rests on his sword. Yudhisthira realizes that Krishna's was the trumpet that blew, that kept Drona from hearing the second half of his sentence: "Ashwatthama is dead, but I do not know whether it is the man or the elephant."

Krishna sets his conch shell down on a map table. "I thought," he says, apologetic, "that you might not be able to carry through your piece. I doubt we needed the trumpet, though, in the end. He had already fallen to his knees."

"I told the truth," Yudhisthira says.

"Of course you did." Krishna places his hand on Yudhisthira's shoulder. Yudhisthira steps back, and feels the strange new pain sharper than before, and embraces Krishna and so stands entangled with his friend, Arjuna's charioteer, the smiling god, when Dhristadyumna draws his sword and cuts Drona's head from his shoulders.

Yudhisthira surges forward, his friend thrown aside, and catches Dhristadyumna's sword arm before the general can put his blade away. Drona's head tumbles to the left and rolls, lying on its side, mouth open. Yudhisthira feels the new pain, and his old rage, and a strange warmth. "Why?" he shouts, and the walls of the tent tremble.

Dhristadyumna pulls back, or tries, but his sword arm will not move. Yudhisthira's grip might as well be forged iron. Dhristadyumna is a brave man, but he feels fear staring into the Pandava lord's eyes. "What did you plan to do with him, once he'd thrown down his weapons? Did you think this would end with you both alive, and friends?"

"We could have bound him. Tied him. Locked him away." Yudhisthira's grip tightens, and Dhristadyumna stumbles. Pain contorts his fingers. The blade falls to the bloodstained carpet.

"You've seen him. I've seen him. He would laugh at prison walls. What bonds could we tie to hold him?"

"He would not have tried to escape. He is a man of honor."

Yudhisthira could close his hand and shatter Dhristadyumna's wrist.

The general spits his words through clenched teeth. "He was a butcher. He was a force of nature. And we will win this war because he is dead."

"Coward." Yudhisthira releases the other man's arm, and stumbles back. "Coward."

"You knew this would happen," Dhristadyumna says. "You knew. And you went ahead with it, and now you blame me."

Yudhisthira feels the new pain again, and the new warmth.

He looks down.

He stands on the gold-thread rug, in a pool of his teacher's blood. He stands, and the rug scrapes his feet, which have not in his many years of life ever touched the ground.

He looks up.

Dhristadyumna's eyes are wide and dark like those of a scared animal.

Yudhisthira turns, and walks past Krishna, out the rear flap of the tent, into the light and noise and death, trailing bloody footprints.

HEAVEN is wheels within wheels, and each turning of every wheel a garden, a palace, a tapestry of light and choice and change. Heaven is a flower, opening.

Heaven is empty.

Drona wanders, calling, crying. "Ashwatthama! Ashwatthama, my son!"

ASHWATTHAMA stumbles from the forest onto the broken battlefield. Above him the sky is a maze of contrails and fire. On all sides the poisoned earth stretches. Soldiers of the king and Pandavas alike clash and war, advance and retreat. Men die, and animals, and their dying looks much the same. This is the war of the world. Ashwatthama's sword is bare, and spotted with dried blood.

He searches the horizon for his father's light, and sees nothing.

This is the war of the world, and its heart is gone.

I first read the Mahābhārata *as a kid, in William Buck's abridged version, and it hit me hard. I found staggering*

moral depth there, not to mention superhuman adven-
ture to beggar any comic book. The tale I've adapted
here, of the guru-warrior Drona's death in a great war
between brothers at the epic's climax, took perhaps two
pages in my childhood edition, but it stuck in my mind
like a splinter and stayed there ever since. I hope my re-
telling conveys a piece of what the story's meant to me,
and encourages people who don't know the epic to seek
it out.

—MG

SO MANY-HEADED GATES
Sheila Heti

Soon, all the trains fell apart. Then all the planes did. Then all the plants did. When the planes and plants and trains had been destroyed, it was time for him and I to show ourselves to each other in our true colors. After all, there was no natural beauty to distract us from each other now. There were no modes of transportation to take us from each other now. Even last year, we could have parted from each other. But now there was no chance of it. Like the fortune-teller said to me, "After March, it will be too late." I had given myself till March 31 to break up with him. The night of the thirtieth I still could have done it. That fight would have justified leaving. But I stayed. Now I wonder if I didn't call that fortune-teller upon myself. Sometimes we do—call upon ourselves, in the form of outside voices, the voices we are hearing from within. How much of life is truly external, and how much of life is our internal life, projected onto the outside, and called to us? Did I call her to me, to tell me what I wanted to hear? What I believed? One thing I do believe is that there are always guardians at the gate—monsters, I should say—to a new level. One must defeat them or go home. There are impulses within us that tell us to go home, to the place of safety and familiarity, that we know well, and love, for knowing it. Always at the approach of a new level, there are these monsters, lions, roaring, with bloody claws. As much in our lives as in any mythological stories. We stand at the gates and get scared. Sometimes these fears send us home. When I saw that fortune-teller, I did not see her as a lion or a gorgon. I saw her as an angel. She was warning me to go home, not on into the future with him, a man, an unknown. I cursed myself for not listening to her, as March turned to April, and I was still with him. I had gone into a dangerous land, not listening to that angel. But now, now it's the end of summer. And I feel like she wasn't an angel, she was a demon I had to pass, to fight to make it to the next level. The next level is now and I am here. There are guardians always to the next level. Every level has its dangers. Every person has their dangers, and the safety of home has its dangers, too. Actually, there are dangers everywhere. The question is whether to proceed or whether to go back. Sometimes one should go back, but one never knows when those sometimes are. The fortune-teller warned me that the longer two people stay together, the harder it is to part. I knew that. I knew it the moment I led him through my garden gate, up into my apartment, for the first time. Even then it was hard to part. I knew it one week later, his head on my pillow; even then it would have been hard to part. And now it is harder than ever. Then, back then, I wondered, "How will I explain it to him? What can I say that will justify my leaving?" Do I say those exact same words to myself now, years in? I do. So all along it has been this way. So that is the way it will always be. A friend of mine feels the same way, about her boyfriend, not mine. She calls that word "love." I had never seen the word spoken of as the bond that from the first understands that any parting would be a serious break. I used contemporary words to describe it, like "codependent." Is that the word we use now for love? But isn't that what love is? He depends on me for his life, and I depend on him for mine. That does not mean I cannot be alone in a day, and I usually am. That does not mean I cannot be alone in my thoughts, for I usually am, and I am usually alone in my body. Usually his body does not come into mine. Only sometimes it does. In the in-between times, which is almost all the time, I am alone enough. So then there are tendrils, then there are tentacles, then there are all the monstrous things that connect us to each other, for the monsters are not only out there. We are the monsters. We are monsters, too. We are guardians to our own inner lands. We are our own gates, keeping each other out. And at every fight, at every sign of the monster in him, I feel as I did with that fortune-teller, "The time is now to leave. The time is ripe to turn around. You should have turned around a long, long time ago! But now you are sure of it!" But I don't. I continue deeper into the wilderness, the darkness, that is him. And he must continue on into me, too. And I think there will always be monsters at the gates. And there are an infinity of levels. And when he dies, or if I die first, there will be more monsters, guarding the level where one continues to love even though the body is gone. And then when I die, after he does, if I do, after he does, still more monsters at the gates, warning me, Do not come into death. But like I've had the courage to go through all these levels in life, I will step through it. I will step into another darkness, being used to the darkness already.

I didn't base my story on any one myth, but the idea of monsters guarding the gates of higher levels seems to cross cultures and time.

—SH

Edith Hamilton's *Mythology*

———— ✥ ————

THE STATUS OF MYTH
Kelly Braffet and Owen King

The day he was born, the Steelers won the Super Bowl. And that's why, every year, our hero eats a football-shaped cake at his Super Bowl party. For many years, his mother made the cake; then, for a few years, the task fell to assorted girlfriends and other designated female intercessionaries. Eventually the ritual settled, with some finality, on his wife, who decreed that the cake would be homemade German chocolate, unless she was really busy, in which case it would be purchased. The year she was on a diet, the cake became cupcakes, for easier portion control. But even the cupcakes were football-shaped, and thus was the ritual offering accepted. When he was an adult, the ritual evolved to include the posting of a cake photograph in a particular album online. Many people saw the photographs, and liked them, and, he thought, recognized in them the passage of another year.

When he was three years old, his Uncle Carl was killed on the turnpike. A steel pipe flew off the back of the truck in front of him and pierced first Carl's windshield and then his head, entering through his left eye. Carl was his only blood-related uncle, not to mention his mother's favorite of her many siblings, and so this was a terrible tragedy for all of them. To this day, when he finds himself driving at high speed on some sort of interstate-like thoroughfare, and there is a car or a truck or an RV in front of him carrying any sort of tied-on, wobbly cargo, his left eye twitches, and he changes lanes. If there is no other lane available, he will often make the next right and go around the block, or pull over and allow another car to pass, so that he is cushioned from the peril. By doing so faithfully, he knows that he has done his best to keep himself safe from flying pipes and bicycles and other things, and death will wait that much longer to claim him. Every year, on his Uncle Carl's birthday, he changes his profile picture to a scanned-in old snapshot of the dead man and tells again the story of Carl's death. Many people see it, and may or may not like it. He hopes that it reminds them of the impermanence of life, and the importance of good knot-tying and bungee-securing skills.

When he was five and he began school, the little boy sitting next to him looked at his paper and said, "You are a bad drawer. That does not look like a horse." And as the little boy spoke them, the words became truth. That truth followed him everywhere and whipped him with self-judgment and recriminations until one day, near the beginning of high school, he rose up and proclaimed that he wanted to draw, and he deserved to draw, and draw he would. He carried a notebook around for years, filling it with sketches of naked women that he referred to as his *nudes*. At first the images were imagined, but many actual women were impressed enough by his efforts that they offered themselves up as models, and as they posed he told the tale of the little boy and the badly drawn horse, and the women joined him in the sharing of indignation and, often, body fluids. As an adult, he began to draw other things besides nudes. Many people see his drawings. Many people like them. Their praise warms him. You, too, he tells them. You, too, can do this.

At seven, he picked up his first baseball, and threw it. And his Little League coach said, in a mildly impressed tone, "Hey, not bad, kid," and the boy realized that unlike football where you had to be strong or basketball where you had to be tall or hockey where you had to skate, baseball was a game where he could take his time and ponder his next move, and not be knocked off his feet by bone-rattling body contact. So he prostrated himself before the altar of the fastball, and served devotedly throughout his years of Little League eligibility, junior varsity, and varsity. As a reward for his devotion he was scouted by Penn State, and offered a small scholarship. He would probably have gone pro had he not blown out his shoulder. He plays softball now, for the fun of it (and it is fun; he has the pictures to prove it). When the Pirates play, he posts live bullpen critiques. He is known, in his online circles, as something of an expert.

At thirteen he had his first kiss: Mary from down the street, at her father's Fourth of July barbecue, under her little sister's back-yard play set. They had both been eating hot dogs. The smell of them was on their fingers and their faces and in the air. And thus did hot dogs, and summer barbecues in general, become very minor erotic focal points—or, at the very least, closely associated with lovely things and good feelings. He also developed a slight prefer-ence for women whose names began with M, or whose names were simple and old-fashioned. Which is how he ended up the husband of a Jane and the father of a Martha. Online, he made a special album for her called *Adorable*, and sweet Mary, from down the street—who was divorced now, with dogs—liked every picture in it.

At twenty-two, he graduated from Penn State and stayed on to earn a master's degree in the visual arts. In the process he learned several things: master's degrees were expensive, and he probably didn't have the talent or drive to really make it in the art sphere, and that girl Jane from his life drawing class—more nudes—man, could that girl slam back some tequila. And by the time the MFA was earned, he was so enamored of tequila-slamming Jane that he had enrolled in a concurrent education program, so that he was soon able to teach art in a junior high, and buy a very nice if not terribly huge diamond for Jane's finger. He discovered that he loved to teach, that he loved to watch his students grow and develop. He did not give up his dream of being an artist; he reshaped it into another dream, that of mentoring a hundred artists, tending them to frui-tion. And that is how he began to grow satisfied with his lot in life, and to tell people that he was happy, that he loved life, and they were glad to hear it, and liked when he said such things.

Because on the Internet, through his laptop or tablet or smart phone, he could collect everyone he knew or had ever known, living or dead—Uncle Carl, his baseball teammates, Mary—in one vir-tual place, and he could say things, and they could all hear them. He could find order in his life: epiphanies that he had not realized had shaped him, rules that he had never noticed he lived by. He could count the people who liked him, his drawings, his thoughts, his photographs. They were quantified and exact.

This is my daughter, he told the assembled masses. Adore her. And it seemed that they did.

This is my life, he told them. Admire me. And it seemed that they did.

This is my experience, he told them. Take it and use it to better yourselves. And it seemed to him that they did.

Sometimes our hero talked with Jane about this, how they began to feel like nothing had really happened unless they'd shared it with everyone they'd ever known: all of those waiting ears and eyes. Because he was more than his profile; Martha was more than a popular post. But those reservations faded and dimmed before the satisfaction of sitting down at the computer, drawing his life in electronic light and invisible transmissions. Telling the world who he was, learning it himself.

Was the world listening? Were they too busy writing their own stories?

Did it matter?

WHAT I wanted to know was, why did we have to burn it?

"Your place is not to question," my brother said.

"Eat shit," I said.

"No," said Chuck.

I was thirteen. Chuck was twenty-six. We had only lived together off and on, because my mother couldn't put up with him. "You just want to light something on fire," I said.

"Haven't you ever desired something?" asked Chuck.

Way in the back of the yard, where it was damp and weedy, there was a corrugated steel trash can. The trash can had been there as long as I could remember. Chuck said we could use that. His girlfriend, Athena Maria Morosco, said she was going to sleep. She lay down on top of the picnic table, but didn't close her bloodshot eyes. Although she dressed baggy in men's shirts and serapes and long flowing skirts, the sinuousness of her body was apparent any time she moved and gravity exerted a drag on her clothes. I often fantasized about having sex with Athena, which also made me afraid of her.

"Lend a hand, fucker," said Chuck, striding into the weeds and toward the can.

I trailed behind him. I was only human; I was excited to see the monk statue; I, too, was curious to see how it would burn, too. It was,

Chuck claimed, an ancient artifact. This was bizarre—a Chuck specialty, the bizarre—and therefore interesting. I had questions: Were we talking about a monk like the kind on old San Diego Padres uniforms? Or some other brand of cleric? Where had the monk statue come from? When he said "ancient," how old were we talking about, really? How hot a fire would Chuck need to incinerate such a thing, an ancient statue of a monk? The last question was obviously the biggie.

The trash can was filled with water and weeds. We grunted and pushed, and the wet earth beneath made a sucking noise. It toppled over, gushing crap onto my jeans and sneakers, and the metal lip of the can left arcs of rust on my palms. With a lot of huffing, Chuck managed to roll the barrel, cutting a swath through the chest-high weeds, and finally reached the patch of lawn. He hauled it upright and delivered a clanging kick to the side. "You know it, bitch," he told the barrel.

"It's going to stink," said Athena.

"Of toasty burning death," said Chuck, and disappeared around the side of the house, presumably to retrieve the statue of the monk from his car trunk.

"It's going to stink," Athena repeated, this time to me. Then, when instead of replying I just stared at her, she asked, "What?"

"My sneakers are wet," I said, and turned so that my boner was pointing away from her, toward the swampy area in the way back of the yard.

"Who cares?" replied Athena.

Chuck and Athena were outlaws. They had escaped from their court-appointed rehab. Now they were back on the hook for their crimes. Chuck had used an axe to fuck up the hull of his ex-girlfriend's father's motorboat. Athena had broken into some guy's mansion looking for drugs, cut her arm on a shard of glass, and passed out on the floor from blood loss. Rehab had been their last chance.

On balance, Chuck was not my favorite person: my mother worked two jobs to pay his debts and cried over him constantly; as a token of goodwill he had given my Wii to a drug dealer named The Jam Man who was reputed to execute his enemies by tying them up and dropping cement blocks on their faces until blood and brains squirted out of their ears like jam; nothing amused Chuck more than telling all of his girlfriends that I wanted to have sex with them. At the same time, he was my only sibling, and I idolized him as much as I hated him. His gleeful criminality had won him the hearts and pussies of a baseball team's worth of beautiful junkies.

The monk left a trench in the grass as Chuck dragged it thudding across the lawn. He stood it straight up by the trash can and stopped to catch his breath.

Grayed by age or exposure or both, hatched over its entire surface with cracks, the statue rose about four and a half feet high. The face was largely obscured by the carved folds of a deep cowl; a clenched, thin-lipped mouth was all that showed. A sheathed sword hung at the monk's hip. His hands were pressed in prayer. Sandals poked out from under the hem of his robe.

"It's a warrior monk," said Chuck.

The cracks were grooves; you could have pressed seeds into them. On the statue's jaw, what was supposed to be skin, the cracks looked like scars. "How old is it?" I asked.

"Old," said Chuck. "Old as the hills."

"Come on, man."

"I don't know. Hundreds of years, at least. It's from an abandoned monastery in Romania. Or maybe Belgium. I can't remember. One of those countries in Europe where it's cold and there are houses like gingerbread houses."

I traced the monk's cruel wood lips with my finger. The wood felt gritty, weathered. You could tell he'd spent some time outdoors. I felt sad for the statue, but I thought he would burn impressively. "What's he called? Is he modeled on a real guy?"

"You know everything I do. If you need a name for him, I think 'Asshole' would work splendidly."

I helped Chuck heave Asshole up into the can, feet-first, so that his cowl just poked over the rim of the can.

"Now all we need is a virgin to tie on top," Athena said.

My brother got me in a headlock before I could jump away. "Yes! What luck! Got one!"

"Fuck you." I flailed at him, landing a few glancing blows.

He slapped my face, kicked out my legs, and dropped me on the ground. "Stop trying to impress Athena. She doesn't want you, or your weeny pink cock. Do you want my brother or his weeny pink cock, Athena?"

"Maybe this is a bad idea, Chuck," she said.

Chuck let go of me and went to her. He took a white pill out of the pocket of his jeans. Athena, still lying there on the picnic table, put it in her mouth, chewed, and sighed. "Thank you," she said. He gave her another one. She chewed that, too.

At the hearing, Mr. Morosco had cried the hardest. "Oh! Oh! Oh!" he'd wailed. "My baby! My baby!" I'd been grossed out by how alike the details of his face were to Athena's—same sharp nose, same deep-set green eyes. Later, I felt bad about that. It was her poor old dad who loved her. Everyone had a dad. I had a dad. Even Chuck had a dad, somewhere. Our dads had dads. Someday, I might be somebody's poor old dad.

"Mom will be home soon," I lied. I slapped the grass off my jeans, and stood up.

Chuck said I could have one of the two cans of lighter fluid to spray. It was the closest to an apology I ever got from him, for anything. "All right," I said.

The lighter fluid cans were tin, painted white. We soaked the monk. The fluid turned him black; I could hear gasoline trickling off his edges, plinking onto the metal bottom of the trash can, and I thought of the rotting house in the woods where people went to have sex. The stench hauled me up by my hair like some gigantic bully, except it didn't hurt. I closed my eyes and inhaled. In my mind, I hung above the ruins of the house in the woods. Water slid along the inverted planes of the shattered ceiling, and I saw through it like it was glass, saw Athena in the bedroom behind the falling water, saw her naked, her ghost's skin, and her face so sad, and the paint on the walls coming off in ribbons. "Travel light," Athena said, beginning to fade into the terrible walls, "and travel alone, and do not ever fucking stop until you reach true love."

Then I opened my eyes and almost fell over. Chuck led me to the picnic table, sat me down. I coughed for a while. He worked on his fuse.

When I could speak, I asked, "Where did you steal it from?"

"The Jam Man," said Chuck. He was sitting on the ground, twisting two pieces of twine together. My half brother had taken off his T-shirt, revealing his gaunt torso, ribs that protruded so sharply you could have played music on them. Over his heart Chuck had a tattoo of a man strapped in an electric chair and a sexy nurse standing by about to throw the lever. "You will perhaps be amused to learn that His Jamness does not lock either his gate or the sliding glass door by his patio."

"Why?" I asked.

"Why did we take His Jamness's museum-quality statue? You might as well ask why I took a leak on his couch and broke his plasma screen television and threw his samurai sword in the pool. Ask enough questions, young man, and you could forget what you want to know in the first place."

"Why?" I asked again.

"Because he's bullshit," said Chuck. "He couldn't even lift a cement block."

"Why?" I asked for a third time.

"Ask Athena," said Chuck.

Athena said, "I did Jam a service, but he didn't keep his end of the deal."

I asked what kind of service. Chuck didn't look up from his fuse. Athena just breathed and breathed.

The blaze was enormous, as high as the house. It spouted upward and curled into a red-black bulb, and the bulb spouted a mane, and the heat hurt my face. My eyes felt as though they were shrinking. The monk's cowl vanished in flame. The way back of the yard wavered, like it was on one side of time and we were on the other.

Chuck put his arm around me. Athena rose from the picnic table, and put her arm around me, too. We stood there, like father and mother and son.

I learned a lot at the trial: that The Jam Man had actually bought the statue of a monk from an auction house in San Francisco; that it was only sixty years old, that its five-figure value was a by-product of its being specially commissioned by a famous Nazi, who kept it in his garden in Brazil until his mysterious demise by arsenic poisoning in 1984; that The Jam Man had been under investigation for three other killings, none of which involved cement blocks; that during the break-in my brother had also stolen a platinum watch, which he had taken to a Mail Boxes Etc. and mailed to my mother as a Christmas gift, three months in advance of the holiday; that Athena had been in the National Honor Society, had dyed her hair from its natural blond; that she kept a diary and it was full of apologies and future plans; that I could sit to the left of a judge and face rows and rows of people, and tell this little story, and hardly break down at all.

———

THE hunters come out at night. You might see the barest hint of them during the day, lurking under the skin of the girl next to you in the grocery store line or the one waiting with you at the prescription counter. But when you look straight at them: nothing. A tired kid who eats badly and doesn't sleep enough. Don't bother searching for their true nature when you're all standing under fluorescent lights. They're invisible then.

But at night? At night, they shine. It's like they emerge from under the very sidewalks, forming in shadows like some demon from a Neil Gaiman story and then tottering away on their ridiculous shoes. Out into the night, out to the hunt. In groups, in flocks, propelled by some fuel that, when burned, smells like perfume and hair conditioner and sugared vodka. Their already pure skin is polished and painted, their hair tortured into perfect straightness or elaborate waves. Every drape and fold of their clothing is carefully considered and yet still their bodies spill out: some plush and velvet, some lean and coltish.

Be careful when you're driving. They're like deer: if you see one, there are doubtless others. They're also like sparrows, changing direction in mid-step as if of one mind, moving like one great perfumed thing. The reflection from their lip gloss can blind like the setting sun. Even driving, even protected by your car, with its many air bags and other modern safety features, it's best to creep through. Let them flow around you, off the sidewalks and into the streets. Because they are also, in many ways, like bees: if you are not a flower, or a threat, you don't exist to them.

Look: stay away from Main Street after dark. If you can.

But if you can't avoid it, and you do find yourself among them, don't look too closely at their faces. If you do, they'll start to resemble people you know. Nieces and neighbors and trusted, beloved babysitters. My goodness, you'll think. That one in the stilettos and the half-shirt—that's Lori's kid, right? That's Kayla. Sweet little Kayla, who was so proud of that pie she made at Thanksgiving. It may or may not actually be Kayla; it doesn't matter. Once you see Kayla in one, you will see Kayla in them all. All the cleavage will be Kayla's cleavage. All the dimples will be Kayla's dimples. There will be no escape after that. Not for you. You will never sleep well again.

Once, our grandmothers' grandmothers told stories of the wild hunt that came from under the hills, that came from across the sky.

Fierce Diana and her otherworldly huntresses, chasing a hart or a stag or a wolf through time and across moonlight. And the many-times-great-grandmothers said the same thing then that we are telling you now: look away. How easy it was for mortals to be swept up in the agony of the hunt, to be dazzled by the beauty of the hunters and entranced by the freedom they promised. The hunters were the shadows of those who died young, the story goes, violently and before their time. Diana drew them to her, those lovely, unspoiled unfortunates, and after that they hunted always. By the light of the full moon, through the silver woodlands. They never aged; they never stopped.

The hunt you'll see on Main Street is the same and also it's different. Now Diana must be subtler: she takes them while they're still alive, and rather than ripping them away from the passage of time she merely erases it from their awareness. And who among these modern young things would be swayed by the pursuit of a hart or a stag? None, so Diana has made her quarry into something more amorphous. Even the hunters themselves don't know what they're chasing. If you ask them—and it's not recommended—they'll use words like *love* and *happiness,* but those words are amorphous, too, and even as they use them they don't know what they mean.

That is the purpose of life; that's why we're here. To find out what those words mean.

Our grandmothers' grandmothers cowered under thick eiderdowns while the hunt raged outside. You will not have that luxury. You might find yourself standing next to three of them in a convenience store, choosing a pint of ice cream, and be lulled into a false sense of benevolence. Ice cream is sweet and safe and so the girls must be sweet and safe. At the register, though, you will meet another three buying far more beer than they can actually drink, and the sight of them will hurt you. Beer is not necessarily sweet. It is not necessarily safe. Neither are the girls.

You think you know. You think you can handle it. You think you remember the way it was, when you were young. These days, we all ride with the hunt at some point. But their hunt is not your hunt is not your mother's hunt is not your daughter's hunt, and you remember yours through thick gentling layers of experience. It's muted and dim. Theirs burns. If you look into their eyes, all of those lovely gauzy layers will burn, too. Instead of taking a stag they take each other, piece by piece, and in turn they are taken, piece by piece. A pair of arms, two staring eyes, a hand. Cut away with knives of disappointment, scalpels of bruised hope. Maybe once you knew the pain of it, this dismemberment, but you don't anymore. Trust me. You don't want to.

And therein lies the trap. Because when you look at them, some part of you will see yourself, and some other part of you will think, *Oh, to be so young, to have it all to live again.* But it hurts to be young. Not just the shoes; the living of it. It hurts.

Some secret part of you still knows that, but that part is safely locked away. The knowledge is unendurable, and the other reason we are here is to endure. You are born. You are young. You get older. You pair off. You breed. You buy a house; you settle in. You amass collections of pets and kitchen appliances and matching no-slip coat hangers. Your children wake up early, and then less early, and then less early. You have many things to do each day and they are all important and there is never enough time. The girls, tottering from bar to bar in their high-heeled shoes—when you look at them, you will think of your small daughter, tottering in the high-heeled shoes you no longer wear. You will think of the days when you tottered in those shoes yourself. You hunted and your daughter will hunt and now it is their turn and to each of us it is as if we are the only ones who ever hunted, the only ones who ever longed, but the hunt is eternal and there is never enough time, there is never enough time.

Do not look at them. You will be hurt, and they will not notice, and nothing will change.

EDGAR and Cassie and Rose and Orion and Lana and Wyatt formed a group at the spot where Irina's dad had come running onto the playground.

"What are you guys doing over there?" called Miss Nathan.

"Making teams," said Edgar, but that wasn't true.

The real reason was that Lana had seen something in the mulch and said they should come over. It was a purple ponytail holder.

"That's it?" asked Wyatt. "I don't remember her wearing that."

"I do," said Rose, and Cassie said, "I do, too. She wore it, like, every day."

The ponytail holder was twisted once so that it formed a small figure eight. It was the kind you could get in any drugstore, inside a pack of all different colors.

Cars blew past on the road. The sky was cloudy and blue. It was just like that day had been. Irina's dad had pulled onto the gravel shoulder, charged across the field, hoisted her underneath one arm, and gone thumping back. He shoved the girl in the car and ran around to the driver's seat, before ripping out into the street. Miss Halifax saw the whole thing—everyone had—but it happened in less than a minute.

Now the playground was surrounded by a tall silver fence.

"They'll find her," said Orion. He resembled the other boys—the close-cut brown hair, the soft knees sticking out from his shorts, the large eyes—but he seemed different, bigger. His parents were artists. They lived at the end of the cul-de-sac in the blue house with the yellow shutters and the elm tree decorated with silver bells.

"Are you sure you guys are just picking teams?" called Miss Nathan again.

Edgar was thinking of his own parents, of the fights they had in the garage where they thought he couldn't hear, about his mother's mean laugh, the one he'd never seen, but only heard. Cassie was secure inside her impermeable personal force field with her baby sister and all of their favorite books. Rose's fingers twitched with the memory of the last time she had braided Irina's black hair into a single, thick rope. Wyatt listened for the thousandth time to the loop in his head of Miss Halifax yelling and screaming, and realized that his favorite teacher's leave of absence would be permanent. Lana imagined hugging her dog and it made her feel a little less cold.

"I mean it. Don't worry," said Orion. "She'll be okay."

Rose brought her hands to her chest and clutched them. "How can you know that?"

"Because I know," said Orion. "Because they'll find her."

Orion's mother had told him he would never die. She'd said, "Darling, when your body's worn out, you'll just go on up to the sky." In his father's study there used to be a massive canvas painted with what looked like an orange hurricane, a terrible burning storm. For months Orion's father had left the center of the painting empty. "I don't know," he said, and smoked cigarettes while he paced around in a stoop, dragging his work boots and tugging at his hair. "I don't know, I don't know, I don't know."

But Orion knew. "Put me in there, dad."

These days there was hardly a museum in the country that didn't sell a postcard with that painting on it. *Storm Born* was its name, and in the middle was this seven-year-old boy, pushing out, cracking open the orange tempest like an eggshell.

Once, Orion had climbed to the very top of the high monkey bars and sat on the crosspiece for an entire recess with his eyes shut and the sun bright on his face. "What were you doing up there?" the kids asked, but he would never tell. They were mortals. It would not do to worry them.

Orion dropped to a knee in the mulch. He picked up the purple ponytail holder. "Irina's going to want this back."

"But what if they don't find her?" The words were so awful Cassie could only whisper them.

Lana sobbed.

Orion rose. He brushed a chunk of mulch off his knee. A semi moaned by on the road. He stuck Irina's purple ponytail holder in his pocket. "Then I will," he said.

THERE was very little that G looked forward to less than meeting a dying child—only rehab came immediately to mind as being obviously less enticing—but you couldn't say no to Make-A-Wish. If you said no, it could end up on the Internet. As far as he knew, a direct connection between declining concert revenues and the blowing off of terminal fans had never been established, but G was well acquainted with the acid results of gossip. He always said yes. Usually it was cancer, although a few of the kids he'd met had been suffering from blood or nerve diseases or AIDS. Hannah Dewhurst, the girl today, was cancer, and her Wish was to meet him, Ganymede, multiplatinum recording artist, pop icon, age thirty-eight.

The private plane set down in Oklahoma City, and a town car picked them up. G's bodyguard went up front with the driver. The drive took about an hour. Outside the car windows Oklahoma slid by, a pale green color that made G think of his mother's dishes a thousand years ago.

"What have we got for crap?" he asked.

Oliver, G's assistant, sat in back with G. From a large shopping bag Oliver produced a poster, a gold record, and a concert headband. The poster showed a younger G leaping, bare-chested and leather-pantsed, in front of a cordon of dancers in yellow domino masks. It depressed G to think of the poster, which he would sign, *Keep Movin', Baby! Love Always, Ganymede*, hanging on the cancer girl's wall long after she died, or worse, of its being transferred to a position of memorial in the family room.

His assistant's fingers traced a curlicue on G's knee. "No," said G. Oliver made a cat hiss noise and laughed. G planned to fire him soon. Something about his hands, the smallness of them, had abruptly begun to repulse G; when he closed his eyes, they felt like independent creatures scurrying on his skin, searching for a place to bite. G knew this was random and unfair, and suspected that it was probably a concoction some corner of his subconscious had created to excuse his libido's wanderlust. G suffered his failings the way that people in old houses suffered their periodically flooded basements; he tried to remind himself of his other charms. It wasn't always easy.

"Sorry," he said, and Oliver shrugged. "No problem, G," said the assistant.

For his next assistant G thought he would go back to having a woman.

The cancer girl and her family were waiting for him at a diner in their town. G didn't catch the name of the town, but the diner was called *The Place*. It had red booths and a checkered floor. G squatted down beside the girl, who was twelve or thirteen, and had a few wisps of reddish hair on her freckled scalp, tubes in her nose, and an IV stuck in the back of one hand. "Hannah," he asked, "may I hug you?"

She nodded quickly, smiled, and blinked back tears, but didn't say anything. G put his arm around her shoulders and squeezed lightly; where his fingers touched the bare skin below her T-shirt sleeve it felt like construction paper.

A photographer from the local weekly newspaper took a picture of everyone surrounding Hannah. Hannah's father wept openly as he shook G's hand. Mr. Dewhurst looked like a town selectman, massively gutted and hugely headed, like the father of the sorts of boys that G—né Leonard David West, born Middletown, New York, 1974—had been afraid of in high school, because the only thing they ever talked about was killing fags. That G had gone on, in the course of time, fortune, and fame, to fuck a goodly handful of these sorts of boys—and, to make a truly accurate accounting, an equal number of those sorts of boys' wives, girlfriends, and sisters—did not engender within him any magnanimity toward them.

"Thank you, thank you," said Mr. Dewhurst. "God bless you, Ganymede."

G sat alone for a few minutes with the little girl at the far booth in the corner of the diner. They clasped hands across the table.

"This must really suck for you," said Hannah. "You must have to meet so many dying kids. You must have to meet so many that you probably barely have a minute for yourself. I bet you've met, like, a cemetery worth of dead kids by now."

G laughed. He hadn't expected that. "I like you, Hannah Dewhurst. You're funny."

"Let me have some of your coffee," she said.

"Should you?" he asked.

"No."

"Okay."

He slid the mug over, peeked around the edge of the frosted glass partition to make sure no one was looking, and told her, "You're clear." Hannah took a sip and slid the mug back.

In the parking lot G's bodyguard was leaning against the town car and doing a word search. Oliver was using the toe of his bright red sneaker to stir around bits of gravel. It looked sunny and dusty out there. G thought about the show the next night, Indianapolis. He felt homesick, but for which home he wasn't sure.

Hannah said, "I wish you could play me something."

"Watch," G said. In the air over the table he ran his fingers over imaginary keys. Hannah coughed hard. He stopped, shrugged. Tiny beads of sweat shone on her mostly naked scalp. She shrugged back. It wasn't, they both agreed, quite the same.

ONE night, when my mother was pregnant with me but not yet uncomfortable, she made a casserole for dinner. The youngest of my three sisters ate her portion voraciously. Before the others had even made a dent, she was nearly finished. My mother commented on her appetite, and the oldest of my sisters laughed.

"The dummy gave away her lunch," she said.

The youngest scowled. "Shut up."

"Wait," my father said. "Why did you give away your lunch?"

The youngest explained that it had been field trip day, and you were supposed to bring a lunch or sign up to get one, and Becky Neman had done neither, so she'd given Becky half her sandwich. Also, the field trip had been really cool. They'd gone to a power plant. (My mother always included that part when she told me the story, that they'd gone to a power plant.)

"So what's Becky Neman's problem?" My father was a factory foreman, an important man in his way, and he faced the entire world with the same brusque authority with which he faced his workers. "Did she forget that she needed to eat?"

Giggling, the youngest said, "No. Her mom made a lunch. She just forgot it."

"Her mother couldn't bring it to her?"

"No, Dad. We were on a field trip. They didn't bring extra school lunches. The teacher felt bad."

She reached again for the casserole. My father said, "So, you're really hungry now, huh?"

"Starving," the youngest said, and giggled again.

With one swift motion, he took my youngest sister's plate and put it on the counter. "Becky Neman is an idiot," he said. "She forgot her lunch. That was her problem, but then you went and made it yours."

My youngest sister frowned. "But she was hungry."

"Wait," my mother said.

He cut her off. "Becky Neman was hungry because she wasn't responsible enough to remember her lunch. You took the food out of your own mouth and gave it to her, and now you're hungry. But nobody's giving you free food, are they?"

"I am," my mother said. "I'm giving her free food."

"I'm trying to teach the kid a lesson, Rhea." He looked back at my youngest sister. "Becky Neman's lack of responsibility is Becky Neman's problem, not yours."

Tears welled up in my sister's eyes. "But I like Becky Neman."

"Oh, I bet Becky Neman likes you, too," he said. "I bet she loves you. Why wouldn't she? You give her free stuff." Then he sent her to her room and told my other sisters not to sneak her food. They nodded their heads solemnly and obeyed. They also teased my youngest sister about it for the rest of the week. *Hey, it's cold out here. Can I have your sweater? I'm bored. Give me that toy you're playing with.* They teased her until she cried.

I don't like this, my mother had said to my father. This is not a good thing to teach them.

Bullshit, my father had said. This is the way the world works, Rhea.

A few months later, I was born. My mother spent that first long night holding me, staring into my crumpled newborn face. Three times before she had spent long nights like this, cradling tiny bundles of new human being in her arms. Swaddled in hospital blankets, we reminded her of lima beans, my sisters and I. Because of the way that sometimes you get a lima bean that's already germinated, the pale green sprout curled around the meat of the bean itself, waiting to unfurl. Holding me as my father slept on the fold-out visitor's cot, she thought of a bumper sticker he'd put on his car: YOU ARE NOT A VICTIM AND NOBODY OWES YOU ANYTHING. She thought of all the bad things that happened in this world, of the bad things that had happened to her and the bad things that might happen to us, to me and my sisters. She thought of Becky Neman, and she thought of me: my just-germinated self, wrapped in helpless, needy infant-skin. My tightly curled lima-bean-ness, and how it was her job to help me uncurl, to give me sun and water and air and love, to fill me with whatever they had.

And that's the story my mother tells, when we ask her why she left my father. All these years later, my sisters remain angry at her. They build thunderheads out of their anger, tall and dark and foreboding, casting thick shadows over their lives and ours. When they finally break, my mother and I can do nothing but weather the storm.

Face the world with hope, she has told me, over and over again. Always hope. Never poison.

SHE found the plate in the back of the cabinet, coated with dust. It was from "The Olympus," a Greek diner in the suburbs of Columbus, Ohio. It was the color of well-used dentures—somewhere between yellow and cream. A small harp was stamped on the center and under the harp were the words "The Olympus." She wiped it down with a rag. The china was heavy and thick.

She remembered the night they stole it. Doug had it under his shirt and dropped it in the diner parking lot, but it hadn't shattered. They had been drunk and stoned and it had been hilarious. Later, still drunk, Weston hurled it against the brick wall of the dorm. Not only did the plate not break, one of the bricks in the wall chipped instead. Nathan dropped the plate from a third-floor dorm window; Annie backed over the thing with her Chevy Malibu; Frieda put it in the stove and baked it on high until it turned red and they were afraid there would be an explosion. Chet even filched a hatchet from a college maintenance van and tried to hack it up—the blows just rang off the plate. Nothing could harm it.

She hadn't thought of the plate in a long, long time.

College was twenty years ago. Some of the old gang was no longer on speaking terms; one had died in a weird accident that still didn't make sense to her; one had become unapproachably religious; one had gone into politics. It was like a legend, the stupid fun of her youth. It was like she was old.

The plate was cool against her cheek.

"What are you doing?" Her son had come into the kitchen. He was sixteen and black-haired and cracked his head on doorways. Girls sometimes called their house to giggle and hang up.

"What?" she asked.

The teenager raised a pierced eyebrow. "You're pressing a plate against your face, you weirdo."

"Oh, that," she said. "I'm having a reverie."

Our notion for "The Status of Myth" was extremely literal: to take some of the stories from Edith Hamilton's Mythology *(Ganymede, Rhea, etc.) and lay them directly atop contemporary characters. What does it mean to be Ganymede in 2013? What does it mean to be Rhea in 2013?*

—*KB & OK*

NARCISSUS
Zachary Mason

Beautiful rooms full of light and fire and everyone pretending not to look at me. I was much desired, by rich boys with their hearts breathily on their sleeves, rich men's wives *d'une age certain* in rather a lot of kohl, urbane and athletic Athenians who spoke of friendship and excellence, spendthrifty wine-factors whose chins trembled when I breathed on them. They offered gifts, which I accepted, and verses, which were always the same—I was perfect, moving and unmoved and flawless as stone, and the like. I never let them touch me, but gave them every chance to sigh.

I'd been in Sybaris forever, it seemed, sleeping through the days, and passing the nights in an endless succession of identical parties that left no more lasting impression than reflected voices, repeated conversations, wine fumes, claustrophobia. I had friends, or, rather, people I drank with, all of whom found inexhaustible delight in the company of louche musicians, noblemen in thin disguise, fire dancers, fire eaters, slaves with interesting histories, the more articulate sort of whore. In the false dawn, on the way home, when the wine was fading, I knew that it was perilous to stay too long, that the demimonde must have a term, that it was, in fact, a banal and mediocre bohemia, but it was home, if home was anywhere, and when I tried to focus on another future my mind wandered.

One night there was a party where someone quenched all the torches and left us fumbling in the dark, which delighted most of the celebrants, judging by the whispers and the laughter. Unseen strangers groped me and moved on; I had never liked to be touched, and was searching for a place out of the flow when a hand closed on my wrist. The fingers were callused, and the ragged, broken nails dug into my skin. "Who is it?" I asked, and tried to pull away, but whoever it was was strong and I found I could smell him, his sweat and unwashed clothes and something metallic. Behind us a bonfire roared into life and I found myself looking into the face of an old man, a stranger, scars where his eyes had been. He said, "Narcissus, loveliest of men, fear mirrors." I was going to ask him why, for I had seen mirrors and been none the worse for it (though, privately, I thought my reputation for beauty was exaggerated), but there was a shriek of laughter behind me and I turned to see a girl standing by the fire with a clique of notably bitchy actors. She was dressed like they were, and stood like them, so much the thespian that I thought at first she must be a boy in drag, but, no, there were breasts, or the beginnings of them—she was about thirteen. She stood between Thyestes the tragedian, who had a patronizing arm around her shoulders, and Bagoas, nobleman and occasional libertine, who was making a show of looking out into the crowd while all his attention was on the girl. Thyestes made most of his money off the stage. She doesn't know what's going to happen, I thought. She caught my eye and smiled, almost convulsively; I nodded to her and turned away but the blind man was already lost in the press of bodies and instead I found Artabazos, nominal playwright, gossip extraordinaire. "Who's the little thing with the actors?" I asked.

"Ah, the ingenue? Echo is her name. Echo from the provinces. Echo had a lover—her first, you see—rich family, vehement objections, but they had plenty of daughters, and it was easier to let her go. He dropped her, of course, and she washed up here. Thyestes found her sitting in an alley, filthy and sodden, hands folded in her lap, staring straight ahead; at first she wouldn't speak, then insisted she was nothing, no one and nameless, but now, as you can see, she is very much at home."

He paused, emotion moving over his face like weather. "Come home and have a drink with me, my dear. I have more to tell you," he said, standing too close, vinous and flushing.

"My excellent friend, I'm afraid I *can't* go home with you—the truth is I don't like you very much and you're too poor to be worth deceiving." Someone next to me laughed wheezily—I was regarded as a wit, on the basis of such remarks, though what I had said was no more than the truth.

The party faded, as parties will, and it was too hot and too dark in the many low rooms, so I decided to go home, but while I was looking for an exit I found myself on a balcony where Bagoas held the girl, Echo, in a sprawling embrace. I would have left them but I saw the rigor in her face, how she clutched her arms to her chest, how her shirt was half torn away.

If I have a principle it's that tricks should be treated genteelly. I said, "Bagoas, you are a pompous and mediocre nobody. No one likes you very much and you are welcome only when you're paying, though you seem not, till now, to have realized it. Also, I hear you're often impotent, so why don't you leave the girl and go practice raping your horses, or, better yet, your dogs?" Such spectacular rudeness can overwhelm the unprepared but Bagoas, to his credit, I suppose, glared at me, fumbled for his dagger, and stood. I should have been afraid but I wasn't, as, in fact, I was never afraid, though I couldn't have said why—I was no warrior. I put on the expressionless mask I wore when I wanted to drop an admirer and said, "The captain of the praetorian said he'd do anything for a smile from me. What do you think he'd do to you if I gave him a kiss? I'm thinking something with a hot iron, and a saw." I smiled pleasantly and watched his face, wondering what would happen next. He gave me a look intended to convey that this wasn't over, that one day he would find me and et cetera, and stalked away.

Echo had neither moved nor blinked. I arranged the remnants of her shirt over her frightfully skinny shoulders and said, "These people. No manners. Very disagreeable."

"These people," she said, in a voice radiant with detachment and inflected with contempt and just a little mirth that, after a moment, I recognized as a fair imitation of my own. "No manners. Very disagreeable." I laughed and asked if she had been hurt, by which I meant raped, but she only looked at me wide-eyed, her need almost palpable, so I stood, murmured what was no doubt good advice, and left.

There were other stations in the night but when the sky was lightening I finally went home. I lived on a posh tree-lined avenue where drunks and vagrants were relatively rare so I was surprised to see someone curled up on my doorstep, apparently asleep, sucking her thumb—it was the girl. I prodded her with my toe and said, "You. Wake up."

She opened her eyes and I said, "I'm no one's gallant, and I'm not running an orphanage, or a brothel, so go home, or, as the case may be, away." She blinked back tears, and then, in the haughty, weary drawl of an empress addressing a beggar she advised me to go and practice raping my horses, or, better yet, my dogs.

I said, "I have neither horses nor dogs, my dear, so it will have to be *you*," and squinted at her with such carnal menace as I could muster. She looked up at me, wide-eyed, considering, and I was about to say something else when she launched herself at me, locking her arms around my waist, her fragile warmth pressing into me, and though I recoiled—I do not like to be touched, and even my most munificent admirers buy themselves only a prolonged agony—she wouldn't drop the embrace, despite my exasperated sighs and ostentatious throat clearing, and, finally, I returned it.

My house was large but I only used two rooms so she had her pick of empty ones. I had almost no furniture so I made her a bed from a pile of my furs and told her she'd sleep like a Scythian princess. I sent the maid out for food, which Echo ate with distressing avidity, and for wine, which I watered when she wasn't looking, in which she matched me cup for cup. I asked her about herself, where she was from, who her parents were, and what had happened with Thyestes, but she only smiled at me, and wouldn't say a word.

It was good to have a pet. She'd be sprawled waiting on pillows in the foyer when I came home from an assignation. I'd show her the haul from that night's admirer and we'd rate it for taste and extravagance. I let her decide how nice I'd be the next time I saw them. And we talked, or, rather, I talked, though I was not naturally loquacious, but she encouraged me, and somehow I told her everything I knew.

I had my tailor cut my old clothes to fit her. I put jewels on her earlobes and on her wrists and on her clavicles. She wasn't beautiful, but her face was broad and blank, all strong planes and shadows; she was an empty canvas for my brush, and I painted her face as I painted my own. We looked like twins, when I was done, or lovers, or both. We were lovely.

When we went out all eyes were on us. Everyone wondered if I had taken a lover, finally, which was good for business, as it gave the marks hope. She was a great social asset, chattering tirelessly while I was stupefied with boredom, and if her opinions were secondhand she had overheard a great many and delivered them all with brio and conviction. We finished each other's sentences, and ate from the same plate, and she draped herself around me. We made a point of snubbing Thyestes. I welcomed each night, and all the nights blurred together, and she was always close by. I thought those nights would never end, and, somehow, at the same time, that we'd leave, one day, and live together, far away, in a quiet house by a river, and never come back to the city.

SOME governor's son paid court to her, which I tolerated, though I insisted that she stay intact, for I wanted neither a screaming infant nor a spotty aristocrat in the household. When he became importunate I told her to drop him but she said she didn't know how. "There's nothing to it," I said. "Just look into his eyes and say . . . nothing. *What's wrong?* he'll ask. *Are you angry?* He'll apologize for imaginary slights, for stinginess, for other lovers. *Do you hate me?* he'll ask. *Have I taught you to despise me?* Why *won't you talk to me?* His sad mouth will tremble, and, if he's not really a gentleman, there may be tears and harsh words, and then it's over."

NEMESIS was a frightful goddess whose name was rarely spoken and the good burghers of Sybaris would have been shocked to learn that there was a party in her temple, which was, I supposed, why we were there. The space made me uncomfortable, all footsteps and shadows and never enough light. It was too dim to see faces but I recognized Rukshana, a minor royal, from her slouch. Rukshana liked a bit of rough, preferring beards and scars to smooth chins and clean lines; she had, to my certain knowledge, fucked her way through the entire praetorian. We were chummy. It was a long way from her to a throne (though never far to a bar stool) but she still had the High Palace manner and their breathy, lisping drawl.

"Slumming, dear?" I asked.

"Oh, no," said Rukshana, "these are quite my people. Salt of the earth, and so on. Who's your little friend?" Echo, lately of an alley, lifted up her hand to be kissed.

I had never been in that temple before and as they talked my eyes drifted up to a statue of Nemesis, larger than life, and her face wasn't what I expected, full of wild pride and terror and desperation, and when I looked back Echo and Rukshana were gone. I searched through the temple but found only strangers, who ignored me.

I had thought she'd be waiting at home but when I got there the house was empty. I waited up for her, supposing she left the party to find her lover, but dawn came and she still wasn't there and finally I fell asleep on her pillows.

I woke in the evening but she still hadn't come back so I went out looking, though I found nothing that night, or the next night, or the night after that, and I hardly slept, and I kept thinking I saw her and being disappointed, and finally at some nobleman's fete I found Artabazos drunk on a divan and he said he hadn't seen Echo but he had seen Rukshana, who had a new friend, a protege, who was little more than a girl. "And it wasn't Echo?" I said.

"No, it wasn't your guttersnipe. I haven't found out her name, yet, but she was clearly of one of the great houses of Persia, not at all your kind."

I flirted my way into the palace and waited motionless in the shadows of the orangery near Rukshana's rooms, watching the courtiers come and go, and when Echo finally walked by in her aristocrat's disguise I hardly recognized her.

"Echo!" I called, sick with relief, but she didn't slow, and I had to run to lay a hand on her shoulder. "You might have told me you were going to be away. I know how it is, obviously, so go have your fun, but then come home." I smiled at her but she stared at me without expression. "Oh, I see," I said, "your new connection with a third-rate demi-royal has put you above speaking. Don't let me detain you—by all means return to your proper palace, or was it an alley?" Her face was unmoving, her eyes cold. "Have I offended you? Neglected you? Is there *anything* I haven't done for you? Look. Have your prince, or your princess, or all the royals in a row, for all I care, but then come back, because it's us against everyone, and we'll take what they have and give them nothing in return and love only each other, so come home. Echo?" I said, but she was already walking away, and I realized then that I had been wrong, that she had always been beautiful.

I looked for her a long time. They barred me from the palace but it didn't matter because from what I heard she didn't last there long. I went to parties high and low, sifted every dive, flophouse, and brothel, every place where the discarded might wash up, but she was never there, and I rarely slept, and drank too much, and ate too much poppy. My new round must have been hard on me because old acquaintances started when they saw me and I finally heeded the seer's advice and stayed away from mirrors. I started waking up in places I didn't know, and the recent past was riddled with dark stretches, and one day it was winter and I was looking for her by the freezing river outside the city walls and it had been a long time since I had eaten, and though it was a bright, frigid day when I closed my eyes it was twilight when I opened them, and there was another river before me, this one swift and black and smooth as glass. I peered into the flow and my heart lifted, for a moment, when I thought I saw her looking up at me.

Echo and Narcissus were separate stories until Ovid combined them in his Metamorphoses. *Their story is famous, these last two thousand years, and resonant, but it always felt to me like the pieces fit together awkwardly, and wanted to be rearranged into another, stabler narrative. In Ovid, Narcissus is warned to fear mirrors; for me, the key change is that the mirror is Echo.*

—ZM

BACK TO BLANDON
Michael Jeffrey Lee

I was given a very warm welcome when I returned home after my trip abroad. In fact, as my ship pulled in, a small crowd gathered right there on the dock, waving their hands and handkerchiefs, crying excitedly, and smiling in my direction. There was one among them who neither waved, smiled, nor cried, so I made up my mind to say a few words in his ear once we were face-to-face, but as we floated closer I was able to see the scene much more clearly, and soon discovered the reason: he was busy fishing: his hands were occupied with his rod, his eyes were fixed on the water, and he was murmuring something softly to himself. It wasn't that he was choosing to ignore me; it was just that he didn't immediately perceive me, and after realizing this, I relaxed again. I drew a deep breath in through my nose, blew it out through my mouth, lifted my arms into a wave, began a high cry in my throat, and turned the corners of my mouth up into a smile.

I didn't have any luggage with me, just the shirt on my back, my pants, and my shoes. I had started my journey home with a nice gray hat, but while passing over particularly deep waters a stiff wind had blown it right off my head and sent it skimming over the waves. The shirt I wore was quite colorful, but also full of snags and splits. Yet it covered me in the right places, in the places I knew I needed the most coverage. My pants, on the other hand, were in much better shape—a family I'd stayed with abroad had given them to me. It was surprising that they gave me the pants, given how tattered their own were, and I almost didn't take them, but after reminding me of all the free literature and life coaching I had given them, they convinced me. I graciously accepted the pants and put them on. They were a little on the thin side, but it was early fall and still balmy back in Blandon when I arrived, so the risk of my catching my death of cold was quite low.

My shoes, no two ways around it, were stunning to see; I'd splurged on them while I was abroad. Nicely heeled, they made a pleasant clopping sound whenever I walked or jogged in them. Also they were shiny, in an admittedly showy way, though I tried not to show them off too often, and if I did, only to those I could trust. As far as finances went, I was not well off, not well off at all, largely due to the fact that I had such an excellent time abroad: eating well, soaking up the interesting cultures, and not worrying about saving the money I made. Since I was without any means that morning, you might think that I was hungry, my stomach busy eating itself for sustenance, but thankfully this was not the case. Before leaving, I spent some money—the last of it, actually—on a variety of snacks, which, just before boarding the boat, I smartly stuffed into the pockets of my roomy pants. This allowed me, during the long journey home, to snap off little pieces of my stash; and while pretending to cough I would bring the pieces up to my mouth and discreetly devour them without attracting much notice. Which was a good thing for me to have done, in the end, because everyone else onboard was starving.

As my ship inched closer, I also noticed that most of Blandon's oceanfront property was up for sale—the words were legible even from my position offshore—and I was overjoyed, though I tried to put on a grave face. Growing up in Blandon, the beach-dwelling people always rankled me because of their luxurious lifestyles, and though my family was by no means poor, we lived farther inland, and didn't go around flaunting our money right there on the beach. However, recent experience had taught me that it was never nice to delight in someone else's property loss, so to change the subject of my thinking I sang a short song to myself, just a little number I picked up when I was abroad:

I will think much of this kindness
From this day forward on
As decay does overtake me
I will sleep through every dawn
I will think much of this kindness
As my life draws to a close
As the nurses they tend to me
Protecting all that I know

With arms outstretched, the wavers assisted me onto the dock. I thanked them for supporting me, they thanked me for thanking them, and after shaking hands and embracing for a while I let them get back to their waving. While I tried to be the bigger person with regards to the fisherman—taking his slight in stride and letting it slide right off me—I just couldn't help myself, so I wandered over to him. He was sitting with his back to me, his hairy legs dangling right over the dock. I prepared to squat, so as to more easily whisper in his ear, but before I could even begin my descent I was struck by the feeling that underneath all that sea-grime lay someone I knew. I smiled thinly at him, just to see what he would do, and much to my surprise he smiled back, widely, revealing his unusual teeth, unmistakable in their curvature, and I then realized, with a certain amount of shock, that I was staring at my father. It had been years since I'd seen him—he'd long stopped living with my mother and me by the time I made the decision to go abroad—but he was still, in his way, a hero of mine, and so I felt compelled to say something.

"Hello." I was hoping to wade in, letting him take the conversation where he wanted. But before he could even reply, something began tugging at his line, and he took his eyes off me and set them on his rod.

"Well, well, well," he said, "what will I eat today?"

"I hope it's something big," I said, though I couldn't put as much feeling into the words as I wanted.

"Thank you," he said. "Thank you for the fishing wishes." Then, because mere tugging wasn't enough, he stood up, and started fighting with the rod. We stared out at the water together. After some struggle, he reeled in his line, then closely examined his catch. It was only a wet handkerchief, perhaps one that a waver had let slip while celebrating. He freed the handkerchief from its hook, wrung it out, and then tied it around his neck.

"Are you going to return that to its owner?" I said.

"Only if they claim it," he said.

"What if it has sentimental value?"

"Distance swells the heart," he said. "How are you doing?"

"Fine," I said. "Trying to get used to Blandon again."

"Well, where are you coming from?" he said.

"Abroad."

"Oh. And how long have you been away?"

"A few years," I said. "Give or take."

"Give or take?"

"I was out of range for a while," I said, embarrassed. "I kind of lost track of the days."

"If you don't track them, you don't miss them."

"I don't know," I said. "I'd say I already miss them."

"I'll bet you made a whole host of friends, didn't you?"

"Absolutely," I said. "Lifelong friends."

"Make sure to keep in touch with them," he said.

"Oh?" I said.

"Or else they'll feel lonely."

"I will," I said, which was a lie. I had forgotten to collect any phone numbers before leaving.

"So, on the whole, you had a good trip?"

"I did," I said, proudly. "I learned a lot."

"Great."

"It was."

"But Son," he said, looking me right in the eyes. "Something doesn't add up."

"What is it?" I said.

"Well," he said. "If you liked it so much over there—abroad, I mean—why didn't you just stay put?"

"Well," I said. "That's a good question. I suppose it never really felt like home—never fully, anyway. Even the moments when I was having the most fun I always felt something calling me back. I missed Blandon. I missed you and Mom."

"Your work dried up, didn't it?" he said.

"How did you know?" I said.

"A father knows," he said. "It's very expensive over there, too."

"It is," I said. "My money just disappeared."

"I must say I'm quite proud."

"Oh?"

"Not many people ever leave their home state."

I didn't really know what to say at this moment, actually, because my father had never told me he was proud of me before, and I was overcome.

"You must think yourself pretty cultured now," he said.

"I guess so," I said.

"Did you hold on to your values?"

"Values?"

"The ones I instilled in you, when you were young."

"Oh, I think so," I said. I wasn't sure what he was referring to.

"Recite them now," he said. "If you don't mind."

I took several wild guesses: "Truthfulness, steadfastness, emotional baldness, transparentness, upstandingness, and willingness."

"You forgot steadfastness."

"Did I?" I said, but went no further—the last thing I wanted to do was fight with my usually absent father. I was eager to leave the conversation anyway, and hoped to end it on a positive note.

"And these values you just recited," he said. "Were you able to foist them onto others?"

"As often as I could," I said. This was the absolute truth.

"And did you find the people receptive to them?"

"Most of the time, I guess. Have you seen my mother, lately?" I suddenly wanted to see her more than anything.

"I haven't," he said. "You know how I feel about sharing beds."

I nodded: it was an issue they fought often about. "I'm going to pay her a visit," I said, and took a high, strong step, which, in hindsight, was a thoughtless thing to do, because my shoe clopped on the wooden dock, and my father's attention was directed toward my feet.

"My," he said. "Those are pretty."

"They're functional too."

"And you bought them abroad?"

I nodded. "An impulse buy."

He handed me his fishing rod, then dropped to his knees. After untying the handkerchief, he spat on my shoes and began polishing them.

"You don't have to do that," I said. I must say I did not like the idea of my own father putting his hands all over my feet.

"I'd be honored," he said. "Especially after everything you've done."

"I don't have money to pay you."

"I wouldn't think of asking," he said. "Never, never, never."

"All right," I said.

"Son," he said suddenly. "How in the world did you make ends meet while you were abroad?"

"I worked," I said. "I was employed. Why?"

"I just hope you didn't sign on any dotted lines."

"No?"

"No," he said. "That's how they get you back."

"It was mostly just work for hire," I said.

"We're in a slump here," he said, "I don't know how closely you've been following the news."

"I've tried to keep up," I said, "but none of my sources have mentioned it."

"Your sources might be biased, then," he said, popping the handkerchief. "Take a look at that beachfront."

I fixed my eyes again on the vacant property. Of course, seeing all those empty and boarded-up homes made me long to see my mother even more.

"Do you know what causes slumps?"

"No."

"One guess."

"Squandered resources," I said. I could not remember where I had learned that.

"Close," he said. "Reckless spending."

"OK," I said.

I decided to make a run for it, and tried putting one foot in front of the other, but my legs didn't properly extend, and I looked down and saw that my father had tied the laces of my shoes together.

"Is this your standard shine?" I said.

"No," he said, "but I'll give you a good price."

"I told you I don't have any money," I said.

"We'll work something out," he said. "Installments."

I wanted to call out to the wavers for help in getting free, but when I craned my neck to look for them, I couldn't find them anywhere.

"What happened to everyone?" I said.

"Do you think I keep tabs on those people?" he said.

Keeping my feet close together, I turned myself slowly around until I saw that all the wavers had lined up single file behind me. Whether they were waiting to get their shoes shined or whether they just liked standing that way, I wasn't sure, and they certainly weren't volunteering information. In fact, they'd given up their waving, smiling, and crying all together, and were now eyeing us silently. My father, oblivious to the queue, continued his polish job—I could see his wrists and hands poking in between my legs.

"I'd like to go now," I said.

"No, no," he said. "Not yet. You haven't asked me whether or not I have been personally affected by the slump."

"Have you?" I said.

"Of course," he said, pointing to an empty cooler nearby.

"Do you usually fill that with fish or with refreshments?"

"Well," he said, "it used to be refreshments, until that got out of hand, and began affecting my fishing."

"Do you miss them?"

"Yes," he said.

"I hope you catch some fish today," I said.

"Me too," he said. "I'd hate to have to hit up your mother."

"She would probably hate that too."

"What are your life plans, Son?"

"I'd like to accomplish a lot," I said.

"Don't you think it's time you found a Sweetheart?"

"Maybe," I said. "It's hard to know."

"But you had your fun while abroad?"

"A lot," I said. I considered mentioning some of my flings, then thought better of it.

"So you lost your innocence, I take it?"

"I think so," I said. "Though if it's still around, I bet it's here to stay."

"Beware the substances," he said. "All substances. Refreshments on down."

"I've always been pretty well adjusted," I said.

"But I gave you the addictive gene," he said.

"I'm not too worried about it," I said.

"Be forewarned."

"I'll try."

"I'm out of advice," he said suddenly.

"And I'm going to see the woman that raised me," I said, without much bitterness. "It's been really interesting seeing you." I turned a careful circle again, so that he could see on my face that I meant what I said. He looked up at me, then smiled, showing his teeth again.

"All done, Son."

"Can you please tie my laces back to their proper shoes?"

"I can," he said, and then he did just as I asked, pulling the laces free from each other and tying two big, beautiful knots, one on each shoe. "Check that rod. Something is nibbling."

As soon as he said it, I remembered what I'd been holding this whole time. Sure enough, there really was something nibbling, and I fought with it for a minute, then reeled it in, but after bringing the catch up to my face, I saw that it was only an old shoe, all worn out and waterlogged, which only added to the guilt I felt about my own. Then I looked down again and noticed that my father had no shoes of his own—his gnarly toes told the whole story—so I freed the shoe from the still baited hook and got down on my knees. Then, taking one of his filthy feet in my hands, I partially shod my father, who seemed grateful, because he put his hand on my shoulders, pulled me up, pulled me close, then brought his mouth up to my ear and softly whispered: "The only reason I was absent from your up-bringing is because your mother and I didn't share the same values that we did before we made you, and I'm telling you this only because I'm very, very hungry and if I'm not able to catch any fish today there's a good chance I will faint and fall forward right off this dock, and except for the small splash my body will make there'll be no evidence that I was ever here at all except of course my rod and my cooler and that part of me that you carry within yourself, and the last thing I would want is for you to live your life hating that part of yourself because I didn't take the time to tell you that I had nothing against you while we were both still alive."

Though he found it necessary to speak with his tongue in my ear, he was still, in his way, a hero of mine, so I stuck out my hand, and he stuck out his hand, and we shook them together, as friends do, and when he released me from his grasp I reached in my pocket and broke him off a piece of what I had. I told him to kneel down and open wide, which he did, his new shoe tucked beneath him, and then I jammed the cracker into his mouth. His eyes lit up, and he seemed to savor it, and it felt so good to see him happy that I ended up giving him a whole cracker, which I really shouldn't have done, because the wavers were still watching us closely. I could have never guessed that they might have been hungry too, but they surrounded my father and me, and closed in on us quickly, smiling wider and crying louder and waving faster than they had when I arrived, and if I hadn't had somewhere else to be I would have gladly stayed and defended that cracker with my father, but my mother was calling me, and it was time for me to be home. I forced myself through the ring they'd formed and jogged briskly down the pier.

This story grew out of an obsession with returning: from death, from duty, from fun, from meaningful existence into something more slippery. It has its basis in half-remembered tellings of Odysseus's return, and in the dreadful projection of Christ's. Other sources: "John Riley," Dostoyevsky's Prince Myshkin, *and* Chicken Soup for the Soul.

—MJL

THE STORY I AM SPEAKING TO YOU NOW
Davis Schneiderman

These are the first words of the story I am speaking to you now:

—ONCE, in the beginning of robots—

THESE words, which I have now articulated, are in fact the first words that the first robot, the first to achieve complete sentience, speaks to its human. A she.

—AND then—the first robot continues.

—THESE are the next words of that story—this first robot continues to continue.

—NOW, I am speaking the story to you—it keeps on—telling you the story that has been told to me and programmed inside me, as software made through the transmogrification of heat-lines in a circuit board to machine language to binary code to a programmed language that comes to you as my speech . . . so when I speak to you, as emotive a robot as there has ever been, I am not only speaking this story, but I am in a very tactile manner speaking the history of speaking.

———

—LET me explain this to you with words you have heard before. With words you may understand.

—ONCE, in the past, before you were born, and before I became the me that I am now—the first robot speaks—when the me that stands or operates or modifies space or exists before you could be called merely information, or at least information in a different form, then, before this, stories and facts lived in separate universes.

—LET me explain this to you with words you have spoken before.

—BEFORE the fire in the human heart became stories—continues the first robot—when put through the plumbing of the mouth and the processing limitations of human existence and the raw data of the experience and the cold outside our caves and the howl of magical animals that hide ready to kill us to eat us to fight us when we hunt and when we sleep.

—BEFORE this.

—BEFORE the speech of our stories, born from the first indistinct moments when the first sounds pushed their way through our windpipe, became these sounds the public sounds that we share together . . . the collective gurgles that we speak we share we understand.

—BEFORE this.

—BEFORE the raw data of experience stood apart and outside of this speech we share together because before the sounds of this data did not exist did not compute itself in a manner that we could hear or understand or live.

—LET me explain in a more clear manner.

—ONCE upon a time, there was an egg. An oval. Along the single axis of the equinoxes, which inside its hard shell contain albumen and vitellus, more commonly called yolk, separated by a sac of thin membranes, storing high quantities of protein and choline.

———

—THIS egg wishes to produce another egg—says the first robot—to reproduce itself and so spread throughout the earth, and so advisedly, by design, calculatingly, consciously, designed, determinedly, in cold blood, knowingly, meaningfully, on purpose, pointedly, premeditatively, prepensely, purposely, purposively, resolutely, studiously, to that end, voluntarily, willfully, with a view to, with eyes wide open, with malice aforethought, without qualms, wittingly . . . the egg produces the first chick.

—THIS chick, yellowish-white, recalls the red and gray jungle fowl of the Indian subcontinent at a time when the Ganges ran like clear viscous sun, and so also thinks ahead to the basements in Brooklyn, where designer breeds hatch under dead fluorescent banks, and back again to René Descartes, over an omelet.

—THE chick thinks not, really, not in a way I use this text-to-speech processor to render the point with the deftly charted acumen of the finest line.

—LET me try to speak this—the first robot says—again.

—TAKE a robot, a robot is just a robot's way of reproducing itself, in that what I say to you now with the words that come from the heat of a circuit board mean very little at all in their apparent content. After all, this is a program, a story, the words are arbitrary and it is only my ability to speak them—speaks the first robot—to repeat perhaps with my own imitable nuances the most delectable tongue-riddles:

—A. Simple word.

—AN. Second simple word.

—AND. Conjunction.

—ANDES. Mountain ranging.

—ANTINOMIAN. Rejecting moral law.

———

—ANADROMOUS. Fish ascending rivers to spawn.

—ANAERECTIC. Destructive.

—ANAPHALANTIASIS. Falling out the eyebrows.

—ANCHORITE. Withdrawing from the world for religious reasons.

—ANENCEPHALIC. Lacking a brain.—

—ANESTHESIOLOGY. Studying anesthetics.

THESE words the first robot transmits. Then continues in this way:

—IF I speak these things well, if I move and vibrate and hum in a way that pleases you, my human master, then there will be more of me in the world in the future. Maybe not me, though. There is no me, really.

—RATHER, the idea of me will stick with the you that hears me speak, or with the you that tells someone about my speech, or with the you that knows simply the idea of the robot, think here of the "unicorn." And so this idea will proliferate in ever-greater combinations through ever more complex thought experiments, AI-Turing Machines, so to speak, as I am doing now.—

THE first robot looks at the human, raises its arms to the sky and slowly lowers these same arms, and then continues.

—ONE day, perhaps long into a future where the stars have begun to lose their heat in a manner palpable to the things on this planet that observe their movements and feel their gravitational intrigues, the idea of the robot will have given way to a new idea that cannot now be spoken, despite the fact that it will close the border between words and facts. What began as the story of life emerging from the primordial nothing, the spark entering and animating the world, will have become merely the originating fact that this new idea not yet spoken has evolved into itself.—

———

THE first robot delights in this monologue, since the human begins to shift her weight as if measuring the mass of a secret. Even so, the first robot continues to continue:

—EVEN though I speak through the words of a distant librettist, I am already condemned to live into infinity.

—LET me tell you how this must end—the first robot pushes.

—I must close my eyes—the first robot says, and you wonder, so many eons distant, if this robot that speaks to you now can also pass though the barrier at the end of the first robot's story:

—AND now the human, an "inventor" of sorts, a type of "tinkerer," perhaps better called a "code maker," should pull out the first robot's hard drive and erase its contents with powerful magnets that the human has collected over many years and at great expense.—

—AND you too, who will speak many eons later—the first robot says— should carefully remove the battery supply—from this robot—from me in the future tense—the first robot means, speaking the story of how the human, perhaps the first human—in a fit of pique, should de- mobilize the first robot—pulling out the wires of the future—fusing them together with a blowtorch into a knot of snarled metal—kissing the once lovingly embedded nails in the sheet-metal body.

AND the first robot says this as its voice falls apart—speaking from its circuits, my circuits too—these are the first words of the story I am speaking to you now—these are the first words of the story I am speaking to you now.—

The story is drawn, in a broad sense, from the oral Ho- meric tradition. In those works, and in the work of many ancient myths, the teller of the tale changes his

position in relation to the gods through the telling. Odysseus exists in large part due to the repetition of the Homeric epics, and we often think of him as the first "modern" man: as one who lives according to a code which is separate from that of the gods. My work here expresses some of this same self-reflexive energy in its telling of the "first robot" by a later robot. The story seeks to demolish the robotic dependence upon human creators simply in the act of its articulation.

—DS

Oedipus

THE BRIGADIER-GENERAL TAKES
HIS FINAL STAND, BY JAMES BUTT*

Imad Rahman

The Brigadier-General wears a frayed bathrobe in a mildewed, smoky nonsmoking hotel room, someplace Midwestern, perhaps Ohio, someplace cheap, perhaps Econo Lodge. To get here you drive through the series of pocketed communities that fray the outskirts of these usual someplaces, someplaces that are like industrial cities that were once more industrious cities. Let's call this someplace Cleveland. The Econo Lodge could be someplace like every other Econo Lodge, mildly convenient.

It's one of those places where primal energy is compartmentalized, where if you avoid the highway and drive up the scenic route instead, a row of bungalow-style strip clubs gives way to a buffer

---

*This is the name you might know me by, if you read the sort of jaded post-postmodern journals I generally ply my trade through, but this is not my real name. Once, before my father died and we moved to the States, I was Jamshed Bhatt. In Chicago public schools, however, I became Jammy-Shed and then Jumbo-Shack and then Love-Shack-At-Bat, etc. It was a hard time, and my therapist suggested radical change. Henceforth, James Butt. A worse kind of torture ensued. My plea to those of you like me: keep your real name! Let all your tortures be honest tortures.

block of boarded-up warehouses before hitting a cluster of split-level churches and then you emerge into the commercial zone. A panoramic sweep of the immediate Econo Lodge area, just a few miles off the highway, reveals a Tommy's Jerky, Towneplace Suites, Subway, Sheetz, Fairfield Inn, Walmart, Target, Chipotle, Hampton Inn, Sonic, Wingate by Wyndham, the Always Retail Center, Bed Bath & Beyond, Best Cuts. Straggling geese dot the driveway to a boarded-up Palm Motel, which is under new management. The place feels less like a rest stop area than someplace the pit bulls of commerce wage a dogfight for the Midwestern paycheck. The air is fragrant with the smell of vegetable oil and diesel and sweat, the sky a blue gas flame patched through with clouds the color of clotted milk.

To get here, you take precautions. Fly in, take the train downtown from the airport, take a cab back to the airport, rent two cars from two separate car rental agencies, then get into a third car you borrow from your old college roommate Gus, or rather from Gus's big brother Tom, who just happens to be from this someplace that we're calling Cleveland, and, because he's a nice guy, is amenable to dropping said car off in the airport parking lot. You don't see Gus, he doesn't live here anymore.

This halfway secrecy,* where things are both named and not named and half-named, is being deployed at the behest of the Brigadier-General, who is a halfway secretive man.† The sight of him in this frayed bathrobe with perhaps a hint of egg yolk and a dab of dried coffee on the lapels is at once disquieting and thrilling.‡ The bathroom door behind him opens and there is a smell that is both lilac and not lilac, lilac and Econo Lodge, perhaps. A woman,

---

*"I have enemies," he says on the phone.
†I have been called secretive myself. The wife/ex-wife/who-the-fuck-knows says there's something CIA about me, an unwillingness to truly share, an inability to remove that final veil of openness, of desire. She has a point. She doesn't even know my real name. I am too self-involved, she says, unable to get outside my head. Push comes to shove, I don't push, I don't shove, I freeze. I'm holding back and that's holding us back. You don't act, she says, you plot, you probe, you recede. Actions speak louder, she says, or else. I promise, I say. Don't promise, she says, shout! Or else.
‡Okay, it thrills me more than it disquiets to see the Brigadier-General in such spectacular disarray, but it might have the opposite effect on you.

a girl-woman, steps out in a towel. She is not surprised.* There is, he will say later, in life as in war, secrecy but no secrets.

He is still imposing at sixty-five. His mustache is waxed, his hair Brylcreemed and most possibly Rogained, his posture military, his erection partially erect behind his partially open bathrobe. In case you don't remember the news from twenty years ago, the Brigadier-General was once news. There was a country, tentatively part of that coalition of that-part-of-the-world, where there was an uprising, which was first sanctioned by our government and yours, and then applauded and then condoned and then ignored and finally reprimanded, and then there was a coup with exploding helicopters and poorly doctored surgical strikes and then, finally, media silence.

The Brigadier-General burst out of the rubble, presidential scepter in hand. There were rigged elections and predetermined contracts and oil pipelines and infrastructural overhauls and political upheavals and assassinations and things thwarted and things festering and things, well, etc. Then the inevitable reverse coup, the hasty retreat, the shadow government assembled, the shadow government dissolved due to lack of funding, a new face emerging with a slightly new agenda and a slightly similar temperament, a new headline, a new headache, a few new late-night monologue bons mots out here in the West that were really variants on the same old not-so-late-night bons mots. In short, a new model of Brigadier-General, one man's punch line, another man's sucker punch.

Few remember this Brigadier-General now, except occasionally as a crossword clue.† There was the ghosted authorized biography, attempts at the HBO movie starring someone ethnic and swarthy but of a different ethnically swarthy persuasion from our Brigadier-General, said attempts stalling preproduction, the light moving from green to red to invisible, a brief sojourn on the college lecture

---

*But I am! I do not have much of a plan, but whatever I do have requires a private audience. Such is the problem with plans.

†Full disclosure: My mother and I left the country of P——, after my father, a former friend and confidant, was assassinated following a failed attempt at assassinating the B-G. The B-G does not know this, I hope, that I am who I am. Hence, here I am. Forty-two, a writer of scraped-together magazine articles, old enough to resent younger successes as opposed to when I was young enough to resent older successes, now both a marginal success and a marginal failure, depending on how you look at it.

circuit, a failed stint as a political commentator on that commentary channel that masquerades as news, and the inevitable fade.

The girl-woman takes off her towel. She is tanned all over. Red welts lacerate her shoulder blades. She is skinny but she doesn't work out. There is muscle and there is bone, and it is natural. Her legs are shaved, the rest of her is not. She puts on a yellow sundress first, then her underwear.

"This is Tanya," he says. "She is my consort."

"He means escort," she says, at the mirror applying makeup. Coffee gurgles in the coffeemaker. The AC kicks on and off. "As in, I provide a service."

"I was important once, young man," he says. "I killed people. I had people killed. I did not have to pay anyone to do so. The promise was enough. People tried to kill me, sometimes from beyond the grave. Rumors of my demise were mostly exaggerated."*

THE Brigadier-General is born outside the small town of S——, the son of a widowed landowner who either lusts after and subsequently rapes, or falls in love with and subsequently rapes, the unfortunately lithe sixteen-year-old who spends occasional evenings in his employ as a kitchen maid. Her parents pay the widowed landowner to farm his land and to live in a shack on the outskirts of his palatial farmhouse. They are part of a team that weeds and waters his vegetable gardens and orange groves daily. In their spare time they grow sugar cane in the plot they lease from the widowed landowner for half of what they make from the weeding and the watering. Most of the other half they pay in rent and utilities, also to the widowed landowner, who might, if the mood arises, offer them a semi-decent price for the sugar cane they grow. If they do not like his price, they are free to walk the sixteen miles to town, or to pay the widowed landowner for the use of his truck and his driver to take

---

*So I've got, in the trunk, a spool of chicken wire, a roll of duct tape, a set of high-end costume-store handcuffs, a variety of bungee cords, a carving knife, and a Walmart-issued Beretta CO_2 pistol, essentially a pellet gun. In the back of my mind, just like in the back of my trunk, I have access to repressed intentions to do the B-G violent harm. Am I capable of this? There is nothing in my history to suggest it, but who the fuck knows. I may not have violence in my limbs, but there is something furious in the soul. Does it help that I picked this week to quit smoking, and now have a nicotine patch on my shoulder, and another on my thigh?

them to town, where they are welcome to try and find a better price, which they probably will not find, since the landowner has pretty much cornered the local sugar cane market, and since he pretty much owns half the town.

The Brigadier-General's mother, the unfortunately lithe sixteen-year-old, dies upon childbirth, as mothers often do in stories like these, and the widowed landowner is gracious and perhaps even heartbroken enough to pay for her funeral and to authorize his driver to take the boy Brigadier-General to town where he will be schooled in the local K–12. The widowed landowner is careful, though, to never allow the boy Brigadier-General into the private quarters at either his farmhouse, where the boy Brigadier-General is employed part-time as a dishwasher, or his townhouse, where the boy Brigadier-General works weekends as the boy-servant to the landowner's real sons when they visit from the city-house. He is never to enter through the front door, always through the back via the servant quarters.

All that changes when he is thirteen and the K–12, as part of an exchange program with its sister city somewhere in the greater Midwest of the USA, welcomes its first exchange teacher, a young and enthusiastically bearded Marxist named James Bell, who comes bearing Xeroxed copies of an unauthorized biography of Che Guevara and an authorized history of Fidel Castro, as well as, for both counterpoint and cultural critique, a year's worth of *Rolling Stone* back issues. He is to teach the children English. James Bell arrives with his family, an enthusiastically evangelical wife named Dolly Bell, who has perhaps given up on evangelically converting her Marxist husband and could be planning to use him as her vehicle for the evangelical conversion of some lucky natives, and a shy twelve-year-old daughter named Simone Bell, who is already unfortunately lithe.

What transpires next is that James Bell takes the young Brigadier-General under his wing and moves him into the cramped quarters his family has been allotted near the main bazaar in town, with the tacit consent of the widowed landowner, who is having a fairly open and lurid affair with the enthusiastically evangelical Dolly Bell, who is no longer perhaps quite as enthusiastically evangelical or is perhaps even more so caught up in missionary zeal. James Bell is so caught up in playing Pygmalion with the young Brigadier-General, and Dolly Bell is so caught up in replaying the beast-with-two-backs with the widowed landowner, that neither notices the attention the widowed landowner is paying to the unfortunately lithe Simone Bell, who has also caught the eye and the heart of the young Brigadier-General.

The young Brigadier-General lives in a roomy closet that can comfortably house a small mattress and has enough elbow room for him to work a flashlight, and which happens to be directly across the hallway from the room occupied by Simone Bell. At night he turns his flashlight off, cracks his closet open and peers into Simone Bell's slightly open bedroom. When she brushes her hair, it ripples off her shoulders in waves. But then the widowed landowner rapes Simone Bell on the night James Bell and Dolly Bell are out for their weekly husband-wife excursion to the local bazaars, while a terrified young Brigadier-General cowers in the closet. Something happens to him then, something that builds and keeps building long after the widowed landowner, his father, has gone and a sobbing Simone Bell locks her bedroom and beats at the walls with her fists, a rage welling up from a strange place inside and the rage hardens and tightens and hardens until it can no longer be ignored.

The young Brigadier-General enters the widowed landowner's farmhouse much later that night with a machete and hacks him into pieces. He spends the night there, next to what is left of his master, his father. He leaves behind a castrated trunk and a decapitated torso, bloody nerves dangling over the gaping maw, and takes the severed head back to the Bell residence to present as a trophy of vengeance to Simone Bell.*

But the Bells are gone, gone, gone. The lights are off, the windows are closed, doors are locked. He knocks and knocks but the sound is hollow. He leaves the decapitated head on their doorstep, just in case.

He walks. The sun is high and blinding in the sky. His filthy shirt sticks to his sweaty back, so he takes it off. His shoes pinch his toes so he takes them off. His pants chafe at his thighs but he keeps his pants on. He walks for three days, sleeping by the roadside. He

---

*Yes, I know. The B-G is, like his father, a cheerful sociopath, and I am not. There is fury in his blood and failure in mine. It strikes me that the one person I know who can best instruct me on how to use my arsenal of violence is the one person I would perhaps like to use it on.

roasts field mice by a fire. He can flex the rage inside him like a muscle. He feels invincible and devastated at the same time. And then he sees it, like a mirage. An army outpost nestled in a forest. Soldiers in uniform march briskly. Officers in uniform bark orders. Guns glimmer in the honey sunlight. There is perfect symmetry to the way they look, a perfect sort of love in the way they fit inside the space the world has made for them. And he knows that he is home.

"I want to go shopping," Tanya says. She is sitting on the edge of the bed channel-surfing. Reading glasses and a copy of *The New Yorker* sit by her side. Her suntanned skin glistens. She plays with a scab on her knee. A thin spool of blood unwinds at the edges. On the TV, infomercials.

In all the media photographs the Brigadier-General always wears crisp forest green military fatigues with a black rope instead of a belt, and a black beret. The usual assortment of medals wink and glitter. His stomach is imposing and looks like a small TV screen under the fabric. Now, he has changed into a large green-and-yellow polo shirt and khaki cargo shorts. Flip-flops flop on his feet.

"People like me," he says, "are either in power and fighting to stay in power, or we are not in power and fighting to be in power." He looks at Tanya and there is something like fondness, or perhaps he is thinking of another conquest from the past or a conquest yet in planning. It is hard to tell. "We shall go to Walmart first, young man," he says. "And then I have signed us up for a guided tour of an authentic Amish settlement."

"He thinks I don't get enough culture," Tanya says. "But I took that course in college."

He uses a small comb to smooth over his forearm hair, trims ear and nose hair with his mustache trimmer. Every now and then his shoulders slump, but not for long.

When he speaks, as his voice rises, you have to picture a podium or a microphone, and, when it drops, in lieu of intimacy, you feel like the outer ring of the inner circle, where a word becomes a suggestion becomes a phone call becomes a career made or a life ruined. "Men like me, we are necessary because we unite those we recruit to keep us in power, and we unite those who have been recruited to put different versions of us in power. It is just like Woody Allen says, in a revolution oppressors become oppressed and vice versa." He looks at Tanya and smiles. "This may not seem like much, this room, for a man of my stature. My per diem, you see, only covers basic housing, but I have an expansive entertainment budget. This is because of loopholes, but that does not need to be written."

The Brigadier-General is no longer in demand on the lecture circuit. He is, according to the PR departments of our governments, both here and not here.

"He likes strip clubs," Tanya says. "And I'm the one who turned him on to Woody Allen. I'm also sort of his cultural adviser at the moment. He acts tough, but really he's a teddy bear with gray chest hair."*

When I look closer at her, I see that her tan is not really a tan, it's just skin.

"She has a graduate degree," he says. "This is the problem with this country."

She looks at the ceiling. "I was going to be a journalist," she says. "Go figure."

"I do not traffic with uneducated women," he says. "Women are the backbone of civilization and if they are not educated, what can we expect of the children? Plus, this way, men and women can work together and work is play and vice versa."

"You remind me of William Alexander Morgan," Tanya says. "I ever tell you that, sweetie?"

"He has a presidential name," he says.

"He was an American revolutionary who fought for Castro."

"What happened to him?"

"I left that *New Yorker* article out for you."

"I do not read narrative. I read summaries."

"Summary: Castro turned on him. Morgan died."

---

*Two days before my father died, he told me one third of a story. It was about a wicked ogre who has imprisoned a village in a dungeon that looks exactly like the real village, except that it's in a dungeon, and as time progresses, a lot of the mommies and daddies forget they're in a dungeon. The ogre wears a handsome mask to hide his ugly face. He takes the daddies hunting in a forest that is really just a smelly part of the dungeon, and the daddies are so happy to be hunting they don't mind the smell. He takes the mommies shopping in a bazaar that is really just a storage room in the dungeon, and the mommies are happy to be shopping, they don't mind the dust and dirt. They are so happy they forget to notice that they can never go hunting or shopping by themselves.

"You must think me very old," he says, "if I remind you of a dead, decaying man." And he leery-smiles and raises his eyebrows, to let her know he's joking. But there is yearning in his eyes.

"The point is, every time Batista or the media declared him dead, he wasn't. He kept coming back from a publicly proclaimed death. That's what I mean."*

"How did he die?"

"Firing squad."

The Brigadier-General snorts. "I do not much care for comedies," he says.

But when she isn't looking, he picks up *The New Yorker* and puts it in his briefcase.

In the car, he insists on driving. He has a learner's permit, because he hasn't had to drive himself in decades, always a bodyguard, always a chauffeur, always a military escort available. There is some gas-brake confusion, some hesitancy to travel any distance in reverse, but he has impeccable concentration and the courage of his convictions. We judder out of the parking lot. Negotiating traffic is like signing a peace treaty with a hand grenade strapped to your groin.

The cashier at Tommy's Jerky wears a black tank top and has impressive cleavage. Mascara streaks down her cheek in a manner that feels deliberate. She could be a carbon copy of the cashier at Sheetz, like in one of those sci-fi movies where the platinum blond clone looks like the cloned platinum blond girlfriend of the mad scientist, only with larger breasts.

"You look like you could be from P——,"† the Brigadier-General

---

*She means: (a) the time rebel troops shot down a helicopter carrying the B-G, only to later discover that they'd blown up the body double; (b) the time the only partially successful assassin, a former member of the B-G's cabinet and former family friend, shot him in the gut, only to somehow miss all essential organs; the media declared him dead, but after a month in the hospital while his doubles roamed the airwaves and declared states of emergency, the B-G made a full and, for some, unwelcome recovery; (c) the time he took a secret vacation to Bermuda and left his doubles in charge, one of whom was subsequently shot by a sniper during a public bazaar appearance; (d) all the other times you may or may not have read about.

†I've met the B-G once, some thirty-something years ago, back when we still lived in P——. I was maybe five or maybe seven, etc., and my father and I were invited to join the president and his wife in the presidential limousine on the way to some official state dinner, a steak and lobster deal in a country where steak and lobster deals were the province

says. "I have spread my seed with vigor, like Genghis Khan, although I regret to say I have not been a father to all my children. You could be one of them, although neither you nor I would know it. I had people in my loop who made sure I stayed out of that loop. How well did you know your father, son?"*

At Walmart, he is expansive, laughing with machine-gun gusto at everything Tanya says, even though she's trying to earnestly summarize the *New Yorker* article about William Alexander Morgan. He disdains public affection and so when Tanya makes as if to put her hand on his, he laughs and clamps a hand on my shoulder and steers us toward electronics while she browses bargain dresses. The cashiers gumming the checkout counters look like older versions of the cashiers at Tommy's Jerky and Sheetz, only happier. They have the genuinely fake smiles of air hostesses, safe and bored in the insulated cocoon of small-talk commerce.

"I have money," the Brigadier-General says. "Those rumors are true. So why the one-star motel for the five-star general? There are bugs in the bathroom, and not the kind with microphones. You stay in a cave long enough for a spider to spin a web across the mouth of the opening, like the Prophet, peace be upon him, or Robert the Bruce, that great Scot. You fly under the radar. Until it is time to strike."

TWELVE years after the murder, the Brigadier-General resurfaces under a different name. He is now a lieutenant in the army, rising swiftly through the ranks. He finds himself stationed in the mountains, commanding a far-flung battalion along the edge of the

---

of the rich and westernized, like us. The B-G was the bodyguard at the time, fresh off a year in the mountains. When the limo stopped at the country club, surrounded in the driveway by garland-bearing members of the what's-steak-and-lobster, we're-farm-to-table-because-we-live-on-the-farm crowd, I stepped, with my new heavy, shiny black shoes, on the brittle toes of the presidential wife. It was to be my last time in a limousine, but I remember, in the melee, the B-G pulling me aside and whispering, "Your reach will always make a mockery of your grasp."

*I feed him some typical bullshit about being orphaned via natural disaster, adopted, colonialized by a couple in Florida. The truth is that I remember my father well. He was a landowner too, but of the non-rapist variety, a gentleman farmer pressed into politics by circumstance, converted into reluctant and ultimately failed assassin by principle. He was, of course, the partially successful assassin. Am I here to avenge him? My instrument of destruction has been the pen, not the sword, which would have both delighted and shamed my father, who like most fathers of P——, would have wanted a son who was both him and not-him. But I have an arsenal handy, just in case I'm not exactly who I think I am. Does circumstance reveal character or create it?

cease-fire line in the outskirts of the strategic glacier area, eighteen thousand feet above sea level. The bordering country of I—— has been warring for decades with P—— over possession of the glaciers, their melting waters the source for the primary rivers and their tributaries veining through each country. Maps have been drawn and redrawn, and the British army, former colonists, displayed an impish sense of humor upon their retreat by playing fast and loose with cartography.

The area itself is precisely what you would expect from a glacier, inhospitable. Both sides of the border are boys from the deserts, the plains, the temperate cities and villages, etc. Some of them have never even imagined snow. Now it bites cheeks, clips earlobes, clamps exposed flesh, drives icicle stakes into their souls. This is the site of more military casualties than any identifiable skirmish for either side over the past twenty years. Death calls occasionally via avalanche or loneliness, but for the most part high-altitude pulmonary and/or cerebral edemas lead in swift turn to swelling, headaches, hallucinations, and dementia. Fluid bubbles and gurgles in the lungs. Oxygen-deprived blood vessels puncture in the brain.

The days blur into frostbite.

The battalion is really just eight men, their post three fiberglass igloos, one for the commander, two for the men, flanked by a machine gun bunker, a latrine, a makeshift mosque, and a tiny observation post on the ridge. Nonstop, two men shovel snow during the day, two men shovel snow at night. They sleep during the day because sunlight unpacks the giant blocks of snow stacked high on the slopes. Blizzards linger, winds hammer-howl, temperatures drop, drop, drop. Snow is a good-bye-forever kiss, a blanket, an ocean of sting and numb. Kerosene is heat and it melts snow, thaws guns. Smoke clots the igloos with a hazy film of soot and some of the men cough up dark grease or pink froth. Unlike the other side with its designer brand gear, their equipment is dubiously contracted knock-off sweatshop, the logos on their parkas a syllable off from the real deal, North Face turned North Farce. At night, they hear banshees in the wind, echoing off crests and crevasses.

They get their supplies by donkey trains. The animals have specially designed glacier goggles. When they stumble, they hurtle shrieking into space. Which is what happens when a supply train times its arrival to that of a minor avalanche caused by a despondent homesick private discharging his weapon into the sky. Half the battalion dies chasing the supply train off a sheer cliff in a moment of Pavlovian abandon, the other half is swept away by the swirling force of everything that is wind and snow and fear. Their bodies pitch down fifty feet right into a jutting serac below.

The Brigadier-General observes from the observation post with his high-altitude kit, which he carries with him at all times, because he is at a very high altitude. He slides down to camp and wades through a chest-high drift. He locates a shovel and shovels snow. When the sun sets he crawls into the latrine with a can of kerosene and sleeps. In the morning, he radios for help. Words fly out, words fly back. Help is two days away. He will be airlifted out. A team will be airlifted in to deal with the bodies, which will then be air-lifted out. In situations like this, casualties double or triple because men die to rescue dead men and have in turn to be rescued. The Brigadier-General knows this. He has four ice axes, six different types of rope, twenty-seven varieties of pitons, and a blowtorch. He descends, digs. Pain blurs into purpose. The bodies he can find are frozen. Faces are grimacing, grotesque, ecstatic. He cannot tell the difference. He understands that families must have bodies. But the bodies are frozen. He makes a snap call. He hacks. He empties his kit and refills it, climbs back to the camp, empties his kit, climbs back down, refills. He does this for days.

It takes them weeks to come. When they find him, they find him sobbing, huddled in the latrine. A kerosene stove shudders and flick-ers in the corner. A pot bubbles over with something dank and sul-furous. The smell is gas and death, sweet and rotten, like perfumed garbage. It's okay, they say. It's okay. It's all over now. He looks up at them. His face is gaunt and streaked black. The donkeys, he says. I forgot about the fucking donkeys.

But this is not the story they tell the newspapers. In that story, the hacked-up bodies are still hacked-up bodies, and the Brigadier-General survived on boiled snow and blind faith.

And in this manner legends are born.

CHEATERS is one of two bungalow-style more-strip-shack-than-strip-club strip clubs on this block, and in not-so-heated competi-tion with the competition, the more provocatively named Climaxx across the street. Both establishments seem to have found their niche; it's Sunday, and a home game for the home team, seven seasons removed from a winning season. There is a festive tailgate-type atmosphere in the Climaxx parking lot, with a steady trickle of high-fiving optimistic brown football jerseys, Climaxx being the place with a chipped neon sign proclaiming, *Home Is Where The Happy Ending Is, Sports Fans, Welcome Home!* Cheaters, on the other hand, caters to the fans who expect to lose; they're sporting high school and college sweatshirts and looking at the tie game on the solitary definitely-not-high-definition screen behind the bar with the grim determination of those who know their history and have determined that the present moment is not to be trusted.

Meanwhile dancers dance on the stage under moderately bright stage lights. They look like the cloned cashiers at Tommy's Jerky and Sheetz and Walmart, only younger and with disproportionate breasts. Everyone here is white, except for us and about half the dancers. The thing about this city is, we are in the suburbs, and in the suburbs, everyone who's buying is white.

We're sitting in a musty booth in the back, turning down the occasional lap dance. The women here seem to know the Brigadier-General and a couple of them mock salute. The men at the bar and at the scattered chairs in front of the stage vacillate between TV and stage with the zombie frequency of those who don't question the source of their erections.

The Brigadier-General drinks middlebrow scotch that is expensive and looks watered down. Tanya's got the special from the kitchen, something like mac and cheese, which can be found on menus everywhere in this city, often double-digit priced and gourmeted up with black truffles, etc. This cheaper, sort-of-classic version appears to be thumping with bacon. She shakes a lick of salt into her beer and drinks it through a straw.

"You might be wondering, son," he says. "About all this."*

---

*But I'm remembering instead that the day before my father died, he told me the second third of the story. The wicked ogre has a best friend, a handsome prince who lives happily with a beautiful princess. Sometimes, to prove they are all best friends, the ogre takes the handsome prince hunting, just the two of them, and the beautiful princess shopping, just the two of them. The prince and princess cannot believe their good fortune. But then one day the ogre is in such a good mood that his mask slips and the prince sees his real face. And it is ugly. And then suddenly the handsome prince remembers his old village with its real air and real water and real forests. So he resolves to slay the beast for the good of his family, his village, his world. The next time they go hunting, the handsome prince hunts

I'm sitting across the booth from the two of them, and suddenly Tanya's foot is snaking up the mouth of my jeans. I look at her and she shrugs.*

"And you must be wondering about the things I have said to you," he continues. "And about why I'm granting this interview of immeasurable circumstantial strangeness to a publication as inconsequential as the one you work for and to a writer as inconsequential as you."

There are strobe lights on the stage now. A willowy cashier-type brunette in a glitter-dusted purple wig sashays to something most people think is sashay-able. Dancers sit off to the side and flip through dog-eared paperbacks and textbooks. The home team collapses down the stretch, blowing a ten-point lead by refusing to throw the ball in the fourth quarter. The game limps into overtime.

Picture the rhythm: Tanya shrugging. Foot snaking. Brigadier-General talking.

"I mean no insult," he says. "I have always been a blunt, plain-spoken instrument. And now I would like to speak off the record[†] for the next three minutes."

He finishes his scotch, and the cocktail waitress brings him another. A copy of something by Naomi Wolf juts out of her back pocket.

Tanya notices the book. She laughs. "In this economy a girl does what they pay a girl to do," she says. "Half the girls in here can't read, and the other half are working on their dissertations."

The Brigadier-General finishes his drink in a gulp, and orders a light beer. "I have become obsolete," he says. "Once I was a roaring lion and now I am a howling monkey. Once, my reach was my grasp, and now my reach has made a mockery of my grasp. But this

---

for ogre blood. Not that hunting for blood is good, mind you, but when it's for the greater good of the family and the village and the world, it's all good.

*As part of my resolve to go full new-leaf, I excuse myself briefly, duck into the parking lot and call the wife/ex-wife/who-the-fuck-knows. "You said, Shout," I say, and I half-shout. "This is a bad time," she says. I stick a nicotine patch, the third one, on my stomach. And what I'm thinking is, what am I capable of?

†I pretend to turn the tape recorder off. It occurs to me that if I do what I would like to do, I am also keeping a record of a crime, but there is something to be said for keeping all options, all possibilities open. I've been taking yoga classes over the past month, and have found value in the moment of being.

old lion will not lie down and die howling like a monkey. Instead, this lion will become a monkey and then the monkey will become a rhinoceros and then the rhinoceros will become a leopard and then the leopard will become a lion." He thumps the table, but not hard enough to turn heads. Soft rock plays loud on the stereo system. Veins on his forehead quiver, dandruff drizzles onto his shoulders. "They have abandoned me," he says. "Like they abandoned my friends. All the old lions, we have been put into the zoo. We can come out only if we promise to be monkeys, because monkeys, everyone loves monkeys, monkeys are the people. So here I am before you now, a monkey in the Econo Lodge, a monkey in the Walmart, a monkey in the strip club, a monkey for the people." He pauses, receives his light beer with a strained smile, continues. "No one I know reads the journals you write for. But no one I know will take my calls either. So now I need you people.* You like Castro, so why not me? What do you want? I'll want what you want. I'll turn the country on its head. I'll privatize everything, educate everyone. Tax the rich, pay the poor. Build hospitals and roads and libraries. Sign a peace treaty. De-weaponize the bombs. Free the press. Have open elections. Stop executing my enemies, put them in prison instead, but feed them well in cafeteria-style settings, and give them free cigarettes. If you give me money, I will give you a kinder, gentler revolution.† And you, my boy, you shall be the official chronicler of my ascent."‡

"Not to spoil this party," Tanya says. "But I don't need a degree to tell you there are flaws in this plan."

"You shall be taken care of," he says. "Flaws and all."

She looks at his beer, sweating untouched. "Sweetie," she says. "If you don't want to drink from the bottle, ask them to bring you a glass. It's okay. Some people drink beer from a glass."

The home team declines a field goal from the five-yard line on third down and calls a play up the middle with the fullback. They fumble the snap, and the visitors run it back for good.

---

*Assumption: Liberals.
†Note to Possible Liberal Revolution Financiers Who May Be Reading: No. I mean, No!
‡Is this dementia, desperation, or Machiavellian mischief? It occurs to me that the course of the world is perhaps set in motion by idiocy so convoluted it is rendered complex.

The Brigadier-General puts his hands on mine and clenches until we've made a fist.

"Just, please, whatever you do, please show them that I'm human," he says.

HIS rise after the incident at the glacier is meteoric and publicly documented. He is now the Man Who Could Not Die. The president takes notice. Promotions ensue. Photo opportunities: the Brigadier-General wears a safari suit, medals glistening on lapels, takes batting practice with the national cricket team, displays sound technique. Accompanies visiting American movie star on a humanitarian mission to a manufactured refugee camp;* she dresses modestly, ties a scarf to her hair, while he rocks the fall military line, no accessory spared. Teaches a mock† religious education class in a strategically local public school, resplendent in the starched white robes favored in the local bazaars.

The president installs him as the right-hand man, secretly hands him the reins to the secret police force, which is really more like a whimsical assassination bureau. Clears out a wing in the presidential mansion. Takes to calling him at night when he needs a wingman, drinking buddy, sounding board, therapist, captive audience for his knock-knock jokes, etc. Makes the fatal drunken mistake of informing him of tentative plans to drastically cut the military budget in order to fund educational and cultural initiatives, since his two sons have unfortunately taken an interest in higher education and literature instead of military history or military governance, and while such interest is regrettable since it is not manly, their being his sons trumps their being men.

The Brigadier-General approves of education and culture, but he is learning the ropes of this world, and they are no less treacherous than the ropes he used to descend into that icy crevasse to hack up the bodies of his dead friends, and he understands that if you are

---

*Real refugees live in real refugee camps. Photo opportunities with celebrities call for movie sets. Army privates, starved for weeks and stuck in the stockade, are conscripted to act like refugees and thereafter either assassinated or promoted, depending on the things that these sorts of things usually depend on.

†These are real children, but they've been handpicked from families of the local landlords, and from the local private schools that these sorts of families usually send their children to.

not in education or culture then you do not benefit from education and culture. He knows that those-with-will have the capacity to convince those-who-follow-will that what is good for those-with-will is first and foremost good for those-who-follow-will. And your will is nothing if not that which sustains you, feeds you, clothes you, keeps your finger twitching on the switchblade of success. He's gone all in with the military. So he calls military friends in other militaries of countries whose factories supply heavy ordinance to the military of P——. He calls military friends in his own military. Everyone calls military friends. Pretty soon, they're all thinking coup. And the Brigadier-General, fond as he is of the old president and his knock-knock jokes, knows that if a coup is to last, you need old blood in new headlines. He installs an estranged distant presidential cousin as the face-man of the revolution, quietly anoints himself chief of everything military.

The old president is hanged in a public square for crimes against humanity. Half of his secret police force is hanged with him, the other half, the ones who pretend never to have worked for the Brigadier-General, become officers in the new secret police force. Half of the old cabinet is exiled, the other half either assume positions of prominence in the necessary opposition* to the new government or denounce the old government and resume lives of renewed prominence in the new government.

A few years later, another coup. And then it is the for-real time of the Brigadier-General.

The rest, as they say, is Wikipedia-friendly.

THE parking lot is empty. The strip mall is abandoned. The streets are deserted. Discarded flyers skitter across potholes. It looks like a video game simulation of a war zone, nothing visible, everything lurking. Across the street, a boarded-up tenement building has a chalked-up sign on the front door that goes, *Beware, Dog.* Broken glass dots the sidewalks. This is the heart of the city at dusk, which spreads purple across the sky. It takes an hour to drive here from where we were. There are livelier spots a few blocks over and downtown, with its revitalized restaurants and nightclubs and

---

*If there is no opposition to the government, how do you know that the government is necessary?

fashionably disheveled hipsters, is a mile or so west, and there's also the possible guided tour of an authentic Amish settlement that we were supposedly signed up for way out in the heart of something very different, but here we are. The Brigadier-General has a point to make.

"This is a metaphor," he says. He's sporting a badly fitted sport coat, something off the rack from someplace with not too many racks, standing in the middle of the lot, next to the car, a plastic glass filled with middlebrow scotch swishing in his hand.

Tanya sighs. "When you promised me the world, sweetie," she says, "I thought you meant, you know, the world."

He puts his hand on her shoulder and they back up to the trunk.* The world is so still and so empty it feels like we're in a city someone built and then forgot about. The wind picks up. Something that looks like tumbleweed skitters across the asphalt, but it's not tumbleweed, it's something else.

Tanya says, "Don't you think this has gone on long enough? Why don't you just tell him?"

And the Brigadier-General says, "Where are your weapons, son?"

Tanya says, "He has the sweetest, most pitiful plan." She looks at me. "Don't leave your keys in the ignition, honey. And don't leave your harmless oddball collection of wannabe weapons out in plain sight." She has the key, she pops the trunk, and the arsenal is summarily laid out in the open, where it doesn't look so much like an arsenal. It looks like a child planning a war.

The Brigadier-General says, "I know who you are."

The Brigadier-General says, "Why do you think your father tried to kill me? He was a gentleman farmer, not an assassin. When do gentlemen farmers kill?"

The Brigadier-General says, "The man who raised you was my friend. Your mother and I were better friends, for a while, although she may have disagreed. But she could keep a secret. Until, of course, the moment she could not. And that moment in the limousine, when you stepped on that ugly woman's foot with your nice new shoes, that was when I knew. You wanted to get out of that door first, just like I did, and you would not let that crone of a president's wife get

---

*At this point, I shiver. I'm resigned to writing the article, to turning my barbaric yawp into a barbaric yawn. Arsenals are for the sort of men who dream about arsenals.

in your way. And I think that was when the man who raised you knew as well. Do you understand now, why then, why now, why you, why us, why this?"

The Brigadier-General says, "If you accept the hypothesis that good and bad do not exist in a vacuum, you also accept that what is good for you is bad for someone else. So it was with me and the man you call your father. So it will be with us and them."

The Brigadier-General says something low and soft and garbled and it is almost like that famous moment in that famous movie.

I'm thinking that what I remember most about my father is that the day before he died, he came back from the fields, smelling like always of clay and cologne. He sat me on his lap, smoothed my hair, and finished the story. I'd waited for this moment, because this was our story, and it was perfect. He said, "The handsome prince kills the wicked ogre. End of story. But before that, the handsome prince is scared. He has a good life with the beautiful princess, and they have a beautiful little prince son, who I have not told you about until now. If the handsome prince cannot kill the wicked ogre, then what is to become of his family? And even if the handsome prince can kill the wicked ogre, what still is to become of his family? They only know the dungeon village. How will they make their way in the world outside the dungeon if all they know is the language of the dungeon? What if they had it better when they were blind? But what choice did he have? What I mean to say, my darling son, is that sometimes you have to make a choice you may not be ready to make, but you are a handsome prince and the handsome prince is expected to kill the wicked ogre."

I thought he was full of shit. He'd gone and ruined a perfectly good story.

Then he said, "Do not try to understand me, son. Just try to love me the way that you remembered me when you loved me."

I should have thought, yes, yes, yes. I should have thought, forever and ever. Instead, I thought, an unhappy handsome prince? Who wants that? And I thought, asshole.

Now the Brigadier-General, arms outstretched, says, "Who's your daddy?"

A slight breeze builds and whispers past me like a blade. And I can feel it then, the thing I am now capable of, welling up inside of me like a cold clay fist and hardening and tightening and hardening until pretty soon I can flex it like a muscle and it will not be ig-nored.

And I open my mouth and what comes out is, Yes, Yes, Yes.

I started with an image of a third-rate journalist in a third-rate motel room with a former first-rate dicta-tor. I discovered the story as I wrote, and I wanted to write something that was both political and personal, to juxtapose the myth of the father along with the myth of the king. I thought of Oedipus and I thought of Icarus, and then both stories became, for me, stories about failure. And this weird hybrid of a story emerged.

—IR

Orpheus and Eurydice

———— ✻ ————

DARK RESORT
Heidi Julavits

Let's assume there's a man on a beach because there is. Let's assume he is a husband because he's wearing a wedding ring. Let's assume he's just been married because he fiddles with this ring perpetually, and as he's on a beach, let's assume he's made the terrible mistake of going on a honeymoon. This honeymoon *will* prove to be a terrible mistake, though of course the husband doesn't know it yet. How could he? At the moment he probably associates honeymoons with happiness, because that's what we'd think in his situation. We can safely, within an acceptable margin of error, deduce his thoughts and feelings based on what we might think and feel if we were him. Guessing is the best we can manage, given the vow that we've taken.

But let's not bemoan our chaste circumstances. Has anyone read *Strategies of Containment* by John Lewis Gaddis? If not, no matter. It has nothing to do with our enterprise—it being a critical appraisal of postwar American national security policy, and also very boring—but the title suggests how we might more positively approach *our* situation vis-à-vis the husband. Just because limitations exist doesn't mean abundant satisfactions can't be gleaned from our enterprise. Consider what they say about blind people, how the lack of one sense strengthens the remaining four. Is this even true? We could do a quick Internet search to find out. Or not. Or we could wonder about it productively in the quiet of our own heads. Or not. The vow we've taken isn't so terrible, see? If we choose, we can know for certain certain things.

So the husband. He is sitting on a beach that appears to belong to a resort. There's a boarded-up palapa hut and a disintegrating stucco wall where the sand meets the palms. Now the husband is joined by a woman in a bikini and a wedding ring and a tiny towel around her hips. Let's assume she is the wife. The sky is gray. The sky is gray because the husband and the wife chose, for financial reasons, to visit this resort during the rainy months (see again the boarded-up hut, probably a beachside bar during the tourist season) when the prices were slashed. It's a decent guess, one also supported by the condition of the wife's bikini—the bottom's elastic has started to sag, the top's clasp is broken, the straps are tied like a halter around her neck— and also the generic bottle of sunscreen they don't need and the small towel the wife has stolen from a resort evidently so inexpensive and unstarred that it provides only small towels. And let's not forget the wedding rings. These are thin and shiny, the sort purchased by people without money or heirloomed relatives, probably through a wholesaler recently relocated from a perishing mall to the Internet. See? Look at how much we can know without being told!

The wife spreads her towel near the husband and sits on it. The ocean crashes in the background; the noise makes it difficult to hear what the husband and the wife are saying, but it appears, from the way she pushes her face into his neck, that despite the inclement weather they are happy. If we were permitted music, this music would be soaring and hopeful and perversely suggestive, in its aggressive optimism, of upcoming strife and hardship; if people begin happy, they cannot remain happy, otherwise who would care about these people? We wouldn't. Except that maybe this happy couple reminds us of being in love ourselves. We might recall how a little precipitation couldn't soak our ardor. We might recall musing how the overcast sky made the day seem *more* romantic than might a cloudless one. Sometimes bad weather is the perfect kind of weather. Maybe the husband and the wife think the bad weather is ideal, or neutral, or maybe just irrelevant to their happiness, happiness which would be blown out of all realistic proportion by the accompanying music (were we allowed music). They are not caring about the weather, is the point, and this is their second mistake. The first mistake was to go on a honeymoon during the rainy season. Or maybe their first mistake was to have been married, or to have fallen in love, or to have left their childhood homes for culturally grander milieus (assuming they did), or to have been born at all.

Regardless, the husband and the wife are unaware of their mistakes. We enjoy, in a vaguely sadistic way, their innocence. Life to them is still a series of lucky intersections. The husband and the wife might fear, really truly fear, that had she not been at that bar or in that grocery queue (for example), or had he not lost his cell phone and needed to make that call, they never would have met. We've all felt thankful for, and also bitter toward, those chance confluences that render our lives saved or ruined. We can imagine that the husband and wife have thankfully reflected on the chance confluence, whatever it was, that brought them to this beach.

Given the calm joyfulness of this scene, we can also understand why—despite gloomy weather that might, under artificial circumstances, be "meaningful" or "symbolic," but under these circumstances is simply the actual weather on that day—they're insensitive to danger. We might even ask ourselves: Is it cheap that we know a tragedy awaits them when they do not? Given the vow we've taken—i.e., now that we're aware of the trickery to which we've regularly fallen prey—isn't their bad end, dangled at us from the outset, the crassest kind of manipulation? Maybe. Probably. But we might also ask ourselves: Would we have remotely given a shit about this couple if we hadn't been forewarned of the terribleness looming on their horizon?

We know the answer. This we *can* confidently know.

So while a hook, if you will, is allowed per our vow, no actual physical hooks are allowed on the beach, neither are fishing lines or ropes or lifesaving buoys or small and slightly leaky skiffs, because none of these items were on the beach at the time. It was the rainy season, remember; the resort staff had probably wisely scoured the beach of possessions that might be swept to sea during a storm, including umbrellas and chaise longues and waiters. The point is: It's not a random act of cruelty that deprives the husband and the wife of useful rescue tools. It is the cruel reality of their situation.

Another cruel reality of their situation is the temperature. It seems obvious, from the wife's shivering, that the temperature is dropping. The husband notices this. He gives her his shirt—an unattractive plaid probably purchased for the sole reason that it was on sale, in fact his plasticky swim trunks, too, appear to have been selected not because they were loved but because they were affordable—but still she shivers. He kisses her and stands. Then he walks down the beach, collecting wet twigs and wet smallish branches, presumably to build a fire. His naïveté about fire-starting suggests he is not the sort to regularly build fires, or to have any outdoors experience whatsoever, further suggesting that he probably lives and has always lived in a city, and has an office job or possibly an academic appointment. His hair is a touch long and his sense of style nonexistent, also we've established that he isn't rich, so probably he is an academic. He's spent his life in libraries, maybe he's even read *Strategies of Containment*, maybe he's a political science professor. Maybe he's struggled over some of the thicker-going chapters such as "Implementing Flexible Response" and "Implementing Détente." Maybe when he and the wife, then the fiancée, argued and made up, he would say to her, while thumbing her breasts through her blouse, "it's time to *implement détente*."

As the husband gathers damp, unignitable sticks, the wife walks to the water. She's still wearing the husband's shirt; obviously she isn't planning to swim. Probably she wants to check how cold it is, because sometimes when the air is chilly, the water, by contrast, can feel pleasantly warm. In fact sometimes the *most* pleasant swimming happens when the air is cold, and possibly the wife knows this, which suggests she is not, at least by birth, a city person. She probably grew up by a lake or a sea, and is teased by her husband for her hardiness and her stoicism, which he possibly suspects to be more of an act than who she *really* is. Maybe she likes to accentuate her toughness to call greater attention to his city-born effeteness, and she does this lovingly, at least for now, but if they had a future together, which they don't, no doubt his effeteness would start to irritate her, as would her theatrical stoicism irritate him. We know, because we've been there ourselves, how a loved one's adorable flaws become drastically less adorable over time. We might even think, "better they never had to experience the depressing inversion of their formerly boundless fondness for one another's imperfections." Since we feel bad and even a little guilty toward this couple, we can't help but wish for them a tiny upside to their soon-to-turn-tragic lives.

The wife, when she reaches the water, walks in to her ankles, then her knees. For a second it appears she really is considering a swim. Why not? She's billed herself as a hardy sort, probably. Sometimes we do things we don't want to do because the person we purport to be is supposed to want to do them. So while the wife doesn't want to swim, it possibly strikes her that when they return home, and report to their friends the crappy weather they endured, it would please the husband to fake-sardonically report, "Of course *she* went swimming."

But then a wave nearly knocks her over. She backs out of the ocean, clearly understanding that this water is nothing to fool with, no matter how tough she might pretend to be or be. The waves are erratic, they are the worst kind of waves, everyone who is not an idiot knows this. The wife is no idiot. She stands now at a safe distance and stares at the ocean. Worry tightens her face. Maybe she's intuiting that life won't always be as blithe as it is now; rough times await, maybe even the second she and the husband return home, when they'll have to face the debt they've accumulated. Now that the wedding's over, she's possibly wondering if it was worth splurging on the extra round of canapés and the auteur photographer. Maybe, too, she's recalling her childhood spent on some dismal coast, and the many times as a girl she stared out to sea and felt the oppressiveness of her surroundings and her life, and experienced a homesickness that made no sense whatsoever, because technically she *was* home. Maybe this is why she married the husband, because when with him she doesn't trend toward her natural gloominess. She needs him near her always. Even when he's a mere hundred yards away, as he is at this moment, clumsily finessing his pyramid of wet kindling, she feels endangered.

She starts back toward the husband. Fumbling with his pyre, he resembles a kid playing pick-up sticks. Anyone seeing him would make this connection and probably so does she. Her eyes crinkle at the edges, which suggests she views his incompetence fondly. Maybe, too, she is imagining the children they will someday possibly have together, and how probably her husband will be such a good father. Despite his age of roughly probably between twenty-eight and thirty-four, he retains a blithe boyishness.

What she likely neither envisions nor intuits, because few in her situation possibly could, is that within three minutes she will be dead.

(Maybe some of us are disappointed to learn that the wife will die, because her death was the most obvious and hackneyed interpretation of the "terrible mistake" made when this couple decided to go on a honeymoon, or to get married, or to be born. Where's the twist, a few of us might be wondering? These days, we are accustomed to more cleverness. But as the vow stipulates, there can only be a twist when there is a twist; as it happened, the wife is the one who died, and there is regrettably no way around this.)

There really is no way around it at all, as the husband will probably tell the local officials when they eventually interrogate him. *It just happened.* What happens is this. The husband has just caught sight of the approaching wife when an aberrant wave rises up behind her, curling over her head like a giant cobra. The wave—surprisingly, given its size—strikes at blink speed. It grabs the wife by the ankle and drags her into the surf. She disappears under the froth. She plain disappears.

Frantically the husband scans the beach, probably for a boat or a person, anything to help rescue her. There is, as we know, nothing of use. It would be charitable at this juncture to put a kayak under a tree or an intrepid surfer, but as there was no kayak and no surfer, there can be no kayak and no surfer. There was nothing and there can be nothing. The husband is, in every sense of the word, alone.

Which is a shame. Because the husband is not, or so we might conclude from his failure to rush into the water, a very strong swimmer. Some others of us might conclude—this would be premature, and also pretty cynical—that the husband is a coward. Whether because the husband is a coward or because he cannot swim, the husband runs in the opposite direction of the water. He runs toward the darkened entrance to the resort, dark because of the giant palm fronds that shade what are probably, if we could see them, stucco steps, eroded by the higher tides, a sign that this beach is not safe, that waves frequently strike at people and things beyond their natural border. Inside the resort, common sense might dictate, there will be a person who can help, possibly a lifeguard who works as a busboy in the resort's restaurant during the off-season. Perhaps I'll find this lifeguard, the husband might be thinking. No, probably, definitely! There *will* be a person who can help!

And possibly there might have been. But as the husband is about to enter the palm darkness, he pauses. He turns to look back at the ocean. To say good-bye, maybe, because a part of him senses that he'll never see his wife again, not alive he won't, and this is as physically close to one another as they'll ever be before one of them is dead.

Who knows why he does what he does. We don't. It's possible the husband has no idea either. This is no fault of ours. Better access, if we had it, wouldn't make the husband know himself any better.

But remarkably, when the husband scans the jagged surface, the wife pokes up just beyond the surf.

She waves.

His face explodes into a crazy mask of relief. He wags his head. Does he think she's laughing at him and his worrying? She is tough, after all, he might be reminding himself. She is tough and he overreacts to nature—they've fought about this in the past, no doubt. Possibly while hiking, and he wanted to turn back when they lost the path, and she wanted to bushwhack to the summit, they argued. Maybe he's thinking how they will chuckle about this new misadventure very soon. What an idiot she was! They'll both agree the fault was hers, even though it clearly wasn't. She'd been a victim of a rogue wave. To acknowledge that chance had nearly killed her probably would be scarier than admitting she'd been stupid. And so they might laugh and concur—she'd been stupid, so lovably stupid.

The husband runs toward the wife, spinning his arms, yelling at her. Again, it's impossible to discern his words over the surf. The ocean really is pounding now; the wind and the rain have intensified. She is not doing well out there, despite her presumed experience with oceans or lakes. If the husband believes the wife is fine, and is waiting for the perfect wave on which to bodysurf back to shore, well, it's hard to imagine how he's reached this conclusion. Absolutely nothing supports it.

The husband stands at the ocean's edge, lamely beckoning the wife to shore. She tries to wave back, quite obviously struggling now. The truth of the situation registers on the husband's face. The wife is dying, she is about to be dead. Again the husband fails to enter the ocean. Maybe he cannot swim, as some of us have posited, or maybe he really is a coward. Or maybe when we call him a coward what we mean to call him—but we don't, given what it might expose about us—is *smart*. No one, not even a decent swimmer, who goes into that water will come out. He will die saving her.

He smartly decides not to die.

Or possibly he just can't swim.

We'll never know.

We can only wonder what's going on in his head after he decides not to enter the water. Maybe he's thinking that he might have saved the wife had he not turned around. If he'd trusted his initial instinct, and run to the resort, he might have found a lifeguard by now, she might have been saved. As it is, however, the water has already dragged her under. She is already gone.

Though the future is none of our business, we can pretty accurately guess that his won't be bright. He'll probably return home and, if he's *really* smart, pay someone to pack up the apartment, and put the boxes in storage, and move to a new place with rental furniture. This is what we'd do under the circumstances. He'll refuse to date for months and maybe years and maybe, if he's the romantic sort, for the rest of his life. Maybe he'll wish to honor the wife—or acknowledge his shameful husbandly failure—by refusing to replace her. A noble act, a truly noble and self-punishing one, but one that might, in the end, make us pity the husband less. Aren't angels rebukes to the rest of us? Because we would march right out, after an appropriate mourning period of course, and fall in love again. We would want, selfishly, to forget about our dead spouse. Memories like the ones the husband is probably forming on this beach cannot be endured over time unless a person is strong, unless a person is strong like the husband might be.

But if he's so strong, why didn't he save the wife? Why didn't he run to the resort for help? That requires real strength—the strength to leave your drowning wife behind. To admit that you need assistance, and fucking just leave her there. Though it's unlikely that the husband was in an emotional position to make metaphors when the wife was first grabbed by the wave, he might, when he remembers the scene, visualize the wave as a giant snake, just as we did. Over years of remembering the wave it will develop a mouth and fangs and eyes, it may even begin to speak to him, calling his name, taunting him, calling him a coward, a total fucking wuss who deserves the pathetic life he now probably has.

Notice how we are starting to lose pity for the husband. Notice how we are starting to blame him for his own misfortune. Maybe the husband, generic as he is, strikes a personal chord with us. Maybe our relationship to the husband mimics a former relationship we had with a person who kept a part of him- or herself a secret, or whose martyrdom threatened us. Maybe, as the relationship disintegrated, we found ourselves blaming the unknowable noble person and convincing ourselves that they deserved to be left, even though our leaving rendered us, in the eyes of some, emotional monsters. This person we left was so good, such a good and pure person! We are clearly narcissists (said our mothers and friends), unable to honor their enigmatic specialness! But a person who remains unknowable can come to seem, over time, a ravenous void. If we're perpetually guessing what this person feels and what they think, in time they are no longer a distinct person but an outpost of ourselves. Pretty soon we're no longer in our own bodies, we're in someone else's body, we've breathed life into a dead person and killed ourselves in the process.

Which is maybe why we feel a little dead right now.

It has been ten minutes now since the wife disappeared. Still the husband does not run to the resort. Instead he sits on the small towel and holds his knees to his forehead and shakes, maybe from the cold, maybe from shock. Shouldn't he want to report the accident? Shouldn't he want to find the wife's body before it's swept out to sea? Why can't he do as we would do? It's incredibly frustrating. It makes us want to leave this place.

And we can. As we abandon the husband on the beach, we have no idea what he's feeling or what he's thinking. Who knows if he was even married to that wife. Maybe he met her last night. Maybe they are married to other people, people who are back home taking care of small children while their spouses cheat on them in the tropics. There's so much we can't know, and in the end, what does it matter? We're either sad or we aren't. We're either implicated or we're not. We're either rubberneckers or we're not. We're either cowards ourselves, or cheaters, or monsters, or we're not. We've either learned something new about ourselves or we haven't. Regarding this person who sits on his towel and weeps into his knees and who is not us, we can be certain of only one thing: a man knows a woman is dead. Beyond his knowledge of this fact, we can assume very little about him.

I decided to write a story with an additional constraint; yes, my story had to be inspired by a myth (Orpheus, in my case). But I also decided to write a story that obeyed the rules listed in the Dogme filmmaking manifesto. How would the Dogme prohibitions against artificial lighting and music, for example, translate to writing? I wanted to find out.

—*HJ*

Paradise

MYSTERY SPOT: 95065

Karen Tei Yamashita

This is someone's paradise, but it's not mine.
—Ronaldo Lopes de Oliveira

Santa Cruz is someone's paradise. Funny thing for a Brazilian to say. Don't those handsome naked bronzed people from the Southern Hemisphere live in Paradise? What about *their* paradise? And what about the Surfer Dude and the Lighthouse, beacons guarding our looking-glass world, long ago left to us by the Hawaiian Duke Kahanamoku. Our looking-glass paradise. Paradise Lost. Paradise Regained. Paradise Central, California. Throne of the most regal female khalifah, Calafia.

In the sixteenth-century Spanish novel, Queen Calafia of the mythical island California fights with her virgin army of black Amazons, their golden weapons and terrible griffins, to regain Constantinople for the Moros, only to be defeated and converted to Christianity. And to marriage. This mythic history was lovingly remembered in the documentary *Golden Dreams,* featured until a few years ago at Anaheim's Disney California Adventure Park, with Whoopi

Goldberg narrating as Queen "Califia" with her mythical griffin, the great extinct grizzly, at her side. In twenty-five minutes, you got the Chumash, the Spanish missions, Japanese picture brides, the Mulholland water scandal, freeways, and Steve Jobs. Whoopi California. This is someone's paradise. And now where are the Amazons?

> Children. *Neofítos. Bestes.* And still it is the same sky, the same night arches like a reed house, the stars of their birth.
> —Louis Owens, *Bone Game*

A birthing ground. A burial ground. Sacred or haunted? Profaned. What happens when you plant a Holy Cross on an ancient Indian burial ground? Layers upon layers of slaughter. Indian author Louis Owens wrote about the curse of mixing blood, churning the earth with dismemberment that produced an appropriated New Age, a new white ecology with its literal pundits and new savage practitioners. New blood to appease an old age. Some hippie dude migrating in from the Summer of Love couldn't get laid for the next decade. It's not that weed slows things down; could be it just makes everything stop. Stop in the name of Love. The next decade after the Summer of Love contained a cycle of murders and dismemberment. Serial murders, meaning this murder is like that murder is like that last murder. Three men killed a family of four and twenty-one women in three years. Seven of the murdered were Asian Americans. A serial poem to death. And before that, Alfred Hitchcock got wind of a newspaper report about thousands of crazed seabirds, sooty shearwaters, that crashed into homes, broke windows, pecked residents, regurgitating anchovies before flopping dead onto the streets. Thousands of stinking dead dark birds were shoveled into trucks the next morning. Talk about ecology for a new age. To continue, Hitchcock put a psychopath in one of the Victorians on Beach Hill. This is how the dark cloud of noir blackened the sunlit California seacoast. But some hippie dude who couldn't get laid said it was an old Indian curse.

> Yet here's a spot . . . Out, damn'd spot! Out I say!
> —Lady Macbeth

Cruz marks the spot, the oracular crossroad, sanctified in these parts because at the cruz, Oedipus fulfilled his destiny, to kill the patriarchy. Whatever happens later (incest) happens somewhere else, but at the sainted Cruz under the shadow of the fog that slips in and out with the moon tides across the mountains, that's the legacy we get left. Cruzians become fatherless Munchkins. *Ding-dong!* they sing, and they query: *Are you a friend of Dorothy's?*

It's Mother's Day, and the grande mother of everyone is Asako, who's made it to ninety. We celebrate at the hillside Chaminade's festive all-you-can-eat brunch at a long table of maybe twenty. The only guy there is our neighbor, the historian, David, but Asako, who's seated at the head of this table, still asks about the twenty guests, *Now, who are all these men?* She's ninety, so she gets to be confused. It's the weekend of the Feminist Studies Conference. How to tell Asako her Mother's Day has been hijacked by the Dyke Ladies Society. *Oh,* she says, but then, quick recovery, *I wasn't born yesterday, you know.* The Chaminade proceeds to take a hit since our table eats out everyone, prime rib to made-to-order omelets, three to one. And how many gallons of mimosas we talkin'?

Overlooking Chaminade's valley with the sweep of May sunshine, feminist scholar Anjali remembers that the Mystery Spot is somewhere nearby. It's the tourist attraction featured on bumper stickers. *You'd better not take Asako there,* Anjali says. *It's not advisable for older people and anyone with a heart condition.*

What are you talking about? For godsake. It's an optical illusion.

No, seriously. I looked it up on the Internet. It's one of eight magnetic spots on Earth. Anjali must be one of the smartest intellectuals we know. Scientific and geographical Internet research reveals this is apparently about a 150-foot-in-diameter time-space antigravity vortex. Or it could be UFO activity. Go figure. *Le Cigare Volant.*

At the Feminist Studies Conference, someone might have given a talk on female ejaculation. There's even a documentary film that goes with it. When you learn about this, you're sitting between two South Asian sisters, Pratima and Prarthana. They might be twins, but their names are differentiated, they tell you, by an *M* and an

N. *Oh yes,* they agree. *When we were growing up, we identified as Caucasian.* Asians from the Caucasus. *But then we came to Philadelphia, and there was all that dotbuster shit.* Now, this Indian lore jams into Cruz.

Spots and dots. Magnetism and ejaculation. Titter titter.

But back to ding-dong. Every night for seven nights at about 3 A.M., some car out there goes berserk with honking. At first, it's just a beep-beep, so you turn over and think, *Get out and catch your damn ride.* But then it goes off like a car alarm, and you snarl into your pillow, *Steal it. Steal the fuckin' thing.* This goes on nightly with a pattern. Serial car orgasms. You check the clock; it's 3 A.M., plus the heating system always goes on. Even the house knows it's too cold to get out of bed to be a witness. The next nights you dream about dead bodies fallen or invasive vermin pouncing on the wheel. Maybe it's the neighbor's cat that's jumped on the car. Could be a coyote or a raccoon or a barn owl. You call faculty housing and complain. Anjali says, *You look tired.* Then, *Dude!* she exclaims. *That's my Mazda. We can't do anything about it. For some reason, the horn just goes off. It's a mystery.* Her partner Lucy says, *Don't tell anyone. It's so embarrassing.*

Years later, make a choice to see this film *Albert Nobbs,* in which Glenn Close plays a nineteenth-century Irish male waiter, and sit in the Nick Theater between two colored homosexuals, in the broader sense of the word, who groan over you like call and response. God knows Close could have done some Cruzin' first before she turned Nobbs into a pathetic simpleton. No relief. Not even the tattered endearment of Charlie Chaplin. Plus, the colored homosexuals are scholars of critical theory. Yammer yammer. The most exciting moment is when Janet McTeer pinches a rolled cigarette between her lips to free her hands to unbutton her shirt to reveal her gigantic bosom. Nobbs gasps the same gasp that the white audience gasped at *M Butterfly* when the Chinese butterfly exposed his penis. It's a mystery, cruising for a bruising. What the fist?

Some mysteries get punished: serials killers go to prison; Oedipus blinds himself; M Butterfly's Frenchman commits ritual suicide; Glenn Close is only nominated for the Oscar. Some mysteries get solved. Turns out the Mazda Protegé has her quirks. When the temperature dips, the horn freezes which triggers the honking spasms. The mechanic explains. *It's sensitive, see. You got to keep her warm. I suggest a hot water bottle and a blanket.* Is someone studying this? You bet. This is that queer technology stuff interrogating the cyborg versus the goddess. Check it out, Queen Califia. This is your dark paradise. This is your mystery spot.

As for a few words on myths . . . paradise, utopia, desire, and the location of a little death.

—KTY

LOST LAKE

Emma Straub and Peter Straub

Eudora Hale spent the warm months in Fairlady with her mother, and the cold months in Lost Lake with her father. That's how it seemed, at least. Now that she was old enough—nearly thirteen—Eudora knew that whatever the time of year the sun would never reach Lost Lake the way it did Fairlady. Some parts of the world were difficult to find, even for beams of light. Sometimes Eudora thought she was the only person in the country who traveled back and forth between the two cities; her train car was always empty, with the uniformed ticket-taker her only companion for the half-day journey. When she reached her destination, her mother or father would be waiting in an otherwise uninhabited station. Eudora assumed that the train tracks still existed as a polite acknowledgment to the days when people still used to go back and forth between the two small cities.

Dawn Hale's white house stood on a corner lot in the neighborhood closest to the center of Fairlady. There were window seats in all the bedrooms. The wide lawn ended at the rounded cul-de-sac. Eudora and her mother were never in the house alone—Dawn had two friends who had their own bedrooms in the house, and their daughters shared Eudora's large room overlooking the smooth asphalt of the street and the houses on the other side of the circle. For half the year, Lily and Jane were Eudora's sisters, her playmates, the ears on the receiving end of her whispers. Sometimes the girls took their pet rabbits down to the cul-de-sac and let them hop back and forth, knowing that they would never run away. A porch wrapped all the way around the house like a hoop skirt with a latticed hem, and when Eudora was in Fairlady, she liked to crawl underneath it and dig her fingernails into the rich dirt until they were black. Eudora loved Lily and Jane, both of them blond like their mothers, but she also loved being alone, underneath the house, where the soil was cool and dark.

The custody agreement was unusual: none of the other children ever left Fairlady, even if their fathers were elsewhere. Eudora had pleaded to go back and forth between Fairlady and Lost Lake, and the judge had been persuaded by her tears. Half the year exactly, split down the middle. Her school in Fairlady had finally accepted the situation, and dutifully handed out reading lists for the months she would be away. There was a library at her father's, in a room they called the fortress, and Eudora knew where to find what she needed. When it was Den Hale's turn with his daughter, he was more likely to show her how to aim a pistol, how to shoot an arrow into the center of a target, how to remain unseen using leaves and branches, how to build a fire using only her bare hands.

THE night before she was due to go to Lost Lake, Eudora sat in the kitchen with her mother and their friends. The women were baking pies; the girls, breaking off the ends of sweet green beans. Lily and Jane sat on either side of her, all of them dumping the beans into a large, shallow bowl in front of Eudora.

"Did I give you the list of books for school? Have you packed your new sweater?" Dawn asked the questions to the whole room, clearly going down a list in her head. "Where is your toothbrush? Do you have clean socks?" Dawn didn't know anything about Lost Lake—she hadn't ever been, but Eudora knew that though her mother had agreed to the arrangement, it rattled her nerves.

"Yes, Mother," Eudora said. Her small suitcase was already packed, mostly with books. The clothes she wore in Fairlady would be of little use to her in Lost Lake. When she was very small—*a pip,* her father liked to say—Eudora didn't notice all the empty space around her, the air in between what people said and what she knew to be the truth, but now she could see it everywhere. She kept snapping the ends of the beans until the room filled with the smell of warm apples and sugar and then she too felt sad about leaving.

After dinner, when the girls had been sent to bed, Lily and Jane climbed into Eudora's bed.

"*Promise you'll come back,*" Lily whispered.

"*Don't stay away too long,*" Jane added, her mouth only inches away from Eudora's cheek. She was the eldest of the three, already fifteen, and tended to worry.

"*I always come back,*" Eudora said, and that satisfied her friends. They slept in a pile with their arms and legs thrown over each other, hearts beating strong and safe inside their chests.

On the train the next day, she was as alone as she had expected to be. The conductor who sat slumped into his blue uniform far back at the end of the car could not be counted as company, nor did he wish to be. Boredom and resentment clung to him like a bad smell. For the first time on one of these journeys to Lost Lake, being alone made her feel lonely. A wave of homesickness rolled through her, though she had been away from home no longer than an hour. She missed the white house, she missed her friends tumbling like kittens around her, and she missed her mother, who started worrying about Eudora as soon as she took her suitcase from the closet and opened it up. You would almost think Lost Lake was a dangerous place, you'd just about have to think jaguars and leopards and madmen with straight razors came stalking out of the forest to flit through the alleyways and little courts of the town. . . . Eudora realized that she felt guilty about having caused her mother such anxiety. She couldn't even talk her out of it, because Dawn refused to hear anything about Lost Lake. If you didn't close your mouth, she closed her ears.

Lily and Jane weren't much better, and their mothers were the same. They all acted like Lost Lake was a childhood nightmare they had sworn to keep out of mind. At home—the clean, white house, fragrant with fresh, warm bread and cut flowers, which she missed so piercingly at this moment—when Eudora spoke her father's name or that of his community, Lily and Jane, and their blond mothers, Beth and Maggie, looked at the ground and swiveled back and forth, like shy bridegrooms. Suddenly errands were remembered;

something in another room, a book or a sewing basket, had to be fetched immediately. No one was going to tell her not to mention Den Hale or his remote northern world; yet it was clear that she was not supposed to say anything about that side of her life. (In Lost Lake, such strictures did not hold. Eudora had the feeling that people in Lost Lake spoke very seldom of Fairlady only because they found it completely uninteresting.)

One other person she was aware of traveled regularly between her mother's world and Den's, and that person made the journey much more frequently than she. It occurred to Eudora that the conductor, as unpleasant as he was, might be uniquely placed to answer questions that until this minute she had not known she needed to have answered. Eudora turned around in her seat and in a loud voice called out, "Excuse me! Hey! Conductor!"

The man opened a sleepy eye and took her in. He shuffled his upper body within the baggy uniform, lifted his cap, and rubbed the top of his head, still regarding her. He appeared to be either shocked or profoundly angry.

"My name is Eudora, hello. I want to talk about you, Conductor. For example, where are you from, where do you live? Which end of the line?" She had never seen him in Fairlady, so he almost had to live in Lost Lake, although he did not much look like the kind of person you met in and around her father's town.

"Neither end. Wouldn't have a thing to do with them places, nope. Don't like 'em. Don't believe they're very fond of me, either. Nope. *That's* been tested out and proven true."

She squinted at him.

"Do you live in some town in between?

"There *ain't* no towns between Fairlady and Lost Lake. All the civilization in this state's a hundred miles to the east. In here, where we are now, this part's pretty empty."

"Well then, where *do* you live?" The second she asked her question, she knew the answer.

"I live here. In the second car up."

"Are there ever any other passengers?"

"Maybe three–four times a year. Someone's car broke down, that's usually the reason. Or sometimes there's official business, where a couple of big shots ride back and forth, whispering stuff they don't want me to hear."

For a moment, Eudora contemplated this picture, trying to imagine what kind of "official business" would demand so much in time and secrecy. Then she remembered the real reason she had wanted to get into the conversation.

"Conductor, you spend your whole life on this train, but most of the time, you never have any tickets to collect because you're here all alone. I'm your biggest customer, and you only see me twice a year!"

He sneered at her. "You think I'm just a conductor, but I'm not. There's more to this train than you, young lady. It isn't really a passenger train, not mainly—did you never look at the other three cars?"

"I guess not."

Eudora could summon only the vaguest, blurriest images of the other cars. Ranked behind the lighted windows of the passenger car, they had seemed dark and anonymous. It had never occurred to her that they might be anything but closed, vacant versions of the car she always used.

"There's *freight*, in there. Most every morning and night, people load boxes into those freight cars. Big ones, little ones. I don't know what's in 'em, I just know it's worth a lot of dough. And I'm the guard over all that stuff. I'm *security*." The conductor checked to see if she had taken in the immense gravity of what he had just divulged. Then he slid off his seat and began to saunter toward her.

Eudora paused, a little unsettled by the conductor's approach but not much caring about the freight. What was the big deal about some boxes? "I want to ask you another question. You must hear people talk sometimes. Have you ever heard anything about a man named Den Hale?"

"Dennhale? No, I never . . . Oh, Den *Hale*. You said Den *Hale*, didn't you?" He had stopped moving. "Right?"

"Yes," she said, wondering. "Right."

"You work for him, or something?"

"No, I . . . no. He's my father. He picks me up at the other end."

The conductor's narrow head moved forward, and his shoulders dropped. For a long moment, he looked as though he had been turned into a statue. Then he wheeled around and moved swiftly down the polished wooden aisle. At the end of the car, he hit the release button and moved across the dark, windy passage into the next car. Resoundingly, the doors clanked shut. Eudora was not certain of what had just happened, but she did not think she would see her new friend again on this journey, nor did she.

JUST past ten at night, eight hours after her departure, the little train pulled into the Lost Lake station. Eudora expected to see her father waiting on the platform, but the man occupying the pool of light from the nearest hanging lantern was not Den Hale but his friend, Clancy Munn. A tough character, Munn was roughly the size of a mailbox, squat, thick, and at first glance all but square. It was funny: when in Fairlady, she all but forgot about Clancy Munn—he was unimaginable in her mother's world—but here in Lost Lake, he felt like reality itself. Clancy's daughter, Maude Munn, was Eudora's closest friend in Lost Lake. She was more fun to be around than the girls in Fairlady, with their sweet breath and brushed hair. It was as if the big strawberry birthmark on Maude's left cheek had cranked up all her inner dials, making her louder, faster, and more daring than most other people. Eudora knew no one more alive than Maude.

When Clancy and Eudora left the shelter of the platform, the slight breeze, already much colder than the air eight hours to the south, whipped itself into a strong wind that cut through the summery jacket her mother had bought for her as though it were tissue paper. Eudora leaned in close to Clancy's thick body.

"It's always so *much* colder here."

"You like it this way, only you forget."

She laughed out loud, delighted. It was true: the details and sensations of Lost Lake were falling into place all around her like a jigsaw puzzle assembling itself, reminding her as they did so how much she enjoyed being here. She *liked* cold weather, she *liked* seeing snowflakes spinning erratically through the air . . . she *liked* the huge fireplaces, and the thick wooden walls, and the great forest.

Clancy turned on the heat in the cab of his truck, and they drove in contented quiet the rest of the way to Eudora's father's house.

Eudora asked for news of Maude, chattered about the conductor, and fell asleep on the last section of the journey. She came half awake only after the pickup had passed through an automatic door and entered a vast underground parking space. "We're here, sweetie," Munn said, and gently shook her shoulder.

Eudora swam instantly back into consciousness and looked around at all the empty parking spaces on both sides. Munn smiled and left the cab. Far off to her right, three men in black coats were dragging long, narrow boxes from the back of an old van and stacking them against the wall. Eudora had seen this activity, or others like it, every time she returned to Lost Lake, but had never before wondered what it meant. She scrambled out of the cab and trotted toward Munn, who was already twenty feet in front of her, carrying her heavy suitcase as if it were empty.

"Hey, Clancy," she said, and he looked back over his shoulder, grinning. "What are those men doing, next to the wall over there?"

"What does it look like they're doing?" He had not stopped moving forward, and was no longer smiling at her.

"Yeah, but what's in those boxes?"

Struck by a sudden, most curious idea, one wrapped in the aura of the forbidden, she stopped and regarded the faraway stack of containers. Eudora thought of the train conductor and his precious cargo. The boxes were long and narrow, each one the size of a person. Munn stopped moving, too, and turned around to look at her.

"Could be anything inside those things. Don't think too much about it, kiddo. Let's see if your old man is ready."

He picked up her case and led her up three flights of stairs, into a wide corridor and past several sets of doors. Asking him anything would have been a waste of time, she knew. As if in compensation, music and the smell of food drifted to her. Munn opened a door, looked at her for a second, then said, "Keep quiet and stay behind me."

She nodded. Her heart was beating faster, and she felt flushed with anticipation.

Munn slipped through the door, Eudora directly behind him.

Over his shoulder, she saw the great fire at the back of the room, the massive table where the remains of a roast sat amidst scattered plates, glasses, pads of paper—the ruins of a working dinner. The fire and the low candles on the table provided the only light.

A group of men, her father's friends and business partners, were seated on stools and sofas and easy chairs off to the side of the table. They were attending to the conversation in progress as if nothing could be more crucial to their futures. In fact, each of these nine or ten men was staring at her father as if he alone were the key to whatever lay ahead. They were dependent upon Den, she saw; he was at their very center. Den turned his head toward Munn and at last found that Eudora had come into the enormous room. Even at her distance from him, even in the dim, flickering light, she saw joy flare up into his eyes. He moved swiftly toward her, his arms held wide. Behind him, the other men watched his progress with the patient curiosity of dogs. Quickly, he pulled her into his embrace and began to apologize for failing to pick her up at the station. The men dared not move until he looked back and gestured.

Imagine, Eudora thought, *it took me my whole life to notice that he's the king around here.*

SIX months later, Eudora and Maude Munn had many times ridden their horses through the town and raced them over the fields. After long secret consultations and hilarious conversations; after luxurious meals and hurried, impromptu meals because she had to get back outside into the cold twilight to track rabbits through the fresh snow; after snowball fights with half the girls in town; after hours of lonely study; after occasions of ecstasy at the suddenly apprehended fact of really being *there,* wrapped in dark furs at the edge of the forest as light snowfall skirled down from the gray, shining sky and the hints of a thousand adventures seemed to shimmer before her; after long conversations with her father; after all of this, it had become her last full day in Lost Lake. Eudora and Maude were taking their final ride together on their favorite horses, and they came again to the edge of the forest no one was ever supposed to enter.

Maude's horse was brown and white, with spots of dirt on his belly that she would have to comb out later on. The horse whinnied, and Maude settled him with a few pats on the neck.

"I don't think even he wants to go in there," she said. Maude shifted on the horse's back, uneasy. It wasn't like Maude to hesitate. When they had leaped off the roof of an abandoned building into a bed of cardboard boxes, it had been Maude's idea. When they had dropped water balloons onto the backs of Den's men, it had been Maude's idea. When they had spent the night together, curled up like she used to with Lily and Jane, but somehow even closer, it had been Maude's idea. But she wasn't feeling bold right now, that was clear. Eudora watched as Maude turned toward her; her strawberry birthmark looked brighter, pinker than usual. It was her stoplight, Maude liked to say, and it didn't like the cold. Eudora thought it didn't like the forest, either. Kids in Lost Lake liked to make up stories about the lake itself, how it was haunted, but Eudora didn't believe them, and Maude had never acted like she did, either. Anyway, she'd never even seen the lake. For all she knew, the lake itself might be a myth, no bigger than a mud puddle after a rainstorm.

"How scary can it be?" Eudora said, and urged her horse on. The forest was thick, but there were pathways—roads, almost—that indicated they wouldn't be the first, maybe not even the first that day. Maude nodded, and squeezed her horse, and into the forest they went.

Dark, empty branches stretched skyward over their heads like the skeleton of a ceiling—all beams and bones, no connective tissue. The leaves were gone. The girls stopped talking, and the only sounds were the horses' hooves on the dirt, the wind in the branches above them, and their own heartbeats. Eudora knew they weren't supposed to go into the forest, but it sounded like advice they'd outgrown, didn't it? She was sure it did. It wasn't safe for children, of course, but she and Maude weren't children anymore. They could take care of themselves. She felt bolder with every step the horse took, until a man in black clothing like a uniform without badges or insignia stepped out from behind a great oak and held out his hand to stop them, and as silently as smoke other men in faceless uniforms, each with an ugly automatic weapon in his black-gloved hands, appeared on both sides, and they stopped their horses, having no real choice, and their audacity momentarily shriveled.

Maude gasped, and Eudora reached out to take her hand. Maude's palm was sweating already. The guards stepped toward them, spooking Eudora's horse.

"Turn around, girls," the guard said. Eudora looked to Maude, who had gone completely white. *What is she so afraid of*, Eudora wondered. They would turn back if they had to, of course, but why was Maude so frightened?

"I'm Den Hale's daughter," said Eudora, "and she's Clancy Munn's daughter. We just want to see Lost Lake." She was sure that her father's name would grant her access to whatever was hidden in the trees.

The guards didn't smile or soften the way Eudora thought they would. "Turn around, girls, and ride back freely, or we'll walk you back, like prisoners," the guard said. "You choose."

Surprised and slightly shaken, Maude and Eudora rode back through the trees and across the ring road and left the horses in their stables, and hugged each other, and promised themselves that the following year they would figure out how to get to Lost Lake. When they parted at Den's door, Eudora thought Maude lingered a little bit, the horse's reins still tight in her hand.

"What is it?" Eudora asked.

"Nothing," Maude said. She shook her head, as if trying to convince herself. "Nothing." Then she clicked her tongue and turned around and went home by herself, back to Clancy's house on the next block. Eudora stayed outside, listening, just in case her friend came back. The following day, when Eudora took the little train back to warmth and Fairlady, a different conductor accepted her ticket, punched it, plodded to the end of the carriage, and disappeared. When Eudora closed her eyes and fell asleep, she dreamed of horses and leaves and men with guns tucked into their waistbands; she dreamed of Maude's hair blowing across her cheek; she dreamed of a vast lake that stretched all the way to the horizon.

Dawn was waiting when the train arrived, a basket of food hanging from her arm. She'd baked biscuits for the short ride home from the station, and brought some freshly made juice the color of a sunrise.

"How was the trip?" Dawn asked, smiling. Her eyes looked glassy, which could have been from the breeze coming through the leaves and the grass. It was spring again, and there was pollen in the air.

"Good," Eudora said, knowing that her mother wouldn't want to hear more. "Fine."

"If it was good for you, it's good for me," Dawn said, and hooked her arm over Eudora's shoulder and turned toward home. After six months in Lost Lake, Fairlady looked like a film set—there was no trash or leaves in the gutter, no eyesore vehicles, not a broken window or an empty building. Even by the train station, the streets were as clean as if they'd just been mopped with bleach.

"How is everyone?" Eudora asked, expecting more of the same, easy answers to easy questions. She loved her mother, but Dawn didn't like to go beneath the surface. Everything was always fine, no matter what.

"Lily's got the bunnies in the living room—there are more of them now, the big one had some more babies. She wanted to show them to you."

"And what about Jane?"

Dawn didn't stop walking, didn't shift her gaze from the clear, even sidewalk. "Jane's living with her father now."

Eudora tried to stop, but Dawn kept moving. "What?!" This had happened to other girls in Fairlady, older ones who were as pretty and blond as Jane. One day they'd be at school, practicing their choreographed routines in the hall, all white teeth and unblemished skin, and then next day, they'd be gone. To their fathers, whom no one had ever seen.

"She wanted to, Eudora. Just like you want to live with your father. Doesn't Jane get to make a choice, too?" Dawn's voice was as even as the sidewalk, with not a single crack.

Eudora thought of Jane's whispered pleas, her soft cheek resting against Eudora's shoulder the night before she left for Lost Lake. That night, Jane hadn't wanted to go anywhere. Eudora wondered when her friend had changed her mind. "Sure," she said. "Of course." When they made it back to the house, all the lights were on and Lily sat in the middle of the living room floor, surrounded by little moving puddles of white fur, smiling as if nothing was different. Even Jane's mother grinned, so happy to see Eudora home again.

THE months went quickly—Eudora went back to school, where she read familiar stories and took familiar tests. She ate her mother's beautiful, rich food and helped clean the kitchen. Lily stayed close to her in bed at night, the two of them singing the kind of children's songs that were harmless until you actually listened to the lyrics, which were about hangmen and rotting earth. The summer came and all the playgrounds were full of children. She washed her hair and braided it while it was wet, which left wrinkles of curls behind after it dried, which reminded her of Maude. In the fall, just before Eudora was heading back, Dawn began to pick at her cuticles, which she'd never done before. Once, Eudora was walking by the bathroom and saw Dawn plucking her eyebrow hairs with her fingers, her sharp nails acting as tweezers. Her mother looked completely unlike herself—Dawn looked pale and frightened, but determined, too. Eudora stepped on a noisy floorboard, and Dawn looked up, catching Eudora's eyes in the bathroom mirror. Instantly her face went back to normal, the corners of her mouth perking back up into a smile. She smoothed her fingers over the reddened stripes over her eyes. "Time for bed!" she said, her voice trilling upward like a happy bird.

EUDORA stayed awake on the train—she wanted to know how far it really was in between the two cities. There were tunnels she'd never noticed before, long stretches of time underground. Eudora stared out the window, sure that she would pass something that would explain the difference between her mother's house and her father's, between the way she felt in her two bedrooms, the difference between Lily and Jane and Maude.

This time, it was her father who picked her up from the train. He walked up the platform smiling at her, and she took in again that he was actually a small, compact man who moved with a wonderful economy and efficiency you never noticed until he was coming straight at you and you had no choice. Den walked, she realized, like a dancer. He sauntered, he strolled, he more or less glided up to her and hugged her close and kissed her forehead. Her father was just about the same height as Dawn. In a few years, she would probably be taller than both of them. Eudora slid her face into the collar of his old brown leather jacket and, to keep her childhood from vanishing completely away, inhaled the fragrance of Lost Lake masculinity, minus the smell of horses—Den never spent much time in the stables—but with some sharp extra smell like that of a winter evening growing dark. It was the smell, she suddenly felt, of cold water.

"Ah, you're glad to be back," he said. "That's always good to know. And you're not too softened up from six months in Fairlady, I hope."

"I'm always glad to be back here," she said. "Last time, Clancy said it used to take me a couple of days to remember that I really *like* being in Lost Lake, but when he picked me up I remembered it instantly. This time, too. But when I go *there*, back to Fairlady, I miss this place so much I think I mope around for weeks."

All in one smooth, unbroken motion, he hugged her more tightly, patted her on the back, picked up her traveling bag, and began to escort her down the platform. Eudora realized that she had never before said so much about Fairlady when in her father's world.

"Must be hard on your mother."

"Maybe. But you know Mom, she's always so cheerful and up-beat. That's what makes her so wonderful!"

"That's true," he said. "Very true. But you always bring some of that cheer to us, you know."

"Jane must do that, too. She's here now, isn't she? My friend Jane Morgan, from Fairlady?"

"I don't know any Jane Morgans from Fairlady, honey. Sorry." He smiled at her, then turned to hoist her suitcase into the back of the pickup.

"But . . . she left to live with her father. Mom said."

Still smiling, Den gestured for her to walk around the cab and get in on her side. "I know a couple of Morgans, and neither of them has a daughter. Abel Morgan is so old he can barely walk, and his son, Jerry, who never married, is a captain in our security force. Your friend probably moved to one of those little towns on the other side of the state, Waldo, or Lydecker, one of those. Or maybe Bates, way south of us, that's a good-sized city. Probably a ton of Morgans in Bates."

Den turned on the engine, gave Eudora a reassuring pat on the knee, and twisted around to back up into the aisle.

"Daddy . . ."

"Something else?" He raised his eyebrows.

"Why do you need a security force? Fairlady doesn't have one."

"That's a big question, honey." For a short while, he negotiated the turns needed to get out of the lot and on the road to Lost Lake. "Fairlady's a special place. There are policemen, but you hardly ever see them, and the town has next to no crime. We don't have much, either, but some of that is due to our security force. We're a much busier place than Fairlady. We do have a jail, and there's al-most always one or two idiots in a cell. All kinds of things go on here in Lost Lake—and besides, this is the *North*. Things are differ-ent in the North. We wouldn't live in Fairlady if you paid us." He gave her a look that was both amused and fond. "I hope you'll feel the same way, next year."

Here it was, thrust in front of her face like a burning torch, the matter she tried never to think about while knowing it could never be very far from her mind. The judge at her custody hearing had ordered that Eudora would have to decide between her mother and her father, between Fairlady and Lost Lake, by the date of her sixteenth birthday, now only two seasons away. After that, her trips back and forth would cease, and she would become a permanent resident of one city or the other, of her mother's world or her father's. There was no in between. This abrupt, unwelcome reminder of the decision she somehow would have to make made her stomach cramp in on itself, and for a moment she feared that she would have to vomit onto the remarkably clutter-free floor of the cab, which Den had almost certainly cleaned up for her arrival.

Some of what she was feeling must have been printed on her face, because her father immediately said, "Shouldn't have reminded you like that. Sorry. I'm sure your mother feels as strongly as I do about this thing."

Eudora thought, *My mother would never have done that to me.* Then: *My mother wouldn't say anything about it even if we were about to go before the judge. Instead, she'd ask how I liked her new brand of oatmeal.* Dawn kept everything locked up tight. Too tight, maybe. Eudora inhaled and said, "How's Maude? I can't wait to see her."

"Maude's probably fine, you know, but she isn't in Lost Lake right now. She won't be back before you have to leave again. I'm sorry about that, too. I know what great friends you were." He used the past tense—*were*.

"No," said Eudora. "No, she would have told me. Where is she, anyhow?" A dreadful thought occurred to her. "Did you do this? Did you send her away?"

"She's on a special trip with Clancy. Town business. She wanted to be more involved! Did I send away your best friend? Of course not. I don't have the power to do that."

"In Lost Lake, you can do anything you like. Last year I finally noticed how everyone acts around you. All those men, they need you to tell them what to do. They look up to you. You're the mayor, or the boss, or whatever."

"Don't you think Clancy decides what Maude does, not me?"

"Clancy especially would do anything you told him to do."

Den frowned at her and without warning swung the wheel sharply to the right, pulling the vehicle off the road and onto the weedy bank. He jerked to a stop, jammed the shift into neutral, and swiveled to face her. His eyes seemed flat, blank, empty. For a second, fear flashed from the center of her chest and sparkled through her nervous system. A gust of cold wind struck the pickup with an audible slap. They were still a mile or two out of town. The nearest building was a little run-down farmhouse about a hundred yards away across an empty field, and it was probably abandoned.

Some feeling came back into Den's eyes. "Look, Eudora. This is how it goes. All right? Lost Lake doesn't have a mayor, and there isn't any boss. When we need to discuss something, we get together, and we work it out. The men in my place, sure, they work for me, but we talk everything over, and everyone has a say in what happens."

"But what do you *do*?" she asked.

"About a million different things." Den paused. "I really thought Maude would let you know, sweetie."

She felt deflated. "Okay. Thanks. I'm sorry. I didn't want to make you angry."

"It takes more than that to make me angry. But if you were thinking, did I send Maude away because the two of you tried to sneak through the forest last year, the answer is no. The guardsman who ordered you back told me about the two of you, however. You were thoughtful enough to give him my name, and *he* was thoughtful enough to come to me afterward. Lost Lake is dangerous, honey, and so is the forest around it. We keep people away for their own good."

Eudora felt her face heat up, and she looked away. Her father was lying to her, she was sure of it. There was no way Maude would have gone away without letting her know. There was something off—first Jane, now Maude. Eudora thought of all the girls in Fairlady who had left school abruptly, all the pretty girls who had never been heard from after boarding the train north. Her father knew the truth, but he wasn't telling.

"Now that we understand each other, let's get into town and have a nice time, okay?"

"If you say so," she said.

Eudora looked through her window and watched scrubby wasteland yield to rows of shacks and pawnshops and liquor stores. They drove between two massive strip clubs that faced each other across the two-lane macadam road. Past the neon of the clubs, the town of Lost Lake began to assemble itself and display what it was really about. A street of morose one-story houses with tiny lawns led to a huge brick structure that ended at a square from which narrow roads wound this way and that through and into a clutter of shops, taverns, restaurants and supper clubs, foundries, courtyards and town squares, movie theaters (all but one shuttered), tiny frame apartment buildings, streets of diminutive factories, a cemetery, and finally, the area on the north end of town where stood Den's huge blank building with concealed vents and hidden windows and multiple entrances, with uncounted chimneys—a building with comfortable living space for twenty people, an underground pool, a shooting range, the library called the "fortress," a dining room, two kitchens, and all of the hearths, fireplaces, and woodstoves beneath the uncounted chimneys. Described this way, the town sounds enormous, but many of the buildings were of no great size, the streets were narrow, and most of the squares had a toylike quality, not unlike parts of Fairlady. Past Den's realm lay the tremendous forest, and within the forest glinted the immensity of Lost Lake itself, forbidden to all but a few of the town's satraps, rajahs, magi, and sultans. Or so Eudora gathered. Maude had promised her to make another foray side by side into that forbidden territory, and that idea overflowed with equal amounts of the fear of capture, the thrill of outrageous adventure, and joy—the blazing joy of sharing both the risks and the adventure with Maude Munn.

It was possible, of course, that Eudora had always liked Maude more than Maude had liked her, that the friendship had been formed out of familial duty. It was possible that Maude was having the time of her life off wherever she was with Clancy, and that if Maude ever thought of Eudora at all, it was with a gentle nostalgia for her childhood, as if she were an old stuffed monkey found discarded at the back of a closet. This consideration had two effects on Eudora: it aroused a sharp, painful shame that seemed centered in her actual heart, and it made her feel that she, too, should move into a more adult phase of her life. Having no choice in the matter, Eudora decided to become a more independent young woman, and took to riding a horse through town by herself; spending hours alone in the "fortress," reading whatever looked interesting, as long as it also seemed unambiguously grown-up: over a single week, she read *Jane Eyre, We Have Always Lived in the Castle,* and *The Bloody Chamber.* All the other children in Lost Lake seemed like simply that—children—whereas Eudora herself felt like nothing of the sort. She was somewhere in between the kids and the adults, and therefore profoundly lonely. Eudora had never before really noticed the extent to which she and Maude Munn had split away from the others to create a self-contained, self-sustaining society of two. She could almost imagine that her friend had been protecting her from the rest of Lost Lake.

ON Eudora's tenth night back in her father's realm, Den and most of his merry men stayed up very late drinking—it was hard to tell if they were celebrating or mourning, the cries and cheers too loud and too blurry for Eudora's ears to differentiate. Either way, she knew that it would be a late morning for all of them, even the guards. It occurred to Eudora that she would probably never have a better chance all winter to slip into the forest unseen. Without Maude did she dare, did she even want to dare? Lost Lake might as well keep its secrets, she thought. Secrets seemed to be the world's principal currency.

Two days earlier, she had been dawdling bored past the big conference room, peeked in through the half-inch opening in the doorway, and seen, far back at a little table near the enormous fire that filled the hearth, her father in the act of counting the money he was transferring from a knee-high metal safe on the floor into a bunch of shoeboxes piled up on the side of the table. He was not counting bills, he was counting stacks of money, bundles of cash held together with thick paper bands. Behind him and closer to the fire, an oversized guard in a black uniform without any identifying symbols stood with his arms crossed over his huge chest. The clearest thing about this tableau was that it *was not supposed to be seen*. A kind of dirty intimacy surrounded it. Eudora had moved away as swiftly and as quietly as she could manage. Yet Fairlady, too, had its dirty secrets. When she sat in her mother's pretty kitchen sometimes, shelling peas or cutting up sweet potatoes, watching and listening as the older women chattered about nothing much—about trivia, really, half of it in that distant time when they had been girls themselves—the empty space she had begun to notice in the air between people's words and what they really meant widened and widened until the kitchen seemed an abyss. As Eudora lay in her narrow bed with the dull clamor of drunkenness booming from the floor below, it came to her that she herself, Eudora Hale, was in imminent danger of succumbing to the depths of the empty spaces, and that she could drown in the emptiness, the meaninglessness yawning all about her. She had this one chance, she thought: *this* one, *now*. And Maude would be with her, too, she thought, not the Maude who had disappeared into "town business" with Clancy, but the other, more real Maude, *her* Maude, who had created meaning with a glance of her eye as she beautifully flaunted her flame-licked face and ran straight at any obstacle that dared place itself before her.

Just before dawn Eudora slipped quietly out of bed and put on as many layers as possible, buttoning herself up with trembling fingers. Carrying her boots to avoid making any noise clumping across the floor, she crept along the hallway and tiptoed down the stairs. At the bottom of the staircase was the entrance to a large room with a concrete floor that Den used chiefly to put up short-term visitors. The sounds of snoring and sleepy mutterings told her that this monastic space was not empty. Alarmed, she moved quietly past the half-open doorway and peered in. Something like twenty men lay asleep on cots and pallets, about half of them in the black uniforms of Den's guardsmen. A stench of flatulence and stale alcohol hovered above the snoring men. Eudora took long, silent steps to a back door and walked outside into fresh, cold air that smelled wonderful to her. The long, flat-roofed stables lay only a few steps on a concrete path away.

Her horse exhaled warm steam onto her palms in greeting, and Eudora stroked his velvet nose, moved down his side, stroking and patting as she went, and like a true girl of Lost Lake vaulted onto his back. With a dig of her heels and a whispered word she urged him forward and stayed flat against his neck while they were still in Lost Lake proper. This was it, Eudora realized with something like shock, she was committed, she would see this through to the end. Never before in her life had she been so flagrantly and willfully disobedient. A ghost-Maude, a shadow-Maude, rode beside her, egging her on with the courage of her own native, utterly out-there flagrancy. That blazing wine-stain on Maude's cheek had demanded more courage than Eudora thought she alone would ever have.

Disobedient? Very well, I will imagine my Maude at my side, and my disobedience will be root, trunk, branch, and leaf.

As she rode the horse at a steady walk past the shuttered taverns and empty inns that lined the empty ring road, she wondered how her parents had ever met in the first place, how they had been in the same room long enough to make her out of thin air. The number of things that had to align to bring her into being! Maude had had a mother too, years ago, and Jane and Lily had both had fathers. Why did no one get to keep both? Surely they did in some parts of the world. Eudora thought that next year, before she was forced to go before the judge and make a choice, she might jump off the train with a bag full of clothes and food and walk until her new, separate journey took her to a nice town that looked like it might be a good place to live. In this place, parents would not get divorced; it would have neither Fairlady's well-swept corners nor Lost Lake's darkness and mystery. Surely such a place existed, somewhere. Didn't it, didn't it *have* to? Yet . . . were she to make her separate journey, instead of losing merely one of the places she already had, she would lose both of them.

Eudora stopped fantasizing about something she was probably never going to do, especially not without Maude, when her horse's steady, one-foot-at-a-time gait had taken her across the ring road's wide expanse and up to the irregular row of oak and birch trees that marked the beginning of the great forest. She was at the exact point where she and Maude—so fearlessly, so confidently, so ignorantly—had entered the forest. This time around, she was fearful, uncertain, and aware that normally a squad of the black-uniformed soldiers would be poised and hidden within the trees, ready to pounce. She nudged her horse into a gentle, quiet walk through the first row of trees and into the forest, where the pale, gray light of the northern dawn almost immediately surrendered to the velvet darkness of the long night. All of the soldiers couldn't have been celebrating with Den, she knew. Probably an equal number had been left at their posts, or whatever they called it. She would have to be a lot cagier today, and softer of step.

The trees seemed sometimes to creep toward her out of the absolute darkness behind them, and sometimes invisible twiggy fingers reached out to dig at her hair, her shoulders, her chest. With better eyesight than hers, the horse did not flinch or panic, but surefootedly stepped around the thick trunks and lacy deadfalls on their wandering path. If it was a path. In daylight, she and Maude had followed some old trail, half overgrown with fiddlehead ferns, but now she had to leave all of that up to the horse. Eudora's only function was to avoid low-hanging limbs and keep the animal moving in more or less the right direction.

She lost track of time. Now and then, she brought the patient horse to a halt and paused a minute or two to listen to what was going on around her. In the darkness and without a watch whose dial was readable at night, a minute becomes a very flexible unit of time. Eudora listened to the forest breathe around her, a faint rustle in the leaves, a quick scurry of tiny feet on the forest floor, a bird's exploratory-sounding call answered or challenged by another bird. Some animal brushed against a tree trunk, and she felt the horse stiffen and shift its legs, and knew it was rolling its eyes in terror. Eudora patted its neck and urged it forward again, grateful not to know what kind of animal it had been, and hoping it was not following them. Then it occurred to her that the animal might have been a human being with an automatic weapon slung across his back. Night vision glasses, and a black uniform with a black hood. Black boots with rubber soles. She let herself be carried another thirty feet, and feeling protected by the darkness no longer, squeezed the reins gently to halt the horse, swung her legs over the animal's back, and dropped silently to the ground.

A faint gray light was leaking into the darkness. Eudora began moving slowly forward through the ranks of the trees and for a moment had the illusion that they grew in straight military rows that exposed her every time she moved into one of the spaces between the neat rows. Far overhead, a squirrel barreled along a slender branch and yelled in squirrel-speak, *I see her! I see her! Here she is, you idiots!* She whirled to look behind her, and the forest, as if by command, snapped back into its old disorder. More carefully, she examined the tree trunks, the bushes, the green sprigs that sprouted from the gray-green mulch, straining to see what she could not see: hidden traps, gleaming wires, soldiers with their faces painted to look like moss. "Okay," she muttered to herself, and led the horse by the reins in the direction she thought she had to go. Ten minutes of patient going later, Eudora heard the unmistakable sound of a group of men moving through the forest with no thought of precaution.

She froze; she listened, hard. The men seemed to be coming right toward her from the very direction she was going. Making as little noise as possible, she led the horse behind a deadfall where a huge broken trunk slanted gray and lifeless through a cobwebby tangle of lesser branches entwined with parasitic vines. She knelt down and as the noise came nearer peered out at the space she had just left. Soon a small troop of the guards, weapons slung across their backs, relaxed and clearly in a good mood, entered the space before her and mooched along through it.

When they had passed, Eudora waited a few minutes, then emerged and listened to them passing away from her, now and then saying something she could not make out. It did not have to make sense to her, she told herself, she should merely be grateful they were making themselves so easy to avoid. Then she resumed walking northward again, toward the lake, the horse treading amiably along beside her.

Nearly an hour later, the sun higher in the sky and sending great shafts of pale northern light down through the trees that were greener and taller than those farther back, she felt the ground beneath her feet grow spongy with moisture. The air was colder and clearer, and she thought it smelled like water. Eudora gave the reins a tug and began to move along faster. Before her, a cluster of matter where none should have been—an unnatural shape, a harsh angle, a brown too red to be alive—resolved itself into a sort of shelter, a hut, a shack. A shack with a dark, glinting window and a wood stove's chimney jutting through the roof. A dark green pickup truck encrusted all over with a rind of dried mud had been drawn up beside it.

Her heart seemed to swing to a stop, then resume after the skipped beat. She thought she knew that pickup. For a moment she could not move. Then: "You stay here," she whispered to the horse, dropped the reins, and set off, crouching and moving despite her terror toward the rear of the shack and its glinting window. It could not be, it had to be. Of course it was. She remembered walking toward it through a blast of freezing air at the side of the station. Since that night, the pickup had known a lot of bad weather.

The real test of her courage was whether or not she could straighten up enough to peer through the window, and as she scuttled across a resilient carpet of weeds murdered by the cold Eudora wondered what she would do when she got to the red-brown wall. Then she got there, and she knew she had to risk taking a look. The shadow-Maude, the silent, insubstantial Maude insisted on it. Yes. A look, really just a peep, a second's glance into that enigmatic space, and off to the next big challenge. Such as, for example, trying to get back home before Den noticed she wasn't in the building.

Very slowly, in fact reluctantly, Eudora came up out of her crouch and plastered herself to the boards next to the window. She inhaled and exhaled, inhaled again and held her breath. It was time. She turned her head, then her whole body, and raised the top of her head and her left eye to the window. Inside the cabin, Clancy Munn sat at a card table, his broad square back to her, counting out bills from one of the stacks Den had been organizing. He placed the bills into three separate piles. Then he waved at someone, telling them to come up to him. Eudora lowered her head again, counted to twenty, then rose up and risked another peep. Two of the soldiers in black were grinning down at Clancy and reaching for the money he was extending to them. Everybody seemed to be extremely happy with the way their lives were going. *Payday*, Eudora thought, *okay, that's all I need*. The guards stepped back from the desk, and Eudora found herself looking at Maude Munn, her radiance considerably dimmed, her face drawn into a scowl, standing there in blue jeans and mud-daubed blue sweater, her hands jammed into the pockets of a dirty-looking duffel coat. She was just thinking that Maude didn't own that sweater, or that ugly coat either, when her onetime darling and best friend glanced up and looked right into her eyes. Eudora froze, and her mouth went dry.

Maude nodded once and looked down at her father, who gave her a couple of bills and waved her off. She backed away and slid her eyes sideways. When Eudora failed to move, Maude frowned more deeply and nodded her head to the left. *Get out of here,* she was saying, and Eudora got out of there on the spot. She scrambled, trying to be as quiet as you can be while scrambling, and disappeared, she hoped, back into the trees. When she got to shelter, she realized that along the far side of the cabin had been a stack of the long, narrow black boxes from the train—from her trains and all the others.

No longer quite in control of herself, Eudora moved aimlessly away from the cabin and finally took in that the trees were thinning out and the ground becoming squishier. And directly ahead of her was a glinting, silvery, molten surface that had to be Lost Lake. She glanced back, assured herself that her horse was within reach and not going anywhere, and turned back to the lake that had been her goal all along. It was vast, but she could see across it, dimly. It looked very cold and very deep, like an enormous quarry. Way off to her right, a truck had been drawn up along a wooden dock. Two of the guardsmen were pulling something from the back of the truck and loading it onto a dolly.

Eudora strained to see what the object was, but the men's bodies obscured it as they pushed the dolly along the pier jutting out from the dock. At the end of the pier, they tilted up the dolly, and something black slipped away into the water and instantly sank from view.

It was enough: it was too much, she needed no more. Eudora stumbled back into the woods, took up the reins, and walked the horse back far enough to feel safe getting on its back again. They plodded through the forest, with every step Eudora seeing before her the shock, as if by flashlight, of Maude Munn's altered face, the face of a gloomy, altered Maude Munn, older, sadder, compromised, another person altogether. The black thing slid into the lake and disappeared. Something had gone away, gone away forever.

It made no difference to her now, but her luck held long enough for her to stable the horse and get into her father's terrible building and make her way to her room unseen. No one had noticed she was missing, no one had gone looking for her. Everyone in her father's employ had been too busy or hungover to notice her absence. She had left muddy boot-prints on her way to her room, but someone would wash them away without ever thinking twice about it. Lost Lake was a muddy place, now and again. Eudora peeled off her clothing and glanced into her mirror to see a filthy body with wild eyes and twigs in her hair glaring back at her as if in accusation.

She fell into bed and seemed to have become disembodied. Being disembodied was fine with Eudora. Her bodiless self rose a foot or two off the bed and became aware that a door, a nice, sturdy red door had appeared in the empty air before her. Behind this door, she understood, was another. It might be larger or smaller, uglier or more beautiful, but it would be different. And after that door would be another, then another, and yet another after that. The journeys opened by these doors were ripe with miseries, splendors, richness and paltriness, with a thousand breathtaking moments and as many of heartbreak and despair, but what she understood most at that moment was that none of these many, many doors would ever lead her back to the first.

My father and I were completely tickled to be asked to write a story together. Taking on an existing story, in some ways, made our job easier—rather than starting from scratch, we went back and forth with myths, talking about the ways in which we could make a story our own. In the end, we settled on Persephone, who travels back and forth between the Gods and Goddesses above and the underworld below. In our version, a thirteen-year-old girl named Eudora Hale travels back and forth between her mother's house in Fairlady and her father's much darker city of Lost Lake. At first, I was worried about being able to edit my father's work, as he has written ten times as many books as I have, but the collaboration was much easier than I expected. If we'd had more time, the story could easily have spilled out of its neat little container and grown into something much larger, with each of us taking unexpected detours along our agreed-upon route. Mythology! Fun for the whole family!

—ES

"Lost Lake" is based on the Persephone/Demeter myth and is therefore divided into two locations that separate out into light and dark, warm and cold, female and male, but only roughly and approximately.

—PS

Phaeton, from Ovid's *Metamorphoses*

WHAT WANTS MY SON
Kevin Wilson

I got to choose the meeting place, so I picked the mall. I tried to think of the one location my dad would most hate, and this was all I could come up with. It made me so mad, as I sat there in the food court, not eating because I wanted him to pay for it, because it hit me that the worst place actually would have been the apartment where Mom and I live. Good god, it would have been the best thing ever to make him sit on the futon with the guacamole stains and have to swat all of Mom's cats out of the way and engage in a real heart-to-heart with me while Mom made us tuna noodle casserole a few feet away from us, snickering at his every attempt to defend himself.

I chewed the edges of my fingers until they bubbled with spit-slicked blood. I used napkins from the dispenser to soak up the blood and then I crumpled them up and set them up around me like a protective barrier. I thought, if he tried to hug me, I would step back and offer my bleeding hand for him to shake. And whatever he did, it wouldn't matter. It wouldn't change my opinion of him.

THE first time my mom told me who my dad really was, I knew, even though I was only four or five years old, that she was just trying to make me feel better. We were alone and poor and other kids, for whatever reason, just hated me. I came home with bruises and cuts and it must have torn my mom's guts out to see that every night when she got off from her second job, me already in bed. She told me that my dad was a god, was something sparkling and beautiful, and, after a dozen times repeating it, something came unhinged inside of me. I began to believe her. And once I accepted the fact that I was half-god, not quite certain of how immortal it made me, it turned my life into a trial, one that, at some glorious point in the future, would be rewarded with all that the heavens could muster.

In the years after that, if I asked my mom about my dad, she would say, "He's so much less than what you'd think, Phaeton," but I kept at it, a steady force, and now that I was about to graduate high school, with a full scholarship to Duke, I guess she decided that it wouldn't ruin me to meet my dad, Helios, god of the sun.

A woman, not much older than me, walked over to my table and sat down. She was wearing a gold skirt suit. "You Phaeton?" she asked, her hand working her cell phone, not bothering to look directly at me. "Yeah," I said. She smiled and finally looked away from her phone. "Good," she said. "That's real good." She punched a few more words into her phone and then stood up. "He'll be here in just a second." She was beautiful, perfect teeth, perfect skin, a goddess, I imagined. "Who are you?" I asked. She looked puzzled and then said, "I'm his assistant. I'm Summer. I work for him." I grabbed her arm and instantly felt like a creep. "Is he a nice guy?" I asked. She snapped her arm from me and then said, "He's awesome." And she was gone, and there was no one to replace her. If I cried, I kept telling myself, I would never let myself live it down.

Ten minutes later, there he was, wearing a purple jogging suit, the material so expensive it looked cheap. This was typical of gods, from what I could gather on the Internet and TV; they were so otherworldly in their level of attractiveness that they dressed like fucking idiots. And it still didn't matter. Every single person in the food court instantly zeroed in on Helios, his peacocking walk, the sound of his gold chains audible over the Muzak piped into the mall. As he got closer, I started to snatch the bloody napkins and shove them into my pocket. I needed the illusion of strength, of having my shit together, much more than I wanted to make him uncomfortable. I could not meet his gaze; my head felt like it weighed a hundred pounds, and then I heard his voice as he said without hesitation, "Give me a hug, boy."

I played Gods & Monsters with the few friends I'd managed to en-snare, latchkey kids who listened to black metal and hated the sun. I'd told them about my dad, his supposed paternity, and, though I could tell they didn't believe me, they loved working it into our campaigns. As a Deity Slayer, I had fought Helios a number of times and, to the delight of Dave, our storyteller, could never muster the mathematically impossible rolls necessary to kill him. "Burned to a crisp," he would say to me, my points finally used up, and the other guys would rag on me. I would simply roll a new Deity Slayer into existence and build up my experience until I could fight him again, my swords so comically large that, under the right set of circum-stances, I could slice the sun in half.

I stood up, could not deny him my acknowledgment, but I merely held out my hand, oozing clear liquid from my self-inflicted wounds. My dad seemed completely unfazed by my refusal of an embrace. "Fine," he said, shaking my hand, not even noticing the blood, "we'll work up to the hug, I guess."

We sat at the table in silence, though Helios seemed not to mind the awkwardness. He radiated light, as if the sun was actually housed inside his fucking body. He glanced at his phone a few times, but, otherwise, he seemed content to just watch me as I vibrated with nerves and tried to think of something mean to say to him. Finally, he spoke up.

"Are you hungry?"

"Not really," I said.

"I'm starving," he replied, scanning the food court, "but I know it's terrible for me to eat this kind of food."

"Mortal food?" I asked, nothing but snark fueling my engine.

"Yeah," he replied, not picking up on my anger. "A slice of pizza is like eating a black cloud of misery. Soda turns my urine blood-toxic. I do it anyways, though. I'm going to do it right now." He pushed away from the table and started walking toward the Sbarro. He left me at the table, and I suddenly realized that I was starving. I wanted to run after him, order a calzone on his dime, but I had already declined food. It occurred to me that I needed to be savvier about this meeting, probably the only time I would ever talk to my dad. I needed him to tell me the secret of my existence, the power I held without knowing it. I needed, I now understood, to be nicer to him, to be a good son.

"HOW did you meet?" I asked my mom. We were touring colleges the summer before my senior year, my mom taking a week off from her jobs, which she really could not afford to do. On the Greyhound bus, nothing but silently grieving people around us, there seemed to be nothing else to talk about. Or at least I thought so.

"Do we have to talk about this?" she said, lowering her voice, turning toward the window and the landscape blurring around us.

"Please," I begged. This was probably the hundredth time I'd asked her, and I hoped that the unfamiliar surroundings, the unsteadiness of the rattling bus, might weaken her resolve.

"How do you think we met?" she asked me.

"You were babysitting his kids?" I said. "Or maybe he saw you at the public pool and took you out for an ice cream sundae."

"You are such a smart-ass," she said. I smiled. I liked it when I got on her nerves. It meant that she wasn't feeling sorry for me.

"I was stripping," she finally said, the wind of her words ragged and quick. "I was only seventeen, but I had a fake ID and so nobody stopped me. He came in a few times and then he paid me a thousand dollars to go into a private room and have sex. I said okay. We kept doing that until I found out I was pregnant and then he became scarce. I could summon him, occasionally, but only for a few minutes. It was clear that he wasn't going to marry me, and I didn't really want him to anyways. After you were born, I stopped trying to contact him; he'd made it clear that he had no interest in us."

In order to stop thinking about my mother in a strip club, fucking strangers in the champagne room, I asked her, "Could you summon him now?"

"Probably," she said. "We're linked because of you. I have some small power over him. I don't want it, but I have it."

"Could you summon him right now?" I asked again, and she looked at me and frowned.

"Honey? Please don't."

"Could you?" I asked, almost crying. The bus lurched to a stop, and people started to file out, but I did not move. "Please."

"CAN I ask you something, Phaeton?" he said. He had finished the pizza in minutes and was now taking his time with the soda, not a care in the world.

"I guess so," I replied.

"What's the point?" he asked. "Why did you want to see me?"

"Are you serious," I said. "You're my dad, right?"

"In a manner of speaking, yes."

"Either you are or you aren't," I said, suddenly terrified that my mom had indeed been lying all these years.

"Fine, yes, yes, yes, I am your dad, okay? I'm your dad. I made you. But I've never been around, never made contact with you. I don't even know your birthday. It was, to my mind, a good arrangement."

"It's why you fuck mortals, right? No responsibilities?"

"Come on, Phaeton. Let's be civil, okay?"

I realized that whatever big moment I was hoping for was not going to happen. I was, in his eyes, just another mortal, a speck of something interesting but finite. Nothing I said was going to move him; he was not going to apologize for something he did not even recognize as needing absolution.

I was his son, fine; at least I knew that for certain, but I wanted more than that. I wanted to have some kind of power. I wanted to be godlike, even a fraction of a god. I wanted my existence to have the possibility of value. And I knew, deep down, that none of this would be my fortune, and so I started to cry, hiccupping sobs. I cried with such vigor that the wounds on my hands opened up and spotted my fingerprints.

"Phaeton," my dad said, looking uneasily around the food court. "Let's not go in this direction, please."

I could not stop hiccupping, the way my sadness kept getting sucked back into me, but I managed to say, "You're my dad, fine. Okay? But I'm not your son. I'm a fucking loser."

"Your mom said something about a scholarship to college?" he offered.

"I didn't say I was stupid. I said I was a loser. Something toxic happened when you and my mom made me."

Helios now seemed genuinely interested in this conversation, amazed at the possibility that he was responsible for anything that was defective. "C'mon, now," he said, handing me some napkins from the dispenser, which I took and immediately plastered to my face. "Look, if I say you are my son, then you're worthy of that title. I acknowledge you, Phaeton. You are special, even if you don't realize it."

"God don't make no junk," I said, starting to calm down, feeling my sarcasm tamp down my true emotions.

"Yes," he said, smiling, grateful. "Yes, exactly. I actually have a T-shirt that says that."

"Not true in this particular case," I replied.

"What do you want, Phaeton? What do you want from me?"

I was totally sober now, the dizziness of revealing true emotions having worn off. Now I had something that I truly wanted. And I was going to get it.

"What can you give me?" I asked, genuinely curious as to how far this might go. If I would continue to be a nonentity in this world, perhaps I could weigh myself down with gold in the process.

"Make a request," he stated. He was grinning now, happy to have something to offer me, the actual request a mere inconvenience in his mind.

"Let me drive the chariot for one day," I said, my future becoming crystalline and perfect.

DAVE and I were waiting for the school bus, another bleak morning without hope or prospect. It being winter, the sun had just barely begun to rise in the east. "Wave hi to your daddy," Dave said. I flipped the bird to the sun and we both giggled.

After a few quiet minutes, the bus running late, Dave told me, "I saw Jupiter once, at a baseball game." None of our other friends were around and I kept looking at his face, so serious, so ashamed.

"What now?" I asked.

"It was the ALCS playoffs two years ago. He had a Cardinals jersey, Albert Pujols, and he was drinking a beer. Every time the umpire called a strike on Pujols, he would shout *bullshit* really loud."

"How did you know?" I asked him.

"Everyone in the stadium knew," he said. "We all kind of stared at him and it was like the Wave, the way it passed around the sections of Turner Field until everyone had figured it out. But we couldn't do anything about it. No one bothered him. Well, one little kid asked for his autograph."

"What did he do?"

"Told the kid to get the fuck away from him. That's the point, Phaeton. The gods, they're just assholes. They're bullies who pick on nerds. Even if Helios is your dad, you wouldn't like him. They live in the heavens and do jack shit; I read somewhere that it takes Helios less than five human minutes to drive his chariot around the world. They come down to earth when it suits them, usually to fuck somebody or make a mess. If he was your dad, in human form, you'd be so happy he wasn't around."

The bus finally came, and we boarded. I pressed my face against the window, trying not to cry, as I stared at the sun as best as I possibly could, wondering if he could see me, if he could at least sense my presence.

IT took nearly thirty minutes of pleading before he finally relented. Now, I was dizzy from ascending to the heavens, a little unsteady on my feet, as he led me to the chariot. He kept jabbering, giving me a lifetime of advice in five minutes. "Just find the middle ground, okay? Not too high, not too low. The worst thing you can do is get too low and burn the earth." I nodded, barely listening to him.

"The hardest thing is fighting the spin of the earth. You'll feel like you're about to pass out. Just hold on to the reins and follow in the tracks I've made, okay? Phaeton? Do you understand me?"

"Sure," I said. "Hold on to the reins, follow in your tracks, don't set the world on fire."

"Shit," he said, realizing the stupidity of his gift. "Your mother is going to kill me."

He rubbed sunscreen on my face, his hands gentle as he streaked my nose and cheeks with Coppertone. It made me feel, just as I was convinced that I hated him, like I was his son and he was taking care of me.

"You're an adult, so I'm going to give you one more chance to back out and then I'm going to shut my mouth."

"It's fine," I said, but he still looked concerned. The stallions were neighing so emphatically that it felt like a riot was swirling around us. "Dad," I said, knowing exactly what I was doing, "it's going to be fine."

"One time around the earth," he said, shaking his finger at me. "Come right back here when you're done."

"I promise," I said.

"Could I have that hug?" he asked.

"WHATEVER happens," my mom said to me, just as I left for the mall, "you have to remember this. I made you. Me. He was present, but I fucking made you."

"I know, Mom," I told her, my nerves skittering across the surface of my skin.

"An empty beam of light," she continued, angry with herself for facilitating this meeting.

"You are my sun, Mom," I said.

"You are my son, Phaeton," she replied, finishing the lines we spoke to each other for as long as I could remember.

"WAIT," my dad shouted as I snapped the reins, the morning arising. "Come back," he said, "let me do it."

I pretended not to hear, the crown of sunlight so heavy on my head, the grunting and gnashing of the stallions ringing in my head. I was off to bring light to the world.

It was even harder than he had explained. I could barely hold on to the reins, much less direct the stallions. I felt the chariot wobble violently as we streaked across the sky; the horses understood that I wasn't in charge, and so they turned angry and frantic. I didn't care. I wasn't afraid. This was what I had wanted, I now realized. I was going to set the world on fire, to turn everything to ash. I was going to make such a mess that every single time my dad stepped into this chariot, every new day, he would be forced to think of me. The other gods would never let him hear the end of it. My mother would curse him for eternity. Everyone would know my name, and it would forever be tied to his. The world would be set aflame.

I held tightly to the sun, white-hot, and let it overwhelm me. I watched as the chariot hurtled toward the earth, a disaster of my own making, and I closed my eyes. When I opened them, I was certain that I would be reborn.

I chose the myth of Phaeton. My favorite myths deal with the interaction of gods and humans or half-humans, the disasters that ensue. That divide seems similar in some ways to the frustrations of a child and parent. And I always liked the idea of Phaeton as a depressed and angry teenager.

—*KW*

Poseidon

THOUSAND
Laird Hunt

One town got a god who carried another town inside of him which locals were sometimes allowed to enter, never to return. Another town got a god shaped like a loaded pincushion who had to be placed on a shelf out of reach of adults and long-armed children because what looked like pins were not pins and what looked like cushion would bubble the skin and boil the eyes and make the bones burn. A third town, I don't know where, got a god who liked to laugh, but was no longer allowed to laugh, so no one in the town laughed either, even though the angels called in a commission which opined that aversion and solidarity were often different spellings of the same word. Other towns got other gods. Once they had been given they were no longer allowed to break the rules by exercising their central powers, not even partially, not even once. The dreaming god dreamed and was taken away by the angels. The smoldering god smoldered and got herself doused.

The doused god came to live in our backyard. She arrived early one morning and woke the chickens and I was sent out in my pajamas to see what was wrong. There had been enterprising weasels in the neighborhood. One morning one week before the doused god's arrival all the chickens two yards over had been found painting scarlet arabesques on the ground. When I got out to the coop I found the doused god. She had let herself in, shut the gate behind her, and now sat slumped in a corner. On the other side of the coop were the hens.

"They will grow used to me," said the doused god.

"You're the smoldering god," I said.

"I *was* the smoldering god," she said.

In those days I knew all the gods. The smoldering god had been small and golden and very beautiful, even after the fall. Now that the smoldering god had been doused she was no longer golden nor very beautiful but of course she was still small. She was the size of a small chicken. As I watched, our brood hen, Handsome, scuttled across the coop and gave the doused god a hard peck.

"They are used to me," said the doused god.

My parents said we could keep her. That if we had her no weasels would come. Still, they never went out to the chicken coop after she had come to live with us. I went every day. Sometimes I brought friends home to see her. At first they came, clamored against the coop wire, but when they saw how small and unlovely she was, and how she let herself be pecked by Handsome, they quickly lost interest. The official fallen deity for our town was the whale god. She had been dropped after her humiliation into the town's square. She lay in a gelatinous heap that we kids loved to bounce upon. Sometimes our parents bounced upon her too. Our grandparents did not often bounce upon her because one of them, in the first days, had bounced too vigorously and had been thrown off and had died. One of the powers of the whale god—only a tertiary power and impossible to turn off—was that it seemed always wonderful to be near her. How lovely it was to stand near her or to bounce upon her. My eyes open wider even now to think of it. I grin. My face pressed against the asphalt, it stops me mid-groan. The doused god had had no such tertiary power and now all her powers were officially gone.

An angel came and told us so. It sat with us in our front room and read to us from an official document that in addition to according us an additional ration to offset what we lost in feeding her assured us that not only were all her powers gone they had been placed where she could never find them. The angel, one of the chiefs of its kind, smiled its unbearable smile at us when it said this and patted its breast pocket knowingly. When it rose to leave I rose too and embraced it and thanked it for letting us keep the doused god. My mother grimaced and my father fainted when I did this but I was not even very badly hurt.

Everyone talked about it for weeks afterward: about my having hugged the angel. When I had recovered enough to go out again the first thing I did was go down to the town's square and bounce on the whale god. I bounced and flipped forward. I bounced and flipped backward. The whale god rotated the salt-encrusted iris of her salt-encrusted eye to look toward me. She blinked and her iris turned turquoise a moment. Of course she couldn't speak. But I could tell what she was thinking. What she had recognized in me. I went home and went out to the chicken coop. Neither the chickens nor the doused god had been fed for a week. Handsome and the doused god were sitting together looking glum.

"You have my powers, now," said the doused god.

"I hugged the angel," I said.

"He will realize what has happened," she said.

"I can pick any pocket," I said.

"He will come for you. He will bring others," she said. Handsome clucked when she said this.

"You can't have them back," I said. "And fuck you too, Handsome," I added. Then I tossed a handful of feed into the coop, packed a bag and went away.

I waited for the angels for years but they never came. My parents grew old and died and still they did not come. Everyone I had known in my youth grew old and died and they did not come. My powers took longer than I would have liked to assert themselves. I had set up my godly shop in a hollowed-out mountain that only very slowly became a volcano. In the early years I had envisioned maintaining a low but significant profile but by and by worshippers with no one but the angels to worship sniffed me out. They built a temple at the base of the volcano and every now and again I would go down and sit with them and drink beer. On one of these nights, as I sat smoldering beside the temple with a bucket of beer in my hand, a new worshipper arrived. He prostrated himself before me, then stood and removed his hood.

"I won't relinquish my powers," I said.

"I am not here to try and take them," said the angel I had stolen the smoldering god's powers from, for that is whom I now saw standing before me.

"You can't have them," I said.

"Do you want us to kill him, boss?" said one of my worshippers, a sturdy fellow named Grok.

"I am here to join you in worshipping this great god," said the angel, addressing himself to Grok.

"I am here to worship you," said the angel, addressing himself to me.

"I'm not even sure you can kill an angel," I said.

"You can kill angels," he said. "But I am no longer an angel. I have not been an angel since you picked my pocket. I was broken and cast down and have wandered the dark ways of the world in hopes of finding you."

The former angel held up his arm. It was crooked. He then lifted up his pants legs and showed me a number of scars on his shins.

"I think you should kill this guy, Grok," I said.

"Unless you would prefer to do it yourself, boss," said Grok.

I had taken, at that period, to wearing velvet bathrobes that my worshippers made for me. The one I had on was a deep, almost electric blue, and went very nicely with the decidedly electric red tinge of my smoldering skin. I took a long swig of beer, belched very loudly, and burned the robe off my skin.

"They'll make me another one," I said, feeling immediately a little foolish because whether they would or they wouldn't was clearly beside the point.

"Yo, Grok, watch this," I said.

I flipped a finger and nothing happened. I flipped it again and the former angel began to burn. It took a while. Then he was dead and a cheer went up and there was some dancing. I tried to dance but was not so into it, couldn't find my godly groove. I drank some more beer, then went up to my volcano. I sat on a rock chair. I did not sleep. I never slept. I felt bad. For what? For not believing the angel? For killing him myself? For burning my favorite blue velvet robe? For not saying good night to Grok before I left? Was Grok, faithful, sturdy Grok, unhappy with me?

"This is the path that lies before you," said the doused god.

"Wait, what?" I said.

She was sitting in the chicken coop. She and the chickens were eating the feed I had just tossed them.

"*This* is the path," she said.

"Jesus, Christ, whatever," I said.

I went into the house. My parents were sitting together on the couch watching television, a show on penguins. I went up to my room and threw a tennis ball against the closet until my father yelled at me to cut it out. I got older. Joined a band. We called ourselves The Other Towns. I played bass and smoked jumbo doobs and forgot about angels and powers. Later I got a job in a bank and fell in love with the branch manager who let me spend time with her in the vault for a while then fired me when a new teller was hired. I went into sales, hawked men's wear, then radiator hoses, then unbreakable plates. Part of the pitch for the plates was throwing them on the ground then catching them when they came bouncing back up. I wore a fake curly mustache and a bowler hat for the job. Sometimes the door was shut before the plate had made it back up to me. Once, in desperation, I pushed one of my pretty salad plates through the mail slot. I heard a grunt and a smashing sound and the salad plate came back out through the slot, in pieces.

Therefore I moved back in with my parents. The chickens and their coop were long gone and the doused god had taken over my old bedroom. She wore a wig now and helped around the house and everyone called her Handsome. This was confusing but that's okay. I was given a cot in the garage. I went to bed early and slept late. In between dreams I played my old bass although my amp no longer worked. Sometimes my father would come out into the garage and share a beer with me. He was very old. Handsome sometimes cleaned in the garage.

"Well," I said.

"Well, what?" she said.

She had taken to sporting a turquoise napkin around her waist— a kind of apron. She looked a little like a tubby gecko. She and my mother had grown close. They played lots of cribbage. My father often sat near them, smiling and offering suggestions. For a while I got part-time work in street advertising. Just a few shifts a week. Obviously you didn't get to choose your sign. I bought a portable CD player and that helped a little. One day, the angel drove by in a Mustang and flicked a cigarette at me. He came by the next day but

I was ready, and his cigarette burned my sign instead of my cheek. Then I got fired and my parents kicked me out. As I was leaving, Handsome called me over. I bent down, thinking, this is it, now I get to go back, finally, fuck, but Handsome only kissed me, rather wetly, on the corner of my mouth and said, "Thank you."

I drifted a while, saw some of the world, did drugs, ate badly, lost a bunch of teeth. When I returned to my town it was unrecognizable. My parents were dead and my house had vanished. In the old town square there was a giant mound of cracked asphalt where the whale god had lain. Rats peeped their heads out of holes in the base of the mound and kids on skateboards patrolled the periphery. They said, "Hey, man!" and jostled me as I made my way up the mound of asphalt. They laughed and threw pebbles when I reached the top, lay down, put my eye against one of the cracks, peered deep into the ground.

The trope of fallen/punished gods is an old one. Add the notion of severe and probably malevolent bureaucracy to the equation and we rejoin Kafka and his parables. I was thinking most immediately here about his image of an exhausted Poseidon, buried in paperwork as he administers the sea.

—LH

Post-Apocalypse

⚭

BELLE-MEDUSA

Manuela Draeger

The other night, someone knocked on the door.

It was late. It was very dark and very cold. Throughout the entire evening, I had listened to the silences and the noises reverberating above the city, in the towers and the crumbling houses, in the empty streets. The meteorite shower had stopped, the fires had finally petered out, and quiet darkness reigned. In the distance, up above the abandoned factories, you caught sight of my friend Big Katz, the woolly crab, in the middle of redoubling his attempts to float beneath the clouds. Against the dark background of the vaulted heavens, you could barely discern him. A little yellow blotch was drifting, not bright enough to light the sky, a sort of rough sketch of the moon with claws and a few tufts of fur. Big Katz still had a long way to go before you would truly confuse him with a heavenly body. He was getting better, it's true, and he applied as best he could the advice of Alfons Tchop, his moon teacher. But, it must be admitted, his technical proficiency was still low. I was seated near the window, under a thick blanket of pleasantly warm wool, and I was dozing. I opened an eye, from time to time, to keep an eye on the trajectory of Big Katz, who was very slowly moving away toward the Jumble.

Someone knocked again.

I wasn't expecting anyone. For a second, I thought that it was maybe Lili Nebraska. We live in the same building, and she often comes to visit me, to entrust me with the investigation of a bizarre case, for instance, or even to cuddle up in my arms, because we are quite fond of one another, Lili and I, and sometimes, when the nights are frightening, we prefer to spend them together, pressed tight against one another. But no. Well obviously, it wasn't her. Lili wouldn't have taken the unlit stairways and the hallways through which tigers roam, slashing at passersby with swipes of their claws and laying down the law. I'm not even mentioning the suffocating odor of pee that they spread in the darkness, and which Lili, like everyone, hates. No, after midnight, Lili tends to take another route to meet up with me. She scales the facade beginning at her apartment on the third floor, and when she has reached the seventh she taps against the windowpane.

Again there was knocking.

Outside my door, on the landing, someone was reporting their presence and was becoming impatient because I still hadn't opened up.

I didn't answer.

It's bad not to answer when someone knocks on the door. You never know if it's an urgent matter or not. What if the person knocking needs help? What if, for instance, it's an unknown woman starved for affection, who hopes that you are going to open up to her with kindness, that you are going to welcome her with open arms and kiss her a little bit all over without making a fuss? Everything is always possible. But as for me, I stayed under my polar blanket and took shallow breaths, so as not to make any noise. You, you think that instead of doing that I should have gotten up and gone to open it, and you are right. I wasn't proud of playing dead, but okay. That night I had very little desire for someone to disturb me, demanding hugs or a cup of tea from me, or even coming to explain to me at length one of those complicated problems that only the police can solve. Apart from Lili Nebraska, that night I didn't want to see whoever it was. Some nights are like that. You're a bit surly. Nothing to be done about it.

At the end of ten or fifteen seconds, the tap-tapping resumed.

"Are you sleeping, Bobby?" a voice asked.

I searched my memory, but this voice didn't conjure up anyone. What's more, there was nothing natural about it. It was a little like when a schoolteacher conducts experiments in acoustical transmission and, to speak with her students, sticks her head in a basin filled with seawater or rainwater.

"Are you sleeping, yes or no?" the voice said.

You really felt a lot of authoritative urgency in this question. I don't know if you've ever lived through a similar situation, but I find that it's always disturbing to be called out to in the middle of the night by someone who insists that you answer them. I started to experience the beginnings of fear. I continued to imagine behind the door a sort of displeased, strict schoolteacher, her face sunk up to her ears in water.

"Yes or no?" the voice insisted.

"Yes," I murmured.

"Okay," the voice said. "You're asleep. That's what it seems like to me."

I stared at the handle of the door. The darkness was very thick. I stared at the place where, logically, the handle of the door had to be located, and I didn't see anything. I didn't move.

"Listen, Bobby," the voice continued on. "Since you're sleeping, it's not worth waking you up. Don't move."

"I'm not moving," I observed.

On the other side of the door, the disagreeable schoolteacher type remained silent, a little as if she were gathering up her sentences before throwing herself into a speech, or as if she were collecting air before again plunging her face into her bowl of water. And then, she started to say things in a voice full of bubbles and with a deformed roaring. She spoke to me of a certain Belle-Medusa, as if this were someone that I knew and as if I were anxious to have news of her, of this Belle-Medusa.

"Belle-Medusa has left her realm in the high seas," announced the voice. "She has gotten to the edge of the ice floe, she traveled along the ice fields and she is in the area. She floats within view of the coast. Belle-Medusa, does the name mean anything to you?"

"Nothing," I said. "Absolutely nothing."

"She would have liked to come closer to town, but she can't. She is too big to enter the estuary."

Too big to enter the estuary! An estuary whose mouth must surely be forty or fifty kilometers wide!

"She could try to squeeze through," I suggested.

"No," explained the voice. "Even squeezing through, she wouldn't manage it."

I attempted to visualize this enormous undersea mountain, gelatinous and vaguely drifting. Even if I added on scalloping, bluish sails, and transparent strands, I didn't succeed in making a pleasant image. Sometimes jellyfish are beautiful, but when they're more than fifty kilometers in diameter, they lose all their charm.

"So, there you have it," continued the voice. "Belle-Medusa would like to visit the city, and since she needs someone to do it in her place, she picked you. She has plugged into you."

"What?" I said indignantly. "She has plugged into me?"

"Don't worry, Bobby. Plugging in is not painful, and if I hadn't told you, you wouldn't have noticed. Belle-Medusa just wants to gather some information through you. You won't have to do anything special. Quite possibly, it will even entertain you."

I let half a minute elapse. I didn't like it one bit, this Belle-Medusa story. And frankly, I don't think you would have liked it either had you been in my place. I will summarize: you're at home, in the heart of a dark night, under a duvet that protects you from the awful cold, you're dozing quite peacefully and you would like to continue to doze until morning, and suddenly an unknown schoolteacher sets up shop on your landing with a basin of water filled to the brim. She shoves her head in it to speak to you, and she tells you that a giant jellyfish has just plugged into you, intending to use you as a tour guide or as a spy.

"I'm not free at the moment," I said. "Ask someone else. The police no longer exist, and we're the ones standing in for them, Lili Nebraska and myself. The investigations are long and they feed into one another, each more absurd than the last, and more often than not, they remain unsolved. It's very exhausting. We don't have any time to dedicate to jellyfish, whether they are beautiful or ugly."

"What are you saying, Bobby?" said the schoolteacher, getting angry, in her washbasin voice. "All this has nothing to do with the police and, in any case, Belle-Medusa is not asking for your opinion. It's best for you to know it right away: nobody disobeys Belle-Medusa. She chose you as an informant and she plugged into you. It's not even possible for you to refuse this task. You will do it, period. End of discussion."

She rattled this off in the tone of someone who won't accept someone questioning her orders, while blowing and lowing loudly

in the water. All the vowels sounded alike and the consonants especially were strange, but, with a little effort, you understood. It must
have been an intermediary language between our own and that of
the jellyfish.

"She could have looked elsewhere," I griped. "For instance, there
are volunteers in the Office of Tourism. For a bit of food and a kiss
on the eyelids, they organize a tour of the city for any travelers who
want it."

"Don't try to make fun of me, Bobby," said the voice. "The Office of Tourism has been closed for ages, and the volunteers departed without leaving a forwarding address. Don't think that
Belle-Medusa chose you lightly. She is like everyone else, she has
heard talk of the strange investigations that you undertake against
your better judgment, and all those muddles that you never manage
to solve. It doesn't thrill her to enlist your services. But there is almost nobody in this city anymore. So she settled for you."

"She settled for me and she plugged into me as if I were an ordinary electrical appliance," I grumbled inwardly.

"And then, what's more, she didn't choose you completely by accident," the voice added. "She knows you have flair. She is counting
on your flair."

DURING the quarter of an hour that followed, the voice explained
to me what Belle-Medusa expected of me, and how I was going to
satisfy her.

Belle-Medusa was hardly interested in urban civilization or architecture and, now that she had traveled around a lot in all the oceans
of the wide world, she thought she had seen enough landscapes to
no longer have much desire to travel. In truth, she only had one passion anymore: she collected smells. Aromas, perfumes, whiffs, and
scents of all types. She numbered them and she put them in tiny special cases in her memory, in a classification system that nobody,
apart from herself, was able to understand. However, her collection
was too limited in data related to solid ground, and she had decided
to complete it. In her memory, she had now set up boxes and even
supplementary shelves specially prepared to receive non-underwater
novelties. And since she couldn't hoist herself up onto dry land,
since she could neither visit it nor even approach it, she had decided
to plug into the residents of the coast and to record the reports that

they would make on the quality of stenches and fragrances. In any case, to begin with she had plugged into me. She invited me on her behalf to sniff around the more or less touristy locations in town, the streets, the houses, the minimarts, the harbor facilities, the burned-out train stations and the factories that hadn't produced anything for years.

"It's quite difficult to describe smells," I objected.

"Breathe in deeply through your nose," counseled the voice, "and then let your imagination run wild. Things will come into your head. And, since you are plugged into Belle-Medusa, it will be directly translated into the language she uses for her classification. You'll see, it's automatic."

"And how will I communicate my descriptions?" I asked.

"Good question, Bobby," said the voice.

For once, she didn't seem exasperated by my objections.

There were many ways to proceed, according to the voice. First solution, they could furnish me with a special mask, thanks to which I would be in turn wirelessly plugged into Belle-Medusa, but it hadn't been invented yet and time was needed before someone could manufacture it and give it to me. Second solution, wait for the darkest hours of the night. The voice behind the door would serve as an intermediary between me and Belle-Medusa, but I might risk being asleep at the moment when she knocked at the door and might not answer, or still worse, to muddle my report with the scraps of my dreams. Third solution, I could go to the end of the estuary and holler the results of my observations to the open sea, but that would force me into tiresome comings and goings, and what's more, if the wind blew in from the water, my words would be carried in the wrong direction and perhaps would never reach their recipient, namely Belle-Medusa. No, the best thing would be to have recourse to aquatic transmission. "Do you understand, Bobby Potemkine?" the voice repeated. "You will communicate through water and liquids."

"How's that?" I asked.

"Yes," explained the voice, "through the water. Rainwater or seawater. Even tap water will do. All you have to do is plunge your head in and speak. Belle-Medusa will hear you. It's the simplest method and the surest."

I was a little stunned by this idea. I didn't answer back, but, since

I am not in the habit of putting my head into water to converse with jellyfish, this prospect didn't delight me, obviously.

"It's nothing out of the ordinary," said the voice in conclusion. "Everyone will do it sooner or later, when they have to speak to Belle-Medusa."

I waited for further instructions. Several long minutes passed, but nothing more came to break the silence. And when I once again heard the tiger-striped cats chasing each other while meowing and with their claws skidding along the tile floor, I knew that there was no longer anyone behind the door. Belle-Medusa's messenger had disappeared.

I stood up, still wrapped in my thick blanket, and went to crack open the door and cast a glance in the direction of the darkness. The hallway was empty, but in front of my door there was a confused, rounded pile, a sort of construction made of cloth, old carpet, and pieces of bark. It looked, more or less, like a teepee. I could have approached it and checked to see if it was inhabited or not, and even tried to slip inside. But the darkness was too deep and I was afraid of a bad encounter, with, for example, an inconvenient tiger who was squatting in it, this illustrious tent.

"Is there anyone there?" I asked.

My voice echoed in the hallway. No one answered.

I closed the door again and drew near to the window. The city slept, overcome by cold and darkness. You could barely see the building opposite and, since at present neither stars nor Big Katz lit the sky, you couldn't even see the nearest bank of the estuary. Over there, at the mouth, floated Belle-Medusa: gigantic, gently brushing aside the icebergs strewn across her path. She was immense and extremely slow. In her memory she had an enormous collection of undersea fragrances and stenches, and she had prepared new special cases to collect descriptions of the smells that wafted along the coast. And she was waiting for me to plunge my head into a washbasin to describe these smells to her one by one.

I had my cheek pressed against the windowpane. Just under my nose, fed by the steam that escaped from my mouth, the frost drew branching ice wisps, which imprisoned the dust. If I had had to specify the smell that lingered on the surface of the glass, I would have spoken of a dusty ice floe, of frozen goose down, of dark sherbet. Wait, I thought, maybe I could send that to Belle-Medusa, in order to check that the communication between us is well established.

I left my observation post. I groped my way to the bathroom and I filled the sink with what flowed from the faucet, water that carried with it cubes and needles of ice. Before immersing my face, I had to stir it with my hand so as not to have to use the end of my nose to break the film threatening to form. The water was horribly icy. I sank my head into it to my ears.

"It's me, Belle-Medusa," I said.

My voice didn't sound like anything. My mouth produced gurglings. It's a complicated word, but it's the most correct in this sort of situation, and, if you want to know exactly what it corresponds to, you could always, you as well, try to recite a poem with your head underwater. You'll see, it's not very harmonious as a noise: a gurgling. My mouth moved at the bottom of the water and therefore it expelled gurglings, sounds which were closed or elongated, bubbles, and lowings. I had foreseen speaking about dusty ice floes, frozen goose down, and dark sherbet but the liquid deformed my sentences, and the automatic translation betrayed it still more. In a language that I hardly understood, I heard myself bellow things completely different from what I wanted to say. The operation of my voice escaped me, I no longer controlled the sentences I pronounced. With all these plug-ins, a foreign speech substituted itself for my own.

"This is Bobby Potemkine, calling Belle-Medusa," I said. "Listen, Belle-Medusa. The first smell that I am going to describe to you lingers on the surface of the cold windowpane. On the other side nothing is lit up. The city is invisible. So, here it is. It's *the smell of a ticket collector from the RER station who has dropped his keys on the ground and who is getting up again*. It's *the smell of a landscape painted in oils by a dwarf painter*. It's *the smell of a chemistry workbook licked by an old lame German shepherd*."

I took my head out of the water and drained the sink, then I rubbed my face with a terry-cloth towel until the feeling of cold went away. I didn't know what else to do. I didn't know if Belle-Medusa had heard me or what she might have retained of my speech. I was ashamed to have come out spouting nonsense into the sink, and I was embarrassed by the idea that Belle-Medusa had already put it away on the special shelves of her memory, this nonsense.

I felt so embarrassed that, in the frigid bathroom, I felt the need to make a remark aloud.

"It didn't work too well, communicating with Belle-Medusa," I said.

My voice shook a bit. It was once again normal, without gurglings, but it was the voice of someone ashamed and very annoyed, and it trembled slightly.

THAT night would have been like all the others if not for that bizarre visitor with her bizarre washbasin voice, and this plugging into Belle-Medusa which had led me to plunge my head into cold water in order to describe smells, and to describe them in a manner which afterward made me ashamed.

Outside, Big Katz no longer shone in the background of the sky. He must have fallen back to earth, or else perhaps he'd gone behind a cloud. A few meteorites whistled from time to time above the city. They would scatter on the terraces of the buildings or in the water of the estuary. Sometimes they had a brief lightning-yellow coloring, sometimes a little sizzling glow, at the moment the nuggets vaporized against one of the surrounding roofs, but mostly the darkness stayed thick. I spent long moments at the window, waiting to see if Big Katz would come from behind his cloud or try a second outing in the heights, then I went back and sat on the sofa.

The meteor shower was approaching its end. Then everything quieted down. In the stairwells of the building, the shadowy ruckus of the tigers increased. Two toms came and went behind the door, no doubt intrigued by the presence of that teepee that had suddenly appeared in the hallway. I heard their dissatisfied growling and the scratching of their claws on the tiled floor.

I was at the point of falling half asleep.

I was at the point of falling two-thirds asleep.

I was at the point of falling three-quarters asleep, and it was just at that moment that the telephone rang. I groped around for the receiver and I picked it up.

"Did I wake you up?" worried Lili Nebraska.

Her voice was a little hoarse, like it was when she'd spent a long while lost in music, in the endless nostalgia of a G-minor impromptu, for example, or in a simplification for violin of a cantata for shewolves and street musicians. When Lili Nebraska starts to perform this sort of piece, you instantly forget everything. You drown in emotion, and, during the minutes and hours that follow, you are always a little bit hoarse. And Lili herself drowned in her own music, in its tears of happiness and beauty, in its shivers.

"Were you in the middle of playing something in G-minor, Lili?" I asked.

"No," said Lili. "I was meditating. I was thinking in the dark."

For a few seconds, I imagined Lili Nebraska meditating in the dark. I saw again her shining pupils, very black, fixed on the vague, sooty reflections of the windowpane or turned toward the heavy and invisible mass of the walls of her apartment. I imagined what I knew of her, her small black-haired figure, her skin brown as gingerbread, extremely soft to the touch, with the black designs embellishing her cheeks and the area surrounding her navel and the curve of her belly. Those designs that I loved to caress and kiss when I had the chance to do so, even when only in dreams. Lili Nebraska is obviously a very pretty street violinist, but, in my opinion, when she thinks in the dark, this is the most moving and beautiful thing of all.

"Is there a problem, Lili?" I asked.

"I have the feeling so," said Lili. "A strange phenomenon."

"I know," I said.

"No, you don't know, Bobby," Lili interrupted me. "It's about the trembling tents."

"The trembling tents?" I said in surprise.

"You see, Bobby. You're not up-to-date. I suppose all the same that I don't have to explain to you what a trembling tent is?"

"No, all the same," I said.

I don't know about you, but as for me, they were something I had already heard tell of, trembling tents. They are a little bit like an ordinary teepee, but with a very large opening at the top. The shamans of the Great North and the Innu Indians go into them when they want to communicate with animals or with other shamans, or with the stars. They function by thought transmission. However, even if they give satisfying results, they are used very seldom, because in fact whoever gets into one hardly has any fun. He sees nothing, he is deafened by cries and growls, animals appear around him, animals trample him or jostle him. When he speaks, he almost can't control the words coming out of his mouth. The tent trembles during the entire session. Nobody goes near it. Several years ago, as the telephone was in the process of working less and less well, it was thought that the trembling tents could be used as telephone booths, but, because of the noises, the animal smells, and the rushing of caribou that you were subjected to during the entire duration of the call, the idea was abandoned.

"Is there a problem with the trembling tents?" I asked.

I thought about the structure that had been erected on my landing, in the dark hallway. It had a dilapidated and disordered appearance, no doubt due to the tiger-striped cats which had tried to get into it, which had horsed around in its vicinity and sharpened their claws on its bark walls, but, in the end, it had exactly the slightly bizarre cylindrical structure of a trembling tent.

"That's what I was pondering," Lili said. "They've started to come and go on their own. But above all, for some unknown reason, it's no longer possible to go into the interior."

"The interior of what?"

"The interior of the trembling tents."

"Ha," I said, "no great loss. It seems that, once inside, you don't have any fun. You hear the howling of animals and stampeding, you get hit by hooves and by horns, and, what's more, according to certain accounts, you are asphyxiated by the strong smells of caribou sweat or poorly washed manes, when it isn't the sulfurous smell of the stars."

I had just conjured up a bouquet of smells, and I told myself that I could take advantage of this, as long as I had them well in mind, these smells, to describe them to Belle-Medusa.

"Hold on, Lili," I said. "I'll call you back in five minutes."

I went into the bathroom and, once again, I filled the sink with what flowed from the faucet, a mixture of icy water and crisp flakes. Just before plunging my head in, I reviewed what I was going to say: the sulfurous smell of the stars. I took a breath and I put my face under the water. I had my sentence all ready, but, in the midst of the gurglings, another sentence came out.

"*The smell of bird of paradise in an elevator,*" I said.

No, it's not possible, I thought. I have to speak of the sulfurous smell of the stars. I have to force myself to say that.

"*The smell of an old granny who is an archery champion,*" my mouth pronounced.

No, it's completely unacceptable, I thought. It's sulfur and stars that it's a question of.

"The smell of a big beanpole in conversation with a little beanpole," my mouth pronounced.

Under the water, I winced. I wanted to force my lips to shape the words that I had on my tongue. Sulfur. Stars.

"The smell of a Ping-Pong ball abandoned in vinegar," I heard myself say.

I took my head out of the water and I dried myself off.

I returned to sit down on the sofa. I groped around to dial Lili Nebraska's number.

"What's happening over there, Bobby?" asked Lili.

"It's not going well," I said. "Ever since Belle-Medusa plugged into me, it's not going very well."

"Do you want me to come over?" Lili asked.

"Yes," I said. "I'd really like you to come."

FIFTEEN minutes later, Lili knocked on the windowpane. I opened the window. While she climbed over the sill, the cold wind rushed into the room, bringing an armful of nocturnal fragrances. The meteor shower had given rise to smoke here and there above the city. The snow and the charred dust had been lifted up by the breezes. The stale smell of the fire combined with winter and they were strong. Lili, though, smelled good. Apart from her violin case, which she wore as a bandoleer, she was wearing a bracelet of varnished wood beads and nothing else. She shivered. I buried my face in Lili's black hair, I kissed her on the magnificent black designs she had on her cheeks and around her navel, I hugged her to me. The violin got in our way. She took it off and put it on the table. I closed the window again. The smells coming from the city had entered the apartment, and they spun around us.

"Do you smell these smells, this fragrance?" I asked Lili. "Could you describe them?"

"It's almost impossible to describe smells." Lili sighed. "You have to refer to images. For example, right now, I have the feeling that it smells like a steam engine stopped in an apocalyptic landscape. You see nothing in this image, which is very dark, but you can imagine a port where all the boats have burned. The train stopped there, at the edge of these areas. And we, we are on the docks, with our own smell of red flags and sweet almond oil bath soap."

"Yes, as an example," I acquiesced. "I'll try to repeat that into the sink."

Lili Nebraska followed me into the bathroom. She didn't understand what I intended to do. I filled the sink and plunged my head in.

"Bobby Potemkine calling Belle-Medusa," I said. "I am going to describe what's floating above the village and has come into the house. First it's *the smell of a playground one June morning . . . the smell of snowy ibis in front of a travel agency . . . the smell of a diving gear merchant . . .* Then, it's *the smell of she-wolf watching a snowy ibis. . . .*"

I raised my head. It dripped. The drops fell back noisily into the sink. I lingered a bit in the same position to regain my breath and to listen to the tinkling song of the drops. I was ashamed not to have been able to stop my gurglings from being automatically translated into Belle-Medusa's strange language. Lili Nebraska went to look for a bath towel and she helped me to rub myself down. She was silent. Then she made a comment.

"It's really strange, what you said under the water," she said.

"Yes," I said. "It's strange."

I started to tell her what had happened since someone had knocked on my door. The voice in the night, the plugging into Belle-Medusa, the water, the automatic translation. We went out on the landing to see the structure of canvas, bark, and hide, upon which the tigers of the building had already deposited an unbearable aroma of pee. Lili tried to go inside. The door, a slab of bark in the middle of rags and skins that had been torn apart and haphazardly stitched back up, refused to open. Since the musky stench increased when you shook it, Lili ended up moving away.

"That definitely looks like a trembling tent," she said, backing away. "And as you see, we can't manage to get inside."

In her turn, she explained to me what she knew about the problem, everything that had made her ponder in the dark during part of the night. The trembling tents didn't stay in place, nowadays. Someone was relocating them, or they moved by their own means and were found at the other end of the city. We speak of them in the plural, said Lili, but they are few in number, these trembling tents. There are two in all. One, collapsed and out of use, at the northern tip of the estuary, and another which Sheewa Gayanlog uses from time to time, on the border between the Jumble and the factory where they made shoe polish, formerly, during a period when they had invented shoes for feet and when they told people that they would look prettier with shoes that glistened.

"Sheewa Gayanlog," I repeated thoughtfully.

"Yes," confirmed Lili. "You know her. You were together at school, from what she told me. You were in the same class."

I tried to remember this Sheewa Gayanlog who had been my classmate. What came to my mind was the image of a polar bear. But yes, of course, I knew her. A big polar bear, with a tuft of mouse-gray fur where her chest began. Not always very kind, very bad in electricity and in manual labor, like me, and interrupting her interlocutors to tell them her dreams as if she had just come out of them. I seemed to recall that one day she had quarreled with our sewing teacher and that she had eaten him, this teacher, but the memory was rather distant and blurry. As distant and blurry as what I had learned about sewing in school.

"I think I remember her eating a teacher, but I'm not one hundred percent certain," I said.

"I don't know what her dietary habits are," said Lili Nebraska. "In any case, she came to complain that her trembling tent has disappeared. She caught sight of it at the port, moving rather quickly in the direction of the minimart. She caught up with it and tried to slip inside, but she didn't succeed in doing so. The tent moved forward alone. She followed it. She followed it to the vicinity of our building, then she lost sight of it."

"You have to wonder why she is so keen on getting into a trembling tent," I pointed out.

"That's how she communicates with her cublettes," said Lili. "Her cublettes are far away, on the ice floe or in the polar waters which slip-slap along the side of the ice fields. The only means of communicating with them is by thought transmission. And the only means of achieving the transmission is by entering a trembling tent."

"Oh, so, Sheewa Gayanlog has cublettes," I said. "Sheewa Gayanlog! . . . Cublettes! . . ."

At the same moment, I felt that it was idiotic to cry out like this in showing my astonishment. She could very well have eaten her sewing teacher and, later, given life to little cublettes. It's not contradictory. I realized that my remark was out of place and I tried to smooth it over.

"Cublettes, ah . . . they're difficult to get," I mumbled.

I was conscious of not having smoothed anything over and, on the contrary, of getting bogged down still a little further in my foolishness. My cheeks started burning. They must have been on their way to taking on the color of tomato juice, but, thanks to the darkness, I remained stationed in black and white. Lili must not have been able to distinguish the crimson tint of my skin, and, in any case, if she did, she pretended not to notice anything. She was a kind person.

"Even if . . . uh . . . that has little to do with sewing, and . . . uh . . ." I continued to falter.

"Don't worry, my Bobby," said Lili Nebraska, drawing near to me.

She came to blow on my very warm cheeks, as if to make them a normal temperature. She hugged me in her arms. It was very loving.

"You know, Lili," I said. "Often I have the impression that I don't control what my mouth says very well. And not only when I emit gurglings into the sink. At other moments, too. For example, uh . . . for the fabrication of cublettes, uh . . ."

"Listen, my Bobby, we'll see about all that tomorrow," said Lili Nebraska while caressing my face with her hair and the black designs of her skin.

It was very loving, very soft.

"We'll begin an investigation tomorrow morning," she added. "For the moment, we're going to try to think about something else."

Lili took me by the hand, made me sit down on the sofa. She held the blanket out to me so that I could muffle myself up in it. I muffled myself up. I didn't dare say another word for fear that clumsy expressions and absurd images would scamper from between my lips. Lili bent down, snatched up her violin, tuned it, and then she played a piece that I loved, an infinitely melodious and infinitely moving pavane in F major. Lili Nebraska is a kind person, she knows that this pavane makes me capsize and that, once capsized, I lose all contact with the worries and strangenesses of the world. I don't know how long Lili played. I was under the blanket in the black thickness of the night, and I floated inside the music. At the end of a time that I was incapable of measuring, Lili joined me. She had set down her instrument. She had also forgotten all the worries and strangenesses of the world. We hugged each other very hard under the blanket as if we had arrived together at a place of happiness far from everything.

THEN dawn broke. It was gray. The colors of the world had difficulty returning to normal.

We took an icy shower. We rubbed against one another so as to not be paralyzed by cold, then we got out. In the hallway, in front of the door of the apartment, the Indian structure was no longer there. Someone had retrieved it, or it had left on its own, by its own means.

Near the entrance hall of the building stood Mimi Schnittke, a former tar-spreading technician. She had become a morning soup seller when she had had enough of covering the streets, which each night were destroyed by frost and meteorites, and now she pushed her cart through the city, offering on demand big ladles of soup, hot or cold according to taste. Since our building was inhabited, she was in the habit of taking a break in front of it, until Lili Nebraska or I approached to order breakfast from her. She served us two bowls of boiling hot potage of squid ink and shellfish. She had a way of holding her ladle which made you think of the spreading of asphalt, and, besides, the potage had a little of this color and consistency, asphalt-y.

"Did you see a trembling tent go by?" I asked Mimi Schnittke while blowing across the surface of my bowl.

Mimi Schnittke looked at me with an expression of surprise.

Her skin had been damaged by spatterings of tar, but her face remained very beautiful, as always with workers and technicians of the Schnittke tribe. Her body was also very beautiful, like cream soup up her legs and on her belly. She had a minuscule diadem of oil-blue feathers on her forehead, a black scarf around her neck, and nothing else.

"Well, yes, exactly," she said. "At the moment when the night was starting to end, I saw a trembling tent moving along on its own, at low speed. You got the feeling that it slipped along one centimeter above the ground. It was followed closely by a polar bear. Both of them, the polar bear and the tent, ran alongside the minimart and disappeared in the direction of the port. I thought I was dreaming. It was too strange."

"In my opinion, you weren't dreaming," said Lili Nebraska. "The bear must be Sheewa Gayanlog."

"Sheewa Gayanlog," I commented. "We were together in a sewing class, but it ended badly. And now she has cublettes."

Mimi Schnittke nodded. She put her black scarf back in place on the front of her very beautiful body.

"I thought that I was dreaming," she repeated, "because it was too strange, and also because that happens to me, receiving in my head outrageous images. It's because of the tar fumes that I inhaled, in the past, when I worked on the roads and the sidewalks. It often happens to me at the moment when day breaks, when I don't really know if I'm still sleeping or if I'm done with sleep."

Lili Nebraska returned her bowl to the morning soup seller. I did the same. On Mimi Schnittke's cart there were two tureens, one hot and smoking, and the other barely lukewarm.

There was a gust of wind. Into the air rushed dust stirred up from the whole district, from the port to the minimart, and, in my nostrils, I sensed that a rich range of smells had settled—mixed, it is true, with the aroma that escaped from the tureens of soup. If I had had to describe it, I would have spoken of a ship laden with fruits and vegetables arriving in a port moderately polluted with oil.

I lifted the cover of the receptacle that contained the barely lukewarm soup.

"What is it?" I asked Mimi Schnittke.

"It's just a light bouillon of seawater," explained the morning soup seller. "I threw into it a spoonful of seaweed, a fistful of arctic wallflowers, and some cilantro root, but, roughly speaking, it's a bucket of salted water, nothing more. Do you want the recipe, Bobby?"

"Excuse me for a moment," I said.

Something pushed me to lean over the tureen. Without my willpower playing a role in it, I knew that I needed to communicate immediately to Belle-Medusa the description of the smells that I had in my head. I leaned forward more and more and, finally, I plunged my face into the seawater.

"Bobby Potemkine calling Belle-Medusa," I said. "It's for her shelves. Smells from the city in early morning."

A boat laden with fruits and vegetables, I thought.

The smell of a cellist who has a toothache, my mouth said.

The boat slowly stirs the dirty waters near the unloading dock, I thought.

The smell of the descent of a bed thrown out the window, my mouth said.

Arctic wallflowers, cilantro roots, I thought.

The smell of the common rat astonished to learn that he is a mammal, said my mouth.

The black scarf of Mimi Schnittke, I thought.

The smell of a cousin from the country, departing, said my mouth.

I took my head out of the water. The salty drops stung my eyes a little. They rolled down me, the length of my chin and my neck, and, since I stayed without moving above the tureen, most of them ended up returning to the tureen.

The drops tinkled.

The wind quieted down.

Lili Nebraska and Mimi Schnittke looked at me. Both of them had magnificent black eyes. They opened them wide, without saying anything.

After a moment, Mimi Schnittke spoke.

She addressed neither Lili Nebraska nor myself. She seemed to be speaking only to herself.

"It's really too strange, all this," she said. "The only explanation is that I am not yet awake. I'm sleeping. And I am in the middle of a dream."

"WE really have to take care of this problem of plugging into Belle-Medusa," said Lili Nebraska. "And soon. But to start with, we're going to try to go examine this trembling tent up close. It was on your landing yesterday evening, in front of your door. The two cases seem to be linked."

Lili must have been right, as she often is. I fell in behind her. We headed toward the port. The sky was overcast, the humidity cut right through to the bone. We moved forward quickly, so as not to be frozen, but, without being able to prevent myself, I stopped here and there to transmit to Belle-Medusa my impressions of the city. Reluctantly, I looked for puddles of water deep enough to sink my face into and to produce gurglings, bubbles, and bizarre lowings. I described smells, and what I said was automatically translated into the strange language that served to link Belle-Medusa and me. I still hoped that what I had in my head would be expressed without distortion, but, each time, something took over my mouth, and what came out had no relation to what I had thought. Lili Nebraska waited patiently next to me and she listened to my washbasin noises. And then, without commenting, she helped me to wipe off my face.

"The smell of a pencil case half filled with raisins," said my mouth (while I remembered the lingering odor of burning in a hallway).

"The smell of a Chinese puppet which danced for two years under the rain," pronounced my lips (while I wanted to speak of a draft of air whistling from a cave).

"The smell of a postman's satchel at twilight," moved my mouth (but I was thinking of a heap of rotten boards nailed over the windows).

"The smell of a cap long worn backward by a bald man," I gurgled (while wishing to make understood to Belle-Medusa the atmosphere of the abandoned RER station, with its mushrooms on the walls and the piles of black dust on the demolished staircases).

And so, smell after smell, I guided Belle-Medusa in a visit to the city. I think that with the automatic translation and the bizarre classification system that she had adopted, the specialized shelves of her memory must have been full. My face was dripping with cold and dirty water, and I would really have liked to be unplugged as soon as possible so as no longer to have to plunge my head into ruts or gutters at every moment. But Belle-Medusa stayed in silent communication with me, attentive, and I continued to sniff out the ruins and the street corners like a panicky animal, then to submerge my head into puddles. This deeply disturbed me, but at the same time I realized that this description of solid ground pleased her, pleased Belle-Medusa. I wasn't 100 percent sure of this, but I had an intuition. That must happen to you, too, I guess: you have the impression that everything has derailed, that you have said only idiocies, and yet, you meet the gaze of the man or woman who is facing you, and it's a benevolent gaze. Finally, you tell yourself that it's perhaps exactly what they were expecting from you, idiocies. And you continue to forge ahead. Belle-Medusa wasn't looking at me and she wasn't settled in facing me, but during my gurglings I sensed a certain benevolence on her part. This made things less disagreeable for me and, even, encouraged me to continue.

The smells translated into Belle-Medusa's language found a place one after another on the shelves.

The smell of mistakenly stolen raft in a raft museum . . .

Or else:

The smell of gravel on which someone has forgotten a sandwich . . . The smell of a bee gathering pollen for the first time . . . The smell of a barn owl having nibbled a cherry . . . The smell of an astronomy chart that nobody consults anymore . . .

We had wandered a little around the port, on the quays, between the back of the minimart and the storehouses, and, after a while, we spotted the white silhouette of Sheewa Gayanlog near an old alternative cobbler's workshop. A long time ago, just after the disappearance of the police, there was talk of inventing shoes other than shoes for feet, and someone had had the idea of setting up this workshop, in case connoisseurs wanted to order shoes for hands or shoes for heads, and even for other parts of the body. In their advertising, the alternative cobblers bragged about soon being able to invent shoes for stomachs, shoes for gall bladders, shoes for buttocks. But, ultimately, this didn't interest a lot of people, and the alternative cobblers didn't make anything at all.

Sheewa Gayanlog paced in front of the corrugated iron shutters that nowadays closed the workshop. She seemed upset. Just beside her were some old piled-up cardboard boxes, but above all there was the trembling tent that had spent part of the night on my landing. Sheewa Gayanlog walked powerfully around the tent, as if to keep a close eye on it, impress it, and stop it from going further. Then she stepped away to swipe at the corrugated iron shutter or to tear up a cardboard box or two.

"Calm down," said Lili Nebraska to the polar bear. "We're here."

Sheewa Gayanlog stopped pacing. She turned toward us. She was like all polar bears in general, not all that white, and very impressive, very big, much more so than in our school days, obviously. She still had her tuft of mouse-gray fur where her chest began.

"Do you remember? This is Bobby Potemkine," said Lili Nebraska, pointing at me with the tips of her fingers.

"Yes," said Sheewa Gayanlog. "We were at school together."

"Hello," I said. "I remember too. It seems to me that you ate a sewing teacher."

"That's nothing but rumors," protested Sheewa Gayanlog.

She looked me in the eyes. She had a very intelligent and very lively gaze. If she had been calmer, you would have wanted to recall in her company childhood memories, but as it was, she seemed rather dangerous, and the intelligence of her gaze didn't improve anything.

"But you know, even if I had really eaten him, it wouldn't have been a great loss for haute couture," she added.

We all laughed without really knowing why, perhaps simply at the idea of haute couture, then, when silence fell again, Lili Nebraska asked the bear where she'd gotten to with her trembling tent.

"I caught it here," said Sheewa Gayanlog. "In any case, it seems no longer to be trying to run all over the place. But the problem remains. I still can't go inside. It's as though it were already occupied. And yet, there's nobody inside."

I leaned toward the interior of the tent and I stuck my head in. Nothing impeded me. The inside was empty, and, when you raised your eyes toward the top, you saw the sky, a night sky, clear, scattered with stars. Not the same sky as that which lit up the port, the storehouses, the workshop for manufacturing shoes for stomachs. In a trembling tent, time, weather, and space are never the same as elsewhere, and in this one, at this moment, it was night. On the ground, there was a puddle. I couldn't tell if the water was seawater or rainwater, and if the puddle was deep or not. The tent had settled above this hole, leaving it right in the middle, as if to incubate it. The stars were reflected in the surface of the water as if in a mirror.

"There's nobody," I confirmed. "And it's midnight in there."

"Try to go in, Bobby," suggested Sheewa Gayanlog. "As for me, when I moved my head forward, I got an electric shock on my snout. That stopped me from going any further."

"As for me, I didn't get anything," I observed.

"That's because you don't have a snout," said Sheewa Gayanlog.

"No," said Lili Nebraska. "It's because he is plugged into Belle-Medusa. That must cancel disagreeable electrical phenomena."

"Ha," said Sheewa Gayanlog, "these are things I don't understand well. At school, I wasn't good either at sewing or at electricity."

"And the electricity teacher, did you eat him?" I asked.

"I don't remember anymore," said Sheewa Gayanlog.

Me neither, I didn't remember anymore, but I thought that she,

Sheewa Gayanlog, would prefer to pretend to have forgotten the details from this period. She was certainly a little ashamed. You only have to imagine how you would feel if you had to admit in public that the teachers of the school had disappeared one after the other in the bottom of your stomach. You would experience a certain embarrassment. And maybe you would end up saying that, on this matter, you had a hole in your memory. That your school days seemed far away and blurry to you.

"It's far away, all that," added Sheewa Gayanlog, fidgeting her big polar bear body. "It's very blurry in my memory."

Since she was moving, no doubt because of the embarrassment that she experienced, she knocked over one of the piles of boxes. The boxes spilled, but there wasn't much inside, armfuls of straw on which seagulls had slept, the scraps of torn clothing, old things that passing sailors had abandoned before leaving again, useless bundles of real or counterfeit dollars. The whole of it had a very particular smell, a little like an open-air museum.

I sniffed that, raising my nose with the same technique as my dog Djinn, as if I really and truly had a snout in the middle of my face.

"Excuse me," I said.

I raised the birch-bark door and I started to go into the trembling tent. No electric shock repelled me back outside. I entered completely. It was night, contrary to what was happening at the same moment in the port, one meter away, but the temperature was rather mild for an arctic night. The sky above me was clear and very pure, with very bright constellations. I had the feeling of having gone into another world, peaceful and silent. I no longer heard the conversation between Lili Nebraska and my former classmate. Lili was no doubt in the middle of trying to explain what Belle-Medusa had been forcing me to do since the previous night, or she was giving her a quick lesson on the subject of electricity, snouts, and bears. I no longer heard their voices.

I leaned forward, toward the center of the tent, toward the thing that resembled a puddle. I had to speak of the smells of old things abandoned by passing sailors, the smells of real and counterfeit dollars, the smells of seagulls. I got down on all fours and I slowly sank my head into the starry sky, or rather into the water that reflected it, this sky. The water was fresh. But as I was going to produce I didn't know what string of gurglings, I suddenly heard a stampede.

Animals were approaching, as always in a trembling tent. I thought that it was a question of a herd of caribou. I don't know what you think about caribou, but when you risk finding yourself in their path, you don't prance around. I didn't prance around, but, since I had started to speak into the water-filled hollow, I continued.

"*The smell of a hair salon at day's beginning,*" I mumbled. "*The smell of a photocopier concealed under a shower curtain . . .*"

"Bobby!" shouted Sheewa Gayanlog.

Her voice reached me, but you would have believed that it had traveled at least three hundred meters before arriving at me. Once inside a trembling tent, you are nearly completely separated from the world outside. You are far away. Sheewa Gayanlog stood right beside the tent, but she must have shouted very loud to make herself understood.

"Do you see my cublettes?" roared the polar bear. "Can you speak with my cublettes?"

I opened my eyes under the water. I found myself seemingly inside an immense image. It was extraordinary, it was another world, it was beautiful. I no longer had the impression at all of having plunged my face into a puddle. I floated upright at the entrance of the image, I wasn't foreign to the image. I was in the image. Facing me was a vast underwater plane bordered by steep sides. Above the water, in the sky, it was night, but in the water a rather clear, early morning atmosphere prevailed, peaceful, with sufficient luminance to see in all directions. And, finally, it was a little as if the day and the night had succeeded in completely canceling their differences. The day and the night, in this place, were exactly the same thing. I stayed almost motionless, looking at this aquatic landscape, then I saw shapes moving in it. On the right was the sea cliff of the ice floe, and, on the left, a second wall that stretched to the horizon. Looking at it closer, you saw that it wasn't made of ice, this second wall, but of an unlimited and gelatinous substance, brownish in its depths, threadlike. Electric clouds traveled slowly through it, and, at certain depths, you made out translucent constructions, racks of sorts that extended for kilometers. No doubt the shelves of memory.

I think it was Belle-Medusa, a little minuscule part of Belle-Medusa.

"Belle-Medusa, I'm here," my mouth said, articulating sounds that were like bubbles of thick mud. "Do you see my cublettes? Can I speak to my cublettes?"

I raised my head to fill my lungs with air from outside. The walls of the tent were shaking with shivers and you had the feeling that invisible caribou went round and round inside, striking with their horns or shoulders against the pieces of painted canvas or birch bark. I knew that I was risking being trampled or manhandled. That's always what happens on the inside of a trembling tent. Not only do you no longer know very well if Sheewa Gayanlog's cublettes belong to her or to you, but caribou arrive and jostle you—not out of spite, but because that's how it's been since the dawn of time and there's no reason for things to change. And, to make matters worse, outside the trembling tent I heard the polar bear getting upset, turning over and destroying piles of boxes. She banged on the side of the tent too. She complained about getting electric shocks.

"Do you see my cublettes, yes or no?" she asked.

"I'm going to try to see them and speak to them," I shouted in Sheewa Gayanlog's direction.

I plunged my head back into the water hole. On Belle-Medusa's side, nothing special was happening, but, on the side of the submerged ice floe, you now saw several swimmers. Considering their size and their appearance, I immediately knew that they were my cublettes, or rather Sheewa Gayanlog's cublettes. Since they were far away and weren't hurrying to draw near, I took advantage of this to continue my communication with Belle-Medusa.

Boxes knocked over in front of a warehouse, I thought. And also the smells proper to the trembling tent: birch bark, buffalo hide, rough canvas, Indian paintings made with saliva and dirt.

"The smell of postcard," my mouth said. *"The smell of a postcard depicting a pillow . . ."*

"And my cublettes?" roared Sheewa Gayanlog, tapping on the birch-bark door. "Do you have any news?"

They were approaching, her cublettes. I counted four of them. They had very slight differences in size but, in summary, you could say that they were the same. Like their mother, they had a tuft of mouse-gray fur where their chests began and, otherwise, they were very white, very elegant, with the black spot of their snouts which they had fun covering with one of their front paws, which made them hardly spottable against the white screen of the ice. They swam toward me seemingly relaxed. They must have been laid-back cublettes, the kind that in class kept themselves busy most of all by telling their dreams to their neighbors, while chewing on gumballs, sticks of licorice, or the remains of teachers.

"I see them," I informed Sheewa Gayanlog. "What do I tell them?"

"Ask them if they have been good at school," hollered Sheewa Gayanlog.

"Have you been good at school?" I asked.

The cublettes started to turn lazily underwater, a little distance away. They frolicked slowly, hiding their snouts under their right front paws and charting underwater loops which made the powerful perfection of their bodies and the beauty of their fur become clear. I don't know if you have ever seen polar bears swim under the surface of the ocean, in arctic waters. It's a sight of which you never grow tired.

"There was a problem with an acoustics teacher," said one of the cublettes.

"A big problem," explained a second cublette.

"What happened?" I asked.

They didn't answer. They continued to chart harmonious curves, spirals and bands, figure eights. I raised my head in the direction of the outside.

"They had a big problem with an acoustics teacher," I shouted.

Sheewa Gayanlog hollered something, but she was in too different a universe and her voice didn't reach me in an articulate way. In any case, I knew what I would have said to my cublettes, if I had been in her place. I would have lectured them.

"When you have a problem with a teacher, don't immediately throw yourself on him to eat him," I said. "Eating teachers doesn't solve anything, whether they be teachers of acoustics or sewing. You have to learn to stop yourself. It's comforting to devour a schoolteacher but it doesn't solve anything."

They didn't answer. They continued to dance lazily under the water. Cublettes are difficult. They're difficult to have and they're difficult to reason with, later, during the years when they attend school.

UNDER the trembling tent, neither day nor night had ended. The stars shone. Around me, I still heard the ground trembling under the hooves of an invisible herd, but caribou neither jostled me nor collided with me. Deep down, when you think about it, to be plugged into Belle-Medusa had its advantages. The electrical power of Belle-Medusa protected me. I assume that a phenomenon must have acted and pushed back the animals that had lost their calm, whether they be the caribou or adult polar bears, furious and dangerous like Sheewa Gayanlog was. An electrical or magnetic phenomenon. I would have difficulty saying more about it. I never learned very well lessons of fundamental physics, at school, even if I had never gone so far as to eat my teachers, out of pique over being a dunce or simply from gluttony.

I lingered a little while in the image. I had ended up becoming accustomed to the din of the caribou and to the breathing of the polar bear circling the tent and, from time to time, lashing out at the door while growling guidance to her cublettes. I didn't always really know if I had my head in the water, in the sky, or between two currents of air, or if I found myself in reality or deep in a dream. It's always a little like that, it seems, when you go into a trembling tent. There is no longer time or space, but only noises, images, and dreams.

Since they didn't appreciate being reprimanded, the cublettes had stopped frolicking nearby. They had put out to sea and, after having slipped along the submerged ice fields which formed a pristine great wall, they had disappeared. I continued to see the ice floe on the right and Belle-Medusa, gelatinous and dense, on the left.

"Bobby Potemkine here," I said. "I'm calling Belle-Medusa."

And there, I started. Not because I had received an electrical or magnetic shock, but because I had just realized that my voice was normal.

"Bobby Potemkine calling Belle-Medusa," I repeated.

The words which came out of my mouth no longer had their bellowed appearance of gurglings, and, in any case, I didn't hear them like that. I don't know what language I was speaking in. Perhaps, from having practiced aquatic transmission, I had improved the basics of my communication with Belle-Medusa. Perhaps automatic translation was no longer necessary between us.

It seemed to me that I was able to address Belle-Medusa directly.

"I would like to be unplugged," I said. "I don't want to stay indefinitely in this image and I am tired of describing smells by plunging my head in cold water. I have done the work I was asked to do. I want to be able to leave this trembling tent to take care of other things."

I was now comfortable speaking underwater, as comfortable as when I chatted in the open air, but that wasn't a reason to continue to be Belle-Medusa's tour guide. I gathered my breath above the puddle, then I went back into the image.

"A few final smells," I said. "*The smell of a nanoctiluphe after a concert . . . The smell of sleep-horseback-riding on a rusty cistern . . . The smell of ferns before an invasion of locusts . . . The smell of a viaduct above a not very busy road . . . The smell of a tom-tom made with a copper boiler and tires . . . The smell of a hat with feathers which falls from the nineteenth floor . . . The smell of pumpkin curry . . .*"

I stopped my cataloging. Under the waters of the ice floe, everything was peaceful and clear, and, in the trembling tent, the agitation had died down. The caribou had gone to gallop in another world. Sheewa Gayanlog had stopped knocking on the door and coming and going nearby. The tent no longer trembled.

Very slowly Belle-Medusa slid toward a part of the image where, little by little, she melted away into the darkness. I thought that she was in the process of leaving the image.

"I would like to be unplugged, now," I said. "The visit is over."

I got back up and I pushed open the door so as to come out in front of the alternative cobbler's workshop. The light of day was a little gray, but a lot brighter than the nocturnal light that I had left behind me. The dock was covered with packing straw and debris. After having knocked everything over, Sheewa Gayanlog kept going after the remains, the scraps of paper and the pieces of cardboard, she had torn them up and scattered them nervously, then she went elsewhere. The unloading dock was deserted.

Lili Nebraska was seated out of the way. She was waiting for me. She was restringing an E-string on her violin.

"That bear's not very controllable," said Lili. "It must not have been very fun to be in school with her every day."

"For the teachers especially it wasn't very fun," I said.

I sat down next to Lili.

My head was dripping. I let the drops run along my arms, down my chest, everywhere. I felt too tired to dry myself off. It seems that that's normal, a feeling of heavy fatigue, when you've stayed for a while inside a trembling tent.

"You see," said Lili Nebraska. "The two cases were linked. Belle-Medusa needed a trembling tent to communicate with you."

"And now?" I asked.

"You've done enough, in my opinion," said Lili. "If all goes well now, Belle-Medusa is going to leave."

"I don't know if I'm unplugged or not," I said. "In any case, the visit is over."

Lili hugged me against her, then she tuned her instrument with its completely new E-string. We looked in the direction of the ocean. The entrance of the estuary was, like usual, grayish and hardly visible under a patch of mist. Down there, under the waves, Belle-Medusa was starting to shake her enormous gelatinous mass to go drift toward another shore or toward the open ocean. She was going to leave, if all went well.

"Please, Lili, play me a cantata for she-wolves of the streets," I asked. "So that the music carries us away and makes us forget everything."

"That's just what I was going to do," said Lili.

She stood up in front of me. In the gray light of the unloading dock she was extremely pretty, with her gingerbread-colored skin, her black hair, and the drawings on her face, on her belly, at the top of her legs, with her mahogany violin, her bracelet of varnished wooden beads and nothing else.

She started to play a cantata in G minor.

We were alone on the unloading dock, both of us.

The music carried us away and made us forget everything.

For a long time, we were far away, and, in any case, we were elsewhere.

And then, holding Lili by the hand, I went back home.

—*Translated from the French by Sarah and Brian Evenson*

Like nearly all of Draeger's work, "Belle-Medusa" takes place in a fragmented world that seems at once to be a possible future of our own world, a realm existing after death, and a dream. Bringing together bits and shards of different genres (the detective story, science fiction, the love story), one of its major purposes

seems to be to generate the new myths of this strange, postindustrial, postapocalyptic society. It does so in a way that, like fairy tales and myths, tries to explain and make sense of the teller's world. Since Manuela Draeger is also a librarian within Antoine Volodine's larger world, these stories are meant to be imagined as stories being told to children trying to understand their lives in containment camps. They allow their listeners both an escape and, in admittedly strange ways, an explanation, and they are full of wonder and delight.

—BE

Raja Rasalu

❦

THE SWAN'S WIFE

Aamer Hussein

I once knew a woman who loved a swan. She loved all swans, and geese and ducks and water hens too, but most of all she loved a swan she called Satin. On Sundays we went to the park to feed the birds that nested among the rushes beside the lake. They'd come running after us and pluck at our calves with their beaks. Satin would wait until she'd fed the rest, and then glide up to her with his mate. She would feed him pellets of bread she'd moistened in her mouth, and often he'd follow her like a pet, as his mate hopped along behind.

Nadja—that was her name—and I lived on different sides of the park, she by the western gate, and I by the south. In summer the park was full of teenagers cavorting, boating, jumping into the lake. Elderly couples strolled in the rose garden, the men with their bellies hanging out of their open shirts over their Bermuda shorts, their wives in thin shifts with their bare arms freckling and their faces flushed. There was a brass band, and a bandstand, with chairs for hire and people selling ice cream.

Sometimes the boys on their roller skates would bully the birds. They'd tempt them with scraps of food; when the birds came over the boys would chase them with sticks and stones. And then the birds would show how strong they were. There was an urban legend about a goose that had attacked a boy with beak and claw and nearly plucked his eye out. But the swans kept to the water, their nests and their own company, and only Satin ever left the lake.

In the middle of the park was a grand house that had once belonged to a rich merchant who had brought back a fortune from India. It was filled with objects he had acquired on his travels; you could see them twice a week for the price of a ticket, but apart from groups of schoolchildren, people barely bothered to visit the house.

As you approached it, the house seemed to be right in the middle of the lake, but that was an illusion—it was built on a piece of land that jutted into the water. They said the merchant had filled the lake with waterbirds so he could look out at them from one of the house's many windows.

Sometimes, when I walked by the water alone, I'd remember the artificial lake I'd read about in a book of old swan tales that I'd been given as a present many years ago. The lake was made by the servants of a king called Karan, who wanted it to be the meeting place of all the birds in the world. At that time the swans had their own kingdom far away in Lake Manasa, in the mountains near Tibet. King Karan had heard of Lake Manasa, and dreamed that his lake should rival it in beauty. In summer the young swans of Manasa would fly overhead and take home reports of this clear lake that rivaled theirs, with fish of every color in its depths and flowers of every color on its margins. They'd swoop down to drink, but they would never linger: they fed only on freshwater pearls, and there were no pearls on the bed of the artificial lake. I looked for the book on my shelf, but I'd probably lost it long ago, or left it behind somewhere when I outgrew fairy tales and other childish things.

2.

Nadja's parents were from a Balkan province that had changed hands and name after World War II. Her father survived the mayhem, but some years after she was born he defected with his wife and his two children. They moved to London via Paris, as refugees. Nadja didn't remember her Balkan childhood at all.

At school she wasn't terribly good at her studies, but she had a flair for languages, music, and dance. She was very pretty, too, with long black hair and almond eyes that changed color from brown to green depending on the light. When she was fourteen her mother put her in stage school. At seventeen she joined a troupe of dancers and played some minor roles on television, and even a bit part in a Bond movie, but she wasn't suited to that life, she said—"too many foul old men with sweaty hands." At eighteen she met an actor and moved in with him. But he was violent and possessive; often out of work, he'd clean flats for a living. She thought he was seeing other women. One night she ran away and went back home to her parents.

I'd moved to live near the park late in the winter of '78, in my twenty-third year. I'd met Nadja a few times, a year or two before; she had once slept on my sister Sasha's sofa for a week, in Sasha's Chelsea flat. But we'd become friends one afternoon when I was walking by the lake and thinking about my life. She called out my name from behind—she remembered my name, though she said it oddly—and we sat down on a bench in the sick February sunshine to talk. She'd moved to a new garden flat a minute's walk away from the park. Her life, she said, was going better: she'd got a job as a buyer in a fashion company, and was designing clothes as well. I worked in a bank and hated my job. It all poured out as we spoke.

We exchanged numbers and started to meet. On Saturdays we walked by the lake and fed the swans and often in the evenings we would stroll down the High Street and eat a pizza or a plate of spaghetti.

Then spring came and she went to Milan for a show. I was alone and had almost no friends in London. Just after my twenty-third birthday in April, I decided to leave the bank and apply to go back to university.

For some months I felt Nadja was avoiding me. But then, that summer before I went back to my studies, she started to call again and we met often. I would tell her about the girl I was seeing; she'd talk about the man she'd fallen in love with. He was about ten years older; a count, she said, from a Balkan state like the one she came from.

"He walked into the store one day and my manager told me to help him," she said. "He bought the most expensive dresses in the store—for his sister, he said—and the day after I received, gift-

wrapped, the one I liked the best, with a bunch of roses and an in-
vitation for a glass of champagne."

She'd been apprehensive at first—she'd met many, many men who
only wanted a brief fling—but he dropped her home and asked to
see her again later in the week.

And then they'd seen each other again, and again.

"He wants to marry me," she said, and showed me her ruby ring.
"Pre-engagement. He's very rich."

And then, with a grimace:

"My mother approves. She says I won't find another man who'll
look after me the way he will."

That's what had been happening to her while I was leaving
my job.

We spent long days in the park that summer—Saturdays,
Sundays—feeding the birds, walking, climbing trees, singing to
each other, or just lying silently on the grass, sharing cigarettes.

In October I was back at university, studying languages. I was
singing again, too, with an acoustic folk group I'd found at college.

In the autumn evenings, if we met after a day's work, we'd either
eat something together at a restaurant—a pizza or a plate of pasta—
or go back to her flat for something exquisitely simple she'd cooked.
But often we'd leave each other on a street corner, and be off to our
other pursuits: she to her nightclubs and five-star restaurants, and I
with my new acquaintances to their student hangouts. Just as often
I'd go to a concert or a film on my own, or home to an evening
alone with a book.

3.

Nadja soon found out that Maximilian, her lover, was married and
waiting for a divorce.

"I'm not making any commitments till his decree is final," she
said.

It was November, and we had our overcoats on. We were striding
rather than strolling.

She'd tried to break up with him after one of their champagne-
fueled nights, and he'd gone away, but he'd rung her bell later, quite
drunk. ("He's fond of gin and of cognac.")

"He swears he'll kill himself if I leave him," she told me as we sat down on a bench by the lake and lit cigarettes.

So the fairy-tale ending wasn't about to be staged yet.

"Another bloody freak," I said. "Why do you always attract freaks?"

(I was retaliating to a comment she'd made once, when she met a Spanish friend of mine: "Is she an au pair?" And when I said the girl was studying philosophy, she said, "Why do you always date such common girls?")

"Max is not violent," she said. "Never ever!"

4.

In winter the park was almost empty after midday. But Nadja liked to go there in all seasons: summer, autumn, and winter, in sunshine and even in snow. Once when I hadn't seen her for some weeks she dragged me out on a Saturday afternoon in early January. It had snowed so hard that the lake had frozen over. She was looking for Satin, but couldn't find him.

"He's probably flown to sunnier shores," I said.

But she knew he'd be there.

And then we heard his call.

He was on the island in the lake, where he had his nest, but when she called out to him he wouldn't come over.

"He's wounded," she said, "I know. He's hurt his wing. Or a foot."

(Was he afraid of the ice? If so, why couldn't he fly? Had his wings been clipped?)

Nadja threw off her fur coat, flung it on the frost-spangled grass, and set off across the glittering ice floor.

(And I'd heard since I was very young that swans never parted from their mates. So where had Satin's mate gone, leaving him stranded?)

"Satin, O Satin, come on boy, come to Nadja. . . ."

She slipped as soon as she stepped on the ice. I grabbed her before she fell. She sat down on a bench, pulled off her boots and her stockings, and set off again, barefoot, to cross the water. I heard Satin crying. Nadja shrieked when her bare foot touched its frozen surface.

"You'll fall," I said. "The ice will crack."

She said: "There were kids skating on the lake earlier. The ice won't give way."

And I don't remember the ice cracking or her falling or whether she ever got to the island. But I do remember her characteristically rambling story about wardens and vets and yes, a swan hospital in Richmond, and three men struggling to get poor Satin on a boat and then into their van. He'd broken a foot and would have to be off the lake for quite a while.

I must have told her, then, about the day the famine came to the swans of Lake Manasa:

The swans, the story said, had eaten all the pearls in the lake. Then the pair that were the bravest among them flew off in search of fresh pearls. They flew over all the world's lakes, but were too proud to stop for food and water. One day, they flew over a lake that was surrounded by pearls that gleamed on the petals of the flowers and on the grass like dewdrops. The male swan swooped down to pick up the pearls: tired, he set his feet on the grass, but soon he found his silver left foot was caught in a trap concealed in a net on which the pearls had been woven. King Karan, who had been watching the swans from a terrace, approached and said to the swan in the trap: "Eat, swan, eat the pearls I laid out for you! Eat and I'll let you go." And the swan replied: "Never! You have tricked me." Karan cried: "Why will you not eat? Have I not made a lake for you that rivals Manasa in beauty? And am I not generous? Have I not laid seed pearls around it for you and your army of swans to feed on?" Then the swan's wife said from her perch in the air: "Kings do not imprison the innocent. Kings do not war against women."

In one version the swan's wife flew away to look for help; in another, the king's men shot her down with a golden arrow. In a third telling, the swan didn't even have a wife; the one who came to rescue him from King Karan was his intrepid friend.

5.

I wasn't serious about anyone I'd met; I'd had flings, too, but mostly I was happy enough to study and listen to music when I was on my own. And I had Nadja. Max only visited for short periods—he'd stay in a smart boutique hotel in Kensington where he seemed to have a permanent reservation, see her for dinner or drop in at her flat, and always bring her gifts: jewels, furs, gowns. Much of the time Nadja was alone and we spent our best times together. More than once I got the feeling she didn't really care when Max failed to turn up. Once the first tide of joy subsided, the old pain came back—her first lover had left her with scars of betrayal that would never heal.

Over the spring we became closer and closer, almost like twins. I felt she enjoyed talking about love, or dreaming of it, more than she enjoyed living it. (Both of us liked to be liked, but once we'd got the object of our affection we were less interested and often longed to escape the possessiveness of our lovers.) Like all dreamers, she was very unpunctual, as she sat for hours in front of the mirror, though I don't think it was herself she was looking at.

She loved eating and cooking (and like most of us who do, she often complained of indigestion and stomach ailments). Once when she was cooking for me at her place—a chicken with aromatic herbs, and a dish of pilaf with nuts and raisins—Max rang and said he'd join us for dinner, because a meeting of his had been canceled. He was a dark-haired man of medium height, with a long nose and very black eyes. He had a slow, hoarse voice and affected mannerisms and didn't seem to be enjoying his food very much. I was waiting to make my getaway when he suggested we should all go to a nightclub called the Saddle Room. I watched while they danced away the night. It was the first time I'd seen him; I hoped it would be the last.

For a woman who loved birds so much and couldn't bear to see a stray dog or cat on a street corner in some southern city, Nadja was unconcerned about the hunting down of wild animals. So she'd put a stuffed tiger in her sitting room to shock all her eco-conscious friends. She took a photograph of me embracing the tiger and giggled because it actually wasn't stuffed at all; it was a mere fake. She loved taking photographs and she loved her Polaroid camera. She took pictures of me: singing, dancing, and posing in every angle one evening when the rain was coming down hard outside. Then she disappeared into her bedroom, and emerged dressed up as some long-gone Hollywood diva: Ava Gardner, perhaps, her favorite. She handed over her Polaroid to me and I took pictures of her too, some out of focus, some quite good, especially one in which she looked like a captive beauty from one of those old ballads I loved to sing, with her arms around her furry black and golden beast, looking out with yearning eyes, dreaming that he'd be transformed into a prince.

Nadja loved dancing. Once, after a drink or two of champagne, she draped a few scarves around her brassiere and tucked one into her panties, put on a record of Arabic instrumental music really loud and undulated like an Egyptian, twisting her belly and swinging her hips, and clashing the cymbals attached to her fingertips, while I lay back on the sofa and lazily kept time with my hands and my feet. Then she dragged me up to dance with her and we wriggled face-to-face, but we never let our bodies touch. She was affectionate but she didn't like being touched and I was afraid of what the touch of her perspiring skin might unleash in me.

She loved music, but didn't really understand the dirgelike folk songs I sang. We both spoke Italian, and when I was a child I'd picked up a lot of Italian big-band melodies like "Volare" and "Come Prima, Più di Prima." I went off and learned the lyrics of those songs to entertain her; I belted them out to her in a fair imitation of Mario Lanza in the kitchen while she baked a cheese and spinach pie, and kept on singing in the doorway of her bathroom as she soaked in her bubble bath before we sat down to supper.

We spent a lot of time in her tiny overfurnished basement flat as autumn approached. We both worked all day; unless we met in the park just before it closed, we didn't have time to meet before dark. And since Satin hadn't come back to the lake, Nadja seemed to want to walk in the park much less often. Once or twice she called out when we did go in search of him: "Look! Satin!" But the swan we saw hadn't approached her, and she decided that it wasn't Satin after all. So we'd stay indoors together on our free afternoons.

But something or someone often came between us: her travels, my studies, her family or mine, but mostly Max. I told myself I didn't mind when Max turned up—I'd feel lonely, but I'd make the best of the time I had for myself. And I had other friends, now. The best of these was Fabi. We'd met on the way home from a university social; he'd called me several times when I'd been busy with her; then one day we met by the French Institute where we were queuing for a concert and sat down together. We both liked French films,

Jacques Brel, and Sartre. To look at, though, we were opposites: smaller than me, Fabi was blond and I was dark, he was ebullient and I was quiet, he was a scientist and I was a student of humanities.

Fabi believed there was safety in numbers: he didn't bother to change girlfriends, he just waited till one or the other of them got tired of his feckless, faithless ways and dropped him, before another one appeared in his life. He liked going out and drinking beer and staying out all night; as for me, it was hard to drag me to a crowded, dark place with loud music playing, except, perhaps, on a Saturday, because I knew what it felt like to be left alone while Nadja was in Rio de Janeiro and the rest of the world was drinking and dancing.

Fabi and Nadja met once or twice; they didn't like each other.

6.

Fall, leaves, please fall! I'd say to the trees when autumn approached. The lull at the start of November was spell-binding, but I was afraid of bare branches and wished the leaves would rain down now so I could get used to the naked trees. By the time the leaves had begun to fall around us and squelch beneath our feet in red and yellow piles, I was too busy to think much about the park or Satin and the other swans on the lake. (For all I knew, they'd all flown off to Lake Manasa.) Apart from my studies, there was the work I did in an office a couple of times a week; my few leisure hours were spent with my musical friends, practicing for our performances in clubs and college halls.

Nadja was on and off planes every few days. Sometimes she was away for three weeks and I wouldn't even hear from her. Or she'd call on a bad line and wake me up at dawn because she was in Hong Kong or Buenos Aires and had forgotten the time difference.

When she was in town, we'd meet just as we always had. But our relationship was enclosed in a glass bubble now. She liked to meet in West End hotel bars, and looked around her a lot as if she were afraid of spies. She'd started to bring gifts for me: shirts, ties, a watch, a lighter. She seemed restless; I felt her loneliness. Max had stopped talking about divorcing his wife; she was completely opposed to the idea of being the "mistress," as she put it, of a married man. Now other names were appearing on her list of suitors. An aging MP. A Saudi princeling. But all of them seemed to be spoken for. She was smoking far too much and complaining of her bad appetite and recurrent stomach cramps.

Once at the Students' Union Bar, when I got there late after seeing her, Fabi, who'd been waiting nearly an hour for me, said over his dwindling second pint:

"When that woman turns up and just crooks a little finger, you dump the lot us, and off you run. What's with you, man?"

And I realized that things really had changed between all of us. I'd fallen into a lot of Fabi's ways, going out carousing till two in the morning even on weekdays, then stumbling red-eyed out of bed to attend my classes. I'd pretend to Nadja, when she remarked on the purple shadows under my eyes, that I'd been studying till late, but she knew me too well to believe that for more than a minute. "You're burning your candle at both ends, darling. . . ." She'd laugh, but there was a brittle tinge to her words and to her laughter, as if I, her reliable friend, was turning into someone she could no longer lean on.

Twice in autumn I'd taken off on a whim, without telling anyone, to spend long weekends in Barcelona and Paris, and been scolded for missing lectures. The truth was that I liked it when she rang and couldn't find me. And when I came back to find that she hadn't called during those days and there was only Fabi to explain my mysterious movements to, I'd be annoyed, because telling her later that I'd been away all the time that she had just didn't have the same impact as her ringing to find me gone.

I felt guilty as I spoke to Fabi now, as if I were betraying her, but I wanted clarity, and I spoke as I'd never done before.

"I'm sick of it all," I said. "I miss her when she leaves. Then just as I get used to her being away, she turns up, and if I can't see her, she sounds offended. She regularly breaks promises she makes. Let's go here or there on Sunday, she'll say, then on Sunday she'll be off to Timbuktu or Ulan Bator. Let's go to the sea, she'll say, but the only waters we've ever seen ourselves in together are those of the park. . . ."

Fabi's mind seemed to wander as he looked into the depths of his glass. And then he said, furrowing his brow:

"Who—or what—do you think pays for those gifts she gives

you? What does she ask for, in return? You're not sleeping with her, are you? You need to find a girlfriend. What are you like, weird?"

He saw my face darken, I imagine. He passed me a Gitane.

7.

If by chance I wandered into the park during Nadja's absence, my mind would wander in different directions. Sometimes I'd feel, Why should I be so attached to one person when the whole wide world deserves my love and attention? Why do I have to put up with an affection that imprisons me in its tight little ring?

We met in the dark Hilton bar. She was just back from Milan.

"Remember those days? How we spent day after day in the park? And how we rescued Satin . . ." There was a kind of yearning in her gestures and her words.

It was Happy Hour. We were drinking foul concoctions of vodka and Tia Maria, the sort of sweet sloppy drink Nadja favored when she wasn't drinking champagne.

"But that wasn't even a year ago. You make it sound like ten years. . . ."

"We were so happy then. It's just that we were so happy. . . ."

"I'm not at all unhappy now, Nadja. Are you?"

"No, no, I'm always happy when I see you."

But you haven't been happy for a while, I thought. Yes, you're happy for a moment when you see me and then you're off somewhere, in some place I can't reach.

Nadja's way of seeing happiness as if it was always something that had happened yesterday made me anxious for a tomorrow around the corner. I wanted to live in the present. Other people's nostalgia made me sad. And then I'd think that though she listened cheerfully to the stories I told her, and asked who I flirted with or even went to bed with, our friendship was—always had been—based on her stories. And my responses to those stories. Her travels. Her troubles. And now, along with stories, there were hopes. A home. Babies. A world that was remote from me and anything I wanted.

And what about my future? I'd take my degree and study some more for a higher one. I'd go traveling in Asia, which I hadn't seen since I left home nine years ago. And I was going to sing again. I hadn't been singing since my second-year exams.

What place, then, would Nadja have in my life? She'd marry and move on. So what was the point of thinking beyond that?

I'd never spoken to Nadja about tomorrow. But sometimes she would say:

"We're going to be together forever. Never let me go."

Come prima, più di prima, t'amerò. . . .

8.

A lonely December Sunday. I was tired of studying and reading and even of music. I took a coach to Oxford to spend a day with my married sister Sasha, who'd moved there the year before.

We went for a walk in the walled university gardens among the deer. She asked about Nadja, who'd once been a friend of sorts.

"Fabi thinks I give her too much time. He doesn't believe in platonic friendships."

"Fabi's right. This friendship's going nowhere, hmmm? Nadja's involved with someone else. You'll be twenty-five in spring; you have your studies to finish next year. And these expensive gifts she brings you . . . have you ever given her anything in return? You don't have a job or a decent income. You study, you sing, you live the life of Riley. Maybe it's because of you that Nadja's not being able to make a decision. Now it's up to you to think of the future. . . ."

We turned a corner by a garden in which roses grew in summer, and came upon an artificial lake. In the distance I saw a single swan glide by. I thought of Satin.

9.

In the coach, on my way home in the winter darkness, I remembered a picture of a pair of swans in the book I'd lost. One was skimming the deep blue water, looking at the sky; the other raised her head from what seemed at first glance to be a tangled nest of thorns in the river. But if you looked again, you could see that she was in the embrace of a giant black bird, his gray beak at her throat, one black talon on her wing and the other on her white and bleeding breast, and what seemed to be water wasn't water at all, it was darkening sky. The body of the swan lay on night-dark soil. Underneath the picture was the legend: *Between you and me there is no kinship.*

They say that once a wounded crow who had flown too high in the sky fell into the swans' nest. The swan gave the hungry, tired crow refuge, but it was an ambush. The crow claimed that he had come to reclaim his mate, the swan's wife. An army of a hundred crows swooped down from above them to peck at the swan's wings and at his eyes; they chased him away from his nest at the lake's edge. The swan hovered in the air above his wife, held off by the army of crows, and the wind was his home and a cloud his nest, and he cried for his mate. (And the cry of a swan is a fearful thing.)

Seeing that swan on the lake had reminded me of the tale. But why, in the picture, was the swan looking away from the crow and from his bleeding wife? From the story I remembered that "between you and me there is no kinship" were the words the swan said to the crow when he offered him refuge. But the intent of the picture left me in doubt. Were those cruel words the swan's farewell to his mate?

(And the cry of a swan torn away from his mate is a fearful thing.)

10.

"I'm going to be twenty-nine on the twenty-second," she said. "I thought I'd have a party here . . . just you and me and a few friends."

We'd finished eating our lobster; we were on our second bottle of wine.

"But you said you were going to see the Nile in winter with Max. . . ."

"Changed my mind. That bastard hasn't done a thing about his divorce. . . ."

And it occurred to me that Maximilian, with his black hair and his long nose, looked just like the crow in the illustration.

"But Nadja, I'm not going to be here. I'm going to Rome over the Christmas break. I'll be gone by then, before the rush begins."

I'd only decided as we spoke that I'd be going to Rome.

For a minute I thought she was going to cry. Then she looked up and said, "But you'll come back for the New Year, won't you?"

It was going to be the start of a new decade.

"Yes," I said. "I'll be back to spend it with you, Nadja."

I knew that by the time I returned things would have changed again.

She smiled. Her eyes in the candlelight were amber.

"I've been meaning to tell you. Satin's back on the lake. I saw him."

A few months ago I'd have told her she had dreamed it all; that she'd seen some other hungry swan and decided it was her old pet who'd escaped from the wily king, the traps, the crows, the wicked boys, and the swan doctors. But tonight I thought I'd leave her with her fancies of the birds on the frozen winter lake.

I leaned over the debris of dinner to kiss her cheek, but it was her mouth that met mine.

"Let me order us a cognac for the road," I said. "Then I should walk you home."

My story began with a memoir I was writing about a woman I once knew, who loved feeding birds and made particular friends with a swan. As I wrote, I realized I was approaching the aims of this anthology, and began reading about swans.

Much as I love them (particularly the Indonesian Manohara), I was determined not to make my heroine a swan maiden: it was real swans (and not shape-shifters) I was in search of.

I was inspired to retell the story of the swans of Lake Manasa by "The Swan Kingdom," which I found some years ago in Noor Inayat Khan's Twenty Jataka Tales. *However, I wanted a pair of swans; a similar tale, though with the swan's wife in a prominent role, appeared in*

"*The King Who Was Fried*" *in another classic collection, Flora Annie Steel's* Tales of the Punjab, *which also brought me closer to my homeland.*

A further search revealed the picture of the wounded swan with the title "With you I have no kinship" that inspired a scene in my story, and the tale of the swans and the crows it was linked to, "Raja Rasalu and the Swans," which exists in many versions.

An echo that was used and discarded was from Donovan's haunting ballad "Lord of the Reedy River"; in the end, I decided to leave my heroine on terra firma.

—AH

Sedna, Inuit

❦

SANNA

Kathryn Davis

I was just a girl and then I wasn't. Many taboos were directed
toward me and I could hear them all! *Pssst pssst pssst.* The
smaller fish expressed themselves with sibilants, the larger ones
with a preponderance of vowels. On the day everything changed, I
was just a girl; hurricane season was upon us, the autumn equinox.
The morning was bright but with a brightness that betokened approaching agitation, like a smile designed to lure you close enough
to strike.

*Streamers of flesh, Sweetness, showers of hair and a hail of bone
and you'll have some supper yet. . . .*

They've always been so poetic, the young mackerel—even when
they're jammed into a bucket together, ignominious, as bait.

THE quay I was born on is no longer there. Or, to be accurate, it's
there, in the sense that it exists, but by now the only things living on
it are crabs and sea lice. In the same sense the house I lived in with
my father is also there, the submerged wood having undergone its
inevitable transformation to slime and then to something more like
nothing, not unlike what he told me happened to my mother. I used

to imagine I could see her adrift in the water along with all the other things. Adrift in the water and coming for me, though my father said she drowned.

The two of us lived together in a house made of southern yellow pine, blackened with age, the side facing the sea composed of panels that could be lifted off at will to let in the elements. Behind us a grove of silver palms swayed like courtesans, and behind them sprawled a giant gumbo-limbo tree with little birds sticking to its branches. I never knew what I'd find in my bedroom when I woke in the morning: a skink, a click beetle, a ribbon snake, a frog. Often my father's discarded cigarette packs would be walking across the floor; once an angel perched at the foot of my bed, lit from behind by the rising sun. "That's a great white heron," my father told me. "As close to an angel as a bird can get." He also told me that hermit crabs like to take up residence in any empty receptacle they can find. It never occurred to me that this was unusual. When I was a girl, like all children, my destiny seemed as inevitable as it was opaque. Of course my father knew it wasn't crabs moving those packs.

He considered himself a nature worshipper, though as far as I could tell a child was a natural object, wasn't it? Naturally produced, living and breathing, radiant with the light Nature infuses in all creation before mowing it down. According to my father I took after his side of the family, my pale skin poured like an afterthought over a towering frame that came straight from him. Like my father I could ride out the worst the sea had to offer and return to shore unshaken. My eyes were large and dark like his, the color of the pitch with which he painted the hull of his boat. *Sanna* the boat was called, as was I—we had both been christened at the same time with a bottle of Veuve Clicquot. My father spilled the champagne over my head before smashing the empty bottle across the boat's prow.

As for my mother, I knew very little about her aside from the fact that the sheet-covered grand piano in the middle of our living room used to be hers. My earliest attempts to draw my father out on the subject were met with a look that suggested the need for absolute silence on both our parts, the kind of fierce shared silence found in an operating theater or a concert hall immediately preceding the scalpel's first incision of the skin, the finger's first striking of the note. There was a suggestion that whatever I wanted was inherent in who we were, in what we added up to, both of us together. The force of his silence required complicity. Nothing could happen without it. Sound was the enemy.

IT'S still beautiful, the house my father and I lived in together, no less so for being on the ocean floor. The entry passage is long and strewn with obstacles—sea wrack and mermaid purse, bones and sponge—the whole place blocked at one end by a black thing that used to be a musical instrument.

Who shut in the sea with doors when it burst out from the womb? my mother says. It comes out *sssshhhhxxgggrrrruggghghghhhhdrmm-maaaahhh.*

Who can catch my girl on a fishhook?

THE first time I played my mother's piano it was my fifth birthday; my father was making jelly omelets to celebrate. At some point when he wasn't looking I ducked under the sheet. It's possible I was playing a game with him even though he would have had no way of knowing that's what I was doing. It's the kind of thing you do when you're a child, even if you've never had someone like a friend to show you how a game is played.

It was a perfect morning, the sky lifting the pale gold off the surface of the ocean, sieving it through the thin fabric of the sheet and onto the waiting piano keys. It was like empyrean turned liquid, spilling over the *ivory ebony ivory ebony ivory ivory ivory ivory ivory* of that row of white and black steps without end. Who could resist? I raised my hands above the keys and then I let them land. I had no idea I was going to make so much noise nor that it would be so terrible nor that my punishment, when it came, would be so swift and without source like an act of God.

My father brought the fallboard down on my fingers. "I give up," he said. "You win."

Even though I was very young I could tell by the way his voice broke when he said "you" that he meant my mother. Immediately thereafter he took me to the mainland where a surgeon set the bones in plaster. I had multiple phalangeal fractures—"a boating accident," my father told the surgeon, who clearly didn't believe him for a minute. During the time my hands were in casts I never wanted for anything. My father treated me like a princess. Jelly omelets were the least of it.

HE came from privilege or at least hinted that he had. In any case, even before the incident with the piano I had never wanted for anything, and our extravagant lifestyle—those spur-of-the-moment trips to the farthest corners of the globe, the exotic foods and wines flown in from places impossible to find on a map—couldn't have been supported by the money he made taking rich sportsmen out on the *Sanna* for a day of deep-sea fishing. I say sportsmen because they were, mostly, men. Occasionally a woman would come along for the ride and then it would be my father, not me, who would help her bait her hook. I can still see him reaching into the bucket and pulling out a furious young mackerel, its flanks shedding rainbows in the early morning sun. He would hold the fish up in one hand so the woman had to watch as he drove the hook through its eye socket with his other. Living bait worked best; the trophy fish he went after were intelligent enough to know the difference.

On the day everything changed I was busy making coffee in the galley. We had three middle-aged men onboard, all of them concerned with the impression they were making or about to make on the other men and on the sole woman; one of them worried about getting seasick, another about the size of the boat in comparison with the size of the ocean. All three of them noticed my breasts, which were, by that time, sufficiently developed that if my mother were still living with us she would have made me wear a bra under the striped jersey my father thought looked nautical. *Poor little thing*, I heard the woman say. *Shouldn't that poor little thing be in school?*

Like most of the women my father took out on his boat, this one appeared to have been born fully formed. He showed her what he'd have to do if she caught "a big one," pressing her down into the fighting chair where she sat splay-legged in her white strapless swimsuit, clearly aroused, as he harnessed her in. "My goodness," she said, tucking a lock of sleek blond hair behind one neat, small ear. The woman had an accent I didn't recognize from some land-locked part of the country I barely knew existed, some place like Nebraska. "Is this really necessary?" she asked, lifting her eyes to his, imploring. "You don't know the half of it," my father replied.

Of course the other men didn't stand a chance. At some point my father's hair had turned snow-white, an occurrence that enhanced rather than detracted from his virility. Due to the tanned darkness of his skin, his hair always looked even more white than it actually was. He dressed like he didn't care—a measure of a man's power to seduce—in an old pair of khakis and a dirty T-shirt, his pack of Luckys twisted in one sleeve. He wasn't exactly popular with the captains of the other charter boats, either.

We'd left home that day at first light, the moment when the sun is still twelve degrees below the horizon. The same rules pertain above as do below; let's face it, the same rules pertain everywhere now that the ocean's busy taking over everything. By the time we arrived at our port-of-call on the mainland the sun was fully visible, a giant red ball far to the east with a curtain of clouds preparing to lower over it. Departure had been scheduled for seven but one of the party "overslept," a euphemism for "had too much to drink the night before," though no one would say who it had been.

"No skin off my back," my father said, weighing anchor. He preferred to depart early when the ocean was at its calmest, a practice designed to help landlubbers adjust gradually to the water's increasing roll and pitch. Don't be fooled, though—he wasn't motivated out of consideration. Sickness disgusted him, as it disgusts most tyrants.

The farther we got from shore, the larger the swells became, while at the same time the water remained quite clear, extravagantly clear, the way it often is before a storm, almost as if you could see all the way to the ocean floor. Later, when the marlin appeared, it was as if there were no interposing medium, as if we were in water or the fish in air, like an image in the mind taking form, as brilliant as immaculate conception.

If you've never seen a marlin, you can have no idea how enormous one of them looks when it swims out from under your boat. It also happens to be beautiful, the shade of blue medieval monks used in their illuminated manuscripts when depicting heaven, with pure black fins and a long pointed nose like a lance. The voice is medieval, too, in the manner of plainsong. *Ho-dee-ee-ay, ho-dee-ee-ay*— "Today," it was saying, *hodie* being Latin for "today." Today. The fish was telling me something was going to happen today, though I still didn't know how to hear what it was saying.

"It must have been his *wife*," the blond woman was telling one of the men. "The girl's *mother*. It was tragic. Don't you re*mem*ber? She was famous—she played all over the world."

They were standing on the other side of the galley wall and didn't know I was there. I often learned things this way that proved useful to my father, such as who was planning to inform the Coast Guard on us for having insufficient life jackets onboard.

"Of course I remember," the man said. "I went to hear her once. At Wigmore Hall. I was there on business and my host had tickets. It's not even the kind of music I like but I'll never forget that night. Whatever she was playing, it went right through me."

He paused, and I could hear the sound of liquid pouring from a bottle into a glass.

"Don't be stingy, darling," the woman said.

By now we were far enough out that there was no land visible anywhere. The sun was still creeping up the panel of sky to the east, growing smaller and harder to see as if our eyes were failing us when really it was the world that was at fault. Meanwhile the boat pushed forward, rocking in the swells, and I could hear a wave break over the prow, splashing spray across the deck.

"Holy shit," the man said.

At last I was able to get a clear look at the pair of them, struggling to keep their drinks from spilling while they stumbled toward where the two other members of their party busied themselves with the task at hand, their rods bent, as meanwhile my father toured the deck, setting lines, scanning the water.

"Didn't they say she jumped?" the woman asked. "I thought that's what I read. It was around this time of year. The sea was choppy, like today. Maybe she lost her balance and fell."

"That's not what I heard," the man replied. "Besides, I can't buy that. If you'd seen her play you'd agree. Anyone who saw her play would know she had too much fire in her to take her own life."

I could tell his condescending attitude was annoying the woman; it was annoying me, too, even though I knew he was right. "Take a life," I thought—what an offhand way to say something so profound.

It was just about then that I caught sight of the marlin. She was approaching the boat from the east, the sun behind her, which is where you want the sun to be if you hope to catch a fish like that.

Before the world's oceans got too hot, even for marlin, they used to prefer the higher temperature of the water near the surface. I knew it was a *she* because of her size—the female of that species is always bigger than the male.

"Well, then," the blond woman was saying. "Why don't *you* tell *me* what happened?"

"I heard it was the husband," the man said. "I heard the husband pushed her overboard. He pushed her into the ocean and when she tried to climb back up he cut off her fingers."

"He *what*? Why would anyone do a thing like that?"

"Keep it down, why don't you?" the man said. "He's right over there."

"The story was they had a perfect marriage."

"Perfect if you think it's easy being married to someone who's so much better at everything than you are."

"I wouldn't know, darling," the woman said, and she leaned forward to kiss him on the mouth.

The sky was still blue but the sea was getting darker, green-black and thickening with intention, a shudder from deep inside it sending forth frills of foam.

"She was a monster," my father said. He had appeared from out of nowhere, grabbing the blond woman by the elbow and leading her—not exactly kicking and screaming but clearly reluctant—to the fighting chair. "Don't be an idiot," he added, baring his teeth. "When else in your pointless life will you get a chance like this? Or would you rather go to your grave knowing that's the best you can do?"

I could tell he was referring to the man with the bottle who, after wandering over to the starboard side of the boat and folding himself across the gunwale, was now being sick into the sea.

My father positioned the blond woman's hands on the rod seconds before the marlin took the bait—it was obvious from the precision of his every movement that he'd been preparing for this moment ever since we'd left the mainland. The rod jerked and he reached around the chair from behind to adjust the gimbal, releasing the catch on the reel and playing out line. "Aren't you going to strap me in?" the woman asked. She was trying to sound flirtatious but she sounded terrified, as well she should—the size of what you hook travels up the line and through your hands and into your nervous system where it's converted into the exact fear the creature on the other end of the line is feeling, drawing you onward and onward and onward—all the way to the edge of the world and, if need be, over the edge into the outer dark.

"Sanna will take care of the harness," my father replied.

The world fell into silence. Even the sound of the engine, the swells slapping the sides of the boat, even the shearwater's ghostly song.

There was no sound at all, absolutely none—

And then all at once I could hear it: my own name, coming from everywhere around me, like two notes struck on a piano, over and over, *Saa naa Saa naa Saa naa,* the sound drawn out like the tidal sound my mother's blood made once upon a time traveling through me.

I could hear so many things then—it was as if I could hear everything.

Who's to say why the harness failed?

AS it turned out there was a system, though it took me a long time to decipher it. The fact that I could never hear my father should have been a clue, but I was young and my world had very little in it aside from him and me. Weeks after the accident the blond woman's body—or a body taken to be hers, greatly decomposed, stabbed through the heart by a big fish before the little fish nibbled it away bit by bit—washed up on a Cuban beach. There was an inquest. Of course there was an inquest. It turned out the seasick man with the bottle happened to be not only the blond woman's boyfriend but also a lawyer. My father was sued for wrongful death; the verdict was contributory negligence. He paid the damages without putting up a fight and his business never recovered from the scandal.

In the meantime we both got what we wanted. I got older and my father didn't. He took to sitting on the beach in front of the yellow pine house, watching the tide as it came in and went out, closer every day until he was sitting up to his waist in water, though he didn't seem especially interested in what the ocean was doing. He didn't seem interested in anything, really, and yet at the same time he seemed like he had never been paying more attention. It's difficult to explain: even though he seemed like he was no longer there, it was also as if he was more *there* than he had ever been, as if he were deeply involved in the process of becoming what he'd been all along, the black emptiness I saw when I looked into his eyes, which was not the color of his eyes but which was Nothing, the end of Everything.

AND then once again my father was in the kitchen, making jelly omelets to celebrate my birthday. You have to understand: we had no choice in the matter. We had no choice in the matter just as we had no choice about the fact that one minute he was at the stove making omelets and the next minute he was lying on the floor like a sock the foot had suddenly been taken out of. The system was monstrous but essential, all the individual parts of the engine that drove it so beautiful you couldn't look at them directly or you'd die. I pulled the sheet off the piano and dropped it to the floor where it floated briefly on the surface of the water there before sinking; when I took my seat on the bench, the ocean was lapping around my ankles. This time I knew there would be no objection, nor did it surprise me that I played the piano as if I'd been playing it my whole life. My fingers were fine. They were better than fine.

Meanwhile in her house on the bed of the sea my mother came to the front door.

As I played I could hear the long, sweeping sequence of disintegrating chords that were the sound of her: *sssshhhhxxgggrrrrugggghghhhhhdrmmmaaaahhh* my mother went; *sssshhhhxxgggrrrrugg ghghhhhhdrmmmaaaahhh,* as she approached me from all the corners of the living room, her ten beautiful fingers coming closer and closer, each filled with the particular genius that was hers, white and strong and at last released to scuttle crablike across the floor to gather me in, finally ready to take a life, to take *my* life, home with her to her house on the bed of the ocean.

The story has Sedna at its heart: the Inuit myth about a girl who either displeases or overly pleases her seafaring father to such an extent that when she's trying to

climb back onboard his kayak he cuts off her fingers and tosses her into the sea. Her fingers become the sea creatures and she ends up ruling the deep. There are multiple versions of this myth and I mixed them to-gether. Sanna is another name for Sedna.

—KD

————— ❧ —————

MADAME LIANG
Lutz Bassmann

Madame Liang is the building's sole inhabitant. She had other names in her youth, seventy or eighty years ago, especially when she was queen of the dormitory and fired a gun alongside the last resisters in the Orbise commune. But afterward she lived in Asiatic refugee camps and zoo-parks for undermen for so long that she practically forgot her initial identities. Over the decades, the adventurous, luscious, and fatal Sofia Marmagadzi, heroine of egalitarianism and role model for several generations of combatants of both sexes, was little by little transformed into an authoritarian and terrifying grandmother, a certain Madame Liang, and her legend changed along with her physique. Nevertheless, there are a certain number of us in the city who respect her both for what she is in the present and for what she was in the past, during the time when you lived through your defeats with weapons drawn. We respect her, we protect her, we obey her, and, discreetly, we help her.

Madame Liang lives on the top floor, the fourteenth. She hasn't left her apartment in years. Several of us have offered to help her relocate, but she insists on remaining up there. She is old and authoritarian, very stubborn, and, on this issue as on the others, her mind cannot be changed. "I don't need to come down to your ruins to know where the world is," she says. It seems like a joke but deep down she is correct. "I tower above the world," she teases. "Why would I mess around in its gutters?"

The material aspects of her existence on the fourteenth floor have been taken care of. An efficient network oversees problems of supply and maintenance. She has recruited a guard, a specialist in close combat who provides her security twenty-four hours a day. He turns away all those who could harm her: prowlers, do-gooders, or squatters. From that quarter she has nothing to fear. The dangers and pollution of the street and gutters don't make their way to her. As for the tower, it stands firm, and, in the end, is less threatened by destruction than the buildings remaining at ground level. The pilots spare it. They prefer to keep a few ghostly buildings in the city to serve as landmarks when they are sent on machine-gunning runs.

To live near the sky is exceptional in our days, and Madame Liang is the exception that proves the rule. When you end up at such heights, it is generally for a very limited time, one hour or two, in a professional capacity. For instance, because you have been employed to hunt the eagles that colonize and dirty the roofs. Madame Liang doesn't ask anyone to get rid of the eagles—just the opposite. Part of her floor shelters enormous birds of prey: lammergeiers, circaetus, wild vultures, eagles. Part of her floor, and also probably part of her apartment. You hear them cry and shake their wings behind the walls, behind the windows. You hear them trample the gravel covering the terrace of the fifteenth floor. Madame Liang tolerates their presence, and although she denies it, I even suspect her of encouraging them to nest with her.

Carrion eaters have immense wings. I suspect her of sheltering them willingly. I have good reason to think so.

The other day, while I found myself in the salon where she receives her loyal supporters, an eagle's shriek shattered my eardrum—strong, strident, so violent that it couldn't have come from outside. From all evidence, the cry had been released by an eagle a few meters away from us, and, to be more precise, in the adjoining room, in Madame Liang's bedroom.

Sitting on the sagging sofa, I gave my weekly report. We were seated face-to-face, with a little low table between us, upon which Madame Liang had put down two teacups and a teapot full of cold broth. Madame Liang entrusts me with material tasks and also with the task of spying on the enemy, and I climb regularly to the fourteenth floor to report. I give her information about the militaro-industrial complex and its henchmen, I bring her the objects and medications that she has asked me for, I describe the state of the Organization to her, its local branch. That day, I had placed between us a bag containing the week's spoils. A frozen uniform on a mummified soldier, a road map, three harpoons, two meters of slow fuse for dynamite, five cartridges of various calibers, a sheaf of carpenter nails. We are reconstructing our forces little by little, yes. And Madame Liang coordinates the collection of materials.

Immediately after the shrieking, there was the noise of a struggle in the bedroom, pecking, feathers being torn out. I interrupted my discourse.

"They're fighting," I said.

"Let them," she responded, shrugging her shoulders.

"They're pests," I said.

I had just signed up on a list of applicants for cleaning the roofs. I hadn't been promised the position, but they had sent me to do an accelerated training course on the subject. The course had lasted two hours and its price would be deducted from my first wages. I had remembered from it that you had to be a good climber, that in the event of a fall into open air no compensation would be paid, and that eagles were pests.

"As if you knew everything about eagles," protested the old woman. "You know nothing, Nathan Golshem. They protect me from intrusions up the façade. And anyway they get rid of the pigeons for me."

In the bedroom, a second strident shriek rang out. During the training course, the instructors had deafened us with recordings. The eagle shrieks or it trumpets. After two hours, we forever hated that cry.

"They're pests," I grumbled anyway before continuing my report.

Perhaps Madame Liang's benevolence toward eagles is due to a genetic complicity. Madame Liang is no longer the breathtaking queen of the dormitory that she was during the insurrections and the camps. Now she hides her wings under her dressing gown, and, from time to time, her face covers itself noisily with feathers. This apparition lasts only a few seconds, and then the feathers retract, with the same disagreeable rustling as at the moment they suddenly thrust out through the skin. Madame Liang does pretty much nothing to conceal this. I think she no longer feels any shame. She turns aside a little and she coughs, sometimes she apologizes by muttering something. She doesn't seem to realize that this abrupt metamorphosis might constitute a repugnant sight, or, if she realizes it, she doesn't care.

I have said that Madame Liang controls the world. Some people maintain not. In their opinion, Madame Liang has only very limited power. In their opinion, she doesn't even control all sectors of the city. When you speak of the world, everything depends, of course, on what you picture behind that word. What is certain is that she controls the district at the bottom of the building, and even several adjacent streets, which go from the burned-out Metropolis movie theater to the Kanalvideo movie theater, where not one film has been shown since the end of the Second Soviet Union. The district represents a considerable human and underhuman area, and, among its hundreds of survivors we are somewhat like fish in the water. We have introduced, on the advice of Madame Liang, a community network which permits us to intervene in all daily matters, and we control ideologically several charity organizations, like the Association of the Semi-Deceased, the Association of Foreign Ants, and the Run for Your Life Club, where the raggedly dressed who turn up receive for free a bowl of soup and basic military training. Which shows to what point we are moving forward in the direction of regaining power on the global stage, or in any case strictly locally. It is a long march, we know. For a long time we wandered haphazardly, but now we are guided by Madame Liang, who puts all the weight of her experience at the Organization's disposal.

Malicious tongues claim that Madame Liang's political commitment is only a smokescreen, that she doesn't care about the problem of reconstructing our armies, that she broke with the Organization and that her activities are not militant, but instead commercial and villainous. That she is in league with a band of scrap metal dealers, with scavengers and bric-a-brac traders to whom she resells our arsenal and our equipment.

That she exploits us shamelessly, cynically, taking advantage of our naïveté and our great weariness in the face of the real.

Those are the rumors.

I can't resolve to think about them. Dirty rumors.

I have never dared consider them. It seems to me impossible not to rely on Madame Liang. We collectively put ourselves in the hands of this woman three years ago, when the state of our physical and intellectual forces had declined to the point that it approached absolute zero. We were eight survivors. Four are dead, one other disappeared. The three who remain are once again operational. We thus again form a group of consequence. Madame Liang helped us regain strength, she permitted us to again become proud of our future as Untermenschen and she succeeded in making us accept that you could draw an equal sign in between our future and that of humanity. Her equal sign was convoluted, but she succeeded in convincing us or, at least, in compelling us to stop recriminating. To have faith in the infamous idle gossip that accuses Madame Liang of duplicity would be to betray Madame Liang, to betray all hope, and to betray the remains of our comrades living or dead. I don't want to believe the story of the scrap metal dealers, the scavengers, and the bric-a-brac traders.

I prefer getting used to the eagles messing about behind Madame Liang's salon wall, to the idea of the eagles, which stink, which fight, which are pests and which she houses in her bedroom, not giving a damn about our opinion, or perhaps quite simply from genetic indulgence. I also prefer to learn to master my disgust when the smooth skin of Madame Liang bristles suddenly with rustling feathers and when, while I would expect from her the breath and stale fragrances of an old woman, I find myself wrinkling my nose at the stench of a dirty cage, of an aviary. But never mind. I'm getting used to all that, I am mastering my revulsion.

On the other hand, Madame Liang's bodyguard is something to which I know I won't manage to become accustomed. It isn't the idea of bodyguards that bothers me. It's the man who is assigned to it, the specialist in close combat who screens visitors and who is all-powerful on the only route leading to the fourteenth floor.

In other words, in the elevator.

The elevator works, but it is in bad condition. It climbs toward Madame Liang's apartment with a despairing slowness, and it often stops between the fifth and sixth floors, then it starts again, then once again it jams, this time between the twelfth and the thirteenth. The stops drag out for many minutes, and sometimes the wait to get going again lasts up to a half hour. You are sorry that you can't climb up by some other route, but the staircase is just a chaotic heap of debris on the first floors, and halfway up the tower it looks like a wide-open chimney. A few rickety ladders take its place, with rappelling ropes, nets that permit any amateur acrobat to pursue the path to the heights. However, for reasons of security, this ingenious ersatz staircase is interrupted many meters before the floor where Madame Liang lives, and, to haul yourself up to the fourteenth floor, someone up there has to throw down the necessary equipment, and this someone can only be Madame Liang or her bodyguard. Apart from exceptional circumstances, you therefore have to entrust your fate to the elevator. But not only to the elevator. You are dependent as well on the moods of this much-discussed bodyguard, who is there, who keeps watch, and who examines you. And who, according to Madame Liang, knows marvelously well how to eliminate unwelcome visitors, an elimination which Madame Liang calls rapid, painless, and definitive.

You always meet this fellow inside the elevator. A certain Bözeg Nicholson. He's a man of hardly impressive size, compact, with a flat face of indistinct expression and with untidy eyebrows. He wears workers' clothing and a black woolen cap. Someone not forewarned might very well enter the elevator car and take him for a lowly and vaguely barbaric neighbor. Madame Liang always speaks of him with a little excitement, with an enthusiasm at once maternal and ironic, while avoiding, it is true, giving too many clues about the route that led him to her and to the essential role of being security guard for the building. The personal history of Bözeg Nicholson thus remains shadowy. I believe that he is the only survivor of a clan of hunters exterminated by the enemy during a campaign to fight against illiteracy, but I don't know anything more about it. One thing is certain: he is devoted to Madame Liang and he will defend her selflessly to the last drop of blood.

Just in front of the building, at a point all visitors, authorized or not, must pass, Bözeg Nicholson from time to time opens a big black suitcase which otherwise he stores on the ground floor, in one of his secret bodyguard stashes. The suitcase exudes the strong odor of venison. In effect, this valise serves him as a stand. He removes from it skins and dried meat, which he exposes to the sun when it's nice out, directly on the pavement, or which he protects under a tarp's corner when it rains, and which he sells. "An entire assortment, even cannibals will find something there," Madame Liang jokes with a greedy expression, though she has never seen the suitcase or its contents, and her information is secondhand.

Bözeg Nicholson's presence makes the climb to the fourteenth floor frankly unpleasant. You would like traveling alone a thousand times better, but it's better not to think about this. Bözeg Nicholson has the key to the control panel of the elevator and under no pretext does he loan it out. For the elevator to move, you have to wait for Bözeg Nicholson to finish with his suitcase and decide to climb aboard. You then stand without saying anything, on your guard, in the flashing half-light of the car, while Bözeg Nicholson searches his pockets and fiddles with the openings of his sacks—because, once his suitcase has been put in a safe place, he carries with him large, half-empty oilcloth sacks. No conversation is possible. Bözeg Nicholson doesn't answer any questions, never reacts to the slightest remark.

The stops between floors are especially alarming. The light lowers, the ceiling light goes out, silence comes, you hear a few creakings of springs and cables, echoes down a dark well. Bözeg Nicholson presses a button next to which is marked: "Wait." And he starts to wait, as if he were alone, or rather as if the second passenger were negligible. Only the tiny green bulb fed by the emergency battery shines.

Only this little light shines, with its cellar glow.

Bözeg Nicholson starts to look for who knows what at the bottom of his pockets and to fiddle with the laces that close his sacks, and, even though you avoid looking in his direction, you very distinctly get the impression you're undergoing an examination, that he isn't just in the middle of checking the strength of his knots, grommets, and buckles. You imagine that suddenly you are mentally weighed, evaluated as a bearer of flesh, bone, and soft organs, with weak points that it would be judicious to strike if a fight began. You try not to think about it, but you know instinctively that the fight would be brief. Bözeg Nicholson is obviously not among those who dawdle during a duel.

You are glued to the wall of the elevator, which is no longer moving, and you feel studied from head to toe. So as not to be frightened by the absence of a response from him, you make no remark about the machinery, about the breakdown, about the now miserable lighting of the car. You try to appear relaxed. You force yourself to think about questions of general interest, about the future of the Organization, about the somnambulism of the masses. But none of these subjects manages to take hold and you are seemingly hypnotized by the motionless shadow, the very close shadow, of Bözeg Nicholson. You are incapable of concentrating on anything else.

It isn't difficult to imagine the appearance you must have then. A livid face, the wide eyes of the hunted, a tensed, wavering smile. You hold your breath—because, without noticing it, you had completely stopped breathing.

Like a dead man. You were no longer breathing.

And suddenly you recognize the smell floating in the confined space, made of odors that you hadn't identified in entering, when, on the ground floor, Bözeg Nicholson had pressed the button to close the door: the smell of blood, of a slaughterhouse scrupulously washed after each slaughter session, of a butcher's knife, of a skinner, of industrial-strength disinfectant, of tendons having ended their resistance under the blade, of scraped bone, of strips of leather set to dry, of moist hide, of a rubber-lined apron, of a salting tub, of distress, and of great loneliness.

—Translated from the French by Brian Evenson

This story is part of a longer work called Dance with Nathan Golshem *which consists of stories that the murdered Nathan Golshem and his still-living wife tell each other once a year when she makes the arduous visit to his grave and dances him back to life. What are myths if not the stories that the living tell the dead, and the dead tell the living? There are elements in this particular story of the Sirin of Russian myth as well as, with the ascent to Madame Liang, a kind of play on the often-told story of the visit of the living to the realm of the dead.*

—BE

SISSY
Kit Reed

To become a man, every first son has to kill his father. Oedipus taught us that, right? Look, you can forget Freud and all those other psychiatric dribblers. In no way is this essential murder about sleeping with your mother. Your balls are on the line, and if you still don't get it, I can't explain it.

For an only son, it's urgent. The lucky ones only have to do it once. Like the coward, my father died a thousand deaths after the first time I tried to kill him. After that I murdered him over and over but only in my mind, until. But the *until* comes later. My bad for botching it but hey, I was only eleven! I hated him. He belched. He drank. He threw the ball around with me all, "Catch," because he knew I couldn't, he threw out my poems without reading them and smashed my violin because he despised me and I knew it. I should have waited, but he pushed me too far!

After that first attempt my father sprang up like dragons' teeth in every room of the country house. He popped up snarling in every room I entered, filling hallways, rooms, closets, the bookshelves and all the cabinets, rising up *in my bedroom* like a monument to contempt. It was my fault, really. I jumped in without thinking. I was too young; it was too soon; I had no plan. No wonder it didn't work. I was eleven! I was overmatched and underequipped and I paid for it.

Mother never forgave me. She loved me, but she loved Father more, and she never let me forget it. It came down at night, on the Grand Terrace; everything about our house is grand. Cook brought bayonets out for Father to barbecue, giant skewers loaded with chunks of raw meat drenched in sauce and dripping blood, and set them down in front of Father. "Seek Kebab," Ali said proudly, which none of us understood, really, although Father pretended.

"The Rottweilers eat last, idiot. Get rid of that shit and bring my dinner."

Ali scowled. "If you want, I'll grill them for you."

"I want this gone!" Father said, shaking a bayonet at him. "Now, or I'm shipping you home to nether Lookbackistan."

Ali flinched. "As you wish, sir."

Mother said, "You've hurt Ali's feelings," and Father gave her a tongue lashing—we knew he beat her, but never out where anyone could see. It was awful. Ali touched his turban but the look he shot my way said it all. I didn't exactly know what *it all* was, but I knew it would be scary.

"And step on it, or I'll . . ."

Mother blanched. We didn't want to know what Father would . . .

"Don't, Dad!" I felt bad for Ali and besides, I knew what he had brought us, I knew!

"Call me Father."

I was so proud: "Don't give that to Rotty and Skanky, Father. It isn't dog food, it's shish kebab," I told him, thinking, *I'm smart, I'm smart, he thinks I'm a re-tard because I can't catch the ball. I don't even want to catch the ball.* I grabbed for the heaviest skewer. "Let me. I can show you how to cook them!"

"Don't even think about it!" Father snatched the thing away and smacked me with the back of his hand, spraying me with vodka-laced saliva. "Pussy." He threw the sword with our dinner on it like a javelin; it landed in the bushes and the Rottweilers finished it. "Take that, Pussy!"

Mother tried to intervene, "Don't call him Pussy, Dearest. That's ugly!"

"Out of my way, Olivia." He swung around and smashed her

with the rings on his left hand while he reviled me, yelling, "OK for you, sissybitch. Here's your new name, get used to it. *Sissy.*"

So both of us got hurt that night, and that was hours before I tried to kill him.

While Father ate the greasy hamburgers Ali set down in front of him with a subservient, murderous glare, I made a plan. I waited for Father to eat too much, which he always did, and watched him sink into the hammock with his bottle of port, which he always drained after gorging. Cook brought tea lights while Mother nursed the bruise on her face and Father fell into his nightly stupor.

Then I did what I had to. You would too! I watched Father's fat throat puffing in and out, in and out, while Ali cleaned up the mess the old man had made of the platter. Seething, I watched until I couldn't stand it. Then I ran at him with the last bayonet.

"Gerald!" Mother snatched my weapon out of my hands before I could fight through the fug of booze and cigar smoke that surrounded his fat form in the elephant hide hammock and plunge it into his throat. "Gerald Edgar Foss," she said in a voice so tragic that it bruised my soul. "How could you?"

I thought to lie. "I was just . . ."

"No you weren't." She was brandishing the skewer. "What in God's name . . ."

I tried, "He was hurting you . . ." That kind of thing, but she was crying so hard that I started sobbing too. "I thought you wanted . . ."

But she didn't want. I wanted, and she knew it. She pounded air with the skewer, hammering guilt into me, word by word. "Don't even think about it. It's like driving this thing into my heart."

"But Mother."

"You have to promise."

Blink. Blink. The tears made it convincing. "Promise what?" Damn you, Mother, damn you for not spelling it out. Instead she was neither here nor there. She warbled, "You aren't hurting him when you do this, lover, you're hurting meeee!"

She knows how to do what mothers do best. Knew.

You'd think I'd gored her instead. Aroused by her grief, Father rolled out of the hammock and charged me, roaring like an enraged rhino.

Mother wailed, but nothing stops the drunken rhinoceros.

Father was fixed on me, frothing with rage, but he was too drunk to hurt me, although from that moment we were sworn enemies. I fled him through the dozens of rooms in our beautiful house, and in the years that followed, no matter where I went in the house, he rose up in every room I entered, cursing me.

The hell of it was, he never forgot and Mother never forgave me. And look at her life! Never mind how powerful he was during office hours. At twilight, drink turned him into a monster. I started hearing thuds in the middle of the night—his fists plunging into her soft places. There was weeping. There were bruises. There were nights when Father's staff doctor came in the town car to treat Mother and once she went away to the sanitarium Father owned, and when she came back she was different.

Shaking, she sobbed in my arms, and I promised that someday she'd have her very own beautiful, safe room, a place that Father couldn't enter. Poor compromises: I wanted to kill him, but, remember.

The first time I tried to kill my father, Mother cried and cried. I felt so guilty! He was rich, he was powerful, he was a thundering bully. We would have been better off without him, but what can you do when your own mother throws herself between you and the man you hate most in the universe, pleading?

Every first son has to kill his father, but Mother? She loved him regardless: if I raised a hand to him, if I so much as remarked on the nocturnal beatings that I wasn't supposed to know about, my mother his wife and defender, my mother the betrayer, started with the reproaches. *Look what you did. You made your mother cry.* I did, and I hated it. All I wanted was to make her happy.

Father never let up. He bought my mother extravagant gowns and jeweled cuffs to hide the marks he left on her. He despised me, and he never let me forget it. I taught myself to paint and he called me a pansy. I sketched rooms to go with every gown Father gave her: Olivia's garden room, with flowering trellises painted on every wall to go with the velvet the color of her bruises; Olivia's salon, with Palladian windows, fishpond; Olivia's morning room, and she smiled, at least a little bit. Every time he beat Mother I sketched a new room for her—anything to make her happy.

If I showed him what I was writing, he snorted. "You write like a faggot, *Sissy*." He tried to make me do sports, but I have issues. It's about hand-eye coordination. He despised me because I couldn't hit the ball. I wanted to learn to fence but he snarled, "Only a pussy plays with toy swords, *Sissy*." He took me golfing and when I failed at that he dragged me home and marched me into his library, with the bordello décor and liquor bottles hiding behind shelf after shelf of fake morocco bindings. "We'll make a man of you yet, *Sissy*." He forced me to make chip shot after chip shot after chip shot on the thirty-foot Afghan war protest runner, a blood-spattered panorama of soldiers shooting and killing that ran the length of his monstrous red and purple room, and whether or not I scored or missed the ball, he raked me with scorn and I despised him.

OK, I thought, *just you wait.*

And I bided my time. And planned. In detail. After I killed him, I'd build those rooms I'd promised her, and she'd forget him. Year after year, insult after insult, Ali and I grumbled and conspired, and when I turned eighteen, we decided it was time. Listen! At that age I was worth a cool half-billion. I could build Mother a Trump Tower, her very own Parthenon, the one place in the universe where she could be happy.

A sissy holed up in the bedroom with his laptop can make a fortune—given the right number of Christmas and birthday checks from Grandma and a knack for investing. I got all As in school. I stayed out of his way. I dug in and refused to catch the ball. I signed off on practicing chip shots, learning martini-drinking or faking good-old-boy language to impress his business friends.

Father decided to boot me into Clemson or The Citadel, but he didn't just come out and say it. Instead he bombed into my room reeking of the last four bars he'd hit on the way up the mountain to our sprawling country house. He pounced on me before I could close my laptop. "OK, this is it. Sissy. Now, *put that thing down*."

"Hell no!" My brain is in that box! I grasped it to me like a breastplate.

He was too drunk to care. "Get moving!" He frog-marched me along to that plushy hellhole of a library and shoved me down on the oxblood leather sofa. He shoved a mess of catalogs into my lap. "Now pick one. You can't keep on laying around in your room like a faggot, Sissy."

That's LYING around, you moronic churl. And watch your language, you mouth-breathing knuckle-dragger. Understand?

"Either you get into one of these schools or it's the Army for you, buddy-boy. I will God damn well make a man out of you."

Mother had a whole mouthful of new teeth, inserted after the plastic surgeons repaired the damage to her jaw. She'd also learned how to sob somewhere that I wouldn't know it was happening, but I knew. She could cry to heaven without making a sound, but I knew. I thought: if a man is old enough to shoot a gun and kill people for his country, I'm old enough to do this.

I said, "The hell with that, *Father*. I'm my own person now, and don't you forget it. You can take those folders and . . ."

"Don't start!" He smacked me so hard that I still bear the marks of those rings. Enough! I didn't fall back; I surged to my feet and I drove the sharp corner of my laptop into the blank spot right between his eyes. Even though she was a dozen rooms away, I could hear my mother's wail.

As though she knew before I knew.

Ali wanted to finish it then and there, but Father's henchpeople came before I could say, "No. Let me." They got the medics here before I could clean the bloody matter off my Vaio, and locked me in a closet until it was clear that Gerald Foss Senior was conscious and howling for blood. All my files were safe in the Cloud, but when I opened my laptop, my *brain* to check, I knew the gods were on my side. Everything on my hard drive was intact.

I could hear them out there, deciding what to do.

I defied the old man and I would pay for it. The price of defiance would be death, but I saw it coming long before I hauled off and let him have it, and remember, I plan ahead. Thanks to medics who could be bought (the very ones who revived Father!) and major advances in cryogenics, I cheated death.

Sure, he had his thugs shoot me with the pistol he bought to humiliate me on the firing range at his club, but death? If you're young and strong and rich enough, death is just a temporary glitch, in addition to which, they shot me in the belly, not the head. Stupid! These days, they don't only freeze the head. A few weeks later I stepped out of that capsule big as life and completely mended.

By that time he'd stopped paying for security around the clock and left the job to the Rottweilers. On the first night the house was silent and untended, Rotty and Skanky welcomed me like the prodigal son, wagging and fawning, even before I threw them the meat. Then I stepped in through the French windows and let him have it with the bayonet I'd kept safe under my mattress ever since Ali brought it to me on, what shall we call it: Shiskabob Night, and yes, I know that isn't how you spell it.

I killed Father at last. I killed him dead.

They hate it when you do that.

Cheat death.

The look in Father's eyes as he bled out on the thirty-foot Afghan war protest runner in his library was one of utter contempt. So I took, I think that thing is called a mashie. I took one of his mashies out of the golf bag and chipped that expression clean off his face.

Mother rushed in, flailing. "Oh, Gerald, how could you!"

I saw the recent bruise on her temple; I saw the zigzag in the wrist he'd broken in a lesser argument. Strong and righteous, I shouted, "I did it for you!"

Oh, Mother! She screamed: "Oh, no you didn't!"

Howling with grief and rage, she spun in place between me and what was left of him, getting louder and louder and wilder and wilder in her frenzy, a whirling tornado of reproach. I tried to stop her but she twirled in front of me with her eyes streaming tears like blood until her face was a swollen blur. I tried to stop her but she just kept spinning, getting redder and redder.

What happened next was astounding.

"I'll never forgive you," my mother shrieked, and dropped like a horse under the knacker's hammer.

Guilt rolled in as she fell, and guilt trapped me here, in my father's house.

I can't leave until I make it right.

You don't know when you defeat death that it's not angry gods that you have to be afraid of. It's your mother. Cerebral aneurysm, the doctors told me, but I knew better. In every room I entered after she died I found my mother, grieving over what I had done, and every time I told her:

"Don't cry, Mother. I can make it better. We'll move on, to a better place."

What's a loving son to do? I built her the Morning Room, where sunlight would find her—in retrospect, at least, that should make her happy—but when the builders and decorators left and I stepped inside to be alone with her memory, I found my mother standing there with her eyes dropping tears like ink and every line in her face dragged down in a rictus of grief and the only thing she said when I approached her was, "I loved him. Oh, Gerald, how could you?"

Never mind. I built My Lady's Chamber off his pagan library; it took a year, but it was gorgeous, and it broke my heart when I found her there on the day I finished, with her mouth filling up with those black, black tears, and the only thing she said to me? "Oh, Gerald, how could you!"

Never mind, I thought, the house is built to expand, Father's acres cover half this mountain. I built the Reading Room, and after that the Art Gallery, the Ballroom, the indoor swimming pool, the Screening Room, but no matter what I designed and executed in her name, every time I opened the door on my newest attempt to make her smile and forgive me, my mother was already there, with her tragic mask firmly in place and no matter what I said or did to her my mother greeted me with the same stark, plaintive words, "Oh, Gerald, how could you?"

After the first dozen new rooms, Ali came to me in the newly completed masterpiece: Olivia's wine cellar. He's old now, but I look and feel the same—cryonics! He said, "You know this is futile."

"Yes," I told him. "But I have to keep trying." I do! I begin each new project with such hopes!

"Please understand." Ali touched his forehead in a mournful salute. "I'm out of here."

"Understand, I'll be out of here too, just as soon as I make a room where my mother is OK with this."

He shook his head, then, "If that ever happens, come visit."

Ali's gone back to Kashmir, where I hope he has grandchildren waiting, and I? My next project is a chapel with a labyrinth on the Chartres model at its center. When it's done, I'll meet Mother there and in the presence of the Eternal, maybe she'll forgive me.

If not, there's always the miniature Coliseum. When they bring in the lions and I grapple them to the death in her presence she'll understand that I'm doing my best; I have for years! I'm doing my best, and I'll keep on doing it until one of us cracks or she gets bored and releases me, but I already know that's an empty dream. There's not a chance in hell that she'll forgive me.

Never mind. There's always the next room.

When Kate asked me to write a story about my favorite mythical character for this anthology, I knew exactly who I wanted to use. Sisyphus makes a perfect

protagonist, probably because his story, in a way, is the story of our lives—well, this writer, who steals time from work to keep the household running, no matter what. Boring! So I took the story of Sisyphus and on the basis of a hasty Google, knew what I wanted to do with him. Yes, "Sissy" is about a guy. He's one of those males who has to kill his father before he can take the throne—and like so many only sons he has mother issues—a guilt trip in the making. As for the rest—there is the labyrinthine, unfinished Winchester house in San Jose, built by the widow of the gun manufacturer, source of another powerful myth. After the death of her husband and son, a medium told Sarah Winchester to leave California and start building: "a home for yourself and for the spirits who have fallen from this terrible weapon, too. You must never stop building the house. If you continue building, you will live forever. But if you stop, then you will die." For me, these two myths fused at tremendous speeds, and "Sissy" is the result.

—KR

The Strix

——— ∽ ———

IN A STRUCTURE SIMULATING AN OWL

Ander Monson

My invention relates to a structure simulating an owl. The object of my invention is to provide a structure simulating an owl as an article of manufacture. A further object of my invention is to simulate an owl as an ornamentation. A still further object of my invention is to provide a structure flexible in part and being colored simulating an owl.

—Grace E. Wilson

United States Patent Office Application
[NUMBER REDACTED], Filed [DATE REDACTED]

1.   In a structure simulating an owl in which are inscribed the eyes of my former husband, having been etched on shook silver foil, serving as a replica of his eyes in his absence, blue dashed with bits of white as if they were in every moment on the verge of dissolving into a simulacrum of eyes, all of us being simulacra, I have been feeling recently, of ourselves from former moments, indistinguishable (as is the way of simulacra) from what others, even our lovers,

our husbands, our dream-sons, our conquerors, our makers, might identify erroneously as ourselves when seen from a distance or even up close if approached quickly enough, in the way that the self can usually be described as two sheets of thin metal folded at least four times and in some complex cases many more (a machine may be required to create this effect) and pinned together by a small bolt, fastened eventually by a nut, the entirety of my history may be included in or at least referred to by a succession of small moving parts.

2.   In a structure simulating an owl in a dream I have had every year on this date from as far back as my memory goes, in which I am in my father's workshop, a word that was among my first (*workshop*, not *father*—though the two are conflated now in memory), watching him from a very great distance which is of course in this structure not geometrically possible except in dreams, as he works above a wooden stove which is burning hot shaping some kind of metal, at which point I kick over a bucket of what must be kerosene or some burnable thing which spills onto the floor where a rope is somehow soaked in fluid, and it is only moments before the rope connects to my father and a number of unidentified canisters and I have no language with which to warn him since as quickly as I try to speak my voice is stuffed with cotton swabs and my breath is somehow fire and my warning turns to flame along with everything in the workshop including my father and his eyes which in every photograph remind me of owls, a human or a memory of a human may be for some time ensconced.

3.   In a structure simulating an owl in which I have been making something for the world that might, in a small way, change it, so as to have an effect on something, once in my life, since I have been recently feeling as if I were a ghost, some combinations of my dreams and waking life and my many so-called sins will be made manifest at last.

4.   In a structure simulating an owl composed primarily of wire and sixteen separate moving pieces designed to spark terror in all creatures preyed on by owls if they come within sight of said structure as it is attached to a post by a rivet or a wishing screw, six feet or higher above the ground, and in some cases it might be suspended from an outdoor ceiling fan or from a series of wire loops attached to a belt-driven mechanism that is activated by the lack of

light so that it moves in an elliptical fashion and makes a sound somewhat like an auk makes, an onomatopoeia, a word I have wanted to use since I was twelve and in eighth grade and discovered it in the oldest dictionary available in the public library where I spent my days fingering my afternoon through pages, in which I learned one might describe one's life or another's by words, not exactly shunned by my peers but hardly invited out, and not engaged in any official after-school activity though I did have tendencies toward delinquencies, breaking into the school bus factory a mile down the road from home to sit in the buses, lonely, my father dead, my younger brother years dead already, dead almost before I knew him, having died when he was two and I was five, my older brother absent, gone somewhere on those days that I could not access, and on these buses I would carve my name along with his or with other boys and sometimes girls in the backs of the vinyl seats, licking all the places where I knew someone's hands might touch in the bus in the next year when it would be eventually deployed and driven, possibly even on the route that terminated in my house after driving past the place of its manufacture, an irony lost on machines and on the drivers of machines and on the many other hands and eyes that resulted in these machines and touched these machines and their sale and deployment on this route, this date, in which they might catch a glimpse in the dying light of the outline of an owl on a high post or possibly moving through the air and wonder what it was in the approaching dark, or thrill perhaps at the fact of owls with their moving parts and soundless flight and outstretched arms that might in another life have entwined with my own, I might find some satisfaction.

5. In a structure simulating an owl, it is incontrovertible that I have been in some way seeking transformation.

6. In a structure simulating an owl, my marriage might be seen closely enough through the attached rangefinders built into the structures simulating eyes, so as the marriage might appear real, not simply as described by law, but in the hearts of both partners legally obligated to each other for the rest of their lives until dissolution or death, a statement neither my husband nor I took lightly at the time, though as with all infinities, or seeming infinities, their true extent is inapprehensible, barely even glimpsable from the

moment in which a marriage can be made and committed to, and from that particular location in which the structure simulating an owl might be placed, one might see over time the way that marriage decayed, due in no way to the behaviors or intentions of the couple but due to the ways a domestic life can drive you apart like a lead wedge placed in a crack and hit with a heavy sledge with a lifetime's worth of force, resulting in approximately two structures that, when held side by side and looked at together, formerly simulated an owl.

7.   In a structure simulating an owl one's life might be understood as if in retrospect, from its very last chapter, as a series of actions and reactions, chemical, biological, emotional, metaphysical, all collected together and held for a moment by the mind, and therein might be seen to be a method to it at last.

8.   In a structure simulating an owl, as the present invention proposes to demonstrate, each moving part or pin being constructed of lines on paper in attached diagram 1, if looked at closely enough with a scanning microscope, one might note that the lines are not solid lines but scattered ink on paper, marks rendered very finely, and not corporeal parts at all, as if to say a physical thing might be actually enacted and made to move and apparition as an animal, we might be in this way terrified by it as we are if woken suddenly enough with enough force.

9.   In a structure simulating an owl, as all structures start to appear if you look at them long enough and hard enough as if they were one of those magic-eye 3-D drawings that only the annoying are apparently able to see, you will see the future of the owl or really the structure simulating it combined with your own future as manifested in your actions; this outcome is what creates the necessity of the forty-four levers that work behind the metal outer skin of the structure that create the illusion of the owl, though if you were, say, an owlet, or another interested owl it's probably plenty obvious by now that this structure only simulates an owl in name and outer shape, and in some of the motions of its wings, not in the scent of an owl, or the way an owl actually flies, meaning that while a structure simulating an owl might simulate an owl it cannot yet fully be

an owl: as long as we understand each other then we can communicate.

10. In a structure simulating an owl that is equipped with increasingly verisimilitudinal scent glands one might secrete the sorts of scents that might fool another owl, a slow one at least, for a second at least, and in so doing, could one actually be considered an owl for a moment, which is to say can a sufficiently advanced illusion be a kind of magic?

11. In a structure simulating an owl which does not account for the amorphous quality and (both wonderful and not) unpredictability of love, and the effect of its loss and slow replacement by the love of another, an impossible love, really, in many ways, not possible, surely, to admit out loud or in writing or in the presence of anyone, ever, if you value your marriage and the pleasing domesticity that it brings, along with the overly alliterative, you understand, damningly dull domesticity that drives me in moments out to the back in the workshop where, in my own world of wire and awl and dictionary and hammer, I can immerse myself for days in the process of producing a structure simulating an owl.

12. In a structure simulating an owl I might more easily understand the ways in which I have transgressed, and another structure simulating an owl might be understood to move of its own volition and driven by its own internal mechanisms, however obscure, containing my estranged husband, who I thought understood how I worked and what drove me to do what I did, but who refused to make allowances for my strange behavior in the last two years, though he said he tried, god damn he did, he said, and I believe from this distance that he did, he did the best he could, and some things end eventually, it's physics, sure, entropy and all, our bonds are only temporary, and in this guise surrounded by this nest of wire I can get some distance from my former self and see history from hundreds of feet above as if aloft and hunting for meaning in the motions of rodents in the world.

13. In a structure simulating an owl ever more closely in this iteration, the machine of one's life can be worked or worked out arriving

at a point, an increasingly fine construction of said structure, and shown to the ones one loves in hopes of expressing the inexpressible to them in the absence of other ways we might show our love.

14. In a structure simulating an owl that entrances animals if they come within 140 feet of it, the cache of stored scents is released in response to various stimuli that in the wild prompt owl-like behavior in owls, because all of us are creatures that respond to stimuli, I am finding in my life and trying to make manifest in the world this fact, because given the collective behaviors of those I come into contact with on a daily basis who try to cloak their animal natures, as if they posit that they are *not* animals, that they are *not* out of control of their own bodies, that they are not like zombies, craven and driven to their desire, but that they are, as my mother claimed to be, entirely self-aware and in full control of her faculties so much that her resistance to every desire became a manifesto, a way of living, a clothing that she wrapped herself with every day of her life and would occasionally deploy to asphyxiate her children and her husband for periods of time: quite obviously it crushed her after years so that you had the sense that there was no inner sense of self, of what she would do if freed from her own restrictions, since she said, for instance, that what civilization is is denying every desire you have in your filthy hearts, and if we do not police our weaker moments, we are not human, and in this way she became like a structure simulating a paragon or a structure of beliefs in which she was housed, in which she might have secreted some small bit of herself away if it was possible to pull the whole thing apart, and that by this lifelong simulation she was making some point to the world, and so even when she was freed, her parents deceased, her husband deceased, all of her other children deceased and just the two of us remaining she might have been free of this, I hoped, and to that end I dosed her several times with psychotropic drops rendered from mushrooms gathered from her own front yard just after a storm, theorizing that by sudden jolt to the senses she might be knocked back into an uncomfortable former shell of self and be forced to fight her way with that small treasure back into the present and what had become of her life: a hollow. Of course this was not possible because until her actual dying moment she persisted in simulating what she had always hoped or meant to be, and apparently

became, at least to all of us who knew her and her capacity to suffer seemingly endlessly, that she could absorb almost anything you could throw at her: all those deaths, sometimes two at once, an alcoholic son, a straying and overly promiscuous daughter, the decline of what she once knew the world to be into a den of iniquity, if that's not saying too much in her own words, or what should have been her words if she was given to those sorts of proclamations, which she was not, which resulted in silence which is the usual result of most stimuli to a structure simulating an owl.

15. In a structure simulating an owl having a flexible covering made primarily of hammered tin adorned with artificial feathers, one might spend one's days perched on one of a hundred points I have indicated on the attached maps around the fair city, these points offering a particular vantage toward a particular view, for instance of my own son among the crowd of beasts released from school at 2:25 in the afternoon, the sun just so in the sky, rushing out to his home with his father which is four kilometers exactly from my own, the separate domiciles due in some small part to my own eccentricities, I have come to understand only too late, resulting in loneliness and what is commonly referred to as my breakdown, though I did not see it that way at all, instead a kind of reboot, a transformation, a shedding of an old skin, a structure simulating a woman, into an entirely new simulation, a pause followed by a subsequent burst of energy resulting in long spans of time spent in my own workshop—and oh!— from this distance they resemble a spray of pressurized water forced out of a crack that might eventually break open and let the whole tank crash onto the ground, or, perhaps better, a spread of mice fleeing some place in which they had been pent up for a time, and in their flight they might easily be snatched up by a creature of such size and floating grace and powerful eyesight such as anyone who might be in the possession of a structure simulating an owl.

16. In a structure simulating an owl one might spend their time roosting on the edge of the gargoyled roof of the bank building at the center of downtown, contemplating the stuffed insides of humans and other animals who built this roof and who spend no time considering their own stuffings, the meat parts that make us up and make the machine of the body work, the bland tours of glands, the

orifices and labyrinths, the complications of our systems, our bodies all being flexible machines for digestion and peregrination and the slow operation of our intelligences, grinding as they do toward a conclusion, like the construction of these carved stone gargoyles, originally meant to frighten off evil spirits, though they now mostly frighten the occasional child who strays her gaze skyward to the perch and is justly startled by the visage of these devilish creatures perched here along with, watching, waiting, thinking, reserving judgment for the moment, planning decisive action, a structure simulating an owl.

17.   If the girl child were to point toward the structure simulating an owl gleaming in the midafternoon sun, she might not understand that the gleam is a result of three sets of interchangeable lenses that can be used to focus and redirect sun into a steady beam that might transfix the object of the structure simulating an owl's gaze long enough to distract said object and to forever hold her there, as if in a sufficiently elongated moment the structure simulating an owl might pass to the object of its strange affection some kind of wisdom about what it is to be a woman in the world buffeted as we are by the actions of those around us, constantly desired or stared at, starred and asterisked in the dreamlives of yearning others, so that it is impossible to look at oneself without the sense of being dreamt of or gazed upon, creating a doubleness, a structure that starts, after a time, to simulate the self and that might be mistaken for the self if the user is not careful.

18.   In a structure simulating an owl either wisdom or killing is a natural outcome of an interaction, owls being understood to be in the possession of some otherworldly wisdom, and owls being the instrument of killing, and sometimes these two things being indistinguishable or at least interlocking, a difficult fact to communicate with others.

19.   In a structure simulating an owl one is always aware that one is wearing a mask, a complicated, lever-operated carefully machined series of metal masks, but a mask nevertheless, and one might consider the ways in which we don and doff a series of masks throughout our lives.

20.   In a structure simulating an owl one might be cold except for the layers of insulation machined initially from gloves purchased at the local Target, and then, after the initial trial run with these layers of repurposed material, the prototype was fitted with up to six layers, depending on the climate you foresee operating in, of asbestos procured from India, though made and exported from Canada, a country that continues to ship out asbestos to India in spite of what is known about its carcinogenic qualities because economic growth is understood to be a universal good, and because an industry operating efficiently gains its own inertia and cannot easily come to a halt, and because warmth is of utmost importance while on location because in a structure simulating an owl it is very difficult to move, except by wire and servomotors.

21.   In a structure simulating an owl one has dreams and must acknowledge those dreams as what they are: shadows of desire, the product of overlapping selves and parental wishes and possibilities for lives understood from early reading of pornographic magazines and women's magazines and many series of effectively authorless teen mysteries.

22.   In a structure simulating an owl I always dreamed—or even thought, assumed, as if a destiny was an inevitable thing, as if there was such a thing as a destiny, as if it could be understood except from the past tense, as if our lives could be seen just from beyond the point of our departures into nothingness or ever-afterness—I would be Miss Minnesota when I grew up, in spite of what I full well knew, though was often told, which was that I was not particularly attractive, my nose slightly hooked, my breasts overlarge and not in the desired way, and my face just slightly too symmetrical to convey the sense of attractiveness that society has decided to validate, not that I let it stop me, begging my mother to enter me in pageants from a young age, I'm not sure why exactly I wanted this so badly—perhaps this was a response to my father's death, in retrospect, and needing some way to cast a long shadow, as I could do walking nights in the old neighborhood when the floodlights from the neighbors' houses would click on at my sudden movement, moving toward their windows and the lives I so desperately wanted to see and understand, as if by understanding their lives I could under-

stand my own, and if at the proper angle the light would cast my shadow that would go on for over a hundred feet until I could no longer tell where there was shadow and where there was just darkness, and my wanting of this brilliant pageant dream increased in proportion to its impossibility, like the lover I fell for so hard that finally split the structure simulating a marriage apart, in spite of that long love spent with my husband, who had and has his faults, and one of them was that he was powerless to stop my drift, geologist that he is, knowing something about continents and their barely perceptible shifting, I would have thought he would understand this better, and I drifted through those pageants in my mask, my makeup face fixed in a dazzling smile that I would later reassess in light of what I had come to learn, in short that by not varying the smile people found me terrifying, spectral really, as if I were not a woman but a mannequin, posed, smooth, but somehow breathing, and this was one in a long string of revelations about the ways in which I have misconstrued others' responses to the way I conduct myself socially, spending weeks poring over etiquette books and practicing responses to common queries to make myself more charming, but in a structure simulating an owl you don't need these things to move or see or appear or terrify a creature at a hundred paces, which may be inevitable anyway the longer we live.

23. In a structure simulating an owl I will have receded successfully from my life, my lives, both before our split and after, finally if not irretrievably, so that I will have no appearance of my own, no face to terrify, no family to be judged by or misunderstood, and in so simulating an owl in said structure for such a long time, in the view of others, anyway, and as such in my own view, since we do internalize the way we are considered by others in our self-imaginings, I will eventually be transformed, and become not just a structure simulating an owl or a woman or a woman simulating an owl, but something else entirely.

24. In a structure simulating an owl I will hope to understand—nay, I will manifest—the desire I have read about in others and seen for myself as in my older brother's drunken state before he died when he would tell me about what he wanted most deeply but never had the courage to achieve, the desires of those who sexually fetishize

amputees (acrotomophiliacs), or, in more extreme circumstances, who desire to be amputees and who might even undergo voluntary amputations (apotemnophiliacs), who feel their limbs are somehow wrong, too long, incorrect, or simply not a fit for them, who may have some version of body dysmorphic disorder, but regardless, want what they want, as humans—animals—do and good luck telling them not to want those things, in that in this structure I might understand that transformation, even if it isn't sexual for me as it was for my older brother, a fact he would not admit to sober, certainly, one reason he was not often sober, that he once said "I will never feel truly whole with legs," though he never had them removed, a fact he called a tragedy, and maybe it was a tragedy, not to get to live one's deepest-held desire, no matter how bizarre or increasingly frustrating or pointless, but maybe it was a sensible tragedy, given the extremity and oddness of his and this desire, and the ways it might have transformed his life—he knew it then, and he said as much, that it might have changed something in the world, in him, certainly, if we can change ourselves, which I desperately hope we can in my better moments even as I am not sure I believe it in my darker ones, though I will not stop trying not ever, in whatever structure or set of clothes or metal exoskeleton I am presently working on—when he died last year, the final straw, as my husband said, ever cruel, overcruel, my mother was the one who cleaned out his home at his behest and when I asked her about the computer and what was on it, trying not to suggest I knew his secret or that he even had such a secret, trying to honor this luminous and folded place that he held within him, that I might have been the only one who knew, that I was wondering what sort of pornography he might have on there, she was of course circumspect, as she always is, and deflected the question, suggesting that she was another keeper of his secret, one he trusted more than me, given her lifelong goal of full-on repression of our other, darker selves, a fact that I took as blame for not going far enough with him, a fact I am hoping to convert to a new understanding of what it might mean or be to become someone else—to become someone else—by silence, by patience, by devious mechanical engineering, and by sheer belief in a structure simulating an owl, to somehow become an owl.

25. In a structure simulating an ow! I mean an *owl* but was cut off midthought and midword in fact by the sight of something swoop-

ing in the darkness from this vantage point and that I was transported by it suggests its efficacy, I will dream again not as human but as owl—featherlight, meatfinding, unthinking—for a time.

26. In a structure simulating an owl I will remain at one of my designated posts for a year or more, removed from life, but not from vision, subsisting on what I can catch and eat, having studied this problem and the many methods owls have of hunting prey and also foraging with my human hands where they extrude from the structure, perhaps in the gardens of my extended family and friends, wondering if they will have forgotten me in a fit of self-protection or if they have written my selfish exit off, or if they are wondering exactly what an owl—what they will misapprehend and is in fact a structure simulating an owl—or perhaps it is an owl, thus the power and point of the extended simulation—might be doing in their backyard at night peering with its set of magnifying lenses into their windows, into their lives, and apprehending the resulting spaces that opened up in there, how they react, how they close and fill those spaces.

27. In a structure simulating an owl I do not expect to die.

28. In a structure simulating an owl I will hereby attempt to know the unknowable.

29. In a structure simulating an owl I will not live as I lived before, in guilt and repression—or in fully giving in to my baser urges and the corresponding renunciation of my former life—lives—and need for light.

30. In a structure simulating an owl in which a complex optical mechanism allows the use of infrared and ultraviolet light to augment and aid perception, an occupant or user can approximate the night vision of owls.

31. In a structure simulating an owl I cannot be my brother, I understand it, nor my father, nor my long-dead younger brother, nor my child, nor my husband, but I can also not be myself for a year or longer and see what that is like, and in so doing I submit that this

invention will be revolutionary and of a deep and abiding effect for certain persons who want to live in what we refer to as a civilization—and occasionally retreat from it via engineered and exceptionally complicated mechanisms like this, in which we might be transported into another self, as in immersive online play or as in Dungeons & Dragons or as in the way we lose ourselves in reading.

32.   In a structure simulating an owl the user might take that transfiguration even further and, by isolation and the fact of one's own diminishing humanity, more bodily embody these transformations into others such as owls.

IN testimony whereof I affix my signature,
[NAME REDACTED]

Myths often explain the transformation from human to animal as a punishment for something, a misstatement, a misdeed, a witnessing. The Strix, owl, bird of ill omen from the Roman and Greek, is the result of such a metamorphosis. Metamorphosis—or the desire for it—is recently the only subject I've been interested in. So this story has our human seeking transformation— perhaps as a kind of respite or maybe delusion or divine intervention via invention. In so becoming we imagine we can leave our old skins and selves behind and emerge as something new, which we usually cannot do.

—AM

Tezcatlipoca

CAT'S EYE
Donají Olmedo

Uncle Sebastián's cabin rose inscrutably above the forest of a wooded town: El Salto, the municipal seat of Pueblo Nuevo, in the state of Durango. Pine trees surrounded it like giant gendarmes. I, a feeble, disoriented boy about to swallow the key to a jail cell and be my own prisoner, drove toward the green, sweet-smelling prison, intending to go through it.

The curves in the Devil's Backbone on the Mazatlán–Durango highway received me with a thin layer of ice on the asphalt carpet. White strings of sleet snaked over the windshield. The solitude of the road kept me company, and in order to avoid skidding, I focused my attention on imagining the spinal landscape, because I wasn't able to admire it. My eyes stayed nailed on the white stripe of the highway, gray sawmills flashing past on both sides.

After I left far behind me the Conafor office, which grants or denies cutting permits, the cold assaulted my bones. Adjusting and hitting the heater proved useless: I was freezing. My eyes turned from one side to the other, searching for a cabin. The dark canvas of the sky hid the moon almost completely. After an hour of cold stabs in my body, distress seeped in and I began to sweat. My breathing accelerated, and the car windows steamed up, entrapping me further. There was no way back, and it was not a good option.

One of the curves opened like a far-reaching tentacle. The car was freed from the inertia force of the curves so suddenly that it shot out of the highway. The white gleam made by a light coming from some unknown place reflected on thin layers of ice on the grass and hurt my eyes. I lost control and crashed into the depth of a glimmer.

It was the third time I was going to the wooded town, and I was supposed to be atoning for two weeks. The cabin imprisoned silence in such a way that it reeked of loneliness and exuded neglect. It was my father's punishment. He sent me there to force me to analyze my faults. Uncle Sebastián helped with my therapy, adding effortlessly the heavy weight of indifference. Soon isolation took the lead. I was going from the hot Mazatlán beaches to the cold mountain range of the Sierra Madre Occidental. I thought maybe the treatment consisted of freezing bad actions and breaking them with a mallet.

Before falling inside the light, a good number of illusions had been shattered. My adolescent fury found no adequate refuge. Music and painting just flew over my head, making me look naïve. Then I dedicated myself to living my way: some days with brightness and people, others so many colors and forms; still others, on a large canvas, I painted scenes in oils, different trips of the same conflict: the forest of my soul in flames. When restlessness made a bulge at the fly of my pants, laziness helped me: getting drunk with friends, I played hooky. Then came the punishment and with it, solitude.

The cabin was my family's hermitage. Uncle Sebastián had made his permanent home there and served as an example of mediocrity and indecision; he lived off his siblings, including my father. For his relatives, he turned into a piece of furniture furthest inside the wooden walls and ceiling, with no electricity, with latrines, with a stove for cooking and a fireplace to counteract the climate. He lived on rabbit meat, beans, and stored and, sometimes, moldy tortillas.

Every day before breakfast, my uncle groomed his scarce hair and white beard, lit his first cigar of the day, and with it in his mouth, put on overalls and shoes; he drew his overall straps toward his breast and adjusted them. Three times a week he wore clean shirts. His jeans were worn out, stiff-looking, and of undefined color.

Then the robust, bearded man walked with long, slow steps toward the first pine trees around the cabin. He put his left ear to the base of the largest tree and remained there for quite a while as if listening to the beating of the aged heart of an immense soldier.

I heard my uncle's voice for the first time during my second punishment.

"What animal bit you last night? You didn't sleep a wink, did you?"

"Cats were crying like dying children," I said. "Didn't you hear them, Uncle? They were heard from inside the chimney flue, as if they had broken in through the cowl; I was about to stick a broom into it through the fireplace."

"Yes . . . yes, I heard their footsteps, sounding like falling leaves."

"Footsteps . . . ?" He got up from the table and left me there with no answers. He went out with his rucksack and some traps to hunt for his food of the day.

Once a week Filemón would show up with his wagon. The vendor looked like a cross between a middle-aged tramp and a pirate. He sold us tortillas, cookies, salt, sugar, beans, some cans of milk, and cigars. He also brought books to my uncle. That day he left Sándor Márai's *Embers*. I bought unfiltered cigarettes; there wasn't any other kind.

"Phewww! You look like you could use some sleep, kid. You look terrible," Filemón said, taking off his sombrero and sticking out his bloated stomach.

"Cats were meowing. I heard them for a long while."

"Did you hear the cat lady?" He opened his eyes in surprise. "Phewww! Well, she visited you, eh?"

"Cat lady? Does she live around here?"

"No, she doesn't. She rather roams around. . . . Ask Sebastián. He knows her better than anybody else." He climbed into his wagon and waved good-bye.

"Do you know who you are? You have to start there before wanting to know who the cat lady is," Uncle Sebastián began.

While he was cooking a rabbit, his severe face came alive, illuminated by the flames. The fiery tongues flickered, making him look sinister; then his voice sounded distant as though he were speaking from the bottom of a well. Yellow hues softened his expression and I felt I was with an indulgent father.

"It took me a long time to understand absolute reality. It was hard to find myself and live. You know? We're strange beings that need to find out what surrounds us first, then understand how to share with it, and lastly know what you are in the middle of all this. To go beyond . . . to look for reality. You, kid, paint canvases, draw images . . . then you look beyond what your eyes can see. It's a kind of another reality, not of man for sure . . . but it doesn't cease to be another. Some people hear the lady, others see her, and still others, like you, hear cats. I . . . see and sense leaves, and feel their steps. She has always lived in my forest. There are various legends: painful stories of unrequited love, others about the solitude of someone who sees her and the good fortune to see her; but the most widespread is one about death. This version is disturbing, but also I find it most beautiful. The cat lady, they say, dreamed of her own death. This happened when she learned who she was because of a man, the day she fell in love with him. Love transformed her, and she recognized her own mortality; this bothered her a lot. Numb with love, the lady shut herself with her man in their cabin, locking the back door. Their acquaintances never saw them again. They lived with insomnia, put their dreams away, and lived through them together. As time went by, the cabin filled with cats. People believe bugs ate them and turned into those animals. I have come to the conclusion that the cat queen is a whole entity, an independent reality. I ask you again . . . Do you know who you are?"

When the car crashed against the light, my skin swelled up. I felt heat, instead of the cold. I couldn't pay attention to what was happening. In a flash I saw my hands and feet bulging and tried to make sense of it. Afterward, it was the pain that drew me. Next, the light. What happened to the car? I wondered suddenly. Then I saw a woman. She was slender, in a beige chiffon dress delineating her breasts, black strands of her curly hair reaching her hips; an urgent look on her face invited me to follow her. Pointing her index finger toward the sky, she showed where the light was coming from. It was a star, fleeing from thousands of dragonflies chasing it. I saw the woman again. The landscape behind her looked familiar. It was my *Volcano*—the oil I painted two years ago. In the background, the volcano spit incandescent bits of brain, entrails scorching the giant's sides. At the bottom of hell, blood was boiling; farther down in hell, stairs emerged and, from there the woman walked toward me with a bouquet of arum lilies in her hands. We left *Volcano* together and took a path thicketed with yellow flowers breathing on our steps. There hummingbirds rained, hurling at us white words showing us the way. The birds led us toward the highway. My car was there, the long-billed birds attacking the windows. Suddenly cats appeared and settled themselves on the ground, without bothering a single hummingbird; they were so numerous, overflowing the road. She walked over the carpet of cat hairs, ears, tails. . . . And I also crossed the strip of fine fur. . . . And I read her eyes. In them, there was me as a young boy, pedaling my dream bike. With pimples on my face, I smoked pot. Lost, I asked Dalí's photo if fate would catch up with me someday. In the fire and in a combination of colors. Oil, pastel, watercolor, ink, collage . . . I was drawing myself.

I lost my purity. It was gone with the blood that almost killed me that day. I also keep changing. My paintings exude moods that seep through the eyes. The interpretation of reality and the meticulous outlining of the conscience keep the contours of my brushstrokes in flux. This has brought me some renown. But I made a name for myself with *Cat's Eye*. In that painting the cat lady is seated on a large misshapen arum with cats raining down around her.

—*Translated from the Spanish by Toshiya Kamei*

The cat is a common feature of Mesoamerican cultures, including the Olmec and Aztec civilizations. The Aztecs were particularly known for their feline connection, dressing their elite warriors as jaguars. Tezcatlipoca, a central Aztec deity, had the ability to transform himself into a jaguar. Therefore, the pervasive stereotype of the crazy cat lady in modern society aside, it's probably no surprise that a cat lady in Mexican writer Donají Olmedo's "Cat's Eye" cuts an attractive figure. In it, the young narrator, a budding artist, undergoes a transformation of his own when he has a dreamlike encounter with the female werecat in modern-day Durango.

—*TK*

Transformation

BETRAYAL

Sigrid Nunez

Whenever I travel I try to avoid getting into conversations with strangers I happen to be sitting with. There is nothing worse than being trapped for hours with a dullard or a chatterbox. Yet it is my experience that these types travel more frequently than anyone else. But with the woman on the train it was different. Partly it was her voice. You're a teacher, she said (I had been grading homework).

I turned and saw an attractive woman on the cusp of middle age with an expertly made-up face and heavy coils of dyed black hair. She wore a tailored wool suit with a peacock-print scarf and several pieces of jewelry—all posh enough to light in me a spark of envy. Her scent—but this I'd noticed before, when she first took the seat next to mine—could have been called something like Dune Rose, or Ocean Blossom.

You're a teacher. It sounded like four notes struck on a xylophone.

I said yes, I was a high school teacher. And just like that our conversation began, as mundane as such small talk usually is, and not worth repeating.

After a few minutes our train emerged from the tunnel we'd been slowly lumbering through and picked up speed, and in the sunlight that flooded our compartment I saw that she was in fact older than I'd guessed—older than myself by a good ten years, I thought (not without a touch of satisfaction)—but, in spite of this, even prettier than she had seemed. I did not think I'd ever seen a pair of eyes such an intoxicating shade of green, like the last drops of some French liqueur swirled at the bottom of a glass.

It turned out that she lived in the city of my destination. She was on her way home from a melancholy errand: a visit to a dying friend. But *I* was on my way to visit a dying friend! To me, the coincidence was remarkable. But the woman only nodded, as if this was something she'd known all along.

After a while she said, You know, I don't usually drink this early in the day but I'd love a glass of wine. Care to join me?

Which is how we ended up in a booth in the café car.

You know that peculiar bond that can form between strangers whose paths cross on a journey, how seamlessly they can pass from small talk to confidences. Almost at once the woman began talking about her husband. In fact, it occurred to me that this was why she'd wanted a drink in the first place: to boost her courage to talk about her marriage. She drank quickly—big, unladylike gulps, it must be said—and as she spoke her entire bearing changed. Not that she became loud or unruly, but there was an urgency, an intensity about her that more than hinted at a soul in distress.

They had been married a long time. She had been just a girl when they met, and he old enough to be her father. He had always cheated on her, and she had always known it. At first they had fought about it; more than once she had threatened to leave him. But when she understood that her husband was simply incapable of fidelity and that there'd be no changing this, she learned to accept it. For she loved him, she said. He was a decent man, and in all other ways a good husband to her.

Naturally, however, she had looked forward to the day when age would slow him down. But, to her baffled astonishment, the old goat was now womanizing harder than ever, and among his lovers were many young and very beautiful girls.

It was at this point that I began to feel sure that she was going to ask me for something. For a scary moment I thought of the famous movie: two strangers meet on a train. . . . And if it wasn't cold-blooded murder this stranger was asking me to commit it was nevertheless something shocking.

What gave her husband such power over women? She confessed that her obsession had reached such a degree that her life had become hardly worth living. Until she knew his secret, she would have no peace.

Why me? it seemed only appropriate to ask.

Well, she couldn't ask just anyone, now, could she. She couldn't ask one of her friends without seriously complicating matters. No, her informer must be a stranger. And you're single, she said. (Was I drunk? I didn't remember telling her this, but I supposed I must have.)

Besides, there's something about you, she said. I sensed it as soon as we started talking. I thought, Here is someone I can trust.

And so the idea had come to her that, after hearing her story, I might be willing to help her.

Perhaps. Yet, to me, it seemed that she'd already planned everything out. She was quick to assure me that a tryst would be easy to arrange. Her husband had a business. I would visit his office, posing as a potential client.

Oh, you'll have no problem, she drawled, in a voice that was not without bitterness. He has a weakness for redheads. He'll invite you to meet him at a certain hotel. . . .

The scheme of a desperate woman—a madwoman, perhaps. But one who had slyly infected me with her curiosity. In fact, I was dying to meet Grampa Casanova. Nor could it be denied that this woman with her sea-nymph scent and musical voice had her own mysterious power, something that made me want to please her and to become more involved with her. Then, too, God knows, I was frantic for a diversion. The friend I was on my way to see was someone I'd known since childhood, someone who was exactly my age, and whose mortal illness had struck me a crushing blow. And just yesterday I'd been given the news: this visit would be our last.

I stared out the window, pretending to think over the woman's request. The world flew past: houses and yards and a shopping mall; houses and yards and a bright, boat-filled lake—like an illustration of how rapidly all things come and go. How long had it been since I'd had an adventure? My days were all routine, spent mostly in the company of adolescents to whom I was invisible except when they remembered to torment me. The thought of the expressions on their doltish, pimply faces if they could have known how I was about to sin bathed me in a warm current of pleasure.

The woman and I had just clinked together our second glasses of cabernet when the lights in the car flickered out and, in the blink before they came on again, I had the illusion that her eyes glowed in the dark.

HE entered the hotel room dressed in a dark suit and carrying a plastic shopping bag. To my surprise, he barely stopped to peck my cheek before shutting himself into the bathroom. In the brief time he was out of sight I considered leaving. Now that the moment had come, I couldn't understand how it had happened. How had I ever agreed to sleep with this decrepit creature? He had palsied hands, a hunchback, and a face so deformed by wrinkles and folds that you couldn't tell for sure whether his expression was happy or sad.

When he came out of the bathroom I saw that he'd changed into a robe. But it was not one of the two plush white Turkish bathrobes that were provided by the hotel. This robe (no doubt it was what he'd been carrying in the plastic bag) was made of some sort of thin, shiny, metallic-looking material, like Mylar, and had a capacious hood.

Very odd that he'd brought his own bathrobe. Odder still that he'd pulled up the hood so that he seemed to be peering at me from the back of a cave. Oddest of all that the robe now began whipping and billowing around him as if he were caught in a storm.

I barely had time to make these observations when the robe blew off entirely and there stood a youth as heavenly-handsome as could be imagined, naked and ready for love, which was what we immediately set about making, and making last (yes, that was part of his secret) for a deliciously long time.

I fell asleep—or swooned, it felt more like—and I could have sworn that it was not a dream but that he went right on making love to me.

When I awoke I found him sitting up, dangling his spindly legs off the side of the king-size bed: an old man, all loose, parched skin, with sagging tits and a belly slopping onto his thighs and concealing so effectively what lay between them that he might have been an old woman. As he bent to kiss me, I shuddered at his old-person's stinky breath. But when he asked me if I wanted to meet like this again I shuddered in a different way and cried *yes!*

If I tell her the truth, I reasoned, she's bound to take action. If she gets her hands on the magic robe, she'll hide it, perhaps even destroy it, thus robbing me of something I would sooner die than give up.

There was no secret. Nothing out of the ordinary had occurred. Alas, I apologized, I tried, but I'm afraid I can't help you.

I see, she said. And although she said no more, I could tell that she knew very well that I was lying. In my agitated state I thought I saw one of her coils of black hair lift a triangular head and wave it at me.

The next time the woman's husband and I met, everything happened just as before. The same hotel, to which he again arrived carrying the same plastic shopping bag. The same immediate dash for the bathroom. The same young god emerging as from a chrysalis to take me in his arms and transport me to paradise.

Again I appeared to pass out, but this time when, shortly later, I woke up I found the man still in godly shape and sleeping beside me. Night had fallen, but the room was not yet quite dark. I needed to use the bathroom.

The hotel was a grand one; the room was like a spacious studio apartment with a particularly luxurious bath, the walls of which were lined with so many mirrors that you could see yourself—you could not avoid seeing yourself—every inch, from every angle, multiplied at least a dozen times. And what I saw gave me a rude shock.

I suppose it had been a while since I'd made such a thorough inspection. I was no longer a girl, of course I knew that. But how had I failed to notice so much deterioration? All the care I'd taken over the years, watching my weight, body-sculpting at the gym—certainly, this had helped. But now, in the form of various bulges and puckers and creases and droops, I saw far less to please than to lament. I saw, with a horror that sent my hand flying to my mouth, *a gray pubic hair.*

I recalled what the woman had told me, about all the young and beautiful girls her husband was sleeping with, and it was like a hot iron pressed to my flesh.

Smarting miserably, I turned out the unforgiving light and headed back to bed. As I did so, I heard a murmur. The man was stirring. Though he seemed to be still asleep, I saw him reach out his arms for me and my heart turned over—only to be gripped in a terrible vise: what if he was really reaching for someone else?

Something crinkled underfoot. I looked down and saw the robe, lying on the carpet where it had blown, a gleaming dry puddle. And I froze, breathless with a question: How did the magic work? Only for him, the robe's rightful owner? Or . . . for . . . anyone.

More rustling from the bed, and I heard him call my name. In a flash, I scooped the robe from the floor and threw it around my shoulders. Shooting my arms through the sleeves, I squeezed my eyes tight and stood, panting and trembling.

I did not have to wait long before the robe began wildly billowing around me. I thought of the famous image of Marilyn Monroe standing atop the subway grate, and could not stop myself from giggling.

He was a decent man. He didn't just leave me lying there. He called his wife. (Why did this not surprise me?)

She came at once, her scent wafting in the air as she paced the room, berating him.

I hope you've finally learned your lesson!

That she had known everything all along; that she had, indeed, planned every step of it; that it had been she, the witch herself, who'd given the wonderworking robe to her husband: these thoughts rose to my mind, but in a whirring and chaotic way, like panicked birds—thoughts of a disordered brain struggling to grasp what had happened.

I was aware of no specific injury but rather of overall pain and weakness—the utter helplessness of a newborn baby—and of the vastly diminished power of all my senses. Moving was out of the question. Even talking was too much: every ounce of my strength was required merely to breathe in and breathe out.

Quick, said the woman. Let's go before the ambulance comes.

POOR thing.

Did she break a bone?

No, she's just old. Doctor says she's a hundred if she's a day. She's reached the end, is all.

Are you sure she can't hear?

Can't hear, can't see, can't speak.

God, I hope I never live to be that old. She looks like a mummy! Does she have any family?

Police are still trying to find that out. She was staying at a hotel, but no one seems to know what she was doing here. Anyway, we just want to make her comfortable.

What's this funny robe she's wearing?

I don't know, but we've got to take it off and get her into a gown. Poor old thing. Looks like she put it on inside out.

When I wrote "Betrayal" I didn't have any one partic-ular story in mind. I was inspired by several elements commonly found in folklore and myth: a chance meet-ing with a stranger who turns out to have supernatural powers; a magical garment capable of physically trans-forming its wearer; the fate of having one's existence changed forever by unlooked-for and unknowable forces; the punishment incurred for vanity, or for fail-ure to keep a promise.

—SN

Trojan Horse

——— ❧ ———

A HORSE, A VINE

Johanna Skibsrud

O unhappy citizens, what madness? Do you think the enemy's sailed away?

—Virgil's *Aeneid*, Book II

I knew I could count on Dean. He was like a brother to me; better than that. Ever since we'd met—our first day of Basic, both of us just eighteen years old. Turned out, we'd both grown up near Houston. Dean was from just north of Sugar Land, in Mission Bend; Alvin, where I'm from, that's just a little less than an hour away. Maybe it was that. Whatever it was, we understood each other. Which is saying something. Dean is not a guy who is easily understood. He's always been nuts—even in Basic. He started picking up "odd jobs" even then. Just to keep things interesting, he said, and mostly—he was right—it was nothing. Just roughing up a guy in town every now and then, for a friend. But after a while he got into some real dirty work, too. I kept telling him he was going to get himself into trouble but he'd just say, *nah*, and when he did get into trouble it didn't have anything to do with any of that shit. He was always pretty good about it—didn't leave a lot of loose ends.

What happened was he got called in for a domestic on account of this girl, Natalie, who he wasn't even serious about. They issued him with protective orders, but that suited him just fine, and for a while it looked like they were going to let it go at that. But then, a year later, when his term of service was up, he was denied reenlistment. If you ask me, it didn't have anything to do with the girl, though that's what they said. Everyone could just sort of tell that Dean was a little—unhinged.

DEAN pretty near lost his mind when he heard about it. You can imagine. I know, because I was the first person he called. That was the beginning of September, 2001. I was home on leave. I told him, Well, come on back home, we'll get you sorted out, and so he came back and calmed down a little. He even managed to pick up a few "odd jobs"—but his heart wasn't in it. He would come over to visit Tracy and me all the time, at first. We'd drink beer and play video games until three or four in the morning and we both fell asleep in the living room—one of us in the La-Z-Boy armchair and the other stretched out on the couch. The night before the twin towers fell was a night like that—we'd been playing *Colony Wars* but hadn't even managed to finish the game. When we woke up Dean said we should finish it out because he'd been winning. I agreed—but only because I still had a chance. It's a good game that way, more like real life. Even if you lose a few battles you can still win the overall—it's just about how everything balances out. Also, it's not like most games where it's either you win, or you die. There are five different endings to the game—two of them good and three of them bad. So that's like real life, too. There's always a chance that things will work out—but more of a chance that they won't.

I was trying to concentrate on the game because I was still losing pretty bad when Tracy came in with Cody screaming on her hip—he was still just tiny then. She just sort of stood there at first, looking at us, letting Cody cry like that. Even if she had tried to say something, though, I probably wouldn't have heard her because of how much noise Cody was making and because I was still trying to concentrate, finish the game, even if I was losing, and because Dean was yelling at me the whole time, too, saying, You're gonna die, motherfucker! You are *so* going to die!

Finally Tracy just walked over, the kid still screaming, and flicked the screen over to the TV, and just at the moment—the Towers fell. It was fucked up. I didn't even know what was happening at first. Like it was a sort of a joke. Or a clip from a movie or something. Dean said, *Damn!* In the same way he did when I beat the shit out of him playing *Blast Radius* or *Hogs of War*.

After that Dean had a job. He got hired on at Blackwater, and he liked it a lot better anyway than he liked the Marines. He told me I should get discharged and join up, too, but I didn't think so. I'd just got back from a six-month tour in Afghanistan and didn't want to go back anymore if I could help it. I wanted to get transferred to the Northern Command. Get posted at Fort Sam, maybe—be closer to Tracy and Cody that way. Plus, I liked the idea of homeland defense. It was an arithmetic thing. Say you blew up three guys over there in Iraq or Afghanistan—you never could be certain if they were the right guys. At home, if anybody tried anything, you'd know for sure when you blew them up you were getting the right guy. If any more 9/11 shit was going to happen I liked the idea of being right here, waiting—couldn't stand the thought of being stuck sitting on my thumbs instead, over at Camp Eggers, or Fiddler's Green.

What, you getting spooked or something? Dean said when I told him about the homeland defense thing.

I shook my head. Nah.

Soft? he said. He poked me in the gut.

I shook my head again. You can see for yourself, I said. No.

The way I said it that time, he left me alone. But the next time I saw him, he brought it up again.

Still spooked? he asked. I said I'd told him before that I wasn't.

It's all right, he said. Everybody gets it sometime. But you got to remember—it's not just about killing and getting killed. You're an artist, he told me. A warrior. Don't forget that. Then he took this book from his pocket and read me something out of it that he said had been written by a Roman general something like two thousand years ago.

For someone who came across like such a special needs case most of the time, Dean was actually pretty deep. He used to carry *The Art of the Warrior* and *Maxims of War* around with him in Basic. Now it was *Meditations,* by Marcus Aurelius.

We were having beers at the Triple Crown in Mission Bend, and when he got up to pay he shoved the book across the table toward me. Take it, he said. You might learn something. Then he made a face as if to say bigger miracles have happened, slammed a tip down on the table and headed toward the door.

I liked the book. It made you think about things. I liked the way it was written, too, in these short little sentences, sort of like the psalms in the Bible—except I could understand them, even with how it was written as many years ago. And when I didn't understand them I would just skip ahead, and it didn't matter. It was pretty cool to know that someone else was wondering about all the shit I was wondering about even two thousand years ago—even though it made me a bit sad to realize that meant nobody had figured anything out in all of that time. Like this one part, where he says that everything exists for some reason—even a horse, he says, or a vine—so why do you even have to wonder about it? But when he says it like that it's obvious he's wondered himself or else he wouldn't have had to ask about why. And then he says, *Even the sun will say, I am for some purpose, and the rest of the gods will say the same. For what purpose then art thou?* I liked that. I'd even sort of repeat it to myself sometimes. *For what purpose then art thou?* Because even though it sounded like a question, it was sort of an answer, too.

THEN, a week or so later, just before I was due to ship out, Dean showed up at my house with a copy of *Rifleshooter* magazine.

This will make you feel better, he said.

I feel fine, I said.

No, seriously, he said. Check it out. If you get blown up over there I'll do this for you—promise. And if I get blown up, you can do it for me.

He flipped open the magazine from the back and read from an advertisement in the classified section.

How about honoring your deceased loved one, he read, pulling a face, *by sharing with him or her one more round of clay targets, one last bird hunt, one last stalk hunt. . . .*

I interrupted. Is this for real? I said.

Ha ha! Dean said. Hell yeah. Then continued to read the advertisement out loud. Only this time he stayed deadly serious.

All you had to do, according to this ad, was send these guys some ashes and they'd turn it into live ammunition for you. One pound of ash was enough for roughly 250 shells, they said. They even did mantelpiece carriers and engraved nameplates.

What better way, Dean read, *to be remembered? Now you can have peace of mind that you can continue to protect your home and family even after you are gone.*

THAT'S the part that got me. I realized sort of all of a sudden what had been bothering me ever since I got back from my first tour. It wasn't that I was scared of dying. The thing that rattled me was thinking about what would happen *after* I died. Not to me. But to Tracy and Cody. I'd start thinking about it, all the crazy shit that could happen, and it would drive me crazy, because there is no end to the possibilities that can happen after you are dead—even more than can happen when you are alive, and that is pretty much anything. I would get so crazy sometimes thinking about this that it got so I couldn't even hardly breathe. I'd get this feeling in my gut like someone had just stuck me with an ice pick, and after that I couldn't breathe or think straight anymore. I'd just have to stand there with that pain in my gut until it passed. Sometimes it would last for a good couple of minutes, which is a long time to go without breathing. It wouldn't happen all the time, but I never could tell when it was going to. After I got back from my second tour it was even worse. I didn't even have to be thinking about anything after a while, and it would happen. I'd be sitting there playing a video game with Cody or eating a sandwich at the kitchen table or Tracy and I would be fucking, and all the sudden I'd feel it. A sharp pain in my gut, first, and then my lungs starting to shut down. I'd try to shake it, but there wasn't anything that I could do. It got so bad I had to tell Tracy. It wasn't like she didn't notice. You can't freeze up like that on someone when you're in the middle of fucking them and not have them notice.

She told me not to worry. Nothing was going to happen, she said. But even if it did, I shouldn't worry, because she could take care of herself—and Cody, too, and I knew it. She was used to it, she said, after all—what with me being gone all the time. And she was right—*I knew.* That's the thing. It was weird. If I thought about it *I knew* I was lucky that way. Tracy was tough, and she was smart, too. We kept a gun in the house, and she knew how to use it. She was even a pretty good shot, and wasn't someone who was likely to lose it and not know how to aim right, or be afraid to shoot, if she needed to. I could pretty much count on that. She would get this look on her face when she was serious about something and you knew that no one was ever going to mess with her.

Like that time when she came into the room and switched on the TV and the twin towers fell. Or the time that Cody nearly choked and died—and probably would have, too, if she hadn't been around to save him. It still makes me sick to think about that, because it was my fault it happened. I was feeding him, and I guess I hadn't cut the pieces up small enough—I figured they were pretty small already. But then Cody got quiet and his eyes got this real scared look to them, like they were going to pop out of his head. It was fucked up because it wasn't even like he choked or anything first. He just stayed quiet and then got even quieter and then his eyes were popping out of his head. I bolted for the phone, and yelled for Tracy, but then before I could get to the phone even, to call 9-1-1, Tracy was there—walking by me like she didn't even see me—that look on her face. She went straight for the kid, turned him upside down, then started thumping him on the back, hard, until pretty soon the little piece of chicken that had got stuck in his throat shot out of his mouth and he was crying and puking all over the floor.

You useless piece of shit, Tracy said, without looking at me. By the time anyone got around to coming over here in an ambulance it would have been too late. Don't you know that? Then she scooped up Cody and took him off to the bathroom to get him cleaned up.

The piece of chicken had flown clear across the room and landed right beside my foot. I remember that after she left, and took the kid, I just sat down on the floor next to it, and looked at it, the way it was lying there on the floor right by my foot, and I thought about how small it was, and how you never knew what it was that was going to fuck you. How you had to be prepared for every little thing.

AFTER my third tour I had that pain in my gut all the time. It was funny, because it didn't happen to me in the field. Over there, I felt strong and I didn't give a shit. A lot of guys get scared. If they've seen combat, or had any close calls, they start to feel like everything they see is going to jump up and bite them. But I wasn't like that. See, I never was afraid of dying—it wasn't that. It was everything else. When I was home I would start to feel it all over again. I couldn't help it. I'd start thinking about how everything was all connected—how every little thing that happened would set off something else happening, I mean. And how that would set off something else, and that if I died there was nothing I could do to stop all the shit that my dying would set off in the world without knowing, ahead of time, what it would be.

I started thinking more about that advertisement Dean had read. I thought about how funny it would be to be sitting up on the shelf. Just ready and waiting up there for shit to happen. To be hard and cold as metal, all loaded and ready inside Tracy's Taurus 1911, which I had got her, and which she knew how to use. I started thinking about it all the time. How it would feel to be inside that gun, with her hand on the trigger. But then when I really did have her hands on me I would get that feeling again and if she was on top of me I'd have to push her off all the sudden because I couldn't breathe. It got to be pretty bad that way, because she would get hurt like maybe I didn't love her anymore, or think she was sexy, and I would tell her, no, that wasn't it, it was just this thing that I couldn't explain and it didn't have anything to do with her—not really. But women always think that everything is about them and so she would turn over and cry and say, for the fifth time, Don't you think I'm sexy, or what? And I would tell her again how she was the sexiest woman in the world, and that she should know that. I knew she did. Everywhere we went people were always checking her out and I knew that she noticed. That she liked it, even. Who wouldn't?

Most of the time, I didn't mind. Sometimes, though—especially when we went to Galveston Island, where her best friend Anelise Hutson's brother, Brian, had a place—I did. She would wear this tiny little bikini, show off, and everyone would look at her—including Brian. There was just something about that guy—the way that he looked at her—that gave me the creeps, I didn't know why. It wasn't like I was jealous. I had no reason to be. He was just this skinny dude with a paunch who didn't do anything all day except sit out on his front porch and answer the telephone. Seriously. He owned a Sea-Doo rental place just outside of town, and then his house was a few miles past that, but he hardly ever went into the store. He had these young guys working for him there, so I guess he didn't need to. Instead, he would sit around at home all day answering his phone. The way he talked about it, it was as if the Sea-Doo rental business was the most important shit on the face of the planet. The ringer on his phone was never turned on—it would just vibrate in his pocket and every time it vibrated he'd jump up and, real exaggerated, mouth out "sorry," then take the call. It was so fucking stupid. He'd actually *mouth* the word, even before he'd picked up the phone.

Except for that, though, I liked the beach. And we were lucky to know someone who had a house literally right *on* the water. The house was stuck up on stilts and sometimes after it stormed or when the tide came in high, the water would rush right up under the deck. I liked sitting out there. Tracy was right—it helped me relax. We'd take chairs and put them in the shallow water and drink beer with our feet stuck in the sand. I'd build sandcastles with Cody and then help knock them down, or take a magazine down with me and stick my nose in it so I didn't have to pretend to care about whatever Brian was saying. He was always saying stupid shit to Anelise and Tracy whenever he wasn't saying it into the phone.

BUT when I came back after my third tour it was winter and so we didn't go to the beach, and I didn't relax. Tracy kept bugging me to see a shrink, but I told her it wasn't that sort of a thing.

Well what sort of a thing is it? she wanted to know.

I was pretty sure she had told her friends about me, by then—about how we weren't even really sleeping together anymore. I just sort of felt it. You know, like when we'd be hanging out with Anelise, I could feel it—that she knew. Maybe even Brian knew. It made me sick even to think about that, and so finally I agreed. I got an appointment with a shrink at Fort Sam and drove up the next day.

It was a lady shrink—a blonde. Her hair was done up real complicated on the top of her head and sprayed into place. It didn't even look real. For an hour, I sat in her office and she smiled at me and nodded her head and whatever I said she wrote down in this little notebook she had. It was all pretty normal, she said, everything I was saying. I said, this isn't any PTSD shit, if that's what you're thinking. I know how I am and I do not even give a shit when I am out there, so it's not that. And she nodded and said that was normal, too.

I started to hate her. The way that she sat there, smiling and nodding, and how, when she nodded not one single hair moved out of place on her head. I figured that all that attention to her hair was probably intended to distract from the fact that she was overweight, and not that attractive overall. After she was done with me she was probably going to drive over to Kroger's to stock up on diet foods. She was probably thinking about that right now. I started to get mad, thinking about it myself. Why was it always fat ladies who dieted? Why didn't they ever get thin?

Tracy could eat anything she wanted. Even when she was pregnant, she didn't get fat—not even a little bit. It wasn't that I cared about it one way or the other, this shrink being fat or not—it just showed a lack of resolve. It was the problem with the whole goddamn country. Sitting there in the shrink's office, it started to become very clear. Nobody really gave a shit. They said they did, but they didn't. Everyone was just sitting around, getting fat and soft, not giving a shit, while all the while—guess what. Everyone else just waiting.

While I was thinking about this, the shrink was setting up a video game on her big-screen TV, and telling me how to work the functions on the control pad she'd given me like I'd never played a video game before in my life. The game was pretty much the same as the ones we'd used in Basic, actually—except a lot cheaper. You know how I could tell? There weren't any shadows. You need shadows to make things look real—the cheap games don't bother.

So I take the control from the shrink and I'm wandering around, blowing shit up, and every time I detonate she says, *how does this make you feel?* And I'm saying, Like this is a cheap piece of shit. My kid still buys the fucking Easter bunny and he wouldn't buy this.

And that's when it hit me. What's wrong with me. How come every time I come home this weird shit starts happening. There's no fucking shadows! You go to Kroger's—or to Target, or the mall, or the fucking dentist office. You stay home even, in your own house, with the fluorescent light in the kitchen and the blinds closed to save on air conditioning. There weren't any shadows anywhere!

I started to get freaked out then, thinking about it. Like maybe nothing was even fucking real, and I just got up, the shrink still smiling and nodding her head, and I went home and Tracy was there and she said how did it go, and I didn't say anything.

I went into the kitchen. I was right. There was not one fucking shadow. Tracy followed me in there, but I turned around and headed into the TV room, instead, where Cody was sitting on the couch playing *Darksiders*. I sat down beside him and started to watch. The game is actually pretty boring, but I guess it's all right for a little kid. You play one of the Four Horsemen of the Apocalypse and have to try to balance the forces of heaven and hell. If you're lucky, you make it to Endwar and you get to punish anyone who's still stuck on Earth. The kid was doing okay, but I didn't think he was going to make it to Endwar. Pretty soon Tracy came in and stood right in front of the screen. She had one hip stuck out, like she wanted to start something. The kid kept playing. He had to lean around sideways so he could see around her legs.

You're not even trying, she said.

Get out of the way, I said. The kid can't see.

She kept standing there. That look on her face.

That's when I lost it. I don't even know what I said. I didn't care half the time because I was thinking, it doesn't even matter, this isn't even fucking real. But then all the sudden it was. Tracy was grabbing Cody up from the couch, and stuffing his arms into his jacket. It was January and it was pretty cold outdoors. She was saying, Fuck you, you know that. Fuck you. I'm sick of this shit. Then she put on her own coat, grabbed her car keys off the little hook by the door, and was gone.

SHE didn't come home that night, or the next. I kept waiting for her, you know. Like an idiot. Expecting her—every moment. But she didn't come. I stayed inside, with the blinds drawn, and I waited. I tried to read some *Meditations* but I couldn't keep the words straight on the page. Nothing made any sense. I played *Darksiders* because it was still in the PlayStation and I couldn't be bothered to change the game, but I kept winning. It wasn't even fun anymore.

When she didn't come home by eight o'clock on Sunday, I called Tracy's mom's place. I was angry by then, and had just started to say something like, This is fucked, she can't steal the kid, when Tracy's mom said she hadn't seen Tracy, and didn't know a thing about it. I was about to call Anelise when all the sudden I didn't need to—I knew where Tracy was.

I don't know how I knew, but I did. I jumped in the car and I drove all the way to Galveston. It took me just a little less than twenty minutes—usually it takes half an hour or more, depending on traffic, but I was driving pretty fast. I didn't slow down till I was past Galveston. I thought at first maybe I wouldn't recognize the street, but I recognized it all right. I turned in and I drove up just far enough so I could see the drive, and sure enough there was Tracy's car parked right out front. Even though I already knew I would find it there, it still felt pretty bad when I did. It felt so bad I got out of the car and puked in the culvert, then I got back in, turned the car around and started driving. I was shaking all over. I thought I should pull over I was shaking so bad, but I kept driving. I drove all the way into town, shaking like that, then I pulled over on the seawall and ordered a beer at this one place, where I could sit outside. No one else was out there, it was too cold, but I sat out there for a long time, and just looked out across the highway to where the ocean stretched out, flat and hard-looking, in all directions. It was sort of hard to tell where it ended and the sky began, and I could see the rigs out there and because it was just starting to get dark their lights were shining so that it looked like they were the first stars, and so I made a wish on one of them. Just like I always had Cody do whenever I was with him and we saw the first star come into the sky for real. I wished I was a bullet, and that I was at that very moment coursing through Brian Hutson's body. That I was that hard and sharp and dark. That I was just then being slowed, only very slightly, by Brian Hutson's cranial bone; just then being splashed with spinal fluid as I severed the connective tissue between his skull and the soft tissue of his brain.

I sat there for a long time, wishing that. By then it had got dark and real stars had come out in the sky and finally I realized I was chilled to the bone and I had only drank half my beer and the kid that was serving me was looking at me funny. So I got up and paid and drove back home and all the time I was thinking—hard.

I knew that Dean was going to be back in town in a few days and when he did get back I figured I had a pretty good plan, and I could count on him to help me carry it off. I wanted to be extra certain, though, because after you are dead it is even harder to make sure that things go according to plan than when you are not.

The first thing I needed to do was arrange things with the ammunition company in Alabama. Make sure that I ordered in advance fifty shot-shells for Dean's Smith & Wesson and two hundred for Tracy's Taurus, so that she could have plenty left after I—and Brian Hutson—were gone. I'd arrange for it all in my will, so there wouldn't be any mistake. Make sure that the shells, when they were ready, would be sent to Dean's address in Mission Bend, and not to Tracy. That way he could go to Brian's house and shoot off thirty or so rounds into Brian's body before delivering the rest of the ACPs to Tracy so she could put them into the Taurus, and still have some left over to put up on the shelf.

The plan was pretty much foolproof, I figured. Dean would call Brian up and tell him who he was—nothing but the truth. He was a friend. He had something to personally deliver, on my behalf. It was my parting wish—some bullshit like that. You could pretty much guarantee that a guy like Brian wouldn't say no. If Dean arrived on a weekday, any time before six, I figured chances were pretty good Tracy would be away at work, and Cody would be at his grandmother's house, like usual. That was important. I would have to stress that with Dean—but I knew he would understand that, too. I would also tell him that he would have a reward for his trouble if, before he did anything, he got Brian to empty the safe I knew for a fact he kept upstairs. That way I wouldn't have to figure out a way to pay him out of my insurance money, which would go to Tracy. The only real risk I could foresee was if anyone happened to be around when Dean arrived, but I figured the chances of it were pretty slim and that if Dean didn't feel right about it, and especially if Tracy's car was there, he could always just turn around and come back another time. Or call up on his cell and tell Brian he was running late, or something—then just wait until there wasn't anyone around. I could just picture him. Pulled off on the side of the road out there, chanting Sun Tzu, or some shit.

But that time of year those roads off the main highway were pretty desolate, especially during the week, so I didn't think he'd need to bother. No one would hear the shots, and no one would see him either come or go. There was always the possibility something else could go wrong, of course, but the more I thought about it the more I saw that you had to take risks in death, just like in life. Now all I had to do was wait.

And even just thinking about it—inside with the lights on and the blinds closed—I start to feel it. It's like I'm already hurtling, 3200 feet per second, to lodge myself behind an ear; to enter at the throat, the belly, the knee, the heart. If Dean discharges thirty bullets into Brian Hutson's body that means that when it's over, roughly .2 ounces of my own body will be left inside his. This is not a lot when you think about it, but sometimes it's the smallest things—the things you least suspect—that turn out to be the most significant.

It's the details, see, the shadows, that make a thing real, and the moment that Brian Hutson feels the first bullet lodge in his chest— in the split moment flash right before it hits—he will know this, too. He will feel, for the first time in his life, how everything has a purpose, and what his own is. Now, as I wait, I think about that. About how at the very end there will just be that question. *For what purpose then art thou?* About how, for a single, unmeasurable moment as I whistle through his body, I will *be* with that question.

Before, in another moment, still less measurable than the first, he will respond to that question with a question of his own. A question, which will seem—for that briefest of moments—like an answer, before all questions are finally extinguished, as it is the nature of questions—and all things—to be.

I had been thinking of ways to retell the Trojan Horse story, which has always fascinated me, when by chance one day I came across an advertisement by the company Holy Smoke LLC, out of Alabama. In order "to help you create a tribute to your outdoorsperson like no other," Holy Smoke LLC offers to fashion rifle cartridges and shotgun shells out of your, or your

loved one's, human cremains. Excerpts from this advertisement have been quoted within my story in full—they were too good to change even a single word. The rest of the story just sort of fell into place from there.

—JS

———— ❦ ————

THE HUNGERS OF AN OLD LANGUAGE
Brian Aldiss

Ken Bekerwire's village was perched between mountain and sea. As the mountain was high, so the sea was deep, in a continuous narrative of geology. In this isolate place, Ken made a living from fishing, as his father had done before that and his grandfather before that.

His grandfather had been killed in a war fought for the country he hardly knew; Ken's father too died in a foreign place, fighting for the country he hardly knew. Ken had been spared war, but now fish were scarce and he felt old age drawing in upon him like a tide.

In the lusty days of his youth, Ken had once been prompted to climb the mountain behind the village. A boulder from the heights had trundled down to land in his vegetable patch, and he had taken it as a messenger. There were messages in all things.

At the top of Mount Greyharn he had found a thatched cottage. From this cottage had come a shy maiden, very slender, whose quiet beauty posted at once to Ken's inner feelings. This was Sheela Bawn Graay. The two of them had talked and talked until he kissed her lips and took her down with him into his village. When the sun cast the shadows of sunset on everything, she cried that she was so thin.

She was starving, starving. What food was there on a mountaintop this far north?

He took her to the little inn and piled her plate with potatoes and the meat of goats. "I am not greedy," she declared. She gave a brave smile. "There is so little to eat up on the mountain. Once I had two hens, but they died of winter cold. Some birds' eggs I can find in season. Otherwise, well, a bird perhaps. Even a snake . . . Or a fox if I am lucky . . ."

All people on earth—and it may well be the same elsewhere—have a secret history as well as an ordinary history, marked by passing years; some folk are barely aware of that inward history. But as he lay in bed with an arm about his slender new bride, Ken listened to what Sheela had to say of her inward story, of which he knew nothing.

And in her story of long ago, this mountain—her mountain—and all the land behind it had been elsewhere, and were joined to the great continent which now stood a long way distant, separated by the deep seas.

To break her fast in the morning, he cooked her the mackerel he had caught previously, and she ate with joy, laughing at her own greed, laughing and weeping because she had grown so thin.

Still her story went on, unwinding over the table.

According to Sheela's tale, great swords of ice had come, sawing up the land, and behind them rushed arms of the sea, and so the two lands had become and remained severed.

"But I, through my long parentage, retain knowledge of those distant times," she whispered to him, pressing her dainty breasts against his great chest. "And I retain knowledge of the Old Language." She gave a little whispered laugh. "It's said you cannot speak the Old Language unless you're starving."

"How's that?" he asked, perplexed.

"I was told the Old Language was never spoken when ruined by fat in the lungs or stomach. You cannot imagine how hard was life in the days when the Old Language was everywhere spoken."

"Speak it to me," Ken whispered. He felt that some vital unknown knowledge was to be passed to him—to him who knew so little beyond the times of tides.

So Sheela—or more properly, she said, Sheelagh—broke into a chant, where vowels were misty and consonants many, and filled with ancient music. The effect was more like a stifled cry than ordinary speech as spoken in the village. And so Ken fell under this lady's spell and feared her almost as much as he loved her. Because this song, this speech, came from distant land and time immeasurable, to be caught in Sheelagh's delectable throat.

He asked her how old was this strange tongue she spoke.

"I only know it's older than is my mountain," she told him.

So they passed many months, body to body and mouth to ear.

As he lay beside his mysterious Sheelagh, Ken was the one who witnessed how her ribs showed under her pale flesh, and how thin were her arms, and how flat her stomach; truly, she was one woman able to speak the Old Language.

And he recalled during the pleasures of their lovemaking something his father had said—his father, gaunt and hairy, sitting in an old chair—"Poverty is the natural state for humanity. Wealth starts in the stomach and corrupts it. . . ."

The natural state for humanity? Ken did not know. Indeed, he knew no one who was not poor—meaning, half starved. It was a fairy tale to him that there were rich people. . . .

At one time, he invited his neighbors to enter his room to listen to Sheelagh singing one of her ancient songs. And two old crones of the village, huddled in a corner of the room, nodded their gray heads and said, "Indeed, yes, it is no less than the tongue once spoken from a distant age, when plentiful fish gleamed like a spill of diamonds in a new sea. . . ."

But the fish were no longer so plentiful. Generations of fishermen, including Ken's father and his grandfather, had diminished the stocks. Many people in the village now went hungry, near starvation, to eat but twice in the week, because of the shortage of fish.

No one could understand where the shoals of mackerel had gone. They could never believe that those same shoals had disappeared into village stomachs. It was that same appetite that had caused the Old Language to die away.

A day came when Sheelagh, obeying a mysterious summons, climbed back up the mountain to her deserted cottage. She went slowly, and when she arrived at that stark old homestead, she lay on the floor and with pain delivered a small baby daughter, showing a wisp of red hair, matching in tone Sheelagh's own ample curls.

And Sheelagh cried and nursed her baby, cried because she had fulfilled a vital part of a woman's destiny—and the baby did not then cry with her, but smiled its tiny unrehearsed smile.

When this dear new child cried to imagine the challenges of life ahead of her, then Sheelagh believed it was in the Old Language that she cried—as her mother had told her she had once done. As she had then needed milk, so did her infant now.

As for Ken, he seized on the opportunity of his beloved girl's absence to launch his boat and sail for deeper waters, where he hoped to find shoals of those elusive fish which were starving his village.

This was an uncertain day, misty, hovering between changing seasons. Ken scarcely knew where he was heading. Rain set in, only to die away toward the horizon like an old blown shawl. But out of the murk ahead, Ken's keen eyes picked out land looming.

He knew there was no land anywhere near, not within half a thousand days, as his father had said. This was just a small island, a wart upon the tousled sea. He made for its shelter with a feeling almost of terror, for here was strangeness indeed.

A gull came and cried its inscrutable regretful call before disappearing into a cloud sailing above the land.

Ken moored in what passed for a bay and lowered his nets—into which mackerel swarmed in joyful abandon. He hauled his catch on deck and then (because he was not as young as he had been some years ago), went and lay down upon a patch of sandy beach to rest, and indeed to sleep.

In his slumbers he thought he heard some words of the Old Language his Sheelagh had taught him. He woke, sat up, and found to his terror a horned beast standing over him, horned and bearded and immense. It backed away, while regarding him with strange goat eyes.

It was a goat! A goat of a kind, with long shaggy coat and immense grooved horns curling backward to its shoulders.

"Fear not, two-legged one!" It spoke in a mere whisper, and the words too were of the Old Tongue, or very like.

So the pair of them were together, man and animal. Other goats came and gathered at a respectful distance. Both male and female came, and one female goat had with her a small offspring, as if to mirror the child to which Sheelagh had just given birth, many a league distant.

The goats spoke only in whispers and imperfectly, brokenly. But Ken's understanding was little better.

Nevertheless, as the great daylights of the noon wore away and the Earth turned its shoulder from the sun, he gained—or thought he gained—an understanding of an old history, as recounted by these animals gathered about him. Long long ago, immeasurable lifetimes past, so they told him in their bleating whispers, the hominids (meaning mankind) had domesticated an animal. That animal was the Ancestral Goat, which voluntarily went into partnership with the hominids. Those were long past golden years, when all the trees in the forests bore fruits—more than could be eaten—and the world was nothing but forests, green, dark green and untrodden.

Alas, in all stories, even those whispered by a herd of goats, what is halcyon must pass away as desolation dawns. So it was in those olden days. Matters could not be understood. Floods, rains, pestilence, starvation—the earth shaking, in order to remove the irritants of life upon its surface.

So survivors had fled, hominids and goats, all. . . . Long whispered talk about this bad time, during which some of the goats present here on this drab spot wandered off to find and eat the seaweed to which their tastes had adapted.

It seemed that those survivors of their early fathers had come in their flight to the end of land. Seas and storms had rushed in. Darkness had prevailed. Those few who lived through this punishing time found themselves—what was that word?—Ken knew it not—"stranded" on this island. So they lived through the harsh centuries, talking the old talk, eating seaweed, or the odd fish trapped in pools. They awaited a hominid who would come and rescue them and restore them to wider pastures.

Much of this Ken understood, or thought he understood. But what was all goathood when set against his lovely Sheelagh? He fancied that if he did not soon get back to his home port, someone would raise the cry "Lost at Sea," and his love would be anguished. So he laced up his boots and stood to bid the talkative goats farewell.

"Oh no," said they, with mighty tossings of horns. "You are the hominid that has come to save us. We will not let you go away. You must take us all to those broader pastures which we crave—which we have ever craved!—where there is no more seaweed, and trees yield the golden pear and little saplings wince to our very sharp teeth. . . ."

And what was more, they showed Ken those very sharp teeth.

Sharp teeth, magnificent curved horns, devil's eyes . . . All set against him, with the horns rasping his thighs.

But Ken had his wits to rely on. He stood firm against his captors and spoke a few words in the Old Language.

"Indeed, I am come to rescue you. But you see that my boat is small. It would sink under your combined weights. I order that two of you are to accompany me now to my land. There we will assemble many boats to sail and rescue you all. You will be welcome in my land, with many green things to eat."

"What does the hominid say?" the horned animals asked each other, shuffling in their confusion.

One said, "Let us kill the hominid now and seize his boat."

Although the suggestion was popular, the wiser goats among the crowd had to confess that none of them knew how to sail a boat.

At last an understanding was reached. Ken was allowed back onto his ketch, with two animals preceding him there.

He stood stolidly in the stern, clutching an oar, staring at the small army of horned animals which now came from the beach to wade into the waters and watch him sail away.

"What if he fails to come back?" one old goat asked. But others immediately set upon him.

"You can always trust a hominid," they said.

The engine started up with a roar, frightening those animals who were up to their hocks in water; they stampeded to safety. Soon the island from which Ken had escaped was lost in a gathering mist. It might seem the little boat now floated alone in a world of water. The two goats folded their hooves under them and crouched flat on the deck, jaws against the planking, evidently affrighted by the immense unfolding of waves surrounding the vessel on all sides.

EVENING was drawing in with a light scatter of raindrops when land came in sight, together with the village in which Ken and Sheelagh lived. Ken cut the engine and they drifted into port. Candlelight showed in a window or two of nearby houses.

AND who should be standing there, awaiting him as he docked? Why, his dear wife Sheelagh, holding in her arms her little newborn child.

Ken skipped ashore, tied up the boat and ran to embrace her, calling her his dearest darling, kissing her and the head of the baby with that ginger curl on top.

Sheelagh caught sight of two goat faces peering anxiously over the side of the recently moored boat. She was momentarily horrified.

She emitted a small shriek, clutching her husband more tightly, asking him with tremulous voice, "What have we there?"

To which, still clutching her, now laughing, he uttered the one word, "Food!"

For much of the time I was writing, I believed that what I was saying might possibly be true. Well, it's not. . . . But there are certain unknown lands and languages contained inside us; they sometimes rise up in idle hours to delight or alarm us.

Could goats possibly have loved us? Well, I have had cats that I loved, cats that clearly loved me.

We are all flesh—even if it comes in funnily different shapes.

Part of our lives, if we are rich enough, are dream worlds, incurably ancient.

—BA

THE WHITE HORSE
Sarah Blackman

Once, through a confluence of events and no fault of his own, a horse fell in love with a baby.

This happened at a busy crossroad where two well-traveled paths met and mingled before going their separate ways. At first the crossroad was a naked X, pressured on all sides by trees. The roads that stretched away from that place were cold and thin, insufficient lines drawn between the mountain and the valley. Over the years many trees had been cut for lumber and the forest pushed back to widen the thoroughfare. Then someone had built a gibbet. Then someone had built a stable behind the gibbet and soon enough an inn next to the stable, a feed store on the other side of the road, an apothecary's shop snug at its side. Soon there were enough buildings and goods to consider the place a small town.

The crossroads was busy day and night but it was not named as a town would be. It was an in-between place. Often travelers were seen standing in the middle of the X, turning from road to road in a state of bewilderment. From each road came the same cool wind. Down each was afforded the same looming view of spruce and hemlock, rock, frosted blooms of lichen, hard dark earth.

———

ONE day, to the crossroads came a white horse ridden by a young and weary rider. They were on their way back down to the valley after a trip to a mountain town to secure the hand of a lovely mountain bride who had been promised but, souring over the months of postal courtship, now refused her betrothed on her father's very hearth. "That cunt," the young and weary man said over and over as they came down the steep road. He murmured it into the white horse's mane as he sank exhausted over the pommel and every time the horse flicked back one soft, sensitive ear as if to agree.

It is impossible to say what the horse thought of all this. At this point he was only a horse, though a handsome one with round knees, strong haunches, a lustrous tail and yellow hairs bristling from his pink, speckled muzzle. He had been born in a barn not so many years ago. He remembered everything that had happened to him since that point: sliding from his mother's quivering vagina and laddering himself upright on his own quivering legs, a whisk of straw scrubbed over his face and in his nostrils, a cold breeze as the barn door opened and someone else came in. After that came many many days that were largely the same.

Immediately after birth, the white horse had been given to the young and weary man as a present and this man had formed the basis for almost everything the white horse knew about himself. For example, he knew he was an animal and that to be an animal was to stand when someone told him stand and go when someone told him go. He knew the sun, which was like his curry brush, and the grass, which was like the bit in his mouth. He knew a sly kind of joke which had to do with his eyes and lips and a quick, sideways shuffle and, if the man were in a different mood, he knew a stupid, towering fear of brown leaves and blowing paper down from which his master could disdainfully calm him.

The young and weary man was mostly patient, but sometimes used the lash. He mostly remembered the horse's soft mouth, but sometimes sawed the reins until the corners of the horse's lips split and bled. In this way the white horse learned what was expected of him and, because he knew nothing but this expectation, came to understand his most intimate self as a figure of what he would do next. Not what he currently was; not what he desired to become.

This is not so strange. Who expects a mule or an ox to have a spiritual life? Who suffers a crisis of self alongside a flea? But the world is full of dawning. The sun comes up. If a man or a woman or a horse is awake to see it, they might mark the very moment when the sun appears to pull itself free of the horizon: shivering like a yolk, bouncing into its shape.

THE horse brought his rider to the crossroads at noon. It was early spring and the sun was small and silver as a coin. They had traveled together all night. At first, spurred by the rider's spleen, they had pelted down the winding, treacherous road, blood in the white horse's nostrils, stones turning under his hooves. Then, when the moon rose, the rider relaxed and they traveled more slowly. There was time to watch shadows slide across the path in front of them. Time to smell the high, thin scent of the pines and listen once and then again as, close by their side, something heavy struck and something small shrieked and fell silent.

When the sun comes up in the mountains the world is very far away. The mountain is black and at first the sun is announced by a deeper blackness, a pooling in the valley. Then the world inches forward in slow shades of violet. Distance is uncovered and every creature knows a specific unease—to see the world unchanged when I have been so changed! to see the world cold and still when I am hot and pounding!

The horse tossed his head and flicked his ears as the sun came up over the side of the mountain. Below them the valley was filled with fog which boiled like the surface of an uneasy lake. Behind them rose the mountain, its face streaming with green water. The horse was small, his great heart beat. The rider leaned against his neck and said, "That cunt. That cunt," in a voice as soft and steady as the new wind kicking up in the leaves. Then the path turned and they wound down again into darkness, quiet under the spreading branches of the pines.

SO. When the horse and his rider came to the crossroads, at noon, weary from their journey, heartsore and ill at ease, their minds were set on vengeance and on dinner, on pain and on a warm, snug place to sleep. This is to say, neither one of them was thinking of love. This is to say, they both nurtured within them a hard dark spot, like a black rock worn smooth by the river, which they turned and turned as if by turning it they would better be able to see. . . .

The crossroads was busy and loud. A man in a red jerkin sold live chickens strung up by their feet. A woman wearing a silver mask was standing on a box waving her arms. Someone was selling meat pies; someone was selling pots. A man tugged on a woman's bodice and her breast popped out. A man sharpened knives on a stone he held between his knees.

The rider dismounted and looped the reins around the pommel. He gripped the white horse's bridle at his cheek and pulled as he used it to balance, standing on one leg and then the next, arching his back like a bow.

"Ten pots. Ten pots," said the man who was selling pots.

"I was buried in the meadow, but I arose," said the woman in the mask. "I was buried on the mountain, but I washed into the stream."

The horse whickered. His hooves felt sore and splayed. He urinated on the ground in a great, steaming arc and turned his head to watch the stream runnel through the dirt.

"Ten pots. Ten pots," said the man who was selling pots. He was walking away from them, a pack on his back hung all about with pots and he clanked as he moved. All in all, he was a funny sort of man, easily dismissible. His hair was black and stood up around his head as if he were wearing a crown. "Buy pots," said the pot-selling man, and no one turned to mark him pass. He was like a slow, clanking shadow, unmoored from the sun, but in between all the pots was a sort of a hollow space and wedged in that hollow space was a kind of a pouch and in that pouch, her face purpling above the drawstring like a furious ornamental cabbage, was a baby girl.

The man turned his stone; he fingered it greedily.

The horse raised his head and pulled against the bridle. He opened wide a protesting eye and, for the very first time, he could see.

OF course, it didn't last. Even as the white horse strained his thick neck forward, the woman in the mask stepped off her box to buy a meat pie from the vendor and blocked the horse's view. When she moved again and he could see past her, the man selling pots had melted away into the crowd.

So it was that the white horse felt joy (her fat cheek! her furrowed brow!), and so it was that the white horse also knew despair and a hunger that came not because something had been taken from him, as his oats must eventually be, as the comfort of his stall sometimes was in the early morning hours, but because something could not be taken from him. Something—this baby! this baby! the wide, clear eye that pierced his own as it looked back at him—was his to seek out, to possess.

"Where else was I buried?" said the woman. She slid the mask back on her head and nibbled at the edges of the pie. Some grease dribbled on her chin and splashed against her white collar where it soaked in. With her free hand she caressed the features of the mask—flat eyes, sharp nose, broad, clashing cheeks. She looked around her dimly. She kept asking questions.

The young and weary man had a terrible time getting his horse into its rented stable. It pulled against the bridle. It locked its knees and braced against him, its neck as long and obstinate as a goose. All he wanted was a meat pie from the vendor. All he wanted was to strike his lovely betrothed in the mouth and then sink to his knees at her feet as the blood flowed over her lips. This would take place in an orchard—early autumn with the leaves on the ground and fruit heavy on the branches, assaulted by wasps and bees. A sweet smell. Her little cries and her fingers in the hair at the back of his bent neck.

He struck the horse on the nose instead and was surprised when it reared up against the sides of the stall and lashed out with its hooves. But all this is temporary. There is something satisfying in turning one's back on a dangerous animal. There is something soothing about being very tired in the middle of the day, the sun on one's skin, people moving about with noise and purpose. If he left the horse screaming in the stable it was one more noise among many. What did it matter which way he turned when all the roads leading from this place looked the same?

"It couldn't have been the ocean," said the woman in the mask. "Where did I leave off?"

The young man bought a meat pie and ate it. Nothing was ever the same again.

FOR the rest of his life the white horse carried his joy and his rage on his back like a second rider. He grew sullen and would disrupt his master's journeying by trying to thrust his head over hedgerows and into open windows as they went. He began to gulp air, to fight the bit. He shied at bits of paper in the road, rustling leaves, the sudden heavy flight of crows, and could neither be calmed nor jollied. His master put him in blinders. He employed spurs and rods, other more inventive encouragements, but the horse was driven, distracted by the weight on his back which was alternately as hard and cold as a ruby, sparkling from all its facets, and as soft and dark as an organ engorged with blood, feebly trying to pulse.

In short, the white horse was ruined. His master, who had passed out of his youth but regained none of his vivacity and so was a stout and weary man, dark as a pudding, fairly steaming, used him to service the mares, but even at this the horse was fractious and unreliable. Eventually, his master put him out to pasture on a deserted, wilding side of the property, bound on three sides by thorn hedges and on one by the rustling forest. He forgot about him altogether. There the white horse languished.

It is impossible to say how much time passed. What did it mean to the horse? Each day followed the next and it was the same sun, the same sky. The grass came up around his fetlocks and he bit it back down. A fox slunk out of the forest and trotted down the hedgerow, its black legs quick as shears. Later it came back with a rabbit slung from its jaws. The horse's knees grew swollen and boxy. His back swayed under the weight of his burden and his coat grew dull and dry. How many foxes? How many suns? The grass came up around his fetlocks and he bit it back down. On his back was a ruby, an organ, a ruby, a great, wet weight. One day, the horse went into the forest.

WHEN a certain kind of girl walks she leaves behind her both the place she has just been and the person she was there. She breaks the new air with her new self and greets around her, with a shining face, all the possible versions of herself to come. Of course, she is caught up quickly. When she stops, even just for a moment to unsnag a thorn from her stocking, adjust the heel of her shoe, all the black weight of her self slams into her back and settles there. Her greed, her fear! Her nervous hands and the dark circles that press below her eyes like thumbprints. She must go on. Quickly, quickly. She must never look back.

A horse is a different sort of animal. The white horse left nothing behind him. He removed himself from the picture and the picture filled in. Simple as a soap bubble: iridescent, then pop.

———

THE forest was not a natural place for a horse to be. The ground under his hooves was spongy and hummocked. Roots arced out of the leaf mold and zipped along a few feet before diving back in like trout choking a stream, the stream boiling with their bodies, he like a horse plashing witless in the shallows.

Was he thirsty? There was nothing to drink, though the forest had the lowering feel of a damp place and around him, at varying distances, he could hear the sound of water plinking against stone. Was he hungry? The horse lowered his head to graze as he went, a domesticate and thus accustomed to meeting many needs at once, but the ground was barren, soft and yet unyielding. Below him were vast hollow spaces. The roots pierced them and traveled on in darkness and in damp. The white horse could not see very well. The forest pressed around him like blinders, at once too close and too far: the dancing motes of light, gold and green, the suggestion past each trunk of a space opening out, the older trees shot like jackstraws, collapsed against each other's shoulders, a bird that called and fell still, called and fell still to listen. Was he thirsty? Was he hungry? The horse went on and on. His back hurt under its weight; his knees swelled and popped. A bird called. Water fell against stone. There was a great, rearranging flurry and then nothing. Silence. The forest drew itself up.

Eventually, as he must, the horse came out of the forest and into a clearing. Here the grass was long and thick. Through the center of the clearing someone had beaten a road; at the head of the clearing someone had built a house. What a pretty sight. A chimney. Rose bushes. There was a vegetable garden sprung with stands of rhubarb and clouded about the edges with pennyroyal and phlox. There was a shape at the window twitching the curtains and two crows perched meditatively on the garden fence. The roses were furled like champagne flutes. A curl of smoke lifted from the chimney and hovered in the still air like the shadow of something larger and farther away.

And yes! the horse was hungry. Yes, thirsty, he was thirsty and stretched out his neck and called, his lips ruffling over his long teeth, for the pail fresh with water to be brought to him at once. Someone was asleep on the job, but he was forgiving. Dimly, the white horse remembered his best-loved joke. Dimly, he bridled and danced beside the path, herky-jerky, all akimbo. The white horse was nothing to see, just another apparition pawing the turf at the forest's edge. And yet, here was someone who had seen him. Here was someone, opening the door, coming cautiously down the cottage path, who had heard and heeded his call. "Cush, cush" said the girl, wiping her hands on her pants and holding one out to him. "Cush" she said, sidling toward him through the tall, damp grass.

(THE sun pulls itself whole from the horizon line. Egg from a hat. Bird from an egg. A burst of doves battering around the ceiling which here is the sky. And the rest of the room? The forest, of course. Oh please, can a horse not lay down his burden? Oh please, can't he just rest it here, here at your feet?)

BECAUSE this was she: the baby who had become this girl. Unmistakable, though her look was entirely altered, and had the white horse the capacity to imagine, he never would have dreamt her so shrunken and ill favored. He remembered the sour bud of her lip, her imperious eye, clouded as marble, her soft round cheek, her corona of hair. . . . Still, there was no mistake. It was she, she!, who braided her rough fingers in his mane, she who wrinkled her sharp, monkey face and said, "Poor thing," as she ran her palm over his ribs. It was she and she was his. He pressed forward to take her. The thick grass. The trembling roses. What a pretty sight at the edge of such a forest. He loved her, he loved her. He reared up to put his forelegs on her shoulders and show her his love.

But she said, "Whoa." She said, "Stop!" She stumbled back a few paces, her feet white in the grass, and as he came after her, she brought up a hand to block the sight of him. She ran back down the path and bolted her front door.

SO, there they were. She inside and he without.

THE white horse was puzzled, but it was not a condition of his being to question. The cottage path wound up to a little concrete stoop, three pretty steps with pots of red geraniums set at their edges, and a wrought iron railing swooping down both sides like extended wings.

At the top of the steps was a green door.

What was behind the green door was his.

This seemed simple enough to the horse; and yet the door was closed; and yet the steps, so foreign to his nature, were unnavigable. The curtains twitched. The sun went behind a cloud, then out it came.

FOR a while the horse grazed in the cottage meadow. When she did not come, he went to the windows and stripped the leaves from the tops of the azaleas. Sometimes, he sensed she was just on the other side of the curtain. Sometimes, he thought he could even see the outline of her body, a shape perhaps like the shape of her eye framed in a minuscule gap in the fabric. At those times he pressed his muzzle to the glass and nipped at it eagerly, but she did not come. She gave him no sign. After the third day the smoke stopped coming up the chimney. After the fourth, as he strolled in the warm dirt of the garden and ate the ferny tops of the carrots, he saw her clearly in a dormer window, fiddling with the sash as if she were about to throw the window open. But when he whinnied with excitement and craned his neck to see her better, she stepped back, a mannequin shape in the dark room and then just a shadow, then gone.

Had the horse the capacity to speculate, he might have suspected she was out of firewood and probably food. Had he the ability to calculate, he might have realized he had almost won. The house seemed still and cold, though in the meadow the sun was warm on his back and the new apples broke like hard, sour eggs between his teeth. Had the horse been his master, or even had his master been there to guide the horse's perceptions, he might have seen how he had trampled the garden, worn ruts from window to window, stripped the flowers from their stems, fouled the waters of the little creek as he slid down its bank to drink, scrambled up its opposite bank to see if it was not so that, while his back was turned, his beloved had come out again to welcome him with open arms.

Had he been a man, the white horse might have recognized all these things as signs of his eventual triumph. He might even have rejoiced, though with regret for all the necessary waste; with annoyance, perhaps, at the silly goose who had caused him to go to such lengths in the first place. But he was a horse, and so lacked subtlety. He fed on roses and carried his burden. He waited patiently for something to change.

ON the sixth day, her father came home.

IMAGINE, for a moment, the scene from afar. Here is the familiar road, one hewn by your own hand. You can remember the trees that once stood there, the squeak of their wood as your axe bit. You can remember your body as it was then—like a machine, each motion foreshortened for greatest efficiency, each muscle in easy relation to the next. To lift and swing. To lift and swing. And then all those years of walking this very same road. Moss and berries in the verges, flowers thrusting up their doddering heads in the spring and in the winter the snow thick and crisp, patterned with the crosses of bird's feet and the hush of their downbeat wings.

For a strange man hung about with clamor, perhaps for any man at all, there is nothing in the world that feels so much like himself as this road and, at the end of it, the clearing he razed, the house he built, the girl who is his, whom he made. She bears no expectation but that he return, and he has!, bearing pots! The rattle he makes is another way the road and the clearing break the forest. His bronze clangor, his clinking tin. He has come, bang a drum, he has come! In this way, the father strode from the forest and into the sun.

For all his oddities, the father was an astute man and not without imagination. He took in the scene before him: the garden ruined, the meadow deranged, the horse, slat-ribbed and broken, stretching the terrible crane of his neck to lip a peachy rose from its vine. Inside the house his daughter pulled back the curtain and stood there framed by eyelet white. She looked like the head of a water parsley. The curtains were the frothy bloom, and she herself the black pip in the center that either says, "eat me," or "beware," he couldn't remember which. In short, she did not seem herself, but a hardened seed of that self. She did not lift a hand to him but merely stood and stared and, as the white horse saw her and rushed toward the glass—his lips coated in slaver, his tail arched and trembling—she slid backward as if on a track and disappeared from view.

It is worth noting that the white horse noticed none of this. Not even when the father, his pack and pots set down at the head of the road, edged around him, up the steps and in the front door. Not even when the sound of voices came from inside, rising and falling, shrill and sharp, or when that sound was replaced by the sound of something heavy sliding and many small doors being opened and shut. The horse was absorbed, blinded more surely than by any blinker, because he had seen her, at last it was her, there in the window, so close at hand. But he had come too late and again the glass was in his way. At least now he could see. The curtains were pulled back, the room behind a sitting room: a couch plaid in broad bands of green and gold, a strange clock, shelves of books, a braided rug. Nothing to see, but something she had seen. Nothing to touch, the glass cold and slick against his nose, but something she had touched, where her arm had lain, her foot had trod. A book she had been reading was slung on the table, a hawk's feather tucked between the pages to hold her place. A pillow she had used to prop herself up was still wadded against the arm of the couch, dented with the shape of her elbow or head.

Without realizing it the white horse began to keen, his voice juddering in his rusty throat. He reared up and struck the side of the house, his hooves denting the clapboard, his back legs uprooting one bush and then another. Red and white azalea petals floated in the air like red mites in a burst of feather ticking. Meanwhile, the father had gotten his gun.

THIS seems a simple story. Why has it taken so long to tell? The gun was in the hall closet, a stubborn shape in the corner, behind rubber boots and oilskins. The bullets were in a kitchen drawer. In any story, the pieces are easy enough to assemble but hard to make move. Here is a woman who must enter a cavern; a man who must move a stone; a monkey who must climb to the top of the tree where the last green coconut bobs just out of reach. And yet they hunker down, stolid and stone-faced. They refuse. The gun was well oiled, the bullets slid home. From where he stood on the doorstep, the father could see both the white horse, still straining at the window, and his daughter who stood in the hall: barefoot, gray, wearing a gray sack dress she had tied at the waist with a dishtowel, her hair on her face like a veil.

Everyone has assembled. Pretty soon, the story will end. But the father balks. A decision must be made. Here is the horse: a pathetic thing, so lonely. He cannot live, but cannot help the way he has lived. He cannot learn from his mistakes. Here is the daughter, grown so long ago out of the shape he made for her on his pack and then kept growing. If he is honest with himself, this is not the first homecoming at which he has found her irreversibly changed.

Indeed, every time he sees her—coming into the kitchen in the morning, walking down the hall to find her sprawled on the couch, one foot on the armrest, her face in her book—he finds he has to blink a few times before it is her that he sees and not just some vague and restless woman-shape dusting his house with flour.

The father stands on the doorstep he himself laid and looks from one to the other. He has a decision to make—here is a man who *must* fire a gun—and after a while he lifts the stock to his shoulder and takes aim.

I had D'Aulaires' Book of Greek Myths *as a child and one of the pictures I liked the most and returned to again and again was Zeus disguised as the snow white bull charging out to sea with an adoring Europa draped over his neck. It was such a sweet picture, but also, of course, sinister. For this story, I was interested in telling something similar but without the element of duplicity: the horse is sincerely in love but also sincerely a horse and so, at the very least, the girl, unlike Europa, gets to see her fate coming.*

—SB

Acknowledgments

⸭

I must thank the gods of this book, who hover over it in so many ways: Maria Massie and Derek Parsons at Lippincott Massie McQuilkin; John Siciliano, Doug Clark, and Rebecca Lang, among others at Penguin; Joyelle McSweeney, Lydia Millet, Karen Mockler, Ann Patchett, and Donna Tartt, and Willy Vlautin, friends and advisers whose words always help; my students—especially those in Spring 2013's graduate fairy-tale workshop at the University of Arizona—who always raise vital new questions; Roz and Wally Bernheimer and Kay Hendricks; and the old myths themselves, too many to name—I turned often, especially, to Edith Hamilton's *Mythology*, Karen Armstrong's *A Short History of Myth*, and The Great Courses' *Classical Mythology* by Elizabeth Vandiver, for doses of inspiration, knowledge, and courage.

Finally, I must thank Brent Hendricks for our late-night porch conversations about myth, apocalypse, Anthropocene, and the Tucson night sky. You and Xia are truly my heroes.

—KB

About the Contributors

Poet, playwright, critic, fiction and science-fiction writer BRIAN ALDISS was born on August 18, 1925, in Dereham, Norfolk, and is the author of more than seventy-five books. Aldiss is the recipient of numerous international awards for writing, including a Kurd Lasswitz Award (Germany) and a Prix Jules Verne (Sweden). He lives in Oxford and was awarded an OBE in 2005 for Services to Literature.

DAVID B. is a French comic book artist and writer.

LUTZ BASSMANN belongs to a community of imaginary writers. Bassmann is a pseudonym for Antoine Volodine, a name which is itself a pseudonym for an author who keeps his name secret. Bassmann is also a character within Volodine's work. Jordan Stump's translation of his novel *We Monks and Soldiers* was published in 2012.

AIMEE BENDER is the author of five books, including *The Girl in the Flammable Skirt* and *The Particular Sadness of Lemon Cake*. Her most recent, a collection of stories, will be out in fall 2013.

KATE BERNHEIMER is the author of a trilogy of novels, concluding recently with *The Complete Tales of Lucy Gold*, and a collection of short stories, *Horse, Flower, Bird*. Her second story collection, *How a Mother Weaned Her Girl from Fairy Tales*, is forthcoming. She received the World Fantasy Award for her anthology *My*

Mother She Killed Me, My Father He Ate Me: Forty New Fairy Tales (Penguin Books).

SARAH BLACKMAN is the author of *Mother Box*, a forthcoming short story collection, and director of creative writing at the Fine Arts Center, a public arts high school. She is the co-fiction editor of *DIAGRAM* and lives in Greenville, South Carolina, with the poet John Pursley III and their daughter Helen.

KELLY BRAFFET is the author of the novels *Save Yourself, Last Seen Leaving*, and *Josie and Jack*. OWEN KING is the author of the novel *Double Feature* and *We're All in This Together: A Novella and Stories*. Both have published stories in *Fairy Tale Review*. They live in New York.

EDWARD CAREY is a writer and illustrator. His novels *Observatory Mansions* and *Alva & Irva* have been published in fourteen countries; the first volume of a young adult trilogy, *Iremonger*, will be published in September 2013.

MAILE CHAPMAN is the author of the novel *Your Presence Is Requested at Suvanto*.

GEORGES-OLIVIER CHÂTEAUREYNAUD has been honored over a career of almost forty years with the Prix Renaudot, the Prix Goncourt de la nouvelle, and the Grand Prix de l'Imaginaire at Utopiales. His volume of selected stories, *A Life on Paper* (2010), won the Science Fiction & Fantasy Translation Award and was shortlisted for the Best Translated Book Award. His stories have appeared in *Subtropics, Conjunctions, The Harvard Review, The Southern Review, Fantasy & Science Fiction, AGNI Online, Epiphany, Postscripts, Eleven Eleven, Sentence, Joyland, Confrontation, Podcastle, The Brooklyn Rail*, and *Café Irreal*. His work is also forthcoming in *Exotic Gothic V*.

RON CURRIE, JR.'s most recent book is *Flimsy Little Plastic Miracles*. His writing has received the New York Public Library Young Lions Award and the Metcalf Award from the American Academy of Arts and Letters, and has been translated into seventeen languages. He lives in central Maine.

KATHRYN DAVIS is the author of seven novels: *Labrador, The Girl Who Trod on a Loaf, Hell, The Walking Tour, Versailles, The Thin Place,* and *Duplex.* She has been the recipient of the Kafka Prize, the Morton Dauwen Zabel Award from the American Academy of Arts and Letters, a Guggenheim Fellowship, and the 2006 Lannan Award for Fiction. She lives in Vermont and teaches in the MFA program at Washington University in St. Louis, where she is Hurst Senior Writer-in-Residence.

MANUELA DRAEGER belongs to a community of imaginary authors. Draeger is a heteronym for Antoine Volodine, which is itself a pseudonym for an author who keeps his own name a secret. Draeger is also a character in one of Volodine's other books: a librarian in a post-apocalyptic prison camp who invents stories to tell to the children in the camp. Three additional Bobby Potemkine stories have appeared in English in *In the Time of the Blue Ball* (2011).

ELANOR DYMOTT was born in Chingola, Zambia, in 1973. She studied literature at Worcester College, Oxford, later working as a commercial lawyer, and as a legal reporter for *The Times* of London. Her short fiction has been published in the United Kingdom and her first novel is *Every Contact Leaves a Trace* (2012). She lives in London, where she plays jazz flute and is writing her next novel.

ELIZABETH EVANS is the author of five books of fiction. A new novel, *As Good as Dead,* will appear in 2014. Her two short story collections are *Suicide's Girlfriend* and *Locomotion.* Her novels are *The Blue Hour, Rowing in Eden,* and *Carter Clay. Carter Clay* was selected for Best Books of 1999 by the *Los Angeles Times.* In 2010, Evans received the Iowa Author Award. Other awards include a National Endowment for the Arts Fellowship, the James Michener Fellowship, and a Lila Wallace Award. She has been a fellow at MacDowell Colony, Yaddo Foundation, the International Retreat for Writers at Hawthornden Castle, and other foundations. Evans serves on the faculty of the University of Arizona's Program in Creative Writing and is a frequent guest faculty member at Queen's University of Charlotte's Low-Residency MFA program in Creative Writing.

BRIAN EVENSON is the author of a dozen books of fiction, most recently *Immobility* and *Windeye*. He has received three O. Henry awards and an NEA Award. His translations include work by Jacques Jouet, Christian Gailly, Gerard Macé, Eric Chevillard, Antoine Volodine, Jean Frémon, and others. He lives and works in Providence, Rhode Island, with his wife, Kristen Tracy.

SARAH EVENSON is the cotranslator of David B.'s graphic novel *Incidents in the Night*. She lives and works in Minneapolis as a freelance illustrator. Visit her on the Web at sarahevenson.tumblr .com.

EDWARD GAUVIN has received fellowships and residencies from the National Endowment for the Arts, the Fulbright program, the Centre National du Livre, and the Lannan Foundation. Other publications have appeared in *The New York Times, Tin House, World Literature Today, Quarterly Conversation*, and *PEN America*. The contributing editor for Francophone comics at *Words Without Borders*, he translates comics and writes a bimonthly column on the Francophone fantastic at *Weird Fiction Review*.

MAX GLADSTONE has taught in southern Anhui, wrecked a bicycle in Angkor Wat, and been thrown from a horse in Mongolia. He graduated from Yale University, where he studied Chinese. His first novel, *Three Parts Dead*, was published in 2013.

SHEILA HETI is the author of five books, including *We Need a Horse* (written for children; illustrated by Clare Rojas), which deals with death, dying, and the meaning of life. Her first book, *The Middle Stories*, includes thirty short stories that have a fablelike cast.

LAIRD HUNT is the author of five novels, including *The Impossibly, The Exquisite,* and *Kind One*. He is on the faculty at the University of Denver, where he teaches literature and creative writing and edits the *Denver Quarterly*.

AAMER HUSSEIN was born in Karachi, Pakistan, in 1955. He moved to London in 1970. He graduated in languages and history from SOAS (University of London), and started writing fiction in his thirties, contributing to a number of journals and anthologies in the late 1980s and early 1990s. His first volume of stories, *Mirror to the Sun*, was published in 1993. He has since published four other collections to increasing critical acclaim: *This Other Salt, Turquoise, Cactus Town,* and *Insomnia,* and two novels, *Another Gulmohar Tree* and, most recently, in 2011, *The Cloud Messenger.* He is now working on a new collection, *The Man from Beni Mora: New and Selected Stories,* which will include "The Swan's Wife." His work is widely anthologized and has been translated into Italian, French, Arabic, Japanese, and Spanish, among other languages. He also writes fiction in Urdu. Recent work has appeared in *Granta, The New Statesman, Moving Worlds, Moth,* and *Wasafiri.* He was elected a Fellow of the Royal Society of Literature in 2004.

SHANE JONES is the author of *Light Boxes* and *Daniel Fights a Hurricane*, both published by Penguin.

HEIDI JULAVITS is the author of four novels, most recently *The Vanishers*. Her fiction and nonfiction have appeared in numerous *Best American* collections and have been widely anthologized. She is the recipient of a Guggenheim Fellowship and a founding coeditor of the monthly culture magazine *The Believer*.

TOSHIYA KAMEI, who translated Olmedo's story, holds an MFA in literary translation from the University of Arkansas. His translations include Naoko Awa's *The Fox's Window and Other Stories* (2010) and Espido Freire's *Irlanda* (2011).

OWEN KING is the author of the novel *Double Feature* and *We're All in This Together: A Novella and Stories.* KELLY BRAFFET is the author of the novels *Save Yourself, Last Seen Leaving,* and *Josie and Jack.* Both have published stories in *Fairy Tale Review.* They live in New York.

VICTOR LAVALLE is the author of four books including, most recently, two novels, *Big Machine* and *The Devil in Silver.* He has been a recipient of a Guggenheim Fellowship, a Whiting Writers Award, and the Key to Southeast Queens.

MICHAEL JEFFREY LEE lives in New Orleans. His collection of stories, *Something in My Eye*, won the Mary McCarthy Prize in Fiction.

BEN LOORY's fiction has appeared in *The New Yorker*, *Weekly Reader's READ Magazine*, and *Fairy Tale Review* and on NPR's *This American Life*. His book *Stories for Nighttime and Some for the Day* (Penguin, 2011) was a selection of the Barnes & Noble Discover Great New Writers Program. He lives in Los Angeles.

ANTHONY MARRA is the author of the novel *A Constellation of Vital Phenomena*. He has won a Whiting Award, a Pushcart Prize, *The Atlantic*'s Student Writing Contest, and the *Narrative* Prize, and his work has appeared in *Best American Nonrequired Reading*. He is currently a Stegner Fellow at Stanford University.

ZACHARY MASON lives in California. His first book, *The Lost Books of the Odyssey*, was published in 2010. It won a California Book Award, the Criticos Prize, was a *New York Times* Notable Book for 2010, and a finalist for the New York Public Library Young Lions Award.

ELIZABETH McCRACKEN is the author of a collection of short stories, two novels, and a memoir.

MAILE MELOY is the author of the novels *Liars and Saints* and *A Family Daughter*, the story collections *Half in Love* and *Both Ways Is the Only Way I Want It*, and the young adult novels *The Apothecary* and *The Apprentices*.

MADELINE MILLER earned her BA and MA in classics from Brown University. *The Song of Achilles*, her first novel, was awarded the 2012 Orange Prize for Fiction. She currently lives in Cambridge, Massachusetts, where she teaches and writes.

ANDER MONSON is the author of five books, most recently *Vanishing Point: Not a Memoir* (2010) and *The Available World* (2010). His work has appeared in *The New York Times* and the Best American Essays series, as well as in many magazines and journals. A finalist for the New York Public Library's Young Lions Award and a National Book Critics Circle Award in Criticism, and the recipient of a Howard Foundation Fellowship from Brown University, he lives in Tucson, where he teaches in the English department at the University of Arizona and edits the journal *DIAGRAM* (thediagram .com) from the New Michigan Press.

MANUEL MUÑOZ is the author of a novel, *What You See in the Dark*, and two short story collections, *Zigzagger* and *The Faith Healer of Olive Avenue*, which was shortlisted for the Frank O'Connor International Short Story Award. He is a recipient of a Whiting Award and teaches at the University of Arizona.

SABINA MURRAY is the author of three novels and two story collections: the recent *Tales of the New World*, and *The Caprices*, which won the 2002 PEN/Faulkner Award. She has been awarded fellowships from the National Endowment for the Arts, the Guggenheim Foundation, and the Radcliffe Institute. She teaches in the MFA program at the University of Massachusetts at Amherst.

SIGRID NUNEZ has published six novels, including *A Feather on the Breath of God*, *The Last of Her Kind*, and, most recently, *Salvation City*. She is also the author of *Sempre Susan: A Memoir of Susan Sontag*. Her honors and awards include three Pushcart Prizes, a Whiting Writers' Award, a Berlin Prize Fellowship, and two awards from the American Academy of Arts and Letters: the Rosenthal Foundation Award and the Rome Prize in Literature.

GINA OCHSNER lives in Keizer, Oregon, and teaches at Corban University in Salem, Oregon, and with Seattle Pacific's Low Residency MFA program. She is the author of the short story collection *The Necessary Grace to Fall*, which received the Flannery O'Connor Award for Short Fiction, and the story collection *People I Wanted to Be*. Both books received the Oregon Book Award. Her novel *The Russian Dreambook of Colour and Flight* was long-listed for the Orange Award (UK). Ochsner is the grateful recipient of grants from the Oregon Arts Commission, Oregon Literary Arts, Inc., the National Endowment for the Arts, the John Simon Guggenheim Memorial Foundation, and the Howard Foundation.

DONAJÍ OLMEDO was born and lives in Mexico City. Her fiction has appeared in the anthology *Three Messages and a Warning* (2012). She blogs at *Casa de Ateh* and edits the chapbook of the same name, where she publishes the work of young Mexican writers.

EDITH PEARLMAN is the recipient of the 2011 PEN/Malamud award for excellence in short fiction, honoring her four collections of stories: *Vaquita, Love Among the Greats, How to Fall*, and *Binocular Vision. Binocular Vision* received the 2012 National Book Critics Circle Award for Fiction.

BENJAMIN PERCY is the author of two novels, *Red Moon* and *The Wilding*, as well as two books of short stories. His awards include the Whiting Writers' Award, an NEA Fellowship, the Plimpton Prize, two Pushcart Prizes, and inclusion in *Best American Short Stories*.

DAWN RAFFEL is the author of four books, most recently *The Secret Life of Objects*. She is the editor of *The Literarian*, the literary magazine published by the Center for Fiction.

IMAD RAHMAN is the author of *I Dream of Microwaves*, a novel-in-stories. His work has appeared in *One Story, Gulf Coast, Chelsea, The Fairy Tale Review,* and *Willow Springs*, among others. He currently teaches creative writing at Cleveland State University, where he also directs the Imagination Writers Conference.

KIT REED is the author of, most recently, *Son of Destruction* and *The Story Until Now: A Great Big Book of Stories*. Reed's 2011 collection, *What Wolves Know*, was nominated for the Shirley Jackson Award. *The New York Times Book Review* has this to say about her work: "Most of these stories shine with the incisive edginess of brilliant cartoons . . . they are less fantastic than visionary." Other novels include *@expectations, Captain Grownup, Fort Privilege, Catholic Girls, J. Eden,* and *Little Sisters of the Apocalypse*.

DAVIS SCHNEIDERMAN's works include *Drain; Blank: a novel*, with audio from Dj Spooky; and *Abecedarium*; and the coedited collections *Retaking the Universe: Williams S. Burroughs in the Age of Globalization* and *The Exquisite Corpse: Chance and Collaboration in Surrealism's Parlor Game*. His creative work has appeared in numerous publications including *Fiction International, The Chicago Tribune, The Iowa Review, TriQuarterly,* and *Exquisite Corpse,* and regularly in *The Huffington Post*. He is an English professor at Lake Forest College and director of Lake Forest College Press/ &NOW Books; he edits *The &NOW AWARDS: The Best Innovative Writing*. He can be found, virtually, at davisschneiderman.com.

AURELIE SHEEHAN's most recent book is *Jewelry Box: A Collection of Histories*. She is the author of two novels, *History Lesson for Girls* (Viking, 2006) and *The Anxiety of Everyday Objects* (Penguin, 2004) as well as a previous collection, *Jack Kerouac Is Pregnant* (1994). Her work has appeared in *Conjunctions, Epoch, Fairy Tale Review, Fence, New England Review, Ploughshares, The Southern Review,* and other journals. She has received a Pushcart Prize, a Camargo Fellowship, the Jack Kerouac Literary Award, and an Artists Projects Award from the Arizona Commission on the Arts. Sheehan teaches fiction at the University of Arizona in Tucson.

JOHANNA SKIBSRUD is the author of the 2010 Scotiabank Giller Prize–winning novel, *The Sentimentalists* (2011); a collection of short fiction, *This Will Be Difficult to Explain and Other Stories* (2012); and two collections of poetry. Originally from Nova Scotia, Canada, Johanna currently lives in Tucson, Arizona, where she is working on a collection of critical essays and a second novel.

EMMA STRAUB is the author of the novel *Laura Lamont's Life in Pictures*, a Barnes & Noble Discover Great New Writers selection, and the short story collection *Other People We Married*. Her fiction and essays have appeared in *Vogue, Tin House, The Paris Review Daily,* and *The New York Times,* and she is a staff writer for *Rookie*.

PETER STRAUB has written three collections of shorter fiction and many novels, among them *Ghost Story, Shadowland, lost boy lost girl, The Hellfire Club,* and *A Dark Matter,* and two novels with Stephen King. He has won nine Bram Stoker awards, four World Fantasy awards, two Life Achievement awards, and the Barnes & Noble Writers for Writers Award.

LAURA VAN DEN BERG's debut collection of stories, *What the World Will Look Like When All the Water Leaves Us* (2009), was a Barnes & Noble Discover Great New Writers selection and shortlisted for the Frank O'Connor International Award. Her second collection of short stories is 2013's *The Isle of Youth*.

Born and raised in Reno, Nevada, WILLY VLAUTIN has published three novels, *The Motel Life* (2007), *Northline* (2008), and *Lean on Pete* (2010). His fourth novel, *The Free*, will be published in spring 2014. Vlautin founded the band Richmond Fontaine in 1994. The band has produced ten studio albums to date, plus a handful of live recordings and EPs. Driven by Vlautin's dark, storylike songwriting, the band has achieved critical acclaim at home and across Europe. Vlautin currently resides in Scappoose, Oregon.

JOY WILLIAMS is the author of short stories and novels, including *The Quick and the Dead*, a finalist for the Pulitzer Prize in 2001. She is also the author of *Ill Nature*, a book of essays that was a finalist for the National Book Critics Circle Award for criticism. Among her many honors are the Rea Award for the short story and the Strauss Living Award from the American Academy of Arts and Letters.

KEVIN WILSON is the author of a story collection, *Tunneling to the Center of the Earth*, and a novel, *The Family Fang*. He lives in Sewanee, Tennessee, and teaches at the University of the South.

KAREN TEI YAMASHITA is the author of *Through the Arc of the Rain Forest, Brazil-Maru, Tropic of Orange, Circle K Cycles*, and *I Hotel*. Most recently *I Hotel* was selected as a finalist for the National Book Award and awarded the California Book Award, the American Book Award, and the Association for Asian American Studies Book Award. She is currently a U.S. Artists Ford Foundation Fellow and professor of literature and creative writing at the University of California, Santa Cruz.

Index of Authors

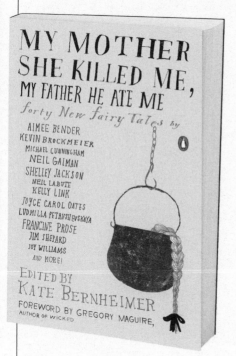